Myra Sims

Also by Janis Owens

MY BROTHER MICHAEL

$\mathcal{M}$YRA SIMS

— Janis Owens —

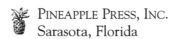
PINEAPPLE PRESS, INC.
Sarasota, Florida

Inquiries should be addressed to:
Pineapple Press, Inc.
P.O. Box 3899
Sarasota, Florida 34230-3899

Library of Congress Cataloging in Publication Data

Owens, Janis, 1960-
    Myra Sims / by Janis Owens.
    p.   cm.
    ISBN 1-56164-177-4 (hc. : alk. paper) —
    I. Title.
    PS3565.W5665M97   1999
    813'.54—dc21   98-24079
                                                CIP

First Edition
10 9 8 7 6 5 4 3 2 1

Design by Stacey Arnold
Printed and bound by The Maple Press, York, Pennsylvania

For the good ole girls: Mama and Katie B, Carole and Helen,
Pat, Shari, Suzy, Joy, and Marcie, and the little ones:
Mimi and Abby and Sweet 'Bel
who've all taught me a thing or two, mostly about love.

I couldn't imagine my life without you.

Myra Sims

I'll tell me Ma when I go home,
  the boys won't leave the girls alone.
They pulled my hair and they stole my comb
  and that's all right, till I get home.

She is handsome, she is pretty
  she is the belle of Belfast City,
She is courting, one, two, three
  please won't you tell me *who is she?*

Traditional Irish Folksong

PART ONE

THE HUNGRY SOUL

*O**n the day my husband Michael died,* I
was too busy with the practical details of death, the funeral arrangement, the notifying of relatives, the soothing of the tears and near-hys-
teria in my children, to take much time out to grieve myself. His illness
had been a short one, relatively speaking, just inside four months, but
I'd been at his side every minute, from the first words of dread at the
surgeon's mouth, till the ICU monitor flat-lined Tuesday morning and
the nurses gave me my hour alone before they wheeled his body to the
morgue. It made for the single hour of my life that was (and remains)
simply beyond recording, when I sat there in that white clinical hush and
watched Michael's still, thin face, without a thought in the world, of grief
or relief or even regret.

Simply shocked to silence; talked out after three days of self-inflict-
ed privacy, when I'd lain beside him in his narrow hospital bed and
chased away the shadow with an aimless mix of stories and anecdotes
that turned, inevitably, to whispered secrets. He was nearly blind by
then, his face hardly registering any surprise at all, only smiling a little at
the children stories he couldn't get enough of, nudging me awake to
whisper, "Tell me about Clay. And the leaf."

I'd oblige him, stifling a yawn and recalling some small childhood contretemps, meaningless to anyone but us, the parents who'd raised him, Michael falling into his final sleep to the sound he loved most: the sound of a human voice.

That was the day of his death.

By the morning of his funeral, after a two-day marathon of arranging for the mountains of food, the placement of the out-of-town guests, the fruitless search for a good black dress, I was too far gone in the reaches of simple exhaustion to do more than drag myself from bed and go about the same old church-going routine I'd endured every Sunday of my married life. There was nothing so extraordinary in it, just the detagging of my new dress (bought at the last minute by my sister-in-law at Parisians), the quick, panicky search for pantyhose, the rolling of my impossible hair in electric rollers. With those preliminaries taken care of, my activities moved out of the realm of my bedroom to the rooms of my younger children, slackers both, who have had to be whipped into action at every dress occasion of their lives. Their father's funeral was no exception.

Missy, the healthiest of us all when it came to emotion-letting and grief expression, was a regular fountain of tears, her eyes an amazing electric blue from the nonstop torrent, her only point of hope a frequently voiced desire that her Uncle Gabe show up for the funeral. It was an echo of her grandmother I found very wearing as the morning progressed, making me snap at her younger brother, who had somehow misplaced his new dress shoes and was blaming, in turn, everyone in the house, even the relatives who'd only come in the evening before.

"Cain't keep *nothing* in this stupid house," he kept whining, as if the house itself were a physical entity, capable of consuming unwary personal effects. It was a complaint I couldn't snap at him too much about, as it was nothing but a mild echo of his father, who'd spent every Sunday morning of his married life stalking around, looking for socks or handkerchiefs, shouting, "My God, Myra, you cain't find *nothing* in this house!"

I enrolled Missy in the search and sent her upstairs while I rummaged around the laundry room, still in my slip and robe, stoically accepting the pats and hugs and phone calls of condolence from my

Louisianan relations who'd hardly known Michael at all. (Maybe they were thinking of the will.) The whole time I listened and searched and murmured my correct replies (*Yes, thank you, of course you do*), I wondered if my mother-in-law would possibly forgive me if I skipped the service altogether in cowardly retreat and joined Sam McRae at Shell Island to fish for reds in kindly remembrance, rather than endure the protracted celebration of death I could expect down at Welcome. The answer, of course, was no. Cissie wouldn't forgive me, not in a million years, and for all her kindnesses to me, I owed her that much; owed her more.

After ten fruitless minutes looting the hamper, I gave up on the laundry room and went back to the kitchen to yell upstairs for Clay to look under the bed, when the phone rang again, for maybe the twentieth time that morning. I paused at the counter to answer it, expecting another New Orleans call, but there was no reply to my hello, just a blank silence. I thought then it might be my brother Ira, and waited for the click of the mechanical recording informing me I was receiving an outgoing call from a state prison, asking if I'd accept the charges. But the silence stretched on, three, maybe four breaths, and still, there was no answer. I had begun to repeat my hellos when there was the soft click of the caller hanging up without speaking, and as soon as I heard it, I knew who it was, I swear to God I did.

Who else would call and hang up, call and hang up, half a dozen times on such a trying day? Who but Gabriel Catts, my long-lost brother-in-law and one-time friend, and the very idea of him out there lurking about the county made me a little unsteady on my feet, having to lean against the counter top for support, thinking *dear Jesus, this is really the end.*

I hadn't seen him in what? Ten years? But knew just that quickly what I was in for at the service: his shattered face, consumed with remorse in his own inimitable style, embraced on all sides by his mother and sister and *my children,* all of them patting his back, telling him it'd be all right. That his brother loved him; that's all that mattered. And at that point, standing there in my slip, a widow at thirty-six, with my son's new dress shoes mysteriously lost and my hair in rollers, I wished I knew where the cowardly little bastard was hiding, because I'd slip out right now, just as I was, and shoot him in the back and be done with it. Either join Ira in the Florida penal system if I was caught, or go on to the funeral if I wasn't, in a hell of a better mood, either way.

But Gabriel was too wily for that. He knew better than to leave his name and number, and I was standing there with the dead phone in my hand, wondering how it had all come to this, when Missy came in with a J. C. Penney's bag held triumphantly aloft, crowing because she, Missy Catts, had (as usual) found the lost shoes and saved the day.

"In the dang car," she said as she handed them over. "Too stinking lazy to bring them in last night, left 'em on the back seat."

She went on to bemoan her thankless life as her brother's keeper, but it was eleven, with the final viewing scheduled for twelve, and I was still running around downstairs in my slip. In a desperate stab at command, I sent Missy to the living room to tell the relatives to feel free to eat if they wanted to, God knows there was plenty, then headed back to the bedroom to slap on a little makeup and try to prepare myself for the ordeal to come.

It was quiet up there, the floors of the old house well-insulated from the rise and murmur of voices below, but as I went about the arduous task of reclaiming a little youth, I felt a small *ping* in the pit of my stomach, the first in a very long time, since I'd gone off lithium for good. It wasn't a bad one, not a call-the-doctor *ping*, just a quiver of horrific unease; butterflies, some people called it, though to my poor wasted mind, it could be a lot more serious than that.

So serious that I sat back and took a deep breath, a *cleansing* breath, they call it, and felt around in the drawer for one of the stray Pamalors I used to take as an antidepressant, though now I only took them for anxiety, because they stayed with me longer than Xanax and didn't have the possible addictive qualities of the older names, say, Valium or Librium. The downside is they don't kick in as fast, and in an attempt to get a grip on things, I pushed aside my worry over the clock and lay down on my unmade bed just as I was, knowing a *ping* was more serious than even Cissie's wrath, knowing she'd understand if I told her.

A full half hour later, when Clay came to tell me Sim had called (my older son, who was staying with his grandmother) to say the limousine from the funeral home was on its way, I was still there, a little dim from the meds and the stress, though the *ping* hadn't taken hold, and I was myself again.

"You're not dressed *yet?*" he asked incredulously, sounding so much like Michael that I smiled.

"Nope."

He didn't appreciate my mellow tone, drawing himself up to all of his four feet, nine inches (he was only eleven when his father died) and informing me that it was *ten* till *twelve,* we were *late* and it was *all my fault.* I guess he was trying to distance himself from the firestorm of blame that would surely fly if they had to delay the service on our account, but his words went far beyond his intent, vibrating uneasily in my mind: *all my fault.*

They prodded me to action, making me rise wearily from the wonderfully crumpled, unmade bed (the same bed my husband and I had shared right up to Saturday night, that still held a vestige of his particular smell) and tell him to go on, I only had to put on my dress, I'd be down in a minute. He turned to leave, but as he made the door, I called him back to add lamely, "And Clay, baby, if anyone tells you anything today that doesn't sound . . . right," I plucked at the covers, "Then don't pay 'em any mind."

It was a silly thing to tell a child on the day of his father's funeral, silly and pretty much indecipherable. But another liability of the Pamalor is that it makes me quite unreserved, imparting a what-the-hell nonchalance to otherwise taboo subjects, though Clay didn't look too shocked. He only stood there watching me a moment out of the deep, hazel eyes he had inherited from his father and used to the same intent, to search and probe. Even at eleven, he saw the effects of the half-hour-old *ping* and asked, "Are you all right?"

"Sure," I told him shortly, even managed a deflecting smile. "Run, call Sim. Tell him we're on our way."

And without doing much more than yanking the rollers from my hair, I slipped on my new dress and the first black pumps I could lay hands on, then hurried down the stairs into the blue haze of the relatives' smoke. I guess it never occurred to them that the family of a cancer victim might not like the aroma of tobacco to assault them on all sides the day of his funeral, or maybe they were too nervous to care, standing and pulling on jackets, taking their glasses of iced tea with them.

The funeral home limousine had arrived out front, but I was feeling a certain need for independence with Gabriel out there skulking around the countryside, and politely declined to ride in it, sending Missy and Clay along with the rest of the family, then driving in alone in the fifty-thousand-dollar Mercedes my husband had bought me for our anniversary. At the time, I'd thought it a criminal waste of money, though the salesman had talked him into a life insurance rider, and as of Tuesday morning, we were paid in full. It was a tiny twist of good fortune he'd crowed about his last six weeks on earth, as if beating the insurance company at their game somehow validated his senseless death, final proof (as if any more were needed) of his old Midas touch.

And I guess I shouldn't complain, for it'd been a spark of victory in a dry white season, and it did drive well, I'll say that for it, the other cars on 90 like children's toys I passed and passed, beating the limousine to the church by a good five minutes, though we'd left the house at the same time. Sim was waiting for me on the front steps, dark and impatient in his good Sunday suit, another echo of his father as he urged me in, telling me they'd already seated the rest of the family and Grannie was having a *fit*.

"Uncle Gabe ain't showed," he said, offering his arm like an usher at a wedding.

Good for Uncle Gabe, I thought, but didn't say a word, just taking his arm and making my way through the tiny vestibule, truly amazed by the sheer mass of humanity that packed the small sanctuary. I'd put the fire marshall's capacity at two hundred, no more, but as Sim led me to the shock of white hair that marked my mother-in-law's possession of the family row, a quick glance showed the place at double that, if not more, so packed Sim and I had to walk single-file through the folded chairs that blocked the middle aisle.

The sense of claustrophobia was heightened around the pulpit by a virtual mountain of flowers and potted plants that nearly consumed the casket: carnations and roses and lilies of every description, even a few poinsettias, some draped with ribbons that bore their sad, glittering farewells: *RIP, Beloved Son; At Rest.* I had seen most of them last night at the viewing and was too busy searching the family row to pay them much mind today, not knowing exactly what to look for, as Gabriel was so changeable, so much the chameleon. In my brief sweep, I didn't see any sign of him, though Sim was pushing me too fast to hardly do more than take my seat next to my mother-in-law, who was not looking so well at all.

I hadn't seen her since the viewing at the funeral home the night before, and then, with the cushion of family around her and the unexpected visit from the lieutenant governor, she had been in her element, charming and controlled, even in grief. It was only in the matter of the open casket that she crossed me, for I've always thought it a barbaric custom, and with Michael's blessing, had planned to greet the guests in the anteroom, then send them on to Candace for the actual viewing, an arrangement that met with everyone's approval except his mother's. She made no overt objection, just sent out these subtle waves of disapproval, and such is the strength of her smallest whim, that before the evening was over, I was chatting over the open coffin as if it were a punch bowl at a reception, though Michael's face was so still and thin and white that I knew in my heart it'd haunt me for the rest of my days.

She had been strong then, Cissie had, but today, wasn't holding up so well, her face flat and despairing above the high neck of the severe black dress Candace had bought her on the funeral junket yesterday, the small hand that reached out to grip mine cold as ice. For her sake, if no other, I felt a small softening toward Gabe, hoping for — or at least, not hoping against — his appearance; it would mean so much to his mother. But though Missy and Clay and the extended family arrived, filling what was left of the reserved seating, Gabe still didn't show, and I was equally relieved at his absence, sitting back and ignoring the service I'd so carefully planned, with Michael's input at first, then the counsel of the pastors, the undertaker, all the proponents of the industry of death.

Brother Sloan intoned his welcome, then the songs began and the speakers, a half dozen at least, all of it spinning out, painfully slow. I thought we'd made it clear that we wanted it short and simple, but Michael had lived in the same town all his life, and the succession of preachers and local pols all insisted on their little stories, a few of them funny, but mostly not. Ben McQuaig, a childhood friend from the Hill, took the podium last of all and as he began his eulogy, I realized that the coffin, not six feet in front of me, was *still* open.

Now, Michael and I had had our share of disagreement over the service, what to include and what to omit, but that was one thing we had both agreed on: sweetheart roses on his coffin, his *closed* coffin, and I whispered aloud, without thought: "The coffin's still open."

Without missing a beat, Cissie glanced at me out of the corner of her eye, and with her natural ability to carry on a conversation in the face of the most compelling sermon, whispered, "Well, I was thinking Gabe — would surely want a see him —"

That's all she could get out, and for the second time in my life, I saw my mother-in-law, this Rock of Gibraltar of a woman, cry. She hadn't even cried at her own husband's funeral and God knows she'd loved him, and here she was, dabbing her eyes with her gloves, making Clay's words in the bedroom come back to me, unbidden: *all your fault.*

But there was nothing I could do about it, pinned in on all sides by death and obligation, and I was too tired, too drugged to worry it, only closing my eyes till Brother Sloan finally brought it to a close, having us stand and sing "Amazing Grace" a capella. Even then, I kept them closed, worried that if I saw much more of Michael's waxy, sallow face, I would forget him as he really was, and spend the rest of my days thinking I was married to the awful, silent man in the coffin, his face so different in death, passive and unresisting, never what it had been in life.

So I wasn't prepared for the great Second Coming, didn't know it was upon me till Missy let out a noise of surprise at the far end of the pew. I looked up; we all did, me at Missy, everyone else at Cissie, who threw off my hand and headed for the coffin, her voice lifted in triumph: "Gabe! Gabe! I knew you'd come — my son, my son — "

The organ continued to play, its muted lament a solemn counterpoint to Cissie's cry of joy as she practically roll-blocked a man muffled in a big overcoat, who gave in to her long embrace. When she released him, I saw that it was indeed the man himself who turned to the far end of the row to hug Missy with no reserve at all, though they'd only met briefly in an airport in New York. Her ceaseless musings in the intervening year had whetted Sim and Clay's curiosity enough that their faces, so shattered these days in the awful confusion of death, were lightened by a slight interest as this figure of legend began working his way down the row, shaking hands like the preacher his mother had raised him to be, with his good hand, his left one.

He took care that Sim understood the reversal, cradling his bad hand against his chest to demonstrate its uselessness, like he did when he was being polite, and something in the sad, protective little gesture went to my heart, Clay's piping complaint echoing back for the third time that day: *all your fault.* It pierced the Pamalor calm with a stinging regret so sharp it made my eyes water, though when he made it down the row and finally faced me, his eyes weren't accusing at all, but unexpectedly Clayton's.

Clayton's and Michael's, too, searching and troubled, his inquiry almost audible to the ear (*"Myra? Are you all right?"*) though he didn't say a word. I dropped my eyes involuntarily, not so comfortable with this man reading my mind, not so happy that my little *ping* was still evident to the discerning eye. Unlike the Gabe of old, he didn't push it, but just turned back to the coffin I'd picked out with such care Tuesday afternoon, solid cherry with brass trim, the little sweetheart roses on top already wilting, though they shouldn't have been, not at what we'd paid for them.

But Gabriel wasn't worried about the roses; his mother was dragging him up to view the body much like she'd done with me at the funeral home the night before, filling me with a momentary jag of fear that he'd call out some irretrievable words of regret, of truth that would embarrass me, embarrass us all. But he only stood there with his back to the line of mourners stilled in the aisle, locals, mostly, who knew as well as I the history of these brothers and were (I think) hoping for a slice of melodrama: a cry of regret, a swoon that would tell its own tale; but it never came.

Instead, with that curious combination of fragility and strength that has always characterized the better qualities of the Catts family (though not so often the younger son), he just paused there a moment, then spoke aloud in a voice that was so familiar, so unexpectedly beloved, that it brought a sharp pain to my eyes, and for the first time that day, hot tears.

For with his unerring instinct, his old Gabe magic, he managed to hit dead rock center at the heart of our awful loss with five grieving words: "*God,* he looks like Daddy."

— 2 —

Now, their Daddy was a yard man and mechanic and a turpentine worker; that, and a whole lot more. He was also a friend to me, and more than a friend: the man I named my first son after, who surrounded me with a light of love when I was a child, a light so bright and shining that I think I've lived my whole life trying to regain it. And though the memory of my own father has been almost completely obliterated by the long march of meds and depression and brain-burning mania, I can remember Mr. Simon to the last hair on his head, even though I was only nine when I met him, that first day on the Hill.

It must have been sometime in the summer of '59, after a cousin got Daddy a job at the local Greyhound bus station doing odd jobs and light maintenance, a position he thought beneath his skill as a first-class shade-tree mechanic that he only took in the hope that it might one day work into a good-paying job as a driver. After two years, it proved to be a hope as false as any other dream he ever entertained, but that was fortunately not so apparent when we climbed out of the city cab that first Sunday on the Hill, all dressed up in our Easter best because Mama was church-born herself and knew the importance of a good first impression.

We had come by bus from New Orleans and expected to meet Daddy at the curb, already unpacked and waiting, as he'd left the previous Monday in a borrowed truck. When Mama found the driveway vacant, the house empty, she had no choice but to fall back on the auxiliary plan given by Daddy in case of emergency: to wait by the fence till he got there.

And that's just what we were doing, standing bare-headed in the scalding July sun, Mama tired and worried, starting at every sound, trying to keep Ira in hand. It was a full-time job on the best of days, the excitement of the trip making him bounce up and down like a red-headed, sixty-five-pound Mexican jumping bean, putting a little more strain on Mama, who kept snapping at him to keep still.

"Your Daddy'll be here," she kept saying, meaning: "You better behave or you know what's coming."

Because even then, when Ira must have been all of ten, the beatings were commonplace and most of Mama's maternal resources were spent separating him from Daddy's wrath. It was the very reason we ignored the shelter of the empty porch and waited so obediently on the curb of the dirt road beyond the gate, because Daddy wasn't fond of disobedience, and all of us knew it. We didn't see any sign of life in the closely packed row houses that marched like dominos, straight up the hill, all with their deep yards and trailing oaks and identical porch swings.

I was standing there wondering what kind of ghost-town this place was, when people finally started coming home from church in old beat-up trucks and sagging cars and more than a few on foot, and though we were standing in full view of the street, none of them gave us so much as a nod. Being fresh from rural Louisiana, where the sin of *not speaking* was grounds for assault, we were unsure of what to make of this big-city snobbishness, Ira returning to Mama's side, trying to get out of the sun by standing in her shade, when a big shiny beetle-shaped Buick pulled into the front yard of the house next door.

With a mighty banging of doors, it disgorged an amazing crowd: four adults, at least, along with a backseat packed with children ranging from a blonde, half-grown girl, to a boy Ira's age with a fat cherubic face and a curling crew cut, dressed in black Sunday pants and a white dress shirt that had come untucked and hung out the back almost to his knees. And in all that strolling, parking, coming-up crowd, he was the only one who made an effort to speak, ambling across the yard with his hands in his pockets, his eyes on Ira, giving him the once-over, then calling across the fence in a curiously high, rolling voice: "Yawl looking at Miss Floyd's house? I wouldn't live in Miss Floyd's house. She died right ther, had her funeral ther and all. Coffin right in the living room, saw it with my own eyes."

He evoked this pronouncement with great relish, then stood there, hands in pockets, waiting for Ira's response. But poor Ira had spent most of his life in virtual isolation on Grandma's farm and was just too overcome to answer, standing, for once, perfectly still, unable to believe that this boy, this car-owning, city-bred boy was actually taking an interest in him, being friendly, calling, "You don't bleve me? Ast my Mama, she'll tell you. She died in the kitchen, fell out on the flo. Mama's the one what found her, you ast her —"

Someone next door — a woman — began calling, "Gabe? Gaabe!"

But he ignored her with no effort at all, his eyes still on Ira, still talking. "Took her out, she's stiff as a board. Michael heped, said —"

"Gabe!" This time, the voice was from the porch, where a young man, still dressed in church pants, but down to a T-shirt and bare feet, came to the top step and called, "Mama says come on, time to eat!"

Now I don't remember much about the boy on the steps, just that he was barefoot and already down to this T-shirt, simply because he was so old, fourteen or fifteen, a man by our reckoning, and therefore outside the realm of my child's world. Besides, he was not nearly as interesting as the little boy with the crazy eyes and pokey hair who was patiently ignoring everyone but my beloved brother, *still* engaging him in the fascinating history of the house we were about to spend the night in: "— she'd got kinda gray in the face, you know, like dead people git —"

"*Gab-riel!*" The young man shouted, and this time he managed to break the spell of the snapping eyes.

The little boy turned and shouted back in what was to us, brilliant, outrageous defiance. "*What?*"

"Time to *eat!*"

At this, the little boy turned and left without a word, running across the yard and up the steps, pausing there as if in afterthought, hollering back to Ira, "Be back in a minute!"

When he was gone, the whole neighborhood settled back to its flat sabbatical calm, the foot traffic dropping off, the old moss-hung oaks massive and silent. Mama walked down to the corner to see if she could get a glimpse of Daddy and the truck, leaving us there at the fence, Ira still in patent shock from the onslaught of interest from the little boy with the crazy eyes, and me beside him so glad, so horrifically glad, that he'd found something to hold onto at last.

Because no one knew better than I what kind of real flesh-and-blood hell my brother lived and breathed every stinking day of his life, and for a moment there, a pencil-thin breath of life had stirred the flat, July malaise with something so comforting we didn't have a name for it yet. Whatever it was, we were immediately intrigued, keeping our eyes on the porch next door till the little boy returned a half hour or so later, dressed in what we would come to recognize as his summer uniform: a big white T-shirt, knee-length cut-offs, and a Timex wristwatch he'd won in a Bible drill at VBS.

He came back to the fence with no word of greeting, just picked up where he left off in that fast, curious voice, his eyes back on Ira. "They had to wait sa long to bury her 'cause they couldn't get in touch with none of her people," he said. "Mama called and called."

The screen door next door slammed again, and the young man who'd called him in for dinner headed down the street in the opposite direction, a baseball glove under his arm. When he was a little way down the road, he turned and called, "Gabe? Wanna come?"

But the little boy didn't so much as blink, still talking to Ira, wrinkling his nose, saying, "Said they shouldn't have made 'em wait sa long, thet the body was gone start stinking, they didn't git it in the ground soon —"

"*Gabe!*" he shouted, and seeing he wasn't making any progress, he bent down and lobbed a pebble in our direction that bounced off the back of the little golden head without any noticeable reaction.

"— and ain't thet just the *nastiest* thang you ever heard of in yo life?" he was saying. "Our dog Wally died oncet —"

That's when Ira finally had to speak, interrupting him to say, "Thet man over ther thew a rock at you."

"What?" the little boy asked.

Ira pointed over his shoulder. "Thet man over ther thew a rock at you. There," he said, as another one bounced off the back of the little boy's head, "he done it agin."

With one hand feeling the back of his spiky little half curls, the little boy turned and looked behind him. "Thet ain't no man," he murmured in a flat, amazed voice. "Thet's my brother Michael."

"You comin?" Michael asked for the third time, and finally got his answer, a wave of the boy's hand and an impatient, "Lea' me alone!"

Ira and I were amazed at this curt dismissal, but his brother just turned and went his way, leaving the rude little boy to return to the subject at hand. "He got the distemper, died right ther under the porch. Michael had to climb under ther and pull him out and he was stinking, *Lawd.* Covered with maggots and stiff as a board, his legs all shooting out like this here —" He stuck his arms in the air to demonstrate. Then, with no by-your-leave from anyone, he climbed over the wobbly, field-wire fence into our front yard, saying, "Come on. I'll show you where the coffin was."

Now, Ira knew good and well we weren't supposed to step foot in that yard till Daddy got there, but the boy's infectious excitement was too much to resist. With one nervous glance down the road, he vaulted the gate, me two steps behind, shouting, "Mama'll be back, Ira. She'll be *back.*" By which I meant: "Daddy's expected down that road sometime today and if he comes up while you're over there, then you know what you're in for and you ain't healed up good from the last time."

But it was no use; the incredible pull of the snapping eyes and the persuasive voice was too strong. Ira was blocking me out like he did sometimes, though the boy Gabe glanced at me from the porch and asked, "Who's she?"

His question caught poor Ira off guard. For a moment there he was in an agony of indecisiveness, running his eyes back and forth between Gabe and me, trying to feel out the right response. I was his sister, of course. Both of us knew that, but we also knew that the truth wasn't always what people wanted to hear, and the secret of civil conversation was to somehow discern what you were supposed to answer before the question was put to you, then supply that answer with all politeness and speed. Ira was unbelievably skilled at this and could usually come up with the correct answer either by simple experience, or reading body language. But there was nothing to the little boy's position, squatted there next to the window, to give him any clues, and since they'd just met, there were no historical precedents to go by, so he was at a dead loss of what to say.

"She your sister?" he asked, and Ira nodded quickly, then smiled in one careful flash, unsure if having a sister was an asset or not.

The boy seemed satisfied with the answer, though, just returning to the window and continuing his monologue. "See? Right in yonder by the fireplace. Had some kind a spell with her heart, Mama didn't find her till she missed church —"

I climbed down off the fence, for there was nothing more I could do. Ira was blocking me out with such completeness that I figured I might as well stay in the road, where I could at least shout a warning when I saw Mama coming. Which I did, almost immediately, and there were chill bumps on my arms when I did it, because Mama wasn't on foot this time, she was driving the old roped-together truck Daddy had driven off in six days ago.

I couldn't see *him* anywhere, in the cab or on the truck bed, but then again, I wasn't looking too hard, just running back to the fence and hopping up on it, shouting for Ira to *come on,* they were *here, Ira! They were here!*

But he'd moved around to the back porch for a better view of the kitchen, and I was unable to get anyone's attention except Mama, who bought the truck to a lurching halt and jumped out. "Where's Ira?" was the first thing she asked, though all I could do was point around back and make inarticulate little noises of explanation. "— boy next door — woman died — little boy — right ther —"

But that's all I could get out, because Daddy was suddenly there, too, jumping off the flat bed of the truck into the street; and before I'd seen him, before I smelled him or heard his voice, I knew he was mad. It came before him like heat on a dry summer breeze, making my words evaporate into the white-hot sky as he began untying the sharp wire that held all our worldly goods in precarious balance on the back of the truck, talking to himself in a low hum of bad temper (*"Stupid no good piece of shit —"*) like he did when he was mad, suddenly looking up at Mama, snapping, "Where's Ira?"

And Mama didn't even blink before she took all that incredible humming violence on herself, saying very lightly, "I sent him 'round back —"

"Did *what?*" he breathed, stopping and staring at her.

She began repeating herself vaguely, wiping her face with the back of her hand, but he ignored her, drawing back as if to hit her, but backing off, his low hum of self-hatred briefly rising high enough to decipher a thin edge of its torment ("— *stupid damn woman got no damn sense* —").

That's when I heard them, right behind me in the yard, Ira and the boy Gabe. They were coming back around the house, their steps preceded by the boy's high, funny voice that cut through the stale heat with its light steady chatter.

"— me and Benny and Albert'll go down and show you tomorror — you gone live here and all —"

Daddy didn't even speak. He just turned, slowly, and when Ira saw him standing there beyond the gate he had been forbidden to enter, there was no reaction at all on my brother's face. This wasn't by mischance, nor was it carelessness, but another concerted effort to give the correct reply. Because Daddy hated fear, would not tolerate it in any of us, and when he was as close to the edge as he was now, any response at all was considered back talk, justifying a backhand to the face.

Ira had lost a few baby teeth from just such cause and effect, and stopped instinctively at the corner of the porch, though the boy Gabe didn't have any better sense than to keep walking, right up to the fence, holding out his hand to Daddy like he was a grown man, saying, "Hey, how're you? I'm Gabriel William Catts, I live right ther next door. My grandaddy's a preacher, thet's his car right ther. Paid six-hundret dollars for it but the bank's gone take it 'cause he cain't make the payments. Lost his church for running around with a woman."

All that in one breath, his fat little hand stuck out over the fence to Daddy, his eyes wide and light in the sun, crazy as a bedbug. I'll remember it to my dying day. Daddy just stood there, staring at his hand, we all did, till a crack of the screen door next door distracted us, and a small, fine-boned man, also down to dress pants and a T-shirt, came down the steps toward us. He was so small that I mistook him for another brother till the little boy saw him and began introducing him in a loud, carrying voice.

16

"Here comes my Deddy. That's my Deddy right there, Simon William Catts — see, that's him right ther."

"*Hush*" was the first thing he said when he made the fence, holding his hand over the wire to Daddy for a shake, his voice so low and flat and country that we were all suddenly relieved to have found one of our own.

"Simon Catts," he said. "Sorry I ain't had a chanch to speak, wife's got some family bidness brewing, she's kindly upset."

"That's what I hear," Daddy answered, tipping his head to Gabe, who was standing next to Ira, his hands deep in his pockets, rocking back and forth on his heels, his voice a clear, confidential murmur: ". . . run around with a woman name Ilene Corbin. Big, fat woman, with titties out to here."

He held his hands a foot or so from his chest to demonstrate, and poor Ira, his face was a study in disbelief. Around our house, words like titty were considered rank profanity and punished accordingly, and here this crazy child stood, talking like that right in front of me and Mama, till his Daddy pointed a quiet finger in his face.

"Gabe? Son?" he asked. "Am I gone have to take a belt to you?"

This dampened his spirits a little, causing him to shuffle his feet and murmur *nosir,* and I think all of us Sims were relieved that in this strange yard in a strange town in a strange state, there was at least one set of good country neighbors who expected their children to behave.

"Why dontchu climb on thet truck and make yo'sef useful?" he told him, sending both the boys climbing like monkeys up like the side of the piled-up truck, wrestling with the ropes, laughing and talking. Once she was properly introduced, Mama took the keys from Daddy and went inside to look around, and I found myself abandoned there at the fence with the menfolk, listening to their men-talk.

"— down to the Greyhound Station," Daddy was saying of his new job. "Nothing much to start with, but my wife's cousin's a driver, that's what I'm shooting for. The hours ain't good, but the pay sho is."

Mr. Catts stood a little slouched on his back leg, his arms folded over his chest, smiling and agreeable. He said, "Good for you," with no trace of jealously, no sign of doubt. I was finely attuned to Daddy's shifting moods, and could detect a tiny thawing, a flicker of solid hope as he aired his dreams and had them confirmed and accepted by this man, this stranger who owed him nothing. Suddenly, the afternoon was full of promise, the sun finally dipping behind the treeline, enveloping all of us in its cool, damp shade. I could smell it all around us, lush and green. Someone was frying chicken nearby; I could smell that, too, taking big breaths of it when our neighbor finally noticed me, interrupting Daddy to ask, "And who's this sweet girl?"

Daddy wasn't annoyed at the interruption, because contrary to some historical accounts, he wasn't a beast with 666 carved on his forehead, but just a tired, angry man, pleased with this attention to the child he was very proud of, indeed, as she was his virtual mirror, with the same oval face, the same dark, brick-red hair. With an effortless heave, he lifted me into his arms, then turned me a little to face the small man across the fence.

"This is Myra Louise," he answered in a proud, possessive voice, "my baby girl. Say hello to Mister Catts. He's yer neighbor now."

I obeyed instantly, my eyes on my feet, though as they resumed talking, I loosened up enough to cast our new neighbor darting looks of interest, instantly attracted to his gentle face, his flat drawl, the small winks and grins he threw me when our eyes chanced to meet. After a year in Metairie with Daddy, I was basically terrified of men — but not this one; and looking back, I can't really say why I dropped my defenses so quickly and completely, why I've so intricately tied my life with his children and his blood.

Was it because he saved my brother a beating that first afternoon with his outstretched hand and his flat country familiarity? Or because he stood there and gave my father a breath of acceptance, a small measure of belief, on a hot July afternoon?

I really can't say. All I know is this chance conversation over a pig-wire fence in the summer of '59 is one of the few memories I have of my father, whose face I cannot bear to remember in the world of reason and control. It stands alone, a persistent memorial to the unarguable fact that beyond the evil he was later to become, he was just a man after all, merely human, with hopes and dreams of his own, and maybe a few for the child he lifted in his arms and introduced with such love. Yes, love — in his hands, in his voice. It's the thing Gabriel forgets, the thing I must insist on remembering. Because how can you explain the depth of the pain and inhumanity into which we all eventually descended, unless you explain the love that came first, and how and why and to what end it died?

— 3 —

My presence in the yard that day —
indeed, my very presence on earth — was the fruit of that love, a love
born in the flat lands of southern Louisiana, a part of the South that is
so similar to west Florida, to me. Whenever I go back on my infrequent
visits, everyone I meet — the old men in the gas stations, the women in
the grocery stores, even the swarms of coffee-colored children playing
in the streets — all seem interchangeable with my west Florida neighbors, with the same poverty, the same Wal-marts, the same incomprehensible sweetness that always reminds me of Michael and his father.

Technically speaking, my own father, Leldon Cantril Sims, was born
west of the river in one of those cotton-growing hamlets that have long
since been reduced to railroad crossings and rural mail routes. I can't
imagine the circumstances of his early life, and since he died young, I
never had a chance to sit down and get the facts straight. He was a man
of rural habits till his death, so I assume he was raised on a farm, and
though he was obviously not Cajun (not dark-haired, that is), as a child,
I remember him speaking a musical, indecipherable language in a familiar, colloquial way, that many years later (when the K-Paul revolution hit
the *Today* show) I realized was Cajun French.

So perhaps there was some Acadian in him, or maybe it was just a legacy of a childhood on the bayou; I really don't know. Whatever his blood, from the evidence of his later life, I'd say his childhood was both brief and violent, and know for a fact that he was forced to leave the comforts of country life for the bright lights of New Orleans when he was still a boy, not yet fifteen. It was nearly a decade later that he wandered into the more accurately recorded history of the Edmonds family when he met my mother at a church homecoming in Sliddell. And though he was already the father of a child in Texas he didn't claim, with a bad marriage and a history of instability under his belt, the moment Mama laid eyes on him, she was in love (or so her sisters say), which wasn't difficult to understand, as my father was a very handsome man, with a sharp, almost feminine delicacy of features that was in odd contrast to his sheer, bulking size. I'd put him at six-three, maybe two hundred twenty pounds, with a high florid color and an overall look of virility, which was another of his quiet deceptions, because, I imagine, even then he was incubating the diabetes and alcoholism that would eventually kill him — though Mama didn't see it back then, not at all.

All she saw was a silky confidence and a way with women, along with that incalculable charm worldly men can sometimes spin with sheltered Christian daughters, which my mother most assuredly was: a tall, red-haired Pentecostal girl, not plain, but not so beautiful either. At twenty-eight, she was still unmarried, and certainly not accustomed to the attentions of a man who'd been going through women since he was fourteen, and knew how to play them. What he saw in her, or any of the other women he was to eventually acquire and discard, I'll never know. I'm sure it was partially physical (there was a well-built body beneath those staid Pentecostal clothes) and maybe it had more than a little to do with her father's wide holdings and her trappings of holiness: her long skirt and longer hair and the elusive air of other-worldliness in her best feature — her smoke-blue, melancholy eyes. Or maybe it was love; I really don't know. Mama wasn't so generous with her own memories and never offered many details, though her sisters assure me it was a swift attraction and a church one, the wedding coming within four months of their introduction, officiated by a justice of the peace, as her own Assemblies of God preacher wouldn't marry a divorced man.

Now, I remember my maternal grandparents very well, her more than him (he died when I was seven) and it's one of those insoluble mysteries that they, pillars of their local church, would allow their daughter to marry a man with such a past, that as far as I can tell, he was never at much pains to conceal. I can only attribute it to the particular charm my father must have wielded (the same charm my brother wields to this day) and can commiserate with them when, a few months after the wedding, they took in their pregnant daughter and kicked out their son-in-law with the request that he never again darken their door.

I don't know the offense; but he was a drinker and a womanizer and a hell-raiser to boot, so the possibilities are endless. It was only after his first (legitimate) son was born that he came back briefly, and after a change of heart that entailed a reconversion and a public repentance, was allowed back in the family bosom just long enough to get Mama pregnant again, with me. He was gone again shortly after, doing time in Angola, I hear, though no one is so open about the exact nature of his offense. Robbery is the most popular theory, though assault would be closer to the mark, and I know for a fact that it was in fear of his expected release that my grandfather kept a loaded shotgun beside his bed every night of his life.

Whenever Ira and I would ask him about it, he'd make a joke of it for our benefit, saying he was *too old to fight and too proud to run,* and it wasn't until after he had died in the summer of '57 that Daddy dared show his face again on the family farm. I remember his homecoming to this day. It was late autumn, the crop pulled, place achingly vacant without Grandaddy around, Grandma talking of selling out and moving to town. Ira and I were shocked at the possibility, for the farm and the river were our home, leaving it, unthinkable. We knew every square inch of the place, from the attic under the rafters that served as our bedroom to the storm house and the flood waters and the corn crib, where we'd play soldier day and night in imitation of the father we never knew, who we'd once heard was a soldier. It was from a cousin we'd gleaned this bit of knowledge that Mama didn't deny, even contributing the name of the place he'd served: *Benning.*

For all we knew, Benning was a country in Europe, a theater of war of world-shaking proportions, and we were high in the loft of the barn that day, parachuting with an old rain slicker into what was left of Grandpa's winter hay, when we realized there was a well-dressed, city-looking man standing in the door below, watching us. We thought he was a drummer at first and sailed down eagerly to check his wares, though he didn't have the quick, solicitous smile of the traveling sales-man. He just leaned in the doorway like he owned the place, looking us up and down, asking Ira, "Whatchure name, *boy?*"

Ira must have been eight or nine at the time, and though he only attended school when the rural buses were running, he was our undis-puted leader, and answered stoutly, "Ira Sims. Who're *you?*"

At this, our visitor threw his head back and laughed. Then with no by-your-leave from anyone, he picked me up by the waist and lifted me above his head, watching my face with curious, reddish-brown eyes that were light and speculative in the afternoon sun, murmuring, "Then this must be Myra Louise."

"Put her *down!*" Ira yelled. During his last illness, Grandaddy had handed the mantle of man-of-the-house down to him, and he took his duties seriously, kicking at the stranger's leg, shouting, "Let'er go. We ain't wanten nothing, just move on."

But the drummer didn't so much as blink, just turned and headed for the house with me in his arms, Ira in hot pursuit, still calling, "Hey! I said put her down!"

He punctuated his words with a kick when he could get one in, though at sixty pounds, he wasn't so effective. He finally gave up when we made the yard and ran ahead to the front door, shouting for Mama to come out, come out right now, this minute!

Mama came in less than a hurry, for Ira was excitable by nature and given to calling her out a dozen times a day on some excuse or another. But this was the real thing, and she came to a perfect halt when she saw us on the porch: Ira, red-faced and prancing, Daddy just standing there with me in his arms, though I wasn't so worried anymore.

For I'd begun to see a resemblance here, and spoke into the sud-den silence with a thin little voice: "Are you his Deddy?"

I meant, was he Ira's Daddy, because that was the clue: they looked so much alike. He just laughed at my question and lifted me effortlessly above his upturned face. "I shore am, baby," he said. "Yours too, or yer

Mama here's got some fast explainin to do."

Ira was struck as dumb as Mama at the pronouncement and went inside the screen to stand next to her, his face no longer red, but pale and bothered, his hand reaching up to grasp the hem of her apron, like he used to do when he was a little boy.

"Leldon," Mama said, her face perfectly immobile till Grandma came to the hall and stopped dead still, speaking quietly to her back.

"I'll call Lacy," she said, meaning the hired man, who was as good and fast as a telephone when you wanted to relay a quick message to town to, say, the sheriff or doctor or preacher. But Mama didn't answer. She only watched Daddy's cocky, knowing smile through the screen, one hand flat against Ira's bony chest, one on the door, then shook her head slowly. "No."

That's about as far as I remember, and it's just as well, because that one-word answer on the porch that October pretty much irrevocably changed the course of all our lives. For though Mama didn't give in to him so easily this time, she did start seeing him again, waking us the morning of Christmas Eve with the incredible news that we were moving into town.

"Your Daddy, he's got him a job," she told us, sitting on the foot of the bed in her old winter robe. It was a sunny December morning, the radiance in her face making her very beautiful as she sat there, her hair no longer pulled back in tight Pentecostal braids, but curled and pinned around her head, like the women you saw in New Orleans. The sun behind it cast it in a golden, copper glow that made her look transformed, angelic.

When I told her so, she lifted my bare foot and kissed it, her face full of that soft, exulting kindness as she continued her fast run of news. "At the Ford place," she said, "as a mechanic. The house is just around the corner, right next to the drugstore. You two can go there after school every day, buy you some candy."

On this wondrous bit of news, she stood up and straightened a hairpin, told us that she and Daddy were going Christmas shopping in the city, but she'd be back before supper, for us to mind Grandma. "She's feeling poorly," she said, dropping her eyes, embarrassed.

You couldn't live in the house this past autumn without hearing their ongoing battles every night in the kitchen over Daddy, Grandma threatening to disown her, disinherit her, even whip her butt, if she kept seeing him.

But apparently, true love had won out, and I couldn't help but being excited, because I was secretly a little in love with my father, myself. I didn't see him too much at that point (Grandma would hardly let us leave the farm, as long as he was around) but was enchanted by the shower of presents he sent us by Mama: candy and ice-cream, even a toy or two.

I told her we'd be good, for it all sounded extraordinary, unbelievably wonderful to me, though Ira was a little less enthused, as he was Grannie's pet and had absorbed her prejudice. When Mama was gone, he told me in a quiet voice that he *drank*.

"Who?" I asked, and Ira was annoyed.

"*Him.* Our father."

Even then, I thought it an odd way to put it: not Daddy, but *our father*. But I was a fairly brainless child and tried to put a happy spin on it all. "But we'll be in town. You can walk to school, ride the streetcars. He'll be our *Daddy*."

But Ira was not to be placated, and that night when Mama returned, still flushed and lovely in a red wool coat her husband had bought her in town, he would not open his early present, nor speak to me when I opened mine. It wasn't until the next morning that he showed signs of thawing, after we burst downstairs and he found his Santa Claus present: a little camouflage soldier outfit, with a matching helmet and machine gun.

My own presents were something of a disappointment, the best of them a red winter coat, a miniature version of Mama's, with a matching hat. But I put aside my annoyance at being a girl, happy for Mama, who seemed to be fitting into the overall scheme at last, finally able to join her sisters on the porch after dinner and watch her children play with their toys, all of them equally gifted and fathered, no difference at all.

And though Daddy still couldn't show his face on the Edmonds property, he came by late in the afternoon and took us for a ride across the lake in a fire-engine red Cadillac. (I have no idea whose, still don't, to this day.) After that, even Ira capitulated, sitting in the backseat in his

little soldier outfit, chattering his head off like he did when he was excited, pretending to shoot dogs with his machine gun, even letting me
have a go with it a few times.

There was only one shadow of unease on the whole glorious day,
when we stopped for gas on the way to town. In those days, attendants
pumped your gas, but Ira was making such a racket that the deaf old
man at the Chevron Station couldn't hear Daddy's instructions to fill her
up. He told him once, twice, then, as the old man cupped his ear to the
window for the third round, Daddy reached over the seat and casually
backhanded Ira across the face in what looked like a light, playful strike
— deceptively light, as it sent him pinwheeling across the seat.

Ira sat up immediately, a little dazed. He'd been so busy running
his mouth that I don't think he realized what hit him, but I'd seen it, all
right, and was shocked. For though Ira had had his share of whippings
in his day, Grandaddy's were to the hind end with a belt, and at least
he'd tell you they were coming, while Daddy didn't so much as blink,
still talking to the attendant through the window, telling him to do the
windshield, too.

"Ira?" I began, reaching for his red cheek, though he pushed me
away, just sitting against the seat, strangely quiet, his eyes on the front
seat, on Daddy, I thought, though when I turned, I saw who he was looking at: Mama.

She was sitting there in her new red coat, staring at Daddy, her hair
still pinned around her head in those movie-star curls, though her face
was no longer full of that crush of good feeling, but tired, empty, much
older. So old she looked like Grandma had that morning when we
charged downstairs and ripped open our presents with such happy
abandon, her face above her starched apron blunted with an elusive
emotion that I could only now identify: hurt.

Simple raw hurt, though when Mama felt my gaze and looked at
me, she tried to smile, quickly, then dropped her eyes, and by the time
we made it home after a swing by the tiny house that was shortly to be
our new home, the moment had passed. Ira was back to *ra-ta-tatting*
out the window, Daddy laughing and sweet, Mama and I just sitting
there, a little quiet in the new coats that had thrilled us so much when
we'd first opened them, though now — now we weren't so sure.

$\mathcal{M}$*y childhood comes to me* in such a mosaic of fragmented pieces that it really is difficult to put a consistent voice to it. Sometimes things are so clear; sometimes blocks of months and even years have vanished without a trace, as that first year with my father in Louisiana has done. With a little effort, I can remember the day we moved into Metairie, finding a cracked Elvis record in a closet and turning it over in my hands, wondering if it would still play; and that, as they say, is it. Later, in the constant reclamation of childhood that is the life of the chronically therapied patient (the insured ones, anyway), I was able to reclaim a few more pieces of evidence, enough to surmise that my erasures were not without warrant.

But for all practical purposes, my life with my father began in a small town in west Florida just below the Alabama line, in an old mill neighborhood perched on a modest hill on what was once the far west end of town, known locally as Magnolia Hill. From what I can remember, in 1959 the Hill looked pretty much like it does today, except there were no trailers back then, and the houses were mostly white. The air of the place was rural, the yards planted fence to fence with all the time-honored favorites: azaleas and Rose-of-Sharons and the faithful old four o'clocks that even today in the Hill's decline still bloom along shaded back gates, tiny trumpets of lavender and yellow and white that fill the twilight with a piercing sweetness.

The grid of the streets was the same as it is today: the slow gradual climb from town, west past the Piggly Wiggly, then one block north to Welcome Baptist, and one last turn up Lafayette into the slanted yards and high porches that mark the easternmost border of the old neighborhood. The fences, now chain-link, were all wire back then, field-wire and kudzu, and the trees — well, the trees were simply magnificent: cupped-leaf live oaks with forty-foot spreads, and magnolias so old they stood fifty feet or more, some straight as pillars, some ornately twisted, like the leg of a Victorian vanity. These, along with the pecan and soft camphor, made up the canopy of our world, while all along the fence-lines and ditches, the mimosa grew like weeds in graceful clusters, huge and drooping, their fronds full of furry pink blossoms or long curling seed pods that would dry out by summer's end and shake in the wind like a thousand timorous rattles. The trees of Magnolia Hill: beautiful all. For many years, they were my most lasting sensory memory of what came to be the death scene of my abbreviated childhood. Even after much of my life there had sunken away into the dark corners of my mind, I'd walk under a spreading live oak and say aloud, without thought: *"Smells like Magnolia Hill."* Not in regret or loathing, but simple perplexity at the contradictions in that brief stab of memory: the smell of Eden, the heart of hell; the cool damp shade, the pound of a fever climbing at twilight; the clenched-teeth fury of my father, and my brother's quiet voice rising above the darkness of a warm, mimosa-scented night.

"— but Miss Ryan says I can make it up," he'd tell me, in those early innocent days when we still shared a bed in the front bedroom off the porch, "Mama says she'll hep, but I don't care. Gabe says I should just skip it, says he sho ain't learned nothing in sixth grade — fifth, neither."

He'd talk with his hands intertwined under his head, his face on the ceiling, sometimes breaking into a smile, but usually just reflective as he told me news of the broader world, interlaced with pieces of sound brotherly advice. "I'd git thet hair cut if I'se you. Nobody in town wears them ole country-looking braids. Gabe says I act like I was born here.

Said you couldn't tell I was country except for the way I talk."

Gabe says. It was the chorus and the refrain of his every breath, the sheer repetition a little wearing, though I will admit I was fascinated by the strangeness of the name that Ira said was incorrect, that his *legal* name was *Gabrielle,* but he didn't like it because it was a girl's name. I knew nothing of feminine spellings, or for that matter, the angels he and his brother were named for, but did like the sound of the name, *Ga-bri-elle,* that rolled gracefully off the tongue, a name as exotic and unfathomable as the funny-talking little boy who owned it, who, for all the love of my brother, had taken an inexplicable dislike to me, early on.

I'm sure it had its roots that very first day, after his planned overnight excursion to the graveyard to show Ira Mrs. Floyd's grave failed to materialize after I mentioned it to Mama, who made it plainly known that Ira would have no part in such an expedition. Ira was disappointed, but Gabe, he was *furious,* and for the first year we lived on the Hill, I doubt he spoke a civil word in my direction, going so far as to forbid me to walk along with him and the other boys to school every day when classes started in September.

From what I could make of my brother's new idol, he wasn't a spiteful child, but if he had set out to create a lasting punishment, he could not have hit on a better one, for I was terrified of walking alone after Mama had sat me down the night before school started and given me the standard mother/daughter lecture about *perverts.* I guess she thought it a necessary precaution since I'd lived most of my life on a secluded farm, and Magnolia Hill was (in her eyes, anyway) little more than a mill slum. But her careful words went far beyond her intent, waking a living fear that made the moss-hung, six-block stroll into town an exercise in agony.

My palms sweated, my heart beat like a drum in my throat as I stopped every third step, looking over my shoulder, sometimes catching a glimpse of movement and breaking into a dead run. I mean, I *knew* the man in the trench coat was out there waiting for me. I could feel his eyes, hear his footstep at my back, and desperately tried to stay close to Ira, to find some shelter in his bony arms, but this Gabe-boy would not allow it.

"Gabe says," Ira tried to explain in the privacy of our bed, "that girls doan walk with boys."

I was probably already a little schizoid by then, and shy to the point of being physically mute, so I had no words to beg, no way to describe the awful, gut-level certainty I had that there was a shadow at my back, a man dodging behind the trees, waiting with hideous patience to catch me alone. All I could do was press my hand to my mouth and cry noiselessly, a habit Ira, who never cried, never, even when he was showing blood, found mighty annoying.

At first, he wouldn't talk to me, just turned aside in disgust, saying, "You are just such a sissy, and you're spoiled. Gabe says you're spoiled. Miss Cissie does too, spoiled *rotten.*"

But I was entangled in a fear worse than anything mere ugly names could dispel, and after a while, he'd soften, turning back suddenly, saying, "It ain't they don't like you, sister. You're just a *girl* is all. Boys doan walk with girls, cain't you see that? Myra? Are you all right?"

I could only shake my head and let the tears fall in silence, and though he couldn't see them in the darkness, he could feel the bed shake, and after a moment, offered a crumb of hope.

"Maybe," he said cautiously, "I'll ast Gabe if you can follow us, just behind. Then if a dog gets after you, I'll be right there — Okay? Myra?"

I slowly released my mouth, feeling a sharp, exhausting relief in this faint possibility. Ira felt for my face in the darkness and when he found I was no longer crying, was kinder. "Sure, I'll tell him tomorrow. I know you're scared of thet old bulldog. I doan blame you. Thet old dog ain't worth shooting. Gabe says Old Man Dailey doan feed him, thet's why he's so mean."

Without giving it a second thought, he went on to fill the night spaces with more talk of the wonderful world outside our fence, content to put a harmless name to my fears: a mean dog. My relief was profound, because mean dogs could be run off. Or cut, or shot, or poisoned. Mean dogs were controllable, and when Gabe grudgingly allowed me to creep along a block or so behind his entourage of friends, my worries were sidetracked for another small breath of peace, and I was able to pick up the pieces of my life there on the Hill.

It wasn't a bad life, not at first, from what I remember. Compared to Ira, who had the run of the town, my own life was pretty limited, not because of Daddy's instability, but rather Mama's reaction to that instability. As he was passed over, time and again, for a driver's position, he grew darker and more morose, making Mama instinctively draw me closer to her side, the practical result being that except for the daily walks to school, I was not allowed outside our yard; though it was a nice yard, I will admit.

All the houses on the north side of Lafayette were variations on the twenties-era row house, ours a simply constructed four-square shotgun house, four rooms straddling a long hallway that opened onto a small, slope-roofed kitchen that had probably once been detached from the house, Cracker-style, but was now an enclosed portion of the back porch. It was older than the other houses on Lafayette, with outdoor plumbing and a backyard that sloped down to a mimosa-lined drainage ditch that was very creeklike to my child's eyes, holding water most of the year, and during rainy season, transformed into a virtual river, full of frogs and watersnakes and small heronlike birds that stalked its swampy margins.

Most of my days were spent down by that water, building dams or floating leaves or catching frogs, my only outside contact our neighbor across the fence, Mr. Simon, everyone called him, who'd come home from work by way of the tracks and sometimes catch me at my daydreams and call over something pleasant. I was too shy to even look at him at first, though as the weather cooled toward winter, I grew to look forward to the late afternoons when he would come up in his old work clothes, a lunch box under his arm, usually alone, though his older son Michael was sometimes with him.

Almost seven years my senior, Michael seldom spoke and never stopped, though Ira filled me in on the glorious highlights of his wonderous life: how he worked at Sanger and dated a homecoming queen and pitched for the All-Stars, details that only made him more inaccessible to my small back world. I much preferred his father, who had no claim to fame and made no bones about it. Who worked at the bank at the time, though when I asked him where they kept the money down there, he just laughed "Oh, sister, I wouldn't know nothing about thet. I'm the janitor. I sweep floors for a living."

That was basically what Daddy did down at the bus station, though God knows he wasn't so lighthearted about it, always going on and on about his boss-man having his boot on his neck. I much preferred Mr. Simon's easy acceptance of life's inequities, and under his good-natured attention, fairly blossomed, waiting for him every day by the creek, then chattering away as fast and mindlessly as Ira, showing him my braids that he always admired, for true to her Pentecostal roots, Mama had a genius for weaving hair. Every morning she sat me down in the kitchen and produced one of an endless variety of braids: reverse; fishtail; Dutch; and the old standby, the simple French plait.

"Well, they're shore purty, sister," he'd always conclude, standing up straighter and giving me his nightly advice to stay out of the water and watch for snakes. "Place is full of 'em."

I sometimes wondered, even then, if he were speaking of the actual little water snakes the boys sometimes fished from the ditch in rainy season, or of Daddy, who had lost the confidence of the neighborhood early on, after he welshed on a few bets down at the burn barrel and beat a much younger man in a fight that had deteriorated to eye-gouging and left his opponent partially blind. That alone was enough to damn him in the sight of our neighbors, that and the ongoing evidence that could be seen any time my mother chose to show her face outside the house: the black eyes, the cut lips, the fist-sized bruises she grew so shy of excusing that she became, as surely as me, a prisoner of our yard, even foregoing church to sit home and listen to services on the radio.

That in itself was enough to seal Daddy's fate as far as public relations went, though I was still loyal enough to ignore the possible implications of Mr. Simon's warnings and drop my face to my feet to murmur "Yessir."

"Good girl." He'd smile and be off, leaving me there at the fence, watching him disappear into the house next door with considerable curiosity, and more than a little envy.

From the outside, the Catts' house was hardly different from the back of our own, a broad back porch that opened onto the kitchen that was always lit that time of night, letting out indescribably good smells of ham and chicken and frying bacon, though it wasn't the food that fascinated me as much as the talk, the movement, the quick laughter.

Sometimes I'd catch a glimpse of Ira over there, his face silhouetted against the light; sometimes it was the daughter Candace I watched.

Even a year older than Michael, she was surely outside the sphere of my closed-in world, though from Ira I heard snippets of *her* wonderful life: how she was a majorette for the football team, dated a boy who owned a car, wanted to be a nurse. The driveway next door pulled around to the back of the yard, and many evenings, while I stood there watching from beyond the fence, her boyfriend would come by to pick her up for a date or a football game. I'd stand there, mesmerized, as she came out the back door, usually hidden in a coat, but sometimes to my everlasting joy, sequined and booted in her little golden majorette uniform, baton in hand.

On at least one occasion, she came out to the fence to say goodbye to her father when he'd paused after work for our little chat at the fence. He returned her kiss easily, told her to be home by ten.

"What if the game's late?" she asked.

He only looked at her. "Ten."

With a roll of her eyes, she was gone, her little brown legs prancing across the yard, setting the tassels on her boots bobbing up and down in a way that made me literally pale with envy. Mr. Simon must have seen something of awe in my face when he turned back to me, as he lifted his face good-naturedly, and asked, "Are you gone be a majorette when you grow up, Myra Louise?"

He sometimes asked me that: *what was I gone be when I grow up?* — a question I found so unanswerable that I really thought it a riddle I was too dumb to figure out. Me? Myra Sims? Grow up? In reply, I'd just look at him blankly, sometimes slowly shake my head, knowing such a life — not just the baton and the sequins and the tasseled boots, but the whole air of relaxed gaiety I saw across the fence — was far beyond me, beyond anything I could possibly aspire to.

He'd always seem bothered by my blank certainty, his smile fading, saying, "Sure you will, sister."

I desperately wanted to agree with him, but his aura of kindness allowed me the unheard-of luxury of dissent, and I'd just stand there, shaking my head, quite unaware of the message I was sending. Having no idea that my little shrugs and occasional bruises (nothing like Ira's, I can tell you that) were being closely regarded by the small man across the fence, till a matter of months later, when summer was once again upon us.

School was finally over, the little ditch full of water, and Ira just as full of life, for after six months of impassioned pleading, Mama had finally allowed him to join himself with the Baptists at the little corner church the Catts attended. *Welcome* Baptist, it was called, and though none of them seemed so *welcoming* to me, treating Mama like a leper and gossiping about her on the porches at night behind her back, Ira pursued them relentlessly.

Once Mama gave him the word, he attended church with the zeal of the convert, going to Sunday School and church and even Wednesday nights, if Mama would let him. He even went down the aisle for salvation early in the summer to universal rejoicing, even from Mama, who generally looked down her Pentecostal nose at these *mere* Baptists and went out of her way to talk Ira out of the nonsense of Eternal Security.

Ira knew better than to argue, for since we'd left Grandma's, her sisters never wrote, never called, and we knew instinctively that the only thing Mama had left was her radio and her faith, and he wasn't about to attack it, taking care to center his conversion around Jesus, and Him alone. And though I personally suspected that the real deity he was worshipping four times a week down at Welcome was a figure of a little less respect, a mite closer to home, I kept my suspicions to myself, not at all enthusiastic when he told me the annual Sunday School picnic would soon be upon us.

"Down at Blue Springs," he said. "Gabe says I can go. Miz Cissie does, too."

He was so excited that I tried to be excited with him, and when the big day arrived, I remember what a *deal* it was, Mama packing him his own lunch, telling him over and over to be sure and keep his T-shirt on. "Or you'll get sunburned," she kept saying.

Ira assured her he would keep a T-shirt on and almost danced out of the house when they beeped the horn for him at nine. I followed him to the porch in my gown and watched the car pull away, packed with children and coolers, Mr. Simon at the wheel, and for the very first time, was washed in a small regret that I wasn't going too. But there was nothing for it; Mama wouldn't let me go so far as the gate, much less the springs, and I spent the morning kicking my heels off the back porch, wondering when Daddy would return, as he'd been gone for almost a week now, which was unusual.

As a rule, he only left us for days at a time, and at first, I hadn't been so eager to have him back, after he'd gone off on Ira so bad he'd nearly cried (unheard of). But with the first of the month upon us, even I knew the rent was due, and at the table, we were reduced to dry peas and cornbread. I was sitting there on the edge of the porch, remembering Ira's stories of Miss Cissie and the wonderful table she laid every day at dinner, chicken and ham and porkchops, when the slam of a car door next door roused me from my thoughts. I went around front to see who it was and was surprised to see it was the Catts, home early from the picnic. They were busy unloading coolers and children and lawnchairs, Ira coming over to use the outhouse, telling me en route that Miss Cissie was feeling poorly, so they'd come home early.

Miss Cissie, the mother of the bunch across the way, was something of a mystery to me at the time, as (I think) she was to all the inhabitants of Magnolia Hill. The youngest daughter of a well-known preacher, she'd spent her early years as belle of the ball out in the country at Piney Grove Baptist, till her tenth birthday, when her father had taken the helm of First Baptist, *downtown*. This wasn't a small feat, as the Baptists downtown were a snooty bunch, as quick to fire as they were to hire, but Brother Tierney had an overabundance of charm in the old-South, Panama-hat tradition, and kept them in line with equal shares of love and brimstone, lovingly applied.

In time, he might have moved his family on to bigger fish in Montgomery or Mobile, if rumor hadn't begun to circulate that some of his charm wasn't as innocent as all that. The whispers finally came into the light of substantiated fact the summer of his youngest daughter's thirteenth birthday, when a fair-haired member of the choir made a confession to her best friend that shook First Baptist to its very timbers. In short order, he was out, lock, stock, wife and seven children, though he quickly rebounded with a public repentance and a lesser congregation in the backwoods below Altha, preaching the mystery of grace to a noisy bunch of hard-shell Baptists.

That was where his youngest daughter decamped at the ripe old age of fifteen, running off with a former turpentine worker twelve years her senior without a penny to his name. It wasn't until all six of his daughters had married and his only son (Case, Cissie's fraternal twin) had taken a job at the heading mill that Brother Tierney took to wandering again. This time, it was with a banker's wife who liked him enough to keep him in Cadillacs and starched shirts till his wife finally tired of it and kicked him out, hats, suits and *Cruden's Popular Concordance.*

At that point, the Southern Baptist Convention turned him over to a reprobate mind and yanked his credentials, though he quickly acquitted himself with mail-order ordainment papers and over the next dozen or so years was in and out of pulpits all over the Panhandle. He held onto a few long enough to attract a following, and at one point even regained the wife of his youth, till he started dabbling in the waters of temptation again, abandoning casual adultery to settle on a full-time mistress, a big stylish woman who owned a hat shop on a back street, who made no secret of her lover's name and went so far as to send his outraged daughters Christmas cards every year. Of the six, only two remained in the area, the oldest, Maggie, and the baby, Cissie, who was the most tolerant of the bunch when it came to lending a blind eye to her father's wild and wicked ways, even allowing him to sleep on a pallet in the living room when he was between women.

Now, that was the factual history of the matter, that everyone, even the Sims, knew to be true, and had Cissie accepted her position as a sadly diminished, working-class housewife, she would have fit in well with all the other also-rans and might-have-beens on the Hill, but she couldn't. After all, she had ruled the poor but proud at Piney Grove, and even the snotty and elite downtown, and simply couldn't make the switch, running her tiny row house like a queen in a conjurer's spell, insisting on sit-down dinners and good china and fanatical attachment to the very Baptists who had spewed her father out with such a vengeance.

Like I say, it made her an oddity on the Hill, but a strong one that no one chose to cross, and as I watched her get out of the car the morning of the picnic, I thought that she did indeed look *poorly* as she made her way up their front steps, one hand blindly gripping the rail, one hand pressing a handkerchief to her face. Ira didn't seem too disappointed, though, having me rub aloe on his sunburned forehead that night in bed and asking me in a small, curious voice what *The State* was.

"The what?"

"*The State.*"

Well, I knew what a state was, but not *The* State, and he was thoughtful. "I'll ask Gabe."

He was out of bed bright and early the next morning and over the fence as usual, helping Gabe build an addition on the treehouse they'd been working on all year in the huge old live oak that nearly consumed the Catts' backyard. I just stayed inside with Mama, sitting at the kitchen table and spinning out a sorry breakfast of cornflakes and water, when there was a knock at the front door. It wasn't a soft, welcoming knock, but a sharp, *ra-tap,* that echoed through the empty house with a challenge that made Mama lift her face with a sudden wariness.

When I rose to answer it, she held out a hand to stop me. "I'll git it," she told me quietly, pushing me out onto the back porch, telling me to stay there till she called me in.

I went out easily enough and took a seat on the steps, looking out on the day that was wilting hot already at nine in the morning, the little ditch drying up in the July sun, soon to be reduced to just that, a ditch, the stalking heron long departed. I was sitting there wondering with a queasy roll of my stomach if it was Mr. Fischer at the door, come for the rent, when someone broke the morning stillness with a "*Hey.*"

Just like that, no particular emphasis, just "Hey," and I looked up to see my brother's idol standing there just across the fence, his light, hazel-colored eyes staring straight at me with a particular intensity. He didn't venture anything else, just stood there at the fence, absently rubbing his stubby little half-curls, and it came to me that he was trying to make amends for his past snottiness, but couldn't remember my name.

In the spirit of reconciliation, I hugged my knees to my chest and returned his greeting, piping over the fence, "Hey, Gabrielle."

He stopped dead still at that, and stared at me with that fixed earnestness that I had no way of deciphering, finally saying something about school, asking what grade I was in. I didn't answer, though, I couldn't, for even as we spoke, the whole texture of my world was changing right at my back, Mama coming to the door almost immediately, calling me inside, her voice harsh and frightened.

I came to my feet in an instant, thinking for one awful moment that it was Daddy, that the knock at the door was the sheriff, and he was back in jail, or drunk, or dead. But it wasn't as simple as that: it was *The State*. And as far as our life on the Hill was concerned, I guess you'd call it the beginning of the end.

$$= 5 =$$

*O*nce inside the house, it was obvious, just that quickly, that something truly horrendous was upon us, though the woman from the State was pleasant enough, sitting primly on the edge of the couch in a white polished-cotton suit with a little medical insignia on the lapel, like nurses used to wear, a notebook in her hand. Mama ushered me into the living room, then left to fetch Ira, and by God, took her time about it. He was just next door at the Catts, but she must have gone all the way to town, as the minutes ticked by, ten, then twenty, the lady from the State talking to me of inconsequential things, how old I was, how I was doing in school.

I can't imagine how I answered her. I spoke so little back then that people sometimes genuinely mistook me for a deaf-mute, so complete was my silence. But she was a trained social worker, after all, with all the whys and wherefores of investigation in her hands, and probably gleaned more from my express muteness than she did from Mama's careful words when she finally came in with Ira, a good half hour later.

It was a painful interview, I remember that much: Mama in her old grease-spotted house dress, Ira in the big white T-shirt he wore in imitation of his idol, me still in my summer gown, all of us nervously glancing around, trying to catch each other's eye. A whole world of unasked, unanswered questions circled our heads (*Who told? Did you tell?*) as we sat there making our little noises of excuse, till the social worker had enough of our evasions and shut her notebook, then politely requested that Ira lift his T-shirt so she could see his back.

Mama's face abruptly fell, then hardened as one of her questions had just been answered (the one about *who told*). But Ira wouldn't do it. It was as if this woman had asked him to disrobe. He crossed his arms and shook his head, his jaw clenched so tightly he looked startlingly like Daddy. When the nurse looked to Mama for support, she just twisted her hands and made some excuse about his going to the springs. Went to the springs with the *Church*, got a little sun burned, feeling poorly —

But, like I say, this woman wasn't wearing a suit for nothing, and with a particularly unblinking look at my mother, assured her that the shirt would be lifted, one way or another, even if she had to call the sheriff to accommodate it. Mama blanched at the mention of the Law, and chewing her lip nervously, told Ira to do as he was told. It's odd, because she left the room when she said it, just got up and walked out, leaving me and Ira there to fend for ourselves, Ira glancing at me, sending another of those fast, unspoken entreaties: *Should I?*

I gave him a small, sad shrug in reply; I just didn't know. His back wasn't such a big deal to me. I was the one who patted cold towels on it when it was fresh and scratched it later, when the welts finally healed and the scabs itched him to distraction. But Mama was always so careful about it, not letting him dress out at gym or go to the doctor, so who could say? He just stood there a moment, vacillating, then, with a roll of his eyes and sigh of enormous indignity, flipped his shirt over his head, facing me, but not meeting my eye, embarrassed at having to stand there like a cow at auction for The State to inspect.

There was an immediate silence in the room, Ira standing there with his face to the window, a picture of adolescent disgust, the nurse slowly sliding her little half-glasses up the bridge of her nose. At first, she just stared, the silence stretching out perhaps as long as a minute; then she touched his shoulder and told him he could drop his shirt. Ira obeyed instantly, then headed to the back door to resume his play in the treehouse. The nurse turned and told me to take off my gown.

Now, I was eleven at the time, and a mature eleven at that, a sad fact of life that was beginning to cause Ira and me both a little embarrassment in our bedroom, getting dressed and undressed for school every morning. Some people have a hard time believing it (my psychiatrist and my husband, to name two), but there was really nothing sexual in our relationship there, sharing a bed. It was a common enough necessity on the Hill, where some of the larger families slept a generation to a room.

But like I say, just lately there was a certain foreboding that times were changing, and I was modest to a fault, standing there looking at her in open-mouthed horror as she politely repeated her request — though Ira, he *exploded.*

"You go to *hell!*" he screamed, bounding back into the room, not attacking her physically, but honing in on her face, shouting, "You leave her *alone!*"

Mama came out in a flash, all dressed up in one of her church dresses I hadn't seen since we'd left Louisiana. She pulled Ira off the nurse the same way she sometimes pulled Daddy off Ira, shoving between them, finally getting the jist of the lady's request and telling her to take me to the bedroom. This was a little more private than the living room, but hardly an improvement, the nurse making me take off my gown and sit on the bed while she looked me over, top to bottom. She was kind enough about it, letting me wad my gown up over my chest and trying to engage me in small talk, asking if my hair was naturally curly, commenting on what an unusual color it was. But I wouldn't respond with so much as a nod, embarrassed at my worn old underwear and the seedy air of the bedroom, sad little tears trickling down my cheeks at the humiliation of it all, till she finally told me to get dressed, that we were going downtown.

The very word had a nasty ring to it: *downtown*, where the sheriff and the jail and the courts were. I dressed quickly, following Mama's lead and putting on my best dress, knowing we were going into battle here, a battle that was somehow connected to Ira, somehow a threat to him. I didn't even bother to braid my hair, but went out in a run, and as we trooped out to the gray car she'd double-parked out front, a few neighbors came out on their porches to watch our progress, their faces flat

41

and unblinking and somehow *satisfied.*

Mrs. McQuaig from across the street was there with one of her grown daughters, and next door, Miss Cissie stood at the porch rail with a handkerchief still clutched in her hand, her eyes on Mama, who met her gaze levelly. She didn't say a word till the nurse slammed us in the backseat and we were alone for a moment, when she quietly spat, "Baptist *snobs.*" Which was Daddy's pet name for our neighbors to the right.

Ira was more distressed by this dividing of his loyalties than anything this day had so far entailed, and all the way to town, he kept telling Mama in a low, desperate voice, "She ain't told, Mama. Miss Cissie ain't told."

But Mama wasn't buying, her face no longer so nervous, but hard and offended, not reassuring poor Ira, who kept up his parrot chatter all the way to the health department, repeating that same light whisper, as if he were talking to himself: "She ain't told."

The nurse drove us to the courthouse, where the pubic health unit was in the basement, down a long, dimly lit hallway lined with benches. She told Ira and me to wait outside while she took Mama into an office and closed the door behind her. We waited there all afternoon long, mostly silent, though Ira still occasionally murmured his defense of Miss Cissie ("Miss Cissie ain't told —"), as if I were arguing, turning once to abruptly ask why I'd called Gabe *Gabrielle.*

"What?" I asked, not remembering anything of the morning, after the humiliation with the nurse, and he was oddly insistent.

"This morning. On the porch. You called him Gabrielle."

"Oh." I remembered, and told him I thought that was his name, *Gabrielle William Catts.*

Ira made a face of great disgust, said, "No — that ain't — that's his *legal* name. His real name's Gabriel. Don't call him that other, he don't like it."

Well, it wasn't the first time I'd ever offended the little snot next door, and I just shrugged, thought no more about it. I was worried about the time they were taking with Mama and increasingly hungry, for I'd only had half a bowl of cereal that morning, and it was drawing on to four when a familiar voice echoed down the long hall.

"Hey! Ira!" it called. "Where's yo Mama?"

We came to our feet in an instant, for it was Daddy, striding down the hall toward us. He was all dressed up in his New Orleans clothes, shaved and cologned, his hair slicked back with water, looking like everything we weren't: confident, controlled, the very personification of power. I was never so glad to see anyone in my life and flew down the hall to meet him with Ira on my heels, both of us hitting him in a powerful embrace, yammering bits of explanation and accusation against the horror that had invaded our home.

"Made him take off his shirt!" I cried, giving in to tears at the sight of his face, which, despite my reservations, I'd been missing.

At my side, Ira echoed, "Told her to take off her gown. I told her to *go to hell!*"

Daddy didn't say anything, but just kept walking with both of us pressed to his side, his face not angry like he got around the house, but narrow-eyed and thoughtful as he stopped at the nurse's door and pounded on it with his clenched fist. The nurse opened it immediately, a little annoyed at the brashness of the knock till she saw Daddy standing there in his good suit and shined shoes.

I don't think she realized who he was at first. I think she thought for a moment that Mama had called a lawyer, for there was a flicker of deference on her face that Daddy neatly erased with his first calculated words that were not spoken in overt anger, but with a friendly, contemptuous venom. "Who the *fuck* are you? And where the *hell* is my wife?"

She flinched like he'd struck her, for casual profanity, especially with a professional woman in an office, was simply unheard of back then, and the f-word not so common outside men's circles, anyway. Even she, who'd withstood Ira's fury without turning a hair, wilted before it, glancing between Ira and me, still uncertain that this man, this well-dressed, good-looking man, was actually associated with such poor, trifling children; and Ira and I, we loved it.

"He's our *Deddy!*" we cried, our arms still circling his waist.

Mama must have heard our voices, for she also appeared at the door, a Kleenex in hand. Daddy just looked at her gravely over the nurse's shoulder, asked, "Eloise? What's this all about?" His voice was absent of the silky contempt he'd used to disarm the nurse, and intentionally so, making a clear distinction between them, showing her he knew how to talk to a *good* woman.

Mama, who God knows had heard that tone seldom enough in the last year, immediately warmed to it, sniffling, "Come by — come by this morning. Says they're taking Ira."

My glee at Daddy's appearance turned to ice at this, though Daddy just let go of us and stalked boldly into the office, said, "We'll see 'bout *that*."

And suddenly he was my hero again. He was the Man who'd show this witch a thing or two, Ira and I returning to our bench, grinning and relieved at his voice that was lifted in a righteous indignation that echoed down the vacant hall. They weren't in there long, and when they came out, he was still on top, opening the door for Mama and turning on the nurse, telling her to go ahead and call the sheriff; that he played poker with him every Saturday night, he wasn't scared of *him*.

The nurse, whose face had returned to its businesslike poise, assured him she would, but Daddy didn't so much as blink, only herded us down the hall, his voice still lifted in a loud, carrying wonder at the *cunts* the state of Florida hired to do their dirty work these days. Mama was recovered enough by then to chide him for his language, and he, cocky enough to take her reproof, excusing himself as we made our way outside into the soaking July sun, thrilling me to the bone by asking if we were hungry. I didn't know about Ira and Mama, but I was. I was starving to death, and we ended the afternoon in a booth in the drug-store, eating hamburgers and french fries and iced Cokes, the first meat we'd had in a month, and I could have eaten a dozen.

Ira, I think, did just that, but for once, his unending appetite didn't annoy Daddy, who sat across from us with his arm around Mama, full of the slick, Irish charm he could turn on when he was reprieved. He told Ira he was the Man for taking up for his sister, told me I should always wear my hair down, that I looked like Rita Hayworth.

Around and about this, he discussed the case, for true to his ex-con past, he was familiar with the ways and means of criminal investigation and repeatedly assured us that they didn't have a thing on him. Mama herself was quiet, not eating much, though Daddy was confident enough to stop by the sheriff's office on the way home to put in his two cents before that *bitch nurse* started making trouble. He apparently did have some sort of relationship with the sheriff, either due to his parole status, or maybe they did play poker together, for he saw him right away, leaving us in the lobby, Mama nervous and jumpy, Ira and I fascinated by the jail and the uniforms, sure Daddy could cut a deal.

But when he came out a few minutes later, he wasn't so cocky anymore; he was *mad*. It wasn't his usual mad, his slinging, slapping, spitting mad, but we were sensitive enough to his moods to *smell* it on him and reacted accordingly, backing off and going quiet, while the sheriff walked us to the door, his eyes on Daddy the whole time, saying, "You heard me, now, Leldon. You heard me."

So maybe they were poker buddies, after all, for the sheriff's tone was not pushy or abusive, just matter-of-fact. And though it was clear that his advice didn't sit too well with Daddy, he didn't make too much of a fuss, just shook his head and made a few more complaints about the nurse that the sheriff all but ignored, only looked him in the eye and repeated, "You heard me, now."

Whatever he'd heard we never knew exactly, though from the evidence of the next six months, it was clear that it was about keeping his nose clean and laying off the liquor, and above all, keeping his hands to himself. Apparently, the quiet little woman in the suit wasn't so easily cowed, and in the months and weeks ahead, we were to see a lot of her on surprise home visits where she'd always make Ira lift his shirt so she could inspect his back. He hated it, God knows he hated it, almost as much as he did the other consequence of her visits: that except for school and visits to the outhouse, he and I were to keep our butts strictly in the house.

This wasn't the nurse's edict, of course, but Daddy's solution to the problem of the nosy neighbors to the right. Either Mama had spilt the beans about the church picnic, or the sheriff had leaked a few details of the investigation, but somehow Daddy knew the Catts were to blame for his humiliation, and around the Sims household, they quickly deteriorated from mere *Baptist snobs* to names considerably more vicious.

In this, Mama and I were not far from agreement, and it was poor Ira who bore the brunt of the conflict, having to listen to Daddy's nasty comments at supper every night, mostly in silence, though sometimes he went so far as to resist Daddy to his face, the only time I remember him ever doing it. With the sheriff's warning so recently upon him, and the specter of Angola still on his mind, Daddy couldn't lay a hand on him. He only dropped his verbal attack to an even more heinous level, so nasty even Mama sometimes tried to intervene with ineffective little noises of reconciliation (*"Now, son. Go easy —"*).

But Ira still wouldn't back down. He'd only stomp to the bedroom and slam the door in clenched-teeth outrage, wouldn't even let me pat his back like he usually did when he was hurting, but just lie there with his face hard against the mattress, set and murderous, intent on sustaining his anger, using it as evidence, prolonging it till Judgment Day.

— 6 —

*S*o began *the next epoch* of our life there on Magnolia Hill, one that had actually dawned the moment I first passed civil words across the fence with the Prince of Lafayette, though I didn't realize it at the time, wouldn't realize it till school started, eight weeks later. In the meanwhile, my brother and I had the dog days of summer to contend with inside a screenless house without so much as a fan to our name, and our father coming home every night sober as a judge, a virtue that sounds a lot healthier on paper than it did to us at the time.

It was harder on Ira, of course, as he was used to a broader range. Since my scope was always fairly limited, I was less stir-crazy, and glad of his company once he got over his pouting and deemed me a worthy companion, passing the time as best we could, listening to the radio, or playing game after game of every poker, snooker, or other card game devised by man. When we tired of that, we'd sit in our bedroom, Ira stretched out on the bed, me on the floor by the open window, listening to the roll of his voice as he went over all the old stories, mostly to do with the family next door whose name we were forbidden to speak.

In time, even those stories ran out, and he went on to speak of future fantasies: of joining the Marines and shipping out to Japan or Korea, and sending me home all the gifts of the Orient, perfume and silk and ivory combs. When he got up enough money, he told me, he'd get an apartment, and maybe they'd let me come over there and live with him, keep his house, cook supper. His voice was hypnotic, and I'd sit there with my arms folded on the low windowsill, mesmerized by the flow of his words, seeing so clearly the sunny apartment on a gay, quiet street, me in the kitchen in a little yellow apron, cooking all the things I smelled from the kitchen next door: chicken and ham and bacon, every night. In my mind's eye I could see Ira coming home in his uniform, both of us laughing; I couldn't have told why, though Ira's face was lost in a dim smile, as if he were seeing it, too.

Our fantasies and our day would end at six when Daddy would come home for supper and we'd make a stab at normalcy, Mama cooking whatever she could pull together, Daddy hot and tired and madder than hell. This was his off-time, his unwind and have-a-good-time time, and he clearly wasn't so pleased at having to share it with a wife and children, complaining about the food, deviling Ira about the Catts, telling Mama to quit putting my hair in braids, to let me wear it down: What was she trying to make me into? Some kind of useless, narrow-assed, Pentecostal *bitch?* They were hard words to a woman whose one alluring quality had been her air of other-worldliness, which was exactly Daddy's intent. He'd always been an angry man, but in his forced sobriety, his rage was like a heat-seeking missile, precisely aimed at whatever he knew to be your particular area of sensitivity.

When September finally rolled around, I don't think there have ever been in the history of public education two pupils more eager to return to school. Ira had the number of days memorized, and every night in bed, after more of Daddy's merciless needling, he'd remind me of the countdown, thirty, then twenty, then ten. Then, finally, the big day was upon us, Ira and me joining the throng of boys who were lately grown tall and thin and stooped. They were all happy to see Ira, elbowing him and rubbing his newly buzzed head, still ignoring me, though I could have cared less.

For I was free at last, and walked along the moss-hung streets at a snail's pace, ignoring the shadows at my back, too happy at seeing faces, hearing voices, even the fast, rolling one of the little snot next door. *Especially* that one, as he not only let me walk with him, but lent me his jacket, carried my bookbag, even offered to kill the bulldog it was rumored I was still afraid of.

"Mr. Dailey doan want him," was his calm rationale. "Doan even feed him. I thank we oughta just put him out of his misery."

I didn't know what to make of his sudden new generosity, attributing it to, if anything, his pleasure at having Ira back, and really didn't think too much about it. We weren't allowed to talk to him anyway, though Gabriel seemed oblivious to our silence, dancing between us like a pixie, sometimes even turning around and walking backwards for blocks at a time so he could face us while he talked, his hazel eyes snapping with an energy I found both fascinating and a little repellent.

The repellence came from his sheer intensity, which in some ways reminded me of my father at supper when he'd pin poor Ira to the wall over some piece of trivia; the fascination with the way he stared at me, eye to eye, the whole time he talked. At first I thought it my imagination, but as the weeks went by, I couldn't help but notice that every time I looked up, his eyes were on me: curious, searching eyes that seemed to be burrowing to the bottom of my soul, looking for the solution to some insoluble mystery.

There were things in my life already that I wasn't so eager for strangers — even friendly strangers, who loved my brother — to see, and I dodged him gracefully, keeping my eyes on my feet, a little afraid of the almost hypnotic quality of his stare, feeling like a bird caught in a python's trance. But Gabriel didn't seem to mind my evasions. He didn't seem to mind anything, in fact, as agreeable a companion as you could ask for, never embarrassing us by bringing up Daddy's foul reputation like some of the boys did, but ignoring our family's shortcomings and treating us as equals. This open-handed acceptance was my first glimpse into the secret of Ira's infatuation with him, and by October, we were a firm threesome, ignoring the others to walk along side by side, so close that when Ira came down with the mumps two weeks before Christmas, I met Gabe at the front gate just like always.

He didn't seem too worried with Ira's absence, or my continuing silence, either, though he did unbend enough to ask if I was allowed to talk. I was a little taken aback at the question, for it assumed, and assumed correctly, so much of the private interworkings of our household. And though we weren't specifically forbidden to talk to everyone, just the *Baptist snobs* across the fence, I could only shake my head, an answer he seemed to find oddly cheering.

"That's all right." He grinned. "I talk enough for both of us. Daddy's always telling me to hush."

I would have liked to have asked about Mr. Simon, and how he was doing. I hadn't seen him in months and months, since the State had overtaken us, and was easing off his memory intentionally, afraid Daddy's radar would pick up on my love, and he'd start in on him at supper, a possibility I couldn't stand.

"Listen," Gabriel said on the third or fourth day we'd walked home alone, "grandeddy give me some money for Christmas. Why don't I buy us a Coke?"

Any kind of food was a treat on our side of the fence, delicacies like Coke unheard of. I nodded so quickly that Gabe laughed aloud, then went in the Jitney Junior and bought us a little eight-ounce Coke that we stood by the wall and shared. There was a particular quality to the afternoon that I remember so clearly: the December sun not the enemy it had been in July, taking on the golden haze it sometimes does in late autumn as we stood there, passing the little Coke back and forth between us. He did the talking, as usual, telling me gossip and stories from the Hill, all of it harmless and most of it hilarious, making me laugh and laugh and even meet his eye for once, even return his absorbed stare with one of my own.

For something in the way he stood there outlined against the electric blue of the north Florida sky was suddenly familiar to me, but I couldn't figure why. It wasn't his voice, that still sounded odd to me, not flat like Ira's, but flowing and gheechie, almost musically Cajun, liberally laced with peculiar Black slang that was sometimes hard to understand because he talked so fast. I had to concentrate to understand him, practically read his lips, and as I stood there that day, listening to him spin one of his outrageous yarns, it suddenly came to me: Mama.

That's who he looked like, that morning in Louisiana when she'd come to our bedroom and told us we were moving to town with Daddy.

The slant of the sun on the tips of his curling hair gave them that same copper glow; his laughing face was lit with the same silky, exulting quality. Once I'd pegged it, I was so amazed at the resemblance I almost broke my silence to tell him. But it was such a silly thing to tell a boy, that he reminded you of your *mother,* that I just contented myself with a reciprocal stare of my own, all the way home.

In bed that night with a sadly ailing Ira, I was the one who broached the subject of Gabe, that he easily warmed to, spinning out the history of the Catts family like it was heraldic legend, all about Mr. Simon and the War, and Michael pitching Baseball and Candace and the Boy-with-the-Car. But for once, I was more interested in the baby of the family and gently steered the conversation back to him, amazed at some of the stuff Ira told me, wondering if he'd told me before, and I'd been too stupid to listen.

Surely this was new, all about how Miss Cissie wasn't supposed to have any more children after Michael, but the Lord told her she'd have one more child, a boy, who would be dedicated to Him.

"Like Samuel," Ira said, though I didn't get the connection and only lay there in a stunned silence, thinking it was the wildest thing I'd ever heard in my life. When I asked Ira what it could possibly mean, he said, well, Gabe was going to be a preacher.

"A *preacher?*" I murmured.

And though he was half-mute from the mumps, Ira managed to rasp, "Sure. Why not?"

I didn't know what to say. I hadn't gone to church since we'd left Grandma's, but seemed to remember preachers as meek and mild and sheep-loving. Something about this Catts boy didn't quite fit the bill, a suspicion that was confirmed the next afternoon when he rocketed into a rage twice in a hour, once with his brother, once, his father, in a way that didn't seem too Christ-like to me, I could tell you that.

The first time with his brother seemed particularly unprovoked, as he'd only stopped by to offer us a ride home from school. It is one of the few memories I have of Michael as a young man: squatting in the back of a beat-up old truck with four other boys, all of them wearing worn practice jerseys and chewing tobacco, obviously just through, or about to begin, a baseball game.

I couldn't take him up on his offer, of course, but didn't see any reason why Gabriel shouldn't, though all he gave him in answer was a quick, furtive shake of his head. Michael (who was never in his life known to take no for an answer) was mildly insistent, saying, "Come on, Gabe, I forgot my cleats. We'll drop you off."

In reply to his generous offer, he got another *no,* this one so stiff and stubborn that I turned and looked at Gabriel, whose face was fixed and red around the ears, as if he were silently digesting a grievous insult. I didn't know what to make of it, and Michael apparently didn't either, only shrugging and turning to spit, pausing a moment when his eyes fell on me.

I returned his look easily enough. There was nothing of his brother's close scrutiny in it, just mild curiosity, though he suddenly seemed to find his little brother very amusing. His face fought a grin as he leaned to spit out of the far side of the truck, while one of the other boys, a big fat Bubba-looking thing with a red face and a ripped jersey lifted his face to the heavens and intoned, "Gabe, Gabe, Gabe, Gabe, *Gabe.* What are we gone *do* with you, son?"

I didn't have the faintest idea what he was talking about, but at my side, it was as though a grenade exploded. "Lea' me *alone!*" Gabriel shouted — no, *shrieked,* pointing a trembling finger at his brother, shouting, "I'm telling *Mama!*"

He was so mad he was *spitting* mad, his face perfectly scarlet, the boys in the truck exploding into laughter, all of them but Michael, who just shook his head as he reached up and tapped on the glass, signaling the driver to drive on.

There were a few more catcalls and teasing as they drove off, ("— take care of it, boy!" and "Don't git caught!") all quite indecipherable to me, though they had Gabriel stomping his foot like a madman. The truck had long disappeared before he came to himself, standing there, chest heaving, trying to offer a sullen explanation. "They just — *bother* me, is all."

I just looked at him, not really knowing what to think. I lived in a household where ferocious displays of anger were commonplace, but never had I seen such a *public* exhibition. After a moment, we started walking again, Gabriel not carrying on his usual monologue, just swiping at his hair and talking to himself under his breath, muttering terse little variations on *telling Mama.* Not knowing Miss Cissie so well, I didn't realize how blood-curdling that threat could be and just walked along in an embarrassed silence till we came to the turn that led back to Lafayette, where he stopped and glanced at me out of the corner of his eye.

"Wanta walk on the tracks?" he asked with a nervous chew of his lip. "It's just a little bit out of the way."

I assumed he didn't want to meet the truckload of teasing boys coming back up Lafayette and agreed, though it was more than a little bit out of the way, more like half a mile. But I only had Ira to look forward to at home, and he wouldn't be so glad to see me, as I had a book-bag full of make-up work. So I agreed, and followed him across the field till we made the steep embankment that led down to the tracks.

Once there, Gabe strolled along more easily, regaining a little of his color, talking and talking, and staring and staring, both of us so caught up in what he was saying that we didn't realize we were being watched till we came upon his father quite suddenly, almost bumping into his chest before we looked up.

"Son," he said evenly, then, "Myra."

There was no one on earth I'd rather have run into, my face breaking into a grin of welcome. He was apparently coming home from work (not at the bank anymore, but another job, painting, he said) and joined us easily enough as we strolled along, taking Ira's place in our threesome. He asked how Ira was getting along, if he was seeing a doctor, obviously not so pleased when I told him no, that Mama was doctoring him herself. He said they might have some medicine left over from Candace's mumps, that he'd send it over later if he could find it.

I thanked him, unconsciously breaking Daddy's edict by falling into my old, quick chatter; I couldn't help it. There were only a few people on earth I could speak to with such ease, and he was like a valve on a pressure-cooker, nodding and smiling, ignoring his own son, who wasn't so pleased with the turn of the conversation, and butted in time and again, telling lies so outrageous that neither of us believed him, growing sulky when we didn't.

He kept up a minimal civility till we were almost home, at the very back of the field that separated our backyards from the tracks, when Mr. Simon paused and asked why we were walking home on the tracks, that surely it was out of the way. I didn't have any better sense than to volunteer that it was Gabe's idea, but before his father could say a word, Gabe was all over it, giving a wildly dramatic recounting of the incident with Michael and the laughing boys, that Mr. Simon didn't seem to think much of, only looking at him levelly, saying, "You doan need to be sneaking around these tracks. Drunks down here. Winos. It ain't safe."

But Gabe wasn't listening, he was going on full steam ahead, retelling his story with an ever more dramatic twist that his father cut short with a sharp, "*Son*. Listen to me. I catch you taking a girl to the tracks agin, it'll be yo butt. You hear me?"

This brought his yammering to an end, though I just looked at my feet, embarrassed at being caught in a family squabble. When I chanced a glance up, I was amazed to find Gabriel facing off his father in the most incredible fashion. He was tall enough now that they were eye to eye, Gabriel almost shaking with anger, though his father just watched him quietly, said, "Gabriel? Son? Didju hear me?"

Still he didn't answer, and I was wondering where in the world this standoff would lead, when Gabriel finally conceded, murmuring, "Yessuh," through clenched teeth, so fast and mad I didn't realize what he'd said before he turned and took off like a rabbit across the field, his stiff, angry back a wordless echo of his earlier threat (— *telling Mama!*) At least, that's where he went, right across the field and up the back steps into his mother's kitchen, leaving his father to stand there and shake his head in honest wonder, much like his older son had.

After a moment, he seemed to remember my presence there at his side, as he glanced at me, a little embarrassed. "He gits kindly — *excited,*" he said, which was a polite way of putting it, I thought. But I kept my opinion to myself, and as we crossed the field, I was quick to apologize for going on the tracks, though he only shook his head, said, "Doan worry it, shug. It'll be all right."

I was glad of his easy forgiveness, but still a little amazed by Gabriel's display, pausing as we separated into our respective yards and murmuring to myself in honest wonder, "And he's gone be a *preacher?*"

I hadn't meant to say it aloud, though Mr. Simon didn't look offended, just shaking his head with a wry, "That's what they tell me."

We went our separate ways then, him up the steps to the lit kitchen, me to our porch, where Ira burst out on me, still in his pajamas, asking where in the world I'd been, that I was late. When I told him about the boys in the truck and the detour to the tracks, he seemed a little unbelieving. "Gabe took *you?* To the *tracks?*"

I was beginning to understand that there was some secret connotation about the tracks that I wasn't aware of. But Ira wouldn't let me in on the secret, just taking his homework and spending the rest of the afternoon at the dining room table, stopping every once in a while to give me another of those quiet, speculative looks. It didn't leave me much to do in the way of entertainment, and when Daddy came home at six, I was almost glad to see him, helping Ira clear the table for supper, when there was a knock on the door, the *back* door.

Ever since the State lady had shown up, an unexpected knock would make my stomach churn, Ira and I gathering nervously at the end of the hall while Mama slowly opened the door on Gabriel Catts, of all people. He stood there sheepishly in the dim porch light, a brown paper bag in his hand, which he offered to Mama.

"Daddy sent this for Ira," he said in a voice that was low and formal and somehow rehearsed. Then, with a great sigh, he added, "I'm sorry I took Myra to the tracks. I didn't have no bidness doing that. I'm sorry."

He didn't look particularly sorry when he said it, only avoiding Ira's eye and backing down the steps, leaving Mama there at the door without a clue in the world to what he was talking about, just opening the little bag and taking out a glass pharmacy bottle.

"Medicine," she finally said, looking blankly over our heads to the hallway.

That's when I realized someone else was in the room: Daddy. He had come quietly down the hall to stand behind us in a moment of stunned silence before he shoved us aside to stride across the room to Mama, shouting, "— tolju not to take nothing from no *goddamn* Baptist *snobs!*"

He was drawing back to hit her when it came to me that she was about to pay the price for my own stupidity, making me speak up from the hallway, without thought. "It wasn't her, Daddy. It was me. I told 'em."

These were words of damnation around the Sims house, which caused Daddy to pause with his fist in midair, then slowly turn to face me, breathing, "You did *what?*"

Mama's face beside him was signaling a clear warning that I back off, *back off.* Ira was doing the same at my side, even plucking at my sleeve. But some of Mr. Simon's light was still shining around me, giving me room to make a stab at the truth, and I answered him clearly, my voice hardly shaking at all. "I told Mr. Simon. Me and Gabe met him, on the tracks —"

Ira audibly inhaled at this. I didn't know why and glanced aside when Daddy hit, crossing the room in two long strides and grabbing me up by the back of my hair, almost lifting me off the floor, shouting, "The *tracks?* The *tracks?* And what was you doing *laying* round the house while yo daughter was slipping off to the tracks?"

He didn't ask it of me, but Mama, who tried to push between us, murmuring for him to *settle down, Leldon.* But he ignored her, shoving her aside to speak to my face in that low patient hum that almost sounded normal, except that he was whispering through his clenched teeth. "— ain't raising her childrun is what I know, let 'em run around like *a bitch in heat.*"

His grip had tightened to a claw on the last words, but I still had no earthly idea what he was talking about, standing there on my tiptoes, my chin lifted straight up at an acute angle, still trying to explain about the boys in the truck and their teasing, but it was no use. He was mesmerized by the sound of his own grievance that hummed along with a rising anger. "And what d'you thank I'll do, *mon ami?* Just sit by and watch? Girl, you thank the State'll stop me? That what you *thank?*"

Whenever Daddy got that far gone into rage, into the humming, shaking, talking-to-himself stage, Ira just stood there and took it; the belt or the cord wasn't far behind. But there was still some thread of connection between my father and me, still some vestige of faith that made me try to talk him out of it, whispering, "Daddy, it was — the boys in the truck, teasin' —"

"Teasin', my *ass!*" he screamed, then turned on his heel and took off through the house, pulling me along by the hair, so high and fast that I was slung along almost in midair, banging into corners and doorjambs.

He stopped once to scream in my face about *defying* him, then took off again, trying to sling me around the corner to the bedroom, but not quite making it, whacking my face against the doorjamb and screaming *shit* when he did it, grabbing me up by the back of my dress and slamming me into the closet, then shooting the bolt behind me.

For a few minutes, his voice was a muffled roar outside, full of violent self-pity at what a man had to take these days from his children. A heavy boot hit the door every now and again, almost bringing it down on top of me, making me crawl to the far corner to escape it, pulling on the skirt of one of Mama's dresses till it fell down on my face. It made for a soft, fragile barrier that didn't provide much protection, but was better than nothing as I huddled there through an endless shouting, then another hollow bang and a gigantic slam of a door.

The house was quiet then, like it always was after Daddy left, everyone checking out the victim, running for ice packs and aspirin. But this time, no one came for me, and I just sat there in the darkness, stunned and nauseated, rubbing the cool material of the dress against my hot face, surprised when it came away wet, because I wasn't crying. It wasn't until I tasted the coppery wetness that was pouring down my face that I realized I was bleeding. I was a little worried about ruining Mama's dress, but the cold silky cloth felt too good against the sharp hot sting in the middle of my face, and I left it there, pushing aside the shoes and clutter to lie with my cheek to the closet floor, gritty and cold.

I was no longer afraid as I lay there, but washed with an exhausting relief that was as close to contentment as I came those days, glad of the protection of that stout little closet. For it wasn't the first time I'd been locked there, and I knew from experience that I was finally safe, that bad things happened all over the house, in the living room, the bedroom, even the kitchen, but never there; and it took more years of therapy to get over my love of that closet than it did the beatings. Even after a truckload of money and pills and a patient file as deep as the Marianna Straits, I simply couldn't be made to understand that that narrow three-by-six space wasn't a sanctuary at all, but a cave, a dungeon, and if I didn't lose my affection for it, it would surely be my grave.

But that all came later, much later. At the time, I was only relieved, curling up with the last of my mother's good Sunday dresses, one for a pillow, one for a shroud, and with the house so quiet and resting around me, fell into a soundless, perfectly dreamless sleep.

— 7 —

*I*t *was a sleep that was to last,* in one form or another, for the better part of seven years, which is not what you'd call a romantic exaggeration on my part, but a psychological fact. For even as my year in Metairie had quietly faded into dust, so my years on the Hill began, at this point, to take on that same dissolving quality. Not entirely, of course, but gradually, the year between the Christmas of '61 and our departure a little over a year later, quietly, inevitably, evaporating to a near blank. The practical result is that except for bits and pieces of vivid memory that can still tear at my heart, it's really like it happened to another person altogether; it hardly touches me at all.

I do remember the whack on my forehead that left a jagged, lightning-shaped scar between my eyes that I bear to this day, and the crisp, cold feel of Mama's dress on my sore face, and the strike of the match at the door when Ira came to check on me later in the night. I remember his face, still pinched and pale with fever, watching me a moment in the brief illumination before he closed the door quietly and left, his tread a soft vibration on the wood floor at my back.

I gathered from his careful stealth that Daddy must be home, but was too blurred to care, waking the next morning when Mama opened the door in the clear light of mid-morning, a white enamel washpan in her hands. She set it on the floor between us, her face as pale as Ira's, but not in the same manner, a fixity there I'd only seen once before, the day the State picked us up, when she'd met Miss Cissie's eye on the porch.

It wasn't a pleasant expression, though apparently not aimed at me, for she was very kind to me that morning, if a little nervous, averting her eyes at the blood, dipping a worn washrag in the panful of water and telling me to sit up. I tried to obey, though I was still a little shaky, having to hold onto her for support, not as concerned with the dull, persistent pain in my head as I was the crinkly sensation of dried blood that seemed to cover me, head to toe, sticking in my hair, soaked into the front of my dress. I was so covered in it that Mama couldn't make out its source, feeling along my hairline, my gums, her face perplexed.

Ira joined us, still in his pajama bottoms, a glass of water in his hand, his face pensive, speaking aside to Mama, asking, "Her nose?"

"No." She answered just as briefly, her own face a grimace as she dabbed at my eyes and forehead, finally coming upon the deep gash on the bridge of my nose, flinching when I cried aloud. "S'all right, baby," she whispered, dipping the rag in the water and dabbing it lightly. "It's okay."

Ira handed me the water and a couple of aspirin that I took automatically, as aspirins were Mama's sovereign remedy for everything from horsefly bites to concussions. He told me to chew them, that it made them work faster. I took his advice, figuring he ought to know, as he was usually the one on the taking end, then lay back down, still a little woozy from the headache, letting Mama wash me off, one section at a time.

It took the better part of the morning, Ira having to empty the washpan time and again when it'd get too bloody, Mama making me take off my dress so she could wash my hair and rebraid it, in simple Indian braids because the French ones pulled at my forehead too much, making me cry. But finally, she was done and had Ira bring me my gown, and except for the dishpan of murky brown water and the pile of dirty clothes and bloodied shoes, everything was back to normal.

Mama brought me a pillow and covers to make me a little nest, because once Daddy put you in, it was up to him to let you out, and he didn't show much sign of returning anytime soon. She piled the shoes up at the far end and was raking out the other clutter when she came upon the dress that I'd used for a handkerchief the night before, that turned out to be her good violet organdy, her last Easter dress before we'd left Grandma's. It was the dress she'd worn uptown when we'd visited the nurse, quite ruined now, the crisp skirt wrinkled and damp, blotched with great smears of brownish red, and I could have cried. Of all her clothes, it was the only real church-dress she had left, though Mama was curiously unconcerned with the loss, just wadding it up and tossing it aside with the other garbage, telling me not to worry about it, that she wouldn't be needing it, *ever again*.

There was something of the earlier hard set to her face when she said it that might have clued me in on changing days, but my head hurt too much to ponder an abstraction. I was content to lie still on my pillow when she left to wash the clothes, my head feeling a little better from the aspirin, though not enough to sit up and play cards with Ira when he came in with the pack. I much preferred just lying there talking, and he was willing to oblige me, lounging in the open door of the closet, shuffling the deck and telling me bits of news: that Gabriel had asked after me over the fence; that Daddy had left that morning and wouldn't be back for a long time.

"How d'you know?" I murmured, and he eyed me speculatively.

"Couldn't stand thet," he said, pointing the deck of cards at my face. I didn't know what he was talking about, so he went and brought me the little shaving mirror from the hallway.

When I held it to my face, a strange, wall-eyed monster stared back impassively. "Oh, my *gosh*," I breathed. "I look like a *Martian*."

Ira burst out laughing, we both did, for the description wasn't so far off base. The bridge of my nose was grotesquely discolored and swollen, with a deep, jagged little half-inch gash in the middle that gaped open when I laughed. But I didn't care; there was always a sense of jubilation in the aftermath of one of Daddy's outbursts, a season of calm, sometimes repudiation. Once Ira saw that I was alive and well, everything was all right again, and my little week-long sojourn in the bottom of my mother's closet really wasn't so bad. I'd sleep and daydream the cold December days away till three, when Ira would come home with my make-up work, along with messages of get-well from Gabe and little eight-ounce Cokes they jointly financed with bottle returns they'd picked up on the tracks.

I was touched by the gesture and ravenous over the Coke, for Daddy's absence was creating its usual famine, the weather turning cold, fireplaces lit for the first time that year. They filled the neighborhood with the wafting scent of woodsmoke, a smell so reminiscent of barbecue that it nearly drove Ira and me crazy. Late in the afternoon of Christmas Eve, just when we were certain that life had passed us by, Daddy showed up out of the blue. He just walked in like he usually did in his old work-clothes and let me out of the closet without a word of explanation, asking me at the supper table what happened to my head. The gash was still there, shrunk to a jagged black scab, only a touch of green-gray left around the hollows of my eyes.

I answered him some way or another. He often asked Ira about his bumps and bruises, too drunk to know he'd been the one who'd done it, though he'd been stone cold sober when he'd slung me into the door. But I accepted his condolences, we all did, and throughout our spare supper, I could feel his eyes on me, pensive and pale, though he didn't say another word and left immediately after, tracking off across the backyard to play poker or drink or maybe go back to work, we never knew.

That night, we didn't particularly care, as he'd left some money in the meanwhile, and we weren't about to argue. Mama just threw on her coat and ran down to Ivey's before it closed to buy groceries, while Ira and I waited on the front porch for her return, yelling like Indians when she came around the corner, a big old box of groceries in hand. She came in and fixed us a second supper that night, a breakfast, if I'm remembering correctly, with biscuits and eggs and bacon, all of us standing around the stove and watching it sizzle in the pan, the cold kitchen full of laughter and relief. It made for a late night, and we had barely gotten to sleep when the church bell down at Welcome started tolling at midnight and Ira woke up long enough to tell me it was officially Christmas morning.

And though we had neither a tree nor toys nor any other present to our name, it really did feel festive there, lying in a warm bed for the first time in a week, my head all better, not hurting at all. When I told Ira it was our best Christmas ever, I really meant it, thinking he was all I needed, that who cared about dolls and coats and tea sets with a brother like him?

We weren't in a big hurry to get out of bed the next morning, as the weather had turned off drizzly and wet, chimneys all over the Hill lit against the cold iron-gray sky, the house still holding the cloying smell of smoked meats that made our life a torment. Ira was already awake when I woke up, looking out the cold, misted window impassively, his hands under his head. I just lay there cocooned in my quilt, glad to be off the cold floor, when our bedroom door opened and Daddy stepped in, a coffee cup in his hand.

It was so unexpected that we just froze, waiting for him to make a move, relaxing when we saw he was both sober and conciliatory. He offered a small smile, tipped his head to the living room, said, "Ain't you two lazybones gone git up, see what Santy Claus brought you?"

Santa Claus hadn't been so generous since we'd moved to Florida, and we just glanced at each other uncertainly. After a moment's doubt, we kicked off the covers and made our way to the living room, where Mama had set out our presents: a fleece-lined denim jacket for Ira (who needed it) and there by the door, a big old red bicycle for me. To tell you the truth, I didn't know what to make of it. Daddy was notorious for bringing home presents after he'd showed himself in a bad drunk, small offerings like candy and ice cream, but this was over the top, and I just stood there, finally glancing at Ira for a clue.

He, at least, seemed happy, mistaking my wonder for fear. "I'll show you how to ride it," he assured me, "Ain't nothing to it."

Mama came in from the kitchen then in her old winter robe, her eyes on mine, searching for a little laughter, a little normalcy in my face, and I couldn't deny her. I ran across the room and hugged her around the waist, told her it was *just* what I wanted, and after that, all was well again. Ira tried on his coat while Mama cooked breakfast, the same thing we'd had the night before, biscuits and bacon and eggs. When we were through, Daddy stood and told me to get my coat (as if I owned one), that he was going to show me how to ride that thing.

Outside, the children of Magnolia Hill had emerged from their houses to compare presents, looking at mine with round eyes of undisguised envy. Ira loved it, told everybody my bike had come from *Sears,* though how in the world he figured that, I didn't know. I was too busy trying to master the contraption, with Daddy running along beside me, yelling a lot of contradictory instructions at my ear. He grabbed the handlebars as I fell over, time and again, dabbed my forehead with his handkerchief when I hit my face on a particularly bad fall that split open the scab, making it bleed all over again.

I remember the day so clearly: the cold slick street, the other children trying out their new gloves and footballs and BB guns, a few like Ira, barehanded, but wearing new jackets or boots or stiff new blue jeans. As the morning wore on, the spirit of the season prevailed, Sister McQuaig sending over divinity, some of the men coming to the gate to offer Daddy a little advice on keeping me up, grimacing at the blood on my forehead. They thought I'd gotten it from the spill on the bike, told me to *go easy, sister,* to keep that wheel steady, to *not look back,* because that was my downfall.

Whenever I'd finally get going on my own, sailing along for a few yards free as a bird, I'd look back to see if Daddy was still holding on, and down I'd go, splat on the pavement. My group of advisors took up the cry: *don't look back, sister, don't look back!* till I finally mastered the urge to turn and was soon pedaling unsteadily up the crest of the hill, Daddy and Mr. Floyd and Brother Kimbrall standing there at the gate, clapping.

It was a magical morning in its way, the only sour note my good friend Gabe, who would not be talked into liking my bike, no matter what Ira said. He sat there on the curb all morning long with a look of profound distaste, saying he wouldn't ride a bike if you paid him, that they were *dangerous.* I was a little put off by his lack of enthusiasm and spoke to him directly for the first time since that day on the porch, telling him it wasn't dangerous, it was easy, did he want a ride?

In reply, he gave me such a withering look that it did something queer to my heart, tapping it with a sharp, unexpected ping of hurt, the likes of which I'd never felt in my life. After that, the new bike lost its charm and I went inside and lay in bed under a mountain of covers while Ira took the box my bicycle had come in and built a fort around it. He tried to lure me out to see it, but I refused, preferring to stay in bed and sulk the afternoon away, pondering boys and their peculiar ways.

So passed the Christmas of 1961, which unexpectedly opened the door on what might be called the Golden Age of our lives on the Hill, a space of almost a year that started out with such promise and quickly widened into a valley of reprieve. It all happened with a suddenness that, to me, seemed nothing short of miraculous: Daddy suddenly (and inexplicably) not so despised by our neighbors, me with a new red bike, Ira taking a job at the corner grocery where the owner let him bring home bent cans and wilted produce and out-of-date bread, so hunger never again haunted our doorstep the whole time we lived on the Hill.

That in itself would have been cause for universal rejoicing, but, apparently, the State's meddling in our affairs had come to an end with the turn of the year when the sheriff dismissed the case. Once the specter of losing Ira passed, we all breathed more easily, especially Daddy, who was able to resume his life doing whatever it was he did for days on end down in jook bottom and the Long Hotel that kept him so relatively easy to live with. By February, he had thawed enough to let us outside, and in the six-month or so interval, the whole texture of Magnolia Hill seemed to have changed.

Not the spreading oaks, or the lap-shingled houses that seemed carved in stone, immovable, but the people, the families. When we went into seclusion in July, we were the outsiders, the lepers, the Philistines in the camp, but suddenly, upon our reappearance, we were embraced on every side, even by the Queen next door, who sent over cookies and cut Mama roses and gave Ira a hand-me-down Sunday suit that fit like a glove. To me, it was a favor as inexplicable and unmerited as the big red bike, but Ira was so happy I didn't ponder it too closely, trying hard to be civil to the boys who were suddenly on every side, offering to carry my books, walk me home, forever nagging me about who I *liked*.

At that point in my life there were precious few things I knew beyond a shadow of a doubt that I *liked*, fried chicken and Mr. Simon and Ira and Mama among them. There was also someone else I liked, but I wasn't telling because he didn't like me, not anymore, and it still hurt my heart when I thought about it. Because I liked him *a lot*, but since I'd been riding my bike to school, he never spoke to me, never waited by the fence, never even waved anymore.

It was Gabriel, of course; who else could it be? Who else had pen-
etrated the veil of silence that I'd taken refuge in, had sent me Cokes and
messages of condolence back when I was stricken with my mysteriously
bruising case of the mumps? Who else did I lie in bed and think about
every night, conjuring the image of him at the wall of the store, his hair
gold-tipped in the sun, his warm, peculiar bread-smell on the collar and
cuffs of the jacket he always let me wear.

But that's all I had to go by: a month-old memory, for on my reappearance in January, he disdained my entourage of tall, spindly suitors to
walk with Ira in a distant, impenetrable silence, surrounded by a hateful
rumor that he was in love with a girl at church named Cassie Lea. It was
a name of infamy around our house, since Ira had been caught kissing
her at a youth rally last summer and called on by the pastor, a kind old
man named Brother Sloan. He didn't make too big a deal over it, though
Mama came close to whipping Ira, telling him he wouldn't be going
down to that church anymore if *that's* what he was up to.

After that, Ira never so much as mentioned her name when we
talked at night, not in bed anymore, because as of Christmas, he'd begun
sleeping on the couch in the living room, for reasons both of us understood, though we never mentioned it. I sorely missed him, the bed cold
and lonely without him, with no one to substantiate the hateful rumors
about Gabe and *that girl,* whom I privately called names I'd picked up
from my father a sight more vicious than *Cassie Lea.*

But there was nothing for it; I was far too shy to approach Gabe
myself, and January had passed into the early reaches of a cool, obliging
February when one of the nagging little boys at my heels clarified the situation and inadvertently solved it, when he asked me point-blank on the
porch one afternoon, *who I liked.* I usually just ignored the question,
knowing the truth about fried chicken and Mr. Simon wouldn't sit too
well with this rowdy crew, and anyway, Gabe was right there, sitting on
the steps petting an old stray cat that Mama had been feeding.

He didn't pay any attention as Ira started playing the fool, pretending he knew who I liked, drawing it out into a big joke. I ignored
him, too, for I was not so enamored with my brother's clownish, public
persona, preferring the Ira of our old bedroom, who hadn't smiled as
much, but had brought me aspirin when my head hurt and let me have

the lion's share of the covers when it was cold.

But that Ira was a world away from the front porch that day, and the clowning, goofy, joke-a-minute Ira in his place, needling me, striking off the boys one at a time: Albert and Benny and Ray; then suddenly, with no permission from me, he let the cat out of the bag, just like that, saying I didn't like boys at all, I liked *angels*.

I shot one panicked look at Gabe, who only sat there with the cat in his lap, absently rubbing its head, though the boys were giving it to him, singing a silly little song about us kissing in a tree, bursting into laughter when I jumped Ira, slapping him for the first time in my life, telling him I hated his guts. They laughed even harder at that, and I went inside with a murderous shake in my breath, slamming the door and going to the bedroom and crawling under the covers, head and all, too embarrassed to show my face on the Hill, ever again.

Ira came in a little later on his way to work and tried to talk to me, apologize, but I gave him such a freeze that he finally left. When I yanked the covers off my head, there was a single Hershey's kiss on the pillow, a peace offering, I guess, and as I sat there and chewed it up in fast, angry bites, I planned to catch that boy when he got home from work and make him straighten this thing out. Tell that little *Baptist snot* across the fence that I wasn't in love with him, no sir, I wasn't in love with nobody but maybe Colonel Sanders, but that was just because he fried good chicken.

It was just my luck that I ran into Gabe later in the afternoon in the backyard when I went to the outhouse, an embarrassing enough meeting, even if Ira hadn't spilled the beans about me liking him. He was standing at the fence watching me with something in his face, some glitter of — I don't know — secret knowledge, that scared the heck out of me, making me practically run back into the house, wishing he had the good manners to leave people alone when they were attending to their bodily functions and didn't have the money for an indoor toilet. But discretion has never been his strong suit (still isn't) and he was back at it again the next day, lounging around the backyard, reading with his back against the old sweetgum that marked the fenceline, almost like he was waiting to humiliate me. I paced the kitchen all morning, putting off the inevitable as long I could.

But you can only go so long and after dinner, I finally took a breath and went down the path, feeling his presence over there. I made it back to the porch unmolested, but as I started up the steps, curiosity got the best of me, and I turned. He didn't so much as look up this time, just sat there with his back to the old sweetgum, his face pink-cheeked from the cool early spring, completely absorbed in the enormous open book on his lap. It wasn't the Bible, as you'd expect a budding preacher to be reading, but something thick and fat in a melon-green hardback that was making him frown with intense concentration.

I stood there a moment, then after a glance inside the screen door at our silent, empty house, curled my arms around the side post and called over to him, asked him what he was reading. He glanced up casually at the sound of my voice, his face bored, but companionable, different than it used to be. No longer so chubby and pretty, but stronger-boned, almost Slavic, the only thing about him that had changed since we'd moved to the Hill, as he hadn't grown tall and weedy like the other boys had, but wider, stocky, his hands and forearms beautifully formed, already a man's.

"*Gone with the Wind,*" he answered with a yawn, laying the book face down against his chest and giving a little stretch. "It's to the good part now, where Scarlett shoots the Yankee in the face. I remember it from the *last time.*"

The title was vaguely familiar to me, and I was trying to remember where I'd heard it, when the implication of that enormous statement sank in. I asked him if he'd really read it before, as it was truly the biggest book I'd ever seen in my life, and he was very modest in his answer, saying sure, he'd read it before; he'd read it *twict.*

I blinked at that answer, wondering when he had time to eat, with all that reading, but he just set aside the book and kept talking, saying he'd seen the movie, too. That his Grandaddy had taken him to Tallahassee to see it, but it wasn't as good 'cause that ain't the way Ashley really looked and it went too fast and didn't I hate it the way they messed up books when when they made them into movies?

I had never read a book in my life and didn't attend movies for reasons of faith, but everything about him — his voice, his eyes, his brown, clever hands — compelled me to agree with him, nodding like an idiot, saying yes, yes, he was right. I hated that, too. That's all he seemed to require in way of reply, his eyes back on mine in the old way, arresting and strange, as he explained the nuances of Scarlett and Rhett in a voice of authority so strong that I could only stand there coatless in the February chill, wondering if he was *kin* to these people, he knew them so well, where they lived, what they ate, the names of all their houses.

The food part especially intrigued me, the barbecues and biscuits and endless platters of chicken. When Mama called me in for my own supper, without even realizing how I got there, I found that I had been drawn off the porch to stand right across the fence from him, dizzily full of Tara and Twelve Oaks and the beastly War, entranced at last, a little bird waiting for the squeeze.

$$= 8 =$$

n short order, he was my life; the hope that got me out of bed in the morning, the last dream before I drifted off to sleep; my companion, my only friend, aside from Ira, who took my defection well, all things considered. For until then, I had been his girl Friday, his confidant, his adoring disciple, and after that spring at the fence with Gabriel, it was really never the same again.

Which was nothing more than inevitable, you might say, as my brother was growing up himself, taking on weight and height so fast that one afternoon when he came up on the porch I mistook him for Daddy. He wasn't even close to him yet in terms of sheer size, though there was something to his walk, a heaviness of tread, a turn of his shoulders, that gave a fleeting indication of things to come. Since our release from house arrest, he had been increasingly going his own way, with work and school and his own love-interests that were expanding beyond the so-called good girls of Welcome to older girls, even high school girls, who came to the door looking for him, bold as you please.

So he didn't have much room to complain about me and Gabriel, and like I say, seemed to take it all right, not the least bit jealous, but quite the contrary, seemingly amazed that I had bagged the Prince of the

Hill. I was equally amazed, and for the first time in my life, I began to study myself in the mirror above the mantle when I happened to pass through the living room, wondering what in the world Gabe saw in me. There must be something there, surely, if he liked me as much as everyone said, but I couldn't have told you what. For the image that stared back had none of the bubble-haired girlishness that characterized the beauty of the day, my hair still pulled back in its severe braids, my face a softer, rounded miniature of my father's, with Mama's distant, otherworldly eyes.

I didn't see any beauty there, in that the spring of my twelfth year, though I saw plenty of it across the fence in the face and person of Gabriel Catts: in his brown, lovely hands, his chin-out smile, his voice when he sang that was a high, sweet tenor. An Irish-tenor, they used to call it, so piping clear that he really did look angelic, standing there at the fence singing me an old, forgotten hymn, after Ira told me he sang in church all the time, and I begged him to sing for me.

At first, he wouldn't look at me when he sang, said he never looked at *anybody,* that it made him too nervous, but only stood there with his arms crossed on his chest, soundlessly tapping one hand to keep time, occasionally chancing a glance in my direction. Whatever he saw there must have reflected back a rare passion, for his voice absorbed it, his tone ringing even clearer, though his voice was low-pitched and wary, afraid the other boys would catch him singing to a girl, and he'd never hear the end of it:

> *Oh, they tell me of a home where no sorrows rise,*
> *Oh, they tell me of a home, far away!*
> *Oh, they tell me of a home, where no dark clouds rise,*
> *Oh! They tell me of an unclouded day.*

It was his mother's favorite song that I never tired of hearing, feeling something in my heart transformed by the sad, lilting melody, a stir of life there more compelling than the tiny wiggle of sexuality that sometimes came to me at night, when I considered undergoing my own conversion so I could slip off to Welcome for VBS and corner him in one of the little basement Sunday School rooms where Ira had lost his reputation with Cassie Lea the summer before.

But singing was as close as we ever moved toward intimacy, and it was just as well, and really just as sweet, standing there in the cool spring sunshine, then the hot summer mornings, Gabriel eventually tiring of the Old South and going on to the French Revolution and Napoleon and Josephine, coming as close to explicitness as he could in his wistful description of their love and marriage and tragic divorce. As the summer passed, his eyes lost a little of their snapping quality, bothered by all this suppressed yearning, sulky in a way that made me nervous, wanting to go back to Scarlett and Rhett and Mammy, who seemed so comparatively safe.

But there was no going back, and it was in such idle dreams that I frittered away my year of reprieve, being in love, though I was careful to keep it to myself. Gabriel and I both were, me because of Daddy, Gabriel maybe for the same reason, not because of Mr. Simon, but his mother, who'd never cared for me much, still didn't, if I read her right when she came out to interrupt our play with chores for Gabe, or phone messages for Mama. Her face was always pleasant enough, but there was something behind it, a particular solidity of expression, that sent me inside in a hurry, full of a vague, nameless guilt that put a little chill in my bones.

As for Daddy, I was as careful to shield my love for Gabriel from him as I had my love for Mr. Simon the summer before, keeping my face carefully blank around him, which wasn't difficult, as he was so seldom home. Since Ira was working, literally bringing home the bacon, we didn't feel Daddy's absence as sharply as we had before, and considered ourselves lucky, for when he was around, something seemed to be eating at him all the time. It was as if the high spirits of Christmas had made a complete inversion, a dip into moroseness the likes of which we'd never seen before. As summer cooled to a dry, lovely autumn, I'd sometimes find his eyes on me at our rare, family suppers, never angry or particularly drunk as he had been the year before, but only narrow-eyed and speculative. It was as if he guessed my days by the fence and didn't like it a bit, though he never made any move of anger toward me, couldn't, with the sheriff still standing in the wings.

I didn't know what to make of it, didn't know what to make of his physical decline that seemed to worsen with every passing absence. He seemed to be losing weight before our very eyes, his usually high-colored face fading to a paste-white, his formerly dandy love of sharp, well-made clothes deteriorating into a slack, uncharacteristic untidiness. If anything, I attributed it to the liquor, though it seemed much deeper than that, as if he were stricken with a mysterious ailment, a secret cancer that was eating away at his legendary strength, filling his face with that blank, apathetic stare that scared the hell out of me. Alone in my bed at night, hearing his heavy step coming or going on the porch, I'd wish Ira were home more often, instead of stocking shelves at the store so many nights, leaving just me and Mama there to face him.

But I didn't realize the head of steam that was building until it blew up in my face, leaving Gabriel and me pretty much disabled for life, though Daddy might be said to have gotten the worse end of the deal. For it cost him everything he had: his wife, his children, his very memory, while all we lost was a hand and a childhood, respectively.

It all came to a head in mid-November, on a cold autumn evening so similar to the day of his last explosion that had left me locked up for a week in my companionable little closet. Just like before, I literally didn't see it coming, hurrying home from school as usual, knowing Gabe would be there shortly, waiting for him by the fence. He came out wrapped in an old quilt like he sometimes did when it was cold, dancing around to keep warm, begging me to go in and ask Mama if I could go in their house to play cards.

I knew better than to bother and only shook my head, my refusal making him exhale one of his huge sighs in a cloud of smoky breath, then stoically stand there in the cold without much left to say. I think that after nine months of nonstop monologue, he was finally coming to the end of his resources, and since I still couldn't leave the yard, it really was putting a crimp in our play. Lately, we'd had to pull out the old standards to occupy us, hopscotch, or sometimes, house, with him the Daddy, of course, and me the Mama of a hungry, fatigued little household that was always eating (my influence) or going to bed (his.)

That day, it was hopscotch, or so I understand, because to tell you the truth, we are embarking on the murky waters of restored memory here, and I am really not so certain that it all happened like this. But it's as close as I can come, and fairly accurate, I believe, based on my own wafts of memory, along with Gabe's recollections and what little other people have offered, including the Queen next door, who came in on the very end.

Apparently Gabriel, in his old bossy, know-it-all glory, decided to enhance an otherwise boring afternoon by designing an elaborate hopscotch board in the sand under the old sweet gum that divided our yards, his design, my labor, as he was careful to stay on his side of the fence. Not content with a multitude of double-squares, he had me draw some of them three abreast, which had me confused, as I couldn't figure how a two-footed person could make such a skip. But Gabriel was as confident as ever, badgering me to work it out according to his directions, both of us so involved that I ignored Mama's call to come to supper. Daddy hadn't been home in weeks, and I didn't figure she'd be in any hurry, as Ira would probably be working late this close to Thanksgiving, leaving just her and me to eat the leftovers from the night before.

So I lingered there by the fence far later than usual, twilight upon us before we finally had the thing drawn. Gabriel leaned on the fence then, his pointer stick tapping our yard, and told me to hurry and find a rock so he could prove the genius of his design before we went in.

"Git you a flat one!" he yelled, sending me kicking through the sand by the ditch. "A roundun'll roll!"

I found one under the live oak and had bent down to pick it up, calling, "Here! Gabriel! A nice flat one!" when I heard something at my back. It wasn't loud, just a soft thump that vibrated down the sagging fence, making me stand, rock in hand, thinking Gabriel had finally leaned too hard and knocked it over.

I turned to laugh at him, my smile fading when I saw it wasn't Gabe who'd thumped the fence. It was Daddy. He faced me across the half-lit yard, holding Gabriel triumphantly aloft by his wrist like the kill at a hunt, his jaw set in a rage so striking that I dropped the rock involuntarily, just like that. It just fell out of my hand, a small shake beginning in my shoulders, the shake Ira and I hated worse than the blood or the sting or the pound of a bruise, because, try as you might, you simply couldn't control it. I remember standing there that night, hating it so much. Not hating Daddy or Gabriel or the twilight that had betrayed us, but the small chicken shake to my shoulders; hating myself for being such a sissy, trying to clench my fists to control it, when somewhere beyond the fence, the evening hush was broken by a sharp, familiar *crack*.

It must have been the *crack* of a slammed door, as Miss Cissie rounded the porch in a flash, dressed in nothing more formidable than a house dress and old apron, but charging the fence like a wild dog, shouting, "Put him *down*, let him *loose* — I'll call the *Law*, you drunk *sorry* piece of trash!"

Just like that, Daddy obeyed, letting Gabriel crumple to the dirt, even offering a mild explanation ("— *in my yard, not given permission to come in my yard* —") that Cissie all but ignored, just poking her small, pretty face within an inch of his, promising to CALL the LAW! To TELL her HUSBAND, who'd SHOOT him like a DOG! Putting a hand on her CHILE!

On that, she picked Gabriel up — not a minor feat of lifting, as he had grown as fast as Ira that summer and was far beyond the toting stage. But Miss Cissie's wrath had drawn her up to Herculean proportions, and even as she carried Gabe around the house, she kept up her aggrieved complaint: "Tired of putting up with trash! *Tired!* Won't stand for it no more!"

When she was gone, the fence line was particularly quiet. Mama came to the back door and called something, I can't remember what, my eyes on Daddy, who was standing at the fence, quietly telling me to go in the house. His voice was different from his usual rage, so quiet and deadly that I simply refused, giving in to a small, pathetic defiance for the first time in my life, wordlessly shaking my head *no*.

"In the house," he repeated quietly, taking a step toward me, then another, but I just kept shaking my head.

I didn't want to go in that damn house, I'll tell you that. I didn't know why, but I knew it was going to be awful, worse than that last time with Ira, worse than anything with Mama, worse than the time he'd killed our little cat, slamming it against the living room wall for peeing on the rug. Worse than even that, and I just stood there, hating the shaking that was infectious, moving down my arms to my hands, making me clench them into even tighter fists to try and still the shaking. I closed my eyes against it, cursing it and me, too, hating myself, wishing I was anybody else, when there was a sound at my back, at the far end of the field.

It was a familiar, welcome sound on the evening chill that made me turn sharply to the tracks, where sure enough, Mr. Simon was coming down the path, a good bit off yet, his white T-shirt barely visible in the twilight. The relief was unbearable, almost as painful as the fear had been, and I had opened my mouth to shout to him when Daddy jerked me up by the back of my hair, his voice a hoarse, honest whisper in my ear: "Say the word, and I'd kill you and him, both. Now *git yer ass* in thet house."

On that, he turned and sent me sprawling to the sand, barely able to get to my feet before he came up behind me and kicked me again, so that I had to practically crawl up the porch stairs. Mama met us there, her voice her old reconciliatory rumble, telling Daddy to *settle down, Leldon*. What was the matter? Supper was all ready, pork chops, his favorite —

But Daddy wasn't buying; he *never was,* slapping Mama bare-handed when she brought up the State, knocking her to the kitchen floor. She sprang up immediately, and it's a measure of his increasing deterioration that she was able to restrain him long enough for me to get to the bedroom and lock the door at my back before he finally threw her off. She hit the wall with a blow so solid it vibrated through the hollow door that slammed in on me when he kicked it open, his face a mask of unrestrained fury, simply indescribable: the last time in my life I ever remember seeing it, literally.

After that night's work, the once-familiar countenance of sometimes-fear, sometimes-affection was sucked into the vacuum of memories so torturous that I eventually lost ten years of my life to the particularly lingering death that is incest: numb and cruel, never what people think it is. Nothing sexual about it at all, like the movies-of-the-week or the dimestore novels sometimes portray it, but a living, breathing emotional death so enduring that I have to count myself lucky to have only lost a *fourth* of my life to it.

= 9 =

$\mathcal{I}$n the recovered memory fad of the
eighties, a few psychiatrists and other counselors of goodwill kindly
offered to hypnotize me so that I might relive every detail of my insuf-
ferable childhood in living color, but I never let them, still won't to this
day. Not just because of Candace's prejudice toward hypnotism, but simply because it strikes me as a psychologically pushy thing to do, knocking down doors best left untouched. So in a world of purged, enlight-
ened survivors, quick to delve into the outer limits of human suffering
in order to make a clean breast of it, I remain a stiff-necked dinosaur, still
sometimes haunted by yet unexorcised demons, but basically too damn
chicken to feel out the extremes of the situation, preferring to leave it in
the hands of the Lord, much to my psychiatrist's disgust.

Which is all to say that I am not lying when I say that I can't ever
remember seeing my father's face again, can't remember ever seeing
Gabriel's either, as a child, though with a little effort, I can recall a few
glimpses of the morning after for a very normal, almost mundane reason: it was the day I started my period. Or at least, it was the day I started bleeding — convenient timing, you might call it, that inadvertently
froze in memory a morning that might well have slipped into oblivion

77

had it not been memorialized by this landmark coming-of-age event, Mama sitting me down at the dining room table with a big old box of sanitary napkins and the little belt that went with them and patiently showing me how to hook them all up. Her own face was yet bruised, her voice a little shaky as she filled me in on the curious bits of myth and superstition attached to menstruation, how you couldn't wash your hair on the first day or churn buttermilk, all of it veiled in a thin, palpable shame that I remember to this day.

I didn't argue with her, didn't question her at all, only leaned over to rest my forehead on the table halfway through, for my father had knocked the hell out of me before he did the worst of his damage the night before. All I could remember with any clarity of the evening was Gabriel and the hopscotch board and Mr. Simon coming down the path, his shirt glimmering white at the very end of the field, but too far away to do me any good. I remembered that and was too sick to care about anything else, sick as a dog.

That's really my most lasting impression of the whole dying end of 1962: of being so damn sick, all the time. I'd feel relatively normal in the morning, but as the day burned on, so would my fever, the chills starting at mid-afternoon, making me shake like a rattle till it was in the hundred-and-five range. That's when the headaches would begin, the likes of which no aspirin on earth could contain. I bet I took a dozen a night, as that was still the extent of Mama's medical arsenal: little hundred-milligram aspirins and cold washcloths that she held to my forehead for hours at a time. I can't remember her face when she did it, just the feel of her damp, worried hands, and her quiet, helpless voice, whispering for me to *settle down, sister,* that I'd be all right.

Ira would occasionally come in the bedroom and pull up a chair for a visit. He was growing so fast that sometimes, toward the end of the year, I didn't even recognize him. I vaguely remember him bringing me a Christmas present, a string of fake pearls he'd bought God-knows-where, unwrapping them and laying them in my hand, telling me that I was going to be all right, that Miss Cissie had sent me some medicine.

When I didn't respond, he leaned close to the bed, said, "Myra? D'you hear me?"

His face was so worried, bunched up in the fleece of last year's jacket that wasn't so big on him anymore, the sleeves ending well above his wrists that had grown like the rest of him, so fast and strong that I sometimes flinched when I woke up and found him there watching me, thinking it was Daddy, but it never was.

"He's gone," I remember him telling me. "Living with some woman in Graceville. Good riddance, I say."

I didn't know what to make of his fast, hard words, didn't know who he was talking about, to tell you the truth, in such poor physical shape when school reopened in January that Mama kept me home. She sent notes to my teacher every week, changing my diagnosis from chicken pox to measles to whooping cough, with never a question raised, unwilling or unable to face the enormity of my real complaint: pelvic inflammatory disease and a nasty kidney infection and a bad case of syphilis on top of that, all courtesy of my father.

A stiff dose of penicillin would have set me to rights, of course, but she simply couldn't chance it, just keeping me home, locked in a haze of denial that I can't very well fathom or explain, apparently preferring to watch me die in my bed rather than open herself up to another public humiliation. I really am convinced that by Easter I would have ended up in a pauper's grave at Riverside if not for Ira, poor Ira, who so craved public acceptance that he was willing to embrace any God, laugh at any joke, bend over backwards to fit in.

Who watched me wither away for a good six weeks, till early February, when he finally blew the whistle, right there at the Catts' dining room table, with a shocking little confession that probably wouldn't have happened at all if our father hadn't broken it off with the woman in Graceville and showed up at our door one night after work, just like usual, no explanation given, none required. Mama apparently let him in without a fight, cooking supper and setting an extra plate, Daddy probably asking her what was wrong with me, as I hadn't gotten up to eat in weeks, down to not much more than bone and hair, having a hell of a time keeping warm that whole endless winter, chattering to death, as it were.

At some point that evening, I remember Daddy coming in to check on me, his face perfectly invisible to my mind, even today, though I think I remember his scarred old work boots pausing a moment at the door before he turned and went back to the kitchen. Sometime later, I rolled over on a penny bag of confectionery hearts he must have left on my pillow, the kind stamped with little messages, *Love, Be Mine,* that I left just as he placed them, the bed so damned cold, no matter how I much I burrowed.

Later, there was another sound at the door, the sound of shuffling boots that wakened me, afraid it was Daddy. But when I sat up, I found Ira standing by the bed in the stained produce apron he wore at work, holding one of the little hearts to the light to read the message. His is one of the few faces I remember from the period, different than it used to be, angular instead of skinny, the brace of lines around his mouth deepening as he made out the message with a curled lip of disgust, then dropped it to the floor and ground it in with the heel of his boot, back and forth, back and forth, crushing it to powder. He didn't shout, didn't make any noise at all, though Mama must have heard something, as she came to the door and told him supper was ready, that Daddy was home.

I was too blurred to pay much attention to her fast, nervous words, though I heard Ira's reply, all right, and knew what he did: he spit at her. I recognized the sound because Daddy was a big spitter when he was mad, spitting on all of us at one time or another, usually on Mama, who would take it from him, though apparently not from Ira, as there was another sound that was equally recognizable around the Sims' house: the crack of a flat-handed slap. It stung the silence of the cold room, made me raise up to find both of them standing by the bed, Ira's cheek dark where she'd slapped him, though he didn't even flinch, just stared at her with that face of cold contempt.

Something in his very resemblance to Daddy turned Mama aside to feel blindly for the edge of the bed and sit there hunched over like an old woman, her silent tears filling me with a terrible pity. I lifted a thin hand to clumsily pat her shoulder, but it only made her cry harder, a dangerous indulgence with Daddy in the house. When his heavy footsteps started down the hall, Mama looked up, suddenly wary, then stood quickly and whispered something to Ira that made his face suddenly alight.

They had a whispered conference by the bed, then he turned and took off out the front door. Mama followed close behind and must have intercepted Daddy in the living room, as her voice drifted through the open door, thin and placating: "— feeling poorly — no, he's a-working late."

I paid them no mind, just burrowed back into the bed to drift into an uneasy sleep, awakened sometime later by a pound at our front door. I no longer flinched at the sound of a knock at the door and just lay there with dry skin and half-slitted eyes till Mama burst in the room, coming straight to the bed and lifting me by my shoulders with no explanation at all.

I tried to pull away, but she wouldn't let go, pulling me off the bed and dragging me through the house, down the hall and out the back door into a curiously lovely evening that was balmy and pleasant, nearing full dark. After so many weeks abed, I could hardly walk, stumbling in the near-darkness, though Mama didn't let me fall, her voice in my ear, whispering little words of encouragement, "Come on, sister — there you go —".

She maneuvered me around the back fence and into the Catts' yard, tripping on the exposed roots of the old oak, both of us almost falling. The jarring made my head pound so hard I had to stop a moment to get my bearings, slumping against her shoulder till I was distracted by a flash of red light that whirled around out front, bathing both houses with a fleeting, melting glare. I realized then that something was going on up there, a knot of angry people gathered beyond the fence.

I tried to stop, to ask Mama what was wrong, but she just marched me resolutely to the safety of the Catts' back porch, when the cluster of people unexpectedly parted to reveal a momentary glimpse of a man lying prostate in the shadow of our yard.

"Mr. *Simon?*" I whispered, and even as I spoke his name, I saw that it was indeed him, hanging limply between two ambulance attendants that gripped him, feet and shoulders, and lifted him to a gurney.

I started for him instinctively, but Mama fought me like a cat, all the way up the steps to the porch, where she paused a moment with her hand plastered over my mouth to speak aside to the deep shadow by the wall, to a pale, grim-faced figure I finally made out as Ira.

"Go on —" she hissed. "*Run.*"

Without a word, he took off across the yard, his jacket melting into the darkness, while just across the fence, I could hear Daddy roaming our house, calling, "Myra? Myra Louise?"

But Mama had me in a death grip, flattened there against the wall by the Catts' back door, her hand so tight on my mouth that I literally couldn't breathe. I was too weak to struggle and was slowly losing consciousness when she finally let go, softly knocking on the Catts' back door that was shut against the evening chill. Gabriel himself answered, opening the screen awkwardly as his right arm was immobilized to the elbow in a white cast that was a little worse for wear, scribbled and frayed around the edges.

I really can't remember his face as he stood there, though I did wonder what happened to his arm as he exchanged a few whispered words with Mama, then motioned us in, running to the bedroom and bringing his mother to the kitchen in a black dress slip. For once, her face was completely devoid of that old snotty fixity, just looking me up and down while Mama whispered ("— going to Texas. Says he's a'taking her, please, ma'am, please —") with eyes that seemed so wounded to me. I can hardly ever think of Cissie without remembering her as she was that night, standing there in her worn slip, grasping my predicament in one horrified glance and practically shoving Mama out the door, her voice a fast whisper: "Go to the church — no — the tracks. No, *run* —"

Mama instantly obeyed, taking off across the yard without a glance back, leaving me standing there blinking in the bright kitchen that smelled like Gabriel's jacket always smelled, of bread, somehow, and even closer, fried meat and smoke from the supper that was still cooling on the table, the ice melting in the tea glasses, untouched. It really was as surreal as a fever-dream, standing there in the Catts' kitchen at last, Miss Cissie calling aside to someone in the dining room, whispering, "Run get Case. *Hurry*."

On that, she snatched me by the hand and started through the house in unconscious imitation of Daddy's forced run the year before. The sudden motion made my head swim so violently that I jerked away when we made it to the bedroom and dropped to the edge of the bed, my face pressed to my knees, trying to get a grip on the nausea before I threw up.

Cissie left me there, turning and turning in place, her eyes huge as Daddy came out on the back porch and shouted in teeth-clenched rage, "Myra? *Eloise!*"

Still she turned, her eyes white and frantic till they fell on the old cedar wardrobe that took up most of the inside wall, when she came to sudden stop. "Here," she whispered, yanking open the doors so hard they bounced on their hinges, tossing out shoes and hose and Sunday hats to the floor. She told me to get in, and Gabe, too, whispering, "Scrunch up. Hold it from the inside, there."

He did as he was told, piling in beside me, and after a moment there was the click of the lock catching, then perfect quiet. The darkness was so complete that at first I couldn't see him, even a foot away, though I wasn't particularly afraid, just sitting there, listening to his breath, which was quick and shallow in the tight, narrow space.

"It'll be all right," he kept whispering, almost to himself, his white cast gradually visible as my eyes adjusted to the light, the first thing I could make out in the darkness.

"Gabriel? Didju hurt yourself?" I whispered, but he didn't answer, and I was too tired to press it, my head pounding so hard I closed my eyes, longing for the comfort of my own little bed, wishing I could lie down there and never get up, never again.

After a while our feet started going numb, and Gabriel wiggled around till I could stretch out a little, ending up lying with my face pressed against his chest, perfectly content. For I hadn't had a human pillow since Ira moved into the living room last year, and it was really very pleasant to lie there rubbing my hot face on his shirt that felt wonderfully cool, his free hand feeling for mine and gripping it in the darkness.

"S'all right," he kept whispering. "It'll be all right."

His short, breathless assurances were so calming that I almost fell asleep there against him, ignoring the crash somewhere in the front of the house that made Gabe's breath even faster, his hand tightening to a hard, panicked grip as the roar moved back out to the porch, then the yard, then was altogether gone. The house was quiet then, Gabe's closeness making my chills stop for the first time in maybe two months, when I felt his breath in my face as he spoke into the darkness, "Myra, listen. I'm gone marry you when we grow up."

There was another silence, as if he were waiting on my reply, but it really wasn't a proposal as much as a statement, and after a moment, he spoke again. "Can I kiss you?" When I didn't answer, his voice took on a

thread of his old wily reasonableness. "I mean, we can wait till we're married, if you want, or we can do it now. It don't matter to me."

It didn't to me either, to tell you the truth, but I obliged and
reached up and kissed him a child's kiss goodnight, then dropped back
to his chest and closed my eyes and almost dozed off, awakened with a
start when the double doors were jerked open wide, both of us recoil-
ing from the glare of the overhead light, Gabe lifting his cast to cover his
eyes.

I tried to burrow away into his shirt, but couldn't, as Cissie caught
me by my shoulders and pulled me to my feet, the pound in my head
returning at the fast movement, and the nausea, too. All night long, as I
was swept passively along, hastily examined by the doctor on Cissie's
bed, then wrapped in a blanket and taken to the ER, I kept remembering the locked wardrobe; how cozy it had been, a safe harbor in a sea of
wall-shaking, head-pounding confusion.

But there was no going back once we made the hospital, for the
person waiting at the admission desk wasn't Mama or Ira or even Dr.
Winston, but the nurse from the State. She thanked Cissie and Case for
bringing me in, then sent them away and followed my gurney into an
examining room where I began a brief stay at Jackson Memorial that really does stand out as possibly the worst three days of my life. Even
Daddy's cruelty paled in comparison, for at least it was tinged with
human emotion, even if that emotion was the same old carousel of rage
and regret — while the hospital was a place of sterile hellishness.

They must have done two pelvics a day on me, the specialist's face
above the raised sheet so tight and revolted, jerking off his gloves when
he was finished and storming from the room. In my weakness, I thought
his hostility aimed at me, and cringed at the nurses' rough treatment of
my mother, who they really did treat like a dog. After that first awful day,
she quit coming to the hospital at all, though Ira visited often, bringing
candy and Cokes from the store, occasionally mentioning Mr. Simon's
progress a few doors down the hall.

After two days on an antibiotic drip, it finally occurred to me that
our simultaneous hospitalizations might possibly be related, though
when I asked Ira about it, he was inexplicably unconcerned. "Sure.
Daddy beat the shit out of him. He's damn near dead."

His light, careless answer was like a kick in the belly, a hollow, breathless horror I could only blink at, worse than the doctors and their probing, worse than the nurses and Mama's desertion. Ira was curiously detached, though, quite unconcerned that this man he loved as much as I did was at death's door. He only sat there slumped in the visitor's chair and let me in on a secret: that we were moving to Alabama to live with Aunt Ross; Mama was making the arrangements right now.

After the horrific news about Mr. Simon, this incredible twist of fortune seemed irrelevant, and I remember just looking at him, whispering, "Why?"

He knew what I meant — not why were we moving to Alabama, but why had Daddy beat Mr. Simon — but was still perfectly casual. "'Cause he's an asshole, that's why."

I was too put off by his silky contempt to even ask him to specify *who* he considered the asshole, Daddy or Mr. Simon, and just watched him out of tired, sunken eyes, thought how big he was getting, not little Ira anymore, but quite grown up.

"So." He grinned. "You excited about Birmingham? Aint Ross has money. She'll buy us some clothes."

But I couldn't return his sudden stranger's smile and only stared at him across the starched hospital sheets, as grieved over the loss of Mr. Simon as I was the loss of my brother, who had never been much of a child before and would surely never be again.

= 10 =

I have no other memory of ever returning to Magnolia Hill as a child, though I understand the State detained us long enough for my blood tests to clear, so we weren't allowed to move to Aunt Ross's for at least a month. That's what they tell me anyway. As far as I can remember, my whole life faded from the time of my brief stay in Jackson Memorial till small glimpses of a very different life began playing out in a very different milieu, in Fairfield, an old working-class suburb of Birmingham, a good two years later.

To my mind, there's not a gap there I can discern, just a smooth transition from my sickly, vivid memories of Florida, then a flicker or two until my conscious life resumed as a remarkably somnolent teenager living a seemingly normal life in the tract houses of North Alabama. The only inconsistencies were the changes in my family, particularly Ira, who in memory seems to jump from a gangling, freckle-faced teenager one day, to a grown man, the next, with no point of transition in between.

He was still my friend, in either case — my only friend, as a matter of fact, always willing to bring along a shy, backward sister to his games, his parties, his whole boundless social life, just as he had on the Hill. Except in this case, there was no magic there to receive me, no Gabriel or Mr. Simon or wistful, childish fantasies to unravel over a kudzu-choked fence, just rock-hard, working-class reality, the kind I have always abhorred. I understand that we lived with Aunt Ross for perhaps as long as a year, till Mama threw off the last tattered remnants of her parents' strict teachings to marry a man she'd met at her job as a cashier at the local Quick Check, a widower twenty years her senior named Carl Odom, who owned his own house and drove a decent car and was within five years of retirement from his job at Gulf Life.

Aside from that, there's not much else you can say about my stepfather. He was a good enough man, a little slow and heavy, quick to adopt Ira and me once the legal hurdles were overcome, equally quick to let Mama wear the pants in the family in a manner so sweeping I can only say that old Leldon had trained her well, which was the other, most irreconcilable difference between my memories of Magnolia Hill and Birmingham: Mama.

In my childhood memories of her, she was our ally, alternately rescuer and victim, Daddy's rage the common denominator of all our lives. Once she was safely entrenched in a tract house in a subdivision in Fairfield (the concrete-block kind sixties' developers rolled out, treeless and bleak, with its mirror image across the street), she was magically transformed into a sharp-tongued, chain-smoking, status-conscious, working-class queen whom nobody crossed any more than they'd crossed Miss Cissie, it just wasn't done.

By then, only Ira could withstand her, and that was because he could withstand anyone, his transition from bony outsider to brilliant insider completed in the summer of his fifteenth year when an observant high school coach noticed him devouring cheeseburgers at a local drive-in. After one look at his sheer size and appetite, he struck up a conversation and all but begged him to show up for practice, going so far as to provide him with cleats when he learned of our reduced circumstances (we were still living on the dole with Aunt Ross at the time). It was a turning point, Ira's entrance into the heart of North Alabama, publically introduced in September with his unforeseen ability to crack heads as that most revered of all players, the six-foot-three, two-hundred-twenty-pound linebacker, who was fast, and *mean*.

These qualities — along with his good looks and a flickering vulnerability (the only vestige of my old Ira, my dreaming boy who wiled away the mimosa nights) — were so appealing that the only friends I remember from the era were from his entourage of girlfriends who took me under their wing. I guess they were hoping that their rehabilitation of a shy, backward sister into a pink-nailed, Doris Day wonder would somehow swing his favor, though they never succeeded with him or me, either one. For we were cast in a mold too hardened to break, our only real bone of contention my fanatical devotion to rock-hard, fundamentalist Christianity.

He and Mama had given up their faith back in Florida, tossed it aside with the last of Mama's good Sunday dresses, and while Ira quickly reinvented himself as a beer-swilling, quarterback-crippling good-old-boy with all the women and hell-raising that entailed, I went the opposite direction, the kinder route of escape: into the arms of the Lord. Now, I don't mean to belittle my choice by calling it an escape, though escape it most certainly was, and every Sunday morning and night, and every Wednesday mid-week service, I'd be down at a small Assemblies of God church which was providentially at the end of our street, since I was the only Odom attending and had to depend on my feet to get me there.

I was so shy I can't imagine how I got up the gumption to go it alone, though I remember the drawing well enough. I still feel it, to this day, the same pull I used to feel toward Mr. Simon at the fence on Magnolia Hill: the possibility of a kinder life out there, a spiritual cement to fill the holes in my poor hungry soul. For whereas Ira and Mama were seemingly restored to perfect wholeness after the pressing matters of housing and clothing and respectability were taken care of, I knew I was messed up; knew it and despaired.

Even at church I was an outsider, sitting quietly in the back with no cushion of family to shield me from the claws of the other girls who were not so willing to let this suspiciously well-endowed stranger in on the few eligible boys, though their disdain hardly mattered. I wasn't there for the boys; I was there for the Lord, going up every night to the altar to pray for Mama, pray for Ira, hardly ever for myself. Why should I? I was strong, I was *saved*. They were the ones going to hell, a calm assumption that nearly drove poor Ira crazy.

He thought it bad enough that I was content to go to school every day and eke by without a word till three, when I'd go home and sleep the afternoon away. But then to go out of my way to embrace not only Christianity, but backwoods, holy-rolling, hard-shell Pentecostalism that deemed everything from pierced ears to cut hair to attending movies mortal sin, that was too much. He was convinced I'd lost my mind, and really wasn't too far off base, as I'm sure my raging legalisms sprang from the same source as his carousing and football fanaticism: sheer survival. By which I mean to seek out a light of acceptance and to run to it with all your might, all your resources.

To take the advice of the good men of Magnolia Hill to not look back, sister, *don't look back!* To forget about Daddy, who we heard via the family grapevine had been sighted back in Louisiana on the arm of yet another wife, though he never made a move of reconciliation in our direction, couldn't very well, with the warrants still hanging over his head in Florida. So we didn't pay much attention when word came in '65 that he was sick, or a year later, when a rumor circulated that he was more than sick, he was *dying,* till I came home from school on the latter end of the year and found Mama in the kitchen in her old winter coat, waiting for me. Her suitcase by the door was all packed; her face was perfectly blank as she made a big to-do over telling me to take care of the house while she was gone, of Carl and Ira.

When I asked where she was going, she was a little vague. "Louisiana," she said, "for the weekend."

I thought it was Grandma, but Mama said no, it wasn't her. She didn't offer anything else, and it wasn't till Ira came home from practice that night that I learned the truth, that Daddy was dying and asking for her.

"Dying of what?" I asked, and Ira just shrugged.

"Shit, I don't know. Got himsef another wife, another kid by some other woman, but soon as he calls, there goes Mama, off like a light."

When Mama returned on Monday night, worn out from the long bus drive across Mississippi, she didn't offer much at supper, though she unexpectedly showed up in my bedroom that night and sat on the edge of the bed.

"Yer Daddy wants to see you," she said quietly and I answered just as quietly, with a shake of my head so instinctual that I didn't even realize I was doing it at first, just felt my head going back and forth. "We're leaving Saturday," she continued, "me and you and Ira. Carl says it's fine. He knows you'd wanta see your Daddy before he died. Knows it's the right thang to do."

She patiently ignored my head that was still moving side to side, just stood and left me there in my little sanctuary that I'd never leave, voluntarily, though after a long night of tossing and turning, I went down the hall to Ira's bedroom and woke him up.

"What?" he said, sitting up against the headboard with a grimace, used to me waking him up at night when I had my technicolor nightmares.

"I ain't going to Louisiana," I told him. "'Kay?"

I don't know why I needed his permission, but I did, and he ran a hand through his tousled hair and gave a huge sigh. "Why not?"

"Because I ain't," I repeated, and he looked at me evenly.

"Mama says he's changed. Says he's dying. Lost one leg, about to lose the other. Says he's got some money for us. And a house or something."

That may have turned Mama's head, but sure didn't mine, and I just kept shaking my head till Ira sighed again. "I'll talk to her," he said. "She'll be madder than hell."

Which proved to be prophetic, though after a few days of shouts and pouts, they left, and Carl and I made out very well on our own till they returned on Monday, both of them tired from the trip. Mama still wasn't speaking to me, leaving Ira to wordlessly hand me an envelope that I left sealed on my dresser two days, till curiosity got the best of me and I opened it. I think I expected money, to tell you the truth, or at least familiar handwriting, but it was just a short note on plain lined notebook paper in a strange hand that read: *Baby, I wished you could of come. I'll call you Sataday night.* It was signed by his own hand: *Daddy.*

I looked at it a long time, feeling absolutely nothing at all, not regret or love or even hate. Just a numb emptiness that didn't stay numb long, not after he started in on the phone calls every week, usually on Saturday nights, Mama or Carl or Ira calling me to the phone time and again. A woman with a flat, Louisianan drawl would always speak first, then hand the phone to Daddy, who didn't sound like himself at all, but weak and feeble, his voice a call back to his rural childhood, that of kindly old cotton farmer.

"Hey, darlin'," he'd whisper. "Whatchu doing, baby?"

That's about as far as he'd get before I'd hand the phone back to whoever had just handed it to me and retreat to the comfort of my bed, or sometimes the bathroom, to meditate over the toilet, poised to vomit, though nothing ever came up. By summer, my stubbornness had cost me the goodwill of everyone in the house. Even Carl couldn't understand my repugnance for the kindly old voice from Louisiana, all of them big buddies by the time Daddy died in late August, after two further amputations and a summer of horrendous suffering.

Mama bought me a new dress for the funeral and talked Carl into letting us take the car to a tiny row house in Sliddell almost identical to the one we'd lived in on Magnolia Hill, with a worn-out easy chair on the sagging porch where his wife said he'd sat every evening to watch the sunset that final summer of his life. We found the place filled with a unexpectedly ordinary mix of friends and family, including black-haired cousins from New Orleans I'd never laid eyes on in my life. Daddy must have indeed had a few roots in the black muck of the Atchafalaya Swamp, as they were Catholic and (at the funeral, anyway) apparently devout, all of them curious to meet me.

"Thought a right smart of you, did Leldon," they told me in their funny, hick-French voices, more than a few commenting on how much Ira and I favored him, focusing all their attention on us, his legitimate heirs, politely ignoring his two or three by-lows who showed up with their mothers, with no mention made of how much *they* favored him.

All of it made for a truly Louisianan tangle, the August heat simmering on the asphalt of the funeral home, the service itself predictable in its overweening optimism. Oddly enough, it was an Assembly of God preacher doing the honors, who admitted he'd only met Daddy in his last illness, but said what a good man he was, always willing to give to the church, so good to his (then) wife, so proud of his children. He crinkled his eyes in Ira's and my direction on that, clearly impressed with the city clothes and wholesome air of prosperity that Mama and Carl had worked so hard to surround us in, a far cry from Daddy's white-trash, row-house poverty.

I wasn't comforted by his pleasantries, just sat there staring at the still, gray face in the coffin with no emotion at all, only wondering if we were talking about the same man, though Ira, he loved it. He believed it, and it was probably there at the funeral that Daddy began his mythic evolution from The Scourge of Magnolia Hill to the harmless gray-faced man in the coffin, the kind old man who was always giving to the church, so proud of his boy.

I never argued, I couldn't, since much of my childhood in Florida was hemmed in by a blank, gray fog, impenetrable in memory. Some things shown brightly — Mr. Simon, the little creek, the fat old oak — though most of it had gone underground, as Florida rivers occasionally do, dissolving into the aquifer without a trace, to reappear miles away, the same running stream. That's what my childhood had done, and continued to do, till the December Ira turned eighteen, when (to the great gnashing of his coach's teeth) he threw over Alabama football to fulfill his lifelong dream of enlisting in the Marines.

He'd signed the papers in early August, and as the date of his departure inevitably approached, there were parties on every hand, him coming home night after night drunk as Cooter Brown, the Recruiter telling him to go easy, that Parris Island wasn't Youth Camp, though Ira only smiled. He was a big smiler, in those days. Not as big a one as he was to become, but even then, people were always commenting on what a good-natured boy he was, with his yes-ma'ams and no-ma'ams and his ready smile. I was the only one who ever saw his darker side, and then only occasionally, in momentary flashes, which I probably wouldn't have thought twice about, except that they reminded me so much of Daddy.

The last incident of that sort happened the Friday night before he left, on what started out as a regular sort of weekend night, me piddling around the house in my housecoat, waiting for some television show or another, Ira fielding a dozen phone calls while he dressed for his last Birmingham blow-out. He kept sending me to answer the front door for the friends who'd showed up to escort him, a little blonde named Glenda, who was his current girlfriend, along with a few football buddies.

All of them had gathered in the living room while Ira paused in the kitchen to answer one last phone call, absently taking a half-gallon of ice cream out of the freezer and eating it out of the carton while he talked. I don't know exactly how the ice cream fit into the scheme of the evening, as I was hanging around the back regions of the house, waiting for them to leave. I didn't mind Glenda, but wasn't so crazy about his football buddies, who'd lately taken to slapping me playfully on the butt when they caught me alone in the hall, all in good fun, though I noticed they never did it when Carl was around.

So I made myself scarce, wandering into the kitchen, where Ira was giving impatient directions to an apparently confused friend, the ice cream carton opened on the bar with a spoon sticking out. I picked it up for a bite, stopping in mid-air when he turned and lowered the phone.

"Leave it alone," he snapped, but I didn't pay him any mind and went ahead and took a bite, not even seeing the backhand that flew back like lightning, hitting me square in the face, so hard it knocked me to the floor. There was an immediate shock of blood in my mouth that I felt for instinctively, while Ira just stood there, phone in hand, his face as shocked as mine. He came around the bar to do something, I don't know what, as Glenda came to the door and told him to hurry, they were late. He just paused there a moment, watching me on the floor, then turned and left without a word, the ice cream carton still sitting open on the counter.

I left it there, and when Mama came in from work much later and found the ice cream carton still sitting there in a puddle of melted goo, she was not so pleased. She gave me hell about it at breakfast, but I didn't bother to explain it any more than I explained my swollen lip, just cleaned up the mess and assiduously ignored Ira when he finally climbed out of bed in mid-afternoon. He was obviously in a reconciliatory mood and followed me to my bedroom when I finished the dinner dishes, to ask if I wanted to go to yet another farewell party with him, this one at Glenda's.

"Her parents'll be there. All square and everything," he said, propping in the doorway as he always did when he dropped by. I just ignored him as I kicked off my shoes and got ready for my Sunday nap, the real marathon of the week, when I'd routinely knock out for five straight hours.

When Ira realized my intent, he straightened up and clenched his jaw. "Dammit, Myra, git out a thet damn bed. You cain't sleep your life away."

I paid him no mind, just scrunched up in my pillows, even when he came in the room and sidled up to the bed, bumping the mattress with his knees, insisting, "Dammit Myra, git up. Come on, git dressed.

It'll be fun — we're having a bonfire at the lake, roasting weenies."

On this bit of uncommon innocence, I opened an eye long enough to answer him levelly. "And whatchu you gone do if I don't, *Leldon?* Kick my ass?"

Ira's face went stiff at that, stiff and twitchy, a far cry from the good-natured ole-boy everyone was always telling me about. He drew his open hand back instinctively, though he caught it in mid-air and held it there a clenched moment, then kneed the bed so hard it slammed against the wall as he turned and stalked out, calling, "I don't know why I fucking bother! Ain't got good sense — lay there till you die, *see* if I care!"

It probably would have been advisable at that point for me to keep my mouth shut, but I hated it when he told me I didn't have good sense. It struck a little too close to the bone and made me jump up and follow him to the door, shouting, "And you can just take your *sorry* ass to Vietnam tonight, for all I care, where I hope it gits blowed *the hell* away."

Ira answered me in kind across the length of the hall, both of us yelling back and forth a few minutes, him about the church, me about who-knows-what, till the phone rang in the kitchen and I went back to the bedroom with a house-shaking slam of the door. I did cry then, long and hard, and refused to attend his sports banquet the next evening, pleading a stomachache and staying home in bed. The next morning, I found the breakfast table cluttered with trophies and certificates and a royal blue letter jacket they'd given him the night before, a year early.

Mama was full of it, going on and on about the speeches and tears, and how the team had all pitched in for the jacket, but I just pushed it aside with a stony silence that lasted the better part of a full day and night, till Wednesday morning, when Mama and Carl had taken off work to drive him to the recruiting office. The weekly bus to Beaufort was scheduled to leave at nine, and I woke hours early to a cold, misting morning, lying there in the semi-darkness of dawn, trying to decide if I wanted to go. I'd been in steadfast denial over losing him for a good year, and even now, on the brink of his departure, couldn't quite fathom it, my pride battling a panicky little voice that reminded me that he was going right overseas and this might be the last time I'd ever see him.

In the end, the panic-voice won out, though I was mighty annoyed when his old entourage began showing up to escort him to town, including a sagging, red-eyed Glenda, who was quietly weeping into a linen handkerchief amid many a pat and hug. I mean, they'd only been dating since August. It wasn't like she'd be his *widow,* or something, though she confided to Mama that he'd proposed at the lake on Sunday and she'd accepted.

Now, Ira has had his share of fiancées over the years, and I can't remember much about Glenda except that her father was somehow professional, a doctor or an accountant, or maybe he was a dentist. Anyway, he was a Name, and Mama was so pleased that it lifted the morning of some of its gloom, all of them sipping coffee at the breakfast table, Ira promising he'd come back in eight weeks before he shipped out, hinting that he and Glenda might tie the knot right then and there.

That was the tone of the morning. The doorbell rang constantly, filling the house with more and more well-wishers (and more than a few Butt-slappers.) I avoided them as best I could, getting dressed and sitting on my bed with his going-away present in my hands, a little New Testament I'd bought after a visiting evangelist told the story of being saved by a bullet at Guadalcanal by a little Bible in his breast pocket. I'd had it embossed with his name and everything, but after his hard words about the church, wasn't so sure he'd take it.

I was sitting there, feeling pretty wretched about the whole thing, thinking maybe it'd be better if I just stayed home, when Carl came down the hall to get me and talked me into going. He and Mama and I rode together downtown, Ira going with his friends, and it wasn't until we had pulled into the parking lot of the Marine recruiting office and I saw the milling crowd and the puffing Greyhound bus, that the unredeemable reality of the whole thing began to take hold. Mama and Carl had to go inside to sign some more papers and left me there by the curb, hunched desolately in a light summer dress that was too thin for the raw December morning, watching Ira and his buddies cut up. They'd obviously brought along a bottle and weren't feeling any pain. Ira was laughing his butt off, on a dare offered it to the granite-faced drill instructor who was standing watch at the door of the bus and laughed even harder when he didn't so much as blink an eye in reply.

"Fuck, he's *Baptist!*" he yelled to the hoots and hollers of his friends. "What *have* I got mysef into?"

I was embarrassed on the DI's behalf and wished I'd stayed home where I belonged, because despite my best efforts to stay stiff and impersonal, my eyes wouldn't cooperate, tears running down my cheeks like an open faucet. I didn't bother to wipe them away, what was the use? I hadn't had a chance to say so much as a word to Ira, much less give him his Bible, and must have made a picture of rare misery standing there in the raw morning chill, for Glenda finally noticed me across the crowd and tapped Ira on the back, pointing at me when he turned.

I was too proud to meet his eye, only shivered in the thin dress, crying like a broken water main, but he detached himself from his crowd and came over, his face a little less confident up close, the whiskey bringing his fading freckles into sharp relief. He wouldn't look at me face-on, but only sidled up next to me, a little hunched in his new letter jacket, and elbowed me around the nose of the bus for a little privacy, his voice quiet and teasing. "Myra, Myra, Myra. What are we gone do with you, sister?"

It was an endearment he'd picked up on the Hill from Mr. Simon that only made me cry harder. Neither of us said anything for a long moment as Ira felt around his shirt pocket and opened a fresh pack of Winstons, tapping one out and lighting up, his voice still a light tease. "So what's all this crying about?"

I couldn't speak at first, but finally managed between shuttering sniffs. "You're leaving."

He took a long draw from the Winston. "Well, hell, girl, you been knowing that for a year." He exhaled with a grin. "And I thought you'se wanting my sorry ass blowed up."

He was clearly trying to draw me out of my little funk with a tease, but I have never liked to be provoked when I'm already at the end of my rope, and glared at him so hard he laughed again. "Shit, girl, you're the one that looks like Leldon now."

"I don't want you to *go*." I finally managed.

He just drew casually on his cigarette. "I'll be all right."

"But you're all I *got*." Which was the truth before God; he was all I'd ever had.

His face sobered a little at that, the twitchiness in his cheek coming back, though he tried to smile. "You'll be all right," he said. "Carl'll see about you."

Which struck me as a funny way of putting it, as if he realized, too, that my many peculiarities had in some private, intimate way, forfeited my mother's loyalty, maybe even her love, and it was my stepfather that I could look to for support. It was the first time either of us had ever alluded to this awful truth, and it only added to my overall misery, though he tried to lighten things with another tease, asking, "Well, ain't you gone give me my going-away Bible?"

I sniffed. "How'd you know?"

"Bible Bookstore called Monday. Said your order was in."

I wasn't too upset my surprise had been undercut, just wiped my nose and slipped the little Testament out of my pocket and tried to tell him between sniffles about the evangelist and the bullet on Guadalcanal, not making a whole lot of sense. Ira was nice about it, though, just turned it over in his hands and put it in the pocket of his jacket till I corrected him. "No, your *shirt* pocket," I said, taking out his pack of Winstons to put it there. "There. Over your heart."

Which was where the evangelist would have been shot if he hadn't have been carrying his, and Ira patted it. "Well, where'll I put my cigarettes?"

"Put 'em in your back pocket."

"They'll be squashed," he complained, though he was smiling, glad he'd pulled me out of my little crush of despair.

I tried to return it with a brave face and a tease of my own. "Then put the Bible in your back pocket. You'll need something to cover that sorry ass."

He laughed louder and longer than the little joke warranted, then made the necessary adjustments and looked me in the eye, and said, "You keep your chin up, Myra Sims. I'll be back Easter. Git you out of that damn bed if I have to dynamite you out of it. Git you a life."

I just smiled, or tried to, as the DI at the bus had suddenly come to life and was reading names off a clipboard, calling them into line. I could hear Mama at the curb, shouting for Ira, clearly not so happy when we came around the bus together, for she'd been waiting for her own good-bye and was more than a little annoyed I'd shortchanged her, snapping that it was too wet to be out in that thin dress, to go wait in the car.

Without a word, Ira took off his letter jacket, the one they'd given him at the banquet, and handed it to me, his face oddly trained on

Mama, like he was sending her a message: she's your child, too. Or maybe it was more of a symbolic covering, I don't know. Glenda looked a little pained at the transaction, as his letter-jacket technically belonged to his fiancée. She politely deflected her disappointment with a sweet Southern smile, though Mama was clearly not amused and told me to go to the car, *now.*

I went without a word, stopping at the car to watch them load up. Ira didn't have a chance to talk to anyone else, though he did cheer Mama by sliding off his class ring and giving it to Glenda. With that ceremony complete, he turned to his buddies and started in on all kinds of nonsensical redneck ritual, rebel-yelling and jumping over each other to slap him on the top of the head, till his name was called, when he extracted himself from their grip long enough to shake Carl's hand.

Then, just that fast, he was gone. Right into the bus, and for all practical purposes, out of my life for good, as the DI called the next name, a Thomas, then a Wallis, then a Williams. Once the final name was called, the DI jumped on board and it closed up and sailed away, leaving the little knots of family standing there desolate in the mist. I was so devastated I was almost disembodied, trying to ignore Mama who was still fussing about me taking all that time with Ira when I'd been with him all week and poor Glenda was so crushed.

"That jacket goes to her," she informed me over the seat, turning to meet my eye. I was too beaten to argue and wordlessly handed it over the seat, not really caring. For what was a personalized, gold-embossed letter jacket to me? I'd lost my best friend.

$$= 11 =$$

My life of inspired somnolence didn't last long without Ira there to shield me from Mama's ambition. By the time he made it home from Vietnam, I'd already flown the coop myself, or more accurately, been booted out of it. The first few months were quiet enough, the Butt-slappers gone, the house no longer full of raised voices, of Ira running around getting dressed for a party or game, begging me to iron his pants or answer the door or make excuses on the phone to some girl he'd made a lot of promises to in the backseat of a car the night before, but didn't want to face again in the light of day.

In a way, Mama was easier to live with without all that frantic activity and one less mouth to feed (and what a mouth that was: I hoped the Marine Corps had laid in supplies). For the first time in four years, her attention fell entirely on me, and she was obviously not so pleased with what she saw. It's hard to describe yourself in memory, but the few photographs that survived the era show a half-baked Pentecostal wannabe, my coarse, brownish-auburn hair hanging at mid-back in a wretched attempt at uncut Holiness, my clothes aiming at modesty, but falling a little short of the mark as I wore a lot of hand-me-downs from an older, petite cousin, whose clothes, owing to my particular body-type, gave the overall impression of tortured seams, especially in the regions of the chest and butt.

That's what the pictures say anyway, my face absent of beauty in its sheer vacancy of expression, though when Liz (the cousin of the hand-me-downs) stopped by the September I turned seventeen, she was fascinated by my hair, my face, my whole humming potential.

"You're a knockout!" she kept exclaiming. "Where are the men around this house?"

Liz was originally a Birmingham girl herself, but had long since thrown over her strict Pentecostal upbringing for a life in the fast lane outside Pensacola in Milton, where she worked as a court reporter, wiling away the year cruising her little VW convertible up and down the beaches of Santa Rosa County. It was her love of a party that landed her at our house one or two weekends a year, as her Grannie Ross wouldn't let her stay out past ten without a fight. I must say that whenever she was home (about as often as Ira) I enjoyed her nonstop babble about the unending satisfaction of her life in Florida — the sun, the beaches, and most of all, the men.

I didn't bother to explain that I spent a good part of my energies separating myself from the Butt-slappers of the world, though I couldn't help but notice that Mama was paying more attention to Liz's chatter than usual. As the visit wore on, she asked pointed questions about job opportunities in Milton and Pensacola, whether there were any openings at the courthouse, how old you had to be to work there. It wasn't hard to see where the conversation was leading, Liz taking the bait with good-natured ease, saying sure, I could come visit, look around, that seventeen was plenty old, she's been on her own since she was eighteen.

Before I knew it, I was on my way, Mama in uncharacteristic high spirits, insisting on taking me shopping at Loveman's and buying me a short, stylish black skirt to wear with a fluffy white angora sweater Liz had gotten from her Grannie for her birthday and couldn't stand, insisting that I, and only I, could do it justice. I assume by justice she meant send shivers down the spine of any man under seventy, but I didn't complain, only tried on the outfit that night at home, a little worried with the tightness of the sweater and the shortness of the skirt, which were not such pressing issues in themselves, except in the message they seemed to be sending about the real purpose of my trip to the coast.

Already, Liz was talking about her men-friends, about one in particular I *had* to meet, an older guy named Bob or Todd or Ted, a *lawyer* with the state's attorney office who loved women with red hair, and you should have seen Mama's face when she said it. After that, she went into overtime, going so far as to loan me a pair of spike-heeled pumps that shortened my shirt by a good two inches and insisting I have my hair done, waving aside my idiotic Pentecostal notions and having her girl clip and cut and puff for the better part of a Saturday morning. When she finally had me shorn of my last pathetic stab at Holiness and swung me around for the final viewing, I didn't know who I was, just blinked at the poofy-haired, melancholy-eyed woman in the mirror, my mother standing there beyond the chair, smiling.

The original plan was that I go back to Florida in the VW with Liz, till a concerned teacher caught wind of my intentions, and I had to wait till Monday, till Mama could produce my birth certificate to verify my age. Mama was annoyed with this interference by a branch of her old adversary, the State, but worked out her angst spending the extra weekend pumping me up for the move, telling me what a good time I'd have. She said I was too young to be sitting home alone, and shouldn't be afraid of meeting *new people,* of having a *good time.*

The Lawyer was the unspoken ingredient here, and though I was a little horrified by the implications, I didn't buck her too hard, as it was increasingly clear that my life of semi-conscious Holiness was coming to an end one way or another. I thought that maybe I'd find a job down there, rent my own apartment, at least till Ira got on his feet in Beaufort, where he was beginning a hitch as a DI himself.

So it was at seventeen, on a cold, blustery day in October, that I caught my own bus to my destiny, though there was no crowd of well-wishers there to see me off, no fiancée to decry my departure, no one but Mama, who had me wait inside the cafeteria to stay out of the cold till the last minute. She had taken off work to see me off, a little pale and worried in her old winter coat, seeming to have a quiver of second thoughts when they made the last call for Mobile, hugging me at the turnstile and telling me she loved me, for the first time in I don't know how long.

I answered her easily enough, telling her I loved her, too, watching her face when I said it, thinking how old she had become, nothing other-worldly about her at all, the lines of suffering etched and deep around her eyes and mouth, the smile lines practically nonexistent. There was plainly nothing left to say after that: the spike heels and tight sweater and chopped hair pretty much said it all, and I had turned and started for the bus, when she called me back, and in a gesture of such helpless regret that in later years it would twist my heart, she slipped off her coat and insisted I take it.

"It'll be cold on the bus," she said, her face suddenly so grieving, though she only repeated herself vaguely. "Cold on the bus."

It was the same old coat Daddy had bought her in New Orleans, a little moth-eaten and worn in the hem and cuff, but still cavernous and warm. I took it easily enough, then turned on my new heels and left without a word, not in cruelty, but ignorance. For I was not used to my mother making desperate, last-minute stabs at reconciliation and didn't recognize it when I saw it, just climbed on the bus without so much as a wave or a nod to nervously embark on a new life with Liz and the beach and the Lawyer who loved red hair.

The drive south was the usual Greyhound experience, prolonged agony, the bus full of servicemen en route to Rucker or Tyndall, with quick smiles for a pretty girl traveling alone, but rough, etched faces that bespoke long nights and short leaves and a complicated war that by the fall of '67, was not what it had been. I returned their smiles, eyes avert-ed, and deflected their attention as best I could by forgoing lunch and supper to stay in the comfortable semi-darkness of the bus, sinking even deeper into the old wool coat that I began to need as we finally drew close to the Florida border, late, near sunset. I had not reckoned on the multitude of South Alabama stops and was worried about getting to Milton so late, swept with a nervousness that was fueled by hunger as much as the increasing twilight, wondering what I'd do if Liz refused to come out at midnight to pick me up.

I had also not reckoned on the Jackson County sign that flashed by at the state line, the reflective lettering glimmering momentarily in the light. I had not realized the bus route cut through that county of old acquaintance and was caught off guard, but not distressingly so, glad to see a familiar name. The distance from the sign and Daddy's old station was not far, fifteen miles at the outside, and as the bus roared down the narrow highway between the sagging trees and fresh-turned fields, I was overcome by a sharp, inexplicable desire to see the old homeplace, maybe talk to Mr. Simon, if he was home.

As I have said, I was shy to the point of virtual muteness, and rearranging a planned journey to accommodate a visit to a man I hadn't seen in five years was certainly out of character in a way that I really can't explain. Even today, I can't tell you from what inner need this deep, instinctive desire arose. Possibly in this last twilight hour of childhood, I was making a desperate reach back, back into days I couldn't so well remember, the scent and smell of the north Florida evening not alien at all, the brush of trees on the bus like welcoming arms, calling me home. Oh yes, that was the plan. Contrary to some historical accounts, Mr. Simon was the lure, the small glimmer of acceptance I was suddenly hungry for, riding that old gray bus to my destiny that cooling October twilight. Not Gabe, whom I had forgotten almost as completely as I had forgotten the sheer distance (two miles, at least) from the bus station downtown to the slanted porches of Magnolia Hill, though I was to remember them both, soon enough. The latter, a matter of an hour later, as I hobbled down Lafayette in my new high heels with many a turned ankle, wondering what in God's name had sent me on such a fool's errand; the former after Cissie opened the door to my timid knock and addressed me, not unkindly, through the screen.

Now, I can't remember exactly how I introduced myself. I'm sure Gabriel came into it in some way, as he was his mother's pet (I remembered that much) and I was in need of her acceptance (and the use of her bathroom). Indeed, at the mention of his name, she immediately softened.

"He's away to school," she said proudly, and (I think) repetitively, though she unlatched the screen door and invited me into the living room I'd only seen once, and on a very trying occasion, and didn't recognize. I was surprised at how small it was, and old-timey, the walls painted beadboard, the fireplace still operational, an anachronism in those days of closed-up chimneys and gas heaters, but gratefully so, as it was lit against the October chill.

When I made a step toward it instinctively, palms out, and mentioned you could smell it all the way up the Hill, Cissie smiled sweetly, and it was Gabriel's smile, closed-mouthed and chin-up. Seeing it resurrected another waft of unfamiliar affection for the smoky west Florida twilight and the damp, camphor-smelling room.

"So he's off to college." I smiled, parroting her shyly in the only way I'd ever learned to communicate, that is, to absorb the good and echo it back in a winning manner. She, the queen of the conversational twist, accepted the volley gracefully and invited me to take a seat on the worn old sofa, then went on for some time without a pause for breath, much less a break for the bathroom I was in desperate need of.

I really can't reproduce her conversation to the word, but can only say that by the time I had finally gotten around to the business of the bathroom a good hour later, I was firmly entangled in the web of myth and innuendo that is Cissie Catts, fully under her spell and charmed into a coma. Without a word of overt bragging, I understood intimately that Candace was a nurse now, an *RN* married to a soldier stationed in Europe, an *officer* in the *Air Force,* and Michael was making money hand over fist locally, though I don't think she mentioned Sanger (how could she spin that?). And last but not least, Gabriel was sweet as ever, handsome, unparalleled in every way, finally coming into his early promise and going to *medical school.*

"*Medical* school?" I repeated involuntarily, and Cissie appreciated my amazement, puffing even broader.

"Well, in a year or so. He ain't got his biology degree yet, but he's hard at it. Workin' day and night and thet ain't Gabe, thet hard work. Michael's the worker, works like a dog down to Sanger, makes *good* money."

If Gabriel had receded a little in the ensuing years, Michael had simply vanished. Dimly, I remembered him chewing tobacco in the back of the truck the day Gabriel had pitched his fit, but that was all. He was the grown one, even then, and I was surprised to find him still living at home, working at *Sanger,* of all places, though his mother was at some pains to explain it, still making her excuses when the sound of footsteps at the back door brought her to her feet with a flutter and a *lord-a-mercy.*

"There's Sim, and I ain't even started supper. Got to talking." She flashed her chin-out smile. "You'll stay, won't you, sister? I'll fry a chicken, won't take a minute."

Well, she didn't have to ask twice. Even as a seventeen-year-old half-wit, I knew that if there was one thing women in shotgun houses could do to perfection, it was fry chicken. "Yes, ma'am," I began, standing up along with her. "I mean, if there's enough."

Something of my sheer hunger must have shown in my face, for she patted my arm as Mr. Simon came through the house. "Why, surely, sister. It's just me and my husband Sim, and he doan eat enough to keep a bird alive."

He came through the doorway just as she said his name, my excitement at the prospect of country chicken instantly checked by a sudden tingle of recognition when I saw his face, not of him five years ago at the fence, but of my own father, of his face the last time I'd seen him, gray in death, and peaceful. It was clear just that quickly that he was a man in serious ill health, his face flaccid and gray, lifted politely as I instinctively crossed the room and held out my hands, saying, "Mr. Catts? My mama says you saved my life once."

Pleased recognition lept into his eyes the moment I said it, his mouth widening to his kind old smile. "Why, Lord have mercy, Cissie," he said, setting down his lunch box and taking my hands. "It's Myra Sims. Look at her now, all grown up."

Cissie let out a cry at this, feeling in the pocket of her house dress for her bifocals, then peering up in my face a moment, exclaiming, "Why the Lord — Sim, I didn't know her! I set here an hour, talking my fool head off, didn't know her from Adam!"

They laughed aloud, and I had to join them, for their laughter was infectious, the shock of his appearance greatly diminished by the joy of homecoming. Looking back, it really does say something about the sheer goodness of the family across the fence, that at the unforeseen return of the child who had so nearly wrecked their lives, they reacted, not with a tight-lipped nod or cool words of reproach, but a cry of joy, as if a prodigal had returned.

"You two come in the kitchen while I git this chicken a-fryin'," she said, asking about Ira, where he was, what he was up to. When she heard he had just come back from a tour of duty slogging through the rice paddies of Southeast Asia, she beamed the same proud smile she'd smiled when she was talking about Gabe and medical school.

"Lil' ole Ira," she kept saying, and when I produced a wallet photo of him in his dress blues, she wanted to keep it. "I know you got more."

Actually, I didn't, but was too charmed to say so, by her open affection for my brother as much as the equally beloved smell of sizzling chicken that quickly filled the kitchen. She fried it in a big old cast-iron pan, alongside a bubbling pot of butter beans and fresh okra that she rolled in pepper and cornmeal and fried whole with the chicken. There wasn't time for biscuits, she declared, and made us hoecakes in the old timey way, fried in the same grease with the chicken.

When she finally finished her frying and discovered she had no dessert to offer, she sent her tired husband back to the Jitney Junior for ice cream. Both of them ignored my sincere objections to his going out again on my account, Cissie following him to the porch to clarify her choices. "Black walnut, if they got it. Plain vanilla, if they don't." She came back inside, wiping her hands on her apron. "We can top it with blackberries if they're out of the walnut," she told me.

By the time he returned, she'd loaded the table with everything she could find tucked away in the refrigerator, even a can of congealed beets she probably had leftover from the Fourth of July. "Now, then," she said as we sat down, "Simon, say grace."

I was to learn later that usually Cissie says grace; I think she considers the realm of the kitchen and dining room her spiritual domain and brings it to the Lord thusly, but on very special occasions, she turns the honors over to the man of the house. On her request, Mr. Simon bowed his head and intoned a longish, formal prayer I thought was off-the-cuff, but later found was memorized. For like many illiterate men, he was uncomfortable with public speaking, and finding himself chained for life with a Baptist, had solved the thrice-daily agony of grace with a properly memorized prayer.

Like I say, I was impressed at the time, with the prayer as much as the food, which was simply above reproach, the chicken fried in perfect simplicity, with a stiff flaky crust a quarter-inch thick around the tender white meat. After the fast on the bus, I think I could have eaten the entire bird myself, one crunchy bite at a time, not to mention the okra and the butterbeans and the tea — sweet iced Lipton's, the only kind served in the Catts household, a matter of doctrine I think, as seriously observed as Communion and Baptism. It was a time in my life when I could (and did) eat till I dropped and never show a pound of it, but neither of the Catts seemed to mind. In fact, they urged me on, seeming to take a solid satisfaction in the sight of a good appetite, a country trait not so often observed in the Sims household, where food was sometimes hard won and begrudged.

When the feast was finished, we retired to the living room for the black walnut ice cream, and, with my feet stretched to the fire, I filled them in on the details of life since I'd left, five years before. They asked constantly after Ira, having me repeat the happier tidbits, the football parts and the commendations, then listened to news of Mama's second marriage with a little less enthusiasm, clearly not so easy with the idea of us being raised by a *stepfather*, when God knows our real one had been enough.

It was late, almost eleven, the fire burnt down to embers, when I finally brought up Daddy's demise, as it was obvious they were curious, and it seemed heartless to let them hang there, uninformed. Made welcome by the good food and half-mesmerized by the rose glow of the dying embers, I went into uncharacteristic detail about the severity and length of his final illness, unprepared for Cissie's response, which was another of her chin-out smiles and a totally unfeigned, "Well, *praise* the Lord."

I can't deny being a little taken aback by her sincerity, if nothing else, for it was the first glimpse I had of the core of blue steel at the center of this kind-hearted Baptist housewife, who spent half a year's Sunday School curriculum teaching God is love but had never been known to take a prisoner alive in her life, if she could help it.

Mr. Simon looked a little pained at her enthusiasm and shot her a look of reproach, which she ignored as she gathered our empty bowls and took them to the kitchen. It was obviously time for me to be leaving, but when I stood and began my good-byes, I think he took it as a reaction to her words of rejoicing at the news of Daddy's death, and was painfully distressed.

"It's sa late, sister, why d'you want to be out sa late?" he kept asking, calling his wife in as reinforcement, and the moment she realized my intent to walk back to the bus station, she put an end to it.

"Right here in Michael's bed you'll sleep," she announced. "Call your Aint, sister. I knooow she'll understand."

I made a few ineffectual attempts to correct her. "She's not my aunt, she's my cousin —"

But like I say, there are deep controlling waters beneath the calm Christian facade of this chicken-frying connoisseur, and in no time at all, I found myself at the phone in the kitchen, listening to her directions on how to call person-to-person, telling Liz I'd be a day late, something had come up. I didn't bother to tell her where I was, or that I'd even left Birmingham, and she didn't ask, cheerful as ever, just reminded me about a party on Saturday that I didn't want to miss.

When we hung up, Cissie was triumphant. "See there? No trouble atall. Cain't think what the world is come to, a young girl out on the road, traveling right by herself."

I was uncomfortable with the implied criticism of my mother, the same old Baptist down-your-nose perfectionism that had so vexed Mama on the Hill, but Cissie was on a roll and couldn't be stopped, bearing me away to the front bedroom in victory, chattering the whole time: "Sleep right here, washed the sheets yesterday. I'll leave Michael a note; he won't be in till late, works long hours, makes *good* money. Have to git Sim to lower this winder — " She paused to yell into the kitchen, "Sim! Come work this winder. I cain't budge it!"

Then said to me, as I set my little valise on the floor, "Boy keeps that winder up, winter frost and summer heat." Then, lest his window habits mar his otherwise perfection, she went back to the same old refrain. "But he's a good boy — or a man. I forgit he's a man, twenty-four last June — been workin' since he was fifteen."

He didn't sound like too much of man to me, still home at twenty-four, when as any self-respecting redneck knew, you could sign up with Uncle Sam at eighteen (seventeen, with your mother's signature) and get out of the poverty squeeze and take your poor old parents with you. It was just a fact of life, a cultural truth all of us postwar hicks knew to be true, the military as revered as Roosevelt in the hollows and row houses of the South. Gabriel must be the one they were pinning their hopes on, I thought, as I watched his thin, gray-faced father wrestle unsuccessfully with the rain-swollen sash. He was the one with the gumption to get out and make his way; he would be their salvation. But medical school was a long affair, four or five years at least, and as Mr. Simon climbed off the bed with a wry shake of his head and an apology, a bone-deep certainty came to me that he'd never live to see it.

"Have to git the blankets out," Cissie decided and quickly had her husband in action, rummaging around in the chiffarobe and under the bed, hunting up the old quilts and ancient electric blankets that had not been taken out of summer storage. She wasn't satisfied until she had piled the small bed with assorted covers, still fussing about the window, wondering aloud if she hadn't better call Case to come see if he could work it down.

I was amazed that anyone would consider raising a brother from bed in the middle of the night to close a stuck window and repeatedly assured her I'd be fine, till she reluctantly gave in and closed the door and wished me good night, telling me to sleep tight and not let the bedbugs bite. There was still a feeling of triumph about the little house, and as I undressed quickly in the draft from the open window, I wondered about it, and why it should be that the return of a virtual stranger should be the cause for such rejoicing. Even when I was under the pile of covers that were cold at first, but gradually warming, I couldn't figure it out, Cissie's words coming back to me, *don't let the bedbugs bite.*

There was something evocative about them, some small, pleasant memory, and as I dozed toward sleep, covered to the nose from the brisk October chill, I remembered Ira, in our bedroom across that very fence, and found myself smiling in the darkness. For that was what he'd tell me every night of our life on the Hill, when he'd run out of stories and gossip and it was time to sleep at last: *don't let the bedbugs bite.*

At the time, I'd wondered where in the world he'd picked up such a silly, childish saying, certainly not around the Sims house. But now I knew, my last waking thought a small regret that I hadn't been a boy, living on the Hill. Because the whole unexpected evening, from the chicken to the ice cream to the chin-out smile on the porch, had finally unlocked the secret of Ira's magnetic attraction to the house across the fence, and I thought that if I had been a boy, and allowed out, I would have been like him, and never come home either.

I slept there peacefully for the first part of the night, at some point embarking on a curiously vivid dream that I was wandering around a cold, cavernous waiting room that seemed to be the bus terminal in Pensacola. It was as if I were waiting for Liz, except that in the dream, I wasn't waiting for Liz, I was waiting for Ira. He was coming home from somewhere, Saigon or Beaufort, I didn't know which, but he was late and I was worried, pacing around, calling his name, when unexpectedly, he got in bed with me. In the context of the dream, it seemed perfectly sensible, wandering around a huge marble-floored terminal that suddenly turned into an equally cold bed, and I drew toward him the way we'd done as children, for sheer animal warmth, my sleepy detachment shattered by a stunned exclamation, right at my face: "*Damn!*"

I sat up, disoriented by sleep and half-paralyzed by the wall of covers Cissie had pinned me under, when the overhead light clicked on, bringing the world of dreams and half-understood motion into brilliant light. I instinctively shielded my eyes, blinking at a man who stood at the foot of the bed, staring at me wildly, like I was an apparition, his voice introspective and incredulous: "There's a *woman* in my bed."

He was mercifully not stripped down to the underwear he usually slept in, but in the rumpled corduroys he'd just worn to work, that were unbuttoned and open like he'd pulled them on in a hurry. I was squinting at him, thinking, *why, he isn't Ira at all,* when his mother walked in with her old chin-out smile and slapped him lightly on the back of the head. "Where's yo manners, son? You been working with thet Sanger trash sa long, you're sounding just like 'em."

He said not a word in reply, just stood there with that look of stunned amazement, while his mother finished her admonishments and finally made her introductions, smiling: "This is Myra Sims — or Odom. You remember, Ira's little sister. She's on her way to visit her people in Milton. Ain't she made into a pretty girl?"

She paused then for his response, and I don't know till this day exactly what she expected us to do. If she thought for a minute that I was going to get out of bed in my nightgown and politely shake his hand, she was in for a disappointment. Her son looked equally obstinate, just stared at her a moment with what looked to be patent disbelief, then turned on his heel and headed for the living room, Cissie two steps behind, again asking him *where his manners were?*

I just sat there in bed, wondering if I should go out and apologize, maybe pack my suitcase and leave early. I hadn't meant to inconvenience anyone and was sorry now I'd stayed. In the living room, I could hear their voices, Cissie's a little louder, saying something about a note, him answering back just as stridently, then, finally, silence. Apparently, they'd come to some kind of truce, as Cissie opened the door and came back to the bed, her face a little sheepish as she took one of my pillows and stripped me of the first two layers of my covers. "Just a little mix-up," she assured me. "Git on back to sleep, shug. It'll all work out in the morning."

She turned off the light and closed the door, leaving me alone in what was no longer so inviting a darkness, the house quiet now, but hollowly so, full of the presence of the newcomer in the living room, who didn't want me there. I snuggled back under the cocoon of covers, I rolled to my side, I might have tried counting sheep, but it was no use. The little nest Mr. Simon and Cissie had built for me had been disturbed, and no matter how much I wiggled and tossed and thought happy thoughts, for the first time in five years, I sought refuge in the mindless forgetfulness of sleep, but was unable to find it.

$$= 12 =$$

ut I did go to sleep sometime that night; I must have, for when I awoke at dawn, I was hot in my flannel gown that was more suited to a crisp Birmingham October than the quick, changeable weather of the Gulf coast. Once awake, I couldn't resist the temptation to lie there a few minutes and listen to the sounds of the awakening morning, a call-back of seven years to other mornings on Lafayette: the barking dogs, the honk of trucks come by to pick up neighbors for work, the spiking song of the birds in the old sweet gum. I couldn't name them, but their fast, rhythmic cries (pretty-pretty-pretty) seemed familiar on the damp morning, as familiar as the dense aroma of fresh-brewed coffee that soon filled the room.

There were noises in the kitchen, and it occurred to me that perhaps Michael needed something from his room and my lingering so long in bed would lead to another embarrassing encounter. It was enough motivation to get me up and dressed, quickly, afraid the door would open with another impudent bang. In my rush, I put on the same outfit I'd worn the day before, the skirt and sweater that was too tight, too hot, for the close, humid morning.

But the mix-up of the night before seemed finally to have been corrected, the house much more familiar in the clear light of day. Cissie was already up, stirring tomato gravy in the old cast-iron fryer at the stove, dressed in an ancient quilted housecoat that added a homey, grannie-feel to the silent house and equally silent elder son who stood at the sink, washing his hands, not speaking, even when I bid his mother good morning. I later learned that it was she he was intentionally ignoring, but at the time, took his stiff back as a pointed snub and wearily added rudeness to the already unflattering portrait I was painting of this much-discussed, but still hardly seen, son.

Physically, he was broader than the slight young pitcher I remembered, not much taller, five-nine at the outside, but bulkier, his shoulders and chest filled out by the work at the plant. I would have surmised had I been one iota interested. I wasn't, and noted when he finally turned to speak that he hardly favored his father at all, with none of his fine, sensitive features, but prominent cheekbones, a wide set mouth, and deep-set, hooded eyes. It was a rough face, darker and more passionate than that of any of the other Catts, and in odd contrast to any of them, in what I was to later learn was a throwback to a not-so-distant Cherokee bride a great-grandfather had picked up in North Carolina on the way home from Appomattox.

With his lack of height, high forehead, and dark, close-cropped hair, he made for an oddly Napoleonic figure as he turned back to the sink and resumed his hand washing, already dressed for work in pressed khaki Dickies, the same outfit his father was wearing when he appeared, wishing me good morning and offering coffee.

I declined, still shy around this silent elder son who was working on his hands with great deliberation, my faint annoyance of the night before quickly bubbling toward a sulky hostility. Not at his open rudeness as much as at the sight of a perfectly healthy twenty-four-year-old man still at his mother's tit when he could be signed up and shipped out and sending home half-pay from some foreign shore, like Ira, like Carl, like any of the other men I knew. All of my carefully honed working-class ethic came to the fore, and I hardly spoke to him as we took our places at the breakfast table, except for another bare nod when he apologized for the mix-up with the bed.

"I left a note," his mother assured us as she took her place at the table, though he was openly skeptical.

"Where's the note, Mama?" he asked. "Show me the *damn* note."

She just ignored him, profanity and all, and the whole time we ate I wished with all my heart that I had the guts to look this sorry excuse for a son in the eye and let him in on a few home truths about the virtue of hard work and honoring your father and mother. I think I might have even made a few veiled references to Ira, and what good money he made, and the gifts from the Orient he had sent, perfume and china. But the elder son across the table seemed more intent on his food than on me, and I finally gave it up as a bad job.

When the biscuits were gone, the coffee cold, his father checked his watch and said he'd better be going, and I stood abruptly and said I had to leave, too, that my bus was due at nine. "I'll walk you to the tracks," I offered.

Cissie set up an outcry at this, volunteering Michael to take me in his truck (*fine truck, bought it brand new*). But I wasn't buying, just gathered my coat and valise and returned her hugs, promising to bring Ira to visit Thanksgiving, then went out to Mr. Simon, who was waiting on the back porch, his lunch box under his arm, just like old times.

"She's a talker," he said of his wife as soon as we got out of earshot, whether in apology or explanation, I don't know, though something in his words seemed to ask my forgiveness for her little slip-up with the note and having to throw a man out of my bed my first night back on the Hill.

I appreciated his tact as much as his kindness and impulsively looped my arm through his. "She ain't changed," I allowed, and we laughed, because it was true: the sun riseth and the sun goeth down, but Cissie Catts reigns supreme on Magnolia Hill, always has and always will. *But we love her anyway,* was the unspoken agreement, and when we came upon the little ditch I used to play in as a child, he held my valise while I broad-jumped it, clumsy in my heels. I took his arm again when we made the other side and paused a moment to watch the clear little rivulet of water that was a lively, trickling run from last night's storm.

"I used to love that ditch," I mused. "Called it 'the creek'."

He smiled. "Yeah, coming home from work, I uster catch you out there daydreaming, uster wonder what in the world you saw in the thang. Worried with snakes."

I remembered his nightly warnings, and as we made our way through the light October haze, I thanked him for that and all his other kindnesses to me, though the biggest one, the fight that almost killed him, we left unspoken. For there was really no polite way to mention it without bringing to mind a few things we'd both just as soon forget.

My shy, clumsy words seemed to please him though, for he patted my arm and told me it was his pleasure, then went on about Ira, how proud he was of him, how he would most certainly have to visit, maybe Thanksgiving, when Gabe was home. I agreed, and when we came to the tracks where our ways parted, he took my hand and told me how glad he was I'd dropped by.

Then, in that same kind voice, though his eyes left mine and darted away across the tracks, he added, "And sister, yo daddy — he wadn't always a bad man."

I couldn't imagine why he was bringing up Daddy here on the tail end of our pleasant walk. Maybe to cover for his wife's tactless response the night before; or maybe he thought that's why I'd come back to the Hill, that it was a deliberate retrieval on my part, an inevitable step in a grief process. But nothing could have been further from my mind and I just stood there watching him search for the right words, finally glancing at the top of my head, saying, "He just took to dranking, baby. Took to drank." Which was the standard excuse in those days for any inhumanly bad behavior, much the same way parental abuse is routinely used today.

And though neither of us really believed it, I understood what he was trying to offer me here: not a denial, but a reason, an excuse for the monster my father had become. A grounds for reconciliation, for peace. I answered him quietly, "Yessir. Yessir, I know."

He smiled then, and with another squeeze of my hand, let go and backed away, meeting my eye now, teasing me, saying, "Run back to the house, sister. Git thet lazy boy of mine to run you to town. Do him a world a good."

He kept up the banter the whole time he backed away, finally turning a good way off with a last wave, leaving me alone on the tracks, watching him disappear around the curve, suddenly aware how fast the morning was burning off to a fine, clear day, as golden as October, as hot as May. I could feel the blaze of the morning sun on my bare head, the pinch of my new shoes, the awful sensation of sweat trickling down my backbone. But there was nothing for it but to pick up my valise and start toward town, feeling a little more diminished with every step, dreading the five-hour wait for my bus at the station (it didn't leave till two — I'd lied) and more than that, my arrival in Pensacola, and whatever slim possibility for a new life that awaited me there.

I shuffled along, having a hard time of it in the spike heels that kept getting caught in the loose rocks that lined the tracks and yanked them right off my feet. I was hopping around, trying to keep my hose intact, without much luck, and finally reverted to a choice selection of Ira-inspired profanity, when I heard someone call my name. For a moment, I thought it was Mr. Simon and straightened up, red-faced, afraid he'd overheard my trash-talk; but it wasn't him, it was his son, Michael. He was parked on the grass verge at the next crossing, leaning against the door of his truck with his arms crossed casually on his chest, watching my progression down the tracks with a poorly concealed, and ill-timed, amusement.

It was quite a change from the brooding general at his mother's sink, but from my point of view, hardly an improvement, a slow red burn starting somewhere in the top of my head that I didn't trouble to hide, calling, "You just leave me alone. I ain't *studying* you." Which was a local phrase, a saltine-cracker phrase, used by disinterested women to interested men, roughly decipherable to *bug off*, or something appreciatively worse.

Michael didn't seem too moved by my outburst, though, his eyes on his work boots, still trying to get the best of his smile, but not quite able. He waited till I was within speaking distance, then tipped his head to the truck. "Hop in," he said. "It's eight forty-five. You're late."

"It don't leave till *two*," I informed him haughtily, as if it were all his fault, me lying about my departure time.

But he still didn't take offense, just took off his cap and ran his hand through his hair, said, "Listen, Myra, I didn't see no note. There *wadn't* no note."

"Oh, *screw* the note," I snapped, not in any mood to be humored. When he had the gall to actually laugh at my ill temper, I threw discretion to the wind and decided it was time to impart a few home truths to this jeering lout, stomping up to him and facing him off levelly, asking,

"And what the *hell* are you doing out of uniform, anyway, hanging round the house, twenty-four years old?"

It came out just like I intended, so barefaced an insult that I knew he'd get it this time, and he did. His rough, aborigine face turned aside a moment, then glanced back as he answered me evenly with a calm, silky honesty: "I'm out a uniform 'cause I fell in a saw when I was nineteen, messed up my arm, made me ineligible for the draft." He lifted his arm to show me the tail end of a twisted scar that ran just below his elbow, then dropped it and finished in that patient, obliging tone. "And what I'm doing hanging around the house is paying my Daddy's mortgage 'cause a neighbor of ours beat the *shit* out of him one time and he ain't been the same since."

That's just what he said, in that smooth, even voice, and I was the one who backed off this time, instantly, as if he'd struck me, dropping my eyes, saying, "Oh."

He didn't push it, just slid his cap back on his head and opened the truck door, said, "Hop in. I'll give you a ride to town."

But I could feel a sudden tingle behind my eyes as if I were about to do something truly humiliating here, like cry, and I turned away sharply and started off toward town. "No, thank you," I murmured, trying to be polite. "I'm walking — I'm walk —"

That's all I could manage, for it was painful enough to see Mr. Simon so old and diminished and hideously gray, but to have the responsibility for the fact thrown in my face right there in the clear light of day, that was too much. I literally fled, not up the cursed tracks, but north along the road, clutching my coat and my little suitcase to my chest and ignoring the noises of entreaty, then apology, then, finally, exasperation, at my back.

I was making good time, a full block away, when he finally shut up and started the truck, but my relief at his departure was short-lived, as he idled up beside me, calling through the open window, "Dammit, Myra! I said I'm sorry."

I just waved him away with my free hand, ashamed of the torrent of tears that I was too proud to wipe away, hoping he wouldn't notice. But he was a persistent devil and finally pulled ahead and jerked to a halt on the grass in front of me. He flung open the door and came around the tailgate with a dark, harassed face, still trying to apologize, without much luck, as I was about at the end of my rope by then. I stomped my foot at him like he was a bad dog, cried, "Leave me alone! Just leave me alone!"

"*Dammit,* Myra," he cried. "I said I'm sorry. Damn, I'm sorry. It was a *stupid* thing to say. He's going on nights in November, taking the night watch. It won't be so hard on him; I got it all planned."

It was the first time in my life I was to hear those fateful words: *I got it all planned.* But I couldn't have understood their significance at the time and was making my own painful reply, my old standard words of excuse ("*I don't feel good, leave me alone —*") when I finally realized what he was saying, that he was talking about Mr. Simon and a better job. I stopped, my chest still heaving. "What job?" I asked.

"Night watchman," he said, his face still harassed. "Six-hour shift. Don't pay nothing, but he won't retire — hell, I don't blame him, my *damn mother* hanging around."

On *damn mother,* he reached over and slapped the tailgate with his bare palm, a blow of some force that must have hurt like hell, though he didn't flinch, just folded his arms high across his chest in that stiff, aggravated stance. I realized then that his disapproving back at the sink that morning didn't have as much to do with me as it did his mother, and was quickly, childishly, relieved to be absolved of my snotty attitude at breakfast. I felt a sudden need to make amends, and ducked my head to stammer, "Well, I'm sorry I said what I did. I didn't know any better. I ain't got good sense." Which was what Ira was always telling me, and after this silly, white-trash fight with a virtual stranger, I was beginning to believe him. "And I'm hot."

This last was a little weeny, but by God, it was true. The sun was coming down the tracks like a microwave, my outfit in shambles, the fluffy angora flat and sweaty, my hair free of the frail hold of the hairdresser's tease and poking out in its natural insanity. Something in my discomforture seemed to amuse him, though, for his somber face flashed in an unexpected grin.

"Well, I offered you a ride," he said equably, and this time I took him up on his offer, too hot to decline even if I would have wanted to, and not so sure I did anymore. Not after I heard about Mr. Simon's new job; not after I saw that flash of a smile, because it was an arresting smile. It wasn't closed-mouthed and charming in the Cissie-Catts sense, nor even necessarily handsome, with a quarter-inch gap in his two front teeth I hadn't noticed before, that made his dark, forbidding face suddenly approachable, full of good-natured appetite for life in general and me, Myra Louise Sims, in particular.

My children, when musing over the idiocy of me marrying a man I'd only known a month, sometimes ask me why I did it. Why didn't I wait? At what point was it inevitable? And I always point to that smile over the tailgate of the truck the first morning I met him. "I liked that smile," I murmur, with a smile of my own, full of congratulatory confidence that even at the ridiculous age of seventeen, I recognized quality when I saw it. Not just in his careful plans for his father, but instinctively, in the space of a moment, in that sudden, gap-toothed smile.

Michael, for his part, used to say his moment of departure was a matter of minutes later, when we were rolling down Washington, both windows open for the rush of breeze that, despite the heat, was still tinged with the sweet autumnal smells of the night before, of burning leaves and woodsmoke. I was sitting there with my head tipped on the back of the seat, glad to be out of the sun, when he made his first stab at conversation, speaking to me in a light, teasing voice that sounded like his father's.

"Why didn't you take off your shoes to walk the track?" he asked, tipping his head at my ridiculous heels. "You weren't making good time in them things."

I answered with my eyes closed, enjoying the wind in my face. "Didn't want to run my hose," I murmured, and he laughed shortly, then looked out his window.

"Well, you ain't gone be thrilled with what they done to them high heels."

I didn't know what he was talking about, and after a moment, sat up and took one of my shoes off, turning it over in my hands. Sure enough, the spike heel was shredded to a blank, ragged gray, all the way to the top. I just sat there looking at it in horror, thinking how much Mama had paid for them and how mad she'd be when I brought them home ruined, but when I looked at Michael, he was shaking his head, fighting another smile till he saw my face.

"Oh, Myra," he began, "forgit them shoes — we'll buy you some more."

"But they cost twenty-five dollars!" I cried. Then, to add insult to injury, I remembered the real kicker, "On sale!"

He finally laughed then; he says he couldn't help it, and I don't doubt it, because his laughter just about derailed what was looking to be the beginnings of a beautiful friendship. The only way he could get me back on track was by taking the shoes and throwing them in the bed of the truck, saying, "Forgit them damn shoes. I'll take you to Daffin's, buy you some more."

"You've got to go to work," I cried, giving myself over to despair, though he just double-parked in front of the post office.

"I got a notion to take the day off," he said. "Cain't send you to Milton barefoot as a yard dog. What would Mama say?"

He smiled when he said it, that same level-eyed smile he'd flashed over the tailgate of the truck, that seemed to be offering me something — asking something, and offering, too. I couldn't have told you what, though there was an unexpected stab of response deep in the pit of my stomach that, had I recognized it, might have clued me to the fact that we were quickly trespassing into waters a sight deeper than mere friendship.

Whatever it was, that brief pinpoint of emotion was so piercing that I didn't argue, didn't even question the propriety of a virtual stranger — and a man at that — buying me an intimate item like shoes. I only glanced uncertainly at my poor tattered feet, murmured, "Well, I don't know. I cain't go in there barefoot. I don't want 'em to think I'm, white trash, or something."

That was his point of departure, he later said, though he never could explain it very well, only shaking his head, saying, "Just something about you sitting there in the truck, barefoot as a yard dog in that tight awful sweater, afraid to get out, worried somebody'd think you were trash. It was too damn funny." He'd laugh, then muse speculatively, "And I liked them little feet."

That's how it was, truly. Like I say, we were married in a month.

$$= 13 =$$

We *married the Friday after Thanksgiving* in a simple ceremony in the Catts' living room, but pretty for all that, the mantle draped with angel-leaf begonias and sago fronds, Michael in a plain black wool suit bought specially for the occasion and worn for many an occasion to come. I wore a borrowed ivory, knee-length brocade, as we had little enough money for the license, much less a wedding dress, with Cissie calling in every favor she'd ever bestowed on any man, woman, and dog in the county to provide the incidentals.

She was enough of an old ward heeler to produce a five-tiered cake and a half-page write-up in the *Floridian* that, to the unfamiliar eye, might have been describing a society wedding in Boston rather than a pulled-together, homespun affair with a mill-hand groom and an underaged bride. I have to hand it to her: it was fast work for four phone-calling, gossip-settling weeks. It was an engagement that in its bare-month tenure withstood my mother's uninhibited wrath, which on at least one occasion threatened to send us all on our merry ways — me back to Alabama, Michael (he said) to the priesthood, whether to get away from me or his mother, I don't know.

Cissie, of course, was the chief instigator; all of us agree on that, if nothing else. She was the note-forgetter, the chicken-fryer; the one who cornered Michael in his bedroom the moment I stepped off the porch and, with no time for subterfuge, instructed him to meet me at the tracks and offer me a ride to town. On this, she was flatly rebuffed, as Michael was already mad about the bed mix-up, mad and humiliated to the extent that he would not so much as deign to answer her.

I imagine his mother saw something of the seeds of her own iron will in the set of his face, for she didn't argue, but backed off in graceful acquiescence, only regretful, wishing aloud that she'd seen more of the girl, whom she'd always thought a lot of — which was a bald-faced lie, of course. Cissie Catts hadn't thought much of any of the Sims, except Ira, whom she loved. But Michael was still giving her the silent treatment and didn't argue, just laced up his work boots while she cleared the remains of breakfast, gathering up plates and coffee cups, stopping to wonder aloud that well, Thanksgiving would be here soon, and when Ira dropped by, he would surely bring his sister.

Then, just as she made the kitchen door, an even wider smile lit her face at the glad realization that Gabe would be home, too, and what a homecoming that would make!

"He always thought a right smart of Myra, Gabe did."

She handed him his lunch then and kissed him good-bye, and Michael (who told me his side of the story much later) told her, good, that he was moving in with Uncle Case, and wouldn't be back for Thanksgiving or Christmas, or Easter, either, if he could help it. But with her arrow set, her point taken, Cissie went back to her dishes cheerfully, humming a little holiday tune, leaving her older son to slam out the back door and go to work in an awful humor.

For though he could have cared less about the Sims girl, whose father he hated more than Satan, her pointed comments at breakfast about the military and the good money to be made there had not gone unnoticed. To a man so focused and ambitious that he didn't get out of bed in the morning without first formulating a Plan, it rankled, and when he stopped for the Ninth Street crossing and saw a struggling figure making her way down the tracks with her suitcase, he felt a certain need to pull over and clarify a few issues.

Parking on the grass, he watched her make her way east, and in the face of her Herculean struggle with the granite verge, began to soften a little; when she got close enough for him to hear her language, he laughed aloud. Clearly, this wasn't the sheltered Baptist flower of his mother's imagination, and, watching her hobble along in such supreme ill grace, an unexpected liking rose up as it occurred to him that perhaps his mother was biting off more than she could chew, playing Cupid with this big-boned, Alabama redhead.

I imagine it was then that he began to formulate his first of a million Myra-Plans: to take her to the bus station, tell her about his arm and how the army wouldn't have him, maybe take her to the café for lunch. He was fairly certain the bus didn't leave for the coast till at least noon, and she hadn't eaten much at breakfast, too worried about his daddy. Oh yes, he knew that, too. He'd seen her face as it followed him around the kitchen that morning, worried, introspective, and, even in his annoyance with his mother, he'd liked what he saw.

For Simon Catts and his ilk weren't exactly the stuff of legend on the Hill, just tired old plow-boys, displaced and disinherited by time, left to slave down at the mill till Social Security and Medicaid jumped in and babysat them till they died. He loved his father and knew his sacrifices intimately, but there weren't many sympathizers for such a life. Certainly not many young women, and good-looking ones, at that, to wring their small hands, and offer to walk him to work, to (probably) apologize for the beating her father had given him years ago, trying to save her life.

It spoke to him of loyalty and gratitude, as loudly as her remarkably contorted sweater was speaking to him of other, equally pressing matters, and made a good enough impression for him go to the trouble of formulating a bonafide Michael-Catts Plan. And though it got off to a rocky start and quickly deteriorated to an out-and-out catfight, Michael Catts armed with a Plan was as invincible as his mother, and I might as well have climbed in the truck and went quietly, as much good as my tears and hysterics would have done me.

Before I knew it, I was sipping iced tea in a booth at the City Café, which was in a state of rare vacancy that time of the day, the early-morning farming crowd long gone, the courthouse sitters just past. On my feet were a pair of sensible white flats, bought on sale at Daffin's as end-of-the-season merchandise, and thankfully so, as they were paid for out of my own meager funds after my conscience had finally rebelled at someone else paying for my mistakes. He'd insisted on buying me a new pair of pantyhose, though, had made the saleslady behind the counter pull out boxes and boxes of tissue-wrapped possibilities, kneeling on the floor to press the finalists against my bare foot, looking up when he made his selection (winter white) with another of those level-eyed smiles.

"You never ought to wear them tan ones, you're too white," he said, as if it were the most normal thing in the world, this rough-faced mill worker advising me on my choice in pantyhose. Another twitch of something — who knew what? — hit me in the stomach, or just below, in the regions of the unknown, between my backbone and the tight waist of my skirt as he came to his feet. "Come on," he said, feeling for his wallet. "I'll buy you lunch."

I remember that first lunch (or breakfast, rather, my second of the morning) very well. It was my first glimpse into the world of Sanger Manufacturing, my first conversation with the man who was very much at home in the smoky enviroment of the café, indeed, at home in every situation we had yet encountered. Everywhere we went that day, he was greeted on every side by waitresses, shopgirls, even an old grizzled black cook who came out of the kitchen of the café to give him a perfectly indecipherable message about Sam and a ride.

Michael apparently understood him, as he answered him easily enough, then went back to his food with much interest, though he had just eaten at his mother's table, not an hour before.

"You ain't hungry?" he kept asking, but I was content to sit in the cool dark corner and sip my tea and thank God for the small favor of comfortable feet. I found myself unconsciously drawn out by his easy, accepting manner, which was much like his father's, telling him about my trip to Liz's with no reserve at all, even mentioning the Lawyer and the party, and shyly, my misgivings at such an undertaking.

"I'm sure they'll be drinking," I said, tracing the condensation on my glass with my finger, dimly assuming a Baptist boy would understand my concern at such a possibility.

Indeed, he was not impressed, eating with his elbows on the table the way Mama used to fuss at Ira about doing. "How old's this fella?" he asked.

I had no idea. I pictured a lawyer as someone old and bald, in a suit, and shrugged. "Old, I guess. Older than Liz, and she's twenty-seven." Which was about the extent of my knowledge of this prospective new suitor who'd given my mother such excitement, adding lamely, "Likes women with red hair."

Michael made a noise of disgust on this and glanced away, said: "*Shht.* I bet he does."

He said it very levelly, every word weighed with concern at the negative possibilities of the situation in a way that made me suddenly self-conscious, afraid I'd put us Sims in a bad light again. I was quick to try and patch things up, lifting my face and trying to look pleased, saying, "It'll be all right, though. Mama said I could go and all."

He made no comment at that, only pushed his plate away and chewed his lip reflectively, as if he were consciously biting back another comment that he really had no business making, only being a friend of an hour.

"Sure you don't want anything to eat?" he finally asked, and I again declined, trying to pull the conversation back into more navigable waters, asking what he did at the plant.

"Not a *damn* thang," a big booming voice answered above my head, so close it made me jump in my seat, looking up to my first official encounter with the world of Sanger Manufacturing in the form of Joe Bates (Joe-Bob to his kin, though by '67, even these west Florida plowboys were dispensing with the hyphens). He stood there with a hand on each side of the booth while Michael introduced me, his light Irish eyes never leaving my chest the whole time he talked, calling to every subsequent customer to come look at what Michael had dragged in.

"Cat dragged in what the kittens wouldn't have," he boomed, at least a dozen times, to the unending stream of sweat-marked, tired-eyed men of every shape and size who filled the vacant seats around us. A few of them were well-mannered enough to reach over the table and shake my hand, but most were content to take their seats with a friendly insult or two, one or two asking what a good-looking woman like me was doing with an ugly son of a bitch like Michael.

He ignored the gibes and looked only mildly provoked at their unashamed stares, not giving my name, but introducing me as a friend from Alabama. When Joe finally left, Michael tossed a few dollars on the table and suggested we find a quieter place to wait, offering a mild apology when we made the parking lot.

"Don't pay 'em no mind. They're pretty good old boys. Harmless." I was used to the stares (who wouldn't be, in that awful sweater?) and tried to be agreeable. "That's all right. At least they aren't *Butt-slappers.*"

He was not familiar with the term, and as we got in the truck I told him about Ira's friends, the good, the bad, and worst of all, the Butt-slappers, laughing at them like the joke I had lightened them to be. But he was not so amused, pausing in front of the steering wheel and bringing my laughter to a halt with another of his level assertions. "Them men don't need to be messin' with you."

I dropped my eyes, embarrassed that, yet again, I'd put us Sims in a bad light — the white-trash across the fence, who couldn't protect their women. "Well, Ira — he don't like it, either." I stammered, though it wasn't technically true. Mostly Ira just looked the other way. I don't think he gave it a second thought.

Michael looked embarrassed in his own right at my stumbled apology. He started the truck, then sat back in his seat, said, "Well, it ain't none of my — *dang,* I'm gitting bad as Mama. Listen, you wanta go to the river?"

I had no idea what he was talking about, but with that three-hour wait in front of me, just smiled, said, "Sure," like I went there every day of my life.

I was as ignorant of the possible connotation of going to the river with a man as I had been of going to the tracks with his brother, though Michael tried to set my mind at ease. "I mean, just to talk," he said. "A friend a mine —" he closed his eyes on that, breathed. "*Shoot,* that's right — listen, I gotta run by and pick up Sam." He glanced at his watch. "Shoot, I'm late. It'll only take a minute."

I told him fine, for everyone on the Hill carpooled to work, a leftover custom from the not-so-distant days when personal transportation was a luxury. As we threaded through the narrow back streets, Michael told me this was the man who was taking his shift, that he'd promised a ride, slowing down almost immediately beside a black man who was walking down the street at a fast clip.

At first, I thought he'd gotten lost and was asking directions, as this clearly wasn't Magnolia Hill. Unless I'd gotten mighty turned around, this was the Quarters, Thurmon Quarters to be exact, though Michael just idled up beside him and called through the window, "Cecil told me. I clean forgot."

The black man turned and snatched open the door, his face hot and annoyed, looking at me a moment in surprise, and what? distaste, I think, checking out the tight sweater and the out-of-season shoes with one fast sweep and not looking too impressed with either.

"Slide over," Michael told me, and I obeyed quickly, suddenly realizing this black man, this *angry* black man, was going to slide into the seat behind me, or on my lap if I didn't get a move on. I slid so far to Michael's side that I was dang near in his lap, so stunned I could only stare straight ahead as Michael continued his apologies. "Just got to talking, got away from me." He paused then to introduce us. "This is Myra Sims," he said, though he hadn't given my name to any of the men at the diner. "Friend of ours from Alabama."

"Sam McRae," the black man intoned, but I didn't return his nod, still in absolute shock, wondering what in God's name I'd gotten myself into, going to the river with a lunatic and a nigger. I mean, I know it sounds harsh, but I just can't describe the shock of him jumping in the truck like that, sitting next to me like I was his sister. It would probably strike me as a little unusual, even today, but in 1967, it was just unheard of. Sam jumping in the truck like that was like — well, it was like going to the grocery store topless, or showing up at a Baptist supper with a couple bottles of good Chardonnay. I mean, moral and ethical considerations aside, it was simply *not done.*

After a moment, I think my petrified unease began to make itself manifest in the truck, conversation coming to a gathered halt, as if it had finally occurred to Michael that he had made a grave tactical error here. It made for a painfully silent little cruise through town, Michael dropping Sam off at the gate with another word of thanks, Sam getting out quickly and leaving just as fast. He strode away at a great pace, though after a few steps, seemed to come to himself and turned, his eyes meeting mine in a manner I can only call defiant (or in that day, impudent), though his tone was polite, if a little ironic, for Michael's sake, I think.

"Nice to meet you," he said, then turned on his heel and left, my ill ease not lessened by the slight shake of his head that could be detected as he strode across the parking lot. When he was gone, the silence in the truck persisted, Michael chastised enough to be cautious.

"Still the river?" he asked.

And though I was no longer at all sure about this man and his intent, I was game enough to repeat, "Sure." My tone was not nearly as enthusiastic as before, my confidence considerably diminished.

On the drive to the river, I remember him trying to regain the easy pitch of our little breakfast, saying what a good man Sam was, how his brother and grandfather were Church of God preachers — echoes of his mother, when she was trying to put an impressive spin on him and Sanger the night before. But he hadn't his mother's hypnotic charm, and I wasn't buying anyway, just sitting there right up against him, a little afraid of that empty space by the window where *that man* had so recently sat.

It wasn't until we got to the river that I began to relax, for I've always loved water, and this was a pretty little stream, spring-fed and crystal clear, too snaky-looking to swim in, but cool to sit beside on a day that was living up to its early promise of heat. Michael parked under the shade of a sagging old water oak and carried the conversation as his mother had at breakfast, making no excuse for the little slip-up with Sam McRae, even mentioning that he was the friend whose family owned the property we were sitting on. It was a revelation that refueled my unease, so that the whole time he talked, I was glancing around uneasily, out the side windows and to the bed of the truck, keeping an eye out for ambush.

But nothing materialized, and after a while I relaxed and made a few comments of my own, growing sleepy in the warm sun after my tossing, restless night, yawning and blinking, and after a long while, coming awake with a start when he shook my shoulder.

"It's one-thirty, Myra," he said quietly. "Time to get a move on."

I sat up, blinking stupidly, not sure where I was, and he smiled. "Took a little nap," he said, starting the truck and putting his arm up on the seat behind me to back up.

"Sorry," I murmured, not really surprised. For I was the sleeping beauty of Fairfield, remember, who routinely knocked out three hours an afternoon, sometimes more. I guess my body hadn't gotten the message that a bold new day was upon me, and I found I had curled around him in sleep, one arm under his back, one around his waist, my head on his shoulder. He made a nice, soap-smelling pillow there, and there was nothing in the world I wanted more than to spin out the rest of the afternoon there by the water; I hadn't rested so soundly in years.

"D'we have to go?" I asked peevishly as the truck ground slowly along the old rutted road, and he smiled.

"If you want to make that bus to Milton."

I could have cared less about Milton and Mama and the whole stinking Florida Bar Association. I was happy where I was, rubbing my face like a cat, speaking bluntly, still half-asleep. "I hate Milton."

He laughed. "Well, hell, baby, come on back to the house. My Mama won't care."

I just rubbed my face wearily. "Mine will," I said.

He stopped at the intersection at the dirt road and grinned at me. "One of these days you'll quit listening to your Mama."

Not any time soon, I would have replied, if I hadn't been so sleepy. After a moment, I realized we weren't going anywhere, just idling at the stop sign in the middle of nowhere, not a car in sight, and I sat up.

"What's the matter?" I asked, as he was strangely quiet, just staring out the windshield a moment before he turned.

"Can I kiss you?" he asked.

It had been a long time since another Catts boy had asked me such a question, and I said the first thing that came to mind. "Why?"

He smiled a little at that, the countryside suddenly even quieter when he answered levelly, "'Cause I been waiting two damn hours for you to wake up. Didn't wanta do it till I asked."

Put like that, it seemed a reasonable request, and I let him kiss me — my first kiss, apart from Gabriel's (if you counted that) — and it wasn't earth-shaking, but it wasn't bad. When we drew away, I just looked at him there, a few inches away, then reached over and kissed him again. I don't know why, not because I was so particularly aroused by the first one, as much as the fact that the horse was out of the barn as far as me being unkissed was concerned, and I thought I might as well try out a second.

He wasn't as untouched, though, drawing back after a moment with a particular noise in his throat, a low groan that sounded like a growl, straightening up and starting us back to town, shaking his head, murmuring, "Myra Sims, you'll be the end of me."

Or something to that effect, I couldn't hear him very well from the far end of the seat where I'd scooted after the kiss, not so comfortable snuggling up to him in such an innocent fashion after we'd crossed the border to carnal knowledge. In fact, the only reason I remember it at all was that he was to say it on so many other occasions that it was to become a standard line, usually just after moments of particular passion, in wonder, and (I think) a little Baptist fear at the arsenal of weaponry the Good Lord had chosen to give woman over any puny man. At the time I took it as a compliment (as indeed, I guess it was) and went back to town, yawning out the window, still sleepy, but suddenly regretting my two-hour nap, wondering if I couldn't have put it to better use.

Michael was silent, though, oddly preoccupied, chewing his lip again and drumming his free hand on the seat. I was too new to his presence to realize I was in the process of being devoured by another Plan, and when he double-parked in front of the bus station was a little disappointed, wondering if that's what this whole morning had been about, a few hurried kisses?

I picked up my little valise that was still clattering around the floorboards and pressed it to my chest, abandoning my mother's tattered heels without a second thought, thinking I'd cross that bridge when I came to it. In the space of an hour, Birmingham and Mama seemed far away, another life, really. I was only sorry I had to go, fishing my ticket out of my purse and letting Michael walk me to the curb where my bus waited, the air conditioner already on, the hum echoing through the vacant parking lot, making conversation difficult.

When we made the turnstile, I tried for another carefree smile, the kind I'd given Mama at the station in Birmingham, while I thanked him for breakfast. But Michael wasn't so easily fooled, standing there with his arms crossed on his chest, his face still thoughtful and absorbed when I told him good-bye.

"Maybe I'll come Thanksgiving," I said, for want of a better parting.

In reply, instead of the usual polite noises of departure, he burst out, "Don't you be messen with thet *lawyer.*" The whole purpose and intent of my trip to Milton was tied up with the Lawyer and the party, and I just looked at him, as he added in that same fast, worried rush, "And doan nobody need to be slapping your *butt.*"

Well, truly, this particular Catts-Plan was coming out a little rough. I wasn't the most experienced person in the world, but even I knew that two kisses did not an engagement make, his tone desperate and protective, as if he were sending a beloved sheep to the wolves. I didn't know what to make of it and just nodded, said, "Sure, Michael."

When he saw my uncertainty, my utter lack of understanding, his face lost that fierce resolve and he took my suitcase and set it on the ground between us. Then, with no further request, he kissed me again, harder and longer and more insistent, sliding his fingers in my hair and holding it long enough for a response, his breath a little quick when he pulled away. He looked me in the eye and said, "You hear me? No lawyer. No butt-slapping. Call me."

I tell you what: I *felt* that one and looked at him with the beginnings of concern, stammering, "I don't — know your number."

He felt impatiently in his shirt pocket for a pen, and while the loudspeaker called for the final boarding, scribbled a number on a scrap of paper and handed it to me with another quick kiss. I picked up my valise and boarded the bus uncertainly, a little dazed by the kiss, while he stood there at the curb, calling out desperate little words of instruction at my back: "— don't go to thet party!" and "Call me!"

He went so far as to follow me down the bus to my seat, shouting further pieces of command that I could hardly hear as the diesel engines came on with a roar and the door compressed in, him just beyond the window, standing on his tiptoes, shouting, "Myra? Didju hear me? *Myra?*"

But there was no way to respond. I was hermetically sealed in the bus that was now in movement, sitting there with my suitcase still clutched to my chest when I noticed a worn-out old country woman who was reading a newspaper across the aisle. She smiled wryly when she met my eye, then tipped her head to the window to comment in a flat, dry voice, "Thank thet boy might want you to call him."

I burst out laughing then, for it *was* funny: the huge purring bus resolutely gaining speed, though Michael was still not sure I'd heard and would obey and, as God is my witness, was running alongside, a tiny voice beyond the compression of the coach, still yelling, "— *call me!*"

= 14 =

*S*o *the trip to Pensacola,* to strike out on a life of my own, garnished with parties and supported by the kindness of strangers, was aborted before it ever got started, for such was Michael's intent. I spent the long drive across the Panhandle staring out the window, turning his scribbled phone number over and over in my hands, thinking about slipping out at the two dozen stops and calling him, but I didn't have the change, and without Cissie's directions, couldn't call collect, I didn't know how.

I vaguely surmised that Liz, with her wealth of worldly knowledge, could surely set me straight; could picture Michael talking to me from his mother's kitchen, standing there with the spiral cord of the phone a lifeline connecting me with Mr. Simon and Cissie and the kindly smell of fried chicken in the high old ceiling boards of the house. The image was so compelling that I sat with my forehead pressed to the window, urging the bus faster, remembering the essence of our time together: the silly, stupid fight (that in retrospect, embarrassed me horribly), the breakfast at the café; plus other bits of memory: his face when I mentioned the Butt-slappers, that first flash of a smile.

That, and the kisses, I remembered them. Today, I think the art of the kiss has nearly been forgotten, but back then, to my Pentecostal mind, it was the peak premarital experience, not to be entered into lightly. I was hypnotized by the memory of his fingertips in my hair, his hard, hungry mouth just like his smile had been: giving something, and asking something, too. Something pressing and urgent, I didn't know exactly what, but the combination of his smile and his kiss was a potent one.

As soon as I saw Liz at the station, sitting slumped on a side bench, reading a paperback novel, I took off in a near-run. When I reached her, I held out the little swatch of paper and asked if she knew how to make a collect call. "Right here in Florida," I said, as if that made a difference in the difficulty of the undertaking.

Liz, who looked a little worse for wear after a long day's work, just put away her book and gathered her purse. "This would be Michael," she said, making me stop stone-still, thinking she was some kind of clairvoyant, though she only stood. "He called. Listen, I don't feel too hot, think I got the flu. D'you mind eating in tonight? We can go out tomorrow."

I didn't mind eating in the rest of my life; I was just speechless at her casual mention that Michael had called, when, as God is my witness, I didn't remember giving him Liz's full name, much less her number. I had forgotten the call the night before and underestimated the sheer bloodhound ferocity of the Catts, though I caught a glimpse of it when we got to Liz's apartment and I bleeped through the long distance operator and finally got Michael on the line.

"Mama remembered the number," he explained. Then, "How was your trip?"

I was sitting just as I'd imagined, at the table in Liz's tiny kitchen, the spiral cord from her perky yellow phone twisted around my hand, a little shy once I actually connected, ducking my face to murmur, "Okay."

"Didju sleep?"

"No," I said, thinking it was his fault I didn't, that I'd been too busy thinking about him, and after a pause, I was bold enough to tell him so.

"Good girl." He laughed, then said quickly, "Listen, what's your Mama's number up in Birmingham? I need to talk to her."

I guess it sounds funny that he needed to speak with my mother, but you could do a whole world of things at seventeen in Florida, but shipping out or marrying wasn't among them, not without your mother's permission. I quickly realized that we were in deep waters here and asked, "Why d'you wanta talk to Mama?"

He was a little hesitant in his answer. "Just to — ah — talk to her. Me and — Mama was thinking maybe you'd wanta come and stay a few days. When didju say you were going back home?"

Well, *never,* if Mama had anything to do with it, but I couldn't tell Michael that, and only made a few circular excuses, though I did give him my home phone number before we hung up. I was still sitting there at the table, turning it over in my mind, when the phone exploded in my hands (I hadn't put it down) and this time, it wasn't Michael, it was *Mama.* I have to say that from her point of view, it must have been the ultimate slap in the face: coming home from work bone-tired on a cold autumn twilight, glad of a quiet house and the knowledge that her children were finally out there, making their way in the world, when suddenly, the phone rings, and from out of the darkest nightmare of her life, a voice speaks. A *Catts* voice, dripping with that gheechie, white-trash, mill-town brogue she so despised, hinting at an unspeakable rebellion in her difficult, least-loved child, whom she'd just put on a bus to a better life with such a tear of regret. Michael didn't have any more sense than to be perfectly upfront and honest, and in a matter of moments, Mama had learned of my overnight stay on *Magnolia Hill,* of my promise to keep in touch, to take Ira there Thanksgiving.

If I know Mama, she'd even picked up on the permission-seeking intent in his voice before she ended the conversation with a mighty whack of the phone and turned her attention to me, and the moment I heard her voice vibrating through a million feet of phone wire, I knew I was in for it, and in for it good. Tired, cornered, and betrayed, my mother could be a very unpleasant woman (I can be, too —), and in her distress, she had jumped to the defense with none of Cissie Catts' charming malevolence, but more along the lines of the bared-teeth, full-frontal attack of a pit bull.

Without so much as a hello, she insisted I cut it off with that boy, that *skirt-chasing* little *snot* of a *boy,* who'd never been up to any good. (To tell you the truth, I think she had him confused with Gabe.) That I never step so much as a foot in *that town* again, and last but not least, that I get my sorry ungrateful tail back to Alabama where I would be greeted home with a whipping that would make *blood run down my legs.* This last was a saying of my father's that I hadn't heard in many years that had me breathing hard before it was over and done, crying when I hung up.

I was still at it when Liz woke up from her nap and found me in the kitchen, the phone impotent in my hand, because I hadn't retained much of her instructions and *still* didn't know how to call collect. Being the woman of the world she was, she quickly grasped the absolutes of the situation and, sitting on the counter in her sadly wrinkled dress, asked what Michael had to say about Mama's little fit.

"I cain't call him. Mama said not to!" I cried with a small earnestness that she regarded quizzically till she realized that I was really and truly not going to defy my mother on Michael's behalf and quickly set things to rights with a plan of her own.

"Then I'll call him," she said, and with all the deep, impenetrable wisdom of a woman living life in the fast lane, took the phone and dialed direct to the Catts kitchen. She and Michael chatted away like old friends as she explained my predicament, calmly nodding when he came up with a solution and hanging the phone up without even asking my opinion.

"What?" I asked, and she smiled.

"He'll be here by ten."

"Ten what?   .

"Ten o'clock."

"Tonight?" I breathed, and she was inexplicably unconcerned.

"Sure. You wanta see him, don't you? He sounds kind of — sweet."

Well, I truly didn't know what to make of that. Sure, I wanted to see him, but with Mama's attack still spinning around my head, I was in a quandary, wandering around the apartment for the better part of three hours. I changed clothes on Liz's insistence, even let her do something to my hair, so when Michael arrived just after eleven (he'd gotten lost) I was all ready for a date, but afraid to open the door.

Liz had long since gone to bed in the single bedroom, but not before mentioning that the couch folded out to a hide-a-bed. I was wondering if that advice was connected to Michael's arrival and got kind of weird about it, thinking maybe Mama was right; maybe I was in a little over my head.

But his face at the door was the only familiar thing about the place, and I opened it gratefully, if a little shyly, glad he didn't try for a kiss, but just asked to use the bathroom. When he came out, he glanced around curiously, "Where's your cousin?"

"In bed," I said, blushing a little at the implication of the dreaded word, though he didn't seem to notice, his face all set.

"We better git a move on," he said. "I have to be to work at six."

I shook my head. "Mama said no."

"*Shht,*" he murmured, glancing around the room and chewing his lip, before he suddenly turned. "Where's Ira?" he asked. "He's stateside, ain't he?"

"In Beaufort, but you cain't get him in camp."

"Sure I can," he said, and without even asking permission, he went to Liz's phone and showed a remarkable knowledge of long-distance dialing, calling information, Beaufort, the Marine Corps information number (the one they had for missing soldiers). I kept telling him it was no use, you couldn't get him in camp, it wasn't possible, till after a good twenty minutes of dialing, his face lightened, and he said, "Hey, bud."

"You got him?" I asked in amazement, but he didn't pay me any mind, though his smile quickly faded.

"She did?" he asked Ira ominously.

I danced around him, begging, "What? What?"

But he ignored me, arguing with Ira, assuring him it was above board, that *his mother* had invited me, that there was a church picnic this week and I'd have a good time. This last seemed a little hokey, even to me, a picnic on the fag-end of October. But Ira must have been softening, as Michael began grinning at me again, winking in a way that set up that old weirdness in my belly, wondering what I'd got myself into when he finally handed me the phone.

I took it gingerly and turned aside to talk to Ira, saying, "Hey," very quietly.

"Hey, yourself," he answered dryly. "What in the world have you got yoursef up to, driving some pore old mill hand crazy?"

I blushed to my hairline, unable to answer with Michael right there beside me, standing with his hands in his pockets, glancing around the room while I talked. "I ain't up to — nothing," I said.

"Well, you sho got Mama tearing up the phone lines, wanting me to go AWOL to run down there and whip his ass."

"Mama called?" I whispered.

He didn't sound too happy about it either. "Shore did. Got me down here on an emergency call, madder than hell. Whatchu doing running back to Magnolia Hill, anyway? Ain't you had yo fill of that place?"

I told him about the bus ride and being hungry, and how happy Cissie had been to see me, but he only sighed. "Well, Mama ain't gone stand for it, I can tell you that. Let me talk to Michael."

So back the phone went to the menfolk, who had another conference, Michael's face finally lightening, telling him he'd see him Thanksgiving. When he hung up, he had that same shameless grin of triumph, though I wasn't so sure, and told him.

"Ira said it's all right," he insisted, but I just looked at him levelly. "Ira ain't Mama."

"I told you to quit worryin' about Mama. How old are you, anyway?" I think he asked it as a hypothetical question, for my answer wiped the smug grin off his face like magic. "Seventeen?" he cried. "You're *seventeen?*"

I nodded my head sadly, and he was truly amazed, walking around the little kitchen, repeating, "Seventeen? *Shit!*"

To tell you the truth, I was finding his incessant profanity a little wearing, and anyway, I couldn't help being seventeen. I'd told his mother how old I was the night before, and she hadn't made such big a deal about it, though when I mentioned that, he was only more annoyed, saying, "Well, hell, she wouldn't, would she? Seventeen! *Damn!*"

On that, he stopped his fussing and looked at me sadly, said, "Well, sister, I don't know what to say. It's up to you. I gotta get a move on. You going or staying?"

At that point, I might have stayed, to please Mama, if nothing else, except that when he asked it, he was standing there slouched on his back leg, his arms folded across his chest in perfectly unconscious imitation of his father. For the first time, it lent him an uncanny resemblance, not in his rough, Indian features, but his face-up way of talking, and I heard myself answer quietly, "I wanta go with you."

He smiled then, and his smile was his own, impudent and pleased. "Good girl," he said, and in short order, my valise and I were back in the truck, heading east to the magnetic little spot on the map that kept pulling me back to the dense oak canopy of my mother's darkest dreams. Michael wouldn't let me sit next to him on the return trip, saying that's all he needed, to get pulled over in Washington County by some big-belly sheriff with an underage minor in his lap. You could tell it was weighing on his mind; every once in a while he'd ask me about my birthday, or what grade I was in at school, grimacing when I said eleventh, for I'd lost a year in Florida and never made it up.

We rode along quietly after that, till somewhere in the inky darkness of the Apalachicola forest, when he abruptly swung into the dirt parking lot of a tackle shop that was deserted that time of night. He turned off the truck and sat quietly a moment, then turned, and in a low, nervous rush, said: "Listen, Myra. Your Mama, she's never gone let you stay."

This certainly wasn't news to me, and I agreed in a quiet voice. "I know."

He paused another long moment, then spoke in that same breathless rush. "Then maybe we need to go ahead, git married. Then you can live with us, and all."

That's just the way he put it, and I didn't even meet his eye, just stared at my ghostly reflection in the window, a clear choice before me: either Miss Cissie and Mr. Simon, or Mama and Alabama and getting whipped till blood ran down my legs. It really wasn't a choice at all, and I didn't hesitate a second before I made some equally romantic reply like "Sure" or "I guess so."

But it was good enough for him, and without even sealing it with a kiss, much less any talk of love or commitment, he started the truck again and off we went. After that, we were both a little quiet and thoughtful, wondering what the hell we'd gotten ourselves into, not speaking again till we were a few miles down the road, when a star fell in the glimmering sky above the highway in front of us. Against the pitch black of the forest, its tail flared out as long as a comet, causing both of us to exclaim aloud. Michael slowed to a halt right in the middle of the highway, his face lifted to the window, watching it streak down the sky in a lovely slow-motion arc till it finally faded back to black. When it was gone, he turned to me, grinned, "Make a wish, baby."

I was young enough to believe him; young enough to close my eyes, and though I do remember wishing for something that night, wishing for it with all my heart, I don't actually remember what I wished for. Happiness, I assume, or peace with my mother, it really didn't matter. Because after that, the ice was broken, and we rode along merrily enough, talking of practical concerns: where we'd live, how we could pay for the wedding — our fate sealed by that random streak of cosmic gas, an omen to my child's eyes.

It was the first thing I told Ira when I finally got him up the next morning with another emergency call to announce my engagement, though he clearly wasn't so thrilled. "Well, hell, Myra, I thank you're gitting your stories mixed up," he said. "This ain't Jesus and the Wisemen, this is real life. You need to thank about this thang."

I assured him I had, though I actually hadn't thought about it much at all. We'd come in so late that I'd slept till eleven, then ate cold fried chicken with a triumphant Cissie. Her open-hearted acceptance had surrounded me in a little bubble of excitement that Ira effectively burst with his first, terse question: "What does Mama thank about all this?"

I told him she didn't have much say-so, that I could run over to Pascagoula if she wouldn't sign (a bit of information I'd picked up from my future mother-in-law, who'd done the same thing twenty-six years ago). On that, Ira sighed. "Well, hell, if you're that set —" he began, then, oddly enough, he brought up Gabe, asking what *he* thought of all this.

"Gabe Catts?" I said. "I don't know. He's gone to school." Which was about the extent of my knowledge of Gabe, still.

For though Cissie had been quick to brag on him that first night, she hadn't been so quick to fill in the details. The only sign of him on the Hill these days was a head-and-shoulders graduation photograph that shared a double frame with his brother's on the television, outfitted in the regulation cap and gown. Both of them stared out with conservative detachment, Michael's photo a younger, thinner version of himself, so void of expression that the picture didn't favor him much. ("Never did," his mother told me.)

On the opposite frame, Gabriel's face was equally flat and expressionless and oddly somber. It reflected nothing of the shadowy memories I had of the lively little boy across the fence, but seemed dim and academic to my eyes, already flown the coop: a doctor-to-be, a Name, far beyond the reach of any of us there on the Hill.

Of his younger brother, Michael himself made no comment at all, except to agree that his graduation picture didn't favor him, either. "Not anymore," he said, with a mirthless laugh and a shake of his head.

I dimly discerned that there was something missing here, some bit of potentially embarrassing information that was being politely withheld. But from what murky, uneven memories I could dredge up of him as a boy, Gabe always was a peculiar child, one that I was willing to leave there on the peripheral, unexplained, though like I say, Ira seemed disturbed at his absence.

On my second night on the Hill, he went so far as to fritter away the last of his emergency calls trying to talk Michael into waiting till Thanksgiving, promising to spend his week's leave on the Hill, maybe talk Carl and Mama into coming. But Michael was oddly resistant to even a week's postponement, and paced the kitchen like a young Napoleon, phone in hand, telling him of our plans to sell his truck to pay for the wedding, to live with his parents till we had a down payment on a house of our own.

He persistently ignored Ira's constant question about what was the hurry and was seemingly relieved when the long distance operator came on the line and told them their time was up. Raising his voice over the crackle of disconnection, Michael assured him it would all work out, then hung up.

"How long do we have to wait?" I asked, but Michael just circled his arms around my waist and nuzzled my neck.

"Wait, hell. We can run over to Mississippi tonight."

But in this, he was sidetracked by his mother, of all people, who didn't seem to mind the impropriety of having an underage, disenfranchised fiancée living under her roof, but insisted we go about this thing with at least the minimal Baptist trappings: the engagement announcement, the bridal shower, and above all, the white wedding gown.

"We don't want people to talk," she kept saying, and with Mama breathing fire in Alabama, Michael didn't have much room to buck his own mother.

So for a good four weeks there, I was the resident bride-to-be, making the Welcome rounds on Michael's arm, feeling like a cow on auction with the stares and not-so-subtle whispers of the neighbors who remembered my father well, and clearly weren't as sanguine about forgive-and-forget as Cissie and Mr. Simon. Such was the stress of the brief month that I hardly remember it at all, with only the barest impression of going to church on Michael's arm and smiling and smiling till my face about froze; of trying on dress after dress in the snooty little bridal shop downtown, none of which we could possibly afford. And last but not least, the enormous bridal shower held in my honor at Welcome Baptist the week before the wedding.

I have uneasy memories of the night, of sitting there in the fellowship hall surrounded by an ocean of punch-sipping, mint-chewing strangers. All of them were humming with curiosity over Michael's infatuation with the Sims girl (yes, *that* Sims girl), checking out my sweater and skirt (the only dressy outfit I had) with looks of sudden enlightenment, as if they finally realized the name of the game here.

The younger ones (including my old nemesis, Cassie Scales) seemed to find it endlessly amusing, and whenever the gift was lingerie, they'd make pointed comments like: "Michael'll love that," in these nasty, simpering little voices that I found positively unnerving, wanting to run back to Birmingham to Mama and ask her what all this giggling was about.

For despite our white-trash reputation and the extramarital tail-chasing in the men of the house, the Sims household was an oddly prudish one, possibly a holdover of my mother's strict childhood, with sex never mentioned at all, never, not even in jest. At seventeen, I didn't even like the looks of the word, skipping over it in textbooks and novels, though I was frightened enough by the women's jibes to mention it to Michael the next night in the privacy of the back porch. We'd gotten into the habit of sitting out there after supper, our feet hanging into Cissie's azaleas, mostly to get away from her unending insistence that I splurge on a real wedding gown.

It was there, under the cover of the companionable darkness, that

I summoned up the nerve to bring up the women and their giggling insinuations, told him I was *scared.*

"Scared of what?" he asked, but I was too ignorant of the whole unspeakable mystery to do more than shake my head pensively. Michael was understandably disturbed by my misgivings, pressing me, asking, "Scared of *me?*"

I only shook my head mutely, not necessarily scared of him, but of the whole hideous bleeding business. I was quietly terrified, in fact, knowing in my heart that it would ruin everything: the laughing, the kisses, the meeting him at the tracks every evening and walking home arm in arm, sitting with him at supper, watching the play between him and his father, constantly reassured by their very likeness.

As soon as the nasty, simpering business of sex was introduced, it would all be ruined, though Michael worked hard to convince me it wouldn't, kissing my hands, assuring me over and over, "I ain't gone hurt you, baby."

I appreciated his assurances, though they didn't come close to striking at the root of the matter. For simple brutality wasn't an elusive subconscious fear to me, but a simple fact of life, something that an ice pack and a few aspirins got you over after a few days. What I was afraid of was a deeper, more nameless violation: of trusting someone who betrayed you in an awful, senseless way; of loving someone intimately who didn't do you justice; who couldn't do you justice, though they tried and tried. And in a more practical vein, of the whole nasty mess of pelvics and steel instruments and disgusted doctors that on some deep, unconscious plane I still connected with the secretive business between the legs, in short, with sex.

Of course, none of it was so obvious to me at the time, all of my fears submerged in a mass of wafting, ill-defined anxiety, so that by the eve of our wedding, I was as pale and quick-tempered as Michael, though his nervousness was for opposite reasons, a lot to do with his inability to quell my ridiculous (in his eyes, anyway) fears. It was a quandary that I'm sure was not lessened by my own snuggling habits, or my boundless sexual naiveté, for I can remember waking him on the couch every morning in my old flannel gown that after five Alabama winters was nearly transparent, seeing nothing at all fearsome or sinful in creeping under his covers to get warm in the cold dark living room.

I'd let him kiss and feel me in the thin light of dawn with no qualm of conscience, a little scared of the delicious sensation of his hands on my breasts, but, as God as my witness, not seeing it as sexual. I wouldn't even jump up or run out in modesty when Cissie turned the light on in the kitchen to fix breakfast, would just stand and wish her good-morning, polite as you please.

Coupled with my tearful misgivings on the porch every night, it must have made for a rare torment, poor Michael nearly frantic by the end of it. He wasn't eating by then, and hardly sleeping, his sheer intensity setting that old fear rolling in my belly again, making me wonder if there was such a thing as a purely platonic marriage, wondering what he'd do if I asked for one. I think Michael might have discerned my intent, which he tried to forestall with an even more ferocious insistence that we tie the knot, with or without the elusive white gown that we simply couldn't afford (and indeed forwent in favor of a borrowed dress of a friend of Candace's).

So the Friday after Thanksgiving, a bare month after I'd first laid eyes on him in his mother's kitchen, we were standing at the Catts' fireplace, the preacher having me repeat formalized vows I'd wager I didn't remember two seconds later. It wasn't Brother Sloan facing us across the Bible. He'd been called out at the last minute on a family emergency, leaving Michael about ready to chew nails until he came upon the obvious solution, and there at the fireplace, all decked out in his trademark seersucker suit, stood his grandfather, who despite his wild and wicked ways, still held on to some sort of religious accreditation.

To the faithful at Welcome, I'm sure Brother Tierney's appearance was as odd a twist of fortune as my unexpected return, as he no longer lived in town, but had tomcatted his way into a second marriage in Memphis. I'm sure fully half of our well-wishers were there to see what had become of this former star of the pulpit, quick to notice the mild air of genteel seediness about his old suit and the tremble in his hand when he made the first toast, though I was too nervous to hardly notice either.

For I'd cried the night away, partly because Mama had signed off my marriage license with a bold, contemptuous hand as if she were glad to me rid of me, and partly because I was dreading the honeymoon so much. Old Brother Tierney seemed to sympathize with my plight and deem it simple intimidation, for he told me in the bedroom before the service not to be afraid of the old biddies at Welcome; that they could kill me, but they couldn't eat me, and if they did, I'd sho make a bellyful — advice I found as fully bizarre as it sounds right here.

On Michael's behalf, he interfered with Baptist tradition enough to make a toast and a benediction in almost the same breath, announcing to the roomful of celebrants that while they might want to hang around for a slice of his daughter's five-tiered wedding cake, Michael and his wife most certainly did not. With no more ado, he hugged Michael and kissed me full on the mouth (the only time I've ever heard of a preacher kissing a bride on the mouth), and just like that, we were gone.

We'd planned to drive to the coast, but didn't quite make it, as Michael had worked till six that morning and was so tired that we stopped at sunset at a little tourist cabin in the flat woods, on what turned out to be the first week of deer season. That's who our neighbors were on both sides, camo-geared hunters who were up at dawn and gone, leaving the place deserted till sunset, when they'd return with their kill and butcher them on our doorstep, with many offers of venison and wild hog that we had to turn down, not having any refrigeration.

It didn't make for the most romantic honeymoon of the decade: the skinned, hung carcasses of headless buck and hog, and the pervasive odor of fresh kill that to me smelled strikingly like menstruation. But it really wasn't so bad, as Michael lived up to his word that first night, taking a lot of time and sweat and shaking effort to get me over the hump (a poor choice of words, perhaps) into the land of marital bliss.

He knocked off immediately afterwards to sleep the night away for the first time in four weeks, leaving me curled against his back with his T-shirt bunched between my legs, not seeing anything even vaguely pathetic or ironic that after my first encounter with marital sex, I had come away unscathed, emotionally untouched — only relieved that despite my runaway fears, this sex-thing really wasn't as bad as they made it out to be. I mean, sure, it was a little strange and sweaty and awkward, but, hey, who was I to complain? I hadn't felt a thing.

$$= 15 =$$

That's how I came to be married at seventeen; a mother nine months and twelve days later, as Michael brought me home from the deer woods with a sight more than a backstrap of venison and a shoulder of wild hog to my name. He brought me home pregnant, and from the very first, I was sick as a dog, moving into his bedroom with no further ado after Mama sent me a trunk of clothes with no message attached, just all my worldly goods packed by careful hands, my Bible laid on top.

The voicelessness of it all didn't hurt me as much as it could have, as Cissie had quickly jumped in to fill the maternal gap, thrilled to tears at the possibility of a new grandchild, keeping tabs on every dizzy spell, every bout of nausea as Christmas approached, a holiday the Catts celebrated with a fervor I found just short of insane. The whole clan baked, bought, wrapped, and consulted as if it were the last Christmas on earth, much of it in preparation for Gabriel's grand homecoming on Christmas Eve.

You'd have thought he was coming back from a ten-year expedition of the Arctic Circle, such was their anticipation, Cissie practically killing the fatted calf, calling on her assortment of nieces and sisters and in-laws to be on hand for the great celebration, the return of the beloved son. I simply couldn't imagine what all the fuss was about, and at night on the porch, Michael couldn't very well explain. He'd let me lay my head in his lap when I was too sick to sit up, apologetic for getting me in the family way so soon, after his father had taken him aside the morning of the wedding and warned him of that very thing. He'd even gone so far as to provide the means of avoidance (an unheard-of intervention in that day and time) and bawled him out the first morning I'd come up sick, though he'd been very sweet to me, standing at the end of the bed and patting my foot, recommending I eat a few soda crackers.

I ate what I could and tried to help Cissie with the holiday cooking, though as I got up time and again to go to the bathroom and meditate over the toilet, I wished with all my heart that when Michael had run out of condoms the second night and kindly offered to run to town to the drugstore, I'd have had the good sense to let him go. But I didn't, too afraid of the hunters and their bloody carcasses, just resigning myself to a life of soda crackers and iced tea and eight more months of the morning sickness from Hell.

Around suppertime on Christmas Eve, after most of the extended family had pulled in the drive with many a hug and tearful kiss, there was a great commotion on the front porch, Cissie calling for me to come on, hurry up! Gabe was home! I went out shyly, dishcloth in hand, and waited by the front door, and had Michael not been walking a few steps behind him, carrying his duffle bag, I doubt I would have recognized his brother at all. For the chunky little boy of my youth had been mysteriously replaced by a hippie-looking malcontent an inch or so taller than Michael and a dozen pounds heavier, with dark blonde hair that hung past his shoulders, sandals (over socks, the strangest thing I'd ever seen in my life), his wide Slavic face lifted in an arrogant tilt to check out what Michael had brought home in a bride.

Just that quickly, the subtle mystery of Cissie and Michael's aversion to discussing him was finally solved: he was queer. I don't mean he was homosexual, but queer in the more universal sense: odd, peculiar, strange. Ignoring the head-shaking of his relations, he took the porch steps in two bounds and extended his left hand, the wrong one for shaking, which threw me for a moment there. I hastily made the adjustment, almost dropping the dishtowel in my confusion, then took his hand and met his eyes, that, contrary to whatever the graduation photograph might have indicated, were unchanged since childhood, snapping and inquisitive, coming to life with a flash of recognition that leapt at me like a line of fire.

"*Myra?*" he cried. "My-ra Sims? You came back?"

There was a blank silence on the porch, as Michael quickly took the steps to join us, his eyes oddly traced on mine, while Gabriel fairly shouted in my face, "You *married Michael?*"

His voice fairly dripped with raw accusation, though I surely didn't know why, wanting to run into the house and lock myself in the bedroom to get away from this raging nut, who turned on Michael without missing a beat and shouted, "You *married her?* You *married My-ra?*"

I really don't know what it would have come to if Cissie hadn't come out on the porch and brought everything back into perspective with a slap to the back of his head and a brisk, "Quit that shouting, honey. Give Myra a hug — she's your sister now."

Gabe obeyed her, blinking like an owl as she herded him inside to his father, leaving the attendant neighbors and relations to break into a speculating hum at the near-scene they'd witnessed. Michael ignored them to pull me to the truck, dishtowel and all, and take me to our old place on the river that had become another of our sanctuaries. I was too stunned to speak on the way out, a little nauseated from all the excitement and shouting, resting my head against the worn seatcovers of the old Ford he'd traded his new truck for to raise the money to marry me.

Michael didn't press it, just parked in our usual spot under the old oak, the sounds of the still, cold evening gathering around us before I finally spoke. "What happened to his hand?" I asked in a small voice, both of us knowing what I meant: not just what happened to his hand, but what happened to *him?* To his hair? His clothes? His *shoes,* for God's sake? Why had he yelled at me like that?

Michael didn't answer right away, only whistled tunelessly through his teeth a moment, then rested his head against his own seat with a quiet sigh. "His hand got messed up when your Daddy broke his wrist," he said. "The hair and all is recent, since he went away to school."

He didn't seem nearly as comfortable discussing his odd brother as he'd been about introducing Sam, though I was too astounded by the news of his wrist to worry it, feeling an unexpected stab of panic when he mentioned my *Daddy* in that calm, matter-of-fact voice. It made my heart beat queerly in my chest, so erratically that I had to lie down with my head on his lap, a thin line of moisture above my lip, finally whispering, "When? After — after we left?"

Michael didn't answer for a moment, and when I opened my eyes, he was watching me, his rough face worried, much like his father's had been the morning I'd first come up sick. "No," he said quietly. "Out by the fence, before you left. A few months before."

I had no immediate memory of the day, and Michael didn't press it, combing my hair off my damp forehead with a cool hand, while I lay there with my eyes closed, trying to remember that day at the fence. The smell and texture of the December afternoon brought it nigglingly close to the surface: the old oak shedding its leaves, the cold autumn wind blowing them up and around into a little whirlwind, Gabe in a — yes! in a quilt.

An old sun-and-shadow quilt, standing there pointing over the fence with a stick. (*"Now, get you a rock, Myra! A flat one — a roundun'll roll —"*)

"I remember," I said, opening my eyes.

Michael just looked at me. "Remember what?"

I sat up slowly. "That day. At the fence. A rock — I was getting a rock — he broke his *wrist?*" I asked in amazement.

Michael nodded calmly, his face reflective, jerking back when a wave of nausea hit me, so violent that I scrambled for the door, barely making it to the window before I was overcome with dry heaves, retching and retching over the door into the dead grass. Michael was nearly as green in the face as I was before it was over, when he let me lie back down with my head in his lap, his hands cool on my forehead, pushing back my hair.

"He scares me," I finally whispered, and it was Michael's turn to be amazed.

"Gabe?" he asked incredulously. "Oh, hell, Myra, he's harmless. Just a little — surprised to see you, is all. He'll git over it."

But when we returned for supper that night, he didn't look like he was over much of anything, his conversation all around the table, with his brother, his aunt, his father, but his eyes inevitably traced on me. Whenever I looked up, there they were, like a cat on a mouse, making me so nervous I forwent the Christmas Eve festivities to go to bed early, with a headache, I said. Michael joined me there, both of us quiet in the darkness, watching the glimmer of the Christmas lights Cissie had strung on the porch that blinked noiselessly in the window, red and green and blue. Later in the evening, they began singing carols out there, an old Catts family tradition, and Cissie cadged Gabe into a solo, his voice startlingly lovely on the cold winter night, making me shiver under my mountain of covers.

"You all right?" Michael whispered.

But I couldn't answer, couldn't describe the awful foreboding that perfectly pitched old hymn awakened in my chest. I just pressed my face to his shoulder, whispered, "He just *scares* me, is all."

But it was a fear that passed as quickly and painlessly as the short, December night, Michael and I waking early the next morning to a fast round of perfectly silent sex (no strain on my part) before we exchanged what small presents we'd managed to scrape together in four weeks. His was a stainless steel pocket knife, mine, a simple navy jumper with a crisp white blouse he'd bought at Daffin's at a price that was the talk of the morning.

After banging around the kitchen a good hour, Cissie finally tired of waiting for us and stuck her head in the door to wish us *Christmas-Gift,* then trooped us into the living room, where she'd laid out our Santa Claus presents. Mine was a bottle of dimestore perfume and a batiste nursing gown, Michael and Gabe's, Old Spice travel kits and identical pearl-buttoned cowboy shirts that they made much fun of, Gabe calling them Howdy Doody shirts, making us laugh and laugh. It was the laughter that finally broke the ice between us, for even his worst enemies (and they abound) will admit that Gabriel Catts is probably the funniest man they've ever met, saying really the most outrageous things to anyone (and I mean, *anyone*) when the mood is upon him. His poor father threatened to take a belt to him more than once that weekend, though Gabriel only wrinkled his face and told him he really *did* need to get over this masochistic need to whip young men.

Fortunately for him, none of us hicks knew what masochism was (or he *would* have got a whipping) though that night at the supper table, after another of his awful comments, I was finally moved to speak to him, not even intentionally, but in unconscious wonder, murmuring, "And you were gonna be a *preacher?*"

My tone of simple amazement caused the whole table (all of us, plus a cousin home from Vietnam and Case) to burst into spontaneous laughter, with Gabriel finally the butt of the joke. He took it pretty well, though, just lifting his chin in his old audacious smile, the dinner conversation moving on to preachers in general and old Brother Tierney in particular, Gabriel amazed that he had performed our wedding. "I thought he lost his papers."

"He did," Case offered, "but he's all set up agin with some outfit out of Memphis. Church of the Blessed Something."

"Church of the Rising Savior," I corrected, as he'd told me all about them the morning of our wedding, what a good solid bunch they were up in Memphis.

His youngest grandson was not so enthused, though, just returned to his plateful of ham, snorting, "Rising *Savior,* my ass. Church of the Rising *Something-Else,* if I know Grandeddy."

There was a groan at that, truly a groan, among the menfolk, at least, for despite my wifely status, I didn't know what the heck he was talking about. Mr. Simon was on his feet in an instant, and politely requested Gabriel's presence in the kitchen, please, leaving the rest of the table (except Michael, who was tilting his chair against the wall, laughing till he choked) to shake their heads in wonder at the sheer depth of spoiling that one woman could do a child.

When they returned, Gabriel made a stab at a mumbled apology, though he went on to say things as bad (or worse) all week long, to my constant amazement. It wasn't that I hadn't heard such ribaldry before; it was just that it was so out of place, in such a *Baptist* household. That, coupled with Mr. Simon's embarrassment, made it doubly hard to take, for he was obviously so proud of his smart-ass of a son, and equally obviously humiliated by my subjection to his raw, steady commentary. I tried to tell him it was all right, that Ira and his friends said things as bad, but Mr. Simon was of the old school where such talk belonged in the bar room, if anywhere at all. They got into it so often that Gabriel finally left early, to his father's obvious relief, though in the weeks that followed, he made a point of echoing Michael's frequent insistence that Gabe was *harmless.*

"Just a little high strung" was the way he put it, and I loved him enough not to argue, just concentrated on surviving a difficult pregnancy and adjusting to my new life on the Hill, not a difficult proposition, as every day was fairly predictable. First, there was the alarm at six-thirty, then breakfast, cooked and served in a manner identical to that first morning on the Hill. When it was done, I'd put on my coat and walk Michael to the truck and kiss him good-bye, hating our twelve-hour separation, sometimes crying when he left.

I'd come back inside with such a look of despair that Mr. Simon, who'd just be returning from his shift as night watchman, would have me join him for his own breakfast. He hardly ate a thing, just sat there sipping his coffee, letting me chatter away as vapidly as I had as a child, till I'd notice him nodding in his plate and send him off to bed.

Once the menfolk were gone and the dishes done, I was left at the mercy of *Cissie-World,* which is what Gabriel calls his mother's domain, in a routine as calculable as clockwork: housework till eleven, then a quick lunch of leftovers, then, from noon till four o'clock, her *stories.* First, it was *As the World Turns,* then *Days of Our Lives,* and so on, one after another, her face glued to the television with a rapt, mystical expression, like an acolyte hearing from God. She would occasionally try to share it with me, calling me in to witness a devilish plot some vixen was hatching, but I have never been much for melodrama and after a few weeks, she left me alone, to drift aimlessly around the house, alternatively sick and sleepy, and as full winter descended, increasingly bored.

For at least in Birmingham I had school to distract me, but after marriage and pregnancy, I'd closed that door, and surprisingly missed it, finding an unlooked-for substitution one lead-gray January afternoon, when I discovered a regular Aladdin's cave of wonders in the little room off the back porch. It was so small, I had assumed it was a storage closet till my bored snooping led me to stick my nose in the door and flip the overhead light on a tiny, windowless room. As it turned out, it had been Gabriel's bedroom before he left for college, that still bore his inimitable stamp, the sloping walls pinned with semi-obscene rock posters, the walls lined with homemade bookshelves, filled with books of every description, everything from biology texts to thin serial Westerns, Baptist hymnals, and freshman literature anthologies.

I was immediately fascinated, slinking into the room like a cat-burglar and closing the door behind me, pulling out a book or two at random, finding them worn and folded, the margins scribbled with penciled, cryptic comment. On a whim, I even felt under the mattress of the narrow bed and came upon the standard adolescent stockpile of carefully concealed *Playboy*s, just like Ira had at home, equally worn. Oddly enough, that's where I began my reading, finding the articles enlightening, the cartoons obscene, the voluptuous women as dreamy and distant as Martians.

When I told Michael of my find in bed that night, he assured me I had the goods to beat them all. "Cain't find tits like this in a magazine," he said with this perfectly innocent appreciation, though he warned me not to dig too deep back there, said there wasn't no telling what I'd come upon.

I told him I wouldn't, but as the weeks passed, I found myself increasingly drawn there, lying on the narrow, lumpy bed all afternoon long, sipping sweet tea and nibbling soda crackers, quickly leaving the women's-tits and men-talk of *Playboy* to slowly but surely begin my two-year consumption of every book in the room. Though I didn't know it at the time, it was a watershed, really, a transition from the escape of virulent Christianity to the escape of the printed word, though I eventually held to both and became the woman I am today: a surprisingly well-read right-wing religionist, or conversely, a suspiciously humanistic Baptist housewife, according to which side you've pitched your camp.

In either case, an oddity, thanks to my insatiable hunger for learning and the unknowing legacy of my brother-in-law, whose taste ran to popular fantasy and Jewish contemporaries, probably required reading for his lower-level lit classes. I eventually devoured them all, only thwarted in a couple of cases, with the biology texts (that were boring) and the plays of Edward Albee (absurd was an apt word), though the book that stole my heart was Daphne du Maurier's *Rebecca*.

I can't imagine how it had come into Gabriel's sphere (I found it wedged between well-thumbed volumes of *Goodbye, Columbus* and *The Two Towers*) but once I read the first wistful line, I was entranced, still at it when Michael came home from work that night at six. I only paused long enough then to heat his supper and slip into my big winter coat, then returned to the unheated little room and dived back into the second Mrs. de Winter's plight, feeling a rare kinship with her unexpected launch into a strange new life, her uncertainty, her every neurosis. It was so real it was as if it were happening to me; as if I had left Magnolia Hill altogether and was walking those sounding corridors, stalked by Mrs. Danvers, drawing near to an awful truth.

I was so involved that when Michael came to the door at midnight to tell me to come to bed, I all but threw the lamp at him. He was amused by my absorption, though, amused and a little amazed, just joining me in bed, having to lie wedged between me and the wall to go to sleep, his breath warm on my back as I drew toward the twisting finale. Around daylight, when the heart of the mystery was finally revealed, I remember waking him to breathlessly report that old Rebecca hadn't been such a peach, after all; that she'd been a whore and cheat and Maxim had shot her, but she had, by God, deserved it. For a man in the middle of a four-day shift, he took the news pretty well, just patted my back and told me he was so glad, then dropped back off to sleep while I thumbed back to the beginning, when Manderley was still intact, and started the journey all over again: the courtship, the fancy-dress ball, the whole nine yards.

I went on about it so much that even Michael got caught up in the story that I tried to explain to him, wiling away the gray winter evenings in bed telling it to him cover to cover, with the actual text in my hands, lest I fall into errancy. He'd lie there with his hands behind his head, his face so distant I'd think he was drifting, though he'd always stir awake when I started to turn out the light with a dim request I keep going, patting my foot, saying, "Keep going, baby. I like to hear you talk."

But it took forever, two months at least, the weather warming, the covers kicked to the floor one at a time, till spring was finally upon us, the old sweet gum bursting into delicate leaf, when I finally came to the passage where they found the skeleton in Rebecca's boat. I had paused a moment to prod Michael's leg to make sure he was awake, when a quiet voice cut through the wall. "Did he kill her?" it asked.

I looked up, open-mouthed, while Michael sat up on his elbows, bursting into laughter when his father sheepishly appeared at the door between the bedrooms in his old pajama bottoms, embarrassed and apologetic, for the question had been his. But I would have none of it, just waved him to the cedar chest so I could finish my tale, not trusting my feeble interpretation to the unveiling of Rebecca's duplicity, but insisting on reading it aloud, verbatim. Michael dosed off halfway through, but his father stayed with me till the end, his arms folded over his chest, his face wonderfully absorbed, murmuring every once in a while in a stunned, reflective voice, "Well, I declare."

It really is my most treasured memory of him, a perfect completion to the circle of our friendship; for we were still teasing him about it a matter of weeks later when he went to bed early with what he thought was a touch of the flu. I paused a moment in the kitchen while he fixed himself a glass of soda and talked about Gabe, as spring break was soon upon us and we were on the brink of another grand homecoming. He was worried about him, as usual, worried with his irresponsibility, his bohemianism, always looking for a way to connect, to make him happy.

He'd been planning since Christmas to take him fishing on the Dead Lakes, though as he finished his soda, he shook his head, told me wryly that he guessed he'd have to pull out the poles and fish from the bank. "Fool boy's too lazy to row a boat."

He laughed when he said it; we both did, for Gabriel's laziness was legend in the Catts' household. Then he set his glass down and wished me good-night, and I went to bed myself, awakened the next morning by a high, staccato shouting that pierced the pre-dawn stillness. I couldn't quite make out what it was at first, and just lay there, blinking, till Michael sat up with a jerk, then lept from the bed, and I finally realized what it was: the sound of my mother-in-law screaming.

$\mathcal{I}$ *found Cissie's hysteria* far more disconcerting than my two-second glimpse of Mr. Simon's calm, sleeping face
when we burst into the bedroom. Michael, for the first (and last) time in
his life, completely lost it, climbing on the bed, shouting, "Daddy!
Daddy! Wake up!"

I wrestled him back to our bedroom while he kept calling for his
father in such an awful, helpless way, though by the time the ambulance
arrived, he was himself again, sitting on the edge of the bed in his
unsnapped, pulled-on pants, his face in his hands, not crying, but in simple shock. Cissie regrouped as quickly, a little off-balance that first awful
day, wanting to dye her clothes black like they did in the old days,
though a combination of church women and her sister Maggie talked
her out of it.

By the time Case finally located and retrieved Gabriel from
Tallahassee, she was back to her old imperturbable self, meeting him at
the door with the calm announcement that he would sing at his father's
funeral. Poor Gabriel, who is given to quick tears on the best of days, had
cried himself into a near-coma on the drive home, so disheveled that he
looked like a transient in his old hippie-clothes. In short order, they got

into the row of the century, Gabe informing her that he could not sing at his father's funeral if she put a gun to his head.

The houseful of descending relations quickly warmed to the fight, splitting equally into two camps: the *is-there-anything-this-sorry-boy-is-good-for?* camp and the *nobody-should-be-made-to-sing-at-their-father's-funeral* camp. I myself stayed clear of both, heartbroken over losing Mr. Simon, but not feeling grief in the normal way, just numb and silent, going out to the little ditch and sitting there all day long, taking *Rebecca* with me, but too hurt to read it; it reminded me so much of him.

As early evening descended, I was reminded of my childhood on the Hill, when Mr. Simon would come home from work every night, his face pinched and tired, his supper waiting on the table, but always taking time to pause at the fence and speak to a lonely child. The memory was so strong on the still blue hush that it made my head hurt, filling my chest with a suffocating tightness. Like Michael, I was still too stunned to cry and just took deep breaths and pressed my face to my knees, jumping a little when someone broke the silence to ask: "Is it just me, or is my mother insane?"

It was Gabriel, of course. He's always been one to sneak up on you and had come up quietly to stand there in the half-light, his hands in his pockets, his voice calm and tired and spent. I didn't answer, for even at that stage in the game, I knew better than to entangle myself in the ongoing Cissie-Gabe Wars. I just sat there chewing a piece of grass till he sighed hugely and flopped to the ground beside me, lying flat out on the grass, his face to the darkening sky.

"Where's Michael?" he asked. When I told him he was making the arrangements at the funeral home, he raised on an elbow to look at me. "So he's left footing the bill?"

I was still too much of a child to have even considered the financial implications of death and only shrugged, making Gabriel drop back to the grass with another sigh, this one of disgust. "Be punching a clock at Sanger till he dies," he murmured quietly, then, without a blink of warning, "How come you two got married so quick? What was the big rush?"

Since rumor of my pregnancy had surfaced, this question had been asked and (incorrectly) answered by most of the busybodies on

the Hill, making me go to some lengths to explain the authorized version, telling him about Mama and her disapproval and how it more or
less forced our hand. Gabriel listened to it all in silence, then commented in a wondering tone, "That is the *hickest* thing I've ever heard in my
life: marrying a man a month after you met him because your *Mama*
wouldn't let you date him. How old are you, anyway?"

I told him, assuring him it was all legal, that Mama had signed and
everything, making him shake his head again in that patent disgust,
though a sarcastic "Good for Mama" was all he said. Then, in another of
his abrupt twists: "So where's the old man?"

I was surprised Cissie hadn't spread the good news of Daddy's
demise, and as the evening lowered to full dark, told him how he died,
not going into much detail, a little wary, afraid of another cry of rejoicing. But Gabriel was only silent when I finished, lying there in the dark,
staring at the new stars, finally getting up when Maggie called us in to
eat.

"You didn't sing at his funeral, did you?" he asked as he held out a
hand and helped me to my feet. When I shook my head, quickly, he
assured me, "And neither will *I.*"

He did, of course. Over the years, I've seen him win a few skirmishes with his mother, but not so often, and after she pulled out the
big guns and had Case take him out to the river with (I think) a bottle to
talk him around, he went down to Welcome with Sister Pumphrey and
spent the morning holed up in the fellowship hall, practicing. His only
revenge was showing up for the service in his good graduation suit, all
pressed and proper, his hair pulled back in a *ponytail,* which doesn't
sound so sensational now, but was pretty damn wild in west Florida in
1968.

The only time I'd ever seen a man in a ponytail was the Indians in
John Wayne Westerns, and from the twitters and elbowing that accom-
panied his arrival at Welcome, I'm sure I wasn't alone, poor Gabriel inadvertently sending a message he's had a hard time living down over the
years, saying in effect: "I *am* queer."

And I don't mean queer in the universal sense, either. I mean, even
in those days an occasional brave soul — a florist or a choir director —
would throw caution to the wind to take a modest step out of the clos-

et, and that's just what everyone thought he was doing. With Candace stuck in Germany, it left Michael as the favored object of condolence, and though he shook hands and made the correct replies and looked so cool and controlled, I knew he was dying inside, lying in bed the night before like a corpse himself, staring at the ceiling without a tear or a snore. He even put me off when I shyly tried to initiate sex to divert him, his rejection rocking my wifely confidence to the core.

For while sex was still mostly a blank process for me, it was really the only thing I had the satisfaction of knowing he *needed* from me, that he loved. His quiet refusal made me even more disoriented the morning of the funeral, with the mob of Alabama relations coming in and a carload of Michael's high school buddies dropping by, even his old homecoming queen girlfriend, whom I could have spit on. They all gravitated to the back porch, dragging dining room chairs or sitting on the steps with glasses of iced tea, and telling stories on Mr. Simon, like people at funerals do in the South. And though all the stories were touching, many hilarious, I found them oddly unsettling, as they somehow resurrected my old feeling of aloneness, as none of them were familiar, even the ones that happened when I lived on the Hill.

Had it been anyone other than Mr. Simon we were recalling, I probably wouldn't have minded, but sitting there in a bubble of my own separate world, I was increasingly weighted by my own memories of him. Not the recent ones, from the past year, but wisping childhood ones that haunted the dark corners of my mind, images so essential to my being that they were more than funny stories, they were foundations of my life. As one or another jumped up to take the stage, I could feel them back there moving around in the darkness, pulsating and alive, but too vague, too distant to hardly remember, much less weave into these compelling, hilarious stories. Try as I might, I couldn't build them into anything more moving than blinks of vague memory that came to me like pinpoints of light, of his face at the fence, his calm country voice, speaking into the twilight ("*And what are you gone be when you grow up, Myra Louise?*").

The sheer frustration of my voicelessness made me feel even more claustrophobic, miserable at the service itself that seemed to go on forever, the sermon alone taking the better part of an hour. I was not only aggrieved, but increasingly overwhelmed with a rising nausea and an urge to pee that was killing me, wedged as I was between Michael and Cissie, who held my hand in an ice-cold grip. I was sitting there thinking that I could only take five more minutes before my bladder burst, when Brother Sloan finally gave it up, ending the service by introducing Gabriel, who'd been sitting up there on the deacon's bench, weeping like a widow.

Brother Sloan made a point of putting his arm around Gabe's shoulder, reminding everyone that he was an old Welcome boy, off to *medical* school, obviously trying to spin him in the Cissie-Catts manner, but clearly not making much headway. That ponytail was just a step over the line, and it was clear no one was buying, the room perfectly quiet as he made his way to the piano and joined Sister Pumphrey on the bench, ignoring us all to watch her play the lead-in of a song that was hauntingly familiar, his voice sliding smoothly after a few bars in a low, even murmur:

Oh, they tell me of a home far beyond the skies
Oh, they tell me of a home far away
Oh, they tell me of a home where no sorrows rise,
Oh, they tell me of an unclouded day

I was trying so hard to place it that I almost squinted as I watched Gabriel sit there slumped on the piano bench, his eyes on the piano keys, his arms folded on his chest, his voice low and controlled, so perfectly pitched that it was eerie. All around me, I could feel the congregation softening despite itself, women dabbing eyes, men reaching for handkerchiefs, something in the sad, patient little melody transforming our grief into something very close to triumphant, Mr. Simon's death no longer senseless, but a good, decent end to a hard life, his soul departed to a kinder place, an unclouded day. Even the suffocating numbness in my own chest was relieved by the sad, sweet chorus that went on and on, Gabriel drawing it out, playing with it, singing it over and over again, Pentecostal style, but carrying it off, Sister Pumphrey right with him.

It wasn't a small feat for a church as stiff-necked as Welcome, and for the first time in my life, watching him sit there entranced, lost in the sound of his own voice, I felt a stirring of understanding for the essence of Gabriel Catts. Not as a hippie or a malcontent or even a profane little brother, but an even rarer oddity in the working-class shoals of Magnolia Hill: a poet, a prophet, an *artist*. I mean, those wouldn't have been my choice of words at the time, but that's what I meant, clearly seeing that there was more to this boy than met the eye; some unfathomable mystery as colorful and compelling as the cluttered little bedroom he'd left behind. The revelation struck me deeply, causing a twinge of response to briefly arise, so potent and overtly sexual that I ducked my head against it, not raising it till the last amen, and even then not meeting anyone's eye.

Fortunately, the end of the service was upon us, the funeral director taking charge, leading us out, and since I was in a delicate condition, no one raised an eye when I forwent the graveside service to walk back up the hill to the empty house that smelled of ham and stale coffee, our bed still unmade since morning. I lay there quietly all afternoon, getting up when the family returned and joining them briefly, even unbending enough to tell a Mr. Simon story of my own, about his last words in the kitchen about Gabe's laziness. Case and the other men loved it, laughing uproariously, though Gabriel didn't take it too well, jumping up and tearing out, Michael close on his heels.

I was humiliated by his retreat and returned to my solitary vigil on the banks of the little creek, where Michael found me later, just after dark, not coming up on me quietly, as Gabriel had, but calling to me from the back porch. I didn't answer, not wanting to return to the rabble of family and friends — including the old girlfriend who'd also made an appearance at the funeral, very sleek and trim in a cranberry-colored suit — and after a moment, he joined me there by the ditch, still in his dress pants, his shirt sleeves rolled to his elbows.

"Come git something to eat, baby," he said, holding out a hand. "There's a pile of food in there."

I declined, and after a moment, he sat on the grass beside me. "You all right?" he asked, which was the standard Michael-Catts question whenever anyone wasn't falling in line to do his bidding: *you all right?* I wouldn't answer at first, and he pressed, "Mad at Gabe?"

I shook my head, but he didn't believe me, and went on to defend him like he always did, till I stopped him, told him *he* was the one who'd hurt my feelings, making him look at me in surprise. "When?"

"Last night. You wouldn't — you *know.*"

I couldn't see him so well in the darkness, but his laughter was clear enough, ringing on the night air. "Myra, Myra, My-ra," he said, "what are we gonna do with you, sister?"

I was annoyed at his amusement, and pulled away. "I'm serious, Michael. It hurt my feelings."

But he only laughed harder. "Why, cain't a man get a break every once in a while?"

I wasn't so pleased at the big joke he was making of my little stab at honesty and tried to stand. "Well, I'll just go in the house," I said, but he pulled me back down.

"You will not. You'll stay right here. I won't tease you namore." We sat there quietly awhile, Michael unbuttoning my jumper on the tight spot over my belly, whispering, "Shhh," when I tried to stop him.

He only opened it a few inches, then leaned over and gently nuzzled my pregnant belly. "Sweet baby," he said, and I felt curiously aroused at the touch of his soft mouth on my belly, much as I had been at Gabriel's song. I didn't quite know what to make of it, and just rubbed my face against the short hairs on the back of his neck a moment, then told him I loved him.

"Do you?" He smiled, sitting up and looking at me. "Why?"

I didn't speak at first, for I'd told him I loved him a few times before, mostly obligatory replies to his own frequent declarations, but this was different. This was a spontaneous response to the little quiver of unknown emotion that was so strange it was unnameable, making me answer honestly, without thought, "'Cause you remind me of your daddy."

He laughed aloud at that, not the least bit threatened, much less jealous, and when our first son was born five months later on the last day of August, he told everyone we were naming him for his father, because that's who I really loved. "Just married me for my paycheck," he said, which was a little short of the truth, though I didn't argue.

I couldn't; I was too whipped, for my labor had been torturously long in those barbaric days of twilight sleep, like a bad trip on LSD, complicated by scar tissue from my last visit to Jackson Memorial that slowed my cervical dilation to a horrific twenty-three hours. I was out of my head by the end of it, calling for Michael over and over again in a nightmare so reminiscent of my childhood stay, Dr. Winston calling for the gurney to take me to surgery for a C-section, when Sim's dark little head unexpectedly crowned.

"Five or six more pushes and we'll have it," I heard him tell the nurse, and from the pit of my drugged stupor, I distinctly remember thinking: *to hell with that.*

Pulling myself up to my elbows, I bore down in one mighty heave, and there he was, my firstborn son, bruised and bloodied and squalling like a cat till the nurses wrapped him up in a towel and handed him into my shaking arms. I was so ignorant I hardly knew how to hold him, though he was immediately quiet, watching me out of beady, ink-colored eyes with what for all the world looked like placid recognition.

Simon Michael Catts, we named him, and I could really go on forever about his birth, about the births of all of my children; they really were the happiest days of my life. Not just because of the sheer miracle of birth, but for less maternal reasons, some of which had to do with simple chemistry. For I had been a depressive since childhood, but it was in the hormonal blitzkrieg of childbirth that I first dipped a toe into the murky waters of true mood disorder, waking up the morning after Sim's birth in that most blessed of all depressive states: mild hypomania.

To the normal soul, this means having a very fast, very productive day, but to the true depressive (of which I am, alas, one) it comes as a rare period of happy normalcy, unfortunate in that it doesn't last too long before you shift back into mild melancholy (if you're lucky) or percolate up into the even rarer true mania. Fortunately, at that point, this complex psychological phenomenon was nothing more than an encroaching cloud like the one the prophet Elijah prayed up, no bigger than a man's hand, and I remember waking up that morning in a light of joyousness that was simply unbelievable. I'd never been so perfectly happy in my life, sitting up and ringing and ringing for the nurse to bring me Sim, though they weren't so obliging in those days about mothers' preferences and wouldn't bring him till his scheduled feeding at nine.

Even then, the nurse looked down her nose at me for breast-feeding him, as bottled feedings had become universally accepted, and whipping out a titty to feed an infant seemed crude and country and ill-advised. She offered no other advice than I try not to drop him, though I had about as much an idea of how to nurse an infant as to circumcise him. I knew it had to do with my nipple and his mouth, but my breasts were terribly engorged, and I couldn't get him to grab hold.

After a few minutes of futile wrestling, I was in tears, Sim squalling and beating me with his tiny fists, when from out of the blue, my brother-in-law strolled through the door like he owned the place. I yanked the sheet to my chin and waved him away hysterically, crying, "Go! *Go!*" Which naturally deterred Gabriel not in the least.

He just stopped in the middle of the room and shouted, "What? Myra? What is it?"

I finally got it over that the nursing wasn't going according to plan, still waving him frantically away, as the presence of a man in the room wasn't doing much for me or Sim, either one, his little face under the sheet nearly purple with rage. But Gabriel has never been one to gracefully withdraw and only went around the little curtain that separated the two beds (the other girl had already left) and stood there shouting oddly accurate bits of instruction: "Lay on your side, Myra! Your side!" he called. "Kind of pinch your nipple so he can get a grip — you feel it? Has he got it?"

It was obvious he had, the mighty wail stilled in an instant, replaced by the most incredible sensation on earth: suckling an infant, though I was a little distracted by the tenderness in my poor chapped nipple, gritting my teeth, saying, "*Yow.* It hurts."

"It'll toughen up," Gabriel assured me through the curtain with his usual authority.

"So how'd you get to be such an expert?" I asked.

I didn't mean for it to sound as provocative as it came out, and there was a pause, as if Gabriel was considering a reply commensurate to the question, but finally, he played it straight. "Shoot, Sister McQuaig had a baby at her tit every day of her life," he said mildly. "Nursed Benny till he was *five.*"

"Did she?" I asked, and the whole time I nursed, we talked through the curtain, Gabriel telling me to switch sides halfway through. When I was facing the other way, he slid the curtain open, and I talked to him over my shoulder, him asking me about the labor, grimacing at the details, tossing over a little receiving blanket that fell lightly on my face.

"It's beautiful," I told him, touched he'd made the effort, though he was his usual contrary self.

"Well, it was cheap," he said. Later, when I told him Sim was asleep, still holding on, but sound asleep, he was pensive. "Lucky dog."

"*Gabriel,*" I said, and he was quickly repentant, talking me into letting him hold him, though it was an awkward transfer, me having to cover myself with the receiving blanket while he picked him up, a little clumsy with his bad hand.

When he finally had him settled in the crook of his elbow, he regarded his sleeping face carefully, even took him to the window to hold him to the morning light a moment before he looked up in honest wonder, murmured, "*God,* he looks like Daddy."

It was all I needed to get started in the bawling; all either of us needed, me using the top sheet as a handkerchief, Gabriel the receiving blanket. He cried so hard he had to give Sim back and lay out flat on the vacant bed to try and get a grip on it, so when Michael came in for the official visiting hours at ten, he found his wife sobbing in one bed, his brother in the other.

"How'd you get in?" he asked, shaking his head at the sight of his ravaged face, half-covered by the blanket.

"Fire exit" was all he could manage, making Michael laugh. For Gabe was six years his junior, in some ways more like a son than a brother, someone to be coddled and teased and protected as a child, when his smart mouth brought on the wrath of the older boys who would have taught him better manners if Michael hadn't intervened. Gabriel repaid his affection with his own particular brand of loyalty, always trying to get him out of Sanger and into a better life, notions of self-improvement that Michael paid no mind to, always of the opinion (shared by virtually all of the Catts) that Gabriel was a little too smart for his own good, kind of an idiot savant, who required delicate handling due to his high-strung ways.

One thing I'll say for both of them is that they were damned loyal, a statement no one questions in the older, or believes in the younger, though in the twenty years I've known them both, I've never spoken a word of criticism of one that the other so much as acknowledged, unless it was some trivial failing, some matter of good humor we laughed about.

It's a bond of brotherhood Ira and I lost somewhere along the way that I must say I envied, even then, as we wiled away the day of Sim's birth, Gabriel charming the floor nurse into not only letting them stay, but even into letting us keep Sim past his regular feeding. Michael had taken the day off and sat there on the bed beside me, holding Sim and listening to a litany of Gabriel's Tallahassee woes: the rent that was past due, the advanced physiology he was failing. And worst of all, the contemporary American history class he'd slipped in his schedule for the ease of the subject that was regrettably taught by a dinosaur of a professor who was drawing him near to armed conflict with his protestations that Vietnam was a winnable conflict.

I listened to it all with half an ear, tired and spent from my labor, but still hanging onto that serotonin high, watching Michael hold our baby in the crook of his arm with a practiced ease; thinking that for a seventeen-year-old half-wit, I hadn't been so stupid about my choice in husbands. I was wondering when Cissie and Maggie and the extended Tierney entourage were expected, when for the second time that day, an unexpected visitor strolled in out of the blue: Mama.

= 17 =

I cried when I saw her, not realizing till I laid eyes on her how much I missed her. Michael was immediately on his feet, a little distant, but trying for compatibility, Gabe openly (and to my eyes, oddly) hostile. He got up and left without so much as a word of greeting, a foretaste of his mother when she came in shortly after, dressed to the nines in one of her hospital-visiting get-ups, her face lit like a Christmas tree till she laid eyes on Mama, and you talk about contact static. Both of them laid back their ears like old tomcats, though Cissie was, as usual, Queen of the situation, crossing the room and extending a fragile, blue-veined hand, drawling, "Why, Eloise, what a *surprise.*" An innocent enough greeting to the uninitiated, though to my ear it fairly dripped with what she left unspoken ("— *that you've quit showing your ass long enough to visit your only daughter.*")

Michael yielded his seat to his mother, leaving me to referee their little parlor game of manners, Mama giving me her gift, a beautiful little wool bunting that Cissie couldn't very well fault, though she did comment to the wall that *her* boys had always detested wool, it was too itchy. Mama politely ignored her little dig, using more subtle means to squash this Baptist snob once and for all, waiting patiently for her full entourage of friends and relations to descend, then *insisting* we discuss my trust.

Oh yes, we knew what trusts were, even in Louisiana, even the Sims, and at the time of my father's death, a cousin in New Orleans (who doubled as his defense- and divorce- and paternity-lawyer) had set up a small one for Ira and me, the kind you came into on your twenty-first birthday. It didn't involve an incredible amount of money, though the way Mama kept going on about it, you'd have thought it was a million in gold. Poor Cissie was impressed despite herself, positively dumbfounded when Mama reminisced about the dissolution of her own inheritance when Grannie sold the farm the year we moved to Florida.

"A much larger amount," she recalled, "but then, *bottom* land on the *Delta* has always been so high."

Cissie's face was a study in disbelief at my mother's intimate use of these old Southern catchwords, unable to reconcile the white trash across the fence with the eight hundred or so arable acres we'd left behind in Sliddell (forgetting, for the moment, the phenomenon of Leldon Sims, who'd gone through a lion's share of the money before we had so much as unpacked a trunk). Mama went on to inquire pointedly about Mr. Simon's estate, and as it was nonexistent, Cissie found herself right and soundly beaten. It was a state she accepted with a modicum of good grace, though she's taken out her angst over the years by assuring her devoted (and clueless) grandchildren that while, generally speaking, Florida farmers are an upstanding lot, this might not necessarily be the case in *other* places.

The strain of their velvet-gloved cat fight had me limp as a dishrag by the time Mama left for Birmingham that night, Sim picking up my stress and whimpering like a puppy when I tried to nurse him for his late feeding. Michael had stayed to watch, leaning his chin on the bed rails and even talking me into letting him sample my breast milk before he left. I was afraid the nurse might walk in and catch us in this deviant act and made sure he pulled the curtains tight before he leaned over the rail to gently suckle my breast a moment.

"It's sweet." He smiled, then kissed me good-bye and took Sim to the nursery, leaving me weirdly aroused by the feel of his soft mouth on my sore nipple, wishing he'd have stayed the night, though with fourteen stitches in my labia, I couldn't have told you why. For I really can't overstate how uninformed I was of the whole business of sexuality, even a year and a child into marriage, eagerly devouring a little sex manual I'd recently come upon in Gabriel's cave of wonders.

It had been there all along, intermixed with the other books, but the title was so euphemistic (*Youth and Development*) that I had passed it over, till I happened to flip open to an illustration of the female reproduction organs. After a sentence or two, I locked myself in and read it in an hour; reread it by supper, and I must say it made for compelling reading, more soul-stirring than Tolkien, more absurd than Albee. There was nothing salacious about it, for it was written in septic purity by a Baptist doctor, half the little volume decrying the dangers of premarital sex, half going through the clinical details. The part about orgasm especially intrigued me, as the little goateed doctor (his picture was on the back cover) really waxed lyrical about the joys of the blessed event, describing the accompanying cries and twitches in a way that made it sound just short of an out-of-body experience. *Achieving* orgasm was the way he put it, making me, Myra Sims, the chronic underachiever, feel pretty small.

I wasn't even sure I was *achieving* arousal, though my attempts at keeping Michael at bay long enough to follow the good doctor's strict instructions had fallen on their face, only moving me forward enough to *achieve* a frustration that unexpectedly peaked that night after he left the hospital, making me feel like a failure in an awful way, truly damaged goods. I cried over my hopeless state and actually sobbed over what a disappointment I must be to my poor husband, all of which were predictable characteristics of what the initiated might recognize as even more facets of the hypomanic state: easy sexual arousal, and equally easy dead-drops into black despair.

This particular downdraft was so devastating that I was nearly suicidal at the hopelessness of it all, and with no one else to confide in, I finally fell back on my old standard, simple prayer, crying out to God that I'd be like all the other women on Earth, and by some miracle I'd *achieve* this mighty act He'd created to vex the common woman. I prayed for hours, literally, till the nurse came by to check on me at twelve and diagnosed my tears as post-partum hysterics, putting me to sleep with a pill. By the time I went home, two days later, I'd forgotten all about it, my hormones leveling out in the intervening weeks, my days resuming their even pitch, hardly altered by the birth of a child.

Michael was still working dawn to dusk, as Sanger had added a third shift, and in his hurry to pay off both the obstetrician and the undertaker, he had taken to working shifts back-to-back, coming home pale as a ghost and eating a handful of aspirin (still Magnolia Hill's sovereign remedy for life) with a chug of whiskey to get to sleep. His unending long hours were my first glimpse into what would become the blight of my marriage: a husband driven by blind ambition — though it was not so painfully obvious in those first years, any more than depression was in me. Both of them crept up on us quietly, hardly visible as long as we were living on the Hill in a life that held little of the responsibilities of adulthood, Cissie still cooking our meals, doing our laundry, my mentor and protector till we parted ways after lunch, when she'd retire to her *stories*, me to the little bed in the back bedroom.

There, I'd nurse Sim to sleep, then read the afternoon away, eventually putting aside *Rebecca* to consume every book in the room, from *The Hobbit* (that I loved), to *Life on the Mississippi* (okay, I guess), to *Goodbye, Columbus* (sad, I thought it.) A few of the authors (Tolkien, mostly) intrigued me enough to pack Sim up and take off to the library on foot, though they had not so much as heard of *The Lord of the Rings.* It was Gabriel who came to my rescue, bringing home a roommate's copy and even explaining the subtleties of plot that I found too esoteric for my taste. I would have put it aside if he hadn't made such a deal of *insisting* I read it to the end, just like the old days, at the fence with Scarlett and Rhett.

We saw a lot of him in those days, as his utter contempt for his contemporary history professor had resulted in a not-so-surprising C in his cream-puff of a class, that had effectively derailed his medical school dreams and thus deprived his mother of her chief bragging point. I'm sure it was galling to poor Gabe, making him exact his revenge on the FSU history department in a sorely intimate way: changing his major to history and spending the next year haunting their august halls in sandals that only got scruffier and hair so long that it was soon past merely queer and into the realm of simple lunacy.

From what I could gather, they were a pretty conservative lot over there, all crewcuts and black socks, and armed with a spice of malice, Gabriel just about drove them insane, applying his natural ability to agitate to the Civil War and coming up with notions so outrageous that only a Yankee would believe them (or so said his mother). But I couldn't complain, as his weekend visits broke up the monotony of the week, and while I enjoyed Gabriel for the exotic he was, Sim simply adored him.

As soon as he could walk, he'd drag me out to the porch every afternoon and peer between the rails like a sentinel, watching the corner for the arrival of the city bus that might signal Gabe's return. We never knew whether he was coming or not, as he was too much of a bohemian to bother with phones or watches, leaving poor Sim in a state of jittery anxiety when the bus swished up and the passengers disembarked. If Gabe didn't show, he'd creep back inside like a wounded thing, but if he caught so much as a glimpse of that golden head, he'd break into a cry of delight that was hilarious to behold and take off down the steps to meet him.

Gabriel would always return his shouts with shouts of his own, then lift him over the gate and carry him in on his shoulders, while I waited on the porch, shaking my head in wonder. For if there's one thing I can say about the Catts men, one thing that has never ceased to amaze me about them, it's their sincere and boundless love of children. I guess it comes down to nothing more complex than they had a good father who raised them to be good fathers — so unlike the men in my family and the string of progeny they leave behind wherever they go, like abandoned seeds behind a furrower's plough, withering in the sun, unkept.

One afternoon on the porch, I remember telling Gabriel just that, though with mixed results. It must have been sometime in the autumn of 1970, as he was home for the weekend, sitting on the porch in his scruffy old hippie clothes, singing some silly song to make Sim dance, a family tradition around the Catts house. Old Brother Tierney used to make the boys dance with his little Irish jigs, or (they say) cry with his teary ballads. And though I never saw the latter, and Michael didn't have the voice to do either, Gabriel would occasionally indulge me, singing verse after verse of his funny little songs, making Sim dance like a dervish, his fat little legs popping the porch boards, his face lit like an angel, the sweetest sight I'll ever behold.

I was sitting on the porch rails that day, clapping and laughing, mesmerized by the image of my happy little boy dancing an Irish jig with the backdrop of our old house behind him. From the Catts' porch you have an unobstructed view of the front of what was never what you might call prime real estate, but lately had fallen on hard times, sure enough, an eyesore in a neighborhood that was clinging to respectability by the skin of its teeth.

But the sight of Sim dancing there made it a happy image, a restoration that lifted my heart, and when he finally fell into his uncle's arms, laughing and red-cheeked, I bestowed on Gabe the greatest compliment I'll ever give any man, smiling at him, saying, "Gabriel, you'll make a good daddy someday. You need to find you a wife."

But instead of a polite smile of assent, that contentious son of a bitch just lifted his face over Sim's head and met my eyes, said: "I did find me a wife. Found her when I was thirteen. Problem is, she married my brother."

It was so unexpected that at first I really didn't understand him, thinking it was another of his shocking rejoinders, though his eyes weren't amused at all, but level and honest, demanding a response the same way Michael's had that first day on the tracks. The difference being that this wasn't a single man and an unattached woman, but a brother-and sister-in-law, the confusion of it all destroying the happy image of the dancing child, making the old house next door loom closer, a living entity yet.

For a moment I just sat there, again little Myra, the voiceless child next door, then I stood very suddenly and snatched Sim from his arms, stammering something about his needing a bath. Gabriel came to his feet as quickly, his blink of defiance gone, his voice fast and apologetic, "Myra, listen — I didn't —"

He tried to grab at my arm, to apologize, but I jerked myself free and ignored his pleading entreaty to run through the house to the bathroom, where I resolutely bathed a crying Sim, who kept trying to crawl out of the tub, jabbering, "Unca Cabe! Unca Cabe!" like a soul in torment.

By the end of it, I was crying, too, huddled on the floor by the tub with a wet, dejected baby in my arms, till I heard Cissie and Maggie come in the back door. I went out then, and affecting a drawn voice, said I had a headache, could they watch Sim? Maggie (who was one of those most blessed of aunts, doting and forever willing to babysit) took the tear-streaked Sim while I beat a fast retreat to the bedroom, locking the doors and lying on the bed, praying to God Michael wouldn't send Sam by to tell me he was working another shift as he sometimes did.

For I desperately needed to talk to him, desperately needed to tell him about Gabriel, and that *look,* but the longer I lay there, the more hesitant I became. I mean, what had he really done, other than make one of his tasteless jokes, trying to draw me out in a tease that for some reason hit me the wrong way? Why had I made such a big deal out of it? Why was I so touchy these days, so quick to cry, so short-tempered and nervous?

That was the final circle of my thoughts, for in true depressive style, my arguments always started with someone else's shortcomings and always ended with mine — yet another flaw in a crippled psyche, a slow death by self-accusation. By the time Michael came in at nine, dog-tired after his Bayer and his chug, I was worked up to a state of outright despair, restless and hopeless, sitting up in bed and raving about life in general. I didn't mention Gabriel at all, so that Michael had no more an idea of the root of my confusion than the man in the moon, though when I sobbed over my most pressing failure, the inability to *achieve* orgasm, he finally stopped me.

"To *what?*"

"Have an *orgasm!*" I cried, too overwrought to be ashamed, describing in sobbing bits and pieces the book and the Doctor, though Michael just shook his head, said he'd *warned* me not to dig too deep back there.

"No! No," I told him, "he's a *doctor,* Michael. A *Baptist* doctor. Everybody else does. I'm just *messed up!* I don't know why you ever married me, I'm *messed up!*"

He tried to comfort me, going so far as to retrieve the little book and read the technical part with a face of growing wonderment, finally murmuring, "*Damn,*" in a way that didn't sound too hopeful, though he assured me we'd work it out.

"Right now, if you want to," he kindly offered. But I was too tired to bother after my little round of self-hatred. I just lay at his side and sniffled him to sleep, getting up late in the night and going to the kitchen for an aspirin, when I came unexpectedly upon Gabriel, sitting in the dark at the table.

I didn't see him till I'd turned on the overhead light, but when I tried to beat a fast retreat, he stood and blocked my way, said: "Myra. Listen, I'm sorry."

But I kept backing away, all the way to the stove, feeling the knobs at my back, the smell of old grease, my heart beating like a drum in my chest while I held out a hand and begged him to shut up, to *please* leave me alone, whispering: "*Don't touch me. Don't touch me.*"

There was a desperate note in my pleading that made him stop in the middle of the room and close his eyes a moment, then tell me he was leaving, moving to North Carolina for his Master's. That they'd offered him a deal, and he was going to take it. And though I loved Gabriel — loved him much the same way my baby did, because he was sweet and funny in his way, poignantly touching standing there with his hair back-lit against the light, a wafting memory of the funny-talking boy next door — I couldn't say I wasn't relieved, holding the neck of my housecoat together with nervous hands and wishing him luck.

"Sim'll miss you," I finally said, and he smiled that sad, bothered smile, then held out his hand for a shake.

"Friends?" he asked, and I was suddenly a little teary, knowing Sim wasn't the only one who would miss him; we'd all miss him, so much.

I gamely took the hand he offered, though it didn't respond to my grip, and I realized it was his bad one. I looked up, thinking it was another of his tasteless jokes, but found his face absent of humor, his dancing eyes stilled and intent, as if he were trying to send me a message, the kind Ira used to send me as a child, wordlessly reminding me that we went back a long ways, he and I. That we both had our share of wounds, and should be more forgiving of one another.

In reply, I just lifted his slightly curled, slightly useless hand to my lips a moment in wordless assent, then dropped it and left him there under the light to rejoin my husband in bed, the face I pressed against his sleeping back wet with tears of what? Regret? Relief? The latter, I think, though to tell you the truth, I didn't know then; still don't, to this day.

In any case, Gabriel was gone the next morning, lock, stock, and barrel. He didn't return at the end of the semester, but moved straight to Chapel Hill, and a year after that, even further North, to do his doctorate at Harvard, to his mother's eternal name-dropping satisfaction. I can't say that I missed him, for in the meanwhile, Michael had set his mind to fulfilling the Doctor's mission with his usual single-mindedness, and with the help of my own as yet undetected, but steadily budding mania, was finally able to turn me into a sexual *achiever,* of sorts.

And though I never could make my way up the ladder according to the Doctor's strict guide, and seldom (if ever) hit the dreamy peaks he promised were my God-given right, I did break through my old passivity enough to partake briefly of the waters of this mysterious river of life that ran like a dirty aquifer beneath my childhood home — though in marriage, I found it a clearer stream. Not a matter of sin or shame or prudish silence, but simple good-natured appetite, as open and unashamed as my husband's proudly imperfect smile.

*Y*ou might say that the most practical result of my fascination with the good Doctor (who spent so much time warning of the evils of premarital relations, but didn't unbend enough to take up the subject of birth control) was that within two years of Sim's birth, I found myself pregnant again. It didn't come as such a surprise this time, as Michael and I were doing it all the time — once a day and twice on Sundays, as they used to say. I would even go so far as to predict that Sunday was the actual day of conception, as it was Michael's only day off, when I got to see him for more than an hour at a time, dressed and combed and scented for church, which, in the light of my increasing mania, gave the Lord's Day a markedly epicurean twist.

With Sunday School not starting till almost ten, we'd sleep late, then stroll down to Welcome for the two hours' worth of unremarkable musing on the ways of the Lord that is Baptist worship, then come home to one of Cissie's magnificent Sunday dinners. Like the daughter of the preacher she was, she went all out on the Lord's Day: fried chicken or pork or best of all, country ham, with her usual river of side dishes and a dessert that for two years running was unrefrigerated banana pudding, because it was Sim's favorite, and he liked it warm.

Once this feast was duly consumed and the kitchen put back to rights, she and Sim would hit the hay for their Sunday naps, and Michael and I would have the house to ourselves, the windows open to the breeze, the layers of Sunday wear coming off one piece at a time, coats and shirts and slips and girdles, till we were naked as Adam and Eve in the garden, and a whole lot happier. No serpents around to tempt us anymore, just Michael and me in the little bedroom off the back porch, that with the thicker insulation of the outside wall, provided the necessary sound-proofing for me to rise to the good Doctor's *oh, baby, baby* heights of passion.

I'm reasonably sure that it was during one of those languid afternoons that Missy was conceived, as the drugstore was closed on Sundays, making us ride pretty close to the pavement on matters of birth control, Michael always pausing at the pivotal moment to ask in a shaky, breathless voice when my last period was. No matter what I said, yesterday or today or a week ago Tuesday, he'd invariably pronounce it safe, and off we'd go, getting away with it for a few months, till the smell of Cissie's bacon sent me flying to the bathroom one morning, and that, as they say, was that.

It was an easier pregnancy, though, me feeling well enough to travel to Birmingham when Ira was discharged from the Marines in August. The weekend turned out to be something of a disappointment, as all of his football buddies plus a bevy of attendant girlfriends all converged on the house, making any conversation difficult; personal ones, impossible. The most I did all weekend was sit around patting a shy, clinging Sim, watching my newly thin, newly tan brother laugh and laugh, never meeting my eye and hardly acknowledging my baby, much less doting on him the way the Catts all did.

It was enough of a rebuff to send me back to Magnolia Hill in a small, sad downdraft, feeling middle-aged at twenty, though I happened to return on a Sunday afternoon, just in time for Michael and my Sabbath solstice. After that, I didn't have any more regrets, only glad to be home, a little hesitant when Michael finally paid off his father's mortgage and began his campaign to leave the Hill and find a house of our own.

He was doing well at Sanger by then, closing in on Danny Langford's job as Thomas Sanger's nigger, which is not a casual racial slur on my part, but the unofficial job title of foreman, and not so far off the mark. For the foreman was not only in charge of production, but also keeping Tom's mortgage paid, his cattle fed, his ex-wives' alimony dispensed, even his liquor cabinet stocked. In all these things, Michael excelled, dedicating three long years of his life to stepping and fetching for this weak, difficult man, till he absorbed enough of the inner workings of the furniture business to make his little backroom alliance with Sam McRae and the vice-president of the Farmer's and Merchant Bank, and so relieve Thomas of his least-productive undertaking.

But that was years in the making, and, in the meanwhile, we needed a house and spent a good part of the autumn scouring the county for a suitable choice, not an easy proposition, as we had precious little money for a down payment, and in matters of taste, Michael and I were more than worlds apart — we were *universes* apart. He had it firmly in his mind that we'd go about it in the time-honored way, buying a little tract house in some up-and-coming subdivision that we'd eventually trade for yet another tract house, the kind Carl and Mama had in Birmingham that still filled me with a chill at their square-roomed, shallow-roofed conformity. At the end of half a year's fruitless search, I was still shooting down possibilities, frustrating husband and realtor alike, restlessly searching for something else, something *different,* and coming upon it thirteen miles and a world away from Magnolia Hill on the last remaining parcel of what had once been Clarence Thurmon's virtual river kingdom.

The realtor had called with the lead late on New Year's afternoon, Michael not too happy to abandon his afternoon of college football to look at another cheap house, till she assured him it was a *find,* thirty-nine acres, zoned agricultural, though it had once had a house on it and she was sure another could be grandfathered in. It was enough of a lure to get him to put on his shoes, though the thirteen-mile drive almost thwarted the deal before we got there, as Michael was local enough to realize we were heading to a very dark part of the county (by which I mean, a very *black* part), east of town, into what had once been the plantation belt.

The realtor, a tough little woman in a polyester suit, deftly sidestepped the issue by talking a mile a minute, about how the land was going for five hundred an acre, full of oak and magnolia, with a twenty-acre stand of mature pine Michael could cut within the month — she'd give him the name of a man who'd buy it. Her dogged enthusiasm was enough to keep us going, the day mild and winter-pale, me a little fat and breathless from Missy's jabs to my ribs, agreeing that this probably was a little too far out, when she turned off the highway into a thick stand of pine, not scraggly little slash pine, but huge yellow pine, their broad trunks going straight up thirty feet or more before they burst into twisted, bristly branch.

Michael, who'd been working in the Sanger woodshop since he was fifteen, immediately recognized their worth and fell silent, though I was as ignorant of the trees as I was the art of the deal and left them at the front of the property to wander off on my own. With nothing better to do, I followed a faint, pine-needled path that curved back a good ways, the pine giving way to a stand of magnolia that was impressive enough, but not blooming that time of year, then to a few truly tremendous camellia bushes that were.

I stopped to pick a handful for Cissie, who was a camellia fanatic (japonicas, she called them) and could tell me their names, my interest piqued enough to study the overgrown brush a little more closely, suddenly realizing that I was standing in what must have once been someone's front yard. You could see the signs of neglected cultivation everywhere in the dim, winter-burnt tangle: sweet-scented Louis Phillipe roses climbing wild in the trees, eight-foot clumps of untended azaleas, and most magnificent of all, a huge old cupped-leaf live oak with a good sixty-foot spread. It was the same shape and smell as the one that reigned over the Catts' backyard till it split in a summer storm and had to be taken out and cut for firewood. I approached it with affection, ducking under the drooping limbs to watch the play of squirrels above my head, who barked their trilling little warnings till I backed off and turned, and there to my left, almost obscured by the unrelenting green, I finally saw the house.

For a moment, I only stood there motionless, my palms flattened against my bulging belly, unsure if I was seeing what I thought I was seeing: an old house, two-storied and forlorn, its windows gaping and broken, for all the world an abandoned Manderley, the ivy on the walls curling in the sun. I literally didn't believe my eyes, for just lately I'd been having little quirks in my brain where in the rush of the day, I'd forget some common information, Michael's name or Cissie's, till my head cleared with a shake, and I was back to normal. It had happened enough that I'd even given these blurs of confusion a name: *pings,* I called them, because they seemed to vibrate uneasily through my mind, like the bounce of sonar off the floor of the ocean.

So I just stood there, perhaps as long as a minute, staring at the obscured outline of the old house that didn't evaporate, the sun-flecked walls stable and real, clearly not a mirage, as I pushed through the knee-high weeds to the front steps, climbing them gingerly, afraid they'd fall in. But they were quite stable, hardly creaking at all, and I had taken a few steps across the old porch when a voice called out behind me, almost making me jump out of my skin: "I wouldn't go in there, Mrs. Catts. The floor's all rotted, I'm sure."

It was the realtor, who'd come up the path a little ahead of Michael. She was clearly not so happy I'd come upon what she obvious-ly considered the property's secret drawback, that awful old house that would have to be demolished, and at some expense, though she assured Michael he could sell the woodwork — she'd give him the name of a man who'd buy it. I was instantly horrified by the prospect and strode back to the yard, arguing for the old house as if it were a beloved friend, blindfolded for execution.

Michael kept signaling me to quiet down, to *back off,* but I couldn't help it; this was the house I'd been waiting for, without even knowing I was waiting, and in the face of my overwhelming enthusiasm, the real-tor suddenly remembered that she, too, loved old houses.

"They don't make 'em like they used to," she smiled, and even went so far as to brave the spider webs and creaking floors to walk us through the downstairs that boasted sixteen-foot ceilings, carved man-tles, and three identical arched French doors off the back, the thick glass panels hardly visible in some places, painted or water-damaged or sim-ply covered in filth. Michael only followed along behind, silent and thoughtful, clearly wishing I'd shut up, as I was transported by every new discovery.

By the time we made it back out on the porch, the realtor was smugly supportive, full of ideas on renovation, recommending we cut the yellow pine and redo the roof and kitchen with the proceeds, though I assured her there was no need; I still had my trust. On the mention of the word *trust,* the realtor's face took on an even oilier smugness, and in years to come, Michael swore he could have gotten the land for three-fifty an acre, house and pine and all, if I hadn't sere- naded them all the way back to town about how *perfect* it was, how I *had* to have it, that I'd give *anything* for it.

To all of his very compelling arguments against living in the coun- try — the cost of renovation, the isolation — I turned a deaf ear, taking Cissie and Case out the next morning for moral support, though Cissie was more interested in the camellias (which were apparently quite rare) than the old house, which she said reminded her of the Bates Hotel. ("I'd be daresome to take a shower in *there,*" she said with a little chill.)

Case was hardly more enthusiastic, deeming the murky, exposed hole in the backyard either a sinkhole or an exposed septic tank, only shak- ing his head when I told him it was the house of my dreams, spitting in the dirt with a wry, "Baby, it don't look like nothing but a pile a work to me."

They were wise words from a man who was a contractor by trade, but I wouldn't listen to him any more than I listened to Michael, begging and pleading and weeping till he finally gave in and signed the papers in late January. It gave me just under three months to get the house in order before the baby was born, thus beginning one of the strangest periods of my life: my one unarguable manic stage. It began innocently enough, when armed with tools and cleansers and any stray relations I could recruit, I worked on the house from dawn to dusk, fanatically intent on proving that beneath the grime and decades of neglect, there was something out there in that unkept garden worth saving.

With Cissie and Case's help (her babysitting, his subcontracting), I had the inside weatherproofed in two months, the window panes replaced, the old floors clean but sadly damaged, a situation I couldn't immediately remedy because Michael wouldn't let me strip them, afraid the fumes would harm the baby. All I could do was add them to the end- less list of other improvements I obsessed over in bed every night long after Michael was asleep, my mind as alive at two in the morning as it was at two in the afternoon.

At first, I only worried over the renovation, though as the winter warmed to an early spring, my nightly dreams began to imperceptively flower into detailed visions of the vivid, luminous parties I'd throw, once the house was complete. In my mind's eye, I could see it so clearly: the house restored to all its 1903 glory, the windows lit with a dozen glowing lamps, the white oak floors shining like mirrors down a broad hall full of antiques and candles, me standing in the center of a laughing, waltzing throng, thin and radiant in a magnificent golden gown.

That was the stuff of my most recurring dream, though as my delivery drew close, these scenes of personal grandeur were expanded to include fantasies of my children and their remarkable lives: of Sim in a baseball uniform, pitching to the roar of an adoring crowd, or equally lifelike visions of the child in my belly that I desperately hoped was a girl. In my fevered night dreams, I saw her as a complete reversal of myself as a child: small and dark like her father, in a crinoline and patent leather shoes, sipping tea at a little table on a manicured lawn, surrounded by a tea party of bears and china dolls. (An image that just now occurs to me as a sad, telling commentary on the loneliness of my life at twenty-one, that even in the mad omnipotence of mania, I didn't people my daughter's fantasy with a tableful of chattering friends, but mute, inanimate objects, their china eyes as blank and staring as mine would shortly become.)

All of which — the grandiosity, the sleeplessness, even the heightened sexuality — put me very close to uncontrolled mania at that point. None of us knew it, how could we? Even if we'd been schooled in the ways of clinical observation, it might have eluded us, for it wasn't classic mania, of the jogging, shopping, talk-your-head-off kind, but molded in the iron restraints of my old passivity, *imploded,* if you like, and damn near invisible, even to the discerning eye.

Thus concealed, I was able to impersonate — indeed, embody — the image of the Ideal American Housewife: wonderfully fit, happy, sexually triumphant, working like a dog to provide my children with a respectable nest. While it lasted, I must say I lived the perfect life, pleasing everyone, even Mama, who didn't lay eyes on the house till it was nearly complete, and after that, never treated Michael with anything other than careful deference, mistaking the sheer perfection of the place (as many people did) as an indication of hidden wealth; not realizing we'd bought it for trash, and even at that, it had cost us every penny to our names.

I went into labor the night I finished the last window in true manic style, having sex, Michael horrified when my water broke, thinking he'd killed the baby, though Dr. Winston assured us it wasn't an unheard-of event. Since the time between my deliveries wasn't long, I didn't have such a difficult labor this time around, laughing and laughing at the sight of the lovely little red-haired girl we named Melissa Anne after her (maternal) great-grandmother. Who, true to her indomitable nature, didn't cry at birth, but just spit out the muck in her lungs like a little blowfish, her tiny face full of distaste, like she was thinking there really *should* be a better way to begin life than this.

I was so eager to take her home to her own little nursery that I hardly slept the whole time I was in the hospital, my heady euphoria dipping into a rush of hysterical tears on the second night, when Cissie brought Sim by to wave at me from the parking lot, as children weren't allowed on the floor. For some reason, the sight of him standing there on the curb, waving like a fool, started me *pinging* like mad, flooding the circuits with a blank, unreasoning horror that I'd abandoned him, left him for Cissie to raise while I took the new baby to the new house.

In a swirl of jagged confusion that was a harbinger of the awful years to come, I ran to the nurse's station and tried to explain my mistake: that I hadn't meant to leave him — what was I thinking? He was only three — or was he two? His name was Simon. *Simon Michael Catts —*

The nurses only put me to bed with a good-natured laugh or two and were still teasing me about it the next morning when they discharged me to a new house and a life that, contrary to the wonder of my night visions, was almost immediately marred by sharp, bitter fights with my one-time ally and only friend, my husband Michael. For, once we left the cocoon of his mother's kitchen, I quickly realized that the man I'd thought so easy to live with wasn't so easy at all, but difficult and hard-nosed, truly managerial material, who counted pennies like a miser and insisted I keep his house in the same state of immaculate order as his mother's.

It was a task that even in my supercharged state, I had a hard time doing, with a toddler and an infant underfoot, and the house renovation still only partially complete. I found the ironing especially tiresome, as Michael was picky about his appearance now that he was on the fast-track, careful to offset his rough, mill-worker's face with a sharp, professional crease, going so far as to make me re-iron a shirt when it didn't come up to Catts family standards.

I'd fly into a rage on such occasions, calling him the hard, half-remembered names from my childhood, even ripping up a few shirts in fits of unchecked fury that came close to ending in slaps and shoves (on my part, not his). Michael would only stand there with his arms folded on his chest, his face hard and disgusted, occasionally unbending enough to make a laconic speculation on my behavior, in which the terms *spoiled, babygirl,* and *white trash* frequently appeared (that's when the slaps would come in).

Fortunately, at that point, our fights still ended up where all marital fights should, in the bedroom, for along with my sleeplessness and delusions and snappy flares of temper had risen an equally pressing need for constant, unending sex. I'm not talking about normal marital relations here, but back-to-back double-headers, my passive indifference having been transformed in the space of a year into a constant, gnawing hunger. After a while, even the high-attitude sex didn't suffice, the pounding need as strong afterwards as it was before, creating an unending craving for my husband's presence that inevitably drew to light the unredeemably weak link in our marriage: his unashamedly workaholic lifestyle.

Blind ambition was such an overwhelming facet of Michael's character that it took on a chameleon-like invisibility in the easy camaraderie on the Hill. It was only when Sim and Missy and I were stranded out in the country that his presence (or absence, as it were) became a shattering reality, one he was never particularly apologetic about, as the very term *workaholic* simply didn't exist when he was a boy growing up on the Hill. The dead-end mill-town inertia had left his father's generation easygoing in matters of provision, content to leave their ambition to their wives, who, baby-rich and cash-poor, saw a whole world of opportunity out there, just waiting for a smart man to grab hold and make his mark.

In this, Cissie was (as usual) the Queen, teaching her children from the cradle to the grave to work, work, work; that the Lord might love a cheerful giver, but the merit of a man was in the dollar amount of his bank account, the make of his car, the cut of his suit. Gabe rebelled in this, as in everything, but Michael, now, he was a machine, his heart where his treasure was, in money and progression and Sanger Manufacturing. Once he had hacked his way through the underbrush of clocked-in slavery and found himself on the side of the money, he was desperate to prove his love for me, for Sim and Missy, even for Cissie, by bringing us home a lion's share of it, simply unable to understand my protestations that I never saw him anymore, that I was *lonely*, wondering what in the world was the matter? Wasn't he bringing home the bacon, restoring the house of my dreams? Wasn't he raising his children, buying me clothes, by God, *laying* me twelve times a week? What else did I want?

The point was, I didn't *know* what I wanted beyond wanting *him*, a need that grew both more desperate and more passive as summer approached, the hot, humid nights gradually losing their flowering delusions, pierced now and again by jagged, irrational fears: Had I put up the side to Missy's baby bed? Did I smell smoke? Was that a noise in the drive? Footsteps on the stairs?

These fears didn't come to me as vague possibilities, but pinpoints of awful certainty that I kept clutched to my chest as tightly as my delusions so that Michael was never the wiser, sleeping in peace while I roamed the house like a thin, nervous ghost, checking windows and locks and gas burners, haunted by a threat of loss so close and familiar I could almost taste it. Looking back, it's amazing how long I was able to trudge along in this tiresome charade of normalcy with no questions asked, no eyebrow raised, at least till swimsuit season was upon us and I appeared at the annual church picnic at one hundred fifteen skeletal pounds.

We hadn't seen too much of Cissie since we'd moved to the country, and I remember how she watched me that day, her face level and worried, pressing me to eat, saying who cared what they said in Hollywood? A man liked a woman with a little meat on her.

I didn't correct her, couldn't even answer by then, just fell back on my old complacent, averted-eye smile for cover, excusing my incredible emaciation with easy agreement, as if it were intentional, saying yes, yes, maybe I'd gone overboard, lost a little too much. By August, I had lost the ability to communicate at all and spent a good part of my life standing at an ironing board in the stifling kitchen hour after hour, ironing Michael's shirts and pants (and handkerchiefs and boxer shorts), desperately trying to compensate for my mental slippage with a veneer of ever-shining perfection. Michael had made foreman by then and was so distracted by his new duties that, at first, I succeeded, though even he was confounded one evening when he came home from work to find me just where he'd left me at seven that morning, ironing in the kitchen in my sweat-slick gown.

"*Damn,* Myra," he said, looking around in wonder at the Aladdin's cave of immaculately starched shirts and sheets and diapers and handkerchiefs. "You don't have to iron my *underwear.*"

But I was too far gone to be saved by mere reasonableness, putting my sleepless nights to good use refinishing every floor in the house to a mirror shine, then moving on to my next project, the hole in the back yard that on closer inspection had turned out to be neither a septic tank nor a sinkhole, but a small, oval swimming pool. Case had spent a month hauling off everything from abandoned tires to a misguided family of water snakes, leaving the final clean-up to me, and after maybe fifty gallons of bleach had failed to remove the pale yellow stain on the oddly hard, oddly slick surface, I realized that it wasn't concrete at all, but marble. Italian marble, to be exact, of a quality that I later learned could have paid for the entire renovation with its retrieval, though at first, it was nothing more than a pain in the butt, as who in God's name knew how to fix a marble pool?

I spent the latter part of the summer cleaning it out, and as August spun out, long and hot and breathless, I became more and more obsessed by that damn hole in the yard, teaming up with our yardboy Tommy to haul in a used pump his uncle had donated to the cause, hoping to get it in order before September, so Sim could swim a few weeks before autumn set in. That was the plan, as far as I can remember, as I'd been running wide open for a good six months by then, making for days that in memory are spotty and uneven, though I do recall a few of the high points (if you could call them that): the day we filled the pool, the evening I was first detected in adultery.

Both came within two days of each other, the first an innocent enough undertaking, me and Tommy and Sim finally getting the pump going and running around the deck like children in our cut-offs and bathing suits, rigging up half a dozen hoses in the empty pool, then sitting back in a fever of impatience to wait for it to fill. I dimly remember how Sim kept shimmying down the steps to check the depth that was to his toes the first time, then his ankles — then, after a long night with the hoses, there it was: a perfect oval pool, shimmering blue as an aquamarine in the hot August sun.

Tommy came early that day to check the pump, and when he found the pool holding, dove in to demonstrate our triumph, the sound bringing Sim down the stairs in a dead run, so excited that I just opened the French door and let him dive in, pajamas and all.

"Come on, Myra!" Tommy called, though I only shook my head.

Later in the afternoon, when I took Missy out to watch Sim swim, Tommy joined us, and with Michael gone so much, and the house so isolated, I didn't mind his company. He was a simple country boy, to my memory, seventeen at the outside, a lot like the crew that used to walk me to school on Lafayette, tall and spindly and crewcut, quick to make jokes, quick to fetch diapers or bottles, and, yes, quick to steal a kiss if he could get away with it.

It was a gesture that a year earlier — even six months earlier — would have horrified me, though now simply seemed part of the summer, and I had no more voice to tell him to quit than I had to tell Michael to forget Sanger Manufacturing and keep his tail home weekends where he belonged. The ability to disagree just wasn't in me, my boundaries melted away with the rest of my mind, leaving me to float along like a feather on a breeze, spinning out the long afternoon rambling on about my plans for the house, or spelling the children's names over and over again, as just lately, I'd had a hard time remembering them.

Tommy just smiled at my nonsense and shared riddles of his own: how he'd had older girlfriends before; that six years was nothing, his grandmother was six years older than his granddad and they'd been married forty years. It was information I really had no way of deciphering, calmly assenting as he gradually pushed his kisses farther and farther, though Sim was bothered by it, coming to the edge of the pool and telling him to *stop*.

He did, for a while, though even I could discern the heat of his presence, the sheer impatience as he begged me to come inside, said he needed to *talk* to me, except that once we were inside, we didn't talk. He just wanted to get away from Sim so he could push me further, and further and further, finally getting me on my back right in the living room, with Sim just outside the door, doing flips off the steps, not a care in the world.

That's just how it happened, the first week in September, with about as much emotional voltage as I've described right here, and so it might have continued, had Sim not intervened, waiting with the patience particular to his nature till his father came home from work that night on time for a change. I remember (or I think I remember) frying chicken in honor of the occasion, moving around the kitchen in a state of happy relief, as Tommy had called, begging me to let him come out and see me that night. I didn't have the voice to tell him *no, don't come,* but was terribly relieved when Michael came in, knowing Tommy wouldn't come if he was home; that he was *scared* of Michael for some reason, I didn't know why.

I couldn't imagine why anyone would be afraid of such a sweet man, who looked so much like his father that night, teasing me about my thinness in a way that would have hurt if it'd come from anyone but him, telling me I looked damn good for a *boy.* I just smiled in reply, feeding Missy mashed potatoes out of a coffee cup while he filled me in on the latest news from Sanger: the misplaced delivery, the man who was leaving, Tom Sanger's latest absurdity.

I just listened politely, without a clue in the world what he was talking about, some of the words familiar, but mostly not, though I made the correct noises of interest, absently watching Sim at the far end of the table, who was just sitting there, his eyes on his plate. Fried chicken was his favorite, and I was wondering why he wasn't eating, when he suddenly lifted his face and interrupted his father's monologue with an abrupt: "*Daddy.*"

Something in his voice made Michael pause and look at him down the table, ask: "What, baby?" Then: "Sim? What is it?"

He wouldn't speak, but just chewed his lip a long moment before he answered his father in one fast rush, the high old ceiling boards of the kitchen echoing back snatches of his thin, piping complaint: "—

don't like Tommy anymore. He keeps bothering Mama — laying on her
when we swim and it scares me, Daddy. I don't want him coming here
no more."

His fast run of words ended as abruptly as they had begun, leaving
the room in a silence so echoing it seemed to vibrate through the tabletop and up the walls to the high ceiling. I followed it, actually lifting my
face to the ceiling a moment, looking for the source of that strange
vibration. But there was nothing there, and as I went back to feeding
Missy, I happened to meet Michael's eye across the table, found him staring at me with a face that had lost every trace of teasing, so hard and set
that I couldn't meet his eye, just dropped my face and stirred Missy's
potatoes, wondering why he was mad.

Why was everyone so mad at me these days? I could hear Daddy's
boots on the porch every night, could tell he was mad, I couldn't imagine why. I tried so hard to please him, ironing and cleaning and never
spending a penny, never telling a soul, but it was never enough. That was
the thing about men: they always wanted more. Tommy, on the phone,
begging me to let him stay the night; Gabriel on the porch: *I did find me*
a wife; problem is, she married my brother. They were never satisfied, and
it was so confusing, my head hurt so much, never any relief. Aspirin didn't
work, I took them all the time; Mama standing at the bed, her face pale
in the moonlight (*"Here you go, sister"*) — and suddenly, it was too much.

I didn't have anything else to give, and just jumped up and ran
through the house, suddenly wanting my bed, wanting to go to sleep
and wake up on the Hill, with Mr. Simon offering coffee, Cissie in her old
housecoat, telling us to wake up, sleepy-heads, that she'd set out our
presents and she knew I'd love mine.

But my bed wasn't on the Hill anymore, it was at the top of a dark
stair in a strange, echoing house that still smelled of stripper and varnish, so strong I couldn't sleep, I never could. All I could do was lie there
night after night and try to remember the children's names, Simon and
— the other one was hard. It wasn't Maggie, but it started with an M. I
used to know it. I used to know a lot of things; I would again if that awful
pinging would stop. I covered my ears and clenched my teeth to try and
still it, flinching when the light came on, thinking it was someone —
something — *awful —*

But it was just Michael, his face no longer so hard and set, just dim and worried as he sat on the edge of the bed, resurrecting a sharp, poignant flashback of his father over the fence at twilight (*"And what are you gone be when you grow up, Myra Louise?"*).

The memory was like a breath of fresh air in that dark, suffocating room, freeing me to fly up like a loosened spring and grab his shirtfront so tight I popped his collar buttons, sobbing, "My mind is going, Michael. It's leaving me, I know it is. I cain't remember Mama's name, I tried all day. I cain't remember how old Simon is. He's my little boy, Michael. Why cain't I remember?"

He tried to quiet me, pulling me to his chest, stroking my hair, but the words kept spilling out as I tried to tell him about Daddy on the porch at night — didn't he hear him? Why wouldn't he come in? And what was the baby's name again? Maggie? Minnie? Marcia? But Michael just pressed me to his chest, and in desperation, I fell back to the calming repetition of spelling their names, till I felt an odd sensation on the part of my hair. I felt for it blindly, my hand coming away wet, a curiosity that made me pull back and see, for the first time in my life, what my husband's face looked like, crying.

$$=\ 19\ =$$

*S*o ended the three short years of plenty, to be replaced, like the corn and the cattle in the Pharaoh's dream, by at least as many years of famine. To me, they are the years of the locust; years I would just as soon forget, though, for the sake of my children, of Clay, surely, I am obliged to try and order as best I can, beginning with that awful night in September when I lost my precarious grip on mania and slid down the greased pole into what the doctors call a *mixed manic state*. It's a condition so tormenting that it really almost defies description, the energy of mania evilly mated with the black hopelessness of depression in a marriage of suffering that could be more accurately called *Night of the Living Dead*.

I am not being overly dramatic when I say that death haunted my steps those first weeks after I was admitted to the two-bed Psych Ward at Jackson Memorial with what was initially thought to be postpartum depression. There, I was bombarded with a hit-and-miss drug cocktail that inadvertently woke the sleeping monster of memory, filling the twilight with horrid little images of Tommy's hands on my poor nursing breasts, his mouth in my ear, murmuring endearments. The mania had robbed me of my old ways of coping, sleep and denial, leaving me to writhe with a near-psychotic self-hatred that peaked on the second night of my stay, when I quietly jerked out my IV and started down the hall in a half-stupor, intent on punishment.

The floor was between shifts, the day nurses gathering their purses and leaving, the night shift standing at the counters, penciling charts and gossiping. I passed among them unnoticed, ending up in a deserted public restroom where I happened upon a small pocketbook mirror on the ledge of a sink. I locked myself in a stall and methodically broke it in two, using the jagged shards to slice at my hands and wrists, feeling a warm, sensual relief at the slice of skin, the spurt of blood, as the numbed deadness of disassociation was finally pierced by sensation — any sensation, at any cost.

Nothing I'd done in months had felt so good, and when the mirror broke to fragments in my hands, I strolled back to the hall, where an orderly was mopping the linoleum, a lit cigarette in his mouth. Something in the glowing tip caught my eye, and with my bleeding hands folded quietly behind my back, I shyly approached him and asked for a drag. With a flick of his mop, he good-naturedly complied, saying something pleasant about the evening as he passed the cigarette that I carefully took between my thumb and forefinger and meticulously applied to my collarbone, the same way I'd seen my father apply them to Ira's bony chest.

Now, I can't remember actually doing the stubbing, though I remember the orderly quite clearly: his coffee-colored face middle-aged and easygoing, his smile turning to horror when he saw my blood-smeared hands, slapping at the cigarette and shouting for the nurses to restrain me. For the remainder of my stay, I was tied, hands and feet, to the chrome rails of my bed, weeping and begging and writhing like a butterfly pinned on a card for the better part of two days, till I finally gave myself over to the relative ease of a nearly catatonic state.

It was a calm that so nearly resembled normalcy that after a week of it, the doctors declared their remedy sound and sent me home to the old house that stood cold and silent among the shedding oaks, my husband at work, my children mysteriously missing (farmed out to day care, I later learned), leaving me to ramble around dawn to dusk like a skinny Norman in drag, *psycho* at last. Dr. Williams was my first psychiatrist, the only doctor we could afford at the time, who treated me out of friendship for Michael and a small personal curiosity, as he'd dabbled in psychiatry early in his career, till his own bout with alcoholism sent him back to general practice in '57 to eventually become the company physician at Sanger.

So his notions of psychiatry were outdated, even then, insisting on the rigors of Freudian analysis along with the newer options that were flooding the market: pills, pills, and more pills, antipsychotics and antidepressants and antianxieties, all in combinations and dosages that today, seem nearly toxic. You might say that he *practiced* psychiatry on me, in the most amateur sense of the word, always quick to stop one medication to start another, equally quick to admit that no, nothing was working, and when my withdrawal deepened to outright psychosis, slap me with the most debilitating of all psychiatric labels: adult onset schizophrenia.

It's a disease that, to this day, I fear only slightly less than the kidnap and mutilation of my children, a place of disembodied voices and horrific suffering, though, mercifully, like the pangs of childbirth, the horrors of that first year have all but faded. I understand from secondary sources (Michael, mostly) that I was the picture of mute suffering for many months, wandering the house, searching for my children with darting, terrified eyes, and nail biting so savage that Michael had to tape my fingers up every morning with gauze and duct tape so I couldn't chew them raw. I still have a few hair-thin scars on my wrist and right thumb from the era, though the sole memory I retain is of lying curled on the foot of our bed one evening, I don't know when, or why. All I remember is that it was early night, which must have crept up on me unawares, as the light was off, the room cast in a dim gray shadow that made me shiver as I lay there, full of the overwhelming terror of insanity that in some ways, *is* insanity. By then, I had no resources left to fight it or deny it or even dream it away, and just lay there shaking like a leaf, my eyes open in a perverse inversion of my old delusions of grandeur, a living nightmare with no hope of relief on waking.

When spring came that year, late, full of unexpected frosts, the blooms on the old pear tree dead before they could set their fruit, my free fall was finally slowed with a monster dose of Pamalor (one of the old tricyclic antidepressants, the kind that slow your heart and give you round-the-clock cotton mouth) and a wide variety of antipsychotics: Mellaril, Haldol, Thorazine. None of them actually worked in terms of returning me to my old self, but only dulled my mind to a state of empty-eyed passivity that I came to accept as a way of life, the dues for simple existence, my every action narrowed down to one desperate goal: keeping my children.

I can't say exactly when, but at some point, I must have recognized the old familiar threat of child removal hovering over my head, which I instinctively tried to avert by trying to please my husband, who as final arbiter of whether or not I was a fit mother, became my own personal *State,* which I tried desperately to appease. With my mind so bankrupt, I had no words to convey to him my terror, and no choice, really, but to fall back on my early training and try to win his favor by becoming his virtual mirror: returning his looks, smile for smile, cleaning house and cooking with the same determination (though not a quarter of the energy) of my old mania.

I even offered sex, with all the accompanying signs and wonders, but in this, failed miserably. For Michael was not fooled by my fakery, sometimes stopping halfway through, gripping my shoulders and shouting, "Myra! *Myra!*" his voice so hoarse and desperate that I'd cover my ears with my fists, wishing he'd stop shouting — I could stand anything but that.

I knew I was failing him, knew it and despaired, and after that first hellish year, there was really nothing left between us but a polite subterfuge, which came easy to me, as I'd spent most of my damn life playacting the part of a human being. I easily presented a polite, smiling face to Cissie and the Welcome crowd, both of us did. Michael more or less insisted on it, too proud to uncover to anyone the depth of shame I'd brought upon us — which is not to say that he was a bad husband, any more than to say that my breakdown meant I was a bad wife. It just happened along predictable lines, no one there to set us down and tell us what was going on, leaving us to navigate these dark waters as most people do: alone, in blindfolds, with many a slippery step, many a nasty fall.

With the help of Dr. Williams, I eventually became functional enough to carry on the routine duties of the house, even retrieve my children from day care, though my nights were still tormented by a psychosis from hell that seemed untouchable by any treatment known to man. The chemicals couldn't touch it; even Dr. Williams lost his early optimism after he'd marched me back to the winter of 1963 and hit pay dirt, psychologically speaking, when he came upon the inexplicable memory loss that heralds childhood trauma.

He was enough of a Freudian to know he was right on the threshold of glorious catharsis, but nothing in his arsenal of analysis seemed powerful enough to penetrate the wall of silence that continued to surround that cold, chattering winter. He tried talk-therapy, he tried meds, he even considered hip new options like hypnosis and Primal Scream, when Michael, tired of his dithering, took matters into his own hands and called Ira, who'd taken a job as a civilian machinist in Jacksonville, and brought him into the negotiations, though with little success.

For Ira and I had hardly seen each other since he'd left for Vietnam, and Michael's shocking little tale of adultery and betrayal was set in the framework of the introverted teenager he'd known in Fairfield, who wouldn't so much as cut her hair for fear of offending God. Against that backdrop, it painted a picture of rebellion worthy of one of Cissie's soap opera divas, and the most he could offer by way of advice was the tried and true method of dealing with an unruly spouse (beating her half to death), which, being his father's son, Michael would not consider.

With that door shut, he returned to his fundamentalist roots long enough to wonder if perhaps this wasn't just a chemical imbalance after all, but something even more scandalous, along the lines of demonic possession. For such was the opinion of Sam McRae, whom Michael was forced to confide in, as Sam was having to cover for him so much at work. The grandson of a Pentecostal preacher, Sam had a certain weighed opinion in such matters that I couldn't very well argue with, as some of my symptoms were bizarre enough to be justly labeled *demonic*. Not just the mutilation and the terror, but actual auditory voices that defied the heavy load of antipsychotics to accuse me of awful sins, everything from the real (what I'd done with Tommy) to the imagined (what I might do to my children).

That alone was enough to convince Sam that we were dealing in the realm of spiritual beings — that and the footsteps on the stairs every night, the *Stairwalkers*, I called them, who continued to roam the house at night, sometimes even pass through the locked door to pause at the foot of the bed and watch me sleep. I'd feel the weight of their hollow, lifeless eyes and shake myself awake to shout at them, and on Sam's advice, even rebuke them in Jesus' name, though my voice was not so ferocious on waking, nothing more than a hoarse, pleading whisper.

But they were a persistent lot, my demons were, and at some point that winter Michael went so far as to send me to an itinerant exorcist, affiliated with no church I'd ever heard of, who was holding tent services a county or two away, just above the Georgia line. I'm sure Michael's chief reason for choosing the man was his very anonymity, as my husband was fast closing in on manager at Sanger and increasingly obsessed with an undefiled image of perfection, buying the right car, the right clothes, even supervising my haircuts.

So it was beneath a cloak of secrecy that I consulted this spiritual specialist, and though I was far too deep in the murky waters of chemically maintained stability to be much more than physically present, I do recall odd little details of the visits. Nothing very telling, just pointless little needle hooks of memory, like the band-box newness of the unskirted doublewide he'd purchased to house his growing ministry, the interior covered in flat, industrial carpet that filled the place with a pervasive new-car smell I remember to this day.

It's funny that over the arc of a dozen years, that smell still lingers. I suppose that at the time, it was the smell of hope, a reflection of the minister's absolute certainty that he could put me to rights, quoting Jesus that first meeting, promising miracles. Of all the people I dealt with in those twilight years, he was (and remains) perhaps the most enigmatic, a wholly sincere, slightly corrupt man who honestly thought he was equal to the task of routing my demons, though in the end, like the sons of Sccva, he ended up routed himself.

With a little effort, I think I remember him as middle-aged and balding, a spiritual Lone Ranger with an obvious charm in dealing with Christians-in-trouble (especially Christians who drove up in shining new Cadillacs, Michael's latest contribution to our undefiled image). To his credit, he didn't gloss over my myriad problems, but took up hours and hours with us that first meeting, talking with Michael, discussing my life, not particularly shocked by any of it as Dr. Williams sometimes was, just assuring us we were *more than conquerors through Him that loved us.*

Aside from the comfort of the scripture, I can remember no other word of the meeting, though I can recall the passion in his voice when I returned alone for my first session, when he implored me to fight! That the Kingdom of God suffereth violence, and the violent take it by force! That was the tone of his ministry and the texture of all our sessions, and I think I was almost relieved when he began making the familiar moves of seduction toward me: the kisses, the assorted promises, all with their predictable end. Because until then, everything he'd been doing, praying and laying on hands and making me memorize scripture, had kept me in a state of virtual uproar, the voices at night screaming like banshees, the Stairwalkers not content with just coming to the foot of the bed, but actually jumping up on it, their voices lifted in hysterical laughter so real that I can recall the contempt in it to this day.

So I wasn't particularly disappointed when my sessions were prematurely curtailed when his wife found a pair of my pantyhose in his office, just returned in abject defeat to the sole care of Dr. Williams, who didn't seem any more outdone with my infidelity than Michael. He just added *extreme religiosity* to my other list of failings and upped my doses of Pamalor and Mellaril so high that the routine duties of ordinary existence became a study in intestinal fortitude, especially the daily ordeal of getting Sim to the bus stop on time.

Michael had enrolled him in preschool in September and for the first half of the year had been around to wake and feed him, till mid-February, when Tom Sanger had appointed him manager, a position that included (among other things) overseeing the plant's nearly round-the-clock operations. At that point, the job of getting Sim up every morning and fed and to the bus stop on time had fallen to me, a challenge of motherhood that I was determined to prove my fitness in. I'd jerk awake with the alarm at six-thirty and take off for Sim's room like a drunken sailor, feeling my way down the hall to his bedroom and pausing there long enough to wake him and set out his clothes and get him moving.

Once I got him going, I'd follow the wall to the top of the stairs and grip the rail all the way down, for in my disoriented state, I often misjudged distances. If I didn't take it slowly, I'd get up a head of steam on the last dozen stairs and slam face-first into the opposite wall, making Sam, who'd been sleeping on the couch since Michael went to nights, jump up like he'd been shot, calling, "Myra? You all right?"

The concern in his voice was so palpable that it brought a little stab of pain to my heart, as it was the same thing Michael used to ask, back when he still gave a damn whether I lived or died tomorrow. But I had no time to stop and chat. I had a breakfast to fix and a lunchbox to pack, and would just wave him away, feeling my way to the kitchen, where I was usually able to get the cereal on the table by the time Sim came to the door all dressed and combed, with a smile that almost broke my heart, and his own words of solicitation.

"Mama? Are you all right? Didju hit the wall again?"

Michael would come home shortly after, no longer in the worn old Dickies he used to wear in the woodshop, but in a style he'd lately assumed in conscious imitation of Thomas Sanger: pressed khaki pants and loafers and button-down dress shirts. Everything about him was so different, his hair shorter than it used to be, his voice brisk and business-tough as he went over the night's work with Sam while he stood at the counter and chewed aspirin, Missy in his arms, giving her to me reluctantly when Sam left.

He'd pause then to speak to me, usually just long enough to go over his whole list of dos and don'ts, most of them connected with the dangers of the unfenced pool. For Missy was walking by then, a red-headed, rambunctious toddler with a will of iron, and as soon as she was old enough to talk, her first word was *ool*. She wanted it, and she wanted it *now,* standing at the French doors all winter long, pounding her fat little fist against the glass, her face crimson with determination, so much like Ira that I'd sit down and kiss her tear-streaked cheeks, promise that as soon as it got warm, she'd have her *ool.*

But her father forbade me to so much as dangle her feet on the steps till one afternoon at the very end of May, Memorial Day weekend, when he woke me from my nap with an amazing concession: that Missy could swim every afternoon, as long as she wore a life preserver.

"Gabe'll be staying awhile," he said, standing at the mirror and reknotting his tie. "Taking off to write a book — told him he could stay over the garage." He turned and looked at me evenly. "Thought I'd give

Dr. Williams a call, see about that new stuff he's been pushing."

I sat up at the news, my usual medicated lethargy pierced by a pin-point of excitement that in retrospect, was probably a very early indica-tion that one of our cures — the doctor or the scripture or the pills — was causing an imperceptible shift in my steadfast depression. I didn't recognize the portent at the time, my flare of excitement not at the news of Gabriel's return, but the fun of waking Missy from her nap and whis-pering into her sleepy little ear that she could go in the *ool* at last.

She was indeed beside herself, kicking off the covers and stripping in bed, then running downstairs buck naked with me (and her bathing suit) three steps behind. Simon and I almost had to tie her up while we scoured the house for the little life jacket, finally coming upon it on a forgotten shelf in the laundry room. Before I could so much as strap her in, she took off through the French door and stepped point-blank into the water, bobbing up immediately in a remarkably efficient little dog paddle. I pulled her out, scolding, but she didn't so much as blink till I evoked the name of her father.

On that, she returned to the steps long enough for me to strap her in the little Snoopy vest, not pausing a moment before she stepped back in without a care in the world, in the *ool* at last, her bubbling little face a sight to behold. Sim lept in beside her and called for me to join them, but I waved him away, preferring to sit on the edge and avail myself of the undiluted force of the hot Florida sun, which was the only thing on Earth penetrating enough to warm my cold bones. I was sitting there, glad of its heat, when Gabriel came sauntering around the corner of the garage in baggy chinos and a Boston College T-shirt, so changed from the last time I saw him that I might not have recognized him at all, had I not known him as a child on the Hill.

Because that's exactly who he looked like: Gabe of the neighbor-hood, everyone's best friend, his hair cut back to nearly a flat-top in a style too short to be stylish, but another of his deliberate anachronisms, his face lifted in his old chin-out smile as I stood to hug him.

"You cut your hair," I murmured, a little confused by the blurring of the past and present he presented, averting my eyes instinctively, though he wouldn't allow it, lifting my chin with a look of mock-reproach.

"You been on some fool diet, woman? You're skinny as a rail."

If there was anything I was used to those days, it was people telling me I was skinny, and I ducked my head again, a little taken aback by his eyes that were also unchanged since childhood, boring down to the soul in a way that was still too intimate for my taste. I worked hard to avoid them as we took our seats on the steps and talked the afternoon away, him doing most of it, me sitting quietly at his side with many a stifled yawn, as Michael had interrupted my nap with his good news, and what with the Mellaril, I was feeling the lack. There really wasn't much to say, anyway, as most of the intervening years were forgotten in the fog of medications, and all I could talk about with any confidence was the house and how much I still had to do.

But Gabriel was very understanding, clearly taken with the beauty of the place, curious about Michael's success, asking how Sanger was doing, how he'd gotten to be manager.

"He works." I said, thinking that about summed up the essence of Michael Catts: he works, he comes home, he eats aspirin and goes to bed. He loves his job and his children, like he used to love me.

Gabriel seemed reluctant to accept so simplistic an answer, though, and pressed me with questions about his brother's ambition that I found a little disconcerting, as I had no idea what was going on in anyone's life these days, much less Michael's. For all I knew, they were cutting up cows on the mainsaw at Sanger, though I made a stab at returning his conversational volleys, his face so open and accepting, a call-back to the funny-talking little boy who used to walk me to school every morning, politely overlooking my inability to reply and filling the silence with his nonstop chatter.

So good-natured, he seemed, always a friend to me. And when I get to this point, sitting there on the edge of summer in 1974, I really am tempted to plead insanity and blank out the next month or so of my life, there at the end of the Great Fall. It would be so easy, so close to true. But what good would it do? What's the use in lying? If we hadn't been so damn worried about being perfect that summer, had opened up to Cissie and Maggie and Brother Sloan, then none of it would have happened in the first place, with Tommy or the preacher, either one.

So I'll try to put a lid on any convenient repression and make an honest stab at explaining with all accuracy and humility the exact nature of my third (and final) foray into adultery, which was a very different proposition from the first two, as I was no longer psychotic, not even depressed in the clinical sense, but actually on the threshold of the first hard steps of recovery.

None of us knew it at the time, how could we? For my tiny blinks of life were nothing more earth-shaking than an occasional twitch of overt emotion, and deeper still, a small, desperate, half-understood hunger in the secret places of my heart that is the seed of every survival: the sudden, insatiable voracity for life. For laughter. For some passing lifeline, no matter how fleeting, to snatch at, at whatever cost. It really is a powerful influence on the tail-end of depression, possibly the propellant that sends bi-polars back into mania, though it didn't go that far with me. It couldn't, for the little med Dr. Williams had finally persuaded Michael to try was none other than that small miracle of modern pharmacy, lithium salts, which meant I wasn't going to ascend to any great heights anytime soon. But lithium, like all the old pharmaceuticals, needed a month or so to kick in, and it was into this small window of opportunity that my unsuspecting brother-in-law unwittingly stepped when he sauntered around the corner of the garage that day with his mother's chin-out smile.

I invited him to supper that night, and even after Michael didn't show, he stayed to keep me company, even helped with the dishes like Ira used to do when we were children. He asked about Ira, what he was up to, laughing when I told him he had unexpectedly married, correctly assessing the situation with a grin and a "How far along is she?"

She was far enough along (eight months) that it wasn't much of a secret anymore. Gabe just laughed, then went on to reminisce about Ira as a child, and how funny he was, always taking dares, always going to the altar for salvation. "Every damn week. Couldn't talk him out of it."

He went on to recall Magnolia Hill with a wistful sweetness that was in sharp contrast to the pit of powerlessness Dr. Williams was chiseling out in our weekly sessions, Gabe skillfully reshaping it into a poor but controllable childhood, with its own glimpses of muted life: the little creek, the fat old oak, our talks every afternoon by the fence. Like the song at his father's funeral, the music of his memories worked to redeem those forgotten years in a way I found immediately fascinating, wanting him to stay, to keep talking all night. To chase away the shadow with his funny, rolling voice that, despite his years up North, still sounded like his father's, milltown and gheechie to the unfamiliar ear, though to me it sang with a entrancing sweetness.

But he didn't stay that night; didn't so much as meet my eye or touch my hand, but left early, kissing the children and promising to teach Sim the swan dive. I only smiled in farewell, then followed him as far as the French door and waited for the light in the window above the garage to come on. After a moment's darkness, it did, and shown there all evening long, a rectangle of light above the inky darkness of the pool, voiceless but compelling, with the unfathomable pull of a new moon. I found myself drawn to it, returning again and again to stand at the door and vacantly stare, till even Sim noticed and turned from the television long enough to give me his verdict: "I *like* Uncle Gabe."

I just smiled a thin smile and heard myself agree in the same voice I'd used to rebuke my demons: the one that in sleep was a mighty shout, though on waking, nothing more than a dim, pleading whisper: "So do I, baby. So do I."

$$=== 20 ===$$

$\mathcal{G}$*abe was as good as his word* about
teaching Sim to swan dive, joining us at the pool the next afternoon and
demonstrating it with a curious perfection you wouldn't expect from a
self-described non-athlete. His bad hand was the only note of asymme-
try that Sim was old enough to notice and young enough to baldly question, though Gabriel spared me the embarrassment of the real explanation by making a face of great regret and spinning one of his outrageous
yarns, telling him on different occasions that he hurt it killing a lion, saving his battalion by throwing himself on a live grenade, getting shot by a
cannon in the Civil War.

Sim was old enough to recognize them all as patently unbelievable,
but there was a note of indisputable authority in Gabriel's wildest utter-
ance that somehow put them beyond question, leaving Sim a little wide-
eyed, saying, "*Oh,*" with great respect.

He even repeated one as historic fact to his father at supper that
night, who warned him that his uncle was not known for his fearless
regard of the truth. "Too much of your Grannie in him" was his diagnosis, though when Gabe showed up for breakfast the next morning,
cowlicked and barefoot, in his usual chinos and T-shirt, he defended

himself with his old bland sureness.

"Oh, don't pay him any mind," he told Sim as he took a seat at the table and let him climb into his lap. "He's just jealous. Weaseled his way out of Vietnam with that fake arm thing, resents us heros who served."

Poor Sim's face was a study in confusion. "I thought you got bit by a lion."

"I did," Gabe easily replied, sipping his coffee meditatively. "Or a tiger, really. They thought it was a lion at first, because of the savagery of the bite, but later decided it must have been a rogue tiger. Jungles of Asia are full of them. Worse than the damn *napalm*."

Michael didn't so much as blink at the spinning of this masterpiece of absurdity from a man who hadn't gotten any closer to the jungles of Vietnam than the camo jacket he'd bought at Army surplus and stenciled with peace signs. He just shook his head and sipped his coffee, leaving Sim in a quandary as he looked to his father for the truth, for assurance that no, Uncle Gabe wasn't a tiger-bitten war hero, and found only bland indifference, though Sim was quickly too enamored with his Uncle's charms to be overly worried with the finer points of integrity — he and I both were.

He because he was a child and hungry for a man around the house, me for nearly the same reason, plus that needling attraction to the light that drew me instinctively to Gabe, to everything about him: his quick smile, his funny anecdotes from the North, even the snapping directness in his eyes that I once found repellent, but now, fascinating. Entrancing, even, always glad to see him when he'd come swinging around the corner of the garage to join us by the pool every afternoon, his northern paleness quickly staining a smooth golden brown that I found oddly appealing, especially fascinated by his brown, shapely hands.

They were his father's hands, and Michael's, too, the one characteristic the three shared, though in Gabriel they were broader and squatter, the bad one not deformed in any way and hardly noticeable from his good one, as he'd compensated so well. I couldn't understand why I found them so remarkable and every day for a week sat there on the steps while he swam with the children and racked my brain for what it could be. It was something about the Hill, some small, pleasant memory that I couldn't quite recall, till late one Friday afternoon while I watched him boss Sim on the diving board, when a fleeting image arose of him as a child standing across a sagging, kudzu-choked fence, his brown, dimpled hands lifted in the passion of persuasion, like a tent-meeting revivalist imploring a sinner to salvation.

I smiled at the connection of memory to fact, not my old deflecting smile, but the genuine article: small-mouthed and bemused. When Gabriel finished his lesson and joined me on the steps, I took his hand instinctively and pressed it flat in my own, alive with the texture, the clinging warmth, so taken with the retrieval that I tried to share it, my true voice emerging, clumsy and halting.

"I loved — your hands," I stammered, meeting his eyes, which were bottle green in the sun, watching me with such singular intensity that I tried to explain. "I mean, I never, understood — why *everyone* said — you *liked me.*" I paused again, for it was almost physically impossible for me to put any emotion to words, much less the visceral comfort of a pleasant memory.

But with his eyes so close, so patient, for once, I tried, closing my eyes with effort, explaining, "'cause I *never saw anything* — good — in *me.*"

I halted uncertainly at that, as another memory unexpectedly arose, the reciprocal one of me at twelve, standing on tiptoe in our living room, peering into the dim mirror above the mantle, searching and searching for some explanation for the inexplicable love of the Prince of the Hill, but never seeing anything there even remotely as wonderful as those clever brown hands. Something in the image bothered me, brought me to a clumsy halt, and though I didn't realize the import at the time, it might well have been the small breakthrough Dr. Williams had been praying for all year: the first time I'd ever entered the old house in memory.

The shock of it made me forget what I was saying, blinking back to life to find myself sitting there on the edge of a marble pool with Gabriel's warm, chapped hand in mine. He was staring at me with such intensity that I was unable to offer anything else, just let go and dropped my eyes, till Sim yelled from the diving board for both of us to *Look! Watch this!* I obeyed, though Gabriel didn't, his eyes still on mine as Sim lifted his little arms and in a small, oddly accurate imitation of his uncle, gracefully arched into the water, slick as a little seal.

I stood then and clapped, my smile wider and delighted in a way that Sim immediately discerned, sputtering up to the ladder and grinning like an urchin, though Gabe just slowly clenched his hand, then lifted it to rub his face in a tired, distracted gesture, as if he were trying to wake himself from a deep sleep. And though he said nothing that day, made no reply at all to my instinctual stabs at integration, his old way of treating me began to imperceptively change in ways I could not so easily explain, though I sensed them well enough, creature of the twilight that I had become.

After that, whenever I'd look up at different times in the day — at the stove in the morning, or in the afternoon with Sim and Missy at the pool — I'd invariably find his sun-tipped face on mine, blatantly posed in question, waiting for my signal. But politely, wordlessly, as all of it was cloaked in a beguiling innocence as we briefly reinvented our lost childhood every afternoon by the pool, swimming and diving and laughing like children at a birthday, till about four, when the fun would wind down and the party would end.

The children would be tired by then, ready for their naps, kissing their uncle goodbye with many promises to see him the next day, then trooping inside the high-ceilinged old house, which seemed vacant and empty and somehow deflated in his absence. I'd put them to bed and read them their stories, then come back downstairs and stand at the French door with my eyes on the little window upstairs, the combination of yearning and vacancy resuscitating even further pieces of scattered memory — brief, fleeting images of the little heron on the creek, of Mama's last good Sunday dress, of Ira's thin, country voice on the crest of a mimosa-scented night (*"But Gabe doan like it, says it's a girl's name"*).

To my numb mind, the memories, calm and unharsh, came to me as glimmers of life that I drew toward desperately, dimly realizing that Gabriel was offering me something — something I'd always passed on before. I couldn't remember exactly why, though with the replacement of the lithium, I was drawing close enough to the surface to actually meet his eye the afternoon he followed me in the house and faced me off evenly, saying we needed to *talk*.

By then, I must have realized (surely) that these invitations by men to *talk* weren't as innocent as all that. But I wasn't afraid, that I recall, or in any way nervous as I told him sure, I had to read Sim his story first, though when I came back downstairs, I found the living room empty, Gabe unexpectedly gone. I called for him a few times, even went to the French door to look for the light, but it was still too early for lamplighting, the thick old glass reflecting back nothing but the bland, merciless sun.

For a moment I just stood there, but it was too early to start supper, too late to take out the ironing board. The children would sleep for an hour, at least, and with nothing better to do, I left the sanctuary of my silent, empty house and climbed the creaking stairs to the little apartment that was hot as Hades that time of day, the door open so that I walked right in, calling, "Gabrielle?"

I used his old name deliberately, a little proud of my retrieval, pausing a moment at the room's unexpected dimness, as he'd draped the west-facing windows with the old nubby bedspread to block out the worst of the afternoon heat, casting the room in shadow. I glanced around at the clutter, the table all but buried under books and scribbled pads, the walls a patchwork of maps pinned side by side, window to door, the little bed under the window stripped to its sheets. That's where he was, still in his damp bathing suit, lying face-up with his forearm thrown across his eyes as if he were unexpectedly ill. When he didn't answer, I went to the bed and asked, "Did you need to talk to me?" Then, "Are you all right?"

Because he didn't say a word, just shifted his arm a little to look up at me with a face that wasn't so unashamedly inviting anymore, but hot and sulky and mad in the heat when he finally spoke. "I love you, Myra. I always have. I'm tired of pretending I *don't.*"

He spat out the *don't* with a petulance so close and familiar that I almost closed my eyes, trying to remember where I'd heard it before. Then it came to me: the little boy Gabe, stomping his foot at a truckload of teasing boys ("I'm *telling Mama!*"). And I answered, not with an explanation of the breakthrough of sound and memory and texture his arrival was flooding into the dry springs of my mind, but an echo of his mother's old words of defense for the orchid of a child she'd bestowed on plain working folk of the Hill: "He *looked* like an angel and I *named* him for an angel."

I even emphasized the same words she did, even echoed her old rock-solid sureness in a way that made me almost smile, pleased with my cleverness, though Gabe didn't return it, but just watched me another long moment in the silence of the still, hot room. Then, with no warning at all, he reached up and with a look of — good Lord, I don't know what — simple bad temper, I think, yanked me to the bed by the front of my bathing suit and rolled me to my back, kissing me for the first time — or no, the *second* time in my life.

But this one wasn't anything like the shy little kiss in the chiffarobe, but as consuming and mindless as the sex that I really wasn't too scared or passive to stop, though maybe I was too damned surprised. For there was none of the groping, tortured entreaty of the earlier drifts into adultery, just a lot of frenzied kicks to get me out of my bathing suit, then whack whack whack and it was over, him lying beside me in the exact same position he'd begun: face-up, with his forearm thrown over his eyes, as if he really couldn't bear to watch the awful goings-on in the dim hot room above his brother's garage.

I myself don't remember any particular emotion, then, or before, or for that matter, *during* the sex, though I do remember feeling cold afterwards, even in the merciless June heat, and reaching up and yanking down the nubby spread he'd draped over the window above us. It fell on the bed, covering our nakedness and filling the room with a blaze of western light that I closed my eyes against as I curled up against him, glad of his heat, as always.

So, yes, certainly, I remember those five short weeks. Like Tom in *The Glass Menagerie,* I have been more faithful to them than I intended and have strangely vivid memories of putting the children to bed every afternoon, then climbing the stairs to the hot, stuffy room that in the humidity of full summer, reclaimed the smell of its old renovation, varnish and stripper and fresh paint. Once there, the routine hardly varied; Gabriel always at the table writing, barefoot and shirtless in the stifling afternoon heat. He'd look up the moment he heard my step always eager to see me, though his face was no longer open in that roguish boy's smile, but bothered, intense, very nearly desperate.

I can never remember him even greeting me, just standing and kissing me without a word, a lover's kiss, long and slow and tender, though his hand betrayed a more pressing urge, jerking at the ties of my bathing suit. The force of his desire was as palpable as a wave of heat on a hot summer day — just like Daddy's anger used to be, now that I think of it — an emotion so strong it took on the qualities of a living, breathing entity. It filled the hot room with its awful burden that he'd immediately try to work out there on the bed, trying to be a good lover, though his haste and very inexperience made it a tricky business, quickly started, and just as quickly over, which hardly mattered, to me.

The part I liked best was that first kiss that was so sweet, like eating a ripe peach, and the talking afterwards in bed, I liked that, too. Gabriel was so animated, so full of plans, surely his brother's equal in that, nudging me awake to listen to some new angle of escape, and though his words were as distant and indecipherable as the quick, laconic sex, I loved lying there against him, listening to the sound of his voice, the texture of his excitement, quietly inhaling his warm breath that still smelled of his mother's kitchen. All of it was so comforting in its very familiarity, returning me to the safety of the old wardrobe, his living body warming my dying one, his fast, breathless run of talk working hard to carve out a sanctuary in the chaos around us, and in that, nearly succeeding, Daddy's shouts at the window gradually diminished to the ineffectual pleadings of a weak, dying man.

So maybe *that* was the part I liked best: the talking and the listening part, which would only last for an hour at the outside before I had to get dressed and go inside to check on the children, start supper, maybe take a shower before Michael came home. At first, Gabriel had no objection to my leaving so soon, though as the weeks went by, he became more and more reluctant to see me go, catching me at the door and kissing me again, not like the earlier kiss, but hard and pushing, sometimes holding my face in his hand so I couldn't look away, speaking to my eyes, telling me he *loved me*. That didn't I understand that? Didn't I *trust* him?

They were words that meant less than nothing to me, though I always nodded; that's all I knew to do. It was the password that freed me to go downstairs and check on my children, to straighten up the house, start supper, brush my hair so I'd be pretty for Michael when he came home from work. For despite everything — the estrangement of the past year, the afternoons spent with his brother — I still loved my husband, still desperately wanted to please him.

As the weeks passed and the antipsychotics leeched out of my system, replaced by the first tendrils of lithium's less opiate calm, I began waiting up for him to come home from work at night for the first time in two years. He still worked later than anyone, not coming in till ten or eleven, or now that he had Gabriel here to babysit, sometimes not at all. But I still didn't have the voice to complain and simply rearranged my life to accommodate him. I'd put the children to bed at nine, then pace around the living room for an hour, sometimes two, till I heard the car in the drive, then meet him at the door with my slowly wakening face, which on the night Ira's baby was born, even Michael began to see glimpses of life in.

Mama had called during supper with the big news, going on and on about how well Ira was doing in Jacksonville and how *proud* she was of her children. It was seldom enough that Mama voiced such a sentiment, and something in her exultant excitement had projected to me, making me too jittery to wait inside when I heard Michael's car in the drive, but run out in my gown to meet him in the garage, yanking open his door and stammering bits of the glorious details: that it was a boy; they were naming him Brian.

"Says his hair's as red as Missy's," I said with such excitement that even Michael noticed, shutting the car door slowly, his face on mine, lifted a little because at thirty-one, he was a touch far-sighted. Not enough for glasses, but enough that a little distance helped him see up close, and something in my exhilaration had finally clicked, making him speak kindly to me, tease me for the first time in maybe two years.

"Another redhead?" He smiled. "Ain't we got enough of them?"

His face was suddenly so young, so much his father's, that I felt a jagged catch in my throat, like I would surely cry as he paused to lift my face by my chin, not like Gabriel did, not pushing and insistent, but carefully, looking me in the eye, asking, "Myra? Are you all right?"

They were his old words of concern, of solicitude I hadn't heard in many years that I desperately wanted to answer, not with the easy answer, the parrot answer, but the truth. I faced him in the close darkness for a long, agonizing moment, then in an effort as taxing as lifting a car, finally managed: "I'm — better." Though I wanted to tell him more, much more. How that in a dozen small, indefinable ways, I was feeling like myself again, sleeping every night, six or seven hours at a time, dreams of peace, no longer so hag-ridden or pursued. But the subtlety of the explanation was far beyond me, and in frustration, I reached up and tapped my forehead, repeated, "Better and better."

After two years of numbed, wandering silence, Michael needed no more explanation than that, just pulled me to his chest and hugged me fiercely, an embrace of hope, of relief so intense that I never wanted to let go, but just stand there in the humid pitch of the old oil-smelling garage, engulfed in his warmth for the rest of my life. He even made love to me that night, not with anything like heat or passion, though afterwards, his sleeping face beside me was so wonderful that I fought to stay awake so I could lie there and savor the vision of him at twenty-four, in those dim, half-remembered days before the house and the Cadillacs and the madness, when we were simply Michael and Myra, in love.

The next morning, Gabriel joined us for breakfast as usual, though it was no longer such a merry gathering. By now the unease in the room was evident to any eye, even Sim's, who forwent his Uncle's lap in favor of *Mr. Rogers* and *Scooby Doo* in a shameless retreat I wished I could join, as Gabriel's good-natured cynicism was increasingly poisoned by a not-so-subtle criticism of everything Michael had become: his work, his cars, his money. I didn't have the wherewithal to connect his hostility to our afternoons upstairs and was only relieved when the phone rang, Ira calling to personally inform me of the birth of his son, along with the less welcome news that the baby was keeping him up nights, driving him crazy.

I must have been on about my third week of lithium at the time, in that weird little transitional period when the world of sight and sound is leveling to a normal pace, which was as disorienting as stepping off a roller-coaster, with that same nauseous unease, when you have to take a few steps, hands out, for balance, before you get a grip on the reality of solid earth. The uneasy note of trapped anger in Ira's voice shook my delicate balance, so much that even Michael noticed and formulated a Plan on the spot that would set it all to rights: that Cissie keep the kids while I went to

Jacksonville a few days, helped Dana with the baby, let Ira get some sleep.

To tell you the truth, it's a moment I kind of hate to recall, for in the clarity of hindsight, I can read between the lines of his practicality, and what I see there makes me very sad, because it shows that he was no longer so ignorant of Gabriel and me. I don't think he understood the physical dimension yet, or wouldn't admit to it, but the suspicions must have been rising, or he wouldn't have tried to separate us, send me off on a two-hundred-mile trip when I was just now dependable enough to navigate a trip to the grocery store.

Or maybe I'm flattering myself. Maybe he just wanted to be rid of it all: me and insanity and uncertainty, and even Gabe and his smart mouth. Maybe he knew all and could have cared less. All I know is that as I stood there by the phone that morning, pondering this outlandish suggestion, Gabe spoke up from the table. "I'm needing to go to Gainesville sometime here soon. Can go today, if you need a ride."

There was a moment's silence at the offer before Michael asked him what pressing business he had in Gainesville? In reply, Gabriel met his eye levelly, mentioned the libraries, how he needed to do some research, and I imagine the audacity of the clear, level eyes momentarily set aside any niggling worries Michael might have entertained. I mean, a son of Simon Catts might be attracted to a married woman, might even cross the line to adultery if he thought he was in love, but he wouldn't join her husband at breakfast, wouldn't boldly offer to take her on an overnight trip, right under his nose. It was unthinkable, beyond immorality and into the realm of simple unbelief. And though it might be in some ways more pleasing to think that the overriding emotion Michael sent us off that day with was *good riddance,* I have a tired, sure certainty that it was probably simple, naive relief.

In any case, with his usual masterful confidence in a Plan, Michael didn't bother to ask my opinion of the matter, just stood and told me that Gabe could drive me over, that I could stay as long as I wanted. Within the hour, I was backing out of Cissie's drive with Gabe at the wheel, Cissie waving us off in perfect innocence, yelling for Gabe to *behave* himself and drive *slow,* though he seemed incapable of doing either, passing car after car on U.S. 90, his face turned to me the whole time, trying to talk me across the seat.

His harping and close shaves had me so jumpy that I asked him to stop just an hour into the trip to take my morning pill. "What pill?" he asked. "Why d'you need a pill?"

There was a sharp, aggressive quality about him that made me duck my head and answer nervously, "I been sick."

At that, his eyes glinted in that old playfulness that was no longer so playful at all, but silky and suggestive. "Crawl over here and I'll make you feel better." He smiled, but I just shook my head, relieved when he stopped at a gas station and bought me a Coke, handing it through the window and watching me take my pill with his old hawklike attentiveness.

"Is it birth control?" he asked in that smooth, suspicious voice. In reply, I simply handed him the packed, quart-sized baggie that held my two-year stockpile of psychiatric drugs, everything from the minor tranquilizers to the big boys, Haldol, Thorazine, Mellaril. Gabriel took it gingerly, turning it over reverently in his hands as he went around the car, then sat back behind the wheel with a face of amazement. "You take this shit?" he asked.

I answered him carefully, telling him no, not anymore, then held up the little vial of lithium. "This is the new stuff."

He took it from me, mouthing the nonsensical brand name that I simplified. "Lithium," I said, which was what Dr. Williams called it: lithium *salts.*

"*Lithium?*" he repeated, and something in his voice made me suddenly wary. For there was a note of outrage there, and satisfaction, too, as if he'd finally come upon the elusive answer of the old insoluble mystery that made him stare at me so much as a child. He shook his head a moment, then turned to me and said in a fast, confident voice: "Listen, Myra: you shouldn't take this shit. It's addictive. It fries your brain."

He paused for my response, and pinned by his hawk eyes, I tried to explain. "But I have to — " I glanced at him uneasily. "Michael *said.*"

And it's funny, because I closed my eyes when I said it, I swear to God I did, knowing what was coming next, smelling it on the hot asphalt, feeling it in my bones, trying to find the same sort of fragile protection in blindness that I'd once looked for in the skirt of Mama's good Sunday dress. But it was no use, it never was. He exploded like a grenade, movement all around me, then a mighty slam of a door that made me open my eyes just in time to see my little vial of lithium shatter against the scarred old wall of the oil pit.

"Gabriel!" I cried. "It's all I brought! Michael *said* —"

"*Fuck* Michael," he snapped, then dropped back to the seat and pinned me to the cushion, speaking to my face, asking, "Myra? Are you gone stay locked up in some asshole's backyard all your life? Walk around like a zombie, wait on him hand and foot?"

He paused again, waiting for my reply, but the steel grip of his hand, the nervous copper smell of his breath scared me to muteness. "You don't need a baggie full of tranquilizers to get you through the day when you got me — I love you. I always loved you — remember? The fence and Napoleon and *Gone with the Wind?*"

He was gripping me so hard I had to look at him, had to answer him with an awful truth: "No Gabriel. No, I can't. Not the fence or Napoleon or *Gone with the Wind*. I lost it."

But he didn't seem too worried with me and my losses, his face lightening as he assured me in his old fast, sure voice: "Well, you did. I loved you and you loved me and it wasn't a game, Myra, a child's game. I never forgot it and you never forgot it and it was *real*."

He kissed me then, while I was still pinned to the seat, and for the first time, it wasn't so sweet anymore. Not like eating a peach at all, but suffocating, nasty, his breath fast and angry when he pulled away and started the car. And though he'd just said he loved me, had always loved me, for a moment there, I could have sworn that he hated me, hated the look of me, the smell of me, hated me as much as I'd hated him, for that blink of a moment.

But whatever split-second visceral reactions might have momentarily surfaced there at the gas station were quickly numbed as the lithium kicked in and encased me with its calm even glow, making me sit there as placid as an owl as the rolling red hills of the Panhandle give way to the flat woods of the Gulf Hammock. Gabriel was still agitated, nervously chewing his lip as he sped on until his headlong, maniacal passing came to an abrupt halt when he swung into the parking lot of a strip motel and turned off the car, speaking into the still, dead heat. "You been a slave too long. You need a rest. To hell with everyone else. We're getting old waiting on everybody else."

213

On those cryptic words, he went in and signed us in as husband and wife and was almost immediately in better spirits, as if the motel register were an official document of manumission. It was as though he'd married me there at the counter, even taking me on a honeymoon that night, to a carnival that was set up just across the highway in a vacant field backing a wide loop in a slow-moving river, the crowd full of crinolined, ringleted little girls who were vying for a crown of some sort, the smell of the sausage dogs and fried elephant ears mingling uneasily with the dank, black waters that flowed smoothly in the light of a thousand Chinese lanterns. It made for one of the strangest evenings of my life: the prancing little girls in their finery, the neon rides that blinked to life at sunset, the hawkers on the midway who kept picking me out of the milling crowd, calling me *pretty lady,* begging me to join them in some exhibit or show or game of chance.

I found their hectoring voices hypnotic and would have been suckered into half a dozen striped tents, but for Gabe, who steered us to the tilt-a-whirls and music-in-motions, the *puke rides,* he called them. I have always been prone to motion sickness and never liked swirling scare rides, but for some reason, they appealed to me that night for the first (and last) time in my life. I can't say why, really, except that the wild mixture of blurred light and slinging motion seemed to bring with it a sliver of waking memory of what it was like to be alive, to *feel* things, even if those things were nothing more passing than the stomach drop of elation that comes before a mighty fall. It was as if I were no longer hermetically sealed in the walls of a private torment, but joined by a crowd of merry revelers in my blurred, swirling Myra-World, all of us laughing and gay, even Gabriel, who was magically returned to the Gabe of old, the bright-eyed boy with a love of a good time.

I think I might have loved him there for a moment, a small moment, when we were high atop the creaking ferris wheel, the carnival and lights and the river stretching before us, a kingdom at our feet. But the moment passed, just that quickly, when we returned to the dingy little room, where he wouldn't leave well enough alone, always wanting more: the bed and the kissing that since that forced kiss in the car had become so nasty to me, nastier than the sex that I could always close my eyes and ignore. But the kissing I couldn't, any more than I could ignore his incomprehensible insistence that I marry him, when he knew I was married already.

I was married to Michael. I'd married him in his mother's living room in a borrowed dress, an event I was reasonably certain was a part of the real world, and not another delusion of the twilight, though by the time he dropped me off in Jacksonville the next afternoon, at Ira's, I wasn't so sure. For I'd been without medication for thirty hours or more by then, my hands damp and a little shaky when Ira came home from work that night and I realized, just that quickly, that fatherhood didn't suit him any better than it had our own father.

Or rather, it suited him the same way, making him nervous and high-strung, most unpleasant company, harassed over the crying baby, irritable with his young wife, and clearly not satisfied with my vague excuse for showing up a day late.

"Gabe and me stopped at a carnival," I told him.

"A *carnival*? Where?"

I gave him as good a recollection as I could of the river, the lights, the little girls in their finery, even the dingy motel room that made him lift an eyebrow, murmur, "How cosy."

But he said no more about it till the next evening, when he came home late from work, drunk from a stop at a local bar and a mite more articulate, pinning me to the wall and warning me with a clenched-teeth sureness that Michael wouldn't put up with much more of my *shit*.

"And I don't fucking blame him" were his exact words, though when I got home after a surreal three days kicking around the backwaters of north Florida with Gabe, Michael wasn't mad at all. He wasn't particularly anything, just his old detached self, tired and matter-of-fact as he sat me down on the edge of the bed and tried to find out what happened to my baggie full of medicine. I tried to tell him about the trip and how strange it'd been, with the carnival and the *puke rides* and Gabriel begging me to marry him, when surely he knew I was already married. Surely time hadn't undone that, too, my fragile hold on this strange new reality slipping with all the new tension that Michael tried to set aside, his face so thin and harassed, assuring me that no, Ira was wrong. He wasn't going anywhere. Gabe was the one who was leaving.

Though apparently not right away, as he showed up for breakfast the next morning just like always, and given my persistent voicelessness and our self-imposed isolation, I sometimes wonder how long our profane little menage would have lasted — a month? a year? ten years? — if not for Ira, poor Ira, whom the Lord seems to have put in my life as the eternal whistle-blower, the scourge of the ungodly. Who finally tired of the disrepute I was bringing on our pristine family name, and with my mother's blessing (I think), put an end to it in true Sims fashion, with fists and broken bones, at, of all things, a family reunion.

*I*t wasn't a *Catts/Tierney reunion,* which were held every other August on the lake up in Florala, but a reunion of my mother's family, the Edmonds, which was held every Fourth of July in the Panhandle at a halfway point between Grannie's people in Louisiana and Grandpa's in Birmingham. I had never actually attended the affair myself, as my own extended family was just that: distant and extended, only Liz and I still in contact via rare phone calls and Christmas cards. She was the reason I went at all, as she had undertaken the odious job of reunion organizer and set the meeting place at a springs in Washington County, had even finagled Mama into coming on the condition that Ira and I would also agree to attend.

When I heard Mama would be there, I suddenly wanted to go, for some of my breakthrough memories were of her as she was on the Hill, younger and kinder to me, braiding my hair with fast, skillful hands then tipping my face up to kiss my forehead when she was done. They were images of a mother I had lost somewhere along the way that I desperately wanted to reclaim, though I suspect Mama's insistence on having me there had more to do with my new Cadillac than anything else. For she'd never had much to do with her family since she bucked them to

remarry my father and would only face them on her own terms, surrounded by her children and their handsome faces and evident success.

It was the kind of wall of protection Mama liked to surround herself with in the later years of her life, though I expect she lived to regret
it, on that occasion, at least, as I showed up all right, with my children
and my Cadillac and, of all the people as an escort, *Gabe Catts,* the one
person on earth she possibly detested more than Cissie. I remember the
day so clearly: the pale even heat of the white-hot July sky, the parking
lot of the springs so crowded with trucks and sagging cars that we had
to park on the grass and lug our coolers a half a mile to the concrete
pavilion that was already filled with a chattering crowd of half-remembered cousins and uncles and relations who were easy to pick out of the
teeming crowd because of the proponderance of red hair. Mama was
among them, standing when she saw the children, her face momentarily soft, till she realized the man on the other end of the cooler wasn't her
hard-working, Cadillac-driving son-in-law, but his worthless, skirt-chasing little snot of a brother (a reputation Gabe had earned in the Sims
household at the tender age of twelve).

In true Edmonds style, she didn't say so much as a word of
reproach, her stark anger only evident in her eyes and cold greeting that
probably no one but her sisters and I noticed, the rest of my cousins
warming to the Catts charm nicely, except the men, who have always
hated Gabriel on sight, I never have figured out why. God knows he was
trying hard enough to please them, the very picture of respectability in
his pressed pants and good-natured smile that after an hour of hard
effort finally had them thawing, a few of them asking after Michael, asking about a rumor they'd heard that he was *buying* Sanger, which was
certainly news to me. I didn't have enough grocery money to so much
as put Missy in disposable diapers, though none of them seemed too
interested in my opinion anyway, their eyes all on Gabe, checking his
measure, as men do, then looking me up and down, invariably commenting on my thinness and how *awful* I looked.

"Like you traded legs with a jaybird and lost your ass in the bar-
gain" was the charming way one of them put it, all of them pressing me
to eat, even Liz, who took me aside and asked after Michael, clearly reading between the lines and not liking what she saw.

I avoided her eyes as best I could and made my usual pretense of eating, sliding the food around my plate with a plastic fork, worried over Mama and her silent rage, wanting to ask her what was wrong; what had I done now? But even if I could have found the words to voice such a query, she wouldn't have listened, the wall around her glacial, impregnable, leaving me to stand by myself in a corner, dreading Ira's arrival, though when he and Dana finally arrived, he was perfectly fine, hugging me and calling me "Bones," but that was all, even letting me hold the baby.

All of it made for a relief, a tiny upwind on the roller coaster of moods I was just lately transversing, up and down, up and down, everything going smoothly, then swoosh, back to black. But this was an upswing, and I enjoyed holding my tiny nephew, who was suffering in the July heat till I walked him out over the water to quieten him, his pearl-white infant's face so small and fragile that it gave me a chill to think of him and Ira living under the same roof.

Dana, who looked at least as drawn as Michael these days, joined me there, not saying much, just making sure I didn't drop her baby, while up around the pavilion, the rest of the reunion wound down, Mama and the out-of-staters packing up and leaving as the sun began to dip below the tree line, casting the deep water of the main boil in a moss-green shadow. I was standing there in the knee-deep water, telling Dana about peppermint and how she could put it in a bottle with a little warm water for Brian's colic, when I realized there was a commotion at my back.

Dana saw it first, biting in her breath with a noise of surprise that made me turn and follow her gaze to a curve in the shallows of the river, where two men were going at it like a couple of pit bulls. Neither of us said a word, just stood there shoulder to shoulder, knowing immediately one of them was Ira. You could see it in the ferocity of the relentless pounding, the sheer contempt when he ended the beating with one wholly unnecessary, wholly vicious kick before he strode away with some laughing bit of comment aimed at his opponent, who was struggling to come to his knees, his face so bloody it was unrecognizable.

I was so emotionally detached that the sheer violence of the scene didn't touch me at all, just stood there next to Dana, jiggling the baby, when suddenly, with no warning at all, I was lifted from the cold waters of the springs and magically displaced to the damp, bumpy sand under a shedding live oak in a transformation so real it was like time travel. I could smell the folksy woodsmoke of a late winter evening, feel the jag of an exposed root that tripped me, the jarring movement creating a firestorm of pain in my head, as swirling and red as the lights that flashed across the small crowd that parted to reveal two men, one crumpled and bloody, the other striding away, laughing and untouched.

"*Myra!*" someone called through the mist, and blinking awake, I saw it was Dana. She was trying to take the baby from me, saying, "Myra? You're dropping him."

I pulled back instinctively and gathered him close, murmuring, "No — I'm all right." And I was, the split-second vision gone, though I could still feel the awful compression of that swirling headache that made my heart hammer in my chest as I repeated vaguely, "I'm okay."

There was a voice at the shore almost immediately, a man standing with his back to the sun, calling my name. With that split-second flashback still upon me, for a moment I thought it was Mr. Simon standing there, his shirt bloodied, his face horribly beaten. I handed Dana the baby without a word and waded in, but when I drew close enough, I realized it wasn't Mr. Simon at all. It was Gabriel.

"Gabriel?" I called. "Are you all right? You're bleeding." But he ignored me to turn and start back toward the pavilion, calling over his shoulder that he was leaving, his voice as mad as Mama, I couldn't understand why.

I waded out of the water and ran to catch up, wanting to ask him what was wrong. What had I done now? But he wouldn't turn, only strode past the pavilion, pausing at the tables to spit at Ira in open contempt. It was a dangerous thing to do on the best of days that made me stop in horror, though Ira just jumped playfully aside and let him go without challenge. When I tried to follow, he grabbed my arm, said, "Come on, shug, leave the boy alone. You'll find you another one here soon. I got a friend at work been wanting to meet you. Got *sevral.*"

I hardly heard him, just turned and asked, "What happened? To Gabe?"

"I beat his ass," Ira answered cheerfully, with no regret, no emotion at all that I could discern, his voice full of that smooth, silky confidence.

"And you're just damn lucky I ain't starting on you. I doan know who you think you are, flashing around here like a *bitch* in *heat.*"

The sheer force of his contempt made me step back, like he'd slapped me, though he wouldn't let go of my arm, jerking me back to his face, jarring another memory, this one purely conscious, of trying to talk sense to Daddy's livid face that would never listen, never. I could feel his hot breath in my face, his hands in my hair, Mama just behind, her face so pleading: *"Hush sister — go easy."*

Why was she always saying that? It never worked. Nothing worked, his jeers stinging like nettles, tormenting poor Ira at supper, laughing as he stomped up the porch steps —

Why was he always laughing? It wasn't funny — none of it was: Mr. Simon's face on the pillow, blue-tinged and silent, Cissic's hysterical screams, Michael climbing on the bed, his face tearless and stunned (*"Daddy! Daddy! Wake up!"*).

"They were people, too," I murmured aloud, right to Ira's face.

His hilarity turned to disgust at my calm, wondering words, making him jerk me up by my arm and spit in my face, "Oh, *cut* the *shit* Myra. I don't know who you thank yer fooling with this crazy shit. Not me or your dumbass husband, either one, who don't give a *damn* about you anymore — letting you lay his brother in his own house, what d'*you* thank?"

I didn't know what to think as I was hit by a sinking, belly-drop of nausea that made me try and jerk myself free so I could bend over, hands on my knees, and try to get a deep breath to the bottom of my lungs. But Ira had me in an iron grip and wasn't letting go so easily, pulling me even closer to his hot, liquored breath, his voice no longer Daddy's, but his own, thin and disgusted. "And what'll you do when he kicks you out? Leave yo childrun for Miz Cissie to raise? Thet what you're thanking?"

And it's funny, because at the mention of Cissie's name, I forgot my nausea and quit struggling, actually lifted my face and met his eye, I really don't know why. Maybe because of the way he spoke it, in our old childhood terms, with an unconscious concern, an abiding respect that unexpectedly conjured a clear image of Cissie at the fence, lifting her face to Daddy and letting him have it with both barrels (*PUT him DOWN, let him ALOOSE, I'll CALL the LAW, you DRUNK SORRY piece of TRASH!).*

The memory saturated me; poured over me in a warm wave so potent that for a moment there, I *was* Cissie, standing at the fence with nothing but my apron and my righteousness to protect me, a wounded child at my feet. I blinked at him once, twice; then, with no more thought than my next breath, drew back and slammed my forehead into his nasty, mocking mouth, knocking him backwards into the drink table in a scatter of bouncing plastic and shattered glass. The men lazing in the lawn chairs came to their feet at the commotion, but I ignored them to dive to the concrete on Ira, managing to evade his fists long enough to bite and scratch and even slap him a few times before my assorted uncles and cousins finally separated us. It didn't prove so easy a task, as Ira was simply insane, shrugging them off like rag dolls, with me nearly as bad, even raising myself off the concrete to kick at him with my bare feet after they had me restrained, screaming things so awful the park ranger had to intervene, or so Liz says.

For in true post-traumatic style, I hardly remember the fight, much less the aftermath. The next thing I remember is zigzagging though the pitch black of the Dead Lakes in an unfamiliar car, holding a baggie of ice to my stiff, useless arm. Sim and Missy were asleep in the backseat, Liz's face illuminated in a faint green by the dash lights, clearly worried, telling me frankly that Ira had been passing around the most awful stories: that I was running around on Michael, that he'd lost his shirt trying to buy Sanger and was about to go under.

All of it was news to me, sitting there bruised and scraped in a damp bathing suit, my head pounding so hard I didn't bother to answer, even to deny it. What was the use? Ira was just mad, and when men got mad, they said the awfullest things. Things that went right into the pink places of your heart, tearing at fragile, tissue-thin foundations, leaving them ruined. It was just the way of men, of the Sims men anyway, and when Liz parked in the drive, she paused a moment to tell me to keep in touch, to call her if I needed *anything.*

Her level-eyed compassion scared me more than Ira's threats, setting up that old unease in my belly, wondering if he was right. Was Michael really through with me? I wanted to ask him, desperately needed his assurance, but he was still at work, the house standing dark in the early twilight, vacant and lonely when we took the children upstairs, both of them still in damp bathing suits and towels, but so exhausted that I just laid them on the covers to sleep.

"I'll undress them later," I told Liz.

She went back to Pensacola immediately, leaving me to ramble around the old house that began to take on more life with my presence: the lamps glowing, the kitchen smelling of the leftover chicken I heated up for Michael's supper. I was standing at the stove, trying to maneuver an iron pan with my useless arm, when there was a knock on the French door that set up a nervous jitter in my stomach, thinking it was Ira come back to even the score.

I inched out to the living room, but it was just Gabe, standing in the semi-darkness beyond the glass, his hands jammed in the pockets of his mud-splattered pants. I opened the door in a small backwash of relief, though when I caught a glimpse of his face, I stopped dead in my tracks, asked, "Gabe? What in the world didju do —"

But he ignored me, just brushed past, snapping, "Where're the kids?"

"In bed," I told him, closing the door at his back. "Had a big day, Mama said."

It was the only polite thing she'd said to me all day that I held to closely, almost smiling till Gabriel turned and I saw his face in the full light. For it was more than merely bruised; it was distorted almost beyond recognition in that old Martian grotesqueness, his left eye nearly shut.

"What happened to your face?" I whispered, going to him and feeling for it instinctively, like I used to with Ira when he was little and beaten and so quiet. (He never cried. I could never understand it; I cried all the time, but he never did. "You can do my crying," he once told me, and I did.)

Just like Ira, he flinched at my touch, but accepted it, his face so helpless, as if mutely imploring me to explain how it had all happened, just like Ira used to do, when we were little, and tried so hard to be good, and *yet* —

But Gabriel's face lost its softness just that quickly, and he grabbed me high on my bad arm, making me flinch. "Did you tell Michael?" he whispered in my face; then: "Why did you tell Michael?"

Everything about him was so insistent: his burning eyes; his hard, gripping hand; even his voice, that was no longer lazy, lost in story, but hard, obstinate, refusing to be placated, posing these riddles that I had such a hard time deciphering. I could never think of the right answer anymore, but in the face of his burning insistence, I tried, thinking and thinking, finally coming upon an evident truth where Michael was concerned, whispering, "Michael is my husband."

"*Dammit,* Myra, I *know* he's your husband," he snapped, jerking my arm so high I cried aloud. "Is this some kind of *game* to you?"

"No," I whispered, standing on tiptoe to try to ease his grip, "it's not a game." Then, in a confession of truth so deep and heartfelt that it almost seemed to come from another person: "I love him."

At that, his ravaged face hardened to a mask of rage the equal of Mama's, of Ira's, of Daddy's even, so terrible that I hardly felt the backhand that flew up, splitting my lip with a shock of copper blood. I was too intent on escape, jerking myself free and making for the stairs, wanting to go upstairs and go to sleep and wake up in a kinder life, like I did sometimes, with Cissie frying bacon, Mr. Simon offering coffee.

But Gabriel was right at my heels, equally intent on keeping me anchored in the awful present, catching me on the couch and pinning me there, making promises and crying regrets, my mouth bleeding the whole time. The ambivalence of the conflicting message was more terrifying than anything these dark years had yet offered, worse than the Stairwalkers or the finger-tearing or even the preacher and his nasty groping hands. For it inadvertently triggered a hair-thin sensation of the deepest, most paralyzing memory of all: of being pinned, helpless and bleeding, in a position of profane intimacy by another angry man. Not a stranger, mind you, but a man I loved — we all loved, so much. One we'd sacrificed everything — our voices, our faith, our very memories — to appease. Who tried and tried to do right by us, though in the end, all he really brought us — and this was my last thought before I was sucked into the mindless vacuum of catatonia — was all he really knew, and that was *hurting.*

PART TWO

EVERY BITTER THING
IS SWEET

— 22 —

*S*o *I did get my wish that night,* to go to bed and wake up in another life, in a manner of speaking, blinking awake the next morning just across the hall from the bed where I'd begun this dark journey two years ago, on the tiny psych unit at Jackson Memorial. It was an easier visit this time, as I had a diagnosis in hand (manic-depression, since the lithium had proved effective) and Dr. Williams to vouch for my harmlessness. So they untied the restraints after twenty-four hours and sent me home, bruised and skinny and silent, but otherwise pretty much intact.

Michael never visited, though. He didn't send flowers, didn't sneak in the fire exit to hold my hand, but only met me in the lobby to sign my insurance forms with the polite distance of a stranger, the business-like polish that even a year ago had been contrived, now, plainly, a matter of routine. Even his hair was different than it used to be: short in a way that made the high bones in his forehead even more pronounced when he finished the paperwork and finally looked up; told me we needed to stop by the drugstore on the way home.

I just followed him to the car and waited there while he ran into Watson's for the prescriptions, noticing that the lithium was the same,

229

but the Pamalor had been replaced by another medicine, a multivitamin. I didn't bother to ask why Dr. Williams had taken it upon himself to change my medicine yet again, though my muteness was no longer involuntary, but a perfectly conscious decision to never speak again, if I could help it. I mean, what was the use in words anyway? Since when had they ever been a friend to me?

Michael didn't seem to disapprove of my resolve, silent himself till we got to the house, when he paused in the drive long enough to tell me I needed to take the vitamin with food, or it'd make me sick. I just gathered my things to go inside, and there in the same garage where we'd broken through to conversation just a matter of weeks ago, he unbent enough to explain, "It's a prenatal vitamin. Dr. Winston says you're too skinny. It'll hurt the baby, you don't get some weight on you."

In just this way, I found out about the impending birth of my third child, that, in the context of the summer's other oddities, didn't strike me as too outrageous. I didn't argue, didn't make any noise of joy or surprise, either one, just went inside, finding the house empty, the children gone. Whether they were farmed out to day care or their grandmother, I didn't know and didn't ask, just took my pills like he said, a gesture of obedience that was as different from my old passivity as my new silence was to my old voicelessness. The dividing factor was that before, it was involuntary, while this was a perfectly conscious resolve to never be drawn out again, never again, as long as I lived.

It was a proposition that was easy at first, as Gabe was mysteriously gone, an absence I would not have minded except that Sim missed him so, actually weeping when his father explained he'd gone back North.

"But he left his stuff," he kept crying, so disappointed that Michael finally closed his eyes and offered a small consolation.

"Maybe he'll come back."

I didn't offer any consolation of my own, as the whole phenomenon of Gabriel Catts had disappeared for the moment in a void of denial so clever and complete that I hardly remembered he'd come at all, except when I'd stumble upon some irrefutable reminder: a towel by the pool; the apartment he left in thoughtless disarray, still crammed full of boxes and books and legal pads. It was as if a hurricane had passed through, papers strewn like confetti, the maps half-torn from the walls, creating a quiet minefield of thumbtacks that I inadvertently discovered when I went upstairs to clean the place up.

I went late in the afternoon while the children were down for their naps, just like old times, not pausing at the door but walking straight into the small, hot room that seemed eerily alive, as if Gabe had just popped out for a moment, his bathing suit still draped over a doorknob to dry. His implied presence made me pause a moment, long enough to make sure he was really and truly gone, then proceed more slowly, my face lifted to the maps that were still partially pinned to the walls, not paying the littered floor any mind till I stepped on one of the strewn thumbtacks with my bare foot, driving it deep into the hard callous of my heel. It was the only time I cried over Gabriel Catts, then or ever, hopping to the edge of the bed and lifting my face to the heavens, howling like a wolf in a steel trap, it hurt so bad.

But that was all: one moment of pure anguish that was hardly remembered, much less dissected and understood as I stayed clear of the booby-trapped apartment and limited myself to the regions below, to days that were quieter, and therapy sessions that had Dr. Williams sitting on the edge of his seat. After two years of fruitless probing, he was sure that we were on the verge of some kind of grand orgasmic catharsis, as I had unexpectedly come upon a mother lode of memories: of Christmas of '61, and even earlier than that, of our first house in Metairie, of finding the cracked Elvis record in the closet the day we moved in and turning it over in my hands, wondering if it would still play.

Dr. Williams seemed to find inexhaustive pleasure in each new find, no matter how trivial, though the only compensation I personally garnered from the grueling marathon sessions (biweekly, now that things were cooking) were calmer nights, my visits from the Stairwalkers becoming increasingly infrequent. They only surfaced now when I was very tired or (for some reason) during afternoon naps, when I'd awaken from a sound sleep, sure I'd heard someone downstairs, knocking on the front door.

After two years of it, I never bothered to go down and answer anymore, but just turned over and went back to sleep, thinking to hell with it, if they wanted me so bad, let them come up and get me. Other than that, my only other curious, psychopathic symptoms were strange (very strange) sexual dreams, when I'd sometimes hear the laughter of the old Stairwalkers in the background, sometimes feel them jumping around on the bed. I was too embarrassed to discuss these flashes of deviance with Dr. Williams, so I really can't say much about them except that they were real all right, real enough to make me come to orgasm the strength of which I've never felt awake.

But other than that, I was increasingly sane. Sane and tired and quiet as a mouse when my sister-in-law Candace flew into town for a couple of weeks in the middle of July in preparation for her husband's discharge from the Air Force in August. Michael had warned me she'd be around, said the children couldn't swim otherwise — a vote of no-confidence I made no argument with — only noting on our first meeting how much she resembled her mother, down to her dark blonde hair and small, wiry frame.

Other than that, I ignored her, even refused to shake the hand she gamely offered after I backed away from her first offer of a hug. As tactile by nature as her mother, she was obviously hurt by my cool reception, though it didn't stop her and Lori (her eleven-year-old, who'd been staying with Cissie since June) from showing up on my doorstep every morning at the ungodly hour of eight o'clock to swim. The only possible good I saw in any of it was that Candace partially made up for Gabe's absence as far as the children were concerned, as she was cut from the same maternal cloth, spending upwards of six hours a day with them out by the pool, cheering for Sim's swan dives and freeing Missy of the cursed life jacket when it was apparent she could swim the English Channel without it. She didn't even ask Michael's permission, just tossed it aside with a confidence I admired, though I admired it from afar, retreating to my sanctuary upstairs as soon as she showed her face every morning and lying there in bed, listening to the laughter downstairs with a sad resignation, feeling like a visitor in my own home, the proverbial crazy aunt, locked away in the attic.

After my first rebuff, Candace pretty much left me alone, her face polite, but as distant as Michael's had become until about twelve days into her visit, when she noticed me holding the arm hurt at the reunion protectively to my chest while I tried to pour Missy a glass of milk, managing to spill most of it on the counter.

"What's the matter with your arm?" she asked with all the confidence with which she'd thrown aside Missy's life jacket.

I only shrugged, though she insisted I hold it out for inspection, pushing up the sleeve of my housedress and making a noise of surprise at the swollen, shining skin that circled my arm a few inches above the elbow.

"How long's it been like this?" she asked, for Candace is a nurse by profession and a nurturer by inclination, not to mention stone-curious over her brother's strange wife, whom she vaguely remembered as the youngest of the raging white trash who in childhood had briefly lived across the fence. A quiet, nondescript child who wouldn't have entered into her attention at all in those last, halcyon days of high school if her goofball of a little brother hadn't gone insane with infatuation over her, if her father hadn't derailed her plans to go to medical school by getting himself damn near killed trying to save her.

"Couple weeks," I unbent enough to answer, as she isolated my shoulder and wiggled my elbow a little, then looked up in amazement.

"I think it's broken," she announced incredulously.

With no more discussion than that, she went to the phone and started making calls that I didn't stick around to listen to, just returned to my bed and lay there in perfect immobility, staring at the ceiling till she came up and told me she was taking me to the doctor. I assumed by doctor she meant Dr. Williams, and got dressed while she gathered the children in hand and piled us all in my car, taking the wheel to drive herself, not turning west at the highway, but east, toward Tallahassee.

"Friend of mine said he'd run a few films," she explained. "Then we won't have to sit around some stinking ER all day long."

I made no argument with that, just rode passively along, listening to the children in the back seat, who were alternately bickering and happy. Sim occasionally tried to draw me out in a smile, poking his head over the seat to point at something in the scenery, a hog or hawk or blooming crepe myrtle, telling Candace in a fond voice, "Mama likes trees."

Candace humored him, smiling aside, asking, "Does she?"

Her warmth was directed at Sim, not sending any particular message my way, of concern or contempt either one, her face quiet and thoughtful as we made the ER. She herded us in with no intimidation at all, leaving Lori in charge of the children and taking me straight through to the nurse's station, where she asked for someone — Gilbert, I think.

After a moment's wait, a young man in a lab coat came out to meet us, hugging her and offering me his hand, though I just stared at it, not in the mood to humor him. (Since when had shaking a man's hand done me any good?) He withdrew it after a questioning glance at Candace that she deflected with a smile, then took me through the tedious routine of X-ray: the gown and tables and hovering machinery.

But the tone of the morning was carefree, Candace and Gilbert standing outside the booth, protected by lead aprons and insulated walls, so caught up in their little reunion that the technician took far more film than was neccessary, not just of my arm, but my chest and legs, even my skull. I didn't complain, just submitted meekly to the flickers of invisible rays, then got dressed and waited in the lobby with the children till another nurse led me back to yet another examining room.

This one must have been in radiology, for it had an entire wall of screens, the bottom row lit with ghostly skeleton films of various joints and bones that were apparently mine, as Gilbert stood when I came in the door and tapped one of an upper arm.

"Clean break," he informed me. "Have yourself a little accident? Bad fall?"

When I didn't answer, he glanced at Candace with a little less curiosity than before, as if some explanation for my muteness had been offered, then kindly overlooked my rude silence to set my upper arm in a plaster cast, offering to do it in a color, if I wanted.

"White'll do," Candace answered, not giving me the luxury of a third stab at snubbing him.

When he finished the cast, he went to the sink and washed his hands, speaking to me over his shoulder. "So what'd you have?" he asked. "Car accident? Multiple fractures?" He jerked a handful of paper towels from the dispenser and turned. "Funny, nothing was set, not even the forearm."

"What forearm?" Candace asked, then turned to me. "Did you have a wreck?"

Before I could so much as shake my head, Gilbert answered, "Not the new one — the old breaks." He went back to the wall of X-rays and pointed at a small inflection of shadow between my elbow and wrist bone. "Unset, I think."

She joined him there, squinting up at the screen while he absently felt in the pocket of his lab coat for a pen and moved over to point it at an X-ray of my skull, tracing a small blur between the sharp bones of my eye sockets.

"See?" he repeated to Candace. "There. Hairline, at least, pretty damn close —" He glanced over at me when he said it, and something in my face made his eyes suddenly alight. "*Ah ha!*" he cried, and crossing the room in three strides, he tapped the little lightening scar between my eyes, then swung back around on Candace. "See? Right on the old noggin. Heck of a hairline. Almost," he mused, "a *crack.*"

He laughed aloud at his pseudo-diagnosis, though Candace seemed suddenly diverted, staring at the wall of X-rays with a particularly unreadable face that didn't revert to its good humor the whole time we waited. To Gilbert's continuing inquiry about old friends, she gave only short, terse answers, till the plaster was set, when she seemed to blink back to life, thanking him with all of her mother's charm, going through all the usual promises of getting together and remembering each other to their spouses.

He responded in kind, even walked us to the waiting room, to the children, who were fascinated by the cast, Lori and Sim painstakingly signing it on the way home. ("Get well!" one of them scribbled; the other, a more appropriate "Good luck!")

When we got home, I did about the only thing I was any good at those days: cooking lunch, hot dogs and green beans that I couldn't have eaten if you'd have put a gun to my head. Candace seemed bothered by my lack of appetite, though, and asked me if it was my arm; if it was hurting. I quickly shook my head, for the cast's hard casing had isolated the soreness for the first time in three weeks, such a relief that I went to the trouble to reassure her.

"It's better," I managed, then after a moment's groping, I tapped it with my knuckles to make my point. "Much better."

She looked at me with even more interest then, picking up on how difficult it was for me to communicate. She smiled a little and said, "Well, good."

She didn't speak again till the children had finished lunch and went roaring to the pool, when she paused in the doorway to turn and ask, "How'd you break it, anyway?"

I just looked at her on that; not in ignorance, or even rebellious noncompliance, but simply unable to describe Ira's iron grip on my arm and the dive to the concrete that really wasn't his fault, as I'd jumped him.

When I didn't answer, she finally asked, very quietly, "It wasn't Gabe, surely?"

I shook my head quickly at that. Gabe did some things, *awful* things, I hated to remember, but not like that. His ways of hurting were more subtle and more lasting, and after a moment's groping, I made another stab at the truth. "Gabe doesn't — break bones."

She just stared at me a moment, then repeated mildly, "Well, good." But she was obviously not satisfied, her face dim and curious, finally settling on an obvious piece of advice, telling me I needed to eat something; I was too thin.

Something about her — her quiet concern, or maybe her sheer resemblance to her mother — gave me the space to offer something further, an explanation of why I couldn't eat that came out as a thin echo of my old words of complaint: "I cain't. I don't *feel* good."

Even that simple statement took a little time and effort, and Candace was almost to the French doors when she turned, her chin lifted, not in Gabe's old audacious smile, but simple interest. "Really?" she said. "Maybe we need to get you some Tylenol or something."

"I *cain't*," I repeated, trying hard to make her understand the weird limitations of my life: the lithium and the pregnancy, the sickness and the cure, but it was no use. It was nearly inexplicable, making me stand there a moment, groping, then finally tell her bluntly, "I'm pregnant." Which was the reason I couldn't take Pamalor anymore. Dr. Williams said the lithium was enough of a risk, any other medication, simply not a possibility, if I intended to keep the baby.

At this simple announcement, Candace's eyes widened to the size of quarters. "You're *what?*" she breathed.

But her shock scared me off, making me drop my eyes and turn away in confusion, gathering plates and cups and busying myself with straightening the kitchen, while she marched back to the phone and started making another round of calls. She stretched the cord as far as it would go to stand in the privacy of the living room, though she was speaking so loud I could hear her openly combatant tone as she told someone, "Yeah? Well, I don't care what he's doing, I need to speak to him *right now.*"

I gave her a wide berth, though snatches of her aggrieved voice occasionally drifted out the open doors: "— didn't somebody *tell* me?" There was a pause, then she spoke with even more heat, "What's not to notice, Michael? She must have had bruises on her the size of *Nebraska* — he almost had to rebreak it." Then a final silence, and a massive sigh, "Yeah. Well, he don't sound like much of one to *me.* Sure. Bye."

She came back to the kitchen then, her face harassed but polite, and told me I could go upstairs and lie down if I wanted, that she'd stay with the children till Michael came home. I left in a flash, wanting to stay clear of what was looking to shape into another Catts War, though Candace stopped me as I made the door and apologized for the X-rays, her voice as close as it ever came to shame. "I didn't — Michael didn't tell me — you were pregnant."

I wondered for a moment what he *had* told her, but it really didn't matter. As long as she kept her distance, I didn't care, not really understanding what the fuss was all about; it wasn't like I'd never been pregnant before. I just waited till it was clear she was finished, then turned tail and escaped upstairs to listen to them frolic around the pool with a trace of my old outsider's melancholy, that awful sensation that everyone in the world was having a party, and I, the only child in class who wasn't invited.

Candace left two days later to go back to New Jersey to pack, leaving me in a six-week void that I hardly recall, though I remember her return in September well enough. Not just because the sight of her waving at me across the crowded vestibule at Welcome brought a little unexpected jab of pleasure to my heart, but because as soon as the crowd parted enough for her to get a full-length view, she just about went through the ceiling, pushing through the crowd and all but collaring her brother, asking, "What is *this?*"

Meaning, what was my arm still doing in the same old ratty cast,

Lori and Sim's jaunty messages faded and dim (*Get well! Good luck!*).
Michael, who didn't like to be second-guessed anyway, especially not in
the crowded vestibule of the church, told her to *hush,* that they'd talk
about it later.

But Candace had her mother's inability to shut up when she was
righteously annoyed, and just faced him evenly. "*Hush,* my behind.
What's your precious Dr. Williams got to say about that? Don't he know
how to cut off a damn cast?"

This last bit of profanity (right there in the open; Brother Sloan a
mildly interested bystander) was enough to draw Michael out in a cold
silence. He just turned and walked away, and that was all that was said
till later that afternoon, when a considerably subdued Candace woke me
up from my nap to cut off the cast with a pair of her mother's old sewing
scissors.

"Lay still," she warned, and with Sim and Missy an interested audience, she hacked and cut and unraveled till the spread was littered with
bits of plaster and snatches of gauze, my arm red and splotched and
bumpy, but otherwise fine.

Sim called dibs on what was left of the cast, wanting to take it to
school for show-and-tell, and with Missy in his wake, tore downstairs to
show his father his find, while Candace slapped the bits of plaster from
her lap.

"Better?" she smiled, and I nodded, for the hot old cast had been
itching me to death. She made a little business of gathering up the
debris, then paused a moment in the afternoon silence and looked at
me. "Myra," she said, then paused a moment, "it wasn't Michael, was it?"

We both knew what she was asking: was it Michael who'd broken
my arm, who'd left me with bruises the size of Nebraska? And with my
arm so wonderfully free and scratchable, I made the effort to set her
mind at ease, shaking my head emphatically, saying, "No. *No.*"

She was obviously not convinced, obviously deserved a little more
explanation, and in a effort to pay her back for freeing me from the torment of the cast, I stammered, "Ira. My brother, Ira."

She was visibly relieved at that, but I felt a need to clarify my
answer, watching her eyes, trying to make her understand. "We fell on
concrete," I said, taking a breath and diving for my little halting details

the same way I delved for bits of memory with Dr. Williams in our biweekly torture sessions, "at the springs. With Gabriel."

I could feel my face twisting at the mention of his name, my voice dropping to a bare whisper as I told her, "Ira beat him. Real bad."

I halted then, remembering Gabriel in the living room that night, his eyes filled with a pain so familiar that I sometimes confused him with memories of Ira as a child, their anguish was so alike. I felt a teardrop, warm and fat, cruise down my cheek that I wiped away, confused with all this remembering — the way I got in session with Dr. Williams, the reason I hated it so much. Because I hated the remembering; I hated the *hating*. Sometimes it was Mama I hated, sometimes Daddy. Sometimes I even hated Ira or God, or even Mr. Simon for not hearing me that night when I opened my mouth to call to him down the path — and it hurt so much to hate them. I really preferred just hating myself, because I was *tough,* I could take it.

That was the secret I held so gleefully to my chest as a child, the bit of divine revelation that had sustained me, though Dr. Williams wouldn't stand for it. He wouldn't let me be strong, he kept taking me back and back and it never seemed to end: the blood and the bruises, the slam of the concrete, the slam of a door, the tack that dug so deep I cried aloud —

"I don't like this *fighting,*" I whispered in as honest a confession as I'll ever make.

Candace just watched me with eyes that weren't particularly hurt or disgusted, just met mine squarely, commenting with her mother's level honesty, "I bet you *don't.*"

She sat on the edge of the bed when she said it and went back to picking at the bits of thread and powder as she spoke in a drier, firmer voice. "Well, don't worry about Gabe. He's all right. Mama talks to him." She glanced up. "And don't worry about any more of that *fighting,* neither. There won't be namore of thet, not while I'm here. I can kick both my brothers' butts in a red hot minute and both of them know it."

She smiled briefly when she said it, then went back to picking thoughtfully at the bits of cast. "That's what's wrong with this family," she mused. "The men're too hardheaded, the women all leave. I been thinking what we need around here is me and you starting one of those *Cissie-Maggie* things."

She went on to explain her logic in the matter, though she really didn't have to explain at all; I knew exactly what she meant. Everyone knew of Cissie and Maggie's devotion to one another, and how it had kept the Tierney family together, even through their father's philandering, their mother's early death. The other girls scattered as soon as they married, but Maggie and Cissie held the fort, kept the old ways, offered a home base for the others to return to, a reunion every other summer. They were more than sisters, they were allies, confidants, best friends. It was a relationship I envied more than any other in my life.

"So what about it?" she asked, holding out a hand for a good-natured shake. "I guess I'll do Maggie. You can be Cissie, God help us."

She finally grinned then, as she and her mother had had their share of battles, the most recent over Candace's infilling with the Holy Spirit (the Desolation of Abomination in Baptist circles in those days). But I didn't return her grin, I couldn't. All I could do was lift a timid hand to finally return her shake, two months after it was first offered, wondering why this smart, professional woman would possibly want to ally herself with someone as screwed up as me. I mean, men I always attracted, one way or another; women, hardly ever.

I simply couldn't understand it, and didn't, for many years to come, till the morning of September 28, 1987, when Candace and I were again thrown together in a hospital, waiting at six-thirty in the morning in a small anteroom off pathology for news we both instinctively understood would not be good. Something in Candace's fixed, nervous face reminded me of the day they'd set my broken arm, and after a dozen years of not giving it a second thought, I asked her what in the world she was thinking that day after Gilbert so humorously lined up the scar on my forehead with the old skull fracture, that had made her go quiet, her face so protracted and dim.

At first, she didn't remember the X-ray at all, then she blinked. "Oh. You mean the ones that fool Gilbert took, with you pregnant." She shook her head in amazement. "Wonder that boy's still in practice," she murmured, then began roaming around the room, tidying up with a nurse's instinctual efficiency, straightening lamps and closing drawers, answering aside with her usual rock-solid honesty.

"Actually, I wasn't thinking about you at all," she told me. "I was thinking about Daddy. All those unset fractures in your arm, your head, they reminded me of the night of the fight when they operated on him, removed his spleen. Dr. Winston had run a lot of film, called Mama in to tell her nothing was broken, that he was fine, except for the bleeding. But I could read X-rays by then and could see these strange little malformations all over his skeleton, *everywhere*. His hands, his knees, his ribs — and right above the hip bone there was this scatter of metal so clear you could see the jagged little perforated edges."

Candace paused a moment, absently regarding unlit boards, as if those shattered fragments were still lit upon the screen. "When Mama left, I asked Dr. Winston what all those malformations were about; he said it wasn't nothing to worry with, they were old. Said most men he saw — mill workers — had tons of unset bone from mill accidents, fights. Said the metal was shrapnel from the war, maybe buckshot. Probably shrapnel, from the jagged edges. He showed me some of them, the knee and hand ones, explained them like he was a forensic pathologist or something. He said," and on this, she took a ragged breath, "that people tend to forget old trauma. The skin closes, the muscle mends. The body forgets — but the bones never do."

She finally turned then and looked at me with eyes that were shiny with tears, already grieving. "And I guess that's what I was thinking that day, looking at that awful crack on your forehead, that clean break on your arm: that people forget. But our bones never do."

$= 23 =$

So began my third and final infatuation
with a child of Simon Catts, a relationship that in some ways has stood
the test of time better than the others, as I tend to get along with women
better than men, simply because I seldom, if ever, fight with them. Men
I scream at and cry over and slap when necessary, women I placate. Not
because of my father's many shortcomings, but maybe his one virtue: I
was always confident he loved me. I mean, it was a perverse love, one
that nearly ruined me, but I never doubted it, whereas Mama's love, that
was so indomitable to begin with, kind of drifted out to sea there, left
me stranded like a fish on a hot rock, an abandonment I've never quite
forgotten.

So despite my sure knowledge of the phenomenon, and God
knows how many years in therapy, I still tend to gravitate toward moth-
er-figures, worriers and nurturers, who join Cissie and Liz in my inner
court to reap the rewards therein: bridal showers for their daughters, a
steady stream of upscale hand-me-downs, prayers and tablecloths, and,
in Candace's case, a quarter million dollars cold hard cash. For such are
the rewards of the righteous, which Candace certainly earned in those
early months of my budding stability when she undertook the tedious

job of reintroducing me to the land of the living. They are months I don't so well remember, the recovery end of depression about as strange and, in some ways, as abrupt as the falling-down part, though Candace is given to fondly (and dramatically) recalling our early encounters.

"Like a wounded animal," is the way she describes me, with her mother's (and younger brother's) penchant for melodrama. "Burrowed away upstairs, skinny and beat-up, your arm in that ratty old cast."

"That was later," I usually correct (for, also like her mother and brother, she doesn't let the facts get in the way of a good story), "after you moved back. It wasn't ratty till then."

"Good thing I did," she always sniffs. "Your arm was about to rot off. That Dr. Williams was an idiot."

Which was not too much of a slur on the good doctor, as Candace had by then firmly made her evolution from a Good Baptist Girl to one of those most curious of all fundamentalist mutations, a Charismatic. Technically speaking, it simply means she's filled with the Holy Spirit with the evidence of speaking in tongues, though practically speaking, it's a whole lifestyle dedicated to family and country and God-knows-what-else, I've never quite figured them out, though I've been speaking in tongues since I was six.

In a nutshell, I guess you might describe a Charismatic as a combination of a Pentecostal and a witch doctor and an Amway salesman, with the legalism of the first, the mysticism of the second, and the hectoring sureness of the third. Thrown into the mix is a raging paranoia that bristles at every threat to the sovereignty of the Word, from Democratic politics to secular humanists, public education, the ACLU, feminists, and perhaps licensed psychiatry most of all — hence Candace's immediate distrust of Dr. Williams.

Fortunately, they are more forgiving of the wounded of the world, and Candace quickly adopted me like a stray puppy, partly because of the similarities between my poor old skeleton and her father's, partly because Michael took her aside the morning she'd publicly accused him, and while the rest of us were singing hymns down at Welcome, set her straight on a few home truths. He took her to the privacy of their mother's kitchen to do it, where he related the highlights of the previous two years in a patchwork of melodrama so astounding that Candace says she only half-believed him, pacing the whole time he talked, only stopping once — to ask her to drive out and check on the children sometimes, now that she was back.

"I'll pay you," he offered, to which she only stared.

"Pay me *what?*"

"*Money.*"

"To be your *sister?*"

"To be her *friend,*" he said, giving her a split-second insight into the desperation that had reduced him to bribing his family for loyalty, an offer Candace could hardly understand, thinking he had grown quite as eccentric as me. But she was pitying enough to extend herself, pro bono, as it were, for despite the narrow-mindedness of her beliefs, being truly a child of Simon Catts, Candace was (and is) fantastically kind-hearted, with an eye for the underdog, which, at the time, I most surely was.

So we did indeed begin one of those *Cissie-Maggie* things, and when I look back on my life, at the multitude of close calls and out-and-out miracles, the reappearance of Candace at that most pivotal juncture of my life strikes me as the most fortunate of all. Because only my own life was at stake in the earlier rescues; in this one, my children, primarily my youngest child, who was yet unborn and likely to stay that way, if not for Candace's intervention.

Aside from her, only Cissie showed any enthusiasm for my third pregnancy coming to fruition, though her support was weakened, as Maggie was in the last stages of lung disease, battling day and night in a way that siphoned off the best of Cissie's time, just as overwork and betrayal had siphoned off the best of Michael's. He never threatened the baby; abortion was never spoken of, except by my mother in shy, subtle digs, and much more openly by Dr. Williams, who even had the name and number of a clinic in Tallahassee that would do it.

"For your own good, Myra," he told me quietly, with none of the aggressive sleaze that usually accompanies such a suggestion, just a simple *let's-nip-this-thing-in-the-bud* common sense.

When I shook my head, quickly, he backed off with no further word of persuasion, unlike Mama, who brought it up every week in a barrage of Saturday night phone calls to check up on me. She was so subtle that I hardly understood her constant inquiries about what week was I in — fourth? Eighth? Tenth? Till I was at the end of my first trimester, when she openly told me it was getting late, I'd better make up my mind.

"About what?" I asked, and she had enough vestige fundamentalism in her to balk at the actual word. "About taking care of that — *pregnancy.*"

It wasn't until years later that I understood her suggestion. At the time, I only replied in perfect innocence, "I *am* taking care of it. Go to Dr. Winston every month."

I'm sure the phrase *ain't got good sense* must have gone through Mama's mind on such occasions, though to her credit, she didn't hound me too much about it after my fourth month when her solicitous calls came to a complete halt. I never complained of her abandonment, for in the same fashion Cissie had once stepped in to fill a maternal gap, Candace now did, in ways that are difficult to explain, they are so routine.

I guess it'd be most accurate to say that she gave me back my voice, for in those early months, I was still very quiet. Not voluntarily, but simply because I'd forgotten what it was like to have an opinion, to voice a preference, and still couldn't converse so easily, having to think and think for the right words. It was as if I'd suffered a massive head injury, Candace my physical therapist, who filled in the empty spaces with all sorts of talk, mostly details of life I'd never quite connected with, always having been separated by that wall of silence and fear.

In a way, you might say it was a replay of my fascination with Gabe as a child, when I was so quickly pulled into his world, for Candace offered the same ringing confidence, the same we're-all-friends-here camaraderie, but with none of the stinging sexual undertones, none of the possessiveness.

And though I don't remember many of the details of life in the months before Clay's birth (wounded animal that I was), I do recall the practical highlights of her hard-headed support well enough: how she'd come by the house nearly every day with Lori in tow, to swim when it was warm, and later, babysit while I went to my doctor's appointments. This wasn't a small favor, as I had Dr. Williams to attend twice a week (much to Candace's disgust), along with Dr. Winston and the high-risk pregnancy clinic in Gainesville, where I'd been referred because my hitherto faithful cervix didn't seem to like the idea of a third child any more than my psychiatrist or my mother.

To their credit, both of my doctors jumped into action at the first sign of miscarriage, though Candace was my main support, even taking me to Gainesville where they did the sonagram in my eighth month, holding Missy to the video screen so she could touch the grainy black-and-white blur the doctor said was another brother.

"How can you tell?" Sim asked, and Candace, whose beliefs have put her at war with most of Western civilization, but thankfully not robbed her of a certain country realness, answered for him.

"'Cause he's got a weenie. See?"

She pointed it out on the grainy screen, managing to turn both Sim's and the young resident's faces bright red, though I was only mesmerized by the wiggling blob of static that was Claybird's first image on earth.

"So what're you two thinking of for names?" she asked me on the long drive home, her casual curiosity making me a little uncomfortable.

"We haven't talked about it much," I admitted in an understatement of Goliath proportions.

The fact of the matter was, Michael and I had gone our separate ways. As of July, he'd taken up permanent residence on the couch downstairs and only spoke to me in routine matters of childcare with the polite distance of a concerned neighbor. I never complained, as the root of our separation certainly wasn't a mystery to me. Unlike my fellow vixens on *As the World Turns*, I had a pretty good idea who the father of my baby was (I was crazy that summer, not *stupid*) and with the help of Dr. Williams' assault on forgetfulness, had begun to retrieve a goodly store of memory. None of it was particularly nasty or explicit, just small, disconnected impressions, of Gabriel's hot, sun-tipped face that would lift in greeting when I came to the door every afternoon, of walking down a crowded midway with him hand in hand, mesmerized by a carnival hawker's carrying tease (*"Hey pretty lady, step right up —"*).

The images didn't fill me with the raging self-hatred the ones of Tommy had, but played out as numbly as the reels of an old movie, and aside from the discomforts of a difficult pregnancy and the side effects of the lithium (a terrific thirst and a constant urge to pee) I really didn't have such a bad time of it that winter. Even the ocean of silence between Michael and me came to me as a space of peace, a quiet death I was no longer so terrified of, coming across a Proverb in my nightly Bible reading that seemed to distill the essence of my contentment: *The full soul loatheth a honeycomb; but to the hungry soul, every bitter thing is sweet.*

It was a complex thought for me to digest, and, at first, only the ending made sense: to a hungry soul like me, every bitter thing — an unwanted pregnancy, a broken marriage, scarred fingers and ears and unset bone — all of them were sweet, compared to the torment of disassociation, of insanity. I even grew used to sleeping alone — reversing my position to lie with my head at the foot of the bed so I could watch the old oak outside the window, slowly waving in the breeze through the dark spaces of the night — awaking in mid-February to the sound of voices in the yard below.

For a moment I thought it was another visit from the Stairwalkers, except the voices weren't filmed in sluggish laughter, but sharp and low on the cold winter night. I sat up after a moment, then rolled clumsily out of bed and went to the window, where just below in the gravel of the drive, a handful of men were unloading lumber in the steady light of a three-quarter moon.

I recognized one of them, Joe Bates, who visibly started when I lifted the sash of the window, though he spoke to the others in a calm, placating voice. "Just his wife —" he said, "s'all right."

He said something else in a quieter voice I didn't catch, then called up a pleasant greeting: "Hey, Myra. Whatchu doing, honey?"

"Nothing," I answered easily, my calm answer bringing a shadow of relief to the stiff backs of the strangers, whom Joe was continuing to reassure, speaking aside in a low, carrying voice. "— mind ain't right. Nah, she's harmless." Then to me, "Where's your husband, darlin'?"

"At work," I answered vaguely. "Or downstairs. Want me to git him?"

He grinned at that, said, "No, baby. Go on back to sleep."

I took his advice, carefully lowering the window and returning to bed. I heard the truck start up a few minutes later, but didn't think too much about it, as Michael was in and out so much these days.

Sometimes, on one of my half dozen trips to the bathroom, I'd hear the television downstairs and peer over the rail to the living room to find him asleep on the couch in his work clothes, surrounded by ledgers and loose paper and an empty plate where he'd eaten a late supper. I'd almost smile at the scene, for he looked rested, his face slack in the forgetfulness of sleep, wonderful to me, still.

But I never went down to turn off the television, never put up his plate or kissed him good-night, the wall between us as smooth and impenetrable as glass, which neither of us had the energy or desire to challenge.

"Does he always work so much?" Candace once asked me, and I was loyal enough to make a stab at an excuse, talking of our expenses: the new baby, the car. Candace was unconvinced. "Then how in the world did he buy Sanger?"

I only shrugged in reply, as my grocery budget was the same as it'd been since we left the Hill: twenty-five dollars a week, including prescriptions and diapers. But even that wasn't the burden it had been, as I was no longer alone in my fight to make ends meet. For Ed was trying to break into the construction business, and as long as Candace had a child at home, she refused to work. Together, she and I fought the good fight of frugality, living our lives on coupons, even going so far as to grow Missy and Lori's hair out because it was cheaper to braid than have cut.

Until then, Michael's budgets had been a torment to me, but with Candace's support it became a game of wits that I evidenced an unexpected precocity in. The only other area I could be said to outshine her was with the one gift my mother had handed down to me from childhood: a genius for braiding hair. It was nothing she'd ever actually sat me down and taught me, my hands seeming to move of their own volition, twisting and dividing and tightening in an incredible array of any braids Candace could describe. She even grew out her own hair out so I could reverse braid it for formal occasions, the results creating enough of a sensation that even the frosty women of Welcome thawed enough to shyly ask if I'd mind braiding their daughters' hair for weddings and proms and family portraits.

And though none of them had really ever treated me with any more welcome than they had my mother, I went out of my way to oblige them, for I was touched by something of Mama's long-lost affection when I'd feel my hands moving according to their own creativity, as if I were conjuring the love she'd once had for me, making a place for her in their circle at last. Before long, Candace and I were being invited to Tupperware parties and showers and mothers'-mornings-out on the same card, a miracle I still marvel at, the mystery of how one connection of love can join you to the rest of the world the way a river joins a solitary raindrop to the sea.

I guess it was nothing more complex than the simple miracle of friendship that struck me with such force because I was so late in discovering it, so taken with it by the day of Clay's birth that it wasn't Michael I wanted with me in the delivery room, but his sister. For reasons I couldn't especially understand, they were planning a cesarean, a silly precaution with my cervix dilated for the better part of three months. But I didn't complain, just went to the hospital at my appointed time as if I were having my teeth cleaned, got prepped and readied, then wheeled into a surgery suite where Candace was waiting, all masked and gowned, joking around with the anesthesiologist.

"Sure you don't want a few more days of peace?" Dr. Winston teased me while they prepped my arm. "He's a bounder, I can already tell."

I just shook my head, and my last memory before his birth was the sting of the IV needle. I blinked awake in Recovery with Lori and Sim and Missy jogging for a position on the bed rail, yelling out bits of news about the baby.

"They done give him a bath," Sim cried, while Lori tried to outshout him.

"— named him *Clayton,* after Grandaddy Tierney!"

Which was certainly news to me. Michael and I hadn't so much as discussed formula preferences, much less naming my son after an old reprobate like his grandfather, and I blinked at her. "What?"

"Clayton," Sim shouted. "Daddy named him. Said he'd leave the last name for you."

For one awful moment, I thought he was making sarcastic reference to the baby's doubtful paternity, and felt sharp, bitter tears behind my eyes, so hard and immediate that I couldn't hold the baby, I was crying too hard. I had mostly recovered when Michael came in later in the evening and clarified the matter with his usual reasonableness. "They needed a name for the bracelet, so I did the first one, left you the middle."

I was relieved, but belatedly relieved, my sadness too set by then, and when I was discharged four days later, I still hadn't come up with a middle name for the fat little cherub who'd made his appearance on Earth unmarked by the birth struggle — as beautiful as, well, an *angel.* (Or so said his clueless grannie, who went on for two years about the remarkable resemblance between him and his Uncle, reminding all the friends and relations who would just as soon have forgotten that *he looked like an angel and she named him for an angel.*)

There was some hospital policy that I couldn't leave until I'd filled out his official registration card, and on the morning of my discharge, while Candace and Lori hauled my stuff to the car, I sat on the edge of the bed with the little paper in my hands, and tried to think of a middle name. I was superstitious about names, determined to offset his first name, which I associated with fast women and wobbly morals, with an upstanding middle one, but with the clock ticking out, I couldn't come up with anything.

Nothing on my side of the family would do, certainly not Ira or Leldon, nor even Grandaddy Edmonds (his character suited me; his name, Edlow, didn't), nor any of the popular choices that were floating around those days: Sean or Chris or Matthew. I was sitting there, teeter- ing on the edge of committing the unpardonable Southern sin of launching a child into the world with one name, when they brought Clayton to me for discharge.

He was a fat little thing, my Clayton was, a favorite in the baby nurs- ery because of his sound sleep and unlooked-for spunk in peeing in Dr. Winston's face when he took off his diaper to circumcise him. But to my eyes, there was a fragility about his clinging good nature, a need for security that bothered me. As far as I could see, he was embarking on a life without a father, a disability no one knew better than I, and I des- perately wished he had one ounce of the Cissie-Catts, know-it-all confi- dence of my Missy; God knows he'd need it.

But he didn't; I knew it as simply and quickly as that. He was a Myra on that account, a searcher and a snuggler with a basic need to belong. And though I was far beyond wasting my fragile resources on useless regret, there was a hopelessness about that blank space between his names that almost made me despair, when someone came to the door, Candace, I thought, but when I looked up, it was Michael.

"Ready?" he asked, looking around for the clutter that usually accompanies dismissal. "Where's your stuff?"

"Candace has it," I told him, his face registering nothing — love for the baby, annoyance that I'd made arrangements without consulting him.

Nothing but a laconic "Well? That it?"

I shifted Clayton around to hand him the registration form. "I cain't think of another name."

He took it from me and looked over it, maybe noting that he'd been presumptuously named as father. It was an inaccuracy he didn't argue with, and I guess I could have been more grateful, though I couldn't help but think it a very different scene from my other hospital dismissals. With Simon, he'd been so in love that he would have let me name him Leldon, if I'd wanted; with Missy, only a little warring (he wanted Renee; I only got Anne after a little persuasion).

This time, there was no discussion at all. He just took the form and dropped it off at the nurse's station, then left Candace to take me home along with the flowers from the WMU and free diapers and a case of soy formula. It didn't make for the most triumphant homecoming of the century, though the real twist didn't surface till a couple of months later after the little registration card cleared vital statistics in Tallahassee and made its way back to the house in the form of a birth certificate, all typed and sealed and official.

I had walked Clay down the drive to get the mail that day, and after a glance at the completed form, was surprised to see that the space designated for a middle name had been filled in after all, in such a way that made me stop dead still in amazement. God knows I hadn't been presumptuous enough to name him *that,* and I didn't know what to make of it, worrying over that little square of documentation all day long, till I finally worked up the nerve to speak to Michael about it. I waited till the children were in bed before I went downstairs in my gown, pausing at the back of the couch, and prefacing my words with a nervous, "Michael."

He was watching a baseball game in extra innings, his attention half-hearted when he glanced up at me, said, "Yeah?"

I didn't know how to tell him that the certificate was wrong, and embarrassingly wrong at that, and only twisted it in my hands a moment. Then, too ashamed to voice the error, I handed it to him over the couch and waited for his reply, which was a quick glance, then a bored, "What?"

"His name," I said. "It's wrong."

Michael glanced at it again, then flipped it back over the couch so casually that I jumped to catch it in midair. "Then change it," he said, his voice so different: not Michael at all, but short and clipped, not giving a damn about anything anymore, me nor Clayton, neither one.

I just watched him a moment, sitting there with his eyes on the game, a lapful of work orders and packaging receipts stacked on the floor around him, and for the first time in maybe a year, tried for contact, swallowing my pride to ask, "How long can this go on?"

I didn't specify what I meant by *this* and I didn't have to. We both knew what I meant: this estrangement, this marriage, this quiet death. He didn't answer, just kept watching the television, till I pressed him. "*Michael.*"

He unbent enough to give me a thread of attention then, his face no longer distant, just tired and defiant, hollow around the eyes in a way that made him look older, oddly vulnerable. It was a face that begged to be comforted, to be touched, but when I made a move toward him, he stopped me with a quiet word. "No," he said, and even lifted a tired hand like a crossing guard, dropping it after a moment and returning to the game with a quiet shake of his head, *no.*

That was all; I mean, what else was there left to say? He wasn't buying anymore, and who could blame him? I didn't argue, just went back upstairs without a word, the little registration form still clutched in my hand. When I called the nurse's station on OB the next morning to vent my rage at their idiot presumption, I was transferred to the unit clerk, an old Welcome girl by the name of Sue Holder, who was inexplicably unconcerned.

"We didn't mess up nothing," she assured me. "Michael filled it out before he left. Candace was kidding him about it — didn't he tell you?"

Well, no, he didn't, and after a stumbled apology, I hung up the phone and stared at the certificate, not quite sure what to make of it. I finally decided that while it might be over between Michael and me, maybe it wasn't over between him and my baby. For in the space provided for a middle name, he'd apparently gone to the nurse's station and filled in the blank himself, with Candace standing there teasing him for being egotistical enough to bestow on both sons his own name. *Clayton Michael Catts,* it read, the only one of our children he named himself.

— 24 —

You might call the spring of Clayton's birth my Last Great Age of Perfection, when I desperately sought to repay Michael's incredible favor in offsetting his grandfather's suspect name with his own sterling one by using every weapon at my disposal to try and make my marriage succeed, an undertaking that around these parts we call trying to *satisfy a man.* It's an art, like the art of a good kiss, that seems to have fallen by the wayside these days, a casualty of feminism, I expect, or simple impatience. For it's a thankless job, even for me, a woman raised in the art of the flattering smile, the well-cooked roast, the clean house, and the deferred opinion. In my day, Alabama girls were schooled in such niceties, and once I had Clayton settled in his own little bedroom, all named and secure, I took up the task of making my husband happy even if I couldn't touch him, cooking and cleaning and even becoming Cissie's assistant in her primary Sunday School class.

When these trappings of respectability still didn't turn Michael's head (or keep him home nights where he belonged), I went to the extreme of buying clothes of my own for the first time in my life. This proved to be an unexpectedly difficult proposition, as my taste in per-

sonal attire was seemingly forever polluted by my mother's expecta-
tions, and at twenty-six, I still gravitated toward clothing in what you
might call the *hot mama* category: tight T-shirts and tighter skirts, hal-
ters and bikinis and spike heels.

I knew Michael had always found my taste a bit on the white-trash
side, even when I had the fragile shield of a good reputation to protect
me. Now, with my sin ever before me (twelve pounds, eleven ounces of
him), I was determined to assume a more conservative facade, though I
didn't know how to go about it till Candace and Lori (who at fourteen,
had the taste of a forty-year-old) stepped in, and by the grace of
Mastercard, introduced me to my new look, which you might call
khakied gentry. It's a style popular in the old-money areas of the South
that sings with pressed khaki and navy and snowy white shirts, Bass
loafers and, in season, white thong sandals. The look was so understated, so country-clubbish that I felt like a clone of Tom Sanger myself, all
pressed and tan and thin, though Candace (who had adopted the look
in college with the zeal of the convert) assured me it was *perfect.*

"Never wear pink lipstick," she told me with the same fanaticism
she advised me to never vote for a democrat, "but rusts and browns and
cinnamons. And never wear red. You ever thought about getting one of
those bust-reducing bras?" (As a matter of fact, I hadn't. God knows that
was one way of *satisfying a man* they never taught us in Alabama.)

But on most things, I obeyed without question, going to any
lengths to satisfy a man who seemed particularly resistant to satisfaction.
Who continued to treat me with the polite distance of a stranger, at least
till he came across the credit card receipts for all that pressed khaki,
when he faced me off with something akin to his old passion. "What the
hell d'you think you're doing, Myra, buying all this *shit?*"

What I thought I was doing was pleasing him. When it was obvious
I wasn't, I meekly chalked up my inability to *satisfy a man* alongside my
list of other failings and eventually gave a lot of it away, the smaller stuff
to Lori, the larger, to my new maid, Louisa. A great aunt of Sam's, Louisa
was another facet of our image that Michael insisted on, who came in
three days a week to clean house, though in my rage to *satisfy,* I didn't
leave her much to clean. She mostly just stood around the kitchen, fussing at the children like she owned the place, as unimpressed with my

new look as Michael, once asking me why I wanted to wear all that tan.

"It's khaki," I told her. She just sniffed at the ways of white folk, though when she found out the price of a good khaki shirtdress from Belk's, she nearly fainted.

"Does it wash good?" she asked in honest amazement.

I assured her it did, but by summer, with the lithium providing a base-level sanity and Dr. Williams finally content with the depth of his burrowings, I began to tire of the charade, all of it: the perfection, the thinness, even the nights alone in bed. I guess you'd say that my soul was transforming from the hungry to the full stage, the stage where you loathe a honeycomb, if that honeycomb is empty enough, all of it coming to a head on yet another Fourth of July, a year to the day from my first dive to the concrete with Ira, at of all things, *another* family reunion.

This one was a world away from the reunion of a year ago, one I wasn't forced to attend out of loyalty to Liz, but loyalty to Mama. After a year of cold silence, she'd finally come down in June to see her newest grandson, though once she got here, she paid him little mind, her eyes so full of everything else: the house, the maid, even me and my cinnamon-lipped perfection. Poor Mama was quite bowled over by it all, and when I walked her to her car that night, she came up with one of the most amazing Plans that had ever been thrust upon me: that I host the July reunion right there, at the house.

"No need to go running off to some crowded spring," she reasoned with one of her thin, fragile smiles. And though I'd just as soon chop off an arm as entertain forty acres' worth of family on the hottest day of the year, I agreed, for it was seldom enough Mama made a request of me, seldom enough that I was able to oblige her. I agreed with an equally fragile smile and set myself to the task that very night, writing out invitations and making phone calls, actually beginning to enjoy myself till Michael came home from work and neatly defused my excitement with his simple outrage.

"A *what?*" he cried.

"A reunion — you know, like Cissie and Maggie —"

"I *know* what they are," he snapped. "Call Eloise, tell her it's off. Tell her I'm working."

On that, he went upstairs for his shower, leaving me sitting on the couch, knee-deep in two dozen invitations and a budding outrage of my own, not at his opposition as much his contempt. It wasn't contempt of the Leldon-Sims variety, not slapping, spitting, tooth-displacing contempt, but dismissive contempt, another aspect of Tom Sanger he'd picked up, of the *shut-up-and-do-what-I-say,-idiot* school of management.

There was a time, and not so long ago, that I would have crept away from such a challenge, and it's a measure of how completely I had identified with my new mentor that I kept on filling out the invitations and sent them out the next morning without a word. So durable was our silence in those days that we simply never discussed it again, even after my relatives started calling in their RSVPs, all of them agreeing to come, even Ira, who had apparently moved back to Birmingham.

I hadn't spoken to him since the fight last year, but after a few stinted moments, we fell back to our old warmth, letting bygones be bygones in the old Sims fashion, ignoring last year's savagery as if we'd been drunk when we'd taken it to the concrete with such ferocity. Michael was rightly disgusted, but I have always reveled in those short interludes of peace among my brother and mother and me, and as the big day drew near, I increasingly transferred my *satisfying a man* energies to satisfying a woman, namely, my mother, cleaning and polishing and pruning, even asking Louisa to wax the baseboards, a request she didn't think much of.

"Why?" she asked. When I told her about the reunion, she was amazed. "With Maggie sick?" I told her, no, it was a reunion of *my* family, the Edmonds-Sims. On the Sims part, she cocked an eye, asked, "Michael know about this?"

Not having grown up around a maid, I didn't understand the complexities of the relationship, nor the sheer gossipy closeness of the entire McRae clan, and had no inkling of just how much of my business they knew (though I'd find out soon enough). I just assured her Michael knew all about it, as he in fact did — he must have, with all the calling and arrangements. He had offered no further word of outrage (nor support, for that matter) but as the big day dawned, his need for a perfected front began to assert itself, as he woke early and took Missy and Sim into town to buy a new blade for the mower. Our guests weren't expected till after lunch, so I put Clay in his swing and took care of the final details, icing a cake and bringing in magnolias and hydrangeas, arranging them on the mantles, strangely exhilarated with the prospect of redeeming last year's disaster with a face of genteel perfection.

In just such kindly pursuits I wiled away the final morning of the Last Great Age of Perfection, happy as a dog (as Clay used to say) right up till the moment Michael and the children returned from town, much later than I'd expected, almost past one. I was just about to pick up the phone to call Cissie to see if she'd seen them, when Sim tore in the French doors with a short new buzzcut, his face scarlet with excitement.

"Missy got her hair cut!" he shouted, and before I could even turn, Missy herself ran in, her brilliant hair chopped off above the shoulders and molded into a stiff, lacquered page boy.

"They cut off a bunch!" she cried. "A yard, I bet." I smiled blankly, though I instinctively recoiled from a smooth helmet cut on my free-spirit of a girl, whose wild, coarse hair so easily lended itself to my intricate braids. "D'you like it?" she asked.

But I was too stunned to answer and just stammered, "Who cut it?"

"Cassie Campbell," her father answered as he came in, lifting his cap to take a swipe at his own newly shorn hair. "Said it'd be cooler for the summer."

My smile disappeared at the news that Cassie (formerly Scales) had taken it upon herself to deprive me of my chief joy in motherhood, though I didn't say a word. I didn't have to; Michael read my face. He must have, as he let out a tremendous *don't-tell-me-you're-going-to-make-a-big-deal-out-of-this* breath, and, suddenly, I was mad. It wasn't my old stomping, slapping, I-hate-your-guts mad, but a dry, quiet rage at this violation of my territory that I wasn't about to let pass, though the words weren't so easy to lay hands on. I just stood there and sputtered while Michael sent the children to change into their bathing suits, waiting till they were upstairs to face him, ask in a fast, angry rush, "Well, who'll pay for it the next time, Michael? I cain't. I cain't afford *diapers.*"

But he wouldn't be drawn into another of our old arguments about his cheapness, and just picked up the mower blade and answered shortly, "*I* will. Don't worry it."

On that, he headed outside to finish his mowing without another word, case closed, end of discussion. But I'd been around Candace too much that year to be put aside so easily and followed him resolutely, catching him on the deck and grabbing his arm. "Well — you could have asked," I stammered. "I don't like page boys. Her hair's too wavy. It'll never stay."

He just stood there, deliberately staring at my hand till I let go, then lifted his face and met my eye, said very evenly, "Well, I don't like her in braids."

Something in his level, unblinking honesty silenced me a moment with a sudden inkling of what he was trying to say, but I pressed him anyway. "Why not?"

He knew what I was doing: pushing him to tell the truth, to get it out. To quit with all this lawn-mowing, pressed-khaki bullshit and face facts, bud, and with a glint of his old Michael honesty, he did just that, meeting my eye and answering in that same level voice: "'Cause it makes her look too much like *you*."

And though I knew what he was going to say before he said it, it didn't lessen the impact that struck like a mule kick, so hard that it made my milk come down with a sharp little sting in my breasts. I was literally struck speechless and just stood there blinking at him, when there was a noise beside us, a car pulling up on the gravel that signaled the start of the reunion. Over the beep of a horn, the shout of the children, I heard myself tell him in an equally honest voice, "I'm going home with Mama tonight. I ain't ever coming back."

I turned on my heel on that and left him there with no further word of excuse or argument or persuasion, for what was left to say? We had each other's number — we'd always had each other's number — from the first smile he flashed over the tailgate of his truck, a lifetime ago on that hot morning in October. And while moving back to Mama's would be awful, anything — moving back on the Hill with Daddy — would be easier than watching this man turn against me, saying those nasty things, right to my face. I'd already shamed him, stolen his honor, his very name. If I hung around much longer, I'd have him turned into a Sims, too.

The car in the drive was Liz, who had a carload of picnic supplies that we lugged around back, her compliments on the house the only ones I appreciated that day, as the rest of the family's comments smacked with a barely disguised envy that was probably Mama's inadvertent handiwork. She must have spent the entire month of June on the phone, building up the house, the car, even Sanger, as my guests knew more about my business than I did myself. It was obviously a hard pill for my Louisiana relations to swallow, all but a few of them making it clear that while I might be rich now, I was still just a Sims, after all, and no one to be taking on airs with people who owned bottom land and honored marriage vows and bore children who actually resembled their husbands.

"How's thet left hook?" a few of the men asked with a grin, as if my fight with Ira last year had been nothing more than a good-natured shuffle. Even worse was the inevitable to-do over Clay's blonde hair that I found a little taxing as the day wore on, as some of them commented on it in front of Michael; one or two said it to his face. "See you finally got yoursef a towhead," one of my Alabama cousins grinned. "What you git for marrying out of Louisiana."

All of it was spoken in a good-natured fun that only made it worse, my face taking on a permanent fixity at their tactlessness, wondering if the idiots thought a house and Cadillac and a factory turned your heart to stone? Michael seemed oblivious to it, though, just went about the role of host with his usual precision, his face equally hard and tired, as if nothing any of my kin ever said or did would ever surprise him again. In that point, if no other, we were in complete agreement, at least until Ira and Mama showed up with a carload of relations I couldn't quite place, till I realized with a little shock of recognition that they were some of Ira's old football buds from Birmingham, two or three of them actual *Butt-slappers.*

"Brought along a few extra mouths to feed," Ira said, hugging me with no reserve at all, then passing me on to Mama's warm embrace and exclamation on how nice the house looked.

"Got a marble pool," she told one of the Butt-slappers with a fond smile, though when I told her I needed to talk to her privately, her smile disappeared. "Later," she said.

I backed off immediately, for I knew it wouldn't be easy, talking her into letting me come home with three children, but where else could I go? Birmingham wasn't my idea of paradise, but it had taken me in as a child, given me a measure of protection, offered a new life. Sure, it was a hard-working, no-frills kind of life, a far cry from the prospects Florida had once offered, happiness as wondrous and fleeting as a fever-dream, that had turned as hollow for me as it had my father, bitter in the end.

Bitter as gall, as Cissie would say, and once I left these sun-scorched shores, I'd never come back, never again. I'd work and slave, save and cajole. I'd raise my children to put aside the illusion of faith and high hopes and fruitless stabs at reconciliation and fight for tangibles, to count on survival, and nothing more. Hard plans, they seem in retro-spect, but if there was one lesson the Catts had taught me, it was the price you paid for extending yourself: broken hearts, broken ribs, rup-tured spleens and nights alone on a narrow couch, comfortless and betrayed. An awful price, I thought, like Polo shirts and Bass loafers, lux-uries none of us poor folk from the Hill could really afford.

With such thoughts I comforted myself that day, though any prospect of a kinder life in Birmingham quickly dimmed as Ira and his buddies took the party by storm. It was obvious they'd made a few pit stops for beer along the way as they were loud and boisterous, elbowing the children out of the deep end of the pool and eating enough for an army, to Liz's unconcealed annoyance. "Who brought along the *boys?*" she asked me privately in the kitchen. When I said Ira, she rolled her eyes. "I might have guessed," she muttered. Then, "Where's his wife?"

Not with him, apparently, and as the day wore on, there was a cer-tain amount of talk that Dana would make no more appearances at our reunions, as she and Ira were no longer a family. But I was in no mood to discuss the matter with my own divorce slowly materializing on the horizon, and just busied myself by counting the hours till sunset, not laughing at Ira or his buddy's antics, nor smiling at their good-ole-boy flirts that included the old standby: "What's a ugly son of a bitch like Ira doing with a good-looking sister like you?"

"Nothing that concerns you," I would have replied if I wasn't so damned tired of it all, dreading a life in Birmingham that with a reputa-tion like mine would be a study in fending off the vultures of the world. You could tell by their smirking familiarity that Ira hadn't been too dis-creet about my past, and far from being repelled by it, they were a wee

bit excited, one of them following me to the stairs when I went to put Clay down for his nap, offering to tuck me in.

I just looked at him evenly, but didn't answer, though I locked the door behind me when I got to Clay's room, not in fear as much as the certainty that if he laid so much as a finger on me, I'd rip his face off, grin and all, which might put a damper on any offer of a ride back to Birmingham.

By the time I got Clay asleep, the shadows of the old pine were stretching out across the yard, the long summer afternoon seeming to go on forever in all its sweating glory. The older guests had all retreated to the shade of the old oak at the far end of the yard, leaving the house itself oddly silent — empty, I thought, till I turned the corner to the kitchen and came upon Michael standing at the sink chipping ice. I hadn't spoken so much as a word to him since I told him I was leaving and didn't then, only put Clay's bottle away in a dead silence that he finally broke with one terse, quiet comment.

"And you're running back to *that,*" he said, his eyes on the frivolity around the pool: the adolescent laughter of the Butt-slappers, the aimless shouts. His voice was weighted with a sad, deliberate challenge like the one I'd offered him on the deck that I didn't rise to, I couldn't anymore.

I was all risen out, and just turned long enough to meet his eye and answer with an equally tired honesty. "They'll just treat me like a tired old whore. So what's new about that, Michael?"

I didn't give him a chance to argue the point, just went back to my lawn chair on the deck, though when I sat down, I realized my face was wet, that I must have been crying when I said it. But it didn't matter. Sometimes in the game of choosing the lesser of evils, you make tough decisions, ones not particularly in anyone's best interest, that you live to explain and justify, deny and defend, the rest of your natural-born life. Alabama was one of them, though Mama still didn't look too interested in our little talk, moving around her sisters and kin, laughing about the pool in a way that simultaneously underscored its quality and its foolishness in one breath.

I just sat there with my eyes closed, feeling the pound of the sun on my face, praying the end was near, when, to my great annoyance, Ira started a pick-up game of baseball in the far end of the field that drew off the young men, primarily the Butt-slappers, and a few odd uncles and cousins, plus little Sim, the youngest of the bunch. The crowd under the oaks gamely relocated their chairs to watch, though I had had enough partying for one day and went back inside to check on Clayton, pack a few things, try to get the house in order before I left.

I was working my way through a mountain of dishes, dreading the last phone call I figured I owed Candace (she detested divorce possibly more than pink lipstick or democrats), when Liz opened the French door and called, "Myra. Come watch the game." I made a few noises of excuse about needing to clean up, but she just cocked her head toward the sound of laughter and cat-calling that carried on the early twilight and grinned. "You gotta see this."

She gave no more explanation than that, just waited by the door till I dried my hands and followed her down to the clearing under the trees where everyone had gathered. The late sun was still blazing away, the players spread out on a makeshift diamond in a conspicuously unbalanced game, Ira and the Butt-slappers facing off Michael and little Simon, who was hopping with excitement out on second base, calling, "Mama! Look! We're winning! They cain't get a hit!"

And they couldn't. With no fanfare at all, Michael was working out his marital frustrations by striking them out, one after the other, whack, whack, whack. Liz sat us down behind first base, laughing her butt off and yelling catcalls at her fellow Alabamans that had them a little red in the face, one or two shouting for her to *shut up*. She just ignored them and explained between pitches that it'd started out a good-natured competition between the Alabama boys and the Florida ones, but the old men had pooped out after a few innings, leaving just Michael and Sim out there in a lopsided contest to see if the young bloods of Alabama could get a run off them. It'd been apparent after a dozen fruitless swings that they couldn't, but instead of admitting defeat, they'd started in on their own catcalls and insults, till Michael had upped the ante and bet that they couldn't so much as take a base.

"Got a hundred bucks riding on it," Liz grinned. "*Ira's* idea."

So it was Michael against the world, but he didn't look too affected by the challenge, his face blank, his hair slicked to his head where he kept taking off his cap and swiping at it between pitches, his attention all on his opponents, none left for anyone else, even me. As I sat there, I began to feel the shape of the scenario forming here, understood why she'd dragged me out to witness this moral victory of the polite over the rude, the sober over the drunk, the wage-earners over the Butt-slappers of the world.

Even the Alabama relations, who'd at first been inclined to grumble over Michael's poor sportsmanship in not letting the Birmingham boys get so much as a hit, began to be carried away by their old Southern love of spectacle, the old men shaking their heads as Ira and the boys kept swinging and swinging. There was no need to swing without a reason; there wasn't an umpire on duty to call strikes, so Michael had to tease them into jumping in on curve balls and low balls and even spit balls, one or two connecting enough to foul, but not much else.

"Didju bring your wallet?" Liz called to Ira, who was really the coolest of the bunch when it was his turn to bat. An athlete himself, he appreciated a rout when he saw one, and only shot Liz a good-natured bird or two, leaving his teammates to carry on in true Alabaman fashion, just about bursting out of their skins with sheer bad temper, calling insults at Michael, even one or two at little Sim.

"Git thet damn kid off the base or I'll knock it down this throat!"

Michael made no reply to their requests, all his attention on the worn out slat that served as home plate, striking them out one after the other, till the sun was nearly gone, the heat finally giving itself over to a tired, soaking humidity. The game was clearly near the end, the Butt-slappers soundly beaten, Michael's hundred bucks in the bag, when he finally turned and looked at me. He didn't say a word, didn't smile, just gave me a quiet, level look that stretched out, four, then five seconds, before he turned back to the last pitch of the game.

It occurred to me then that maybe he was working hard on his own that day, going about the only task possibly more frustrating than *satisfying a man: satisfying a woman,* and a hard-headed damn woman at that. But I didn't quite understand his look, couldn't see how a little bad-tempered baseball wager could possibly play into it till the next batter took the plate, one of the Butt-slappers of old, the one who'd offered to tuck me in.

He obviously didn't have a clue in the world that he was the paschal lamb about to be sacrificed to a woman's need for revenge, just stood there, legs-astride, shouting for Liz to *shut* the *hell* up, his eyes pinned on Michael like he held the secret to a long and happy life, as I guess he did. Or at least the secret of *satisfying a woman,* when he drew back in his slow motion rewind, then let go of a blur of a pitch that cost him a hundred hard-earned bucks when it connected, all right, not on the wood of the bat, but six inches below the belt, tha-*whack.*

The Butt-slapper fell like he'd been pole-axed, while all around him the game broke into pandemonium. The Alabamans let out a roar of victory while Liz bounced to her feet, shouting, "A hit! A hit! Not a *bean,* you *idiots!*"

Ira shouted back in kind, though I hardly heard them, just sitting there with my eyes on Michael, who ignored the commotion to stride toward me with great purpose, yanking off his glove and flexing his hand while he walked. He didn't stop till he was right in front of me, his voice raised to be heard over the commotion.

"Missy went over the fence again at Mama's," he shouted. "She's having a big old time over there playing in the ditch. Looked so much like you it was — scary."

He stopped then, his face red in the heat, a little harassed, as if he were afraid he wasn't making himself clear, though I knew exactly what he meant. Missy was always sneaking over Cissie's fence to play in our old yard, and it was a torment to me, a constant battle. Not just because the place was full of snakes and rotten boards, but because the dappled shade would sometimes play tricks with the light, darkening her braids, clouding her face, bringing to life another little girl, the one who haunted us all.

"I'm sorry," he said, not really saying what he was sorry for: his hard words about my family, or cutting her hair, or saying she looked like me.

But I didn't worry it, just echoed his apology; three little words made it out as Ira and his buds descended: "I am, too." By which I meant: I'm sorry, too, for Gabe and Clay and Tommy and the Preacher, for ruining your Plan with my sorry mind and my sorry family and my white-trash ways. He didn't answer, though. He couldn't, for Ira and the boys were quickly upon him, slapping his back and demanding their money while Liz called me over to comfort Sim, who was near tears.

"It's just a game, baby," she told him as we went back to the house. Ira and the Butt-slappers (all but the crippled one, who was moving slowly) jumped back in the pool, while I went upstairs to check on Clay, who'd been awakened by the shouting and was screaming with abandon.

"Hush, baby — there's my boy," I murmured as I picked him up, having a hard time nursing him back to sleep as Clay has never been one to overlook a slight and kept casting me these sniffling little looks of reproach for not having heard him sooner. I finally got him down and went to the bathroom to wash up when there was a quiet tap on the door at my back, and it's funny, because I knew who it was the moment I heard it. I mean, I knew it wasn't Mama or Ira or even Liz. I knew it was Michael and let him in without a word, then locked the door at his back and went for his mouth for the best kiss of my life. It was even better than the one that night in the garage, as he wasn't in his preppy Sanger clothes, but hot and sweaty and *Michael,* coming home from work on the Hill, meeting me at the porch steps with his lunchbox and his father's kind smile (*"There's my girl"*).

It was a kiss of such wonder that, like Jacob, I would have worked seven years of my life for it, forgetting Mama and Ira and every Sims on earth to stand there and feel his hunger, his old Michael-appetite, nothing like theirs, nothing they could aspire to in a million years. With no more talk, we worked ourselves free of every parcel of cloth that restrained us, and with one knee jammed against the sink, one against the door, he came into me for the first time in a year, his breath hard and quiet, like he was about to blow apart from the intensity of it all, me rubbing my face in his hair the whole time, whispering I loved him, loved him, loved him. Not just because of the sheer hard sensual relief, but because it was by God true if anything was, him knocking me against the sink at the end so hard I hit the back of my head on the mirror and cracked the glass — bad luck, some people say, though I wasn't complaining. Neither of us was, not drawing back, but just rested there a minute, face to neck, not meeting each other's eyes when we finally parted, a little afraid of what we might see there.

For it'd been often enough that we'd stretched out hands to each other these past two years that had come back empty, and neither of us could stand another desertion, not now, not after that. So he washed up at the sink, me at the tub, quiet and efficient, till someone started calling for me downstairs.

I dressed without a word and went downstairs, meeting Ira on the landing. "Mama's ready to go," he said, looking me up and down. "Said you wanted to talk to her."

I just blinked at him, still kind of dazed and breathless, with a curious sureness that he knew I didn't need Mama anymore. In a wandering voice, I finally managed, "It's all right. Tell her I'll call her. Sometime."

I looked away, for he grinned when I said it, his old mirthless grin that managed to put a nasty spin on my little reconciliation, like he'd caught me up there with one of his buddies, though he only turned and went down the stairs, calling over his shoulder, "Okcy-dokcy. Tell your husband to git thet check in the mail."

I told him I would, then went back downstairs, and with even less patience than before, began working my relations toward the door, especially the Louisianans, who looked like they could have stayed a year with no encouragement at all. After a good hour's effort, and many promises to call and write and see them Christmas, I finally had the house clear, Missy asleep on the couch, Sim on the rug in front of the fireplace.

I went back upstairs then in search of my husband and found him sitting on the edge of the bed tying his shoes, all showered and dressed for work. And though I hadn't cried when he cut Missy's hair, I could have cried then, for it was clear nothing had changed. He was Michael, *he worked,* and I hated Sanger so much I could have burned it to the ground, him in it. I didn't say anything, though, just went back downstairs, ignoring his attempts to tell me he'd be back by eleven, pretending I didn't care. He finally gave up and left me to work out my angst trashing styrofoam and crushing aluminum cans, putting the children to bed and stewing till eleven, when I heard a car in the drive, just like he'd promised.

I softened a little then and waited for him to join me in bed, but he never did. Finally, after a good twenty minutes, I kicked off the covers and went to the top of the stairs and there he was, lying on the couch in front of the television like nothing had happened between us at all. I wasn't hurt as much as I was rightly annoyed and marched down the stairs in a huff, though he didn't hear me till I was right at his back.

"Michael," I said, and he jumped like I'd shot him.

"My *God,* Myra!" he cried. "Don't sneak up on me like that."

I hadn't meant to sneak up on anyone and just looked at him. "Come on to bed," I told him. "It's late."

In reply, he just looked at me with an expression I could not so easily fathom, chewing his lip thoughtfully, then finally shrugging. "I cain't, I'm busy. Go on back to sleep."

But there was no heat to his voice, and I knew him well enough to know that even if our little episode in the bathroom hadn't been the grand reconciliation I imaged, once he'd jumped the fence, he wouldn't be turning me down so easily. I mean, he *never* turned me down — it was against his religion, I think — and in a sulky little voice, I actually insisted. "I don't care what you are. Come on to bed. You're *tired."*

Which was a polite way of saying what we both were, and he knew it. He just watched me a moment with another nervous chew of his lip, then tipped his head upstairs. "Go on up. I'll be there in a minute." Just as I made the stairs, he added, "And turn out the light, 'kay?"

Well, I didn't know what to make of this, but wasn't in too much of a position to argue, just flipped off my gown and turned off the lamp so the room was pitch black when he came in a few minutes later and paused by the bed to slide something under it before he stripped and climbed in, kissing me before he touched the sheets. Like I say, I wasn't in any position to complain, just reveled in the miracle of forgiveness, the miracle of good hands, the miracles of, well — a *lot* of things, the inky darkness reducing them all to the wondrous basics of touch and smell and taste. Sweet, it was, with Michael sometimes calling my name like he used to do in the twilight years, "Myra! Myra!"

It was only now that I realized that the voice I'd thought so accusing was only tired and worried and searching, as if he were out on his mother's back porch, calling for me late in the evening, hours after I was expected home. Calling and calling into the shadow of that kudzu-choked fence, and after three years of turning aside, I finally answered, pushing back his hair to whisper: "Hush, baby. I'm here. Here."

And I was, right there to the triumphant end when he fell asleep just as he used to, my chest to his back, our separate breaths rising and falling in perfection syncopation, a living duet. In a way, it was a relief as passionate as the sex: laying there heart to skin with someone you loved, so wonderful I didn't want to waste it in sleep. I only got up once, the whole night long, to slip on my gown and nurse Clay, though I paused when I came back to our room and went around to his side of the bed to feel under the fringe of the spread for what he'd slipped under there. I laid hands on it immediately, cold and metallic in the darkness, but couldn't quite make out what it was, turning it over quietly in my hands — when there was an audible *click* in the quiet room.

Michael jerked awake at the sound and came off that bed like a spring, hitting me in the shoulder and sending me sprawling on my back before he realized it was me.

"My *God,* Myra!" he cried, snapping on the lamp and bringing to light the tousled bed, the discarded clothes, and me, laid out flat on my butt in my inside-out nursing gown, a battered old shotgun still clutched in my hands.

═ 25 ═

*I*t *was a sawed-off shotgun,* in fact, and crudely done, the barrel nicked, the wooden butt cracked and pitted like a Civil War relic. I just stared at it till Michael took it from me and broke it open with a look of infinite patience.

"Myra? Baby, don't *ever* cock a loaded gun in a house with children," he said, as if that had been my intent. "It'd go right through the plaster."

I hardly listened to this sound bit of advice, for in that first moment when the light had come on, I'd had a split-second realization that the end had finally come: that Michael hadn't called me back to love me; he'd called me back to *kill* me. The revelation had come to me with such a gut-level certainty that I couldn't speak, even after he pulled me up to sit beside him on the bed, the old involuntary chicken-shake starting in my arms that made him look at me with a shadow of his old concern.

"You all right?" he asked, but I couldn't answer; I was still too shaken.

After a moment, Clay (who hardly ever went back to sleep unless you rocked him) started his squalling next door and I got up without a word to check on him. I found him sleepy but spoiled, pulling himself up by the rails to climb into my arms and settle like a little bird between my elbow and my chest, his sweet little face content at last. I felt my way to the rocking chair and sat there in the silver darkness rocking him till Michael came to the door.

"It ain't you, baby," he said in a quiet voice. "It's the men at the plant, Joe and Ricky and some of them. They're mad at me. They're making trouble."

Now, there were still many unalloyed terrors in my life, insanity and psychosis and child removal among them, but Joe Bates and the boys from the plant were about as fearsome to me as a clutch of squirrels. My unbelief must have shown on my face, as Michael went to some lengths to convince me, pacing around the room and telling me about Sam's promotion to manager, which I already knew about, plus other things I didn't: how they'd pressed for a union to keep him out, and when that failed, had actually burned a cross in Sam's front yard.

"A *what?*" I asked.

"A cross," he said as he finally sat down on the bed beside me, his face tense in the half-light. "It's the Klan, baby. The *Klan.*"

He said the word as if he were afraid of them, and I'll tell you what, I just didn't get it. Having lived in Birmingham in the mid-sixties, I knew all about the Klan, or as much as anyone did in those days. To my mind, they were relics of another decade, like beatniks and narrow ties, a dim branch of a half-understood religion, like a Masonic Lodge with a bone in their throat over black people. Sure they wouldn't want Sam manager of Sanger, but who the hell cared what they wanted? Like my father used to say: *they weren't buying me breakfast.*

I think Michael sensed my inability to grasp that this was trouble, as he went on and on about how they'd politicked Joe Bates and others to join, had turned the city against them, had the code enforcer on their backs, the sheriff on their side. "Cecil says they been coming in the café every morning, passing out newsletters, crap like that."

But I was still curiously unconcerned and just watched Michael with a faint rise of relief, thinking no wonder he was so tense, so quick to snap lately. It wasn't me and my blonde boy at all, but, of all things, the *Ku Klux Klan.* I was sitting there pondering the strangeness of it all, when I suddenly remembered the night I'd seen them in the yard unloading lumber, had words with them through the window.

"They were here!" I exclaimed. "That was the *Klan?*"
Michael's face jerked up like a hound on a scent. "*When?*"
I thought a moment. "Before Clay was born. February, I guess."

On this, Michael jumped up without a word and took off downstairs. When Clay finally returned to his thumb-sucking bliss, I went down to the kitchen and found him talking on the phone in a fast, excited voice. He dropped the receiver when he saw me, said, "Run git dressed, baby, sheriff's coming." He returned to the phone, pieces of his conversation following me up the stairs: "— trespassing, if nothing else — *hell*, yes, I will."

I didn't hang around to hear the details, but went upstairs and got dressed, even put on lipstick. When I came back down, Michael was outside, standing in the driveway in his bare feet, talking to a deputy who looked me up and down as I approached, as if it weren't the first time he'd heard of me, and what he'd heard before wasn't so good.

At the sound of my step, Michael swung around, said: "Tell him, Myra."

I complied, telling what I could remember of the odd sight of them in the front yard unloading lumber, till Joe caught sight of me and called his pleasant greetings.

"Any idea what they were up to, Miz Catts?" the deputy asked, causing Michael to exhale hugely.

"Hell, what d'you *think* they were up to?" he asked quarrelsomely. "Building a damn treehouse?"

The deputy just ignored him and repeated, "Miz Catts?"

I had no idea then, nor really even now, what they were up to and shook my head. "Nosir."

Michael let out another explosive breath at this and swung back around on the deputy. "Well, I know what they were up to," he said, "and I'll be downtown tomorrow, file a complaint if I have to call the *state attorney.*"

At the mention of a higher power, the deputy tipped his hat off his forehead and faced him evenly. "You can do what you want, Mr. Catts. There wasn't no harm done, far as I can see. They threaten you, Miz Catts? Any rough talk?"

I shrugged at Michael, then shook my head, for the scene had been odd and dreamlike, but not threatening — not by Sims standards. The deputy looked vindicated at my answer and closed his notebook. "Well, you see anything like that," he said as he backed away, "— any rough talk, breaking things up — give us a call."

Michael actually spit on the ground at this, the old Magnolia Hill sign of contempt that brought the deputy to a halt. He met Michael's eye coldly, said, "Y'know, Mr. Catts, there's some people thank you oughta work out yo own problems, quit expecting the law to come into it." He added archly, "This ain't the first time we been called out here on some wild goose chase."

He didn't so much as look at me when he said it, but I dropped my eyes anyway, remembering the nights, and not so long ago, that I used to call them about the Stairwalkers; the deputies good-natured at first, though after a while, no matter how much I pleaded, the dispatcher would only laugh me off. Michael didn't look embarrassed, though; he didn't particularly look anything at all, his anger suddenly gone — or not really gone, just hardened to a silent rage that was only evident in his eyes that glittered in the dim light.

"Fine," he said, then turned abruptly. "Come on, Myra. Let the boy git back to work."

The *boy* was not accidental, of course, but caressed with a particular mill-town silkiness that stung the darkness, making the deputy pause as he got in his car, call, "I'd take care, now, Mr. Catts. Doan go doing something *stupid.*"

He tried to spin the *stupid* to sound as insulting as the *boy*, but was not quite able as Michael just smiled at him across the darkness, said, "Oh, I won't be *stupid.* They show up around here and I git a clean shot, I'll blow their damn heads off. But I won't be *stupid.*"

The deputy stiffened on that. "It's against the law to threaten bodily harm —" he began, and Michael just feigned surprise.

"Is it? Well, hell, why don't you run down to the café tomorrow. You could fill the damn jail with what they been threatening me."

And that was about the end of it. The deputy left with an angry squeal of tires that still didn't quite even him up on the *boy,* while Michael went back to the kitchen and called Sam back, told him they wouldn't file a complaint. Sam must have set up an outcry at this, as

Michael held the phone away from his ear a moment, then turned his back on me, though I could hear fragments of his quiet explanation. "— not a reliable witness — oh, hell, no."

I waited for him by the French doors, embarrassed at the deputy's little jab, knowing it was all my fault, that I'd ruined our credibility. When Michael hung up, I tried to apologize, but he wouldn't let me. "It ain't you, baby," he said. "Denise saw 'em, Darryl did, too. Darryl saw 'em light the damn cross. Crill's up for reelection this year. He won't go against them."

His old Catts sense of fairness was clearly outraged with all these sleazy goings-on, but it wasn't the first time a sheriff had let me down in this county, and I just slipped my arms around his waist. "They'll get over it," I told him. "Come on back to bed."

But Michael was not so easily drawn off the scent and pulled away. "I cain't just lay up there, baby, pretend nothing's happening. They come in this house, they'll come up on me first, down here, with a gun."

For the first time, the horror of the situation began to dawn on me: not the idea of Joe Bates getting it in the face with a sawed-off shotgun, but of me lying alone in bed every night while Michael kept a vigil downstairs. I tried to talk him out of it, even pointed out that our bedroom offered a better lookout. But he was adamant about the couch, and I finally realized he wasn't protecting me or the house, but the staircase that led upstairs to his sleeping children.

"I'll stay with you," I offered, but he was adamant about that, too, sending me back to bed, where I sulked the night away, till a Plan of my own began to emerge with the coming day. It wasn't a Michael Plan, a well-thought-out Plan, but a Plan, nevertheless, and as soon as it was decently late, I picked up the phone and called Candace. It was so early that it took a few rings to arouse her. When she finally answered, I told her I knew where I wanted to eat breakfast the next morning before our weekly shopping junket.

"Where?" she yawned.

I smiled into the thin light of dawn. "The City Café."

With just that much malice and foresight I embarked on what you might call my civil rights period, one I'd slept through in Birmingham and was forced into in Florida as a simple act of survival. Like I say, there was nothing too premeditated about it, just a small insistence on eating breakfast at the café every Monday with my clueless sister-in-law, who'd left Welcome in its latest Charismatic split in May and was too busy keeping her mother from disowning her to worry herself with city gossip. Every Monday, while the children were filed away in VBS and mothers'-morning-out, she'd stroll in behind me with the easy swing of a small-town princess, greeting everyone with the same open smile. She'd occasionally ask what was going on with Joe and the boys; why were they sitting around the café at nine o'clock in the morning?

"They quit," I told her, and Candace just lifted an eyebrow.

"Really? Good for them."

I think I might have seen a few actual Klansmen there, sitting around drinking coffee with the same bored intensity as the others. At least they weren't local and had a look of hardened resolution about them when Joe or one of the others nodded in our direction. I can't imagine what they were saying and couldn't have cared less, really, as I wasn't following one of those Michael-Catts hard-and-fast Plans, but a vague intuition that was hard to explain, even to Louisa, who cornered me one morning in the kitchen and asked me plainly what I thought I was doing. "Cecil says you been showing yousef at the café. Whatchu think you'll prove, messen with thet trash?"

She said it with some authority, as Cecil (the same grizzled old man who'd given Michael his indecipherable message that first morning in the café) was her uncle, who'd run the place time out of mind for our old landlord Buddy Fischer. I was embarrassed that he'd caught me in my maneuverings and a little afraid of Louisa's disapproval, stammering, "Nothing. Nothing stupid. Just making sure that whatever they do, it'll be out in the open. Not way out here at night, me in my nightgown."

What I meant to say was that I was trying to strip them of their *Stairwalker* status, rob them of their anonymity, though Louisa warned me off. "You best be leaving it alone," she said. "A woman ain't got no bidness in the café with the likes of them."

By then, Louisa had moved up a few notches from casual acquaintance to the closer circles of my heart, nearly mother-figure (which I seem to go through life collecting, the way some people haunt flea-markets for Hummel figurines and Blue Willow), making it harder to disagree with her than go hand-to-hand with every Klansman in the state. I really couldn't meet her eye, just shrugged my old Myra-shrug, to which she breathed an aggravated *"Shht."* Then, "I doan like to think of what'd happen, they catch you there alone."

I warmed to the concern in her voice and tried to reassure her. "Candace goes with me," I said, and she was a little mollified.

"Well, you make sure it ain't just you. You go in there alone —" she didn't finish, just nodded her head at me, sending a message we both understood: if I went in there alone, the unspeakable could happen. The thing that wouldn't happen with the Cissies and the Candaces of the world, not in a million years, but the Myras and the black women, the voiceless and the wounded — sitting ducks for that kind of thing.

I just answered her nod with one of my own, my eyes on my feet, for I was creeping along in the twilight here, following my nose, sustained in my quest by a sermon Brother Sloan had preached recently, that came to me often: *there is nothing hidden that shall not be revealed.* I think his angle was about personal failings, secret sins, but the phrase caught in my head, becoming my motto, my new credo. It was the bit of confirmation that drove me forward every Monday, quelling Candace's distaste for the smoke and grease of the café by professing a craving for Cecil's biscuits (lard and water, nothing to write home about). Though the real motivation was this quasi-insane need to rip off the covers! Throw open the doors! *Nothing hidden shall not be revealed!*

Michael was too preoccupied by money worries to even suspect that I was up to any such nonsense, clearly at the end of his financial rope, having to sell his car when school started, and ten acres of the yellow pine in late October, holding off on the rest, not able to get a good enough price. It was sad day for both of us, the loggers doing their work in maybe six hours, chop, chop, and the front of the highway was cleared to slash stumps, the cold morning full of the sharp, pungent smell of cut pine.

"It'll grow back," he said with all his old optimism, though his face told another story: hollow-eyed, very nearly aggrieved, as he'd taken a liking to the old pine, bragging about their worth, their great age. Cutting them so cheap seemed to cut the heart right out of him, harder by far than selling the car, or even my wedding band, that probably brought in all of twenty bucks.

"I'll git you another," he promised, though I only told him it was better to sell it than lose it down the drain (which is where most of my rings ended up). He didn't argue, but only told me he loved me (worth more than a hundred rings, now that I think of it), too distracted to pay me much mind, as the chill, gray days of autumn were upon us, when the old boys at the café finally tired of my encroaching on their turf.

Until then, they had made no overt threat, had hardly acknowledged me at all, till the Monday after Halloween, when they waited for Candace to go to the bathroom, then rose as a group and made their way down the aisle toward me in a slow, ominous procession. They didn't say much then, just paused at the end of the table long enough for one of them (maybe an actual Klansman, dressed identically to the others, though his eyes were oddly gray and opaque) to lean over the table and warn me to *stay clear.*

I only sat there and worked hard to meet his eye, thinking how funny it was, that after twenty years, the silence-mongers of Jackson County were still using the same old lines: *Stay clear. Go easy.* You'd have thought they'd have come up with better material by now. But I said nothing in reply, just met his level gaze till Candace came back from the bathroom and pushed between them with her old good nature, patting Joe's belly, telling him he better lay off Cecil's biscuits.

Her open teasing deflated the tension, making them back off and head out en masse, only the hard-eyed stranger keeping his face on mine as he backed away, pointing a quiet finger at me to make sure I got the message: *Go easy. Or else.* It wasn't the first time I'd ever been sent that message, my shoulders replying with their cowardly little shake, though I just sat there clenching my hands. I had to; my mouth was so dry I couldn't have spit if you paid me.

The moment they hit the door Cecil came striding out of the kitchen with a dishtowel slung over his shoulder that he slapped down on the tabletop, making Candace sit back with a little yell, say, "Gosh, Cecil, it's pure bleach. Sit back, Myra, you'll get it on your shirt."

I sat back obediently, though Cecil paid me no mind, just wiped the table with fast, angry swipes, his face on the door till he was sure they were gone, when he straightened up and he met my eye, said, "Time you ladies was leavin'."

"We haven't even ordered," Candace complained. "Myra's taken this great liking to your biscuits."

He just flipped the dishtowel back over his shoulder. "I burnt the biscuits," he said. "Go home." Then, "No, not home. Miz Cissie's. Go ther."

He didn't leave much room for argument, and something in the set to his jaw made Candace lose her good humor and glance back and forth between us as I gathered my purse and stood. She followed me to the car without a word and let me drive her to Cissie's, staring impassively out the window till I parked in the carport, when she finally turned and gave me one of her mother's dry looks. "Well? Are you gone tell me, or Mama?"

"Cissie doesn't know," I said lightly, the old chicken shake giving way to a limp-noodle exhaustion that Candace wasn't about to take for an excuse, marching me up to the porch and interrogating me there, as Cissie was still staying at Maggie's, the house locked and empty.

"Let's have it," she said, and got her money's worth, all right, as I told her everything, not just about the Klan and the café, but the whole steaming decade: the hospital and the medicine and the preacher; the Klan and Sam, even Gabe and his inadvertent handiwork, my six-month-old son.

"Good *God*," she murmured on this last bit of news. "No *wonder.*"

I don't know if she meant no wonder he favors him, or no wonder he left, and didn't ask. Both of us just sat there in the golden autumn light, till I glanced at my watch and stood. "I need to go pick up the children."

Candace came back to life then and sat up, said, "Myra." Then, "Lou's right. You don't need to be going down to the café anymore. They could do anything and get away with it, with your —" She paused a moment, searching for the right word. *Reputation,* I think she was going to say, but softened it to "history."

I just shrugged, my unheard-of defiance making her look at me with a growing amazement. "Myra?" she asked. "Didju hear me?"

Sure, I'd heard her; I'd heard them all, for years — *Hush, baby. Go easy* — and only met her eyes levelly, quoted: *"There is nothing hidden that shall not be revealed."*

For an old Charismatic, she was oddly hostile to my little scripture, bringing the swing to a halt by planting her feet firmly on the porch boards and saying, "This ain't a joke, Myra. Does Michael know?" When I shook my head, she let out a noise of impatience. "Well, that's just *great* — I'm going down to Sanger and tell him this minute."

"You are *not*," I cried, pressed enough to actually face her off, stammer, "You cain't, Candace. See — it's just that, before — it was done in darkness."

I stopped in frustration then, having a hard time laying hands on the right words till I happened to glance aside at the sagging old house that stood across the fence, desolate and silent as it had always been. It brought it all back to me, making me stride across the porch and point at it, say: "See? That was the thing, Candace: the silence, the darkness. That's their strength, the Stairwalkers. You can't face them, can't fight 'em alone. Michael can't, neither can Sam. I couldn't, I *never could*. They need a Cissie, a Mr. Simon, a *witness*. They need us to go there, look 'em in the eye, say: this is wrong. This is a terrible thing you're doing. *See?*"

It was obvious she didn't as she just sat there, arms crossed, watching me with that obstinate Cissie-face, and it was so frustrating. For I knew the lessons I'd learned in the twilight were accurate, it was just so hard to apply them to the lighted world. I stood there trying for a better explanation, but the silent old ruin next door was about as good as I could do, and I finally just threw up my hands and picked up my purse, said, "Well, I don't care. Go on and tell him. Then he'll pitch a fit, make me stay home, and I'll be right back where I started — the crazy woman upstairs, *harmless.*"

The very word was so bitter it was almost physically painful, making me stomp off the porch and pick up the children in a stomach-churning silence, absently listening to news of their day. I took them straight home to an empty house, expecting a phone call of outrage from Michael any moment, asking me what the hell did I think I was playing at? But it never came. I just went about my afternoon routine, cooking supper as twilight fell, gray and cold, the smell of cut pine still strong in the air, when there was a knock on the French doors.

I was cagey enough by then to make sure the shotgun was on the mantle before I answered it, finding Candace standing there bundled in a big jacket, Lori behind her, a wiggling little beagle in her arms.

"What in the world?" I asked as I opened the door. Lori dropped the wiggling dog that galloped in like a mad thing, barking and circling the room in crazy little circles with the children in fast pursuit, screaming in delight.

"It's a dog!" Candace shouted over the commotion.

"Well, I see that!" I hollered back. "Whose is it?"

"Yours! From Uncle Case!"

I led her to the relative calm of the kitchen, where she leaned against the counter and absently scratched her arm. "I wanted a pit bull," she said, "but he wouldn't send a hog dog here with the children. Said a beagle would do you better. You might want to dip him or something. He's like, covered with fleas. Don't see how Uncle Case stands it."

Case had thirty-seven hunting dogs at last count, walkers and beagles and hog dogs and every conceivable combination thereof. "How much does he know?" I asked, meaning Case, but she just twisted her arm around, looking for flea bites.

"You know Uncle Case," she murmured. "Knows all and sees all. Said the city was backing the boys, hanging Sanger out to dry."

"Didju tell Michael?" I asked, and she didn't answer a moment, just pensively scratched her arm.

"Nope," she finally said.

"Why not?" I pressed, till she met my eye and answered with all her brother's wily reasonableness.

"'Cause he wouldn't let us go to the café tomorrow if he knew."

I almost smiled, then said, "Tomorrow? Tuesday? What about Missy and Clay?"

Candace just shrugged and scratched her arm. "Take 'em with us. Why not? I mean, they can kill us, but they cain't eat us, and if they do," she flashed that old indomitable Tierney smile, "we'll sho make a bellyful."

*S*o began *what you might call* the second
phase of my civil rights period, one a sight more tedious, as I added the
wild card of Tierney-defiance to my quiet rebellion, to everyone's dis-
comfort, especially Cecil, who was momentarily expected to blow our
cover. Any day I expected a phone call of outrage from my husband, but
as the golden days of November stretched into the grayer, colder days of
December, no call was forthcoming. Candace and I ignored all good
judgment to continue our trek downtown for breakfast every morning,
with Missy and Clay in tow, unless Cissie happened to be home from
Maggie's and could babysit.

"Don't see why you wanta go running off to the café every morning,"
she told us every morning. "I could fix you up a baker of biscuits in a jiffy."

We'd make noises of excuse, eyes on our feet, as Cissie was no fool
and could smell a lie a mile away. It was only her worry over Maggie that
had her sidetracked now, sending us off to breakfasts that were growing
subtly more hostile by the week, Joe and the others joined by men
who'd forced a walkout the week before Christmas. Albert Tierney was
among them, a third cousin of Cissie's, one of the crew of lanky boys
who used to walk me to school. His presence in the back booths

brought it painfully home just how close to the bone this thing was cutting, his eyes never quite meeting mine when they'd rise to leave, coming down the aisle in a noisy herd.

If Candace was there, they'd pass by with a big show of casual laughter, but if she happened to be away from the table, they'd pause to look me over with a lot less tenderness than they'd watched me from the yard that night in February. They'd occasionally make some sort of comment, nothing particularly threatening or nasty, but clothed in a good-natured malice, Joe once nodding at Clay, who was strapped in a highchair, grinding eggs in his mouth, and asking the others: "Now boys, which one of the Catts brothers would you say this chile favors?"

There was a silence then, my face hot, though I didn't look down — I couldn't. Looking down was saying: take whatever you want boys, it's on the house, and I couldn't do that, ever again. So I just faced them off evenly, my heart going boom-boom-boom in my chest till Joe cocked his head playfully to the side and offered his stinging punch line: "The good-looking one, I thank."

At the sound of their shout of good-old-boy laughter, Cecil appeared at the kitchen door as if by magic. He didn't even wait till they left, but crossed the room in three long strides, not asking, but telling me: "I'm calling the plant."

Sure enough, not ten minutes after Michael left that night (they were battling wild acts of weekend vandalism, Sam watching one week, Michael the next) there was a knock on the French doors. I had already put the children to bed and crept to the door, only able to make out a squared-shouldered, angry back beyond the glass. It set my heart to beating erratically, though when it turned, it was just Sam, who wasn't looking so hot these days — more harrassed than Michael, if possible.

His face was set, his eyes an amazing bloodshot red as I unlocked the door and let him in. "What d'you thank you're doing, Myra?" he asked as he stomped in without so much as a hello, just turning on me, asking, "You thank this is a game? The shurff's gone step in, put the bad men in jail? Thet what you're thanking?"

"Hush," I told him, nodding upstairs where the children were sleeping. I led him to the kitchen, then turned and asked, "Now, what were you saying?"

But he was obviously in no mood to barter and just lifted a quiet finger to my face like I was a kindergartner caught peeing in the cloakroom. "Whut I was saying was for you to keep yo butt out of the City Café. Thet's whut I was saying. Cecil says you're provoking 'em. S'at right?"

I just leaned against the counter and faced him off evenly, wondering why I'd ever been afraid of this man. Sure, he was big, even by Sims standards. Not tall, but solid, his width from chest to backbone maybe two feet, not sculpted muscle, but not fat, either. Just genetically engineered *big*, the way the Sims got red hair, the Catts runaway idealism. But there was nothing of threat about him, nothing I had the slightest fear of offending, or need to appease. For by some fluke of relationship, of knowing him chiefly through Michael (who loved him more than he loved me), Sam had become one of those rare people I could afford to be myself around; tell him I loved him, if I wanted, tell him to go to hell, if it suited me.

"I go there for breakfast," I told him mildly, my calm deflection making his eyes even redder.

"The hell you do," he breathed. "You're provoking 'em is what you're doing — and just what good d'you thank'll come of gitting in a pissing contest with the likes of them?"

Now, a *pissing contest* was the old Sanger term for when two shift workers got into a disagreement about missed breaks or slacking off and took their grievance to the public arena of the break room to gossip behind each other's back, play dirty tricks, generally kill the monotony of the week. I didn't think it an entirely accurate portrait of what I was trying to do down at the café and tried to explain about the *Stairwalkers* and how they worked in darkness, but Sam was as resistant as Candace, his finger still jabbing in my face.

"You doan know what yo messen with, Myra! Yo *playing around!*" Which was yet another Sanger term. *Playing around* meant goofing off, being stupid, and at that point, I began to get a little annoyed myself.

"I ain't playing at nothing —" I began, but he ignored me, his voice still lifted in its pained, rolling complaint.

"— doan know how bad it could git!"

And suddenly, I'd had enough, tired of being told what I knew and didn't know when God knows I knew more about the silence and the night than a Catts or a McRae would know in a thousand long years. I came off the counter and poked my face so close to his finger that it was about an inch from my nose, asked, "Really, Sam? Then, tell me: how bad does it *git*? They gone break my arm, crack my skull? Beat the *shit* out of me? *Rape* me, Sam? Is thet how bad it *gits*?"

"Aw, *Myra!*" he cried, *howled,* as if the word itself hurt his ears. "Why you wanna talk like thet?"

But I didn't show him any mercy, still closing in, saying, "'Cause, Sam, I been there, done that." Then, after a moment's pause: "*Resist the devil and he must flee.*"

Which was particularly low of me, as it was the same scripture he'd taught me to rebuke the Stairwalkers with, one he recognized all right, that made him turn aside to the window with a disgusted jerk. He stood there a long moment with his arms crossed tightly on his chest in a gesture of stiff-backed defiance, though when he finally spoke, his voice was as tired as his eyes. "You just come out of a dark time, baby. Why you wanna go back?"

The concern in his voice was irresistible, the particular caress of the *baby* almost making me say: *Sure, Sam. Whatever you say.* But I couldn't, anymore. To go back was to return to the darkness, and I only whispered yet another scripture imperative: "*To him that knoweth to do right and doeth it not, to him that is sin.*"

He made a grunt of annoyance on this and glanced at me out of his tired eyes. "Yeah. And to them that quote scripture to justify doing *silly-assed* things, to them that is *stupid.*"

But there was no heat to his voice when he said it, and I knew I'd won. That we might fuss and name-call and get into a pissing contest of our own, but he wouldn't tell Michael. He just exhaled mightily and turned, asked, "Where's thet dog Case give you? It didn't bark when I come up."

I went to the living room and whistled and called till Speckles came to the top of the landing, wagging so hard he was about to throw himself down the stairs.

"A *beagle?*" Sam asked in amazement. When I told him what Candace had said about it being good with children, he rubbed his face, asked, "Where's the gun?"

I obediently retrieved it from the mantle, holding it by my fingertips, scared of the nasty thing. Sam broke it open and checked the chambers, then snapped it in place and lifted the sight to his eye, making me kind of nervous, to tell you the truth.

"Michael said not to cock it in the house," I offered.

Sam just dropped the sight and looked at me dryly. "It ain't loaded, Myra."

"Oh."

He handed it back to me, rubbing his face meditatively while I slid it back on the mantle. "You ain't got no people up in Alabama you could go stay wid till this thang blows over?" he asked.

When I shook my head, he made another noise of wonder, then looked at me levelly, said, "Then listen: this is the way it is. You can take yo stubborn butt down to the café all you want, but you make dang sure Candace's wid you. You hear me? Doan you go down there alone. You hear me, Myra?"

I nodded obediently, and he added, "And thangs git outta hand — they start somethin' with Cecil — you git yo butt to the counter. He keeps a pistol there, in a sack under the registry. You git thet pistol in his hand, you hear?"

I nodded again, and he seemed satisfied, leaving as abruptly as he'd come, though he paused a moment on the deck that was cold as a tombstone and called, "And put thet dog outside. What good'll it do you in there?"

"He sleeps on Missy's bed," I explained, making him close his eyes a moment, like Louisa did sometimes, as if the ways of white people were really beyond the comprehension of the Godly.

"Well, put him outside. Ain't gone do nobody no good in there."

I obeyed, calling *Speckle-Speckle-Speckle,* bringing him down the stairs in a twisting, wiggling delight, thinking he was in for a dog biscuit. Sam watched him caper around with a face close to despair, then looked at me a final time. "Well, tell Missy not to worry it," he said. "I'll let you in on somethin' yo husband doan even know: we're closing January first. Got to. No money, no juice. The city's citing us and we cain't pay the fine. So you just sit tight. Two mo' weeks and it'll all be over but the crying."

On that, he turned and strode away, one hand lifted in silent farewell. With a little dodging, I managed to get back inside without

Speckles, who was outdone at my duplicity, climbing up to paw at the door, whining to be let in. The cold night had turned off wet, the pelt of rain on the windows turning to thin, cracking ice, with poor Speck caught in the thick of it. He was smart enough to follow my light around to the front of the house and position himself beneath my window and try to talk me out, finally resorting to a keening wail that pierced the twilight like the whine of a disappointed child.

It made for an eerie evening, lying there alone in my cold bed, wondering what we'd do after the first of the year. I had no idea how far in debt we were — a lot, if Michael had cut the pine, sold the ring and his car. Aside from the rest of the pine and the house itself, we were down to little more than a car payment and a closet full of preppie clothes. Try as I might, the only other possible resource I could think of was Cissie. If worse came to worse, we could always move back with her, at least till Michael found another job, maybe down at St. Joe at the paper company. It'd be hard on him, going back on the floor at his age. Maybe both of us could get on, work opposite shifts, so the other could keep an eye on the children, like some people did.

That was the circle of my thoughts that night: making do, looking ahead, not panicked as much as I was relieved, almost like Sam had been, glad it was all coming to an end. Because though I wouldn't have confessed it to anyone, the breakfasts at the café were beginning to wear on me. I couldn't sleep at night without medication, and sometimes I'd feel a little ping beneath the lithium calm, my own body warning me: *Go easy, sister. Stay clear.*

I lay there till nearly dawn and turned it over in my mind, tired and nervous from Speckles' whining complaint, finally going to the window and raising the sash on a cold, misting sunrise, shouting for him to *hush up!*

Poor Speckles drooped away in a sad little pout that made me relent a little, call, "I'll be down in a minute, goofball."

But I didn't. I was too cold and just crept back under the covers, knowing I'd have to get up soon enough, as it was Sunday morning and I was teaching Cissie's Sunday School class. I had taken over in August, since she was staying out at Maggie's so much these days, warning us the end was near.

"Ain't long for this old world" was the kindly way she put it, refusing to send her back to the hospital and mostly refusing anyone's offer of help other than Uncle Pete's, saying it was quieter there, with just the three of them. ("What d'you do all day?" Candace once asked. Cissie looked at her calmly. "We talk.")

Taking on her primary class was the extent of my support, and I usually enjoyed it, but not with an icy December dawn upon me. I was lying there dreading it, wishing Candace hadn't bailed out with the Charismatics, or I'd call her, beg her to take my place. But she was gone for good, leaving me to toss in my bed, though I did begin to doze off just as morning dawned, cold and wet, poor Speckles annoyed that I'd forgotten him, letting out another wail that ended sharply, with the slam of a car door.

I vaguely remember thinking: good, Michael's home and will let him in before Missy wakes up, the sudden silence giving me a little space of relief to pass into sleep, waking up in the full light of day to the sound of children's voices downstairs, calling; *Speckle-Speckle-Speck-les.* The bedside clock showed nine o'clock, and without bothering with a robe, I took off downstairs in my gown and met Michael at the kitchen door, still in his work clothes, chewing his aspirin.

"Why'd you let me sleep so late?" I asked him. "It's nine o'clock!"

Before he could answer, Sim came shivering to the French doors in nothing but his pajamas. "Where's Speckles, Mama? We cain't find him."

But I was more concerned with him walking around barefoot in the frost and pulled him inside, said, "I don't know, baby. Run call Missy — we're late."

I went into immediate action, having Michael punch out my Wisemen and Shepherds and dress Clay while I herded Sim and a whining Missy upstairs. I had them back in the kitchen by nine-twenty, gathering my lessons and a neatly dressed Clay, who hadn't had breakfast and was letting us all know about it, wailing and grabbing at my blouse.

"I'll nurse him on the way," I told them, as I'd already deemed it less dangerous to drive around with a baby at my tit than the screaming siren of a wail Clay could produce when he was hungry.

Michael walked us to the car, barefoot in the cold, and kissed me through the window, looking so whipped that I was tempted to tell him what Sam had said about it being over soon enough. But I didn't, just told him to get some rest, while Missy called over my shoulder for him to keep an eye out for Speckles.

In reply, he just looked at her a moment, then glanced away. "He's probly got off after a squirrel, baby," he said vaguely. "Probly after a squirrel." And it's funny, because that's when I knew Speckles was dead.

Because Michael was adept at a lot of things, but he was a lousy liar. He just didn't do it often enough to build any proficiency, and sitting there, watching his pale, averted face, I suddenly knew what happened, just like that. That's what that last wail had been about: they'd caught him on the porch, killed him in some quiet way, right about the time I would have opened the front door to let him in, if my warm bed hadn't been so inviting.

I didn't say anything, just started the car and backed out, mechanically going about the morning's routine as if nothing were wrong. When we got home, Michael was crashed on the couch in the same clothes we'd left him in, so exhausted I talked the children into taking a long nap, promising we'd look for Speckles when they woke up. Once the house was sleeping, I sneaked down to the kitchen to make one hushed phone call, then took my own nap courtesy of a blue Valium, and woke in better spirits, cooked supper, and took the children on a walk around the ice-stiffened yard, calling for the dog.

I was still zonked enough on the Valium to stay pretty calm about it all, just asking Michael one small favor: that he drop Missy off at mothers'-morning-out the next morning so I could sleep in.

He agreed, and shortly after they left the next morning, Case showed up, knocking on the French door in an old quilted hunting jacket, his weathered cheeks beet-red from the cold, a huge beagle sniffing around his heels.

"Didju bring him?" I asked, meaning Domino, his best nose dog.

Case jabbed a pinch of tobacco in his lip and nodded at the beagle. "Brought Dixie," he said. "She's his mama. She'll find him."

"Let me git my coat," I told him, my feet numb as I followed him around the frost-stiffened yard to the front porch, where Dixie suddenly lost her wagging good spirits and let out a worried, keening whine. With her nose pressed to the brick, she circled wider and wider, till she trailed off into the bushes and let out a sharp, plaintive howl. There was a human note to her keening that made me stop just short of the porch, my heart in my throat as Case fought his way through the waist-high boxwoods, stooping down a moment, then calling: "Here."

"Buried?" I asked lightly, as he would have to be, if Michael had found him. Case just grunted, having to fight Dixie back, her howls so loud I had to lift my voice to ask, "Could you — ah — dig him up, please?"

After sixty years of life with Cissie, Case had grown tolerant of feminine whims, just looking up a moment, shifting his tobacco around his cheek as if he were thinking of a reply commensurate to the request. But he didn't argue, didn't ask what the hell I thought I was playing at, just picked up Dixie and handed her over the bushes, told me to put her in the dog cage. I got hold of her as best I could and half-carried, half-dragged her to the truck, her howling grief strengthening my resolve, so that when Case came around the corner toting a dirt-caked, foul-smelling grocery bag, I told him to put it in the car.

"The Cadillac?" he asked incredulously.

"The trunk."

He obliged me, slamming it in, then looked at me evenly. "I'm gone take Dixie home. Make a few calls. You sit tight till I git back. You hear?"

I just nodded, dropping my eyes when I did it, because I wasn't any better a liar than Michael, and what I had to do, I had to do quickly, right now, or I couldn't do it at all. I had to do it while it was all still with me: Dixie's howls, Sam's red eyes, Missy's tears in bed the night before. ("But it's so cold, Mama. Where'll he go?")

I didn't even bother to change clothes, just slipped on my houseshoes and zipped Clay up in the little wool bunting Mama had given Sim, nursing him on the way to town, my heart beating so hard that the bump-bump-bump made his cold little cheek pulse against my breast. My hands were shaking so hard by the time I made the café that I could hardly unlock the trunk, the keys slipping from my cold grip, clattering to the asphalt.

I finally balanced Clay on one hip and got it open, then took a big breath and with the rotting old bag in one hand, Clay in the other, stode resolutely across the parking lot and backed into the café's double doors, afraid I'd missed them, coming this late. But they were there all right, and why not? They didn't have a job to be late for, filling the big booth in the corner with a low, furtive conversation and a palpable cloud of cigarette smoke that hit me face-on as I strode down the aisle toward them, not stopping till I was at the opening of the crowded booth.

I had a split impression of stilled conversation and upturned faces — Joe and Albert among them — before I made out the stranger's face in the din and spoke to him across the table in a voice so thin it seemed disembodied. "I thank you left somethin' at our place the other night."

Joe was making some attempt at reply, dropping his cigarette to grin, "Myra, darlin', I thank you're mistak —" when I slung the bag across the table, so hard the seams ripped, sending what was left of poor Speckles sliding to the wall in the stiff, dirt-caked obscenity of death.

The booth exploded like I'd thrown a hand grenade on the table, Joe leaping to his feet, shouting, "What the *hell?*"

But I'd slung my courage away when I let go of poor Speckles, shocked to speechlessness at the hideousness of his twisted little death and shaking like a leaf, blinking at the stranger who pushed Joe aside to shout some unheard abuse in my face. Something in my blinking immobility seemed to enrage him, as he reached back and backhanded me so hard Clay slipped from my hands, hitting the linoleum face down with a mighty howl, a grave miscalculation on the stranger's part, clearly the work of a man *not from around here*. I mean, the boys from the mill might side with Joe on the matter of Michael leap-frogging over the foreman to give the manager's job to a nigger, might even be talked into paying dues or extending a little political pressure. But they hadn't quite worked their way up to slapping scared women, one of them (Joe? Albert?) grabbing the Klansman's arm with a terse, "Hold on, now —"

But I hardly felt it, hardly heard them. I was shaking so hard I couldn't pick up Clay, but just squatted down beside him and patted his screaming back while Cecil came striding down the aisle with nothing but the dishcloth on his shoulder for protection.

"Thet'll be enough of thet," he said shortly, picking up Clay by the back of the bunting and lifting his voice over the wail to say, "Time you all was leaving. You ain't welcome here no mo."

They all looked a little stunned at that, someone saying, well he didn't own this place, what would Buddy Fischer thank of thet? But Cecil just faced them evenly. "It'll either be me or you. If I'm cookin' tomorrar, doan bother to darken the door."

On that mild piece of advice, he herded them down the aisle and out the door, Clay's face scrunched in a purple wail at the *horror!* The *horror* of what had happened! A suckling infant! Dropped on the floor! His brilliant outrage was probably what drove them so docilely to the relative peace of the parking lot, Cecil turning the deadbolt at their backs and striding back down the aisle, handing me Clay with a gruff, "Give thct chile a tit." Then: "Where's Candace?"

I just looked at him blankly. "Home," I finally managed for lack of a better answer, unbuttoning my coat and nursing Clay, who was hardly able to suckle he was so mad, his dimpled little hand compulsively rubbing the angry lump on his forehead, as if to say: "Look ahere, Mama! Look what they done to me!"

The café was deserted that time of the morning, though soon enough, the lunch shift started banging at the door. Cecil was occupied in the back and let them bang, one more strident than the other, so hard I thought it'd crack the glass. I finally got up to answer it myself, tell them the café was closed, and found myself facing my outdone uncle-in-law, who was peering in the glass with a shotgun under one arm, a pit bull, the other.

=== 27 ===

"*I toldju to stay put!*" was the first thing Case said when I turned the deadbolt and let him in. Cecil must have heard the jingle of the front door, as he strode out of the kitchen with a face like a thunderbolt till he saw it was Case.

"Where's Candace?" he barked.

Case just dropped the sniffing dog. "I doan know. Home, I guess. What'sat stink?"

"Speckles," I told him as I rebolted the door and returned to the privacy of my booth, ignoring the rising hum of indignation in the handful of men who gathered as word of the confrontation began to make its rounds downtown.

None of them bothered to knock on the front door, but came in by way of the kitchen, city clerks and shoeshine boys and even Buddy Fischer, who covered his face with his hat as he strode in, shouted, "Case! Git thet stinking dog out of here. Health Department'll shut us down!"

When he discovered it wasn't a living dog stinking up the place, but a dead one, he was even more outdone, striding out the door and straight into the mayor's office, chewing him out like it was *his* fault.

He'd apparently gotten the story a little confused and thought the Klan had brought in the dead dog to intimidate Cecil, the talk mounting so hard and fast that it was really impossible to keep it straight. I was probably the only one there who could put things to right, explain Speckles and Dixie and *nothing hidden shall not be revealed,* but I was too whipped to do anything but sit there quietly in my booth and nurse Clay, unnoticed and unapproached till it was time to pick Missy up at mothers'-mornin-out.

The mystery of Candace's whereabouts was solved as soon I got home and found her little Subaru skidded up in the gravel behind the garage alongside Louisa's old Buick. They must have heard me in the drive, as they abandoned their coffee to meet me at the French door with a volley of fast-breaking news: "Where've you been? Cecil and the Klan had a big free-for-all — threw a dead dog in the window! Buddy Fischer called the state attorney!"

All of this was shouted in one communal breath, so fast and excited I could hardly decipher it as I took Clay upstairs for his morning nap, wishing I could crawl in with him and go to sleep, sleep forever. But I had Missy to tend to and went back downstairs and listened with half an ear to Lou's glowing speculation that this was the turning point! The straw that broke the camel's back!

Though Candace was a little more subdued, saying that rumor had it the dog was a beagle. "Missy says Speckles is missing," she said quietly, with a quick glance at Louisa.

I just rubbed my eyes. "He is."

They made faces of horror at that, their outrage a foretaste of the whole town's reaction, which was odd, as the cross burnings, the vandalism, even the severing of Sam's civil rights never chilled anyone as deeply as the murder of the little dog. Even my public slap and Clay's tumble were lost in the shuffle as I withdrew into a shell of silence, haunted by the image of Speckles' twisted little death. During the day I could put it aside, but at night, I'd lie in bed and wish with all my heart that I could turn back the clock to that night and let him in, no matter what Sam said. That who cared if they'd caught me on the porch? What could they do to me that hadn't been done before?

Poor Speckles. I could see him pawing the glass, see Dixie making her agonized little circles on the porch. Maybe if I'd listened to everyone, kept my butt home where it belonged, none of it would have gone this far. The plant would have just closed, and that would have been the end of it. Michael would go on at the paper mill; I'd find something for myself, surely. That was the circle of my thoughts, my defiance gone, just like that, replaced by a jittery nervousness, thinking for the first time in a year that I heard things out in the yard at night, or on the stairs while Michael was at work. Even during the day, I'd sometimes turn sharply, thinking I'd felt a hot breath on my neck, or caught a glimpse of a man in a trenchcoat, dodging between the trees, pursuing me with his old relentless focus, the threat I could not confront because it marched in the shadowland of my mind.

I was well-versed enough in psychology by then to recognize the slide of my thoughts from rational to irrational, even apply a clinical name to my fears: *paranoia*. But there was nothing I could do to halt it, just take my pills and keep busy, an easy enough proposition with Christmas so quickly upon us, Michael indulging in his usual over-the-top generosity, buying his mother a television, me a diamond solitaire to replace the plain little wedding band he'd sold in September.

This financial double-standard — me strung out on the budget from hell while he played Father Christmas — was always a sore spot with me, but he gave no indication that anything at work was amiss, even went in Christmas afternoon, returning home late in the evening and taking me upstairs to the bedroom, saying we needed to talk. His face was unusually somber when he said it, and I thought he was finally going to tell me about Speckles and the Klan; about the plant closing in a week, and how we'd have to sell the house.

But all he did was set me down on the edge of the bed and say, very quietly, "Baby, Mama called. Aint Mag went into a coma. Mama's there, said it'll be — anytime."

He blinked when he said it, his eyes red and watery, not from overwork, but simple grief, as he was Maggie's favorite, the baby Cissie had given her when she'd had her last miscarriage during the war. Her dying on Christmas day seemed a bitter end to a bitter year, making me cry and cry, so hard Michael wouldn't leave me alone, afraid I'd plunge into a black despair. He ended up spending the evening sitting up in bed in his worn old shop clothes, talking to me while I went through my closet, weeding out my skinny clothes to give to Candace.

For we weren't the only ones facing hard times that year. What with the unusually wet December and the bleed-over resentment over the Catts' nigger-loving ways, Ed wasn't having too hot a year in building, leaving Candace (who celebrated the holidays with all her mother's insanity) to wring her hands over Lori's sparse presents. I could commiserate and was casting about for some odd piece of jewelry I could pass on when I remembered the closetful of clothes I'd bought last spring that were still in style, just too small now that the lithium was puffing me back into my old ten/twelves.

I made my offer to universal rejoicing, but after the Slap, was a little slow in the follow-through, too damn tired to keep at it, though Candace wasn't letting me off so easy, calling every morning, even offering to go through the closet herself. I told her no, I could manage, and after Michael came home with the news about Maggie, set myself to the task, sorting through a world of shoes and shirts and *good God*, the dresses! There were two dozen, at least, most still tagged from Parisians and Gayfords and Belks, navy and white and (of course) khaki, some identical, bought the same day, on the same ticket.

I was finally to the point of stability where insanity could amaze even me, and looking at the duplicate dresses, I said the saleslady must have thought I was *crazy*, buying three identical dresses on the same day. Michael, who was lying there with his hands behind his head in a near-doze, just commented, with all his dry reasonableness, "Baby, you *were* crazy when you bought them dresses."

He didn't even say it as a joke, just a calm truthfulness that made me smile, then laugh aloud, because it was true: I *was* crazy when I bought those dresses, the distance between the then and now suddenly palpable, something to rejoice in. The realization turned the mood of the evening a little more festive as the children came upstairs to be with us, Simon practicing casting his new reel down the hallway while Missy and Michael played on the bed with Clay, who'd come up empty-handed that morning, as the money was so tight and he was too little to know he was being stiffed. The knot on his forehead had faded to a sickly gray, though I'd made light of it to his father, saying he'd had a little bump on the floor (he had; I just didn't mention where).

"He's a tough old thing," Michael had teased, as Clay was anything but: a fat little cuddler, lazy as the day was long, at ten months not showing the slightest interest in so much as sitting alone, much less crawling. But he was a good-natured baby, an *easy* baby, Cissie called him, and when the children tired of their new toys, Michael showed them how to blow on his belly to make him laugh and laugh in a high baby chortle that was probably the sweetest sound I'll ever hear in my life.

Later that night when the clothes were all packed away and the children asleep, Michael and I sat on the couch in front of the lopsided Christmas tree, not really talking, just sitting there holding hands, an unspoken agreement between us that we were waiting for Cissie's call, saying it was over with Maggie. Every once in a while the phone would ring, the bell turned down so it was barely audible. Michael would always hear it first and jump up to answer it, saying it was just Sam at the plant, calling about business.

I didn't argue, just sat there, mesmerized by the blink of the Christmas lights, finally unbending enough to ask what we'd do after the first of the year when the plant closed.

"Who said we were closing?" he asked sharply. When I told him I'd just heard it, I couldn't remember where, he grunted, "Shtt. I bet. You tell *Lou* we ain't doing nothing, first of the year. City took back the complaint. We're all right. Doing fine."

I wasn't so convinced by his old Michael-optimism, only glad the city was backing down, no doubt the fruit of Buddy Fischer's stomp into the mayor's office. I was glad some good had come of my little stab at civil disobedience and sat there against him, listening with half an ear as he went on about his plans for saws and orders and production, technical stuff I could never follow, when he added in an offhanded way, "Albert come back."

"Albert *Tierney?*" I asked, sitting up in amazement, and he looked at me mildly.

"Yeah. Come back Monday night, clocked in like he'd never been gone. Ricky did too — said Joe'd be calling Monday."

"Joe *Bates?*" I breathed, so astonished that he went to some lengths to justify talking to him.

"Yeah, Joe's all right. He just got his head down over Sam. Manager always goes to foreman, and he just got his feelings hurt. I tried to tell him, to explain, but he got to foolen with the Klan, listenen to that shit, till he started to see, that, you know — you lay down with dogs, you git up with fleas."

Which wasn't exactly how I saw it, though I didn't argue, just sat there with these little tendrils of happiness beginning to work their way down my veins, wishing it wasn't so late, or I'd run upstairs and call Candace, tell her about Joe and Albert, say: *See? See?* That was the thing with the darkness; it needed a light, a witness. A Miss Cissie, a nurse in a suit. A Mr. Simon, standing at the fence at twilight. (*"And what are you gonna be when you grow up, Myra Louise?"*)

For the first time in my life, I had an answer, and could actually see myself lifting my averted face to answer him over the fence: *"I'm gonna be just like you."*

The image was so lucid, so powerful, that I closed my eyes, not hearing the phone when it rang again; it must have, as Michael rose to get it. This time, he didn't hang up immediately, but talked a moment, then came back to the couch rubbing his eyes, and told me it was Cissie, calling from the hospital, that Maggie had died.

"Peaceful in the end," was the way he put it, and I didn't even cry this time, just stood and hugged him, even talked him into sleeping in his own bed for once.

When I awoke the next morning, he was (as usual) already gone, the rain finally broken in the night, the December sky clearer than it had been, and colder, the children able to wear their new winter coats, a major item on this year's list, with hard times looming. I spent the day packing up the car with Lori's boxes so I could drop them off at Cissie's when I took Sim and Missy into town for two respective parties (Missy's a slumber party, Sim's at the skating rink), anxious to talk to Candace, tell her about Albert and Joe.

She was supposed to meet me at Cissie's at four to try on a dress for the funeral, her car already in the drive when I pulled up a little later than I had intended, caught at the corner by the train. I noticed that Cissie had her fireplace lit against early winter twilight, the wisping smoke tinting the air with the sweet smell of burning oak. It gave the chilly afternoon a feel of restoration, of life returning to normal, Michael back in his bed, the café back to stale coffee and lard biscuits, Cissie apparently back in her kitchen, as her living room was brimming with the company smells of ham and boiling potatoes when I went to the door and called for Lori and Candace to help me unload the car.

They came out in a clatter of excitement, Lori in a rush to get her hands on the loot, though Candace knew something was up the moment she laid eyes on me, stopping just inside the door to ask, "What?"

I crossed my arms and lifted my chin. "Guess who showed up for work yesterday?"

She just looked at me a moment. "You're lying," she said.

"Am not."

"I don't believe it," she muttered, taking Clay and stepping out on the porch. "What'd Michael say?"

"He's a happy man," I grinned as I flipped out my keys and went to help Lori unload the car of its burden of dresses and shoes and shirts and skirts and sandals, feeling lighter with every step, free at last: of perfection and khaki and silence and skinny, free to the bone.

Lori was equally excited, dancing around the porch with a shirt or skirt held to her waist, exclaiming, "Oh, I love this. I remember when you bought it. Oh, Myra, you are so *good.*"

When we were finally done, the porch scattered with boxes, I paused long enough to dig out the funeral dress for Candace, assuring her it'd fit. "It's a big six, more like an eight," I told her, then took Clay and followed her as far as the screen door to call through the house to Cissie, reminding her I wouldn't be at the funeral (Clay wouldn't let me out of his sight long enough), but we'd sent flowers, white roses, Aunt Mag's favorite.

Cissie came to the kitchen door to answer me, wiping her hands on a dish towel. "Doan worry it, shug," she called. Then, as I stepped away, "Come back when you git Sim. Gabe's here. Come in for the funeral." Her face softened to its old Mama-smile. "Wanten to see thet baby."

I was almost to the steps when her words hit after their little four-second lithium delay, like a mule-kick to my chest. I couldn't move, couldn't breathe, just stood there paralyzed, till I caught a flicker of movement at the bedroom curtain where, sure enough, not six feet away, a pale, introspective face watched me over the old window fan, dead-eyed, intent.

The image was distorted by the sun on the thick old glass, so nasty that I almost blacked out, right there on the porch. I could literally feel my eyes rolling up in my head, feel Clay slipping from my grip. His sheer weight brought me back from the depths to turn and take the steps in one jarring bound, then run like a thief to my car, not strapping Clay in his car seat, but keeping him clenched to my chest as I keyed the ignition with a roar. Candace came out on the porch and called something about the dress, but I ignored her, slamming out of Cissie's drive and streaking to my house like a fleeing animal.

Once inside, I locked the place up like Fort Knox and sent Sim upstairs for his bath while I started supper, banging around the kitchen with Clay still clenched to my chest. I tried to fry a chicken, but kept starting at every sound, actually jumping in fright when I heard someone at the door. But it was just Michael, home early for once, who stopped the moment he laid eyes on me, just like Candace had, asked, "What?"

I wouldn't answer him, just shook my head and went back to the chicken, for this Stairwalker wasn't a stranger in a robe, but an insider, a brother, protected by his mother's winning smile. I couldn't touch him. I couldn't do anything but stand there and try to turn the chicken with one hand, shaking so hard I splashed my hand with the hot grease, though I didn't even feel it, didn't flinch.

Michael set down his briefcase and pulled me to the sink, turning on the tap and holding my hand under the water. "What in the world's the matter?" he asked, searching my face with worried eyes. "You look like you seen a ghost."

"I did," I whispered, with such conviction that he closed his eyes, thinking: *here we go again,* with the Stairwalkers, the laughing deputies, the twilight. But it wasn't that. This Stairwalker was real, he ate and drank. He made jokes, he fathered children. He drew you into his web, time and again. "It's Gabe," I whispered. "He's here, Michael. *Here.*"

"Here?" he breathed, jerking his face to the living room.

"No — Cissie's. Wanten to see the baby, Michael. Wanten the *baby.*"

"Aw, Myra —" he began with his tired old exasperation, though I wouldn't be put aside this time and jerked away, abandoning supper to take Clay upstairs and lock both of us in his room, refusing to open the door. For losing him wasn't merely a psychotic gnawing in the night, but a genuine threat to me, one particularly close to home, as Ira had lost Brian in September in a bitter custody fight, the verdict going against him in a big way, no visitation, nothing. I could think of no more horrifying a scenario: the judge calling the court to order, looking at me from the bench over his half-glasses (*this woman was taken in adultery, in the very act*) and pronouncing his judgment with a rap of the gavel, case closed. What would I do? Go home, pack up Clay's stuff, his pillow and his toys? Zip him up in his wool bunting, the only real winter clothes he had, put him on a plane to Washington when he hated to leave me. He cried and cried, he held my leg —

I couldn't sleep that night, couldn't be reasoned with, just paced the house, dry-eyed and desperate, a sleeping Clay clutched to my chest, searching, searching for an answer. I thought of every angle: escape, murder, legal loopholes. I even found myself conjuring insanity before the night was through, could actually feel my hysteria beat against the glass ceiling of the lithium, I swear to God I could. It was like a moth beating itself against a window, *tap-tap-tap*, wanting to break free into something, despair or mania or catatonia, I didn't care which — anything to relieve me of this hellish confusion.

I thought of what Sam had asked me in the kitchen that night, about how I'd just come out of a dark time; why did I want to go back? At the time, I'd almost laughed in his face, it was so absurd. Who wanted to go back? Back to the abyss, the thinness and the void? But pacing the house that night, I had to admit that there was a sanctuary there, a hard, solid floor, a haven of rest. I would have gone there if I could have, but somehow, I couldn't, waking the next morning on a chair in the living room with no memory of falling asleep, no idea how I'd gotten there.

When I realized Clayton wasn't with me, I came to my feet in a flash and ran upstairs to find him right where he should be: asleep in his baby bed, his thumb corked safely in his mouth. I stood there a moment in the half light, watching him sleep, was about to pick him up when Michael came to the door in his work clothes and said very quietly, "Myra. Leave him be."

I didn't even turn, but just stood there wavering, wanting to pick him up so bad. To hold him tight against my chest, where nothing could touch him, ever again. Michael finally had to come and physically lead me to the little twin bed in the corner, squatting down beside me and speaking quietly into the half light, "Myra. Baby, you need to settle down. You're pushing yoursef to break and there ain't no need. Nobody's taking that baby."

"They took Brian," I whispered.

"Yeah," he agreed. "They took Brian. They had to. Ira ain't fit to raise a chilc. Baby, you know that."

I knew it, but I didn't want to, hardly comforted by the knowledge that we were failing, my brother and I. "Neither am I," I whispered, dropping my face to my hands. "That's what they'll say, Michael. The judge will —"

"Aw, Myra," he said, taking my hands and speaking earnestly to my averted face. "There won't be no judge. Gabe ain't after thet baby. Gabe just keeps coming back — it's like he cain't hep it. He ain't after Clay — he's after what he's *always* been after."

He spoke with such certainty, such utter confidence, that I looked up, curious despite myself, wanting to find the key to the enigma of Gabriel Catts, of his snapping eyes and lifted chin, his stinging slaps and his bitter regrets. But something in my face made Michael stop short, his eyes on mine, just like they'd been that first day on the porch on Magnolia Hill, as if he were searching for something — disappointment or regret, or maybe simple understanding.

Whatever it was, he must not have found it, as he dropped his eyes to our clenched hands and finished lamely. "He's just a sad, lonely man, Myra. He's harmless."

They were the same words he'd excused his brother with that day, when I'd felt that first breath of unease: *he's harmless.* I'd wanted to disagree, even then, for I wasn't a stranger to the Hill. I knew what it was like to be strung out between two desperate men. I knew how bad it could get, but hadn't said a word, afraid I'd sound like a fool, afraid I'd compromise his love.

I couldn't say it then, but I could say it now, and corrected him in a low, sure whisper: "Harmless to *you*, Michael — and Cissie and Candace — but not me. Not *me.*"

Michael didn't argue it, just squatted there before me, his face introspective and resigned, like he was digesting a painful truth, an awful one he could no longer resist, and it was a terrible thing, making him bear witness against his own blood, the worst thing, really. Worse than Tommy and the Preacher; worse than Clay and his blond little curls. But he did it all right, not saying a word, just coming to his feet and kissing my head, telling me to get some sleep, let Louisa watch the baby.

But it must have played heavily on his mind, as he called me when he got to work, back in action and trying to build a Plan, wanting to call Gabe and set a meeting with a lawyer so we could talk this thing out. But the possibility of facing Gabriel, with or without a lawyer, filled me with the most amazing terror. I cried, I paced, I even loaded the nasty little shotgun on the mantle and asked Lou to come in on her day off to set watch like a sentinel in the kitchen.

"What'll I do if he shows?" she asked.

I didn't blink an eye. "Shoot him."

She seemed to find this a perfectly reasonable request, though she declined on the grounds that it would kill Cissie, leaving the shooting up to me, if any was to be done. Given the desperation of the moment, I don't doubt that I would have, had the opportunity arisen, though as it turned out, there was no need. For Gabe's visit stretched out four, then five days, with no attempt at contact, Sim a little hurt he'd been so easily forgotten. He begged me to take him to his Grannie's so he could show Gabe his new reel, though I kept stonily silent on the subject, leaving the excuses to Michael, who was getting better at this lying business, telling him smoothly that Uncle Gabe was sick, that maybe we'd go see him later.

"When?" Sim cried, and Michael just looked away.

"Later."

And that was really about all there was to it. Gabe flew out of Tallahassee on New Year's Eve with Cissie apparently none the wiser, as she caught us on the church steps the next morning and bragged about his visit in her fast, proud Mama-voice, only disappointed he hadn't taken the time to run out and see the baby. I think she was afraid he'd hurt our feelings, as she made a great point of telling us how busy he was these days.

"Working his fool self to death," she said, "and thet ain't Gabe, thet hard work. Worried. Holler-eyed. Hardly left the house, whole time he was here. Thet terrible cold ain't never agreed with him — doan know why he wanted to go tearing off up North in the first place."

We just nodded, Michael and I, careful to keep our eyes on our feet, though I finally unbent enough to say, "Sim'll miss him."

I said it in perfectly unconscious echo of the last time he'd left, hot tears stinging my eyes when Michael added mildly, "So will I."

$$=== 28 ===$$

I *remember to the very hour* the incident that marked the end of my great fall, after which I could say, with all honesty and precision, that I was back to my old self — or rather, my *new* self. For I never really returned to the woman-child I was previous to 1972, I couldn't; like Manderley, she *is no more.*

It happened at a roadside park in North Carolina, where Candace, in one of her brilliant vacation schemes, had taken us to see the rhododendrons bloom. Ed was away on a reserve weekend, Michael (as usual) too busy to take off, leaving just Candace and me and the children to make the long drive up, and being an established Floridian by then, I hadn't packed clothes nearly warm enough for a cold mountain spring. It made for four days of shivery torment, with me finally reduced to going to a country store and paying big-city prices for ski jackets, though through it all, Candace was intent on having a good time, at one point *insisting* we have a picnic.

The spot she chose was one she remembered from a high school 4-H trip, just outside Cherokee at a public picnic area at a juncture of a river and a mountain, with a scenic overlook that was stunning on nicer days, but that day swathed in a ghostly mist, the wind hurling through those mountain passes at about sixty miles an hour. The children were willing to brave the elements to climb to the overlook, but after a few minutes of it, I admitted defeat and returned to the car to scrunch up in my new jacket and watch Candace lay out her picnic with all the finesse of a cat: paper plates and sandwich meats, two-liter drinks and chips.

She was the very picture of domestic bliss in her purple coat and muffler, when suddenly, with no warning at all, the wind gusted between the mountain and the water like a bellows, blowing her carefully appointed table upwards thirty feet in the air, scattering plates and bologna and rolling drinks, with Candace in hot pursuit. She was particularly intent on getting her hands on this rebellious roll of paper towels that was unraveling in the wind, tantalizingly close. It danced ahead of her, hurling itself to the river just inches beyond her frenzied grasp, and sitting there in the shelter of the car, watching her chase after it like a mad thing, I did something I hadn't done in so long that my face felt strangely stretched, my chest hollow with effort: I laughed. I mean *laughed.* I mean, threw my head back and kicked the floorboards and laughed till I about peed in my pants, trying to go out and help her, but hardly able to walk.

Candace, of course, was not so amused, and turned on me like it was *my* fault, shouting and stamping her foot in a way that just made it all the funnier. "It's all ruined!" she kept shouting, as if we'd lost our children to a hurricane. "All ruined!" Till I finally got enough of a grip to help her pick up the pieces and settled her angst by kindly offering to take everyone to Dairy Queen for lunch.

And how long did it take for this magnificent transformation to take place? How long did I walk this earth without the relief of one sincere episode of hilarity? Well, if the dozen or so pictures we took later that afternoon at the Indian village do not lie, Clay must have been two, which would put it close to three years after the first Sims reunion, when I finally said to hell with passivity and turned to fight. And to what do I owe this miraculous recovery? Well, it's hard to say.

Or rather, complicated to say, as everyone holds these wildly differing opinions of the exact nature of my breakdown, and where credit for my recovery lies. Candace, of course, owes it all to the hand of the Lord, Dr. Williams to Freud, Sam to Michael's faithfulness, and Michael to lithium salts, a drug he invested with almost mythical powers. To his mind, it was the presto-chango difference after two years' worth of fruitless searching, a fact no one had reason to argue with till 1983, when I committed the unpardonable psychiatric sin of going off lithium AMA (against medical advice) to Michael's great teeth-gnashing fear it would precipitate another breakdown.

But it didn't, and after three years of lithium-free stability, my diagnosis was changed for a third and final time, to two diabolical-sounding diagnoses: post-traumatic stress syndrome, and clinical depression, bipolar (sometimes unipolar, according to whom you're talking to). I don't doubt that I fit the DMV-III criteria for both, though I personally go to my indomitable mother-in-law for the most accurate summation of mental status.

Cissie, who lost nothing over the years in terms of spunk or kindness or sheer hard-headedness, has a virtual dictionary of cracker-catchphrases to describe most of human experience. There is nothing of science about her explanations, just color and compassion, which tend to lighten the grimmer realities of life. She calls death *going to be with the Lord;* the entire spectrum of female suffering, from migraines to menstrual cramps to endometriosis, *female trouble.* She even has a kindly description for the complaint I suffer from that she applies to every shade of nonstandard thinking from Down's syndrome to outright psychosis: *"Their mind ain't right."*

She only uses the term when someone is way out there, *not among us,* not viciously, but in kindly excuse, as in: "He broke in the church agin, slept on a pew. They called the Law, sent him to jail — I kinda hated it. His mind ain't right — wadn't wearing nothing but pantyhose and an old coat. Told the deputy he lived there."

For the less far-gone, she has a lighter version of this excuse: "Their mind ain't *altogether* right." I assume by this, she means they have moments, maybe years, of relative lucidity, living among us as equals, but still, something isn't quite right there. Not *altogether* right. And after half a dozen years in therapy — on pills, off pills, back on them again — I can say with some pride that I have worked my way up from the former category to take my place as a proud citizen of the latter, by no means a minority around here.

I mean, I'm not sleeping in the church, wearing nothing but pantyhose and a coat, but I'm not a Catts by any means; still just a devout convert to normality, only remarkable in that I went drug-free for four and a half years, till my husband was diagnosed with cancer in 1987, when right back on the carousel I went.

But I'm getting ahead of myself and would really be as amiss as the little Baptist doctor and his soliloquy on orgasm if I went into such glorious detail about mania and depression and didn't give a little time and effort to the years from roughly 1976 till 1987, when I lived the most golden of the Golden Years of my life as a seminormal housewife, cleaving to life and finding a voice. They are the kind of years that almost seem diminished in the telling, as there are no catchwords to describe them, the Klan leaving the county shortly after the death of the little dog (which was indeed the straw that broke the camel's back), Crill defeated in the sheriff's race (possibly due to a concerted effort by the whole McRae family to unseat him or possibly due to his innate sorriness that the episode with the Klan merely brought to light).

I really don't know the details of the matter, as Gabe's unexpected return pretty much cured me of my compulsion to reveal hidden truth, living out the next decade with a less taxing credo, something along the lines of letting sleeping dogs lie. It wasn't scripture, but it was, by God, effective, all our accursers likewise scattered to the wind, Ira moving back and forth between Birmingham and Jacksonville till 1983, when he made a more or less permanent move to Union County.

Now, at this point, I guess I could make a stab at unraveling the twists and turns of my brother's decline, but I won't. Let it suffice to say that he's not likely to ever darken my door again, as his residence in Union County isn't by choice, but compulsion, as he is an inmate at Union Correctional (which he much prefers to his previous residence across the river at Florida State Prison, more commonly known as Raiford). The tale of how he got there makes for fast reading, but you'll never hear it from me; his story is his own, and that it will remain. My sole contribution to his decade-long legal battle is in the form of the depositions I've been subpoenaed to attend to bear witness to his sorry childhood, though to little avail, as the good citizens of Florida have tired of hearing sob stories from criminals and prefer a straight eye-for-an-eye justice.

The only glimmer of good fortune in the whole ugly mess is the fact that though he'd (apparently) long been under investigation, his actual arrest didn't come about till after Mama had gone to her own reward in 1981 via a particularly virulent form of ovarian cancer. It's a matter that I also don't have much to say about, as I wasn't notified of her year-long, life-and-death battle till precisely two weeks before her death. Even then, she apologized for having to bother me with the trifling matter of her funeral, for such was the depth of our eventual estrangement that it wasn't a matter of bitter acrimony or angry accusation, but a slow, gradual drift, another of my father's lasting legacies.

As for Gabe, after that brief Christmas visit in 1976, he was simply gone, vanished from our lives like an uneasy dream, leaving a few odd bits of flotsom and jetsam in his wake. Primarily, one son, plus an apartment full of Civil War memorabilia, maps and books and scribbled legal pads that never quite got taken down and put away, as if, even then, we dimly surmised his departure would not be of an everlasting nature. In a way, you could say that he never really left us at all, his memory haunting us as surely as Rebecca taxed the de Winters. Not in the form of a malevolent housekeeper, but in the affection of his niece and nephew: Sim, who faithfully repeated his many jokes and stories (including the lies about his hand), and Missy, who insists with all the sureness of her very sure nature that she never forgot his laugh. ("Kind of a high *akk-akk,* like the scream of a woodpecker.")

As for Michael and me, we simply never spoke of him again, never told his stories, never conjured his childhood or youth, his unsmiling picture atop Cissie's television as voiceless and unchallenged as a son lost to war. For the first few years, we heard rumor of his wanderings second-hand from Cissie, till someone (maybe Louisa, or possibly Case) saw fit to clarify the details of her favorite grandchild's paternity, when poor Gabe was plucked out with a vengeance for the better part of seven years.

It was an abandonment that was never justified, much less explained, any more than the fact that though I was obviously a partner in his sin, I was never indicted in Cissie's wrath. I really don't know why; possibly because my mind wasn't right, or more likely, because Cissie, as daughter of a flagrant womanizer, always tends to blame the man —

reason number four-hundred-and-one that she really is worthy of mother-figure status. In keeping with my new credo (the one about sleeping dogs), I certainly never asked, the drama of the previous decade gradually fading against the passage of the mild Florida seasons that were not marked by snow or turning leaf, but rather an unending succession of children's sports.

For whereas lithium had once provided a baseline stability in my life, now there was autumn football that gave way to the winter sports, soccer and basketball, then Little League and Babe Ruth, half my weekdays and most of my weekends spent on a hard bench or echoing gym, making a true ass of myself yelling for my children on some field of play.

· That's really how the years come to me, not through death or estrangement or bitter loss, but the growth of my children: Simon, dark and sinewy and eerily like his namesake till he was thirteen, when he underwent an amazing teenage transformation, growing six inches in a year, till he towered over his father by a good three inches (to his father's everlasting delight, I might add). His face changed, too, losing its angles and bones, his quick smile unthinkingly robbed of its potential when we put him in braces when he was nine, not realizing at the time that once that Michael-like gap was gone, it wasn't ever coming back.

Personality-wise, he was the prototypical first child, with all the pressure and promise that entails, ridden hard by his father — too hard, I always thought, as Michael tended to most identify with him and expect great things. On this, he was hardly ever disappointed, as Sim worked hard to achieve in just about anything he undertook, from playing baseball to making grades to learning the furniture business, a perfection that used to bother me a little; still does, now that I think of it.

As for Missy, there was certainly no danger of my falling into the trap of over-identification with her, as she was my opposite in everything but height, a peculiar combination of her two missing uncles, with Gabe's verbal agility (not to mention love of gossip and nine best friends), though physically, she was clearly (and in her eyes, tragically) a Sims.

"Face it, Mama," she told me on her twelfth birthday, when she was already half-a-head taller than her beloved Grannie. "I'm gonna be this red-headed Amazon warrior and it's all your fault."

In time, that's exactly what she became, her size and coloring exacerbated by a personality that was as flaming as her hair, her IQ testing out at 148, her athletic prowess predicted by an observant T-ball coach when she was all of seven years old. When I asked him how he could tell this young, he looked at me like I was an idiot indeed.

"Look at them arms," he said. "They're a dog-gone yard long."

When I pointed out that *my* arms were a yard long and *I* wasn't an athlete, he'd spit out a cheekful of tobacco. "Maybe you ain't got the heart. That 'un there. She's got heart."

Well, I couldn't argue with that. She was all heart, my Missy was, heart and mind and a will of iron that was fortunately not so often set against me, unlike her wee brother Clay, who seemed divinely ordained to take the place of his dearly departed uncle as the Catts family pet. Blond, cowlicked and amiable, he looked the part early on, and though he was never his uncle's academic equal (fighting a losing battle in the classroom till he was diagnosed dyslexic in the third grade), he had all his hard-headed determination, not a difficult child as much as he was an amazingly sensitive one.

Sim and Missy were fairly tough emotionally, as I guess they had to be, given the subterranean turmoil of their early years. By order of his birth, Clay had mostly avoided all of that, the shadow of insanity and depression and betrayal all passed into history by the time he was galloping around on his sturdy little legs, the baby in a family who loved babies. It made him soft, as youngest children sometimes are, and easily wounded, his first full sentence a cry from the heart: "You hurt my *feelings!*"

He'd shout it at one or the other of us about twice a week, the *feelings* an absolute howl of outrage at the very idea of anyone disciplining him, disagreeing with him, or otherwise thwarting his pursuit of a life of amiable leisure. To say that we spoiled him is a vast understatement. The truth of the matter is that we coddled and mimicked him and laughed our butts off most of the time, as even aside from the dyslexia, Clay was cut out of a different cloth, christened *Claybird* by his father for no very good reason — perhaps a tribute to his soaring imagination, or (now that I think of it), his very fragility.

I really don't know, as Michael and I didn't have the luxury of sitting around and pondering the abstractions of our children's personalities, all our time and effort spent raising them. My part was mainly on the homefront, cooking and cleaning and taxiing them around in the eternal triangle of school and sports and church, while Michael and Sam worked sixty-hour weeks, trying to salvage what was left of Sanger after the Klan left it alone.

It was a task five years in the making, and not altogether successful till they hit big-money pay dirt in 1980, when they second-mortgaged everything they owned to buy out the failing South Georgia Furniture Company in Waycross and rework it to specialize in supplying ready-made furniture and fixtures to the burgeoning mobile home furnishing industry. That's where they really made their money, on cheap pine headboards and couches and loveseats — not what you'd call heirloom furniture, though God forbid one of them to hear you say it.

The Golden Years were literally golden in that sense, our net worth beginning at maybe fifty thousand, house, pine, factory and all, and ending at closer to five or six mill, though to tell you the truth (and Candace hates me to say this) it really isn't the fortune it sounds. I mean, it's not like it's free cash and gold coin like Scrooge McDuck keeps locked up in his safe, but all tied up with accountants and cash flow and renovation. It really doesn't affect me much in the daily wear and tear of life, as I've always been crucified on the cross of a household budget that even in 1986 (the year Michael bought me a fifty-thousand-dollar Mercedes) was right at seventy dollars a week, and I only got that after I threatened to divorce him. Because that was the thing with Michael Catts: he never changed.

I mean, I married a hard-working, hard-loving, penny-pinching poor boy in 1967, and for all practical purposes, I buried the same, twenty years and six million dollars later. He put on a little weight in the meanwhile, lost some hair; went from playing sand-lot baseball to country club golf, but that was about it, a loyalist if there ever was one, still set in the old ways, with nothing of pretention about him.

He was just a working man who'd hit it big, who still ate with his mother every Sunday, still sent his children to public schools — small rural schools, predominantly black, so that all three of them sound like they grew up on the Hill, with that fast, rolling, gheechie slang that I still love. We figured they'd get as good an education there as anywhere in town, though Candace was appalled, not at the racial angle (or not altogether; it's hard to tell with Candace), but the spiritual. For at some point in their varied development, the Charismatics threw over public education in favor of private Christian schools, where their children could be educated in the ways of the Lord with all comfort and security, free from the Mongol hoards.

Candace, who only got holier with the passing years (and could sure enough run your life if you gave her a leg), nagged me day and night to rescue my children from the clutches of the secular humanists, filling me with all sorts of horror stories of rape and pillage, mandatory sex education, rampant drug use. She constantly held up for example the Zen perfection of Lori's life: the chapel, the creationist texts, right up till 1984, when Lori herself showed up on my doorstep three months before her wedding with the little dipstick out of a home pregnancy test in her hand, wondering if the blue meant yes or no (it meant yes).

At that point, a less stubborn woman might have admitted that a semester or two in Human Growth and Development might not necessarily have been a bad thing, but not old Candace. Like another sibling I could name, she has never liked being second-guessed, and just threw up her hands in the time-honored fundamentalist fashion, wondering how and oh how could it have happened?

It was a question I was particularly suited to answer, as Lori had been seeing the same boy for the past three years (Curtis by name, son of an old hunting buddy of Case's), car dating for two of them. But Candace was so devastated that I just bit my tongue and stood by her as God knows she'd stood by me, throwing them the wedding of the season on the front yard under the magnolias, with a harp and golden chairs, so posh and *chi-chi* that not a murmur of accusation arose from any of her Charismatic brethren, or Curtis' wide-eyed folks.

The reception afterwards was also a Myra-affair, as I seem to have a knack for that sort of thing, out by the pool, equally posh, though the whole thing was complicated by a prearranged student trip to France that Missy had talked her father into, one of those if-it's-Monday-this-must-be-Paris deals that fell right smack in the middle of the wedding crisis. Her departure the night of the shower had me a little anxious, though the week went fast enough with all the wedding hype, Michael and I both picking her up at the airport in Tallahassee on Friday night, pacing and anxious when her plane was late.

I was entertaining visions of burning aircraft and strewn debris when they finally announced the arrival, Missy popping out first, running across the tarmac and through the gates in a froth of excitement, clutching a present to her chest that she said was for the wedding. I didn't know how she'd come up with the cash for a gift, as her spending allowance had been pretty tight, but she was very secretive about it, suddenly all right about the wedding that she'd been fussing about before she left, a little jealous (as was Clay) that the whole family's attention had been diverted to Lori.

But all that was apparently past, her grousing about the bridesmaid dresses lost in the excitement of the gift! Wait'll we saw what she'd gotten them! We'd die! Which, in fact, turned out to be nearly the case, for when Missy triumphantly read the card attached to the little gift, I nearly choked to death on a wedding mint, making for possibly the most embarrassing moment of my life.

It happened late in the afternoon of the wedding, the harpist gone, the food long devoured, Lori already changed into her traveling clothes in preparation for the run through the rice. That's when Missy gathered us all in the living room and insisted Lori open her present before she left, dancing a little jig of impatience as she unwrapped the little box and dug through a mountain of tissue paper to unveil a pretty little china egg.

"It's *Lemonges*," Missy cried, and before her father or I could open our mouths to ask her where in the world she'd come up with the cash for such a gift, she insisted, "Read the card! It's from *both* of us!"

I was standing in the French doors chewing a handful of wedding mints while Lori obediently ripped open the envelope and read it, then, oddly enough, shot a fast, embarrassed little glance at me. I met her eye evenly, wondering what in the world was the matter, while Missy practically stamped her foot with impatience, crying, "Read it, Lori! Read it!"

Still, Lori didn't comply, and Missy finally snatched it from her hand and read it herself: "Congratulations to Lori and Curtis. From Missy and *Uncle Gabe*."

She read the last name with a proud little lift of her head, bringing an immediate hush to the room, Sim jumping up immediately and trying to grab the card from her hand, saying, "You're *lying* —"

But Missy jerked it away, snapped, "Am *not*." Then, to her father, "I met him in the airport in New York. My plane was late and I called him, Daddy, just like you said."

I was dumbfounded when she read his name, actually choking when she said the part about her Daddy telling her to call him. One of the little mints must have gone down the wrong way, and all I could do was stand there helplessly coughing these dry little coughs as everyone in the room turned to stare at me while Missy went on and on in a rush of undisguised infatuation.

"And he came right away, dressed like this nutty professor, wearing this big coat over his pajama top, and I said: 'Gosh, Uncle Gabe, I said the plane was *late,* not *on fire.*'"

I guess I'd have stood there and choked to death in front of them all, if I hadn't been so intent on getting the hell away from Missy and her shining face, staggering to the kitchen and gulping down a handful of water while everyone else moved out to the porch for the rice-throwing that signaled the end of the wedding.

We'd long ago made plans to go to the beach *en famille* for a few days to divert Candace from the trauma of losing her only child, and as soon as the bride and groom left, everyone was ready to go, coming in to change clothes and make arrangements of who would ride with whom. I just stayed in the kitchen and nursed a glass of water, told Candace to go on, that I'd be down in an hour or two, after I'd straightened up a little, wrapped up what was left of the wedding cake.

When they finally got off, I kicked off my shoes and sadly surveyed the wreck of the house, the living room littered with punch cups and half-eaten food, the floating candles all upended where the groomsmen had thrown Curtis in the pool (this was a Southern wedding, remember), the delicate fairy lights we'd draped in the trees sagging dangerously close to the water. I went out to unplug them, when I noticed the window was lit in the apartment upstairs. Curtis and the boys had gotten dressed up there and must have left it on, the rectangle of golden light hanging over the pool like a quiet moon, a silent call-back to another May evening that stopped me dead in my tracks.

Over the years, I'd occasionally come upon some reminder like this, which didn't upset me as much as it perplexed me, made me wonder: what *did* happen that summer? Of course, by now, it was all ancient history. Michael had even told Sim, and soon (very soon, with her spouting his name all over the place) I'd have to set Missy down and tell her the bare-bone facts of the matter. I wasn't exactly looking forward to it, but figured that sooner or later she'd inevitably hear it somewhere, and I wanted it to come from me, though to tell you the truth, even now, none of it was so clear. Some things I remembered very well: the fight with Ira, the day at the springs. Other things were less precise, like those cursedly faithful little slivers of memory of the lazy afternoons in the apartment upstairs, Gabriel always looking up when I came in, shirtless and barefoot in the heat, always glad to see me. I have to say I remembered them, though they seemed very far away, like they'd happened on some continent light-years from home, not those tiny rooms right up those creaking stairs.

Standing there in the doorway, I couldn't help but think how odd it was that tonight of all nights the light should be left on, as we hardly used the old apartment anymore, except to store Christmas ornaments and odds and ends: ski equipment and fishing gear. Somewhere beneath the clutter, boxed and forgotten, were the books and legal pads, companions to the curling maps that still lined the walls. Sim or Missy, or (worse yet) Clay sometimes asked why we left them up, though I never answered, simply because I really didn't know. Maybe because Michael wanted to retain that last tie; maybe because I'd stepped on a thumbtack the day I went to tear them down and never went back.

I shook my head, the coincidence of it all striking me as an omen, as if God were saying: *Myra, baby, it's time to deal.* It wouldn't be the first time He'd ever told me that, as most of my breakthroughs had come that way, in the form of tiny, accidental triggers that were like clues at the scene of a crime, that could be reconstructed to even greater discoveries, though Candace said there was nothing accidental about them at all: it was the hand of the Lord.

So maybe this was, too, and I was standing there, pondering the strangeness of it all, when someone spoke behind me, "I don't feel so hot."

I jumped like a cat, but it was just Michael, still in his dress pants, but down to a T-shirt and bare feet, who laid himself carefully on the couch, said, "I thank those oysters were bad."

"You scared me to death," I breathed, taking a step on the deck to pull the plug on the lights. "I thought you took the boys."

He just laid there on the couch, his forearm thrown across his eyes. "Mama took 'em."

"Cissie drove?" I asked in amazement, but he just rolled to his side.

"Yeah — listen, baby, I'm dying here. We got any Maalox or something?"

I looked through the medicine cabinet and dosed him with whatever bellyache medicine we had on hand, then rubbed his feet, as thirty years of working on concrete was finally beginning to tell on him in leg cramps and sheer fatigue. I didn't say anything, didn't mention Gabe, and how he was surely the reason Cissie had made the unheard-of trip to the beach, to hear more of Missy's joyous sighting, though after the Maalox and the foot rubbing had eased him a little, Michael offered, "You mad?"

"About what?" He frowned at my evasion, opening an eye to look at me wryly till I played it straight. "No," I said simply. Then, "You might have told me."

He just shrugged. "Didn't think nothing would come of it — but maybe it's for the best. Maybe it's time you two got over your little pissing contest and grew up."

I would have been on my feet in an instant, except that he had me pinned with his feet, sitting up a little, saying, "Myra? Would you please sit down? Mama's gitting old. She ain't gone be around forever, and when she dies it'll be too late. Uncle Case and me was talking. We thank it's time he was coming home."

Case was hardly changed over the years, though he'd moved out to the fish camp now that he was retired and only came into town occasionally, to take Cissie to the doctor or drop by to see the children or supervise my little renovation projects. He was probably closer to Cissie than anyone on Earth now that Maggie was gone, and I couldn't very well argue his point, just sat back and rubbed my eyes with that same tired sense of inevitability I'd felt when I saw the apartment light.

"Has he talked to him?" I finally asked.

Michael just shrugged. "He doan know where he is. Candace give me the number. Says he's teaching again — doing all right, she says. Still ain't married."

Well, I could have done without this little dig and came to my feet, shoving his legs aside with such force that he couldn't stop me, though he made a grab for my dress, said, "Myra, would you — *damn,*" he breathed, curling up and gripping his belly. "*Damn,* that hurts."

He was genuinely in pain, so obviously that I stopped, asked, "Where?"

"Here," he said, feeling for his side and wiggling around for a better position.

I pushed up his T-shirt and inspected his smooth brown flank, murmured, "Maybe we need to call Dr. Williams."

"I already talked to him," he said, which wasn't so unusual, as they golfed at the same country club, and around here, professionals ply their trade anywhere you can catch them. "He says it's gall stones."

"Gall stones?" I cried, amazed that he'd gone as far as a diagnosis, though Michael just grimaced.

"Yeah. He's been after me to git 'em out, but who has time to sit around the house six weeks? I don't."

"You do so. You'll go tomorrow," I said, with such conviction that he smiled.

"No, baby, shhh," he said, pulling me back to the couch. "Come 'ere and sit down. I'll do it after Christmas," he promised. "I already talked to Sam. In January. When things slow down."

When things slow down had become another of his sayings, as in: *I'll string that clothesline for you when things slow down.* Or: *I'll take you to Jamaica when things slow down.* Unfortunately, things never did, and 1986 was no exception, the summer flashing by and then the autumn, Lori going into labor in December four weeks early and safely delivering a tiny five-pound baby boy whom she named Ryan Dylan, to her grandmother's unending amazement.

"*Rine?*" Cissie exclaimed. "Like a watermelon rine?"

"Like *Ryan's Hope,*" Missy told her, and Cissie — who'd named her own sons for archangels — shook her head sadly.

"Poor little thang. Going through life with a name like *thet.*"

She set the tone of the year that all in all, comes to me as one of unending triumph, except for Michael's continuing bouts with the recurring bellyache that Dr. Williams insisted was cholecystitis. He kept at him all year to have those stones out in elective surgery, but Michael steadfastly resisted till the following September, when he concocted a Plan that would enable him to wile away his recuperation during Missy's softball season.

Around these parts, girls' softball is a serious concern, the local girls having gone to All-Stars six years running. The city had started an autumn league to keep them in form, and though it was just a county-wide thing, the competition was red hot, Missy her team's star catcher/hitter. She'd been at Michael all summer long to come on board as pitching coach, and he'd finally agreed, thinking that he'd run in for the surgery the last week in September, then spend the rest of October hobbling around a baseball diamond before he returned to work for the Christmas rush.

It was a sound Plan, I must admit, and I remember how lighthearted we were the morning I drove him to the hospital, him giving me a hard time about how messy I kept the Mercedes. I'd only had it a few months, and already the tufted leather seats were strewn with straws and coffee cups and stray cleats, even a pair of wadded up pantyhose Missy had left there the Sunday before. Michael, who'd only gotten neater with the passing years (and was making five-hundred-a-month payments on the thing), didn't fuss too much, just shook his head, said, "Myra Louise, you'll never change."

He closed his eyes when he said it, for he wasn't feeling too hot these days, the little episodes of cholecystitis growing more frequent, so that he wouldn't eat much, afraid it'd make him sick. "I'm glad you finally broke down and penciled this in," I told him, reaching over and feeling his face. "You're white as a sheet."

He just smiled a thin smile, his eyes still closed. "I'm all right," he said. "Git some color during softball."

Candace met us in the lobby, as she had gone back to work that spring to help pay for Ryan's month in the incubator. In four short months she was already ruling the roost in ICU, the very personification of modern nursing in teal scrubs and running shoes and the wire-rimmed glasses she wore to work. She gave her brother a good-natured hard time as he checked in, though something in his face must have caught her eye, as I noticed she lifted her face to look at him through her bifocals the whole time she talked.

She said nothing of it to Michael, but waited till the orderly came to wheel him away to surgery, then asked me in a light voice, "How long has he been that sallow?"

"That *what?*" I asked, concentrating on a small mountain of insurance and release forms they'd left me to sign.

"Sallow," she repeated, watching the double doors close behind him, then turning. "You know, pallid. Yellow."

I shrugged. "I don't know. He won't eat. Says it makes him sick."

She just folded her arms on this bit of news and thoughtfully chewed her lip, finally offered, "He almost looks," she paused a moment, "jaundiced."

I had no idea what she was talking about, and she didn't explain, just chewed her lip a long moment, then flashed another vague smile, this one purely mechanical, said she had to get back on the floor but would come down for the surgery at six.

"Don't worry about it," I told her. "Brother Sloan or Carlym'll be by. Dr. Azuri says it'll just be a couple of hours."

But she studiously ignored me, said, "I'll be there at six."

As it turned out, she actually talked herself into the operating suite as a scrub, not showing up till nearly nine, when she appeared at the door of the waiting room in a pair of maroon surgical scrubs and told me to call the children, tell them I'd be staying the night. I'd been sitting around all evening, skimming magazines and making small talk with Carlym, the new associate at Welcome, both of us coming to our feet on her news.

"Why?" I asked immediately. "What's wrong?"

"The surgery went fine," she answered smoothly. "They're stitching him up right now."

"They got the gallstones?" I pressed, and she nodded, but didn't offer anything else, just took off her glasses and wearily rubbed her eyes. It was clear that I wasn't getting the big picture here, but I couldn't quite figure it, just glanced between her and Carlym, then finally stammered, "Well, that's good, isn't it? I mean, he won't keep getting sick, will he?"

In reply, Candace just slid her glasses on and looked at me with her old tired confidence. "No. He won't keep getting sick like that. Never again." She started backing to the door. "Dr. Azuri'll be wanting to see you when the lab work's in. Tonight or tomorrow. The lab's closed, but I'm calling a tech, see if he'll come in early. 'Kay?"

She smiled when she said it, another quick, fake flash, but I didn't return it, mysteriously chilled by the eerie permanence of the innocent little reassurance she'd given me: *never again.*

A s it turned out, I never left the hospital, but stayed right there in the waiting room all night long, arms folded, staring at the wall, knowing something had gone very wrong, but too stiff and paralyzed to ask. Candace came in twice — once to sneak me into recovery to get a peek at my peacefully sleeping husband — then later, just before daylight, to take me down to pathology. We didn't say anything on the long walk down the hall, just made our way to the little anteroom and stood there staring at the X-ray sceens, the examining tables, till the lab tech finally came out with a stack of yellow slips in his hand.

He paused a moment when he saw us, said he was taking them straight to Dr. Azuri (who was also staying the night, asleep in the doctor's lounge), and though Candace accepted this with a nod, I couldn't help but ask, "Is it all right?"

"The doctor'll be speaking to you," he said very kindly, in a flat, south Georgia drawl, though my face must have been too pleading to turn aside, as he paused to add with a face of terrible compassion. "It doan look good, Miz Catts."

On that, he turned and strode away without another word, and it's funny how that little phrase has stuck in my head. Even now, someone will ask me about things as innocent as softball scores or weather predictions, and I'll hear myself mimicking his flat, wiregrass accent exactly, saying: "It doan look good."

I don't know why I do it — maybe to rid the words of the hideous, blunting weight that settled in my veins like plutonium, making me go very still, very quiet. I didn't press Candace any more, just followed her to the little consultation room they had set up for such interviews where Dr. Azuri was already waiting. Yet another friend of Candace's (he went to her church), he was a young Lebanese doctor, the father of three children himself, obviously a little shaken by the news and trying to be optimistic, but not having much to offer by way of hope, except to say that he was calling in an oncologist from Tallahassee, the best guy around.

I just watched his face and nodded on cue, too sane to be comfortable with the disassociation of shock and not even recognizing it for what it was, just flowing along its quiet stream, acting and reacting out of a numb void, just like the bad old days. When the little interview was over, we all stood and shook hands as if we were concluding a business deal, taking care of a few incidentals as we made our way to the elevator: the post-op visit, the care of the stitches. Then back Candace and I went to ICU.

The hall and lobby were empty that time of day, the clerks and secretaries not yet arrived, just the night shift nurses, all friends of Candace, who turned when they saw us step out of the elevator, their faces wary, knowing the news wasn't good. Candace stopped to speak to them while I went down the corridor to Michael, who was still asleep in his curtained little alcove, face-up because of the IV, not drugged, just sleeping in, a luxury he didn't so often allow himself at home.

There were no chairs there, so I just stood by the bed, my purse on my shoulder, watching him sleep, my mind as blank as if the doctor had whacked it with a hammer. Candace stuck her head in the curtains after a few minutes, her face as stiff and tearless as mine, and whispered that maybe she needed to make a few phone calls. It was like she was asking my permission to do me this most incredible favor, refusing the quarters I began rooting for in my purse, saying she'd use the phone in the doctor's lounge.

She was gone in an instant, but our whispers must have awakened Michael, as he began stirring on the bed, his face corded from the pillow, blunted with sleep. I didn't say anything, just stood there while he did his little stretchings and rubbings, something in my face making him pause after a moment to mutter: "What'sa matter?"

When I didn't answer, he sat up a little and glanced around at the IVs, the blinking console. "I thought you went home," he said. Then, "What is this?" Meaning, the curtains, the machinery.

"Intensive Care," I whispered.

He leaned back then and scratched his chest with his free hand, still a little disoriented, his eyes on my face, repeating, "Myra? What's wrong?"

I just shook my head, not able to say a thing. For it had only been four years since Mama died, and I had a pretty good idea what it was all about: the thinness; the pain; the gray death. But I couldn't say the word and just stood there with my purse on my shoulder, till he patted the bed. "Come 'ere." he said, "Come lay down."

I set my purse on the floor and with a little maneuvering was able to lower the bed rails enough to lay beside him, my chest to his shoulder, my shoes up on the top sheet that smelled of bleach and many washings. "There we go," he said when I got myself situated. "I didn't sleep worth a dime in this place. I'm talking to Azuri, tell him to send me home."

There was a petulance to his voice that made him sound like Clayton, and I finally whispered, "I'll speak to him."

That's really all I said, all either of us said for a long moment, just lying there side by side, the nurse coming in to check on us after a while. Yet another friend of Candace's, she was cheery and professional, checking the IV and saying the doctor would be in shortly, though she never met Michael's eye, the whole time she talked.

He must have noticed the omission, for as soon as she left, he spoke levelly into the silence, asked, "Myra? What is it?"

I still couldn't answer, just pressed my stinging eyes to his shoulder, till he pulled away and looked at me across the pillow. He didn't say anything, just looked at me eye-to-eye for a long moment, then lay back, the silence running on, I don't know how long, till he finally spoke again, whispered, "You won't leave me, will you?"

Looking back, it seems so strange that he asked me that, because at that point, he didn't know a thing. Only Candace and I knew about the ammonia levels and the liver failure and the five months, and yet, that's what he asked, and it was a funny thing with Michael, his fear of abandonment. Sometimes I think it was the root of his ambition, his overwhelming generosity, the Mercedes and diamonds. He didn't want to be left, had a certain need to bribe, to hedge his bets, to keep you on the hook.

God knows where it'd come from. As far as I knew, he'd never been abandoned in any sense of the word, and yet he feared it so. Maybe the seeds had been sown in his babyhood when Mr. Simon had marched away to war. Maybe it rested there, the first loss that became his last fear, and though I couldn't give him anything else, I could surely give him that, having a hard time speaking, finally whispering, "Never."

And I didn't, that day or any other, always at his side, always waiting. Waiting for Dr. Azuri to come and give him the actual word, waiting for the MRIs and X-rays and ultrasounds. Waiting all week long for a three-way consultation with Candace and the oncologist from Tallahassee who finally showed late on Saturday morning, not in surgical scrubs, but (of all things) khaki pants and a maroon FSU polo shirt, as he was stopping off to see us on the way to the big game. He'd already seen the assorted lab results, and since Michael wasn't buying the odds on chemo, was in complete agreement with Dr. Azuri, offering nothing, not a crumb of hope, basically just telling us to make our arrangements, the end was near.

"Three to five months," he said, trying for a professional compassion, but by God excited about them 'Noles, his face relaxed with a weekender's relief as he gave us a brief rundown on the vicissitudes of pancreatic cancer, at one point fishing a little flashlight from his shirt pocket and clicking it in Michael's eye, saying, "See? It's jaundiced already."

I had no earthly idea what he was talking about, just sat there in the same clothes I'd been wearing for four days, having a damn hard time feeling the ground under my feet. It was like I was receding into the atmosphere as he gamely fielded Candace's many questions, a few words cutting through the fog, one of them: *liver failure.* The other: *coma.* The last: *morphine,* while all around us the click and chatter of the hospital routine continued, the nurses coming on shift, orderlies emptying trays, a continuum of life I could not understand, wondering how they could go so merrily along? Didn't they realize the world was coming to an end?

But at that point, I didn't cry, didn't do anything but nod like a trained dog, standing and shaking the doctor's hand when he left. I think I might have told him to enjoy the game, I wouldn't doubt it. I hadn't felt so disassociated in years, Michael or Candace occasionally looking at me, asking: Are you all right? I'd just nod; I was fine.

This wasn't really happening, was it? It was psychosis, wasn't it? Because there really was a queasy unreality about the bright, golden day, Candace finally breaking down and sobbing when the doctor left, Michael closing his eyes, still tired from the surgery. Tired and dying, it seemed — at least that's what I *think* the doctor said.

Even after Candace got a grip on herself and had us pray, growing more militant and Charismatic by the moment, rebuking cancer and almost visibly retreating beyond the curtains of her faith, even that seemed surreal. A little part of my heart was sure that Dr. Williams would come by in a moment and say: "Myra, honey, you're tired. A little stressed out. I told you about going off lithium. Told you it'd seem real to you. I warned you, baby."

Later in the afternoon, the children came by as arranged. Michael had been in the hospital four days by then, long enough that none of it was so strange anymore, though of the three, only Sim knew the truth, from Candace. She'd sworn him to secrecy, for we hadn't quite decided how to tell Missy and Clay, smiling and faking it when they showed up just after four. Sim was quiet and stunned, Missy and Clay having a big old time, bringing their father a vase of carnations from the lobby gift shop and a Whitman sampler they ate on the spot, Missy all alather about her game that night, begging Michael to come.

"We're gone whip butt and take names," she assured him, fighting Clay for the caramels and talking baseball. "Grace Burke's pitching, but I don't care — *pleeease* say you'll come, Daddy. I *promise* we'll win."

When I told her it was too soon for him to be out, she begged even harder, sensing a thawing in her father and going for it, promising to hit him a homer. She was getting up to leave when she said it and pointed majestically over the bed like Babe Ruth did for the little boy in the movie, not even telling me good-bye, just doing her usual little begging dance to see if Joanna could spend the night. "Sim won't be there and Clay's going to Kenneth's — *pleeeease,* Mama?"

Clay was going home with Kenneth as a planned diversion to give us time to talk to her alone, so I just kissed her and told her no. I wanted to say something to Sim, but was silenced by the other two, just walked them to the elevator and kissed him good-bye, told him everything would work out. He just nodded in reply. Poor Sim, lately he'd been looking older and older. Now, suddenly, he was so very young.

When I returned to the room, I found Michael sitting on the edge of the bed in his little hospital gown. I pleaded for him to wait for the doctor, to lay back down, but he was possessed with his mother's hardheaded determination, calling for his clothes, saying, "Hell, Myra, you heard the man. There ain't nothing for me here — where's my stuff?"

It was only with some pleading and finally, tears, that I got him to wait long enough to get an official discharge, as it was his iron-clad intention to go to Missy's game. In the regular course of events, this might have been impossible, but at this point, there was nothing Dr. Azuri could refuse him. He just signed him out with a shake of the head, reminding him to go easy on the stitches and come back Tuesday to have the staples removed.

I promised he would, and once I got him into the parking lot, into the slanting September sun, it really was better, smoky and autumnal, if still a little surreal, for nothing had changed here, either. The traffic through town was the same Saturday afternoon tangle, the car still littered with McDonald's wrappers and cleats and pantyhose, though Michael didn't comment on it this time, just rode along with a tired gratefulness, glad to be going home.

By the time we made the turnaround back into town, Missy's game was well under way, the early darkness tinted with a hint of a Halloween chill. With a little hobbling effort, we made our way around the fence to our place just behind the bullpen, one of the parents coming over to help me with the lawn chairs, a few asking Michael about his surgery, none of them any the wiser. We made the correct replies without saying much of anything, then settled in our chairs, the score two to four at the middle of the fifth, our girls up to bat.

After a week cooped up in the hospital, I was glad of the clear night air and grateful for the diversion of the game that had Michael's attention immediately, the Cottondale team a tight bunch, our girls' work cut out for them. I just sat there like I'd done many a night before, with the same old nervous jitter in my stomach when Missy was called on deck, grinning at us through the wire without an inkling of the day's discoveries, only glad we'd made it, after all.

The batter up was Tiffany Campbell, who grounded right and, by savage pumping, managed to hit first base a blink before the ball, to the wild cheering of the crowd. It put the count at one on base, two outs, when Missy came to bat, cocky as Babe Ruth, but a mite more attractive, her calves a yard long in her knee socks, her face snapping with that old Missy confidence. She forgot all about us once she made the plate, her entire attention narrowed down to the ball in the pitcher's hand, her elbows raised high, passing on the first pitch and jerking in disgust when the umpire called it a strike.

She stepped away from the plate and caught her father's eye, the message as clear as if she'd said it aloud (*"Low and inside, my behind,"*). Then, with that — I don't know — inexplicable confidence, she was cocky enough to lift the bat and point it at left field, just like the movie, and mouth to her father: *homer, left field.*

Everyone saw it and laughed, for this was classic Missy Catts, full of life, and I'm only glad she connected with the next pitch, because I couldn't have sat there for four balls and two more strikes, stomach churning, legs weak. My mind was still rushing headlong over Dr. Azuri's hard sympathy ("You could try Houston or Turo, spend a hell of a lot of money, but it won't matter much, in the end"), my thoughts not so organized, though for a moment there a small childish petulance washed over me and for the first time that day, I closed my eyes and genuinely prayed.

Not like Candace, not for a miraculous recovery, but what seems in retrospect a particularly silly prayer: that she hit the ball, that He owed us this one. When I opened my eyes, Missy had turned back to the plate and assumed her tight, high-elbow stance, waiting on the ninety-mile-an hour underhand pitch that went so fast I couldn't see it. All I heard was the crack of the bat and the shouting, watching in wonder as the small, white blur went up in a clear, soaring pop to left field, over the back-peddling outfielder, over the sagging chain-length fence, gone.

The crowd came to its feet to a man, except for Michael, who sat there in his lawn chair, shaking his head in a tiny, barely perceptible shrug of disbelief, not even clapping as she ran the bases to the roar of the crowd. This was the stuff legends were made of, high good times out on the old ball field, the stadium lights white and streaming, the first-base coach high-fiving her as she passed, a dozen hands reaching out to pat our backs and congratulate us on *what a girl!*

All that fierce exulting victory, set against the day's silent defeat, produced, I'd say, the most exquisite pain I've ever endured, ever hope to endure again. Michael's white face beside me was still set in that determined, easy smile that was only betrayed by a small wetness in his eyes, which he reached up and touched as she bore down on home plate, jumping on it with both feet and bouncing high in the air, her eyes no longer on her father at all, knowing he'd always be there for her; he always had before.

She just disappeared into the dugout, still high-fiving and fighting hugs, leaving us there with nothing left to say, for we wouldn't tell her that night, we couldn't. It had become one of those hard things, like second-mortgages and orthodontist bills, that you bore in secret misery when you had children, the burden of the silence sapping what was left of my strength, so that I hardly remember the rest of the game — the final score, the victory trip to Dairy Queen. I can't recall a single moment till we got home, the house quiet, Michael white and exhausted, sitting at the kitchen table and punching the blinking light on the answering machine while Missy kicked off her cleats.

She was still full of game chatter that turned to squeals of delight when she heard the quiet voice that filled the kitchen with an odd familiarity that I could not, at first, place. "Ah, Michael, this is Gabe," it said, and I closed my eyes. "Candace called and I'm — ah, thinking about flying down." There was a pause, then a brief, "Call me."

That was all, then the click of the receiver and the sharp beep of the next message that could not be heard over Missy's yelp of joy. "Uncle Gabe?" she cried. "That was *Uncle Gabe?* He's coming? That is so — I gotta call Joanna —"

She left in a swirl of excitement, her cleats in one hand, pulling her jersey over her head with the other. I followed as far as the door and watched her go upstairs, knowing this might be my last glimpse of the perfect childhood, knowing we'd have to tell her tomorrow, that Sim couldn't be farmed out forever. When she made the top of the stairs, I turned and looked at Michael, who was sitting at the table, ignoring the beeps and messages that continued to play on, his face no longer white and strained, but cool and speculative, with an expression I could read easily enough.

With no discussion at all, I said quietly above the trill of the rewind, "No, Michael."

He looked up at me a different man, his old color rising, his face lifted to speak, but I shook my head. "Never," I said, retreating upstairs to the bathroom, to the medicine cabinet and the little orange Pamalors that, early on, affect me like a tranquilizer, producing a heart-slowing, mind-dimming calm.

Missy was in the shower, and as she got out, wet and happy as a seal, I had to ask her how she could be so sure about the homer to left field. Michael could sometimes explain his magic to me and his daughter was as generous, wrapping herself in a towel, saying, "Wasn't nothing to it. Old Gracie ain't what she used to be. Got that displaced cuff, always low and inside, low and inside. They need to change her out more. She's fast, by gosh, but she's too stinking predictable." She straightened up, her head framed in the white turban. "So I hit it hard and out and *wa-la,* a homer to left field. Did Daddy like it?"

I assured her he did, and she gave me a quick hug as she went to her room, still brimming with excitement, telling me as she passed, "I just can't believe Uncle Gabe is really coming — you'll like him, Mama. He is so stinking funny. I can't wait to tell Sim. He'll die —"

Then she was gone, leaving me there in front of the mirror, staring at my reflection face-on: the pale skin, the dark shaggy hair that glinted red in the vanity light, my eyes hollow, larger than usual, already showing the effects of the Pamalor. It gave me an eerie feeling, reminding me of another visit from a beloved uncle, another vacant woman there to welcome him, and with a shutter of foreboding, I hurried to bed, hoping for fast, immediate sleep.

But the reaction time wasn't long enough. Michael returned his messages too quickly and followed me to bed like a hound on a scent, trying to broach the subject again, to explain it, as if I hadn't read the depth and audacity of his latest Plan the moment that strange/familiar voice had spoken from the tape like an echo from the grave, sending Missy into her raptures.

I could not listen — I refused to listen — rolling to my side and covering my ears with my hands till he was finally quiet. He didn't argue anymore, just drew close behind me and slipped his arms around my waist like God knows he'd done a thousand nights before. He lay there quietly until I had finally begun to drift into the calm, dreamless world of tricyclic sleep, when he whispered very clearly in my ear, his voice full of his old flat honesty, "Myra, baby, you may not like it, but you cain't fight it. What'll be, will be. You hear me? It'll be."

That's all he said, not bothering to explain the quiet, confident sincerity in his words, not specifying the exact nature of the inevitable he was alluding to, whether it was death or Gabriel Catts. Which was just as well, as I was too far gone by then to protest, dim and drifting, my heart slowed to a bare beat, his words a small, sure echo as my mind finally shut down for sleep: *what'll be will be.*

— 30 —

H *is words proved prophetic,* and quickly so, as he only lived twelve weeks beyond them, weeks that weren't as painful as some people suppose, Michael being sick (that is, nauseated) rather than pained, spending most of his time at home in bed, so fast was his decline. The collapse of his hepatic system was years in the making, but it wasn't until the moment he was diagnosed that his body finally seemed to get the message that the jig was up, his weight falling off at the rate of maybe five pounds a week. I guess you could say that he never really recuperated from the surgery, the staples removed in time, and the stitches, but the scar a red cat's hair on the smooth, familiar landscape of his well-known flank that I never got used to; I didn't have time.

Once we broke the news to Missy and Clay (who took it better than we'd feared, being children, and not understanding the sheer permanence of the word), death, for the most part, became the unspoken facet of our new life. It was like an unwelcome gentleman caller who gravely receded to the parlor until called for, allowing us the breathing space to fight the smaller skirmishes: the battle to keep Michael comfortable, to get him to eat, to take his medicine and quit worrying about the damn money and get some sleep.

Those were the boundaries of the little world I lived in those final twelve weeks that I must say I miss so much. Even now, some small reminder will occasionally surface to briefly resurrect a glimpse of memory — an anniversary, a story, the particular smell of a cold November morning — and for a moment, I smile and think: Oh! That was then, the autumn Michael was alive — he was right up those stairs!

I don't know why they come to me with such piercing nostalgia, maybe because it *was* the end. Or maybe because it was the fraction of my marriage that I finally had my husband right where I wanted him: at home, with me. Not doing much of anything, either of us, just lying in bed, sleeping and talking and (of course) making love, sometimes going to town for a doctor's visit or a run to see Peter, our lawyer, till even that was too much, and Peter had to come out here to work on the Grand Strategy.

It was the only time I'd leave Michael's side, when Sam and the lawyers were there, talking money and investment, tax strategies and wills, Peter sometimes asking me to stay, though I never did, for it was just too permanent, this tax talk, this disbursement. Michael parting with his money spoke irrevocably of endings in a way I couldn't stomach, as the other unspoken ingredient of our life was a terrible fear: the fear of the unknown, worse in him than me. As long as I was physically with him, he was fine, strong as Ulysses. It was only when I made a move to leave, to run to the pharmacy, to pick up the children from school, that this terrible fear would percolate up, an aspect of my husband that I'd seldom ever seen.

For Michael was a good man, no one would dispute it, and a Christian with all the comfort that entails. His problem was his very nature, which was so earthbound, so *Indian* to me. I once read an article in *National Geographic* (I think) where an anthropologist was talking about the religion of the Peruvian Indians, and how practical their spirituality was. He said it had no provision for the afterlife — that, to their mind, if spirituality didn't produce better corn, then it was useless — and that was the heart of Michael Catts. That's why he clung to me, I think, because I was nearly his opposite in such matters. If I had any love for old mother Earth, it had been wiped out early on by old father Sims, and like the hymn we used to sing at Grandma's church in Louisiana: *this Earth was not my home.*

It was the inverted faith of the melancholic, the faith I shared with him at the end, not with sermon or scripture, but my very presence, which, like that of every other survivor, was a living memorial to the triumph of life over death, faith over doubt. That was the strength I offered him, my last gift. My only gift, I think — that and the stories I'd tell him as we lay in bed every day, much the way I'd once buoyed his heart on the Hill with *Rebecca*. They were nothing so moving, just childhood anecdotes, shared memories, the sound of my voice like a cloud of opium that kept him afloat, that and the Plans that he never lost faith in, and there in the end, obsessively spun around all of us. The general scheme was that Sim should work as Sam's personal assistant for a year after he graduated to get in a little practical experience before he got a degree in business at FSU, and Missy should go to Stetson if they offered her a softball scholarship, or Samford (the Baptist Samford in Birmingham), if not, for no other reason than to land her a good Baptist husband.

Sim was perfectly content with his arrangements, though Missy, who'd been bit by the traveling bug in France and had secret hopes of one day returning, just looked at him with a face of simple wonder. "Why would I *possibly* wanta do that?" she asked, and he'd been outraged.

"'Cause I doan want you bringing home some heathen son-in-law that'll go through my money and drive yo Mama crazy, that's why."

As for myself, it was clear from the very first that he had equally hard-headed Plans for me, though he was wily enough to keep them to himself till later in the illness when he knew his weakness would win me over — I swear to God he did. I mean, the genius of Michael Catts was that he played his cards as he was dealt them, not bringing up my future at all in the early negotiations, just moving from Missy to his beloved Claybird, who was the wildcard, to tell you the truth, too young for Michael to imagine his life, to even guess at how it might unfold.

For that reason, he was the child who worried him the most, the one Michael lost sleep over, built trusts and investments to protect. But still, it wasn't enough, and it was about midway through, when the money was disbursed, his skin turning perceptibly yellow, that he once again began to bring up Gabe in sly, cunning little asides, as it was his (apparent) intention to bring the bad boy home to finish the job of raising his children and deliver me from the horrors of widowhood. It was an utterly Michael Plan, one that appealed to both his raging reason-ableness and his latent romanticism, that had the benefit of assuaging a nagging little guilt he'd nursed over the years for marrying me before Gabe came back for Christmas, though I'd made it abundantly clear that had his younger brother met me at his mother's door that smoky autumn evening with his long hair and glittering eyes, I would have run back to the bus station in my mother's high heels and straight into the arms of the Lawyer Who Loved Red Hair with never a look back.

But Michael remained unconvinced, and I was too tired to argue by then and would only get up and leave the room if he so much as mentioned his brother's name, which was a cheap shot, as he was too weak to follow me down the stairs and would have to yell through the house: "Myra! *Myra, dammit!* You are the stubbornest damn woman I ever met in my life! *Myra!*"

But I'd ignore him, just go out on the front porch and sit in one of the rockers, watching the leaves fall in their solitary little circlings till the children came home at three or someone dropped by for sickroom visits, which were fairly frequent — Ed or Case, Sam or Louisa or one of the men from the church. I'd take them up to the bedroom where he'd be sitting up in bed with his TV tray of medicine and juices and a face not unlike his youngest son's, though he'd never argue in front of people, just cast me these little looks of reproach that were kind of pathetic, to tell you the truth.

I'd sometimes burst into tears under their weight, our visitor (especially if it was a man) coming to his feet, saying he'd best be going. I wouldn't argue, just show them out, then go back upstairs to Michael, who would be lying there with his eyes closed, thin and frail and sallow, though when he'd hear my footsteps, he'd raise up like Lazarus and snap, "Dammit, Myra, quit running out on me! It ain't fair!" Then, in a smaller voice, "Come lay down. I doan feel good."

He never did, after one of our rows, and I'd lie beside him, sometimes taking off my shirt to scrunch up, bare-chested, at his back, knowing what it was like to be dying in cold weather and trying to keep him warm. Even then, he'd try to slip in some bit of argument, murmuring, "Doan know why you wanta be sa damn stubborn," or, "Just give it a chance — all I'm asking."

That's about as far as he'd get before I'd kick off the covers, say, "I need to run to Wal-Mart. I'll pick up Clay while I'm out."

At this mild pronouncement, he'd be beside himself, trying to sit up, pleading, "Aw, Myra — baby, come on, lay down. I promise I won't talk about it namore."

And he wouldn't for a while, just lie there till the children came home from school, which was the high point of the day. Clay, who was still in middle school, would always get there first and come straight up, bookbag in one hand and a snack in the other. He'd sit on the end of the bed and talk his head off about his day, Michael back to his old self as long as he was there, though when he'd leave to go downstairs to work on his homework, he'd rub his face meditatively, whisper, "It's a hard thing, Myra."

He didn't mean the dying, either, but the leaving of his children, and it was. God, it was hard, fueling even more Plans — crazy Plans, that had his accountants chewing their pencils, to leave half a million dollars to Candace and Gabe in a not-so-subtle bribe they remember his children. The original Plan had Candace, Gabe, Cissie, and Case splitting it four ways, but Cissie and Case had refused to take so much as a penny as a point of honor. Candace was waffling on taking the high road herself, till I pointed out that the money could be trickled down to Lori, to build them a house and pay off her hospital bills from Ryan.

She grudgingly accepted it then, leaving Gabe the unwitting recipient of a quarter million unearned dollars, an irony that might have annoyed me had I not been too whipped to argue, as we were into the last month by then, with Michael increasingly overtaken by all these little peripheral illnesses. The worst of them was diabetes, not in terms of difficulty to treat (just a shot a day), but because it was what my own father had died of. Until then, Cissie used to say it was God's vengeance for his sorry life, and it seemed a senseless twist that Michael should be struck down by the same complaint.

But like I say, it was easy enough to treat, a hell of a lot easier than the ascites that began to devil him after the fluid from his nonfunctioning hepatic system started draining into his abdominal cavity, giving him a bloated belly and a sagging Martian weirdness around his eyes. The pressure of the fluid on his diaphram also made it hard for him to breathe, and the first week of December, Dr. Azuri readmitted him to the hospital to have it drained.

Michael was down to maybe one hundred twenty pounds by then, visibly yellow from the jaundice, and except for the children (who oddly enough, never commented on, indeed hardly seemed to notice his deterioration), he refused to see any more visitors outside of the immediate family. Cissie came every morning, bearing biscuits and pound cake and whatever else she could tempt him into taking a bite of, her face so hollow and stretched and artificially happy that I told Candace that one day my heart was going to break in two at the sight of it, *crack* in my chest.

We kept up an equally false face of happy nonchalance for her benefit, telling her it was just a routine procedure, nothing serious at all, though Dr. Azuri had privately told me that the color of the fluid was a good diagnostic tool as to life expectancy. If it was clear, we were good, but if it was cloudy, then, well, it wouldn't be long. He also mentioned that in the light of Michael's increasing deterioration, he simply might not wake up at all, but die right there on the table, and had Hospice bring up the Do Not Resuscitate orders which Michael carefully signed, the scratch of the pen the only sound in the room.

It was clear that our gentleman caller was getting restless there in the parlor, the pacing of his footsteps sometimes audible to the discerning ear, my separation from Michael that day the hardest I ever endured. I stalked around the hospital all morning long, getting more agitated by the hour, as they were running behind in surgery and had to keep bumping him later and later in the day.

"But he hasn't eaten," I kept trying to tell the nurses, who knew they were dealing with a woman on the edge, and kindly suggested I go home and try to get some rest. Candace finally came up from ICU and made me promise to wait in the room, said she'd call me the moment he came out, and though I obeyed her and returned to the room, I still couldn't lay down or sit still, pacing beside the bed for a good hour, till the phone finally rang late in the afternoon, about four.

I leapt on it, snatching it from the cradle, shouting, "Yes?"

But it wasn't Dr. Azuri, wasn't anyone I could immediately recognize, just a man's voice that was low and nervous, hesitating a moment, then asking, "Myra?"

"Yes?" I repeated.

There was a small pause, then, "This is Gabe."

I closed my eyes then and sat on the edge of the bed as he pressed forward nervously, speaking quickly, saying, "Listen, is Michael there? I need to talk to him."

"He's in surgery," I heard myself answer, my voice calm and flat and far away.

"But I just talked to him — he called me, not ten minutes ago."

"He must have called from pre-op," I said, and could picture him so clearly, waiting around down there, bored and restless, worried about me, worried about the children, finally asking for a phone to try his luck from another angle. "They're in there now," I said, "draining the abdominal fluid. Doctor says if it's clear, he's got till Christmas, but if it's cloudy," I paused for a long breath, "it could be tomorrow. Or tonight. Or while he's on the table."

He didn't say anything for a moment, then spoke in a light voice. "I'm sorry, Myra. I don't know what to say. Tell him I love him. That I said *yes*. He'll know what I mean."

Well, hell, we both knew what he meant, and I just sat there, engulfed in that old hollow disembodiment, thinking, *My God, can this really be happening?* while Gabe rolled on without turning a hair, his voice suddenly animated, as if he'd hit upon a Plan of his own. "And listen, Myra — tell Michael to let Clayton come up there and see him. I called your house and talked to him and he's hurting, Myra. Don't leave him out of this."

He issued this order with all his old righteous conviction that made me hold the receiver away from my ear and stare at it, literally unable to believe my ears. "You did *what?*" I asked, and he didn't hear the outrage in my voice, or at least didn't acknowledge it, but droned on and on in his neat little explanation while I slowly came to my feet, anger like a bubble in my chest that grew and grew till it finally burst in one clenched-teeth question, spoken in a low, deadly earnestness: "And who the *hell* do you think you are, calling down here, talking to my son, trying to tell me what to do?"

It was the first — no, the *second* time in my life I'd withstood him, the novelty of it making for five stunned seconds before he went off like a rocket in all his stomping, spitting *telling-Mama* glory. "Your son? *Your* son? *My* son, too, woman!"

And it really was fortunate that we were separated by half a continent, or I'd have killed him for that, put a bullet between his eyes and laughed while I did it. As it was, I had to content myself with screaming like a harridan, "He's no *son* of yours! Don'tchu ever say that again — don'tchu even *think* it!"

"Oh cut the shit, Myra!" he cried. "I can't believe you're still playing the injured virgin here. Listen, you can pull that shit with Michael, but I was there, I *know.*"

"Well, I'm glad you were, 'cause I sure as *hell* wasn't!"

"Oh bull*shit* — don't even try that with me. Listen, I know crazy when I see it and I know guilty as hell, and you were the latter. You can save your lines for the WMUs —"

"— wasn't a line, and you *know* it. You used me like a field whore — you never cared for nobody but yourself — me or Michael either one!"

"Used you?" he howled. "*Used* you? I am *sick* of this babygirl bullshit! Sick of it, d'you hear me? I haven't seen my brother in ten years because of you and it was the worst night's work in her life when mama hid you in that closet —"

"— got that right!" I shouted back. "Locking me in with a horny little *snot* like you!"

It was right about then that I realized Dr. Azuri was standing in the door in his surgery scrubs, his eyes so wide that I dropped the phone to my chest to cry, "*What?* What is it?" For I was sure it was Michael; that he'd died on the table — my heart jumping with this little jerk of unbelief that shouted, *No! it wasn't time!*

But it must have been my screaming that had him so white-eyed, as he dispensed with his usual courtesy to say, "It's fine. It's clear. They're sending him up right now."

I just nodded, my brilliant rage gone, just like that. I didn't even thank him when he left, just felt for the bed and sat down, forgetting I had the phone in my hand till I heard this faint little begging on the line. "What? Myra?" it pleaded. "For *God's sake,* was it —"

I lifted the phone and whispered, "Clear."

"Thank God," he breathed. Then, after another pause, "Tell him I love him, Myra."

"Yes, Gabriel."

"He won't let me come," he said in a small, petulant voice that sounded amazingly like Clay. "I wanted to see him, but he won't let me."

"No," I said, wiggling a handkerchief out of my pocket and blowing my nose. "Not like this. He's right. Listen, I gotta go. I gotta call Cissie."

"Oh, yeah. Well, call me. Promise you'll call me, if you need anything."

"Yes. Of course," I said. Then, as I hung up, "I love you, Gabriel."

"I love you, too."

I called Cissie and gave her the news, then sat there, slumped on the bed, till they brought Michael up from Recovery. He was still pretty drugged, not opening his eyes as I climbed in beside him, and worked myself around the tubes till I was right at his back, so thin! When I had myself situated, he managed around a nose tube, "Went good. Feels better."

He took a deep breath to demonstrate, and I pressed my face to his shoulder, not in grief, but relief, for by then, we'd take our victories where we found them, we weren't choosy. After a moment, I whispered, "Gabe called."

He opened his eyes at that. "Did he?" he asked, and I smiled the same fake smile we'd used on Cissie that morning, the everything'll-be-fine smile.

"Yeah," I said. "He said to tell you he loved you."

"Anything else?" he pressed, and I tell you what, I can be a hard-hearted woman at times, but not that hard.

"Said to, ah, tell you yes. Said you'd know what he meant."

"Good," he said, relaxing against the pillow and closing his eyes.

He looked so thin and fragile, I hated to argue, though I had to tell him the truth about me and Gabe in a small, honest voice. "Baby, it's just — I don't love him like you do. You have to know that."

But he seemed curiously unconcerned and answered with his old sure confidence. "Thet's all right, 'cause he loves you so much. I figure it'll take up the slack."

Such was the unfailing practicality of Michael Catts that I didn't argue, but just let him go back to sleep and sleep the day away, having an ambulance take him home that evening so he could spend his last weeks in his own bed, surrounded by his children. And it's funny, because after that, he let up on Gabe, hardly ever mentioned him again, diverting the end of his dwindling energies to his very last Plan of all: his funeral.

I understand (from Candace) that terminal patients tend to fall into two categories: the ones who can't face it and the ones who can, and Michael fell firmly into the second, just about driving us crazy those last two weeks with his insistence on nailing down the hard-headed details. In death, as in life, he wanted something with a little show to it: a cherry coffin ("Why not pine?" I asked, and he was outraged. "Slash pine? Hell, Myra, why don't you just pitch me in the ground and be done with it?") and an equally ornate tombstone.

And though I agreed to the first, I refused the second, for a reason he couldn't very well argue with: "Because your Daddy'll be right there next to you, and I don't want people a hundred years from now thinking he was any less a man because Cissie couldn't afford a nicer stone."

He'd sniffed at that, then asked, "Well, have you thought of what you're gone put on it?"

I shook my head, for we had yet to come upon a suitable inscription. I was usually pretty good with that sort of thing, but after twelve weeks of round-the-clock nursing, I could think of nothing at all, not a thing. None of us could, though after two hours' worth of nagging about Samford and marrying Baptist, Missy had suggested, *"Thank God He's Gone."* (Which sounds kind of gruesome in retrospect, though at the time, it was drop-dead hilarious, all of us laughing till we choked, Michael most of all.)

As the week of Christmas approached, he finally nailed it all down, asking Ben McQuaig to do the eulogy after Sam regretfully declined, said he just didn't have it in him. It was the last detail to be taken care of, and once his funeral plans were set, Michael seemed to find a place of peace at last, his heart weakening so rapidly that I was forced to take him by ambulance to ICU, so he could be put on a respirator, if necessary.

That's where he spent his last days, half a dozen doors down the hall from the rooms where I'd borne our children, just him and me and the patter of rubber-soled nurse's shoes, Candace's among them, as she was working nearly round the clock to be near him. He was very weak by then, the morphine succeeding in doing that which neither therapy nor prayer nor nagging had ever been able to achieve in nearly twenty years of marriage: it turned him into a talker, there at the end.

Cushioned in its haze, he was finally able to put into words so much of what had gone on between us that until then had been simply unspoken, insisting, among other things, that he'd married me for something other than my mammary glands. "Liked everything about you," he confided in the quiet, level murmur that had become his speaking voice. "Liked the way you smelled. Like corn. Liked the way you stayed on your side of the bed in summer, mine in winter. Kept it warm. Always kind to me. Always smiled when you'd see me coming, run to the fence. Nobody ran for me, back then. Nobody but Myra Sims, and that suited me just fine. That's all I wanted, anyway."

That was the way of it: calling some people by their full names, as if he were watching it from some higher plane, his soul already half-departed, the part of him left a sure, quiet voice, which in the end was reduced to bits of disconnected musing, frequently over his children. "Sim'll do good, with Sam. Sam'll kick his butt, he needs it." And of Missy: "She needn't git married so young. Let her finish school, do what she wants. Needn't ever leave the house, far as I'm concerned." Of Clay, he mostly reminisced of his funny sayings and odd ways that meant nothing to anyone but us, the parents who'd raised him. ("Remember Clay? *You hurt my feelings!*")

When he finished with the children, his talk turned, inevitably, to secrets, the most arresting of which was his insistence that on the night my father broke Gabe's wrist and ordered me in the house, that it was he, Michael, coming home from work, whom I tried to call to.

"I thought it was Mr. Simon," I said in amazement. "I could see his T-shirt, coming down the path."

And though he was very weak, Michael was adamant. "Thet wasn't Daddy," he said, "thet was *me*. Daddy was working in Bonifay, painting for Smith Keller. I could hear Mama way down on the tracks, shouting. Knew something was up, started to run — time I made the yard, it was all over. Found Mama in the kitchen, raging like a wildcat, Gabe on the couch — wouldn't tell me what happened."

He paused a moment, his eyes narrowed, his thin, ravaged face dim in the telling, as if he'd bodily returned to that chilly November day, so long ago. "He was laying face down," he continued, "wouldn't turn over. I finally had to grab him by his shoulders, heave him over, and he was soaking wet. I thought he'd fell in the ditch, but it wasn't water. It was sweat. He was *sweating*, it hurt so bad."

He was so intent on his story that I became a little lost in it myself. It was like *I* was the one who'd come home from work that night; I was the one who turned him over — Michael's voice going on, dim and level. "But he wouldn't say a word. Scared of Mama. Scared she wouldn't let him see you no more. You could hear yo Daddy over there, beating the shit out of somebody, but Mama wouldn't let me go. Said I couldn't take him. He's too big. Too drunk."

Michael seemed to come to himself on that, losing the thread of his story, his thin, sallow face mad with the righteous thoroughness of a child, petulant with his mother for steering him wrong, and for some reason, it struck me as funny.

"You look just like Clay," I smiled.

"It ain't no joke," he pouted. "I was eighteen years old. Too old to be listening to my damn *mother*."

"He'd a killed you," I told him plainly, though Michael just snorted.

"He'd a *tried*."

This huffy brag, from a man who in 1962 had probably tipped the scales at a hundred thirty pounds, sounded so much like Clay that I had to rub my face against his shoulder to keep from smiling, finally getting enough of a grip to lift my face and say, "Well. You beat him in the end."

For a moment, he didn't say anything, then he grudgingly allowed, "Yeah. We beat him in the end."

His breath was more labored by then, his pauses to sleep more frequent, though the heart monitor bleeped bravely on, a comforting counterbeat to his slow slurred words, when he finally tired of his secrets and went back to minding my business for me. "Never fire Peter," he told me, "even if he moves to N'Orleans. Stay with him. He'll see about things."

As the morphine drip was changed more frequently, the walls of his promises to not mention Gabe cracked and fell in, and he returned to his old arguments in a wandering voice that I could not very well defend. "Come by that night, after Aint Mag died. Wanted to see you. I said *no*. He's so damn stubborn. Never would listen. Just give him a chance. Let him know the children. He's the only one that'll do right by 'em. Him and Sam and Candace. Sam the bidness, him the children, you and Candace, everything else. Left them fixed, they promised. Don't disappoint me in this thing. Myra?"

He'd keep at it, repeating, "Myra? Myra?" till I answered, (*"Yes, baby* —") then lie there quietly, taking these deep, labored breaths. They were soon such an effort that I found myself trying to help him, taking deep breaths of my own, so obviously that he finally opened an eye and looked at me with a shadow of his old dry humor, said, "You cain't breathe for me, baby."

I didn't argue, just smiled a dim smile, and changed sides when the nurses moved us to the far end of the room for a little more privacy. At some point, I remember a technician coming in pulling a cart with some kind of apparatus on it, asking if I'd filed the Do Not Resuscitate orders with Hospice. I nodded to him over Michael's sleeping chest, and he took the cart away, pulling the curtain and leaving us alone for another long stretch of time.

Whether it was a day or an hour or a week, I couldn't tell in that quiet, windowless void, the nurses sometimes waking me with a sandwich or a Coke, putting it in my hands without a word. I looked up to say thank you once and found Candace standing there in her scrubs and wire-rimmed glasses, changing the IV. She smiled at me with a glitter of wet eyes and kissed Michael when she left, leaving me to lie there and feel his last, slow breaths when he went into a coma at last, with no words of departure, no last revelations — God, I hated him for that.

It seemed such a small thing to ask: a vision of heaven, an alighting dove; one last smile. Something to recount at his funeral, a final word to comfort his mother. But death came upon him quietly in the end, nothing more than a long sleep that finally didn't break, his skin cooling, cooling to cold, the monitor setting off, not with a jarring hum like they do on TV, but a sudden unbroken silence, as one of the nurses (maybe Candace) had turned off the alarm. When it flat-lined at six o'clock on Tuesday morning, there was no running, no shout to revive him, just the soft rubber pad of nursing shoes on the linoleum and a kind, faceless form above me, quietly dropping the bedrails and telling me to wake up, Miz Catts.

It was time to go home.

I *remember little* of the subsequent weeks
and months, even the funeral we'd planned with such care, down to the
roses on the coffin, antique Cecil Brunner's — *sweetheart* roses, they
call them around here. I had such a thorough support system that I was
spared many of the agonizing details, returning home Tuesday afternoon to a house that was magically restored to pre-cancer normalcy, our
bedroom stripped of the sickroom clutter, the oxygen and pills and bottles of morphine.

Basically, all I had to endure was the social niceties, perform the
awful role of widow that I made a fairly good job of, for Michael's sake,
and Cissie's, though I must say that my heart wasn't in it. Left to my own
devices, I would have fled the whole funeral ordeal and joined Sam at
Shell Island, where he spent the day fishing for reds in Michael's memory, to the larger McRae family's collective horror. Louisa (who'd long
since retired to her daughter's in Quincy) had threatened to disown him
if he carried out this massive Southern insult, nagging him so much that
he called me the night after the viewing to explain that his absence
hadn't been mischance, but deliberate.

"Couldn't stand it," he said with all his old forthrightness, that only got more forthright with the years. I told him to by all means stay away. "You'll be there, won't you?" He knew me well enough to ask, and I said sure. For Cissie.

"Good woman," he said, and that was the end of that.

The funeral itself comes to me in memory oddly similar to the bad old days on the Hill — in some ways so weird: Michael's still, thin face, the stiff, waxy smell of the florist shop; in some ways so routine: the houseful of tea-sipping relatives, the quick, panicked search for a suitable dress. Since it was December, the stores were full of black dresses, but they were party dresses, velvet and sequined and (as was the fashion that year) even crinolined.

It clearly wasn't the season for death, and I was toying with the French custom of wearing a pastel, when Cissie caught wind of my intent and sent Candace to Tallahassee on a ten-hour shopping junket, returning home tired but triumphant with a simple black dress that had cost an arm and a leg at Parisians. I could have cared less at that point, for after two days of drugged, restless sleep, my numb shock had finally given way to a querulous exhaustion that made me snap at Clay before the service for misplacing his new shoes and want to stand up and scream at Ben McQuaig during his endless eulogy. Everyone else went on and on about how wonderful it was, how moving, but all I remember was a petty aggravation when he couldn't find the word to describe Michael's down-to-earth candor, his complete absence of airs, even after he started bringing in the bucks.

The word he was looking for was *unpretentious,* but Benny couldn't quite put his finger on it, even stopping to scratch his head and ask us, the audience, "You know — how he never forgot who he was — "

I was about at the end of my rope by then, about to oblige him by standing up and screaming, "Pretentious! *Pretentious,* you idiot! He wasn't pretentious or anything else! He was *Michael Simon Catts!*"

But I didn't; I just closed my eyes and took deep breaths and prayed to Jesus it'd be over soon, when just like that, it was. Brother Sloan had us stand and sing "Amazing Grace" a capella while the funeral director gave his ushers hushed instructions, having them start the mourners up the aisle for that final (unplanned) viewing. Even then, I kept my eyes closed, gripping Cissie's hand and using Clay's shoulder for support, till Missy let out a little noise of recognition that made me look up in surprise. Cissie threw off my grip and all but roll-blocked a slumped man who stood just ahead of us in a big winter coat, crying, "Gabe! Gabe! I knew you'd come, my son, my son!"

He returned her embrace that was long, many moments, then drew back, affording a two-second glimpse of his grief-ravaged face that was still wide-boned and Slavic, his hair darker than it used to be, and thinner in a way that made his forehead much more distinct. It gave him a brief, unexpected resemblance to his brother as he turned and hugged Missy long and sincerely, then moved down the aisle to shake Sim's hand with unconscious good manners, with his good hand, his left one. He took care that Sim understood the reversal, though when he drew back and found himself facing Clay, he didn't offer his hand at all, but just stood there and stared at him with an expression that was — indescribable.

On it went, four, then five unblinking seconds, till his glance finally moved to me, his breath smelling of whiskey and exhaustion, though his eyes were his own, worried and searching, asking, "*Myra? Are you all right?*"

The question was so clear I thought he'd asked it aloud, though Candace later told me he hadn't spoken a word, but only stared at Clay and me in our turns, till Cissie dragged him to the coffin to utter his plaintive cry: *God, he looks like Daddy.* There was something so evocative in his words that they made me actually close my eyes as I stood there, trying to remember. Then it came to me: the shining morning Sim was born, when he'd taken him to the window and held him to the August light, then lifted his face and said the same thing.

How happy we'd been that day, how young — the stabbing sweetness of the connection succeeding in doing that which neither death nor sickness nor exhaustion had done: it made me finally break down and cry, and I hated it so much. People said it helped, but it didn't, burning like gasoline in my eyes, my chest, till I finally made it to the privacy of the limousine and took two Ativan, and after that, I was gone. Not disassociated, which isn't a genie that you can conjure on demand, but simply worn out. Tired of trying to sort a little meaning from something as patently meaningless as death, and spending the rest of the afternoon shaking hands and accepting hugs and hearing myself repeat like an automaton all the idiotic things you say at funerals: "Didn't he look good?" and "Didn't it go well?" and even the old standby, "He's gone to a better place."

I remember only glimpses of the evening: the packed house, the blur of faces, Gabe's appearance the talk of the day, Candace alternatively excusing and angry that he'd made a cowardly retreat at the corner and left without a word, everyone amazed he hadn't stayed. I didn't offer any opinions of my own, though I couldn't understand how they'd missed that long protracted look he'd given Clay. Why would he have looked so desolate if he hadn't been going, quickly and forever?

I wouldn't have been surprised to hear that he'd died in the next few days, drank himself into oblivion or put a gun to his head, for that had been the smell of his intent. But I was too exhausted to worry it and resolutely marched myself through the final details, the hostessing and child-comforting and scribbling thank-you notes that Candace privately told me were illegible.

"Maybe you ought to wait a while," she said, a piece of well-meant advice that I ignored, for my shaky, trembly scribble sent a message more powerful than my frail words of thanks. It said: I am only just hanging on. Look how much I loved him. This is an awful thing.

It hit closer to the truth than any message I could possibly write, though the weeks and months that followed Michael's death were really not the hellish torment some people imagine, simply because of the mechanisms of denial that I seemed to have come equipped with at birth, like the airbag and antilock brakes on the Mercedes. While Sam and Candace and Case suffered terribly, like orphaned children, I was the Strong One, even stronger than Cissie, for the first (and last) time in my life, behaving as stoically as Michael would have, had the circumstances been reversed.

The difference was that he would have done it out of strength, while I held up because I simply couldn't convince myself that he was really dead. Gone. Six feet under down at Riverside, though I visited his grave every morning, early, before dawn. I'd awake with the alarm at four-thirty and dress in the silent house, then drive through the vacant countryside to the silver darkness of the graveyard and follow the winding path to the top of the hill just as the five-o-five from Perry came clattering down the tracks, the roar and whistle familiar backdrops to the cold, etched stillness.

The white winter sunrise would always find me there, muffled and oddly peaceful, glad of the bitter cold that made my ears tingle and my fingers ache, for it made me feel like a thing of sensation and life, not another pale disembodied ghost, haunting the paths of the dead. I'd sit there among the graves and watch the slowly lightening sky, feeling an odd closeness with Michael's bones, sometimes even lying down on the cold ground to be closer to them, though God forbid if Candace ever found out. She was scandalized enough that I went to the cemetery alone every morning; she'd have really flipped if she'd have seen me do that.

But she didn't, no one did. My time at the grave was my own, something I looked forward to every day, I really don't know why — maybe to somehow convince myself that he was dead. Because I really did have it fixed in my head that any moment he'd come walking in the door with his briefcase in hand, yelling at Clayton to put up his bike, telling me he had to run up to Waycross, did I want to ride along?

No matter how many times I told myself, reminded myself, stared at his *grave:* there it was, this false expectation that made me run to the stairs every time I heard a key in the lock, or save him a seat in church and spend half the service craning my neck, watching the double doors, wondering what in God's name was keeping him.

Now, I didn't need the benefit of a psychiatrist to diagnose my complaint; the problem was, I couldn't fix it, pulling in the drive every morning and idling in front of the still, dark house, telling myself that Michael was dead. He wasn't there anymore. He was gone. I'd wait a moment to see if any grief, any sorrow, any tendril of loss would rise up, but it wouldn't. My head said he was gone; the rest of me just didn't believe it.

So while everyone around me battled the Dark Night of the Soul, I rose effortlessly to the role of comforter, taking Cissie to lunch at the steakhouse every Sunday and drying the children's tears, though what I was really doing was dropping into automatic pilot in my old pattern, spending a hell of a lot of time in bed, sleeping. The meds were partially to blame for it, as Dr. Williams had tried to forestall any plunges into despair by putting me back on Pamalor, along with a preventive dose of Tegretol, a drug more commonly given epileptics to prevent seizures that's now used to prevent mania.

I'll say this for it: it could, by God, becalm you, especially in combination with the Pamalor and Ativan. Come to think of it, it's a wonder I ever got out of bed at all, but I did, for my daily visit to the grave, that would only last till full light, when I'd come home to wake the children and send them off to school. I'd return to bed then and sleep till three, when I'd finally get up and take a shower and start supper, so that when Clay came home from school, he'd find me right where he'd left me that morning: in the kitchen in my robe.

It was a strange life, a callback to my twilight years in Alabama, though at least now I had the comfort of my children, who'd join me in bed at night, huddled there for warmth like a litter of puppies, Clay and Missy on the bed, Sim too big for that, preferring the floor. We'd lie there and talk about school or church or the future, or anything that came to mind, even Michael. It hurt me to hear them speak of him in the past tense, but I didn't want him to become surrounded in this grieving secret curtain and encouraged them to remember him, to laugh about him, cry if need be, privately a little sad as the months passed and the weather warmed toward spring, when our collective grief began to move on out to sea.

I mean, it's the nature of life to grow toward the light, to heal and recover, and that's just what happened, Sim and Missy returning to their own beds by summer, only Claybird there to lie with his face to the ceiling and sniffle at the hideous permanence of loss. He didn't say much, just huddled there like he used to do when he was a baby, comforting himself in his strange little Clay-ways by describing what a blowout of a funeral they'd have for me when my time came.

There was nothing morbid about it, just these fantastic descriptions of the flowers and the food (catered, he said) and the coffin, solid cherry, with a plush velvet lining. It would be the funeral to end all funerals, he told me, sometimes coming with me to the graveyard to point out likely tombstones, as he was apparently disappointed with the modesty of his father's stone, though he had come up with the inscription himself: *He Walks With God.* Cissie had objected to it on the grounds it wasn't technically scriptural, till Case (who was as churched as she, though he didn't make as great a show of it) pointed out that Enoch had walked with God, and if it was good enough for Enoch, it was good enough for Michael Catts.

So the inscription stayed, and Clay worried night and day over what they'd put on mine, sometimes getting down on his hands and knees to decipher a faded inscription on one of the old moss-grown slave graves that dotted the hill. ("*Well Done, Good and Faithful Servant?*" he asked hopefully, though I shook my head. "I don't think so.") I didn't find his new-found obsession too strange, for it seemed to help him bridge the gap between the living and the dead and did as much for him as it did for me, though as the cool spring days lengthened toward summer, Candace insisted that all this death-talk had to come to an end.

"It's morbid and not good for Clay," she announced after he'd spent a lazy Sunday afternoon with his Grannie, describing *her* funeral in some detail, also down to the flowers and velvet linings.

"So d'you still think he's alive?" Candace asked, meaning Michael, as I'd once tried to explain the denial thing to her, though with little success, as Candace was so damn literal-minded; I think she thought I was carrying on conversations with him at supper like a dotty old Southern belle.

I tried to allay her fears, even halfheartedly agreed to give Clay the word on the funeral plans, without too much regret. For by then, the continuum of life was beginning to nip at my own heels, most evidently in the sudden barrage of dinner invitations I began to receive from a dozen different men, divorced, single, and (I am afraid) happily married, all really most intent on making a stab at taking Michael's place as man of the house. It just beat all I'd ever seen, though Liz, who had once divorced in a small town, had warned me it would happen.

"Lot of lonely people out there," she said, though I wasn't prepared for the volume of the calls, much less the sincerity.

For these men were dead serious, trying to sweet-talk me as if I were sixteen years old, and like I say, I just didn't quite know what to make of it. I mean, I'd spent a good part of my youth fending off the *Butt-slappers* of the world, but at thirty-seven, my butt wasn't what it used to be, nothing to write home about.

I couldn't understand what the fuss was all about till I put the question to my all-seeing sister-in-law one morning over coffee, who answered with her usual blunt honesty. "Well, you're still a good-looking woman," she allowed, "and the bucks don't hurt."

"They're after my *money?*" I breathed, though Candace just looked at me as if I were an idiot.

"Well, sure. All they have to do ask you out, take you to Sonny's and buy you a pork special. If you happen to hit it off, they could theoretically nab a marble pool, a new Mercedes, and seven million bucks, all in one swoop. Not bad, for one night's work."

"That's the most disgusting thing I ever heard in my life," I said, though Candace just shrugged at my naiveté, going on to talk about other things: Lori and the baby; Cissie and how lonely she'd become, spending a good part of her social security check calling around Boston, looking for Gabe.

"I thought you had his number," I said, and again, she shrugged.

"He moved."

But that was all that was said of it, even after the most serious contender of all stepped up to the plate, Carlym Folger, the assistant pastor at Welcome, who'd been hired the year before to take over Brother Sloan's more odious duties: the youth and visitation and Sunday School. Michael himself had been on the hiring committee, along with his mother, whose summation of this particular applicant's qualifications was, "He's the best-looking man I ever seen in my life."

It was a comment I was to hear from many other quarters, one I thought that fell a little short of the truth when we were finally introduced in June, though I had to admit he was right up Cissie's alley, tall and even-featured and suspiciously muscle-bound, like he had a Soloflex secreted away in his closet. Originally from north Atlanta, Carlym was vastly qualified (indeed, overqualified) for the job, as he had a degree in chemical engineering from the University of Georgia, where he'd played second-string quarterback for the Bulldogs till he got saved at a Fellowship of Christian Athletes meeting and was called into full-time ministry.

His hiring had added a little spice to the summer, as the presence of a good-looking bachelor in our parsonage had caused a wide-spread conversion all across the county, our Sunday School attendance jumping from ninety to a hundred twenty the second Sunday he preached; though to be honest, as a preacher, Carlym made a fine engineer (but with a butt like that, who was complaining?). I, myself, found his sheer perfection a little off-putting, as it gave him the glossy untouchability you see in a lot of preachers these days, a legacy of televangelism, I expect, as if Christianity were a Madison Avenue production. Though, to be fair, Carlym's shine had more to do with good breeding than a good publicist, for unlike the rest of us redneck wannabes, he was the genuine article: a Buckhead boy, son of a well-known judge. You might say he was born into his khaki; we came into ours by attrition.

So he made an interesting study, if nothing else, and I sometimes wondered what career choice had landed him here, the humble assistant in a church that had split so many times that it was holding onto its congregation by the skin of its teeth. But I never got a chance to ask, as any social interactions I might have had with him were swiftly curtailed by Michael's illness, when I must say that Carlym proved his weight in gold, always there when we needed him, to pick up children or meet us at the ER, to hold Sim's hand the night Candace gave him the news about the cancer.

It created an immediate bond between us, so that by the time I was forced from hibernation in June, we were fast friends, though there was nothing of intimacy about it, sexual or otherwise. We just happened to be thrown together a lot, always ending up talking at the skating rink or the steakhouse or the springs, conversation that came easily enough to me, for in some ways, Carlym reminded me of Ira, not as he is today, feral and caged, but in his younger years, growing up in Birmingham. He had the same natural athleticism and love of football — indeed, the same entourage of adoring women, now that I think of it.

But there wasn't any sexual chemistry between us, really no physical attraction at all, at least on my end, though when Liz dropped by for a visit in late August and caught a glimpse of him in a bathing suit, she urged me to strike while the iron was hot.

"I don't think we *click* that way," I told her.

Liz, who had never quite gotten over her love of a good man, looked at me with the same astonishment that I had when Candace told me about the money. "What's not to *click?*" she asked. "He's gorgeous."

I just shrugged. "I don't think I care for gorgeous."

"Good *God,* woman, you been on lithium too long," she cried, then leaned over the table and pointed her straw at me (we were sitting in Dairy Queen) like she was imparting the secret to a long and happy life. "Listen, baby. Men been calling the shots for you all your life. You're finally in a place to call a few of your own. I say: go for it."

"He's five years younger than me," I complained, and she turned her face to heaven.

"My God, Myra, that's my point exactly. He's five years younger than you. He's good to your children. He's got a job and looks like Christopher Reeve. What's not to like?"

"Candace says these men are after my money," I said, but she just laughed.

"Well, who the *hell* cares? You think Michael Catts married you for your personality and *rapier* wit?"

"Said he married me for my little feet."

"*Shht,*" she breathed, then pointed her straw. "He married you for your tail, baby. You need to turn it into a family tradition."

I just laughed her off, even after school started and Carlym began a subtle courting, offering to take the boys places with the youth group, or showing up for Missy's softball games and sitting with me on the bleachers. It was still all pastorly and innocent, though every once in a while I'd catch him watching me with a reflective, contemplative face, like a farmer at auction, eyeing a prospective bull.

But like I say, at that point, I just wasn't buying, still heading out to the cemetery every morning, not as happily as I had before, but increasingly depressed, the emotional bankruptcy of the previous winter finally giving way to a tired, bitter melancholy. The meds kept me from any plunges into despair, but even with their shield, sometimes there in the warm, muggy dawn, I'd find myself thinking of my own death with a wistful sweetness, how peaceful it could be, how very right. After all, the children were almost grown now, their future secure, all the money tied up in trusts and wills, Candace the executor. I figured that if anything happened to me, she and Ed could move into the house, take care of

Clayton till he came of age. I could picture them laughing and splashing around the pool on a warm summer evening, while Michael and I rested in our plush velvet coffins, six feet under the companionable earth, together at last.

I'd get so caught up in the sweetness of the little vision that I'd lose track of time, coming to myself in the full morning light, having to shake myself awake, a little scared of the seduction of the thing. For suicide idealization wasn't a stranger to me, but a marked, recognizable enemy that would creep in when I was particularly down, always had, since I was a child. It was a serious matter to a woman who had in her purse enough tricylics to kill an elephant, and I rebuked it with the same vehemence I used to rebuke the Stairwalkers, then hurried home to get the children off to school, though they'd already be gone by the time I got home, the vacant, echoing house only fueling my unease.

It happened so often that October that I stopped going to the cemetery for a few months there, promised myself I'd return in December, when the cold would numb my fingers and sting my ears, the steady ache a reminder of what it was to be alive — to think, to feel, to *hope*. I looked forward to it like a summer vacation, spinning out the warm, humid autumn clinging to life by the skin of my teeth, occasionally wondering if Liz was right, maybe Carlym was the man. I don't mean the man who'd make it all right and set my life in order, but the man who'd help me raise my children and keep me warm at night, maybe help me remember what it was like to feel things, to be alive.

Though even aside from the glossy perfection thing, there were other things about Carlym that just didn't click, like the age difference, that despite Liz's assurances, made me a little uneasy, as I was used to being the babygirl of the Catts household and didn't much like the idea of giving it up. I mean, it was petty, it was childish, but there it was. And there were other things, too, like the way he always brought me frozen yogurt at the steakhouse every Sunday.

Carlym had taken to joining us there for the blue plate special, with dessert included in the price of meal, either ice cream or frozen yogurt that was served from a self-service island on the salad bar. Since we ate with a boothful of old people, one of us younger ones would always go and get it for the whole table, and I couldn't help but notice that whenever Sim or Missy or Clay got mine, it'd always be ice cream. Whenever Carlym got it, it'd be frozen yogurt, though he always (and this was the kicker) got *ice cream* for himself.

On one occasion, I'd unbent enough to ask him what was the deal with the frozen yogurt, and he'd answered with unthinking honesty, "Oh. Well, it's low-fat, you know."

Well, poor Carlym, being new to the area, he had no way of knowing that the f-word around the Catts household these days was *fat,* and woe to the poor sucker who used it. "Yeah, and *screw you,*" I wanted to say, but didn't, though maybe I should have.

Because it kind of ate at me, provided as good an example as any of what life would be with a closet Solo-flexer, who'd always be wanting me to exercise and watch my fat, and at that point in my life, I just didn't have the strength. I mean, I'd done my time in Alcatraz as a child and wasn't studying on going back. I just returned to Michael's grave once the first frost fell, cold and tired and listless as the anniversary of his death approached, thinking there had to be more to life than this — when suddenly one morning, just like that, there was.

— 32 —

*I*t happened on a bright Saturday morning sometime within striking distance of Christmas when I went to the graveyard to put a little holiday wreath on Michael's grave. I was going later than my usual crack-of-dawn visit, as Clay had asked to come along, a rarer occurrence than the year before, as he was no longer a tag-along little boy, but in the very early stages of bursting into his own amazing teenage transformation. At twelve, his feet were suddenly as big as Sim's, though physically he was still on the short and chunky side, his hair more ash than blonde, his face momentarily unfocused, as if uncertain of which way to go: Sims or Tierney, Edmonds or Catts.

He and I were on our own that weekend, as I'd sent Sim and Missy out of town to distract them from the first anniversary of their father's death. Missy had left the night before to go to north Georgia for a few days with the Chapins, while Sim went down to St. Joseph's on a flounder-gigging trip with Carlym and a handful of Welcome boys. Clay was invited, too, but had declined, preferring to stay home and fish the local circuit with Curtis, whom he'd grown close to the past year, turning subtly redneck under his influence, converting to Wranglers and cowboy boots, even chewing Redman when he could slip it by me. (Not often, as I wasn't above checking pockets and whipping butts.)

I had dreaded rattling around the empty house alone and was glad of his company, taking him through the drive-thru at Hardee's on the way to town that morning and buying him a bagful of biscuits that were reduced to crumbs and wrappers by the time we made the graveyard. I parked on the drive below, then sent him up to the family section by himself, for along with his big feet and crackling voice, he'd been plagued by these waffling mood swings and would sometimes cry up there on the hill, which in light of his new redneck toughness, embarrassed him terribly.

So I took a seat on a marble bench in the lowlands by the path and waited, a little annoyed at the mildness of the December morning, the trees still holding their leaves, the grass still green all the way down the hill. I was sitting there wondering at it, trying to believe it was a year to the day that I'd taken Michael back to ICU, when from out of the silence of the grave, a low, familiar voice asked, "Myra?"

I jerked my face up at the sound of my name, and if I had a weak heart, I'd have fulfilled my death wish right there. For the shock was like no other I'd ever had in my life, the blood surging in my ears as I faced the owner of the quiet voice, who stood not ten feet away, dressed in the same overcoat he'd worn to the funeral, his face red-eyed and pale in the clear morning light, not unlike a ghost himself.

"Gabriel?" I whispered, and his face clouded with concern.

"Damn, Myra, I didn't mean to scare you —"

That's about as far as he got before I came off that bench like a spring, hitting him with such force that I very nearly knocked him flat, holding on to the front of his shirt for dear life, and crying and crying for the first time since the funeral, I really don't know why. Maybe because of the little leap of love in my heart when I looked up and saw him standing there that meant the end of the confusion of wondering if I could ever reconcile myself to a life of frozen yogurt and gold-digging men.

Or maybe because when I looked up and saw his pale, haunted face, my heart was finally relieved of the hideous burden of doubt, the dead weight of denial that had hung around my neck, a stinking albatross, these twelve months. For as soon as I laid eyes on him, I knew just that quickly that Michael was gone, he was dead; I'd never talk to him again. I'd never hear his step at the door, never see his face, dark against the sheets, transfixed in passion, like a happy Indian, I used to tell him. *Never again,* the truth like a knife in my heart that made me cry and cry, thinking that maybe that's what I'd have Claybird put on my tombstone: *The Truth Hurts. The Silence Hurts More.*

We eventually made our way back to the little bench, him still holding me tight to his chest till I finally got a grip on myself and sat up a little, fishing the handkerchief I'd brought for Clay from my pocket and using it myself. Gabriel immediately launched into an involved apology for the hard things he'd said the last time we talked, though to tell you the truth, I've been known to forget things shouted in anger and hardly remembered our little cat fight. I just sat there, wondering what all this jagged remorse was about, till he confessed the most grievous Baptist sin of all.

"I was drunk. I'm an alcoholic," he said, though he hastened to add, "but I haven't had a drink in ten months. Well, nine, really. Nine months and eighteen days."

I just wiped my nose and nodded, smiled a little at his honesty, for who was I to judge? I was a Tegretol, Ativan, Pamalor-chomping fool, and admitted, "You're doing better than me. I'm back on meds. Will be till I die, Dr. Williams has anything to do with it."

He smiled then, his old *you-still-love-me* smile, and was confident enough to be generous, saying, "That's not the same, though."

"Mama thought it was," I said, finishing with my nose and stuffing my handkerchief back in my pocket. "She thought I was a drug addict or something."

His face lost its charm in a flash. "Damn, your mother was a *bitch,*" he snapped, which kind of annoyed me, as he'd never liked my mother, for no particular reason I could discern, other than she didn't take to him running around with her married daughter.

It brought to mind a few memories I'd have just as soon forgotten, and I sniffed at him. "Don't curse my mother, Gabriel. You always hated her and you never even knew her."

He looked away on that and mumbled an apology, though he didn't loosen the grip on my hand, both of us content for the moment to sit there side by side in the golden December sun, me thinking how stunned and amazed Cissie would be when she saw him at the door. I'd already bought her Christmas present, an Aigner purse that had cost me a pretty penny, though it sure paled beside this. I finally stirred, asked, "Where've you been, anyway?"

He looked a little surprised. "New York. Didn't Michael tell you?"

"I mean, this year. What took you so long? Your mother's been worried to death."

At the obvious concern in my voice, his eyes took on that old glint, and he lifted an eyebrow. "How about you?" he asked in a silky little voice. "You been worried?"

Well, I'll tell you what: I was glad to see him, I won't deny it. I was glad to get a faceful of that old Gabe-smell, even glad to see that chin-out smile. But at the surfacing of his old Gabe cockiness, I was filled with the most overpowering urge to squash that roachlike ego once and for all, dropping my face and answering with a careful nonchalance, "Oh, I knew you'd turn up sooner or later. Michael said you would. And I been busy myself."

He was sitting there with his chin still lifted in that self-satisfied little smile when I went in for the kill. "Got married last week," I said with a shy little smile of my own. "Married your cousin Randell. He come down for the funeral and we hit it off. He divorced Cynthia, took a job at Sanger, doing real well."

There was a stunned silence on that, and when I chanced a glance at him, I found him staring at me with an expression that reminded me of a stray cat I'd once trapped in a Humane Society cage for Cissie. Usually the old strays on the Hill went easily enough, but this one had gone into these Tasmanian Devil-like circlings the moment the trap sprung. By the time they came to pick him up the next morning, he was perfectly bald from all that whirling, glaring at me through the wire with this truly crazed expression of the wildest unbelief, that I, a mere mortal woman, had actually trapped the King of the Hill.

That's just how Gabe looked, so funny that I leaned over and pressed my face to his chest, laughing. "I'm teasing you, Gabriel. I'm teasing. You should see your face — Gabriel?"

But he wasn't so easily soothed, not making any reply, just shaking his head and hunching deeper in his coat, even when Clay came down the path with a telltale redness about his eyes that he was at some pains to conceal. I introduced them, then went up and put my wreath on the grave, not lingering like I usually did, but coming back immediately, finding them standing there hunched in their coats, Clay quietly sniffling, Gabe still looking like thunder from my little joke.

"Well, Gabriel?" I laughed. "What's got into you? You used to tease me all the time."

"Must have lost my sense of humor," he muttered, not looking so hot in the clear morning light, his eyes gray-smudged and hollow, his hair not as wavy as it used to be, but darker and thinner and kind of crazy, as he kept rubbing it nervously with his good hand. It made him look kind of vulnerably loony, an unexpected callback to a funny-talking little boy I used to know. (*"Hey, I'm Gabriel William Catts. I live right ther next door."*)

The memory filled me with a sharp little affection as I looped my arm through his and offered to drive him to his mother's, though he demurred. "My car's on the other side of the hill," he said, glancing between me and Clay. "Where're you two going?"

"Home," I told him. "Clay and Curtis are going fishing."

After a moment's indecision, he asked if he could tag along. "Sure," I said. "Need anything from your car? A suitcase?"

But he just climbed in the passenger's seat and felt for the seat belt. "All my stuff's in New York," he said. "Come to think of it, I might have left the cat in. Remind me to call my landlady when we get to the house."

I shook my head at his old Gabriel craziness with such affection that Clay began to show a little more interest in this figure of legend, checking him out from the back seat with these cunning little glances, and finally unbending enough to ask how long he was planning to stay.

In reply, Gabriel glanced in the rearview mirror and answered uncertainly, "I don't know. Depends, I guess."

Clayton just nodded, not quite sure what to make of it, and after a few unsuccessful attempts to charm him in the usual manner, Gabriel quite unconsciously began to draw him out with a story, a funny little anecdote about an ill-fated fishing trip to the Dead Lakes when he and Michael were children. He had a whole cherished repertoire of these family things, Case-stories and Granddaddy-stories and now, finally, Michael-stories, spinning them with the gift of the Irish poet, bringing Mr. Simon back to life before our very eyes, and Michael, too, as a child, before I knew him.

Such was the spell of his words that I could see Michael so clearly: thin and dark and tough, a skinny little fighter; though I wasn't as spell-bound as poor Clay, whose eyes were almost to trance-size by the time we got to the house, where Curtis was waiting in the drive. Clay was so charmed that he didn't want to leave by then, edging back to the car and inviting Gabe along, though I declined on his behalf, as he'd been driving all night (apparently sixteen hours, straight through) and needed to go to bed.

"He'll be here when you get back," I promised as I waved them off and took Gabe inside through the front door, anxious to call Cissie and tell her to kill the fatted calf! Her son had returned.

I smiled at the thought, figured I'd nip in the car and go pick her up while Gabe took a nap, maybe call Candace and Ed too, take them all out for dinner, if Gabe was up to it. For he was looking kind of dazed and lost as he followed me down the hallway in his big coat, glancing uneasi-ly at the photographs that lined the wall, asking, "Where's Missy?"

It was kind of sweet the way he asked it, like he was the new kid in school, looking for a friendly face. "She went to Helen with the Chapins," I told him. "And Sim's camping on St. Joseph's with some men from the church."

He nodded, still looking around the high-ceilinged old room, tak-ing in the carved mantle, the line of French doors, till he saw me punch-ing in Cissie's number. "What's this?" he asked. "Who're you calling?"

"Your mother," I told him over the receiver. "I'm serious, Gabriel. She's been worried to death."

He didn't even answer, just came to the couch and took the phone away from me, tossing it aside and kissing me with all that old eating-a-peach sweetness that I couldn't very well resist, lifting my face to get it all, every bit of it. I don't really remember how long it lasted, a happy lit-tle interval, till he started messing with the front of my shirt, making my collar jump around.

"What're you doing?" I murmured, pulling back a little and looking down to find my shirt open to the lace of my good Bali bra. It was fast work for a one-handed man that made me step back and cry, "Gabriel?" "D'you think you can just blow into town and hit the hay in half an hour?"

He just stood there gaping at my bra like he'd never seen one before, "What about the bed? You told Clayton we were going to *bed*."

"I said *you* were going to bed," I corrected. "*I'm* going to get your mother, who's been spending half her social security check every month calling around Boston looking for you!"

"I been in New York three years —" he began, but I was just about fed up, not to mention a little wired and shaky and mad.

"I don't care if you been in *hell* three years! I'm going over there to get her right now while you take a nap."

"A *nap?*" he cried, like I'd stabbed him dead, staring at me a moment with a face of genuine anguish before he dropped to the couch, patting the cushion beside him. "Myra, honey — here, settle down. Mama's fine. Here, sit."

I obliged him, not sitting on the couch, but the edge of the coffee table, just across the rug. He didn't argue it, just leaned forward a little and watched me a moment with that hypnotic steadiness, then told me in a smooth, quiet voice, "I love you, Myra. I always have. I came back as soon as I could, to marry you. You know that, don't you?"

I was amazed at his forthrightness that, by God, rang true, like he really meant it — and maybe a little hypnotized, as I heard myself answer in a small, clear voice, "I know."

He smiled a little at that, rubbed his chin, asked, "Well? Do you love me?"

You really did have to have the audacity of an Heir Apparent to so baldly ask such a question, and I couldn't help but smile. "You know I do," I said, though it was really kind of a revelation on my part. I mean, I wasn't so sure myself till I heard myself say it, though Gabriel accepted it with his usual massive sense of entitlement, dropping his face to his hand a moment, crying, I thought, till it popped back up like a jackknife.

"Then why the *hell* aren't we in bed?" he shouted, "I'm thirty-*eight* years old, too old to be putting up with any more of this *shit!*"

Well, I'll tell you what: I might be too polite to tell the preacher to screw himself, but I sure wasn't afraid to tell the likes of Gabriel Catts, jumping up and meeting him face on, shouting, "I don't care if you're a *hundred* and eight! You can act right or you can *hit* the *door!* Who d'you think you are, coming in here, acting this way?"

"*Gabriel William Catts!*" he shouted in brilliant outrage, heading out the door with his coat flapping like a conductor's tails, leaving me standing there, clenched-fisted and chest-heaving, perilously close to tears. I was reaching for the phone to call Cissie and *tell Mama!* when he came back and hammered on the French door.

"I left my son-of-a-bitch car at the cemetery," he shouted. "Gimme a ride to town!"

I can't think now why I didn't just spit in his face and recommend he walk. Maybe I really was hypnotized, or in shock or something, as I grabbed my purse and chauffeured his sorry ass back to the cemetery, annoyed by his bad-tempered muttering and snorting, finally telling him to *shut up.* He hushed then, though he kept nervously jiggling his knee like he was a bomb about to go off, casting me these mad little glances that began to soften as we slowed for town, because I had, by God, started crying.

I wanted to tell him it had nothing to do with him, that it was like the shoulder shakes, one of those old post-traumatic-stress things I couldn't control. But we weren't on speaking terms, so all I could do was sniffle and drive till we made the cemetery, when I unbent enough to fish a Kleenex from my purse and wipe my nose.

I idled there, waiting for him to get out, but he was quickly undone by my tears, sighing a huge sigh and saying, "Myra," then, "listen. I'm sorry. I didn't mean to yell." I didn't say anything, just sat there wiping my nose, and he reached over and took my hand, lifting it to his lips in our old gesture of truce. "It's just that I love you so much and I've waited so long."

I just gave a mighty sniff and whispered another one of those incredible revelations that I didn't know was true till I heard myself say it. "I know."

He smiled then, not his old audacious smile, but quite sweet and gentle, his voice that same light drawl. "And listen, baby, I'm an alcoholic. It's not easy for me to stay celibate and sober, too. I mean, I can handle one or the other, but the combination's killing me."

He lifted his chin at this heartfelt confession, and I'll tell you what: I can handle a certain amount of sorriness from some people. People who have had hard lives, like Ira, or just don't know any better, like, say, Joe Bates. But I sure wasn't about to take it from a spoiled Baptist Mama's-boy like Gabe Catts and just retrieved my hand and wiped my nose while I felt around in my purse for my wallet.

Gabe just sat there with that quiet, expectant face, like he was proud of himself for making a clean breast of it, till I located a handful of crumpled dollar bills that I flipped into his lap, one at a time. "Here's your liquor money," I told him after the third bill, "and here's your whore money," after the fifth.

I snapped my wallet shut and flashed a credible imitation of his old chin-out smile, drawled, "Welcome home, *Gabriel William Catts.*" Then, before he could even howl, I kicked open his door and told him with a clenched-teeth earnestness, "Now, you get the hell out of my car, you manipulating little piece of *shit,* before I throw you out."

I think at that point, I was channeling enough of my father that he feared for the safety of his other wrist, for he got the hell out of there, all right, and so did I, squealing out at the corner and heading home, stomping upstairs and trying to return to my bed to sleep like I usually did every morning after my trip to the grave. But like all those years ago on the Hill, no matter how much I tossed and turned and thought happy thoughts and sought refuge in the mindless forgetfulness of sleep, I was unable to find it.

I finally just lay there, face up, and thought what a sniveling middle-aged fool I had become. Had I really told Gabriel Catts I loved him? Had I really opened my mouth for one of his poisoned kisses the minute he blew into town? I'll tell you what: it was behavior unbecoming a manic-depressive and kind of deflating, making me lie there and sigh and sigh, even try to daydream a scenario that would put things to rights. Maybe he'd just stay till Christmas, I thought, then leave like he used to. Or maybe he'd left already, in his old runaway glory. Maybe I was done with him once and for all, and Michael couldn't very well fault me, for I'd given him his chance. A good chance. One kiss. A good kiss.

I closed my eyes and sighed again, even more hugely than before, then just lay there, thinking what a pathetic creature I had become, when the phone rang on the bedside table. I thought it might be Missy, calling from Georgia, but it was just Candace, her voice full of this Jesus-has-returned glory, breathing, "Guess *what?*"

"What?"

"Guess who's back in town?"

"Gabriel Catts," I said flatly, and she was amazed.

"How'd you know? Mama just called."

So he had gone to Cissie's after all. Well, good for Cissie, I thought, though I couldn't help but sigh at this final evidence of a passing era, the end of the Golden Years. Candace must have heard me, as she paused a moment, then said very carefully, "I thought we'd all get together for supper. He could see the baby and all."

"What baby?" I snapped.

"Ryan. How many babies we got in this family?"

"Oh," I said. Then, "Well, I don't know. It's just me and Clay here. I was thinking we might go down and see Sim." I had thought of it that very moment, in fact, and tried to sound less threatened. "I mean, you all have a good time, we just —" I paused, then sighed for maybe the fiftieth time that day, "we won't be coming."

There was a long silence on that, so long that I finally asked, "Candace?"

She stirred on the line, said, "Gosh. I didn't think you'd be this, *hostile.*"

"I'm not hostile," I lied. "I'm tired. I was taking a nap. You woke me up."

"You sleep too much," she said, just like Ira used to, back in the Dark Ages in Birmingham. And while I gladly would have told him to go to hell, with Candace, I just waffled.

"It's the Tegretol."

"You need to get off that crap," she said with all her old quarrelsome, Charismatic sureness, and I thought: *yeah and you need to mind your own damn business,* though I just sat up and wearily rubbed my eyes.

"Listen, Candace," I said, "I don't have time to go into all this. I ain't going off anything till the doctor tells me, I ain't going to Cissie's for supper, and I ain't marrying your damn brother, okay?"

This last had come out of its own volition, one of those old passive-aggressive slips, my face kind of hot when I heard myself say it, though Candace didn't sound too offended, just breathed, "*Married?* Who said anything about marriage? You two are getting *married?*"

I was even hotter at that, sitting up, stammering, "No. That's what I said: No, we're not."

"Why would you want to *marry* him?" she asked, almost to herself, then, in this voice of utter amazement, "You *love* him!"

"I do *not!*" I cried.

But she was just quietly speculative, muttering, "You do, too. Well, there's a nasty twist. Did Michael know?"

Well, you talk about post-traumatic stress. I slowly came to my feet, shoulders-shaking, breath-labored, said, "Candace. Listen to me. Don't you *ever* talk that way to me again." Then, in this truly pathetic stab at bribery, "I've got that jacket for Lori, and I want to give it to her. It's suede — but I'll throw the damn thing in the pool if you ever talk to me that way again. You hear me?"

She was quiet a moment, kind of stunned, I think, for her voice was calm and placating when she answered. "Sure, Myra," Then, in a weenier voice, "Maybe you need to settle down. Take a pill or something."

"Don't you *patronize* me," I snapped, slamming down the phone and bursting into tears for the third time that day, maybe a record.

The phone started ringing almost immediately, but I ignored it to go downstairs and lock the doors and pull the curtains, because if Candace couldn't get you by phone, she'd jump in the car and catch you at the mailbox. Sure enough, not twenty minutes later, there was a knock on the French doors that I ignored, feeling a small satisfaction when she finally gave up and left.

When the phone started ringing again a little later, I had to answer it, in case it was Sim or Missy, surprised when Clay said, "Mama?"

"Claybird?" I asked, "You all right?"

"Yeah. The trailer got a flat and I came home, but the back door was locked. I couldn't get in."

I sat up guiltily. "I was sleeping, baby. Where are you? I'll come get you."

There was a small silence on the line. Then he said, "I'm, ah, over at Grannie's. Watching wrestling. She said I could spend the night."

I bet she did, I thought, but seized on an obvious snag. "What about church? You don't have any church clothes."

"I got some old stuff. Grannie says it'll fit." Then he got to the heart of the matter. "Uncle Gabe's here. He's asleep, but Grannie says he'll git up later. She says that you should come to supper. She's baking a ham."

Now, it took a hard-hearted woman to withstand Cissie and one of her homecoming hams, and I closed my eyes. "That's okay, baby," I said. "I'm kind of — busy. But you can stay. I'll bring you some stuff to church. You can change there."

"I'll come early," he offered, "at nine."

I told him fine, to meet me at my class, then hung up and tried to occupy myself as best I could. I did my Sunday lesson, even wrapped a few Christmas presents, since the children were gone and I had the house to myself. When the early December twilight had finally set, I went to the bathroom for my nightly handful of pills that I'd been looking forward to, as they always knocked me on my butt. But standing there, looking at the handful of shining orange and blue and baby pink capsules, I got kind of disgusted with myself. I mean, I'd only planned on going back on them for six months, and here I was a year later, still running to the medicine cabinet every time the phone rang.

"Chicken," I whispered, and instead of taking them, I flushed them. Not the whole bottle, because I knew from bitter experience that flushing whole bottles in one dramatic swoop was an expensive, presumptuous habit. It was more humble just to flush one handful at a time. Then, if you backslid, or had any little chemical storms or panic attacks, you could always jump back on the wagon without having to call your doctor in the middle of the night in a lather of sobbing repentance.

But there was a price to be paid for even that little handful, and I took a book to bed and read the night away, *The Hound of the Baskervilles,* as I'd lately been indulging in a little love affair with Sherlock Holmes, who in terms of sheer know-it-all bossiness, reminded me of Michael. I ignored the phone when it rang at eleven-thirty when Candace got off her shift, smiling a little when there was yet another car in the drive and another pounding on the French doors, this time harder and more insistent than before.

I just lay there reading, glad I'd never given her a key, a little surprised she didn't come around front and throw pinecones at the bedroom window (she had once before, the night Ryan was born). But maybe this wasn't such a big deal, or maybe she figured she'd leave me for her mother to finish off at the church the next morning, though as it turned out, Cissie was crafty enough to drive in her nails right there on the Hill where it'd all started, twenty-six years before.

$$=== 33 ===$$

After a decade of teamwork, Cissie and I
had our Primary class reduced to a science. She was the storyteller, the
Queen of the Peepbox (these little felt-covered shoeboxes with strategic
light holes that illuminated stand-up scenes of every major event in the
Bible). I was the junior member of the firm, supplying the snacks, the
birthday presents, the bankrolling of our more ambitious projects,
including strolls down Lafayette to McDonald's for breakfast when we
were too burnt-out to teach.

I must say that it made for a Sunday School class without peer,
though as I drove into town the next morning, I couldn't help but be a
little nervous over Cissie's reception, praying to God that Candace hadn't
spilled the beans about my unwonted hostility toward her younger son.
I'd marry the son of a bitch before I'd hurt his mother, and in a truly
weenie attempt at out and out bribery, drove five miles out of my way to
drop off the suede coat at Lori's, though I got there too late and she was
already gone.

So I was going into the ring barehanded, a little shaky when Clay
met me at nine with the sad news that his uncle never woke up, all night
long. "Grannie says the cold don't agree with him," he explained.

I just smiled a perfectly fake smile and sent him to the bathroom to change, still smiling when Cissie herself arrived a little later, not mentioning Gabe at all, just telling me I *looked sa pretty*. It was the same thing she told me very Sunday, though I must say that I warmed to the flattery, as I'd gone to some pains that morning to reclaim a little youth, even went through this three-step Mary Kay beauty routine with stuff I'd bought at a party five years ago that I'd never even opened. I was supposed to have used it something like twice a day for the rest of my life, so I wasn't expecting any miracles; I'd just slapped it on, hating myself while I did it, telling my reflection just how truly pathetic I had become.

But maybe it did some good, as Clay also told me I looked nice when he came by to drop off his fishing clothes on his way back to class. I kissed him in reply, told him maybe we'd drive down to St. Joseph's later that day, see Sim and Carlym and the others, maybe take them some food.

"Can Uncle Gabe go?" he asked immediately, and I just maintained that frozen smile.

"I'm sure he'll want to see Ryan."

Clay accepted the excuse easily enough, though Cissie couldn't quite let it go, talking to me in a light patter as we got the class ready, mentioning in an offhanded way how good Gabe looked. "Losing his hair," she admitted, though she was quick to add, "but it suits him."

She mentioned other things, too, his job, his car. "*Nice* car. Got *New York* plates."

She said it with a significant lift of her face like this was a feat of some proportion, though I just nodded and smiled and made my correct replies. "How nice" and "Is that so?" and "How *nice*."

It must have been clear that her old Cissie-magic wasn't taking, as once class was under way, she abruptly shifted tactics, going to the supply cabinet and making a noise of dismay, saying she'd forgotten the peepbox. "And you know how hard it is to teach Creation without the peepbox."

Well, I'll tell you what: I wasn't born yesterday and just offered to send Clay, though she was quite adamant, saying, "No, baby, it's sa cold — just slip on your coat and run on. It's right under the bed, you know, where I always keep 'em."

She didn't look within a mile of my face when she said it, a transparency rare in an old campaigner like herself that struck me as kind of pathetic. I mean, maybe Michael was right; Cissie was getting old. Maybe it was time Gabe and I got over our little pissing contest and grew up. Maybe I'd go over there, talk to him, we could be friends. Good friends, like we used to be — one of the best friends I'd ever known.

Without any more argument, I pulled on my coat and smiled a thin smile. "Be back in a minute," I told her.

She smiled quickly and (I think) involuntarily, as it was her old smile of triumph that she must have realized was a tad premature, as she was at some pains to conceal it, ducking her face, saying, "Thank you, sister."

I'll say this for the old girl: she was wilier than a serpent when she had her mind made up; it's no wonder she raised such wily children. But I didn't realize how primed I was for battle till I walked in the closed-up bedroom and found Gabe still in bed, sitting up when he saw me, asking, "What? Myra? What is it?"

You'd have thought I'd walked in with a shotgun, though I just hoisted the hem of my coat and knelt by the bed. "The peepbox," I told him. "Cissie forgot it."

Well, he *would* have to laugh, though it wasn't too damn funny to me. For I'd lost a little of my friendly resolve when I'd charged through that front door and was hit, face-on, with the savory smell of Cissie's Sunday ham, intermixed with the camphor smell and the oil heat of the tightly closed house. After twenty years, it was still the smell of lazy Sundays in the little bedroom off the porch and coats and shirts and girdles coming off, one piece at a time, till we were naked as Adam and Eve in the garden and a sight more happy.

My poor old body responded accordingly, my face flushing, my voice not so steady when I paused a moment to point in his face, say, "Don't you start that crap with me."

But he just laughed harder. "Oh, Myra — baby, don't you see what she's doing? Mama's fixing us up here. She knows I'm still in bed, so she turns up the heat and sends you over here dressed for the kill. I tell you what, if that woman'd been in the Pentagon, Vietnam would be our fifty-first state."

I didn't have any doubt Cissie wanted us to talk, though I doubted very seriously she meant for us to end up in the sack and just ducked under the bed and began tossing peepboxes up on the covers. "What d'you call these?" he asked.

He sat back on the bed with a face of great disappointment, turning one over in his hands, and I told him, "Look for *Creation*. The whole Primary class is waiting."

He sighed hugely at that, though he gave in without a fight, obediently peeping through a dozen or so boxes, till he came upon Creation. "Here you go," he said.

While I stuffed the other ones back under the bed, he sat up against the headboard and held the peepbox to his eye, his voice regaining a little of its old sparkle. "You ever notice how there's always a lion standing here in front of Adam?" he mused, "And that very convenient limb hanging there in front of Eve's —"

I just grabbed the box and stood, "You ever noticed you need therapy?" I snapped, starting for the door, when I realized what he'd said and paused to peep in the box that sure enough, was Adam and Eve. "This ain't Creation," I said in disgust, thinking it typical Gabe Catts narrowmindedness, to think the world began with naked people. "This is Adam and Eve."

"That *is* Creation," he asserted with his old authority, though I just tossed it back on the bed and hoisted my coat.

"It is *not*," I said, ducking back under the bed. "Creation's the black-and-white one with sun and moon cut-outs."

I ignored him this time while I snatched out two dozen boxes and held them to the light, with Gabe still stretched out on the bed above me like a lazy old lion, bare-chested and kind of warmly inviting, if he would have kept his mouth shut. Which he couldn't, of course, just rolling to his side and murmuring these pleading little invitations. ("Come on, baby. Why d'you wanta be sa stubborn?" Even the old stand-by, "Baby, you know I love you.")

I found it a little wearing, especially as I couldn't find the Creation peepbox. I finally gave up and went to the living room to call Cissie and make sure it was supposed to be under that damn bed, but with Sunday school already under way, I couldn't get her. I finally had to send Brother

Dorsey down to her class to ask, and took a seat in her easy chair by the phone to wait. It was a good five minutes before he came back on the line with the comforting news that Sister Catts had found the peepbox the *minute* I left the parking lot — but for me not to worry, that Brother Sloan wasn't preaching, some missionary was, so if I was detained, everyone would *understand.*

Gabe had come to lean in the doorway to listen to my conversation, wearing nothing but a pair of wrinkled khaki pants that were unbuttoned at the waist to make room for the swell of his belly. "What?" he asked when I hung up, his eyes all a twinkle.

For a moment, I just sat there rubbing my eyes, then lifted my face and relayed her message, making him practically stamp his foot with glee, say, "See? See? You were supposed to find me in bed and wake me up, and we'll be dressed again by the time Mama gets back, wrestling with the *guilt* of the thing, promising it'll never happen again."

Even after twenty years with the Baptists, they still have the capacity to amaze me, and I just dropped my hand and looked at him. "You're serious, aren't you?"

"Of course I'm serious!" he cried, "It'll make up for the time she set you up with Michael. Oh, come on, Myra. Quit being so damn stubborn. We got time, *hours.*"

I just looked at him, truly amazed this fool thought he was actually going to beg me into his bed. I mean, if the smell of baked ham hadn't gotten me there the first ten seconds I'd walked in the house, he sure wasn't going to *whine* me there. I was tempted to ask him as a matter of purest curiosity if he'd ever tried to seduce a *sane* woman, but softened it to, "Has anyone ever told you your mind's not right?"

Being Gabe, he grasped the duality of the messages, both the spoken and the unspoken, and fell back on the couch like I'd shot him. "My mind's fine," he muttered. "It's my liver and my prostate that's got me worried."

I just kicked off my heels and got comfortable, ready to talk to him like the friends we once were, though being a Catts, he couldn't quite let it go, opening an eye and looking at my snakeskin pumps with the same disgust he'd once used to dismiss my new red bike. "That lithium hasn't made you *frigid* or anything, has it?" he asked.

After twenty-five years, his contempt could still ping my heart with a ringing little hurt, making me suddenly restless. I stood and wandered around the tiny room in my coat, thinking maybe I'd drive down to St. Joseph's after all, though I answered him evenly, "No. Why? Did the liquor make you impotent?"

Well, that brought a little life to him, making him sit up with a thread of his old pained, self-righteousness snap. "I tell you what, Myra, alcoholism is nothing for you to be making these smart-assed jokes about."

I just turned to face him. "And manic-depression is?"

He wilted a little at that, then capitulated with his usual grace, dropping back on the couch and rubbing his eyes. "I thought you were schizophrenic."

"I been upgraded," I told him, "to PTSD. With manic components."

"What the *hell* is that?" he murmured.

"Bad nerves."

I strolled into the bedroom on that and paused by the window that looked out on our old house that had just that summer been officially condemned, the roof partially caved in, the front door stickered with orange warnings from the city inspector. It's funny, but the whole time I lived on the Hill with Michael, shared this very bedroom, the old house never gave me pause; I don't think I ever saw it. Now, in the bright December light, it looked as worn and decrepit as I felt, making me slump there in my coat, think maybe I'd forget about St. Joseph's and leave Claybird here with the Catts, go down to the cemetery by myself. Maybe it'd turn cold tonight and I wouldn't leave, but stay there all night long, feel the ache of the frost on my fingers and nose, remember what it was like to feel things, to be alive.

Curiosity must have gotten the best of Gabriel, for he came to the door and paused there, watching me a moment, then sat on the foot of the bed with a sigh. "I'm sorry, Myra," he said.

I just glanced at him, then nodded at the old house. "For this?" I asked, but he tapped himself on the chest.

"For this."

I turned back to the window then, and watched the dead leaves circling off the old sweet gum, thinking of another winter I'd looked out the same window, one house down, at the same blowing leaves. It was the winter I was closet-bound, the winter of my fractured skull. But I didn't dwell on it, I never did, just shrugged and made light of it. "Don't worry about it. I'm used to it. I mean, I've heard more lines this year than I did when I was sixteen."

Gabriel's face jerked up in a flash. "From *who?*"

I ignored his outrage and answered vaguely, "Oh, men I been seeing."

"You been seeing *men?*" he cried, with such amazement that I looked at him.

"What'd you think I been seeing? Dogs?"

I wished I'd kept that bit of sarcasm to myself, as it landed us right back in the old song and dance — about how Michael was lying dead in his grave this year, and he was puking Antabuse in New York, while I lived it up down here with the rednecks. I just watched him, really wondering if the idiot believed this stuff he spouted, finally asked, "Well, what was I supposed to do? You left the funeral in a huff, so drunk you couldn't *walk.*"

"I did *not,*" he snapped. "I drove all the way to the airport. I was perfectly fine." He plucked at the quilt, asked, "Who've you been seeing, anyway? That *idiot* Randell?"

Sitting there wrapped in a quilt with that pouting, sulky face, he really did look amazingly like the little boy across the fence who'd once so entranced me. I shook my head at him, said, "Good Lord, Gabriel, forget poor Randell. He weighs about three hundred pounds, has a wife and two grandchildren."

"Then *who?*"

I was toying with the idea of not telling him; but with Cissie on the trail, it wouldn't stay secret long, so I told him the bald truth. "Mostly the new pastor, Carlym Folger. He's a good man, Gabriel — the children love him, but he's only thirty-one —"

His face darkened on the *good man,* positively sneered on the *thirty-one.* "And he's been giving you a line?" he cried, "A preacher? *Damn* I hate these hicks. They always got one hand on the Bible, the other on their fly."

The heck of it was he really meant it, sitting there radiating these little waves of moral outrage. "You are the most outrageous hypocrite I ever met in my life," I told him, though he just dropped back on the bed and went back to compulsively rubbing his eyes.

"I'm Episcopalian," he muttered. "We can do these things, we're allowed."

"I bet," I said, turning back to the window and watching the circling leaves a moment, then sighing, "Yeah, ever since the obit hit the papers, they been calling, all kinds of men, all kinds of lines. They love me, love my red hair, love my — how do they put it? Strong convictions." He made no reply, and I tired of the circling leaves and went to the bed and sat down wearily beside him, dropping back to lie face-up in my coat, staring at the high ceiling and finishing wryly, "Love my *Mercedes*."

He turned at that and beaded me with a serious eye, said, "Hey, don't look at me. I drive a Volvo. Sixty-thousand miles and new tires. I ain't hurting."

I burst out laughing then, for the first time in what? — sixteen months, at least. Because God knows it was true — that whatever else his personal failings, this was one man firmly entrenched in the Catts family marry-for-tail tradition. After a year of being chased by the money-grubbers and the yogurt-pushers of the world, it really was a relief, making me roll to my side and laugh and laugh. "Oh, I do love you, Gabriel. I do, I do. Maybe Michael was right. He said to wait, to give it a chance."

"Did he really?" he asked, and I answered easily enough, absently rubbing my fingertips against his golden chest.

"Well, I don't think he liked the idea of some stranger stepping in to raise his children —" I began, till he reached up and grabbed my hand.

"Myra, honey," he said with an equally friendly confidence, "if you aren't planning on being naked here in the next few minutes," he lifted my hand, "then don't be doing this."

He was right, of course. You couldn't have it both ways: the snuggling and the friendship, too, not in this house anyway. I rolled to my back and lay there a moment, then sat up. "Sorry," I said, hunching deeper in my coat and glancing back at him. "I'm really not just being a tease here," I told him. "I mean, I am a Christian, and I do have some convictions it's the right thing. Anyway, Missy's fifteen now. What am I supposed to tell her? It's all right for me, not her?"

This perfectly reasonable explanation briefly aroused him to rise up to his elbows and argue, "You're a grown woman, Myra. She's a child —"

But I just waved him aside, and stood. "Michael waited," I said. "So can you."

Just like that, we were back in the ball game. "You were a seventeen-year-old Baptist virgin with Michael. Of course he waited. We're adults. This is different."

But I was a little tired of all his pushing and just went back to the window and stared at the pale winter sun. "You're forgetting your ancient history," I told him. "I was seventeen-year-old damaged goods. I'd been treated for syphilis twice when Michael met me."

This was a deliberate admission, a bit of my history that I'd come upon, oh, four years ago, after Mama died and I went through her papers and had found my original discharge from Jackson Memorial. I couldn't understand all the medical jargon and had taken the forms to Dr. Williams, who noted that in the space listed for treatment for venereal disease, syphilis was noted, along with the cryptic little message: x2 — which in medical terminology meant: times two.

It was a shocking discovery, to say the least, one Dr. Williams thought accurate, as the little house in New Orleans was still impenetrable in memory, work for a hypnotist, if I ever wanted it to divulge its secrets. Which I didn't, not particularly, because it was really too nasty for words. I mean, being raped at twelve was bad enough. Seven? Eight? God knows, I didn't.

And it's funny, because I never let Michael in on this bit of revision, nor Candace either one; I figured they bore enough of my sorrow. Yet here I was, telling that jackass Gabe, who closed his eyes when I said it and kept them closed as I finished. "And he respected my wishes, and so can you." I turned and looked at him. "I think."

For a moment there, I really wasn't certain he would. I thought he'd fall back to subdividing the proposition, and if he did, I'd walk out that door and go back to Welcome and tell Cissie: Sorry. I mean, I love you, but not that much. For it's like I say — I'd done my time in Alcatraz and wasn't studying on going back, not even for her.

But maybe this Gabe wasn't the wily little trespasser I'd once known, as he lifted his chin and met my eye, said, "Of course I can."

It was a sweet way of putting it, kind of made him sound like a man. I found myself smiling brilliantly, my first real Myra-smile in a long time that made my face feel kind of stretched, as I went to the bed and held out my hands.

"Well, we don't have to wait long," I told him, taking his hands, the good and the bad, and pulling him to his feet. "I mean, what's to stop us? I'll just have to call the children and you'll have to go see Peter, our lawyer. Michael left you some money, but it's all tied up. You'll have to talk to him. He'll have to explain."

"What money?" he asked, coming to his feet and encircling my waist in a perfectly innocent fashion, his hands on my back.

"The bribery money to lure you back to marry me."

"Bribery money?" he repeated, tilting his head back a little to look at me. "What? A couple thousand bucks?"

I just shook my head at his totally sincere, totally clueless face, confided, "I think I might be worth a little bit more than that."

$=$ *34* $=$

*B*y *the time Cissie returned home* from church that day, unusually late (they'd gone to the steakhouse for dinner), my fate was more or less sealed, Clayton obviously excited by the news of my second marriage, though in keeping with his new redneck stoicism, he just pointed out that my last name would still be Catts. And though he was technically the only person we told, Cissie must have sneaked in the kitchen to make a few calls of her own, for by the time I got home that night, the red light on the answering machine was flashing with a tapeful of messages.

I stood there at the kitchen counter and made twelve calls in an hour, to friends and relations who really couldn't quite believe their ears, their reactions ranging from Missy, who screamed like a crazy woman ("*Yes! Yes!*"), to Liz, who had only one question, spoken in the wildest disbelief: "*That* Gabriel? The horny little snot that got his tail tore up at the reunion?"

Put like that, I kind of hated to own up to it, shuffling my feet and making little noises of excuse. "He's really *nice,* when you get to know him."

Of the twelve, only Candace didn't react with any surprise at all (damn her), just came by the next morning to congratulate me, a gesture of support that I could have appreciated more had I not been so nervous about telling Sim, who was still away in the wilds of St. Joseph. I would have jumped in the car and checked every campsite on Cape Sandblast, but apparently they'd broken camp to chase the flounder further down the coast (to Destin, as it turned out) and weren't where they were supposed to be.

So all I could do was pace the house till Thursday night and try not to analyze my motives too closely, lest I back out at the last minute and break Cissie's heart. For once the wheels were moving, the pre-nups signed, the license in hand, I started having serious second thoughts. I mean, sure I loved Gabe, I always had, even when I hated him. I just wasn't so sure it was *love* love. That is, *Simon-Catts* love, because I really do have a problem opening my heart to people. Offhand, I could only think of maybe a dozen people I really and truly loved: Ira, of course, and Michael and our children; Candace and her brood, Cissie and Case, Brother and Sister Sloan; Liz and Lou and the assorted McRaes — but that was about it.

I think the list is so short because in order to love someone, I have to implicitly trust them, and poor Gabe: he was sweet, he was funny, he loved my children more than he loved himself; but still, he was never what you might call trustworthy, always ready to cut and run at the first scent of trouble. Try as I might, I just didn't feel any particular settling of *love* love for him deep in my heart, and it kind of ate at me, made me wonder if I was just doing this to please Michael or Cissie or the children.

On the other hand, I couldn't deny that we had sexual chemistry, and that in abundance, as my poor old body had never quite gotten over the shock of walking into that ham-scented living room and coming across a willing Catts man in bed. I think it actually made me ovulate, because I've never gone into heat like that in my life, and hope I never do again. I couldn't eat, couldn't sleep, fell into such a vile temper that Missy and Clay retreated to Cissie's, where their uncle was living the life of Riley, eating ham and holding court with his assorted nieces and uncles and cousins without a care in the world.

I couldn't complain, as my isolation really wasn't his fault, since I was the one who'd forbidden him to come over, even less sure of his resolve than my own. To his credit, Gabe didn't argue the matter, most of our contact via Candace or Cissie or Clay, who ran messages back and forth about the incidentals — the meeting with Peter, the time of the ceremony, all of it hinging on Sim's approval. If he didn't cater to the idea of welcoming his uncle back into the fold, then it was just too bad. I'd go back on Pamalor and take a cold shower every night, and that would be the end of that.

The uncertainty of it all made for one hellish week, me chewing Tylenol and picking fights till Sim finally made it in late Thursday night, his voice reduced to a barely audible rasp from camping in the cold. Carlym brought him by himself to apologize for moving camp without letting me know, and I think he might have been planning on making an official stab at asking me out, for when I gave him the news on my upcoming nuptials this very Saturday (the Catts men weren't much on long engagements, especially when they weren't getting anything in the way of compensation), you would have thought I'd announced I was marrying a woman.

He was literally struck speechless, just got in the car and drove away without a word, so amazed that I had a sad little feeling in my heart that maybe this wasn't the first he'd heard about me and my infamous brother-in-law. But there wasn't much he could do about it at that point, as Sim was as excited as Missy, insisting on going over to Cissie's bright and early the next morning, to shake Gabe's hand and creak out in a barely audible voice, "I remember you. You taught me how to swan dive." (And you should have seen Gabe's face when he said it.)

After that, it was all over but the crying, though we came upon yet another snag Saturday morning when Brother Sloan woke up with bronchitis and couldn't perform the ceremony. By then, Gabe and I were entertaining so many doubts that the ever resourceful Catts women had to step in to fill the gap. Cissie badgered Carlym into performing the ceremony, while Candace and Lori dropped by with a little Fredrick's of Hollywood outfit for my trousseau.

"Get Gabe in the mood," his sister said. "God knows it's the only kind of lingerie he's ever seen on a woman. Of course, she was probably *dancing* in a *cage* at the time."

It was the first inkling I was to have of the next round of Catts Wars, the Candace-Gabe conflict, though I was too harassed to worry it, glad of their support, though neither Missy nor I could quite figure out how the little two-piece feather and elastic thing went (or how the little dangling whistle came into it). We spent the morning of the wedding speculating on it, me so jittery that I finally broke down and took an Ativan after lunch, leaving Missy to pack my going-away bag as we'd decided to drive down to the beach for a couple of nights.

After a practically sleepless week, the Ativan knocked me on my butt, sleeping so soundly I almost slept through my own wedding, waking up late in the afternoon and finding a note on my pillow informing me that my children had tired of waiting and went to spend the day with their Beloved. Their abandonment made me a little sad, and as I got up and dressed, I fought this waffling little rebound depression, swamped by that old feeling of outsidership: that the whole world was having a party without me.

I could picture Gabe at his mother's, the children following him around like puppies, hanging on his every word, Cissie in the kitchen, baking her Christmas cakes, all smiles. Hers was the only happiness I didn't begrudge as I took a shower, then trudged to the closet to pick out my wedding dress — with just that much forethought and consideration. I opened both the louvered doors and sat on the edge of the bed and surveyed the possibilities, but I hadn't shopped for a year and half and found the swatches of sleeves and shirts and flowing scarves oddly unfamiliar.

I finally narrowed it down to two finalists: a navy acetate pantsuit and an ivory suit dress, though the black silk I'd worn to the funeral caught my eye, as it most clearly articulated the spirit of today's festivities. It actually looked pretty good on me and I considered wearing it, but thought no, the irony would not escape Cissie, and would hurt her.

So I chose the navy suit, which had the one asset I had come to value (indeed, require) in an outfit: it was slimming, and a little formal, a tad uptight. It said: I'm doing this with my eyes open, and I ain't so happy about it. Furthermore, it was shirred in the front with a tightly fitted bodice, a wee bit sexy in an understated, Casual Corner kind of way, the kind of clothes that, despite Candace's many years of effort, I continued to gravitate toward: an aging Hot Mama, but a Hot Mama yet.

After an hour's hard effort with a blow dryer and rollers and the Mary Kay stuff, the results were not so bad. I could still see a few years' hard living in the thin lines around my mouth and eyes, but, overall, I looked like what I was: a well-off, melancholy descendent of the Emerald Isle, who really should have settled in a climate more conducive to maintaining ivory skin. My hair was kind of strange when I took it out of the rollers, bigger and poofier than usual, and I tried to remember the last time I had it cut. It must have been around Thanksgiving, for Cassie Lea had talked me into buying a raffle ticket for a turkey shoot. That couldn't have been more than a month ago, and I was wondering how it had grown so fast — then I remembered: it'd been a year ago Thanksgiving that she'd cut it, so it'd be easier to care for in ICU. I'd forgotten all about it till just now. No wonder it was so long.

But there was nothing for it now, and with the clock hastening on, I sprayed it in place, gathered my stuff, and took my suitcase to the hallway, where I was stopped dead in my tracks by a sound downstairs, one eerily reminiscent of an earlier day. I thought I was alone in the house, but apparently I wasn't, as someone was downstairs watching a — baseball game? in December?

The hollow call of a good-ole-boy announcer ("— a strike, left field, look at it go!") gave a ghostly sense of retracted time as I went slowly down the hall to look over the rails to the living room, where sure enough, the television was on, blaring ESPN. I paused a moment, then took the stairs quietly, a small part of my mind reasoning that, well, Gabe had finally done it: driven me clean out of my mind.

For the ghost of Michael Catts was as real as any Stairwalker, his Bass loafers poking off the end of the couch, the tassels tapping a beat to the fast action on the field. I was too numb after the last week to be really anything but curious about this apparition and approached the high back of the couch slowly, my heart beating a little hard at what he'd look like after a year in the grave. He must have heard my heels on the wood floor, as he sat up just as I made the couch, his calm, even face making me scream. "*Sim!*"

He jumped like he'd been shot. "*Mama!*"

I really nearly swooned, my head so light I had to lean it against the back of the couch a moment, finally lifting it to ask faintly, "Why aren't you at your Grannie's?"

He was still a little scared and unfolded himself slowly. "She sent me over to drive you in."

I should have known the Catts Woman wouldn't leave anything to chance. "Why?" I asked, "I been driving myself to town for a right smart of years."

I was quoting Cissie with the *right smart*, though Sim didn't acknowledge the parody, just came to his feet, his voice still a little hoarse from the camping. "I don't know. I'm just doing what *you women* tell me. You ready?"

It didn't take a Sherlock Holmes to figure out where he'd picked up the *you women*, and I just closed my eyes and thought, *my God, what have I done?*

I stood there so long that he finally offered, "You all right? You look kinda — white."

"That's because I'm a white woman," I told him, then wearily picked up my suitcase. "Let's get this thing over with." Though on the drive to town, I couldn't resist asking, "So how's your uncle holding up?"

Sim was old enough to grin at my careless words. "Oh, about as *happy* as you," he said. "Him and Grannie got in a big fight."

"What about?"

"Clayton wearing Wranglers to the wedding. Boy, you shoulda heard 'em."

"Oh, I've heard 'em," I assured him and didn't bother to ask who won.

Sure enough, when we made the parking lot at Welcome, Clay was slouched on one of the front pillars in a pair of black dress pants he must have left at his Grannie's sometime in not so recent memory, as the cuffs came right to his shoe tops. It was clear that a grievous wrong had been done him, and I stopped to kiss his outdone face, told him, "You look handsome, baby."

"I do *not*," he snapped, sliding off the pillar. "Gabe said I could wear Wranglers and it's *his* wedding."

I had a feeling that this had been the Cry of the Defenders and took his arm as we went in. "Well, it ain't," I told him. "It's *my* wedding, and I think you look handsome. Whose stuff is it, anyway?"

"Mine, from the funeral," he said with that same tone of deep disgust. "Wearing *funeral* clothes to a *wedding*."

From the sound of it, this had been the secondary attack that I circumvented as I knocked on Brother Sloan's office door. "Well, don't worry it," I told him. "I almost wore black myself — *Gabriel.*" I smiled as he opened the door, all dressed up in the navy suit he'd brought by the house for my approval, his hair kind of crazy as he kept swiping at it with his good hand.

"Where is everybody?" I asked, and he answered distractedly.

"Decorating the car, I think."

The boys went out like a light to join in the fun, but I just looked at him. "Whose car?"

"My car."

"Why aren't we driving my car?" I asked.

"Why your car?"

"'Cause it's a better car —" I began, but he just threw up his hands.

"Hey, forget it," he said. "I'll take the bus before I git in a fight with another damn woman."

He looked it, too, pale and distraught, nervously chewing his lip in a way that was wonderfully reminiscent of another husband I used to know. It made me kind of love him there for a moment, forgetting my own misgivings to slip my arms around his waist and ask, "So when'd you turn into such a pussy?"

He relaxed a little at the naughty word, his face taking his old teasing glint. "Matter of survival, my dear," he said, then spoke over my shoulder, "Didju find it?"

It was only then that I realized someone else was in the room: Carlym. He must have been standing at the filing cabinet when I came in, and I could have dropped dead when I saw him there, not two steps behind me, his face very polite, very tight when he nodded. "Myra."

I cannot overstate the hideousness of my embarrassment. It was like I'd used the f-word in front of Billy Graham, or worse — for he was a stranger, while Carlym hovered somewhere between good friend and brother status, obviously deserving better of me than this. For an awkward couple of minutes, we were forced to stand there and make small talk, till Candace and the rest of the crew finally showed up, bright and churchy in their Christmas best, Lori bringing me a small bouquet of roses, though I was too flustered to be properly grateful.

I just took my place in front of the desk and repeated my vows in a pained undertone, working hard to avoid Carlym's eyes the whole time and not even offering Gabe the traditional kiss till Missy reminded me. When it was over, we didn't stick around for the congratulations, but took off straight to the car (my car, which set up a wailing and gnashing of teeth in the children, as they'd decorated his), where I lit into my new husband the moment the doors were slammed. "Why didn't you *tell* me?"

"Tell you *what?*"

"That Carlym was standing there. You let me walk right in and say that *awful* word right in front of him."

Gabriel just looked at me evenly. "Hey, if I'm gone get bitched out everytime *you* use an ugly word, then I'm going in and getting this thing annulled right now."

Well, he did have a point: the ugly word had been my own, one of those awful white-trash words I only used with my husband. It hardly seemed fair, working your whole life to build some semblance of middle-class, country-club, navy-suited respectability, only to have it undone in two unguarded seconds. "Why'd it have to be *that* word?" I kept moaning all the way to Panama City, though Gabe ignored me, steering with his good hand and chewing his lip, as if we were driving down the old four-lane to our Doom.

By the time we'd made it over the bridge to the beach, we'd given ourselves over to damnation, pulling into the first little motel that had a vacancy, him making the arrangements while I lay back in the seat, my arm thrown over my eyes. It made for a honeymoon about as romantically inclined as my first, as we'd landed on the old part of the strip, a treeless, concrete stretch frequented by soldiers and their prey — dirty, two-storied block, with a parking lot that came right up to the front windows. In July, the asphalt would steam like a waffle iron, though the mild December air was kinder, the afternoon sky cloudless but calm, the place deserted when Gabriel returned with the key.

"How much?" I asked, when he came back.

He answered distractedly, "Twenty-six."

"The whole night, or by the hour?" I asked, but he didn't answer, just handed me a suitcase and took the key up to the second floor where he opened the door on a long, narrow room that was furnished with maroon shag carpet and an enormous king-sized bed topped with a velvet heart-shaped headboard. "Now this is what I call a honeymoon suite," I said dryly, looking around the room that was bare except for a built-in dresser topped with an ancient television and the usual little HBO pop-up that I glanced at absently. "Oh, good," I said. *The Terminator*'s showing."

Gabriel didn't answer, just sat down on the edge of the bed with this slumped-shoulders dejection, as if this truly was The End Of The Road. I left him there to go out on the little balcony, the ocean a clear, unsullied emerald this time of year, the air salty and mild and oddly comforting. "D'you wanna take a walk on the beach?" I called inside, but there was no answer.

After a moment, I came back in and found him fallen backwards on the bedspread like someone had shot him from the doorway, his good hand rubbing his eyes. "You all right?" I asked, but he just kept rubbing his face, finally dropping his hand to look at me sadly.

"Myra, darlin', I hate to tell you this, but after a week's worth of suppression and an hour's worth of venomous stares from Knute Rockne, I ain't at all sure I can do this magnificent bed justice."

It was hard not to laugh, but his face really was pretty ravaged, so I just lay down beside him and patted his belly, told him, "It'll pass."

He zoned in (as usual) on the kindness, his face taking on a little of his old Gabe glint (the same slide it'd taken when I'd said the Ugly Word in front of the preacher, damn him). "Was Michael ever impotent?" he asked.

Now, Michael Catts was impotent about as often as he was lazy, and with a little glint of my own, I answered evenly, "Michael? *Never.*"

He rolled away on that. "You git away from me."

"Oh, hush," I said, lying there a moment staring at the water-spotted ceiling, till I remembered the Fredrick's of Hollywood stuff and raised up. "Here. We needn't despair. I come on this trip prepared. You haven't seen my sleazewear yet."

He made no reply as I dug them out of the suitcase Missy had loaded with every bubble-bath, perfume, or pair of silk panties I owned, as if I were vacationing at a brothel. I found the little bag of elastic and lace in the pocket and took it to the bed, shaking it out and trying to make sense of it. I still couldn't figure out the leg holes, and finally nudged Gabe. "I cain't figure this stuff out. Me and Missy tried all morning." I held up one of the pieces, the one with the whistle. "Is this the top or the bottom?"

Gabe lifted his face a moment. "That's a g-string, you hick."

I just looked at him. "Well, what's that supposed to mean?"

"It means it's the bottom."

"Oh," I said, stretching it out as far as it would go (not far enough, I'll wager —) "Well, what are the feathers and the whistle for?"

But he'd burrowed into the pillows, his voice muffled and aggrieved. "I don't know. I'm just a fat, overeducated, latent homosexual who can't even get it up on his wedding night. Run call Knute, he probably knows."

"Idiot," I said as I went to the bathroom, which was fortunately too old to be affixed with that great twentieth-century squasher of self-esteem, fluorescent lighting. I didn't look half bad stripped down in the light of a dim, forty-watt bulb, till I stretched myself into the little bands of elastic that were probably two inches too small below, maybe four, above.

"Good God," I murmured at the sad showing I made in the sleazewear, the little patches up top not doing their job in any sense of the word, the back view not much of an improvement.

"I tell you what, my butt ain't what it used to be," I called out in warning, though Gabe answered in a lighter, slightly more interested tone.

"Come on. Let's see."

But I wasn't in the mood for any more humiliation and sadly regarded my reflection. "Who wears this kind of stuff?" I called. "I look like a circus horse."

"Oh, come on, Myra," he begged, then, in an even lighter voice, "*please?*"

My reflection rolled its eyes at that, and with a little adjustment of the patches, I stuck my head around the corner to the bedroom, where he was sitting up against the headboard, still in his suit, though he'd kicked off his shoes and loosened his tie.

"I look like an idiot," I told him, but he was in his magnetic mode, his hair still spiky from all the head-rubbing, though his face was calm and hypnotic.

"You do not. Come 'ere."

"You better not laugh," I warned him, inching around the door to stand with my butt to the wall. "I wish Candace would get over this fantasy I weigh a hundred twenty pounds," I said sadly, popping the tightly strung bodice. "This one-size-fits-all stuff never works for me."

Gabriel didn't argue, just looked at me with a misty-eyed appreciation, commenting in a light, wandering drawl, "It was one of my boyhood ambitions to marry a woman who could say that." He patted the pillow beside him. "Come here."

But I stayed there against the wall and waved a hand at the bed. "Kick off that nasty spread," I told him. "I ain't going home with body lice."

He obeyed, kicking off the spread, his eyes on me the whole time, sitting back when he was done and tipping his head against the headboard. "Come on."

"Well, I'm taking this stuff off," I said, shimmying out of the elastic, then joining him on the pillows, neither of us touching at first, though his face was suddenly relaxed, like he'd taken a shot of whiskey while I was in the bathroom.

"I *love* naked women," he said, his voice that distant, storytelling murmur. "I mean, women in clothes, they're nasty, they're controlling. Naked women? They're harmless and cuddly as little kittens. Little fuzzy biddies we used to get in our Easter baskets —"

"I don't want to hear about your other naked women," I told him plainly, but he just smiled absently.

"Well, there have been so *many*," he said, leaning over to kiss me lightly on the lips, so light it was a little electric, my whole circulation system moving up a few notches, though he drew back lazily, still fully dressed, asking in that wandering tone, "Why is that?"

"You're a misogynist," I told him, and he grimaced.

"Oh, Myra. Baby, I hope to God I doan go home and find your bookshelves full of that Betty Friedan crap."

"Arthur Conan Doyle," I said, as he kissed me again, then pulled back.

"*Who?*"

"Sherlock Holmes. Watson said he was a misogynist. I looked it up."

"She's a smart old girl," he said lightly, tugging at his tie and tossing it off the bed with other pieces of clothing, a slow proposition, with his one hand. I finally sat up and helped, though he was a little taken aback by my (how shall I say it?) *level of participation,* his hesitancy making me laugh and laugh, filled with a lightness of being, the way sex does me sometimes — the joy of the Lord, the Charismatics call it.

Because it was funny: Gabriel damn Catts, the big-talking sinner of Magnolia Hill, a man so debauched he was exiled to New York for ten years — all stripped down, he turned out to be about as sexually astute as he was at thirteen, trying to lure me down to the tracks. It's not that it wasn't good (I was ovulating, remember, a fairly full-proof recipe for achievement) — it was almost *too* good, Gabriel deviled by that old adolescent problem of (how shall I say this?) *control,* his tender endearments limited to breathless variations on, "Myra, baby, *be still —*"

Which only made me laugh harder, because it was good, for one thing, and kind of sweet, to tell you the truth, as I'd been a little afraid I was marrying a jaded old womanizer who'd try to boot me up like a computer with the same old moves that had driven his girlfriend-before-last wild. So you might call it laughter of relief, which goaded Gabriel into showing a little of that old Catts stamina there at the end, which I couldn't argue with, doing a little begging of my own before it was over and biting the crap out of his shoulder, a nip of pain that took him over the edge, though at that point, neither of us was complaining.

When it was all said and done, the room dim in the afternoon light, the sheets a mess, he lay there like a dead thing, finally opening an eye to look at me with a shadow of his old hurt defensiveness. "What's all that *laughing* about?"

I yawned. "You're funny."

"Funny how?" he asked, rubbing his shoulder where I'd bit him.

I scrunched up next to him and mimicked, *"Myra, baby — lay still, darlin'."*

He closed his eyes at that, said, "Well, you needn't be complaining about my lasting power if you ain't willing to *cooperate.*"

I just laughed, then shared a patented truth I probably should have mentioned before we tied the knot. "Well, baby, it's like this: I quit laying still for men in 1974, and I ain't ever going back. Not even for you."

He was quiet for a moment, then murmured, "What an evil woman you are." Then, in a tone of open sorrow, "You'll be running back home tomorrow, telling my nosy damn sister."

"I will not."

"You will, *too,*" he moaned. "Every damn woman at Welcome'll know in a week."

"They will *not,*" I said, pressing my face to his shoulder. "We'll go home suffused in this rosy, sexual glow, like Marilyn Monroe and Arthur Miller. They'll all be scandalized."

"You think so?" he asked in a voice that was a little more hopeful.

"Sure. The Awful Man Who Stole His Brother's Wife."

The phrase settled on him like a blessing. "Knute hates me already," he pointed out, and I lifted my face.

"See there?"

He seemed reborn at the idea of scandal, rolling to his back, asking, "Well, are you gone let me make love to you again?" (Actually, he used the old Magnolia Hill term; this is the country-club translation.)

"Sure," I said, and he smiled a beatific smile.

"Well, I think I'm gone like this marriage stuff," he said, and I just smiled.

"I always did."

*W*ith just that much thought and foresight
I entered into the holy state of matrimony with a recovering alcoholic just five days after I'd begun weaning myself from the cushion of three different psychotropic drugs. I'm sure that when Dr. Williams heard news of my nuptials through the Sanger grapevine, terms like pattern thinking, co-dependency, not to mention *stupider than shit* must have flittered through his mind, as he made a point of leaving a message on the answering machine while I was at the beach to remind me that he was always there if I needed him.

Gabe was outdone at the good doctor's doubt, though I'm not sure he was so far off base, as those first few weeks made for such steep undulations of agony and ecstasy that I sometimes wondered if I'd inadvertently slipped back into a mixed manic state. For in true manic form, the ecstasy was mostly between the sheets, the agony creeping in when I began the more challenging task of learning to live with a man who was as stubborn as his mother, not to mention jealous, self-absorbed, and seemingly determined to return me to the empty-headed passivity of my youth.

Fortunately, none of this was so obvious as long as we were

cocooned away from the real world in a cheap motel on the beach. There, I saw the best of Gabriel Catts — the lover, dreamer, storyteller Gabe, who kept me held hostage in that bare room for the better part of three days. Such was the sweetness of his particular charm that I hardly thought to complain, just lying there, mostly just talking, with my face against his wonderful chest that was not what you'd call chiseled by any means, but wide and comfortable, dusted with a coverlet of graying, golden hair that made for a nice pillow.

He told me of his jobs, his teaching, the cities he lived in and how much he hated them, while I filled him in on news of the home front, of Case and Cissie and Candace, Michael and the children. I hadn't realized how lonely I'd become until I had him there as a listener, chattering on as mindlessly as I once had with his father, till the short winter days drew to full night, when our talk turned, inevitably, to secrets. That's when I told him of the other decade, the unspoken one, everything from Mama's final weeks to Ira's sorry little arrest and conviction.

Now that Michael was gone, only Candace and Cissie knew the whole story, and they pretty much kept it to themselves, though Cissie was (against all good judgment) still a vociferous supporter, sending Ira scrawling letters and tins of cookies he claimed were more valuable in trade than Marlboros. Gabriel, who had as good a reason to hate my brother as anyone, was equally generous, not dwelling on the prurient details like most people did, but just shaking his head with his old bleeding-heart compassion, muttering, "Poor son of a bitch. Is he a sociopath?"

I explained the terminology such as I knew it, and it's really a shame we had to pack our bags and return to the real world the next morning, for I was feeling so many loving thoughts toward him that I began to think that maybe Candace was right: maybe I *did* love Gabriel. Maybe this wasn't merely a marriage of lust and convenience. Maybe it was a perfect fit.

I was so buoyed by the possibility that I sailed through Christmas on a wave of laughter and contentment, all of us going over to Cissie's on Christmas Day, stuffing ourselves on turkey and Lane Cake, Cissie's face a sight to behold. It was a magical restoration in its way, though you'd have thought that an old manic-depressive like myself would have realized the euphoria couldn't last, it never did. This one was no exception, all my dreams of love and happy endings crashing down in this awful domino effect that began bright and early Sunday morning when Gabe refused to go to church.

Now the going to church part wasn't such a deal in itself, as I knew Gabe wasn't your average communicant. I mean, his faith wasn't the faith of Michael Catts, that Peruvian pragmatism, but something a lot more complex, in a way that's kind of hard to explain. Suffice it to say that I was certain he believed, though he was kind of ashamed of it, kind of a closet fundamentalist, you might say. I wouldn't have been so hard-headed about him going to Welcome if he hadn't been so adamant himself about the importance of us maintaining a *continuity of life* for the children.

I don't know where he'd come up with the phrase, but he'd waxed pretty eloquent about it when we were still naked in bed at the beach — about how they'd had enough upheavals in their young lives and we needed to *work together* to smooth his transition into our household. He's a convincing old soul when he wants to be, and his arguments (as always) had a ring of truth that made me wholeheartedly agree: they *had* had enough upheaval; we *did* need a continuity. It wasn't until we returned to the real world that first Sunday that I discovered that in the world of Gabe Catts, intent is light-years away from reality, when I had to interrupt my own church-going routine to tell him to get dressed.

I had to run up to his old haunts above the garage to tell him, for his first order of business upon his return had been to restore the tiny rooms to their old 1974 glory, cleaning out the fishing gear and odds and ends, leaving nothing but the desk and boxes and narrow bed, which was returned to its place of honor under the window. I didn't complain, as he was a historian by profession and needed a place to work, though that light above the pool every evening still gave me a queasy little foreboding, making me avoid going up there as much as I could.

So I wasn't too thrilled with having to run up Sunday morning and whip him into shape as if he were one of my children. I just went as far as the door and called, "Gabriel? It's nine-fifteen. You better get a move on. We don't live on the Hill anymore. We're ten miles out."

He was standing at one of the maps in his reading glasses and old robe, and paused to look at me through his bifocals and ask, "You need me to drive you in?"

"No, I don't need you to drive me in," I told him. "Come on. I got your suit laid out. Where're your shoes?"

"My shoes?" he repeated absently, then seemed to realize my intent, as he actually flinched, as if I'd shocked him with a live wire, then waved an arm at the wall of moldering maps. "Sunday's the only day I have to work on my book," he said, for as of last Tuesday, he'd been going into Sanger a few hours every day to learn the basics of the furniture business at the hands of Sam McRae.

It was an undertaking he was proving fairly adept at, though his real job (and I hoped he realized this before I had to baldly tell him) was to show up at golf outings and board meetings and look white, since being perceived as a minority-owned business was proving to be a thorn in Sam's fiercely competitive flesh. He was convinced it was costing him orders and had appointed Gabriel chairman of the board, hoping to send the message to our mobile-home manufacturing friends that no matter what the color of the man in charge, this was still just a good-ole-boy undertaking after all, and Jesse Jackson wasn't getting a penny of it.

Gabriel didn't complain and actually undertook his new duties with considerable zeal, though being a professional White Man was just his day-job. His real vocation was the completion of the book he'd left boxed up over the garage twelve years ago, in which, on closer inspection, he saw the clear signs of his own young genius. Every morning, he got up at six and worked on it a few hours before he went into Sanger, which was fine with me. I just wanted him to take off Sundays and go to church.

For Welcome, like many small congregations, had shrunk over the years, losing its young people to the varied programs of the much richer First Baptist downtown, or worse, to the upbeat goings-on in the local Charismatic movement. Men, in particular, were a rarity, far outnumbered by the children of the Hill who faithfully trooped in with their dimes and ragged Sunday best, and the old folks, contemporaries of Mr. Simon and Cissie, who'd known Gabriel all his life. Over the years, Cissie had kept them abreast of his amazing accomplishments: the degrees, the colleges, the big-city names: New York, Boston, Washington, D.C.

They had taken great pride in a local boy doing well and weren't even particularly shocked when I up and married him out of the blue, some of the ladies going so far as to sacrifice a few dollars of their social security checks to buy us a little wedding present, a doily or set of tea glasses from WalMart. I must say I was touched by the gesture, as they seemed to be sending their own message: that if Gabriel was willing, they were ready to welcome the bad boy home. For they'd loved his father, they'd loved his brother — they'd love him, if he'd give them a chance.

That was the message, though Gabriel was too wrapped up in Gabe-World to so much as acknowledge the offer, much less answer it, just leading me to the bed that Sunday and setting me down like a dim-witted child. "Baby, there's a whole new market now for Civil War books," he explained, "a lot of interest in reenactments. I need to strike while the iron is hot."

Like I say, he can be a very persuasive soul when he wants to be. The problem was, he'd already convinced me about the importance of *continuity* and life going on, and I just stood. "You can borrow Sim's if you can't find yours," I told him, making him lift his face to heaven.

"No, no," he said, pulling me back to the bed and scattering me with a peppershot of excuses. "I'm Episcopalian. The pants to that suit are too big. Brother Folger hates me."

"I took the pants up last night," I said, and he groaned aloud and fell to his secondary defense: outright begging.

"Myra, baby, listen. I attended Welcome three times a week the first seventeen years of my life. I've been saved, I've been baptized, I've been rededicated every time they preached hell. I know every hymn by heart, I can quote more of the King James than Jerry Falwell, and I will gladly, *gladly,* give whatever is the going rate in tithes, up to and not exceeding ten percent. Okey-dokey?"

I just detached myself and headed for the door. "I can't find your socks, either. They must be in your shoes."

There was a groan at my back that I ignored as I went inside to get dressed, though when I came back to the kitchen, there was still no sign of him. I sent Sim and Missy on to town in Michael's (now Sim's) truck and had Clay run up for one more try, thinking that the sight of his slicked-back hair and obvious eagerness to show him off might lure Gabe out, though after a few minutes, Clay returned, disappointed and apologetic.

"He ain't coming," he said, and in the face of my obvious aggravation, tried to offer an excuse. "He's already saved."

"I wouldn't be so sure of that," I muttered dryly, and as I drove into town, I wondered what the hell he thought constituted continuity? Did he mean he was going to reprise his former role as the Catts' family pet? Live above the garage, just show up to eat breakfast and hit the sack a few times a week? Hell, I thought I'd married him, not *adopted* him.

His mother looked equally miffed when I told her he was concentrating his sabbatical energies reconstructing a hundred-twenty-year-old war, though she kept quiet about it through Sunday School and church and dinner at the steakhouse, which was a pretty squelched affair. Until that moment, I hadn't realized how much my and Carlym's dour little courtship had invigorated the whole group.

Now that I was an old married woman, none of us had much to say to each other. Clay went with Cissie as usual, leaving me to return to a perfectly silent house and a husband who had given up his historic labors and returned to bed to read the paper.

"How was church?" he asked easily, as if he really were an angelic being, not in need of spiritual ministration like the rest of us mere mortals.

"Fine," I said flipping out of my church dress in a sad, sleeply little slump, as the loss of the Tegretol cushion had seriously screwed my nocturnal clock. "Brother Sloan preached, lost his place a few times, bless his heart. Carlym really needs to go on full time."

He made no reply to that, for not having entered the world of Welcome Baptist, he didn't know of the raging debate of whether or not Carlym should be put on as a full-time associate. Brother Sloan really did need to surrender the pulpit more often, but no one (including Carlym) wanted to hurt his feelings by hinting that his sermons were getting kind of wandering and confused, difficult to follow and painful to watch.

But like I say, Gabriel was above all that, just skimming the paper, asking, "Where're the children?"

I told him how they'd scattered as I crawled into bed in my underwear, as Sunday afternoons were still peak sexual interlude time around the Catts' household, one of the few times in the week when you could let go without fear of having a child knock on the door and ask what all that *groaning* was about. But I was still kind of peeved about him dodging church and just punched myself into my pillows and prayed to God I could get in a few hours' deep sleep and restart my internal clock.

Gabe, who'd been bone-idle all day, was naturally in the mood for a little conversation. "So y'all ate at Mama's?" he asked.

"The steakhouse. We go there every week with the old folks. Clayton loves to hear them talk. It's just something we do on Sundays."

"Just you and Clay and Mama?" he pressed.

"Yeah. And a few others."

"What others?"

I yawned. "Brother and Sister Sloan. Candace and Ed, sometimes. Carlym. Just the usual."

He finally left me alone on that, and I did indeed go to sleep, deep and dreamless, waking up a good three hours later, finding my husband all showered and ready for the evening service, standing at the mirror, knotting his tie with angry little jerks of his hand. "You're coming to church?" I asked, and he gave me a sliver of his attention.

"Yes."

"Why?" I asked, for it was obvious he was doing it under duress. I wondered if Cissie had come by and given him the word, though he just finished with his tie and turned.

"Because I'm whipped, that's why."

I just stretched. "Well, you don't have to. Nobody's putting a gun to your head."

He didn't even reply, just turned and gave me and my good Sunday bra one of his amazingly withering looks, then went downstairs, his pained silence making his homecoming at Welcome a pretty sad affair. Mostly, all he did was sit there with his arms crossed in a mad little pout, not giving much indication what his funk was all about till that night in bed, when he tried to talk me into converting to Catholicism.

"To *what?*"

"Catholicism," he said with all his old wily reasonableness. "It's the last bastion of true Christianity in Western civilization. I mean,

Protestantism is weeny, it's watered down, it's been intermingled with lesser beliefs."

"What lesser beliefs?"

"The Charismatics. Calvinism. Not to mention the sleazeball evangelical circuit. I mean, really, anything goes in the Baptist Church anymore. Look at Jimmy Swaggart."

I knew enough about Louisianan spirituality to argue this one, though he ignored me to go on and on about the rot of the Protestant church, predicting that in ten years they'd be bleeding chickens on the altar. I really couldn't imagine what in Carlym's rambling little sermon on the fishes and the loaves had brought on this withering storm, and only blinked at him as he sat up on his elbows and really went in for the kill.

"And if you want to raise Sim and Missy in that decay, well that's fine," he said, "but Clay needs to be somewhere they really believe. You know, hold fast to the teachings of Christ. Not swayed by society mores."

I was thinking for one wild moment that he was going to suggest we join Candace at Living Water Assembly, for the tone of his disgust had the smell of her old Charismatic contempt as he lay back with a snort, said, "I mean, look at Welcome. Unashamed racists, cheat on their taxes, run around. The divorce rate is the national average, if not *higher.*"

On that, he chanced one of his cunning little glances, and I finally realized the name of the game here: simple jealousy. Peter (the lawyer) had told me he'd been a little weird about having to sign a prenuptial agreement ("I'm an asshole, not a con artist," he'd complained). Furthermore, he was *convinced* Carlym was still secretly lusting after me, just waiting for an opportunity to pounce. He'd gone on about it quite a bit during the honeymoon, even had the boys calling him Knute (as in Rockne) in one of his silly Gabriel-games, but I hadn't paid him much mind. I mean, if Carlym hadn't gotten into the pouncing mode when I was a merry widow, I doubted very seriously he'd endanger his career (not to mention soul) by attempting it now and just rolled my eyes.

"Gabriel, you idiot," I said as I punched myself into my pillows. "You had me going there for a minute. *Catholicism.*"

But he couldn't let it go, actually grabbing my shoulder and rolling me to my back, saying, "No, no, listen. They have a centralized government. They keep a balance between the spirit and the letter of the law.

They let the alcoholics meet in their basement."

"They don't believe in divorce," I added with a grin, and he glared at me with that old stray-cat craziness.

"What's wrong with that?" he demanded. "Read Matthew! Read Mark!"

It's part of his closet-fundamentalist thing that he really does know the Bible, and I just laughed. "I'm not arguing."

"You're not arguing," he cried, "but you're running around with a preacher, taking him out to dinner while your husband starves."

"While my husband *pouts,*" I corrected, which was a little below the belt, as it was one of those trigger words with Gabe. Whereas *Babygirl* and *White Trash* can make my blood boil, Gabriel really and truly detests any allusion to his padded childhood, the very word making him rise up in brilliant outrage.

"I was not — I was reading the paper," he began furiously, lowering his voice when I jerked a warning nod at Clay's bedroom, "But I'll tell you one thing, Myra — I don't think it's too damn funny the way you're doing it *right in front of the children.*"

Well, you talk about trigger words. Just like that, I lost my laughing patience, rising up on my elbow and telling him with a level-eyed honesty, "I've been going out to dinner with Cissie and Clay and the others for years, and your presence or your absence isn't going to stop me from having a perfectly innocent —"

"Innocent, my *ass,*" he snapped. "Does he or does he not pull out your chair, pour your tea, ingratiate himself to Clayton?"

"The waitress pours my tea," I told him mildly. "Carlym and Clayton are friends, yes, and he does pull out my chair, as he does for your mother and all the other ladies —"

"— I bet he doesn't enjoy looking down Mama's dress half as much as he does yours," he snorted, which might have struck me as funny, except that it was so insulting to Carlym, who, aside from the frozen yogurt, had never treated me with anything but respect.

It was more than you could say for the lunatic across the sheets, and after facing him off a moment, I finally lay back, said, "Gabriel? Honey, if I was you, I'd spare myself the agony of applying my own lack of sexual maturity to every other man I met."

He catapulted out of bed at that, though he paused at the door to fling back his own deadly bit of advice. "Yeah, and if I was you, Myra, I'd remember a little more of my ancient history, and how the last time you indulged in a little casual adultery, you not only wound up pregnant, but *catatonic.*"

He stormed away, and I didn't bother to follow, but just threw a pillow at the door, shouted, "Yeah, and it wasn't any damn good, either!"

But he was gone, and good riddance, I thought, just rolling over and going to sleep, kind of glad to have the bed to myself, as I'd gotten used to sleeping in the middle. The deep little afternoon nap had indeed reset my clock, and I slept like a brick till just before dawn, when someone shook my shoulder. "Myra," a voice spoke into the darkness, making me sit up.

"Gabriel?" I blinked. "What's wrong? Is it the children?"

"They're fine," he said, his face barely visible in the dim half-light, his voice tired, but conciliatory, saying, "Listen, I'm sorry I said that about adultery. It was a cheap shot."

I just looked around, disoriented, asked, "What time is it?"

"Five-fifteen," he said. Then, "Listen, baby, you can go to church all you want, but those sleazy bras and underwear have got to go. You hear?"

For a moment there, I really wasn't sure I had, for I still have this weird thing about being abruptly awakened at night, an ear still cocked for a return of the Stairwalkers. This odd little piece of advice struck me as nearly as strange. "You woke me out of a sound sleep to lecture me about my underwear?" I asked, and he nodded firmly.

"Yeah. That's exactly what I did. No woman wears underwear like that unless she's asking for it."

He said this awful phrase without a flicker of ill-conscience, and I just looked at him. "That all?"

"Yes," he said, a little weenier, and after a moment, I rolled over and started snuggling back into my pillows. He lay down beside me and slipped his arms around my waist, everything okey-dokey — though after a moment, he asked in a small, hopeful voice, "Well? Are you gonna get rid of them?"

I just settled in and told him plainly, "No, Gabriel, I'm not. They cost too much just to throw them out. Furthermore, I've got some that don't even have underwear. They're just garters, and I'll wear them too, when it suits me."

There was a silence in the room as if I'd stabbed him dead. Then in a small, sad voice, he asked, "Myra, honey, why d'you want to do me this way? I love you."

"I ain't doing you no way," I assured him. "Whether or not you trust me is your business. It's nothing to do with me one way or the other. You want an enabler, you get yoursef a dog."

He sighed hugely at that, and after a moment of silence, murmured the same thing he'd said on the honeymoon in that tired, sad voice. "What an evil damn woman you've become."

There was a day when such a heartfelt pronouncement would have cut me to the quick. Now I just yawned. "Matter of survival, my dear."

— 36 —

*Y*ou'd have thought that would be the end
of it, that the lines would be drawn, the boundaries established.
However, this wasn't a mere mortal I was dealing with, but Gabriel
William Catts, and as it turned out, the vetting of my underwear was just
the beginning of what you might call the clash of Myra-World and Gabe-
World, though I didn't know it at the time, just went back to sleep and
slept soundly, all things considered, till the alarm rang at seven.

Gabriel was already up, working on his book, I assumed, as he was
due to meet with Sam at the plant at nine. I woke the children with a little feeling of lightness in my heart, glad of the return of the old Monday
morning routine, for I'd learned long ago that a firm schedule is the stuff
emotional stability is made of. It gave the cold January morning the distinct smell of returning life, as I'd agreed to throw a baby shower that
night for the first time in a year, and Missy had suddenly, just that weekend, announced her intention of attending the annual Sweetheart
Banquet at Welcome.

I counted her capitulation as a domestic victory on my part, as
Missy was having a hard time breaking into the woman-thing, still preferring to hang around the softball field instead of having much to do

with dressing up, and who could blame her? On the field, she was competent and talented; on the dance floor, a good half-foot taller than most of the boys, too smart and mouthy and redheaded to be anybody's little sweetheart. It was just a sad fact of life she never seemed to mind too much till she started high school in town and had the misfortune of falling in love with a boy in class who couldn't be bothered with her, preferring petite blondes, as a lot of rednecks do.

His open-handed rejection cut her flaming confidence to the core, a double whammy, emotionally speaking, as it had come within months of her loss of the one man in her life who'd pushed her to be the best athlete she could be, who'd rejoiced over every inch of her five foot nine and told her she was beautiful every day of her life: her father. Without his support, she seemed to lose her compass, talking of throwing over softball in favor of cheerleading, spending her weekends cruising the mall in search of the perfect outfit, even acquiring an uncharacteristic slump, as if trying to physically shrink herself into more acceptable proportions.

It cut at my heart more than any of the other fallout from Michael's death, possibly the reason I put aside my unease and went ahead and married Gabriel Catts, whose first words when he saw Missy getting out of the Chapins' car was an exclamation of honest wonder, "My God, Myra, she's grown a foot. She's gorgeous." (The Catts all have a great affection for height, not having so much of it themselves.)

Sure enough, in just one week, I'd seen a remarkable return of Missy's old bounce and had gladly shelled out a small fortune on a magenta blue formal for the banquet that really did look stunning on her. Yesterday, she'd found the perfect shoes and was bright and excited for once about dressing up, with none of her usual wailing over the injustice of being a redheaded Amazon. I couldn't help but think it a good sign, as if our little self-imposed isolation might be ending at last: Missy coming out, me back to a normal, unmedicated life, and the bathroom smelling of men's cologne for the first time in a year.

It put me in a mellow, forgiving kind of mood, at least until I came downstairs to find Gabe in the kitchen giving Missy hell about spending ninety-six dollars on her new shoes. I had heard their raised voices upstairs, but didn't come in on anything but the last line, spoken by

Gabriel with all his old socialist-liberal glory: "Well, you can wear 'em if you want to. I mean, they're your feet. But as far as I'm concerned, ninety-six-dollar shoes are an abomination before God, and people who wear 'em will burn in hell."

He made this (absurd) pronouncement with the aggrieved right-eousness of a prophet of old, though he did have the grace to shoot me a guilty little glance when I walked in, effectively bringing his tirade to a halt. Fortunately (for him), Missy still had too much of her father in her to be so easily cowed, and only put her shoes back in the box with a laconic "Maybe I'll donate them to the March of Dimes when I'm done."

He just shook his head in disgust, making me rightly annoyed, not at his outrage at the price of the shoes (that *was* kind of disgusting), but the fact that he was taking our little pissing contest public. It sure didn't sit well with me, but in a try at civility, I didn't tell him to go to hell in front of the children, but just requested his presence upstairs in the bedroom, please. He was equally civil, saying sure, just let him finish his coffee, and I'll tell you what, it was a good thing the Pamalor hadn't quite left my system, or I'd have had a good reply to that.

As it was, I just sent the children on their way and went upstairs to my own Monday morning routine, jerking the comforter off the bed and stripping the mattress, when he finally sauntered to the door, coffee cup in hand, and asked, "Myra? D'you need to talk to me? I'm supposed to be at Sanger at nine."

I didn't even turn, but just yanked at the pillowcases, still trying to make a stab at reasonableness, saying, "D'you know Gabriel, I never had anything growing up. Nothing that didn't come out of a bag of hand-me-downs, or off the sale rack at the Dollar Store." I paused to see if he was with me, and he was, his face lifted politely, still sipping his coffee as I tossed pillows and continued. "So when I had my children, I promised myself that one day I'd provide for them better than was provided for me —"

"Ninety-six-dollar shoes?" he burst out. "Come on, Myra, you're turning Missy into a Cracker American Princess here."

"*And,*" I continued, "if it takes ninety-six dollars to make Missy feel pretty enough to go to one of these stupid banquets, I will spend it. In fact, I will spend five-hundred-and-ninety-six dollars if that's what it takes. She's my child and it's Michael's money and it's nothing for you to worry with," I tossed the stripped pillows back on the bed, "one way or the other."

He just shook his head in patent disgust, but made no further objection till I'd gathered the bedclothes and passed him in the doorway, when he lifted his face to heaven and murmured in this arch, singsong little voice, "Once a *babygirl,* always a *babygirl.*"

I stopped as soon as he said it, not two feet in front of him, and he really did have the audacity to face me off mildly, even take a sip of coffee, till I lifted my own face to heaven and intoned in the exact same voice, "And once a *Mama's boy,* always a *Mama's boy.*"

I didn't wait to see the knife go in, just went on to Missy's room and stripped her bed, hearing the stomp of feet on the stairs and the French door being slammed with great offense. I figured he'd left for Sanger and went about getting the house ready for the shower, kind of jaded and tired, telling an outright lie when Sam called at ten to ask where Gabe was.

"He's sick," I said, feeling like a fool, wondering where the hell he'd gotten off to, till I left for Winn-Dixie later in the morning and saw his car was still in the garage. He must have gone upstairs to pound out his frustrations on the War, not showing his face all day long, as I stuffed mushrooms and decorated the little front parlor with crepe paper and silver balloons.

The children came home briefly after school and left about as quickly, except for Clay, who was still carless and homebound. With nothing better to do, he followed me around two steps behind, whining about not having anything to do.

"Go upstairs and torment your uncle awhile," I told him, but he was still too shy to go up there alone and just hung around the kitchen staring at the garage window, trying to wish him down. I kept (literally) bumping into him every time I turned a corner, and by seven, was about ready to whip him and send him to bed when I came upon Gabe leaning against the kitchen counter eating grapes.

He was about thirty hours into his little pout by then, still in the clothes he'd put on to wear to Sanger, studiously ignoring me till Clay came to the door and started whining about being hungry. At that point,

I'd heard about as much Catts-whining as I could stand for one day and turned on him, telling him to get his butt upstairs, when Gabe intervened with his tired old Tierney charm, straightening up, saying, "Run get your coat, son. I'll take you to a movie."

Clay froze at that, clearly interested, though he tried to sound reasonable. "I already seen it. Me and Keith went Friday."

Gabriel just went to the sink and spat seeds in the drain. "This is different," he said. "It's in Tallahassee, about Vietnam. We'll have to hurry, it starts at eight."

Now, all my children have gone though their little seasons of infatuation: Missy with softball and Cabbage Patch dolls, Sim with various sports; but of the three, Clay was the true obsessive. Once he got fixed on something, he, by God, didn't let it go, everything from wrestling to fishing, to just lately, Vietnam. It was odd to me that such an easygoing child was so attracted to warfare, but then again, liberal-hearted old Gabe had devoted his life to casualty rosters and camp conditions of a hundred-twenty-year-old slaughter.

So I (privately) figured that maybe it was genetic and allowed him to see a few of the recent surge of Vietnam movies, the Rambo and Oliver Stone stuff, in the hopes that it would spur him to inch his way through a few books, as he was still struggling with the dyslexia. At twelve, he'd compensated enough to be literate, though he still transposed words and notebook papers, even affixed posters to the wall upside down, a small disability he was ashamed of, which is probably why he was still a little shy around Gabriel and his legendary brilliance.

However, the lure of Vietnam was enough to make him turn tail and run upstairs for his jacket, leaving Gabriel and me in the kitchen in a small silence, him still leaning against the counter eating grapes, me feeling these little waves of affection for his kindness to my child. I mean, he basically was an asshole, but a sweet one when he wanted to be, and I swallowed my pride enough to ask in a small voice, "Are you hungry?"

"No," he said shortly, knowing he had me right where he wanted me and not giving an inch, till I finally broke down and went over and slid my arms around his waist.

"I'm sorry I called you a Mama's boy," I said in his ear, but he was still an iron man, just leaning there, eating grapes.

"Don't worry it," he said. "I been called worse."

I was liking the feel of his neck enough to find his tough-man thing kind of sweet, and whispered, "Not by me," which was about as far as he could hold out, finally giving in with one of those wonderful Gabriel-kisses, his good hand fighting for position under my sweater, so that I was holding his face with one hand, trying to keep him from unhooking my bra with the other, whispering, "Gabriel. Gabriel, here. The ladies are in the living room — your Mama's here —"

But he didn't stop till Clay came back to the door, his face alight with the prospects of an evening of Uncle Gabe and Vietnam, dancing attendance to the car with an exuberance that was wonderfully reminiscent of another little boy I used to know.

There was something enchanting in the moment, and after I kissed Gabe goodbye and sent them on their way, I paused on the cold marble by the door and enjoyed the little spark of magic: the night clear and cold, the stars like diamonds this far from town. For a moment there, everything seemed to be falling into place: Missy babysitting for Ryan, Sim in Waycross with Sam, Claybird heading to the movies with Gabriel. There was an innocence there, a kind of life-after-death perfection that lifted my heart as I rejoined the chattering group of women in the living room, Cindi getting a fairly nice shower, thanks to the old guard who resolutely marched out to showers come sleet or snow or winter rain. I had a good time eating carrot cake and counting down the hours till Gabe returned home when I could consummate that kiss in the kitchen, though I fell down on the job and went to sleep before they came in, waking in the morning to an empty bed, Gabe already downstairs with the children, dressed for Sanger.

"How was the movie?" I asked Clay at breakfast, and he was oddly hesitant.

"It was," he paused a moment, "interesting."

It was about as much as he cared to say about it, unusually quiet and absorbed, though when I asked Gabe if they'd had fun, he was quite nonchalant, saying sure, though the movie was kind of intense, real footage from the war. "Not that Hollywood crap."

I could hardly see how the genuine footage could be any more gruesome than the stuff they were showing in the theaters these days, which I never could stomach, not seeing the need for that kind of graphic glorification of destruction. I mean, if I wanted to demonstrate the reality of violence and darkness and death to my children, I'd drive them over to see Ira behind the wire in Union County, not pay five bucks a head at the local multiplex.

Clay never fought me on it, as he wasn't such a tough little cookie himself about the gore and blood, really preferring the fairy-tale spin of the Rambo stuff, where the evil was punished and the good prevailed, which was fine with me, as I'd already seen one starry-eyed boy grow up too fast and wasn't so eager to let Clay go.

So when Gabe assured me nothing was amiss that morning, I had no better sense than to believe him, until the real scoop on the movie came to light in the worst possible way: from the mouth of a fellow mother, on Sunday morning after church. That's when Susan Brown (Keith's mother) cornered me in the cold little corridor of the Sunday School wing and asked if Clay was feeling better.

"I know he was upset," she said, and I just gaped at her.

"About what?" I asked, immediately thinking that it was the marriage: that Clay had secretly objected, but was too shy to say so.

Susan, who was a pretty good old soul, a single mother raising two sons alone, just gave me a curious look, said, "You know, that awful movie he saw, with his," there was a small, imperceptible pause that everyone at Welcome used when giving Gabe his popular title, "*uncle.* Kind of pornographic, Keith said — mangled bodies and something about — ah — soldiers with actual — ah, prostitutes — you know, having sex — and you know how sensitive Clay is."

I just stood there with my mouth open, for I knew all about how sensitive Clay was. Despite his budding redneck persona, he didn't particularly like to bait hooks and had given up hunting after Keith had (accidentally) shot a little rabbit that cried like a baby (he said), sending Clay into a two-week funk that everyone (but me) thought was so hilarious.

The news that Gabe had seen fit to deflower him with the real world did something strange to my brain, igniting this glowing red anger that blotted out everything else, though in a devious twist of timing, church had already begun when I finally caught up with Gabe. It left me no choice but to sit there passively through one of Brother Sloan's wandering, hour-long sermons before I could foist the children off on Cissie and finally face him in the privacy of our car.

As soon as he laid eyes on me, he knew the fat was in the fire, though he didn't say a word, just sat there behind the wheel, staring at the milling throng of fellow Baptists as I put on my seat belt and commented in a perfectly calm, reasonable voice, "So it wasn't that Hollywood crap. Just simple, straightforward, real-life *pornography.*"

He didn't say anything, just sighed hugely, and I slowly turned to look at him. "Why didn't you tell me?"

Which possibly wasn't the best way to phrase the question, as Gabriel was the king of dissimulation and answered with a bland, honest face, "'Cause I knew you'd bitch me out."

Well, poor Gabe. Having been exiled to the North these last few years, he didn't know that the other f-word around the Catts household was *bitch,* an inconsistency that I will admit to, as I spent the next sixty seconds giving new meaning to the word. He tried to argue, but couldn't get a word in, and finally drove us over a few streets to the parking lot of the Piggly Wiggly, where he tried to talk me down in this loud, hectoring voice. "It was — would you shut up for one damn minute? It wasn't porno — Myra, for God's sake, SHUT UP. It wasn't a pornographic movie. It was two minutes of bare-breasted women —"

"— why he'd been so quiet!" I cried. "You messed him up, Gabriel! You messed him up!"

"— couldn't even see what they were doing!" he insisted, and I really shouted at that.

"What they were *doing?* He's twelve years old! He gets embarrassed at tampon commercials!"

He finally tired of the trenches then and tried to take the moral high road, lifting his face to the heavens and wailing, "Well, I toldju it was too intense, but no, you don't care about a little death and destruction, just a little sex has you uptight, you hypocritical —"

But I'd reached my saturation point by then, and had we been facing each other, probably would have gone in for a Sims-style head-butt of the sort that had almost cost Ira a tooth. As it was, I had to content myself by (literally) kicking him out in the parking lot with one last shout of advice: "Don'tchu ever even *talk* to my children again!"

I meant it, too, leaving him to stand there and stamp his foot in magnificent outrage, shouting, "Myra! Myra! *Dammit!*"

But I paid him no mind, just drove home by rote, till I pulled into the empty garage and thought, hell, what was I doing here? I used to love the solitude of an empty house; now I couldn't stand it and just sat there in the idling car a moment, then backed out and headed to the graveyard. It seemed odd, going there that late in the day, the brilliant midday sun glittering off the rough-cut marble as I made my way up the path for the first time since I met Gabriel there, two weeks ago.

You could already see small signs of neglect, the grass around the graves scraggly and weedy, my jaunty little Christmas wreath faded and splattered, half turned on its side. There was something sad and abandoned about it still being there the week after New Year's, knifing me with a small sliver of guilt. I knelt down and pulled the weeds from Clay's inscription (*He Walks With God*), briefly resting my forehead against the rough edge of the tombstone, but not finding much comfort there, just thinking how funny life was, how seductive. It was always drawing you out, calling to you from the fence, so charming, so harmless. But once you answered its call, it really was hard to go back to the solitary comforts of closets and isolation and death. When you tried to return, there was nothing left for you there but cold stones, empty, echoing houses.

Maybe it was the price you paid for life, for love; you couldn't have it both ways, and I closed my eyes wearily, wondering whatever had possessed an old Stairwalker like myself to think I could choose the light, when there was a sound on the drive below, the slam of a car door. I looked up and saw the familiar broad hood of my old Cadillac that we'd passed on to Cissie when we bought the Mercedes. It made me sit up quickly and wipe my face, wanting to make myself presentable before she made it up the path, though it wasn't Cissie at all. It was Gabe.

He was still in his church clothes, his dress shirt rolled up to his forearms, his face tightening when he saw me kneeling there, not in anger, but pain, knowing I was indulging in my old necrophilia and kind of sad about it. He didn't say anything, though, didn't start in on another round of Catts-Wars, just took a seat on his father's tombstone and sat there rubbing his eyes a moment, then lifted his face to say: "This isn't working out so well, is it?"

His quiet words pinged my heart with that old stinging hurt, for I thought he was about to suggest that we call Brother Sloan, see about annulment or divorce or whatever the legal term was for getting out of two weeks' worth of undiluted aggravation. But he just sighed and said, "Listen, Myra, I'm sorry. *Hearts and Minds* was a stupid choice for a twelve-year-old. I'd forgotten it was so intense. It shook me up, too, and the way he talks, he's seen more nudity at twelve than I have at thirty-eight."

"Where's he ever seen nudity?" I snapped, and he shrugged.

"Don't ask me. Ask Mama. She'll probably have the goods on him by the time we get home."

I stood then and slapped the dirt off my hands. "Well, I'm sorry I screamed," I said, sitting down beside him. "I tell you what, I'm thinking about getting Dr. Williams to put me back on lithium. I get so crazy anymore."

Just like that, we were all right again, him taking my dirty hand and kissing it lightly. "It's because you're in love," he told me with all his old wily confidence, though I wasn't so sure.

"I been in love before, and it wasn't like this."

He smiled a ghost of his old chin-out smile. "Not with me, you haven't."

I didn't argue the matter, and it really was kind of pleasant, sitting there in the golden sun, holding his warm hand in mine. It wasn't like we'd actually resolved anything; we were just basically too whipped to be lured into any more border wars, just talking of routine matters, of church and the children, Gabriel asking how the primary class liked the Creation peepbox he'd made to replace the one Cissie really had (apparently) lost.

"The moon's too low," I told him. "The children thought it was a beach ball."

He promised to fix it, then stood, saying we'd better go see about Clay, that Cissie had once made him write John 3:16 twenty times for inspecting one of Candace's bras. "I can't imagine what the punishment is for blatant, unashamed voyeurism. She might have stuck him in the microwave or something."

"She'll probably sic Carlym on him," I smiled, though at the mention of the Dreaded Name, he came to a complete stop and looked at me a moment, then made a grunt of annoyance and kept walking.

He waited till we were on the flat land by the car before he paused to ask very casually in this uninterested, nonchalant voice, "D'you really think I lack sexual maturity?"

"Gabriel —" I began, tired of the fighting and wishing he'd leave well enough alone, though he couldn't, of course, just stood there, trying to look unconcerned.

"No, really. I won't get mad."

I was tempted to roll my eyes at this, but there was something a little touching in his uncertainty that made me stop and give the matter a little thought before I answered slowly. "Y'know, to tell you the truth, I think you lack maturity all the way around — don't get mad —" I added as he gave a quick little shake of the head. "I mean it as a compliment. I think it's why I love you, why I always loved you, even when we were children."

He quit his wigglings then and was quiet, and for good reason, I thought. For we'd known each other what? Twenty-six years? And this was the first time I'd told him I loved him without being led or cajoled or passionately engaged, his face very still as I stood there in the sun and tried to explain. "I mean, you were so innocent, so sheltered. Cissie and Mr. Simon had made you such a happy little world with your friends and your books and your church. It was like you were a prince in a castle, enchanted, like nothing could touch you at all."

For a moment, I thought of him as a little boy, strolling up to the fence and offering Daddy a fat little outstretched hand, with Ira left behind, stalled out by the porch. I could feel my own smile faltering as I tried to explain. "I mean, Ira and me, we were never that way. No protection, no enchantment. But you were, and I think just knowing you showed me there was a better life out there, a salvation, if I'd just hold on."

Which is what one of Ira's forensic psychiatrists had once told me, and I felt my face sharpening as I added this bit of scientific confirmation. "I had a psychiatrist tell me that once. She said the difference between me and Ira was that he'd accepted cruelty as the norm, but I never had. I'd disassociated before I'd accept it — and it makes sense to me, because insanity is curable, but inhumanity? I don't know."

Gabriel didn't answer, but just let me chatter on as we started walking again. "And I don't know what you've been up to all these years, but you've never changed, you *never will.* That net Simon and Cissie wove around you is still there, and it kills me when you and Candace talk about war and hate and viciousness — you don't know what you're talking about. You're both just so naive, so protected — it's never touched you at all. That's the world I've tried to make for my children. Every child that's born should have such a world."

I turned then and looked at him. "That's why that movie bothered me. I mean, sure it's true. Nobody has to convince me of the reality of evil, but why not let Clayton find out on his own? Why rush it? He'll see the underbelly soon enough. Let him be a child a little longer. Let's all be children. It'll be over soon enough, anyway."

I found my eyes going back to the cedars atop the hill that cast their cold shadow over the graves, and I felt that old sharp arrow of reality, so painful. God, it almost paid to be a Stairwalker in a world so hard. My voice lost its glow and dipped back to Earth: "I mean, look at my poor Michael. Forty-three years old. Worked every day of his life, worried and struggled, and why? So his widow could drive a fifty-thousand-dollar car, his daughter wear ninety-dollar shoes. While there he lies, dead and turned to clay."

Gabriel blinked at the suddenness of my descent, then lifted my chin and spoke in his father's teasing voice. "Dead and turned to clay? Woman, I'm gone have to make you a new Resurrection peepbox, you keep talking like that."

There was something very Michael-like in the way he looked at me with that old optimism, that bottomless faith that made me smile in the thin winter sun, say, "See? It hasn't touched you yet. It never *will.*"

$$= 37 =$$

We made peace that day in the graveyard, Gabriel and I, for the first time in, oh, eighteen years, since he left the Hill and headed north in '71. There was nothing else for it, as we weren't so young anymore. If we didn't want to wind up back at AA and Dr. Williams' respectively, we knew we'd better let up and allow each other a little breathing space, which was about as close to true love as a couple of old war-scarred veterans like ourselves could aspire to these days: the comfort of a warm body in a bed, along with the luxury of a little dissent.

That was all we asked, and once we'd made that hurtle, you might say that Myra-World and Gabe-World converged to produce a whole new Creation. It was admittedly a Strange New World, one dedicated to the proposition of raising our children with some semblance of continuity through their last years of childhood, that thrived, even within the iron restraints of Welcome Baptist. For once Gabriel broke down and returned to church as God (or at least, his mother) intended, he really proved to be as wily a Baptist as he was anything else, custom-fitting a struggling, unimaginative little congregation to fit his own insane needs.

His first creative act was to take over the men's Sunday School class, which was really nothing more than a collection of half-a-dozen old reprobates who'd never gone to church voluntarily in their lives and were only there (like Gabe, now that I think of it) because their wives had tired of playing good-hearted-women-in-love-with-good-timing-men and put their foot down. I'd always gotten along with them myself, as, despite their great age, they were basically nothing but a bunch of Butt-slappers at heart, who'd never quite gotten over the love of a redhead-ed woman.

Every Sunday they greeted me with winks and ancient old come-ons ("*Hey, good-lookin*") though they'd fortunately lived long enough to know better than to follow up their winks with slaps or pinches (which might have resulted in the displacement of their dentures). So we got on just fine, at least until Gabe blew in like the proverbial ill wind that blew no one any good. After that, I only pitied the old boys, because despite his best intentions, Gabriel really is a garden-variety asshole, and there just isn't much anyone can do about it. I have never in my life met anyone more attracted to the love of battle, and in short order, he'd taken this group of semi-invalids and turned them into a roomful of rav-aging wolves, standing at the podium every Sunday and screaming at them like Mussolini from a balcony, taking whatever stand he deemed would provoke the most acid response.

One week he'd be a straight bleeding-heart liberal, one, a near-fas-cist, always probing for whatever nerve was most tender, once pro-claiming the apostles to be charismatic, which at Welcome Baptist, was like striking a match at a gunpowder factory. Poor old Brother Sloan had literally almost had a heart attack, someone having to run to the par-sonage for a nitroglycerin pill while that idiot Gabe stood there at the podi-um like a nut on a street corner, shouting for him to *read Acts!* Read *Acts!*

Now, I didn't mind him going after the other old boys, I figured they could damn well take care of themselves, but Brother Sloan was my bud. He and his wife (one of my second-generation mother figures) ate dinner with us every week at the steakhouse and whenever it was his time to get the dessert, it was always ice cream, straight down the line. He'd also known my family, had actually stepped foot in the Sims house (when he'd come to tell on Ira and Cassie Lea) and had never held it against me — not a small favor, as around these parts, people aren't so forgetful about what side of the tracks you are from.

So when Gabriel helped me out with my primary box after Sunday school, I warned him to go easy. "He's eighty-one years old," I told him. "Leave him alone. Welcome's split six times over the Charismatics. Even Candace left. Don't torment him about it. He's too old."

"Not too old for the truth," Gabriel answered with his old self-satisfied smile.

"Must you always win?" I asked, and he just slammed the trunk.

"Only when I'm right."

Unfortunately, he considered himself to be in that exalted position about a hundred percent of the time. Though on that occasion, at least, he found himself right and soundly beaten, when Brother Sloan took the pulpit a half hour later and with a dead-level stare in Gabriel's direction, announced his text: Second Samuel, chapter 11.

As soon as he said it, I ducked my face, not in embarrassment, but to bite my lip to keep from smiling, for as everyone knows, this is the story of David's depressing little backslide into adultery with the fair Bathsheba. It's a sad, cautionary little tale that Brother Sloan roared out with the righteousness of a prophet of old, spinning the sermon to dwell on the consequences of David's sin, primarily the death of his beloved son Absalom, Brother Sloan's trembly old voice braying out the last verse like a cantor: "Absalom, Absalom, my son, my son. Would God I had died for thee, oh Absalom, my son, my son."

Gabe studiously ignored him to play War on the back of the bulletin with Clay, though his neck was as red as a beet before it was over, hardly able to contain himself till he could get back to the privacy of our bedroom and rage like a madman. "I can't believe it! He nailed me from the pulpit, the ruthless old son of a bitch!"

"Don't you *ever* —" I began, but he waved me aside.

"Oh, cut the shit, Myra!" he shouted. "He cursed me was what he did. Didju hear him? *The thang thet Daavid had done displeesed the Lawd.*"

Gabriel really is a brilliant mimic, never more wickedly accurate than when he's mad, and I lay back on the bed in my slip and laughed till I cried, which only made him madder, storming around, threatening to sue! Defamation of character! Libel! Till I finally got enough of a grip on myself to sit up and say, "Gabriel, honey. It's just your own guilt talking."

"Guilt, my *ass!*" he shouted. "Everybody knew what he was talking about, and I'll tell you one thing: that'll be the last time I ever step foot in Welcome Baptist, me or my checkbook either one — I can grant you that."

"Suit yourself," I said, privately a little relieved, as his love of needling was beginning to bring on a backlash of resentment on my own head, a few of my old mother figures (saintly wives of the old reprobates in his class) beginning to wonder aloud at the wisdom of a woman who'd pass up the attentions of a man like Carlym in favor of a Gabriel Catts. It was a question I didn't like to ponder too closely myself, as his career as a Professional White Man had also come to an end after he'd dared to publicly disagree with Sam in the hearing of a vendor.

Sam had maintained his usual cool till the vendor had left, then politely informed Gabe that he'd better never do that again. Gabe, who is constitutionally unable to resist a challenge of this sort, just met his eye and mildly asked what would happen if he did? What would Sam do? Tie him to a cotton fan? (Which, he later explained to me in the privacy of our bedroom, was what they'd done to Emmett Till, and where he'd come up with the parallel, God only knows —)

In reply, Sam (who apparently understood the Emmett Till connection very well) just met his eye with equal honesty and said: "Yaasss."

Which, like I say, pretty much squelched Gabe's desire to return to Sanger in any capacity, so that the mantle of Heir Apparent was passed on to Sim at the ripe old age of eighteen. It was probably just as well, though after a few weeks around the house Gabe began to get cabin fever, and one morning in early March announced at breakfast that he was looking for a job of his own.

"Why?" the children asked, as they'd gotten used to him being the family pet, always underfoot.

Gabriel looked a little hurt at their response, explaining with his usual goofball logic, "Because I'm the Big Man, the Daddy. I go to work. Bring home the bacon."

Sim and Clay took this on face value, nodding sagely, though Missy just looked at me with the beginnings of concern. "We don't have to actually *live* off it, do we?"

I had the temerity to laugh at this, though Gabe was not so amused and went about job hunting with the same massive sense of entitlement he went at everything else, starting at the top at the university level, sending out resumés and making calls, prepared to be hired on the spot. When no offers were immediately forthcoming, I pointed out that it was the middle of the semester, and that maybe he should wait till summer and go about this in a more professional manner.

In reply, he just looked at me like I was an idiot and went on and on about what a catch he was, professionally speaking, with his degrees, his experiences, his various writings and grants and awards. "Yeah, but that was up North," I argued. "This ain't Boston, baby."

He rolled his eyes at that, then went into even more elaborate detail about how superior his Northeastern credentials were. He said, academically speaking, that the South was to education what sand fleas were to flounder-gigging, which naturally offended my sensitive little Louisianan heart, making me suck my teeth a moment, comment, "Guess that explains all those offers that keep *pouring* in."

He kept to himself after that, not letting me in on any more of the details of his fruitless search. By March, I figured he was crapped out and ready to wait till June or July and go about it in a more reasonable fashion, though as it turned out, he had something else up his sleeve. I didn't know what, but knew something was incubating one afternoon when he and Clay invited Cissie to join us for supper at the steakhouse.

Throughout dinner, Gabe was smooth and composed, though Clay was about to burst in his seat, hardly even eating, he was so excited. I couldn't quite make out what was up till supper was finished, when Gabe stood with his tea glass in hand and announced that after careful examination of career options in north Florida, he had decided to accept a position of great responsibility shaping young minds at Lincoln Park Middle School.

"Doing *what?*" I cried, as Clay let out a yelp of victory and jumped up to clink his glass.

"Teaching American history," Gabe said, upending his tea glass the way he probably used to upend a glass of whiskey. "I'll make eleven thousand a year. Missy will have to shop at Wal-Mart."

Missy let out a roar at that, though I stood and kissed him lightly on the mouth, for his kindness for my child, if nothing else. For apparently, this was all Clay's idea. His history teacher, Mr. Nair, had been sidetracked by a nasty collision on I–10, and after a little begging, Gabe had agreed to go to the school board and personally apply for his job. Clay, of course, saw nothing ironic or unusual in a man leap-frogging from a tenure-track position at NYU to teaching remedial history at a country middle school, but I certainly did, and it made me kind of love him there that night.

That night, and many nights to come, as he went about custom-designing his class with his usual gonzo brilliance, all but banning the state-approved text and in its stead, instituting what he called an Oral History Project, to the poor remedial students' unending gratitude. It was probably the first time in their lives that they weren't made to trudge through those hideously boring texts, but sent home to fish up old gossip and stories, quilts and home remedies, even a lynching or two, to their old professor's never-ending delight.

I told him he'd missed his calling as a reporter for the *National Enquirer*, for he really did have a nose for scandal and spent the end of the year collecting private little recountings of murders and adulteries, rogues and mob actions. But I never complained, as Clay was so visibly blooming under his tutelage, making the honor roll for the first time in his life and talking of becoming a historian himself. As far as I can remember, it was the first time Clay had ever voiced a life plan, and when he began his final project in early May, Gabriel talked him into making Michael his subject.

"But won't everyone think it's *stupid,* doing my own father?" Clay asked, though Gabe just beaded him with his crazy, genius eyes.

"Why not? Michael lived in time; he was born, he died. He's got as much right to historical preservation as *Ronald Reagan,* for God's sake."

Clay only looked at him with the dazed, blunted face of the entranced, a look I knew so well, having once been so completely in his spell myself, because the fact of the matter was, once he'd gotten over his initial shyness, Clay loved Gabe so much he was damned close to being *in love.* He repeated his every joke, maneuvered to be at his side, most of our own conversations prefaced by those faithful old words: "*Gabe said.*"

"He loves you so much it's scary," I told Gabe one night in bed, late in the spring, close to the end of school.

And though it was too dark to see his face, I could tell he was pleased. "Why d'you sound so surprised?" he asked. "I'm universally loved, wherever I go. With a few exceptions, of course."

He said it with a touch of his old petulance, for he knew I loved Michael more than I loved him, though it was only on our honeymoon that he found out that his father took top billing even over Michael. ("We're in some deep Freudian shit here," he'd muttered darkly.)

Now it was my turn to be a mite jealous, lying there in the darkness and offering a mild warning, "Go easy on him, Gabriel. He's a sensitive old soul. A lot like his father."

Which was about as close as we came to the truth those days about Clay's true paternity. It wasn't a deep, dark secret; of course, it couldn't be, since Sim and Missy knew, as (it seemed) did everyone else: Cissie and Case and even newcomers like Carlym. I think that in all of Jackson County, maybe Clay was the only one who *didn't* know — or maybe wouldn't admit he knew, for the evidence was as close as the bathroom mirror.

Except that his hair was darker and smoother, his eyes down-tilted like Mama's, he and Gabe were nearly identical, always had been, and Clay had grown up on the comments, some made innocently, some pointed, about their very likeness. So maybe he knew, but didn't want to know, the same way that I'd always known something unspeakably awful had happened on Magnolia Hill, but I didn't want to know exactly what, the truth diluted with the bittersweet wine of denial. Because the fact of the matter was, Clay also loved Michael and clung tenaciously to his memory, for, having lost him as a child, he seemed to be losing him even more with every passing year in that little dead-zone of adolescence, when the immediate past seems to slip away, forever lost.

I'm sure Gabriel understood this phenomenon very well, he must have, as he insisted Clay choose him for his final project. Under Gabe's supervision, he went about documenting Michael's life in an amazingly orderly fashion, first gathering physical evidence, baseballs and check-stubs and childhood pictures, then making the rounds to interview his closest relations: his uncle and mother, his partner and his sister, even his wife.

When his tape was finished, I sat up one night and listened to it in its entirety, amazed at what an accurate portrait it painted of a man who worked hard and died young; whose life was an ordinary mix of triumph and failure, only dramatic in the amazing love and loyalty of the people he left behind. You could hear it in nearly every voice: Sam's compelling and strong, Cissie's teasing and dry at first, though as she spoke, it began to break up, a painful thing to hear.

Candace's was as concise and practical as Michael's would have been, with a little flair of the dramatic when she recounted how he'd tried out for the Reds in the summer of '65. Case's was good-old-boy hilarious, poor Gabriel's the weakest of the bunch, even worse than mine. For at least I'd made a stab at telling a halting story of our first meeting when he crawled into bed with me that first night on the Hill, and the mysteriously forgotten note. All of the children had heard variations on the story before, but it was only now that the sexual implications of climbing in bed with a woman finally hit home, making Clay laugh and laugh.

So at least my contribution was funny, whereas poor Gabe, the master storyteller, just hemmed and hawed, talked about how neat Michael was, of all things; how they used to fight about it as children. How he went off the college, Michael didn't.

"Stayed home," he said in a halting little voice, as if he were still perplexed by the decision. "Stayed home."

Clay didn't pick up on his sudden voicelessness, his stumbling regret, didn't find it unusual or disconcerting, and didn't complain, as he got an A on the project and sailed through the term with his name in the paper for Honor Roll for the first time in his life. But I noticed it, and it worried me, made me uneasy in a way that was tame and well-behaved during the day, though it came to haunt me in the still reaches of the night, waking me from a sound sleep the way the Stairwalkers used to do. Except this time, it wasn't the ghost of Leldon Sims come to haunt me, but the ghost of Michael Catts, pressing me to do the thing he always insisted: Tell the truth, Myra. Tell him *now.*

But I resisted, I really don't know why. Probably for the same reason my mother denied ever living on Magnolia Hill: because the truth is more than a two-edged sword, it's also awkward and embarrassing and it hurts like hell, whereas silence, as they say, is *golden.* And things were going so well that summer, Gabe and Clayton inseparable, going fishing with Case every week, goofing around the house, Gabe talking of taking him up to Washington to show him the Smithsonian. It was so innocent, so loving, so — well, I hate to say it, but so *perfect.*

So I put it off, thinking maybe I'd tell him when school started in September, or on his birthday in March, or maybe when he was sixteen. Or maybe, *maybe,* not at all. I mean, maybe he *was* Michael's son. I mean, there was that brief reconciliation the night of Brian's birth, and wouldn't that be a shame, if I went to the trouble of confessing five weeks' worth of senseless, pleasureless stupidity and it turned out to be a moot point? Why poison his mind with doubt? Why, indeed? That was the flavor of my musings that whole summer long, till the very end, when of all people, Cissie herself saved me the agonies of confession when she let the cat out of the bag quite accidentally on the last weekend of the summer, Labor Day, 1989.

She did it right there at the dining room table, where we always gathered for summer holidays, as she still had the old backyard barbecue pit that was yet to be equaled in its smoking of pork. Usually Candace and Ed and their bunch joined us, but they'd decided to run up to North Carolina for the weekend to get a little relief from the heat. I couldn't say that I missed them, as Cissie's house hadn't gotten any bigger with the passing years, and when she filled it with all her offspring and their growing broods, the tiny rooms were filled with boots and elbows and size-twelve Nikes, so loud you couldn't hear yourself think.

Just our branch filled the tiny dining room to overflowing, the table packed plate-to-plate with barbecue and cole slaw and baked beans, green onions and french fries and tea glasses, the chatter loud and constant, the children excited about the school year that was so quickly upon us. As of Tuesday morning, Sim was starting work as Sam's official protégé and gofer for one year, till he went to FSU in accordance with Michael's master plan, while Missy began her junior year in town, finally able to drive herself in every morning in Gabe's old Volvo. As for Clay, he was making the big leap to high school in town, a landmark I was a little amazed at, sitting there wondering when I'd gotten old enough to have a baby in high school, listening with half an ear as Missy nagged him about his awful table manners.

"Don't you even *think* about talking to me in the cafeteria," she said, afraid her little hay-seed brother was going to ruin her cool-girl-ath-lete reputation with his redneck ways. She'd spent the summer lectur-ing him about his clothes, his friends, had even talked him into putting aside his cowboy boots in favor of Nikes. Clay took her advice good-naturedly enough, even when Cissie jumped on the bandwagon and offered a little advice of her own.

"Never talk with your mouth full," she said sagely as she rose to get the dessert, "and when one hand is on the table, the other one ain't."

"Where is it?" Sim asked mildly.

"On your crotch," his younger brother offered in a wisecracking voice that was amazingly like another snot-nosed little brother who'd once graced this table. "That's the polite place to rest your hand while you eat."

Sim laughed much like his father always had, though Missy just pointed her fork at him. "Do me a favor and never talk to me again," she said as her Grannie rounded the table, passing Gabriel on the way to the kitchen and wagging a finger at him.

"He's a-getting more like his daddy every day," she said in a tone of open sorrow. "Now you'll see what I went through a-raising *you*, Gabriel Catts."

There was an immediate blank silence, though Cissie was, as usual, an innocent, going on to the kitchen for the ice cream, leaving the rest of us sitting there, stunned. Sim and Missy recovered first and started chattering again almost immediately, trying to cover for us, though I didn't speak; I couldn't.

I was too busy watching Gabriel across the table, who wasn't pay-ing me any mind, but watching his son, and it was only then I realized that he wanted Clay to know. Subconsciously or not, that's what all the fighting and historical revision and needling the old men was about. He wanted to provoke the truth, force it up from the silent depths, his eyes across the table fixed and supplicant, and poor Clay, I pitied him. For I knew that look, over this very table, and could sympathize as he did exactly what his mother used to do: he ducked his head to his plate, his face flushed and introspective, though he said not a word. I guess I should have stood then and dropped my napkin on the table, fended for him the way Mr. Simon used to fend for me, and said, "Clay? Can I speak to you in the kitchen?"

But I didn't. I couldn't. I really didn't want him to know. I didn't want to let him go, leave his boyhood here at the table as Ira had all those years ago, for my sake. I was tired of sacrificing the innocence of everyone around me and just sat there, stomach churning, letting Cissie come back and dip me a saucer of ice cream, though I didn't touch it.

All I could do was sit there in silence and stir it till it melted, while Missy and Sim tried to keep the good times going, teasing Cissie about something, though it was so forced and painful, awful really. I was almost relieved when Curtis came by to take Clay out for one last trip to the river. I didn't even tell him goodbye, just went to the living room and sat there on the couch in a light paralysis, only speaking when spoken to, till it finally got dark and we could leave.

It was a strange drive home, Gabe and I in the Mercedes, neither of us saying a word. I felt his eyes on me, curious and concerned, making a stab at a smile when I glanced at him, though he was pale and hunted around the eyes, as if he were bleeding from a slow wound, and I didn't want to talk. I wanted silence. As soon as Missy and Sim came in, I sent them straight to bed, Missy making an outcry, though I couldn't be bothered with her protests and just made my way to the kitchen, sitting there at the table in deliberate immobility till Gabe came to the door.

"You coming to bed?" he asked, though it was only eight o'clock, the long summer evening barely given over to twilight.

I just shook my head, and he joined me at the table, a little timid, as if he realized that I'd finally figured out that he'd been more faithful to the truth than he'd been to me, though even then, he couldn't voice the inevitable. Neither of us could, just sitting there a good while, till I finally unbent enough to say, "You talk first."

He nodded easily enough, just sitting there a little away from the table, arms crossed, like a man ready for anything: the charge of a bull, the rout of an army. We didn't say anything for another long while, till he took a deep breath and said, "Myra." Then, "Does Clayton know —" He paused again and nervously chewed his lip, "Does he know about your father?"

I made no reply to this, though it certainly wasn't the first time anyone had ever asked. Sim and Missy knew the bare bones of the matter — that my father was a drunk, violent and abusive, but not much more. Candace and Dr. Williams were always after me to share even more of the wondrous details, though I just shrugged, thought, what did they want me to do? Set my children down by a cozy fire one night and tell them how he used to beat my brother unconscious, used to grab my butt when I was old enough to have one, and sometimes come into the bedroom when he was drunk and kiss me goodnight with nasty, open-mouthed kisses, and slap the hell out of me when I pulled away, so hard Mama used to tell me to go easy, sister. That he was my father. He loved me. Till I was — how old? twelve? — when he finally made his move, though mercifully, the door whacked me unconscious before he could do the worst of his damage.

So I didn't even answer him, just shook my head slowly, a quiet tear rolling down my face untouched, because I'll tell you what: I'd put a shotgun in my mouth before I'd tell my children the technicolor details of such horrors. "I don't want him to know," I finally whispered. "I told Missy and Sim, but not him, and I don't want to, Gabriel, none of it. None of it."

"It's all right," he said, just like Mama used to, and I could appreciate their concern, but couldn't agree: it wasn't all right. None of it was. None of it. "Here, baby," he said, standing and helping me to my feet as if I were an invalid. "You go on to bed, get some sleep. This'll be better, one on one."

"No," I began. "I'll talk to him —"

But Gabe was adamant about telling him by himself, and with a little persuasion, I let him escort me to bed and give me something, God knows what — maybe one of the old Haldols that I still came upon in medicine cabinets and stray drawers. Whatever it was, it knocked me on my butt, and I woke the next morning in a disoriented daze, not knowing who I was, what I was. I just lay there a moment, blinking, till I saw the clock that read seven-fifty, when a spark of my old get-the-children-to-school panic brought me to my feet.

I took off for their bedrooms, but found them empty, and had started down the stairs, clutching the rail as I used to, calling for them, when the phone in the kitchen began to ring. I ran for it, catching it on the fourth ring, and it was Candace, her voice dry and quiet, speaking very levelly. "Myra. Listen. Clay's here. He's asleep on the couch."

I didn't say a word, just stood there blinking, while she continued in that firm, reasonable voice. "He showed up here at five o'clock, walked all the way to town. Somebody told him about Gabe. He's real upset. Promise you won't call till I talk to him. 'Kay?"

I took a breath and tried to adjust myself to her calm pace, said, "Sure, Candace."

At the sound of my easy compliance, she exhaled. "Let me speak to Gabe."

I dropped the phone obediently, but the kitchen was empty, the coffee pot unplugged, with no sign of anyone. "He isn't here," I told her. "He must have left for work."

Candace made a little noise of exasperation at that. "Then listen," she said. "Call the school and tell him, Myra, to stay clear. You hear?" I nodded, but she couldn't see the nod and kept driving in her point. "Tell him that if he calls him, or corners him or tries to see him, he will lose him. You understand? Myra?"

I didn't answer, just lifted my face at the noise of a car door in the drive. "He's here," I said, seeing a tip of the hood through the window, and Candace was very firm.

"Then go tell him, right now, before he goes to town. Okay? Myra?"

I told her I would and set down the phone to go out on the deck and call for him. When I got outside, I heard a tapping on glass and looked up and saw him standing at the window upstairs over the garage, his face distorted by the glass, oddly like the time I'd seen him on Cissie's porch when Clay was a baby. I wasn't afraid, though, just went up the creaking stairs and found him at the window. He turned when I came in, his face very pale as I told him in a light voice, "He's at Candace's. She's on the phone. She says he's very upset. She made me promise I wouldn't call."

He closed his eyes in relief, then nodded in wordless assent and rested his forehead against the heavy glass. I went back to the kitchen to tell Candace and was crossing the deck when I heard something upstairs, a crack, then a shatter of broken glass that made me look up in horror to see the window breaking up in a rain of blows, the glass tinkling down on the marble.

"*Gabriel!*" I shouted as I ran back to the stairs and burst in the room, where Gabe was still at it, standing at the window and viciously hammering his forehead against the broken jamb in conscious, senseless destruction. I pushed between him and the window and pressed his bleeding face to my chest, both of us sliding to the floor and huddling there as Ira and I used to do as children, seeking refuge from the harsh judgment of an exacting world. Gabriel's voice was no longer lifted in hilarious mimic, but broken and grieving, reduced to a dim whisper: "*My son, my son.*"

$=== 38 ===$

So *ended the Era of Sleeping Dogs,* that
ended as most such eras end, in the ER at Jackson Memorial, which was
fortunately deserted that time of day, as it took twelve stitches to close
the gash in Gabriel's forehead that pumped blood like a severed artery.
It looked like we'd gotten into a fist fight and I'd taken a two-by-four to
him, though I hadn't. I had no need; he'd gone into the destructive
mode on his own.

All I had to do was hold his hand while the doctor stitched him up,
trying not to look too disbelieving as Gabe explained between grimaces
that he'd slipped on the deck and hit his head on the edge of the pool.

"Must be one hell of a deck" was all the doctor said, though Gabriel
was, as usual, master of the situation.

"Well, it's Italian marble," he explained with this amazing believ-
ability. "Kind of slick."

The doctor immediately lost his cocky skepticism, curious about
the pool and how it had come to be constructed of Italian marble. Gabe
answered with his usual authority, and I didn't argue, just filled out the
insurance forms, then drove him back to our empty damn house, wishing for the first time in my life that I'd taken Michael's advice and bought

430

something in town that would be less isolated, less silent.

Gabe didn't seem to find it too desolate, though. I guess he was used to coming home alone, as he just went to the phone and called in sick with the same lie he'd told the doctor, that he repeated to Sim and Missy when they came home from school that afternoon. And though the evidence of the shattered window was up there for all to see, they didn't dispute it, just made small jokes, Missy saying *thank God* he'd landed face-first. "Otherwise, you could have done some *serious* damage."

Gabriel just laughed, or tried to, as the laugh just wasn't in him, not with Clay steadfastly holed up at Candace's refusing our calls. We did what we could to return the household to some semblance of normalcy, Gabe returning to school the next morning, me calling Case to come out and look at the shattered window, asking him how much it'd cost to cover it with sheet rock.

"Close it up?" he asked in amazement. "No winder atall?" When I nodded, he'd taken off his cap and rubbed his neck, surveying the damage with a wry, "Well, that's a hell of a note."

I don't know exactly what *note* he was referring to: Gabe's head or the blood-splattered window ledge or Clay's desertion, and didn't ask, just had him board it up for the time being, telling him I'd give it some thought, which I did: much thought, with little result. For there just didn't seem to be any way to settle Clay's outrage other than to go over to Candace's and face him off, and for some reason, I instinctively shied away from doing that, I really didn't know why.

Gabe, of course, was biting at the bit to go over there and fight it out with the same energy and inventiveness that he'd fought it out with the old men in his Sunday school class, but I wouldn't let him go. I couldn't exactly think why, as I was fighting my usual rear-action battle with runaway fear, waking up every night, *pinging* like crazy. By now, these night-things were no longer so mysterious, long ago diagnosed as nothing more than garden-variety anxiety attacks of a particularly potent nature. They didn't send me running around the house checking the gas anymore, though they did send me back on Pamalor, which was doing its usual magic, not solving a damn thing, just making me too blunted and sleepy to care. It made it awfully hard to come to a decision, and I bet I picked up the phone two dozen times a day to call Candace, call

Clay, go over there and make it right.

But something stayed my hand, and it wasn't until late one night after the *pinging* defied the meds to jerk me awake with its heart-thumping panic that it finally came to me: Candace was right. He did need room. I don't mean room for persuasion, but room to come to his own conclusions in his own time and not have them thrust upon him the way Mama and Ira had thrust their little revisions on me in Birmingham.

I mean, in a small way, he was facing the same thing I had: parental betrayal of a sort not so easily understood. What if Gabe went over there and shouted and cried and made it right, and Clay bought it just for the sake of keeping the peace, and ten years down the road, it ate him into a depression? God, I'd have rather have died in '74 than pass on that curse to my Claybird, and sometime in the night I made up my mind and picked up the phone and called Candace's house, holding my breath while the phone rang and rang. Ed finally answered and took a message for his wife to come over the next morning as soon as she could.

Now, Candace is nothing if not confrontational and was knocking at the French door at the stroke of eight. I led her to the kitchen table without a word, where we sat facing each other, much as Gabe and I had two nights before, though this time I was ready to deal.

"You remember," I began carefully, having to work my way up to it, "when I was pregnant with Clay?"

She nodded slowly, her eyes kind of wary, as if she thought I was on the verge of another awful confession: that Clay was really Case's, or something. But I just took a breath and pressed resolutely on. "Michael was — he was not so excited."

It was a hard thing to admit, but there it was: he didn't love Clay till he saw him, though his sister was quick to defend him. "Understandably," she inserted, and I conceded the point.

"*Understandably* not so excited. No one was." I lifted a quiet hand and pointed at her. "But you." She just nodded again, still worried with what this was all leading up to, and I finally got to the point. "I need you to do me a favor, Candace."

I took another breath then and tried and tried to think of a way to explain, but like I say, Candace isn't the easiest person in the world to explain things to. I finally settled for the bald truth and told her plainly, in a light, halting voice, "I need you to — take him — for a month. A year. However — long — it takes."

I closed my eyes then, I had to, for they really were the words I never thought I'd hear myself utter, the room very still, as if I'd shocked it to silence at last. When I finally opened them, Candace was just sitting there across the table, not particularly mad or shocked, just a little teary. "It's for the best, Myra," she finally managed with a mighty sniff. I nodded, couldn't speak, and she repeated, "— for the best."

And with just about that much discussion, I forfeited my youngest child, much the same way my own mother had forfeited me, though God knows I hadn't out of choice — and it only came to me then that maybe Mama hadn't, either. Maybe it was just another one of those survival things, picking up the pieces and making do. Without another word, I pushed back my chair and went upstairs to pack his stuff up in whatever I could find: suitcases and boxes and finally, paper bags.

Candace tagged along, trying to help, but she's never been too domestic and kind of got in the way, as her sniffles had given way to a mighty storm of tears. She was crying so hard she was literally blinded, though I wasn't. I mean, what was the use in crying? Would it bring my Claybird back? It never had Ira. It never had Michael. It was another thing about men: when they got ready to fly, they flew.

So while she staggered around weeping like a widow, I kept going up and down the stairs, piling the couch with bags and boxes, everything I could think of, though I couldn't find his new shoes, the pump-up Nikes Missy had talked him into for school. I crawled under the bed, I rifled the closet, but could find nothing but the empty box, and finally went downstairs with his ragged old gym shoes in hand and found Gabe home early from school, standing by the couch with his book satchel in hand.

He looked up when he heard me, his forehead still snaked with his twisting black stitches, though I ignored him to speak to Candace. "These are his old ones," I told her, laying the sneakers gently on the stack. "I can't find his new Nikes. I just bought 'em last week. He won't wear 'em; they hurt his feet."

Candace's tears had run out long ago, replaced by a determined cheerfulness as she chided me in her old dry, teasing way, "They're on his feet, you idiot. But pack the old ones too. He'll need 'em for fishing."

I just nodded, not quite able to meet Gabriel's eye, as I'd given his son away without even asking. It hardly seemed fair, but I was too beaten to argue anymore and just went back upstairs for one final glance around the room, finding it stripped and empty of everything but the Rambo posters that were child's things now, nothing he'd care to take along into adulthood. There was plainly nothing left to pack, but still, I stood there, blinking in the midmorning sun till Candace came to the top of the stairs with her purse on her shoulder and said she and Gabe were taking the first load, that they'd be back in a while.

I just nodded again, heard the slam of the French door below, the car in the drive, then the silence that seemed to permeate the empty house. After a moment, I sat down on the bottom bunk of the cheap pine bunkbeds and closed my eyes, thought of the night Michael had brought them home from Sanger when Clay was four. He'd been so excited, dancing around in his little footed pajamas while we assembled them, though Michael was worried about him falling off the top bunk, told him he had to sleep on the bottom till he started school. He said if he caught him sneaking up there, he'd disassemble them, turn them into twin beds.

Clay had solemnly promised to stay below, though he never had, and every morning for a year I'd run in while Michael was still in the shower and slip him down one level into his rightful bed so his father was never the wiser. I threatened him, too, but to no avail, for Clay couldn't help himself. He could see the window from the top bunk, the sky and the trees, the white of the old magnolia, and it drew him like the moon draws water. I finally just told him to stay away from the edge, and sure enough, every morning when I ran in to transfer him, he'd be scrunched up on the top bunk with his back to the wall, sleeping like an angel.

Now, just like that, he was gone. Flown the coop. Glancing around at the looted closet, the strewn drawers, I spoke aloud to the streaming morning sun, "Fly back to me sometime, Claybird. Fly home."

I stayed there in his room till Candace and Gabe came back for a final load, which Candace took by herself as Gabe's head was bothering him so much that he had to take a pill and lie down. His inactivity broke my paralysis, and I spent the rest of the day setting the house in order, washing sheets and making beds, restoring Clay's room to an uncommon neatness. It gave me a curious satisfaction, folding and dusting and sweeping, probably the same satisfaction it used to give my mother, cleaning up Ira and me with her dishpan of bloody water: everything's all right now. Nothing wrong at all.

When I finished, I took a pill of my own and went to bed, and I think the most you could say for those first hard months was that we survived. For Clayton proved to be well-visited with that old Tierney defiance and didn't make any indication that he missed us, wanted to see us, had one iota of forgiveness for anyone. And though I'd promised Candace that I wouldn't press the issue and make any obvious effort to see him, I secretly thought that surely I would — it's not like we were living in New York City. I was sure that sooner or later I'd run into him at Wal-Mart or Winn-Dixie, or maybe a church picnic, and concocted a whole little plan of action: how I'd be kind, but not pushy; interested, but not fawning. It was also very important for me to be neat and pretty when I saw him, thin, if possible (good luck), I really don't know why.

I guess I was trying to restore my image of perfection, though my efforts were in vain, as I never saw him, not once. The closest I came to actual contact were occasional glimpses I'd catch of him around town in Curtis' truck, or in the handfuls of wilted flowers I'd sometimes find on his father's grave — roses or camellias he'd probably picked from his Grannie's backyard.

But that was about it, and after a month of ceaseless searching, I finally gave up and returned to the twilight of psychotropics and deep sleep, while Gabe submerged himself upstairs in his historical meanderings. There wasn't much else for it, with Candace working hard to smooth the transition with her usual single-mindedness. Every Sunday afternoon, she'd call while he was visiting his Grannie and give me updates of his new life in town: the ankle he sprained in gym, the trouble in Latin (tough on anyone learning-disabled, damn near impossible with the dyslexia).

I commiserated, offered what advice I could as an uncommonly cold winter crept by, complete with snow and ice, the Pamalor returning me to a base-level calm, and Gabe's forehead finally healing. To this day, we have matching little lightning-shaped scars between our eyes, *Marks of the Beast,* you might call them, though Missy sometimes tells people it's where we had our third eyes removed.

She was a comfort to us, my Missy was, she and Sim both, who'd lately grown disconcertingly adult, their faces finally breaking free of their imposed genetics and veering off into their own unique looks. Sim ended up medium-tall, still very much like his namesake around the nose and eyes, but dark like his father, too soft in the chin to be drop-dead handsome, but every (Southern) mother's dream, polite and easy-going — a *good-looking boy,* his Grannie called him.

As for Missy, she was still her flaming Amazon self, though at the last moment, her old wiry slenderness had popped out with these hot-Mama curves that made me kind of sad. The job of driving Clay back and forth to school had fallen to her, and every morning at breakfast she filled us in on the juicier details of his new life: the girl he loved in alge-bra, the high school crowd he was hanging with (still Keith and Kenneth, thank God), how he was rapidly leaving behind his staid Baptist teach-ings for the emotional lure of Charis-mania. ("As if he wasn't goofy enough already," said his loving sister.)

And as the icy winter lost its tenuous grip to the warmer winds of March, she began to report an even more peculiar development: how he had cashed in his redneck persona for an even more unlikely image: the jock. Suddenly, he wore nothing but Nike and Adidas shirts to school, had spiked his hair, even tried out for freshman basketball.

It was one transformation I could hardly fathom, stammering, "But Clay isn't a, you know —"

"Any dang good?" Missy offered.

"An *athlete,*" I said.

"Well, Mama," Sim confided, "just between you and me, it ain't like he's going to the Olympics anytime soon."

Though when I asked Candace about it during our weekly call, she was full of her usual boundless confidence. "Of course he's not any good," she said with her mother's bristling defensiveness. "He just start-ed. He didn't make the cut in basketball, but track's starting soon. He might do cross country."

I'll tell you what, it made me wonder about the rumors you hear about Charismatics and mind-control, because the old Claybird wouldn't walk down to the mailbox without a shotgun pointed at his head, and here he was, running circles on the old track field. I didn't quite know what to make of it and found Gabriel equally quiet on the subject. Too quiet, I thought, always upstairs working on the Cause, mostly just showing himself in the morning before breakfast and late at night, when he'd knock off precisely at ten and wander upstairs and join me in bed. We'd talk then for a while, then go to sleep with nothing more than a kiss, much less our old muffled groanings.

I didn't analyze it too much, just figured he was too whipped to extend himself; both of us were, though I kept an eye out for signs he was seeking solace in other places, occasionally slipping up to the apartment while he was at work and looking for bottles. But he was either wilier than I thought or keeping himself clean, for I found nothing but his old creative disarray, lit by the brilliant light of the old window that I'd finally let Case replace.

So the light over the garage once again shown out every night, golden and compelling, till sometime in the very early reaches of a cold spring, when Gabriel didn't come in at his usual time and I finally went up there to see what in the world he'd gotten himself up to. What I found was a sight more unsettling than an empty case of Jim Beam: a stack of legal pads and a brilliant smile as he proudly announced that he had *just that night* completed the first draft of his most ambitious, most fantastic oral history of all. This one not of anything as mundane as a civil war, but a memoir of the life and times of Gabriel Catts, particularly of his love for his brother Michael and his brother's wife, yours truly.

"For Clayton," he said, "so he'll know the Truth."

It was a coupling of opposites that I found immediately unlikely: Gabe and the Truth, and without giving it so much as a second thought, I crossed my arms and told him plainly, "Well, you can write all you want about your own life, but not mine — nor Michael's, neither."

"Why not?" he asked with his usual amazement that anyone would even *think* of being so presumptuous as to disagree with him.

"Because you ain't" was about as concise an argument as I could offer, and after half an hour's impassioned pleading, he finally just handed me a quarter-inch of typing paper.

"Well, at least read it," he said. "Then use it for fat-light, if you want."

I stood there a moment, vacillating, then took the handful of scribbled, marked sheets to bed with a cup of hot tea and a pretty good idea what he was up to: the authorized version of *The Life and Times of Gabriel Catts and How He Made a Few Purely Understandable Errors in Judgment in His Quest for True Love.* It wasn't what you might call a classic theme, though as I sipped my tea and read the first few pages, I began to sit up straighter and straighter, thinking: *My God, what has he done?*

Because what he'd written wasn't a matter of dry dates or tortured excuse, but a dive headfirst into that most wondrous of all Florida destinations, *Gabe-World,* wilder than Busch Gardens, more fantastic than Disney. He began with Michael's funeral, then dipped back into his childhood on the Hill, and it was astounding, really, how well he'd captured his magical reign as the Prince of Lafayette: the smell of an icy December morning, the slam of a screen door at twilight. It was like necromancy, how he brought them back to life: Michael and Mr. Simon, Cissie and the boys from the Hill, whom he knew much better than I, being their beloved leader.

Ira, in particular, was a marvel, not yet hardened in the concrete of childhood horror, but still a skinny little fighter, buoyant in his early, desperate scratch to survive. It tore my heart out, seeing him come back to life, made me want to throw on a robe and dash over to the Hill and brave the rotten boards of our old house to pound on the door and demand to see my brother, *right now, this instant.*

I could see him so clearly, coming through the shadow to answer my call, thin and wary, though I'd be kinder than the nurse from the State. I wouldn't make him lift his shirt, reveal his wounds — I wouldn't have to; I knew all about them. I'd just look him in the eye and tell him in a low, convincing voice, "Pack your stuff, Ira, and come on. This is Myra, grown up. I'm rich now. I got a house, and food, *trust me.*"

I was lying there, mesmerized by the sweetness of the hopeless little vision, when Gabriel sat down on the edge of the bed, his face bereft of his usual spunk, tired and thinner, oddly vulnerable. I blinked back to life and shook my head, murmured, "Gabriel, Gabriel. You almost made me miss Magnolia Hill. Lord, I never thought anyone could do that."

He closed his eyes when I said it, told me he loved me, though I was too full of his little story to return the sentiment. I just tapped the paper in my lap, sniffed, "Poor Ira. He never had a chance, Gabriel. Never."

I started crying then, which was ironic, as Clay had been gone, what? Seven months, now? and I'd never cried for him. Twenty-seven years had passed, and Ira was still the boy I reserved my tears for. ("You do my crying for me," he'd once told me, and I did.) Gabe just let me cry, moving the papers aside so he could lie down beside me. His very warmth was, as always, very comforting, and when I'd gotten the best of my tears, he lifted my chin with his brother's teasing playfulness and asked, "Poor Ira? What about poor Myra?"

I sniffed. "I haven't gotten that far yet."

He smiled a tiny smile. "Well, save some tears for Myra Sims. She never had a chance, either."

He was right, of course. In my little rescue vision, I hadn't given a thought to the other child of the house — the quiet one who wouldn't speak. She was still back in that closet, dammit, easily forgotten — or willfully. For I'd have to make my way through that dark, cobwebby old shack to loose her and I was scared of that old house, afraid of the creaking boards, afraid I'd hear a silky, bayou-tinged voice at my back ("*Whatchu doing, baby?*").

Or maybe because she'd already flown the coop herself, run off with a penniless millhand on a starry October night, and in a small voice, I corrected him. "She had Michael."

Gabriel unexpectedly agreed, his eyes very kind. "Yes. She had Michael."

I was touched by his generosity, touched and a little amazed, for — who would have thought it? — Gabriel Catts, a man. "And she had Gabriel," I smiled.

"She always has Gabriel," he said, leaning over to kiss me with one of his sweet, peach-kisses. We made love then, for the first time in a long time, and it was good; it was more than good. It comforted my soul, setting off a string of late-night lovemakings of a quality really above reproach, with none of our usual fight for dominance, but just tender and relieved and finally, at peace.

All of it made for a loving little interlude there while I read his truly heartbreaking account of my own aborted childhood from the Catts side of the fence, so moving that I offered to type it, as he was proceeding so slowly with his one hand, at a rate of about a page a night. Even I could do better than that, and as I sat there and pecked my way through the long spring twilights, I began to wonder if maybe I *had* returned to Florida to see Gabriel. I mean, I *thought* I'd made that painful trek up the Hill that night to see Mr. Simon, but maybe I was deluding myself. Maybe Gabriel's love really was the rudder that steered my ship, both of us going around in this golden romantic glow for a few weeks there, till I typed my way to the end of the childhood years and found myself undergoing a peculiar transformation in print.

I mean, until then, I was the good-natured girl next door, kind of used and abused (ideal rescue-bait, which is what these Baptists do best) and the perfect foil to my Prince-of-Darkness father. But as of my return to the Hill in 1967, whenever my name was mentioned, an image was evoked of those full-figured hillbilly women lolling around the porch on *Hee-Haw* in cut-off shorts and midriff tops.

"How did I make this quantum-leap from childhood innocence to this Redneck-Temptress-Butt-Waving-Wonder in one chapter?" I asked my beloved creator one afternoon when he came home from work.

"I don't know," he said, ignoring my sarcasm to answer equably. "Genetics, I guess."

Well, there weren't any soaring spirits in the old bedroom that night, or many nights to come, as my image really plummeted when he returned the summer of the Great Sleep and I was found to be lolling around the pool in a transparent bathing suit. That's where I finally drew the line, going up one Saturday morning to the apartment and facing him on his own turf, telling him plainly, "I have never worn such a thing in my life! You made it up, Gabriel, you made it up!"

He was unusually calm, just sitting there at his desk like a scholar in his bifocals and old robe, arguing with his old pedantic surety. "It was only transparent when it was wet. I noted that very clearly, see?"

"But it's a *lie,* Gabriel! I never owned such a thing."

He just shrugged. "You were loony that summer. You don't know what you owned."

"Well, I know I didn't wear a see-through bathing suit around a horny little snot like you. Michael was busy that summer, he wasn't *stupid*."

But it was like talking to a wall. He would not be budged, and I had to sit by and helplessly watch my life unroll before my eyes in all this sweating, panting, copulating glory that came to its glorious climax (perhaps a poor choice of words) right there in the little room upstairs. It was as if those five short weeks were the defining moments of my life, and it was useless for me to protest that I was *psychotic* that summer, Gabriel! I was just off *Haldol!* That I was in fact, not even a particularly willing accomplice.

I threatened, I wept, I finally stooped to pointing out that he'd lost his tenure up North and should I choose to divorce his sorry ass, the pre-nup would leave him penniless, but to no avail. By April, I was about at the end of my rope, toying with the idea of sneaking up there while he was at work and shredding the damn thing, when once again, Candace came to my rescue with an innocent little phone call one Saturday morning, asking what I was doing that night.

"Punching out Daniel and the Lion's Den for Sunday school," I told her. "Why?"

She paused a moment, then asked in a sly little voice, "So are you in the mood for a little baseball?"

$$\underline{\qquad} \; 39 \; \underline{\qquad}$$

"**W**hat baseball?" I asked.

"The Civic League," she said in this smug little voice. I thought Ed must be sponsoring a team till she added, "Clay's playing left field."

"For *who?*" I asked in amazement, and she took her usual calming, everything's-cool-here tone.

"Sanger."

"Sanger *Manufacturing?*" I breathed, and she was a little annoyed.

"How many Sangers we got in this town?" she asked peevishly. Then, "Tonight's their first game. I thought you might want to tag along. Discreetly, of course," she added, lest I forget my place and be actually caught speaking to my own son. "And for goodness' sake, don't tell Gabe."

I found this an easy enough proposition as we were hardly on speaking terms these days. He was still spending his nights and weekends holed up in the apartment scribbling out The Gospel According to Gabe Catts, giving me the space I needed to shower and slap on my Mary Kay stuff and even roll my hair without raising too much commotion, though by the time I got to Candace's, I was overcome with a hot-handed guilt.

"I feel like I'm meeting a man at a motel," I told her on the way to West Park.

She just glanced at me across the seat. "You *are* meeting a man. Clay's grown up. Prepare yourself."

I hadn't seen him since Labor Day and wondered what the heck she meant by prepare myself? Had he grown a beard? Become a hunchback? It made me even more nervous as we made the park and maneuvered ourselves into a parking space right up against the fence that offered a wide view of the entire field: the orange diamond, the Sanger jerseys, the umpires in blue shirts.

"Where is he?" I asked immediately, straining to see out the tinted windshield.

Candace gathered her purse and gave me my orders in this concise, sergeant-major's voice. "Listen. I'm going over to talk to him. You just sit tight. I'll get us something to drink, be right back." Then, before she shut the door: "If anybody comes by, kind of scrunch down, cover your face. 'Kay?"

I nodded, keeping my sunglasses on and just about crawling into the floorboards whenever anyone passed. I tried to keep an eye on Candace as she made her way to the concession, though she was hard to follow as she kept stopping to talk to people like a politician working a barbecue. She paused before several players, but they were all grown men, and I couldn't find Claybird anywhere, on the diamond, in the dugout, nothing.

I was about ready to chew the dash before she got back to the car, a Coke in each hand, a bag of popcorn hanging from her teeth. "The game's starting," I hissed. "Where is he? Is he here? I don't see him!"

She just handed me a Coke and pointed out the windshield. "There. See? In the dugout. Nervous as a cat, bless his heart." She sipped her Coke reflectively, said, "Y'know, I think Clay's kind of — sensitive."

Now, there's a news flash, I thought, still trying to see into the dugout, but not quite able, though Candace just sat there munching popcorn, her voice a patient rumble. "Keep your pants on," she said. "He'll be up to bat in a minute — see? In the dugout? Number twelve?"

"No!" I said, taking off my sunglasses and squinting through the glass. "No! I don't see nothing — damn, Candace, am I losing my mind?"

Because it really was so bizarre, staring at this whole team of grown men, looking for my Claybird, knowing he was there, but not able to make him out.

"There!" Candace finally exclaimed. "He's coming on deck! That's him! It really is," she insisted when I dropped my sunglasses to stare at her in open-mouthed amazement.

I finally turned back to the windshield, murmured, *"Jesus Christ."* Not in blasphemy, I don't think, but petition, though Candace was on it like white on rice, telling me I'd been hanging around Gabe so long I was sounding just like him. I hardly heard her, too intent on watching number twelve stand on deck, tapping a practice bat on his cleats.

"That's *Clayton?*" I asked in amazement, but she was still annoyed and answered me shortly.

"Yeah. That's Clayton. I told you he'd grown."

"Grown," I repeated in a small voice, thinking it hardly seemed an adequate word to describe this amazing transformation from a maybe five-foot-four, hundred-and-fifty-pound roly-poly of a boy to this six-foot-one, hundred-eighty-pound man. It was the same growth spurt Sim had gone through at that age — I don't know why I was so stunned — and just sat there in open-mouthed wonder as he took the plate and struck out one-two-three, though who the hell cared? I didn't, though Candace was disappointed, asking if maybe I'd talk to Missy, have her work with him.

"Sure," I murmured, watching his every move and occasionally throwing out a bit of comment that Candace fielded casually, suddenly the big expert. "He's another Ira," I said at one point, though Candace just made a face.

"He is *not.* He's a Tierney."

I didn't argue the matter, though when he took off his cap later in the game for a swipe at his hair, I pointed triumphantly. "See? His hair's going dark."

"That's because it's so short," she said. "It'll lighten up this summer."

Again, I didn't argue, because stare as I might, I couldn't quite put my finger on what it was about him that reminded me so much of Ira. It wasn't his height, really, or his face, that in the shine of the stadium lights was still very much like Gabriel's, but something else, something hard to pin down. Certainly not his athleticism, that despite his amazing new size, really wasn't what you'd call Olympic material.

Every night, Missy would come home from her forced practice sessions tired and disgusted. "Mama, he cain't *catch* the *ball*," she'd groan in this pained, hillbilly drawl she and her uncle used to mimic the rest of us.

"He's just starting," I told her, with a little less confidence than her aunt.

"But, Mama," she insisted. "He *cain't* catch *the ball.* You cain't play ball if you cain't catch it. He cain't catch. He cain't hit. The only way he'll ever stop a line drive is if it konks him on the head and *kills him daid.* I thank you need to pull him off the team. *I* thank it's dangerous."

"Hush," I told her. "You sound like your idiot uncle."

"Where *is* the famous author?" she asked. "Up working on *The Book?*"

She asked it with a twinkle in her eye, as she'd gotten wind of the great project, making fun of it in a way that really was painfully hilarious, needling Gabe with all the surgical skill he once needled his own father. After he'd given her and Sim a pretty serious summation of his intentions one night at supper, telling them it was about him and Michael (he knew better than to say it was about me), she'd looked at him with this face of great admiration.

"Gosh, Uncle Gabe, that's so neat. I thank I saw a movie-of-the-week just like it. Yeah," she said. "It was *Rich Man, Poor Man.* I guess if they make it into a movie, Nick Nolte'll play you."

You had to pity the man, though he was master of the situation, ignoring their laughter to suck his teeth a moment, say, "Missy, darling — have I told you lately how much you resemble an old childhood buddy of mine, name of Ira Sims?" He shook his head meditatively. "The resemblance is, uncanny — except that Ira was much *thinner,* of course."

She just shot him a good-natured bird, something they were always doing to each other, even (I am afraid) at church, where Gabriel had finally returned that summer like a whipped puppy. He'd even taken back his old Sunday school class, though without a tithe of his old spunk and bluster. For the old men knew what had happened with him and Clay and were oddly touched by his loss, going easy on him, sometimes even bringing him presents, jars of Tupelo honey or bits of memorabilia (including a piece of the rope that hanged Leo Frank).

I was glad of their ministrations, which distracted him from the fact that Candace and I were suddenly so inseparable, sneaking off to ball-games twice and three times a week. After a month of it, I began to evidence my own mother's genius at excuse, pretending that I was going to church, going to Cissie's, babysitting Ryan so Lori could take a night class. Gabriel accepted them all at face value, too involved in teasing out the niggling details of The Book to pay me much mind till sometime in mid-May, when he came upon me sitting at my vanity, rolling my hair at four o'clock in the afternoon.

He paused in the door a moment, then asked in a mild, casual voice, "Myra, baby, let me ask you something. That you are running around on me, I know. That it's making you a very satisfied woman, I also know. What's got me curious is: who is it? I mean, there aren't too many Catts men left to hit on anymore. Case? Is it Uncle Case?"

I just kept rolling my hair, a guilty little flush creeping up my neck, though I answered in an equally mild voice, "Good Lord, Gabriel. Case is seventy years old."

"Then it's Knute," he sighed hugely. "I knew it. It was just a matter of time."

"It's Clayton," I told him plainly, though he hardly looked less aggrieved, just standing there in the door, relieved, I thought, till I realized he was, by God, crying.

"It's just baseball," I told him, going to him and slipping my arms around his waist. "I go with Candace. She didn't want you to know."

"It's all right," he managed, though I led him to the bed and sat him down, concerned. I mean, it wasn't like Gabriel to be so fragile. He just sat there, rubbing his eyes, then looked at me with a tired, honest face. "You ever think that your whole life has been nothing but a endless series of pointless screw-ups?"

"Sure," I told him. "But then I blame it on Daddy and take a pill and feel a whole lot better."

He didn't even smile at my jibe, just sat there in a slumped silence, then looked up. "Can I go?"

I was immediately wary, "Go where?"

He just looked at me with the same small patience his brother used to, till I played it straight with a little shrug. "Candace says no."

And maybe he wasn't beaten yet, as he exploded in all his old foot-stomping glory, shouting, "Well, who the *hell* does Canadasier think she is these days, telling me when and where I can go?"

Now, Canadasier is Candace's legal name, which she despises almost as much as he despises his own, and I just looked at him levelly. "She thinks she's looking out for Clay," I told him. "And I think you better *stay clear.*"

That was about far as I got drawn into it, knowing old Canadasier could damn well take care of herself, which she did the next afternoon during our weekly phone call, telling Gabriel in no uncertain terms that he was *not* welcome. It was like the Clash of the Titans, listening to them go at it, but in the end, she prevailed, much to my relief. For I'd come to enjoy those twice-a-week intervals of Gabe-less peace and knew that the moment he stepped foot on the old ball field that peace would be irrevocably shattered, because the fact of the matter was: Clay wasn't any good.

Even I, his mother, would admit it, and sitting there every week, watching from the privacy of my own little tufted-leather world, I couldn't help but ponder the random cruelty of genetics that would give Michael Catts the heart and soul of a Jackie Robinson, but not the reach (his downfall in the big league, he always thought), while poor Claybird got Ira's shoulders and massive hands but Gabriel's totally nonathletic nature that made his contribution to the team minimal, to say the least.

Once the novelty of having him on the team wore off, neither the fans nor the other players were too patient with his indolent ways. The coach (in a devious twist of fate, none other than Joe Bates, lately grown huge and choleric) chewed him out after every missed ball in a way I tried to be patient with as I'd seen Michael chew out his share of players in his day. I just made a mental note that Gabriel never be allowed within a mile of the place, as he would jump that fence in a New York minute, and Joe was of the *too-old-to-fight-too-proud-to-run* school of thought, who carried a pearl-handled revolver in his pocket.

So unless I wanted to go through the banalities of another funeral here soon, I had to insist on going alone, and poor Gabe, it ate him alive, being left home alone while I openly cavorted with another man. (Which, now that I think of it, is exactly what the prophet Nathan told King David about him and Bathsheba: what David had done in secret would be done to him in the sight of all of Israel.)

And so it was with Gabe — done in the sight of all of Sanger Manufacturing, at least — a turning of the tables he didn't find much to his taste. On game days, he'd creep around the house like a shadow of his former self, even offering a few wily concessions on The Book to win my favor, toning down the Daisy-Mae aspects of my young life and making a stab at presenting me in a slightly more intelligent light. God knows if it was accurate, though I had to admit that in some vague, Gabe-ish way, it did have a ring of truth, though it still tended to make Michael look like a rough-talking thug (using the f-word on a couple of occasions, which aside from my father, *no one* uses as casually as Gabriel Catts).

Even more annoying, it went into pointless detail about Ira's decline, coming to a variety of conclusions that were so obvious and elementary that I finally told him, "Gabriel baby, I think you've studied too little Jung and too much Donahue."

He didn't speak to me for forty-eight hours on that one, though after a few more nights left at home while I cavorted with my Younger Man, he made the grand gesture of trashing the Ira-chapters and downgrading Michael's language to what was probably a pretty accurate account of the matter. My own concession was to allow him to tell it in his own inimitable voice, which made it kind of down and dirty, to my way of thinking, after he agreed to lock it away till Clay's fortieth birthday. "By then," Gabe predicted, "nothing will shock him."

I guess he was speaking from experience, as he was quickly approaching his own fortieth birthday on June sixth, wanting to get The Book tied up by then and salted away in the safe deposit box down at the bank with the will and trusts and other documents of good will. I was feeling so guilty about the baseball that I agreed to retype it, and was correcting typos in bed when I paused to wonder aloud, "It's funny."

"What's funny?" he asked, as he always hovered close when I was doing my reading, afraid I'd carry out my oft-repeated warning to torch it.

"That you don't ever mention your hand."

"What hand?" he asked in this incredulous voice, as over the years, he'd told so many lies about it, I don't know if he remembered the truth of the matter himself.

"Your hand," I said, reaching over and tapping it. "You never mention it."

It was one of the few times in his life that I've ever seen him literally struck speechless, staying up all night to reread the whole damn thing. When I woke up briefly at dawn, he was still at it, pencil in hand, slashing and correcting, muttering, "How could I have left it out?"

"I don't know," I yawned. "Maybe it doesn't bother you."

But he was obviously amazed that an old campaigner like himself had overlooked this potential mother lode of pity. "But it was such a wonderful symbol to overlook," he mused. "I'm gonna have to rewrite the whole damn thing."

This woke me up enough to sit up and look at him. "Well, I ain't retyping it, I'll tell you that."

"I'll hire a typist," he muttered, going back to his pages.

"You will *not,*" I said. "You'll do it yourself. I don't want some stranger reading my life."

"It'll take ten years to type it myself," he complained, but I just dug into my pillows.

"Make a footnote," I said, and could hear his voice, thin and petulant. "I hate footnotes."

"Then make an addendum" was my final offer. "It won't matter, anyway. Just explain why you're so easy to beat up."

He just grunted in reply, and I didn't argue it, just trailed off to sleep. When I woke up, much later, a little disoriented from the Pamalor, I squinted at the clock a moment before I reached over and shook his shoulder. "Wake up, Michael. It's nine. You're late."

He didn't turn a hair. "It's Saturday and I'm Gabriel," he answered smoothly, then charged right back in, saying, "Listen, Myra: my hand's the reason I yell at the old men."

"What?" I asked, sitting up and blinking.

He held up his curled hand. "My hand. It's the reason I yell at the old men."

I lay back and took his poor beleagued hand, which really didn't look useless at all, and really wasn't, as he'd learned to compensate so well. I pressed it flat against my chest, said, "Don't blame your poor old hand. You'd probably yell at people anyway."

"I would not," he assured me with his crazy old logic, then went on for some time about how his hand had dictated his life, using words like cripple and handicapped, the first time I'd ever heard him speak of himself in such a way. When I didn't react with an outpouring of sympathy, he began to get annoyed, said, "You just don't want to retype it. You're just lazy. And practical. God, I hate it — it's like I'm married to Mama."

I just yawned, my indifference making him roll over and pin me down with his old snapping-eyed surety. "Listen, Myra: I've never been able to *shake hands* with other men. And *your father* did this to me, and listen: I used to be afraid I couldn't *perform sexually* because of my hand."

I found this a little baffling, but he forestalled my inevitable question with a great breath of resolve, said, "I'm sorry. I'll have to revise."

In reply, I just lifted his hand to my cheek and thought of him as a child, eyes snapping, hands lifted in the passion of persuasion, like a camp-meeting revivalist calling a sinner to repentance. Well, at least he'd bagged one convert before he lost it, and after a moment, I sighed, "Gabriel." I paused again to take a breath before the storm, then asked, "Have you ever thought that all this fuss over your hand could be nothing more than a try for the sympathy vote? Have you ever thought of that?"

He jerked his hand away, said, "Go on, Cissie."

I didn't argue, just got up and went down the hall to wake Missy, as we were running over to Graceville to the VF Outlet with Candace and Lori to check out the sixteen-buck Jansen bathing suits. When I came back to the bedroom, Gabe was still lying in bed, the big old manuscript tossed on the floor by the bed. He didn't say anything, just rolled to his side and watched me dress in silence, finally asked, "Don'tchu even remember your youngest son anymore?"

I paused a moment, looking at him in the mirror, but didn't hit at his little piece of bait, just said, "Ah, yes. I think his name's Clayton. I'm watching him play baseball tonight."

He grunted at that and rolled to his back, said, "Well that's a tight relationship for you. Sitting in your car while he ignores you on the field. Boy, I wish I was that close to *my* children."

But I paid him no mind, just kissed him and went downstairs, for just these past few weeks, I was beginning to see signs that Claybird might be softening at last. Sometimes I'd catch him watching me from the outfield, his face reflective, thoughtful. One night he'd even waved when he'd taken his position way out there in left field, though he couldn't see me there behind the tinted glass, waving back like an idiot.

"He knows I'm here," I told Candace when she dropped by to talk to me, as she was too social a creature to stay with me in the car and had long ago rejoined Ed and the others in the stands.

She smiled a sad little smile, as if she knew her days of surrogacy were coming to an end. "Yeah. He knows. You can come around and sit with the rest of us if you want to."

But I was perfectly content to watch from the car with my calm, outsider's eyes, shouting along with the others the night he finally made a clean hit, a small pop that took him to first base for the very first time. Candace couldn't let the moment pass, running around to the car and piling in, shouting, "Didju see it? Didju see him? I toldju he was getting better!"

We sat there holding our breath while Ricky Vaugh came to bat and whacked one out of the park, everyone in the stands, including Joe Bates, coming to their feet when Clay crossed home. It really was a magical moment, Candace and I crying so hard we had to use the Dairy Queen napkins on the floorboard for handkerchiefs as Clay ignored the shouting in the stands and the back-thumps of his teammates to turn and look for my car, to see if I was watching.

It was so wonderful that I didn't know if Candace and I could stand it, though when I got home and told Gabe, he just sniffed, "Good for Clay."

But I didn't let it bother me, lying in bed that night and reliving the scene over and over in my mind, finally speaking into the darkness of the bedroom. "My gosh, Gabriel, I think he hit it for Michael. You should have seen his face when he crossed home. You know, Missy hit him a home run the day he was diagnosed. I think that maybe, this was Clay's."

"Of course it was," he said into the darkness, his easy agreement making me turn.

"How can you be so sure?" I asked, not in challenge, but simple curiosity, and though I couldn't see him very well, his voice was full of its usual authority.

"Why else would he go out there and sweat his ass off and make a fool of himself, if not for Michael? He's marking his turf. He's sending a message."

I just lay there, kind of stunned, then asked, "You don't mind?"

He made a noise of derision, "Mind? Mind what? That he loves my brother? That he's fighting to keep him alive? Hell, Myra, whatchu think I've been doing upstairs all year? You really *do* think I'm some slick-talking, skirt-chasing, Donahue-watching dumbass that makes a stab at being human every once in a while when it suits him."

"I used to," I admitted in a small, perfectly honest voice. "I ain't so sure anymore."

For a long moment, he was silent, then admitted, "Neither am I." Then, in an even smaller voice, "It's a hard thing, Myra," which was the same thing Michael used to say about dying, and losing Clay.

The blank loss hurt my heart just like it used to, and suddenly, I wasn't mad anymore. "Baseball'll be over soon," I promised, rolling over and drawing him close. "It'll be all right. It'll be okay."

My words of comfort were fast, instinctual, quite heartfelt, quite familiar. It was only when he'd gone to sleep that I realized they were the same words he'd comforted me with in the chiffarobe, when we were right on the brink of disaster as children. It struck me as funny that they should come to me now, for we weren't endangered in any sense of the word, but heading into calmer waters, with Clay giving me his little nod, the walls crumbling down. I couldn't figure out where this little thread of panic was coming from and finally wrote it off as my old baseless paranoia and went to sleep.

But I should have known better, and did the next morning when I woke up on Curtis and Lori's fourth anniversary, which coincidentially also marked the anniversary of the day that Michael had first complained of his recurrent bouts with a mysteriously debilitating bellyache. It was an anniversary that might have passed unnoticed had his brother not woken up with an even more terrifying complaint: a bedful of rumpled sheets spotted in bright red blood.

— 40 —

"*It's just the ulcer, baby,*" Gabriel told me when I tracked him to the bathroom, where he was brushing his teeth with a calm, tired face. "It's nothing. I'm fine."

I held the blood-spotted pillow up for evidence. "It is *not*. I'm calling Dr. Williams."

"What's he gonna do?" he asked as he sauntered back to the bedroom. "Interpret a few dreams, put me on lithium?"

"He's a medical doctor," I informed him over the receiver, though I couldn't get Dr. Williams himself, just his nurse, who recommended we go to the ER. I thanked her, then threw on the first thing that came to hand and tore downstairs, where Gabriel was about to pour himself a cup of coffee. "Put it down," I told him, grabbing my purse and scribbling Missy a note. "We're going to the ER."

He set up an outcry at this, but I paid him no mind, just marched him to the car and drove him in myself, casting him these little sideways glances that scared the hell out of me, as it was so evocative of another drive I'd once made to the hospital. Just like before, my passenger was sitting there with his seat tilted back, rubbing his forehead, with no inkling of how pale he looked in the clear May sun, how very pallid. He even closed his eyes halfway there and absently pressed his hand to his stomach, the small gesture bringing on such an unreasonable panic that it was hard for me to speak when we finally made it to the admissions desk.

"He's *sick*," I told the nurse, for want of a better description. "He *has* to be seen *today*."

Before she could answer, Gabriel butted in with a face of great exasperation, said, "Listen, I got an ulcer. Just call me in a prescription for Tagamet and I'll be out of your hair."

But I insisted he stay to see the doctor, and he submitted to the various preliminary examinations with his usual small grace, still groaning about losing a day's work, about how much this was all going to cost.

"We'll sell some shoes," I told him absently, roaming around the examination room while we waited, feeling that old strange disembodied numbness begin to creep into my bones at the familiar hospital smells of alcohol and astringent and Betadine.

The doctor, when he finally appeared, turned out to be the same one who'd stitched Gabe's forehead in September. He lifted his face with interest when he recognized Gabe. "Mr. Catts," he said, flipping open his chart. "Having trouble with that marble deck again?"

Gabriel was opening his mouth with an equally acerbic reply when I put an end to their foolishness. "He's bleeding from the mouth," I told him. "The pillow, it was *covered with blood*. I told him he can't ignore it. It won't just go away."

The doctor cut the clowning then and had Gabe lift his shirt and lay back on the examining table so he could look him over, though Gabe still tried to downplay it, saying, "Listen, she's exaggerating. I got an ulcer, had it for years." Till he pressed his stomach, when he let out a howl. "*Damn*, boy, that hurts."

The room lost its teasing air just that quickly, the strange little shake beginning in my shoulders as the doctor resumed his examination with a new seriousness, his voice thoughtful. "Have you had some kind of blunt trauma recently?" he asked. "A punch in the belly? A fall?"

Gabriel denied it, but I remembered the nasty fall on the marble deck and grabbed his arm, said, "Tell him the truth, Gabriel. He has to know —" Till I suddenly realized, *my God, that wasn't true.* He'd hit his head on the window ledge. He never slipped on the deck. That was the lie he told the children.

It brought me to a clumsy halt, though Gabriel began to play it a little straighter, admitting, "Well, I did puke Antabuse Christmas. Ate some — uh — fruitcake with rum in it."

The doctor made a little noise of alarm at that, and I was glad we were finally getting down to business and clutched at Gabe's arm. "See? They can do things for you. They can fix you up. They've got medicines now," I looked to the doctor for support, "don't they?" But he wouldn't answer, just watched me over the table with a face of speculative concern, just like Dr. Azuri used to, and, hell, I didn't need their pity, I needed their help and tried to reassure Gabriel. "That's all right, though. Because they can do things for it now. Nowadays it never kills anyone."

Even to me, the words came curiously weighted, a half-remembered echo from some ancient sealed vault, tinny and strange, that made me go very quiet, very still, even turn aside to the wall, wanting to deflect the doctor's attention, his level stare. At my back I heard Gabriel ask him if he'd please call his mother? Cecilia Catts? Her name was on the chart, the next-of-kin. The doctor said he would; then with a final comment that he was ordering *lab work,* he left, the very word like a knife-stab of terror that made me close my eyes quickly, as if I'd been struck.

Gabriel stood then and pulled me to his shoulder, whispering that it was fine. He was fine. Those bloody sheets were nothing. I don't know why he brought them up. Maybe he thought they'd set off some kind of post-traumatic incident, but God knows they hadn't — how could they? I'd never seen a bloody sheet in my life; my mother was too good a housekeeper for that.

I pulled back and tried to explain. "It's not *that,* Gabriel," I said. "It's never *that —*"

But he just looked at me the way Candace sometimes did, in total noncomprehension, the frustration of it all finally forcing the truth up from the depths in a fast, panicked rush. "Michael died here! He came in just like this. He had the flu, we thought; then it was just gallstones, but he was never the same again. He got so thin, so weak. He *died,* Gabriel! He *died!* He'll never talk to me again."

Thus, for the first time in two years, I uttered the most profane word of them all: the d-word. Because the fact of the matter was, to voice it was to relive it, to face the brutal fact that Michael wasn't merely gone; he wasn't in Waycross, staying the night, or over at Cissie's, asleep on the couch. He was dead. He died right here in the hospital. He was so thin, without breath. You could see the outline of the tumors that had spread to his neck, could count his ribs before they finally came for him; they covered his face; they took him to the morgue.

He wouldn't dance at Missy's wedding or cry over his first grandchild or ever grin that audacious grin again, the awful permanence like a slam in the forehead, but a hell of a lot more painful, because cracked skulls eventually healed, left tiny little scars, while death! Death went on and on! Why, it wasn't a gentleman at all, the terrible finality making me cry and cry, so hard and comfortless that Gabriel was close to tears himself when his mother came strolling in as if she owned the place.

She didn't so much as nod at me, just came straight up to the table, tipping her face back to peer at her son through her bifocals. "Well, son?" she said. "What in the world's the matter? You ain't *slipped* on that *deck* agin?" she added in a voice that dripped with insult at having been fed such a lie.

"I got a bleeding ulcer," he said in a fast, scared voice, though his mother just looked annoyed.

"Well, son, I tolju to quit eaten sa much of thet hot sauce." Then, with a dropped voice and an even leveller eye, "It's the whiskey what's done this to you."

At this grim unveiling of the wages of his sin, Gabriel's face lost its perplexity and he laughed aloud. "Hell, Mama, I haven't had a drink in two years."

"It was the dranken *before* two years what done *this*," she murmured with a sure Mama-confidence. Then, with a kinder eye to me, "Well, Myra? Baby? While he's a-getting these tests and whatall, why don't you come home with me? Clay's coming by after school, heping me move my azaleas and cut back the kudzu."

I was amazed at the casual way she said it: *Clay's coming by.* It was like it was all water under the bridge, this past year: him holed up at Candace's, me sneaking out to see him in sunglasses. I didn't know quite what to make of it, but must say that her old Mama-sureness made it mighty tempting. "We get done in time," she continued, "you can stay to supper. I got a ham and potato salad and we'll send Clay to the sto for ice cream or frozen yogurt or whatever it is you women eat these days."

At the mention of the ham, I forgot all about last year's unwelcome gentleman caller, and just stammered, "I need to stay with Gabe."

But he was having none of that and pushed me off the table. "Oh, go, go —" he said. "I'll be fine. Listen, when he gives me the Tagamet, I'll pay him his thousand and go grade my finals."

I made a few more noises of uncertainty, though arguing with this pair was useless. I could barely withstand either of them, on a good day, with the wind at my back. Together, they were like biting a granite rock, and after Gabe promised to call the moment he heard anything, I gathered my purse and left.

Cissie wouldn't let me take my car, but insisted on driving me to the Hill in the old Cadillac that was a heck of a lot cleaner now than it had ever been when it was mine, the dash all shiny, the carpets vacuumed and neat. Once there, I wiled away the morning in my old newlywed routine, peeling potatos and dicing onions, beginning to yawn as the kitchen grew warm and humid from the steam.

When Cissie caught me in one, she insisted I lie down and take a nap. "Right in your old room, baby," she said. "I'll be here to answer the phone, anybody calls."

Clay wasn't due for two hours, at least, so I took her advice and lay down on the same old bed Michael had so innocently crept into my first night on the Hill. I was thinking how narrow it was, not even full-sized, but three-quarters, how we'd had to pile up like puppies after we married, though we never thought to complain — why should we? We were happy piled up here, warm in winter and hot in summer, the old window fan keeping the air flowing over us, shielding our nocturnal groanings from the rest of the house.

The constant old rattle lulled me sleep, to wake much later in the day, blunted and disoriented, with a niggling sensation that I'd forgotten something, something important. I just lay there yawning a few minutes, till I suddenly remembered — my God, I'd left Gabe at the ER with a bleeding ulcer!

I leapt from the bed and stumbled to the living room, where Cissie was curled up in her old easy chair watching the last few minutes of *The*

Guiding Light with her usual absorption, her eyes never leaving the television as she told me, "He's fine. Had to operate. Sewed him up. Be home Tuesday."

"*Why?*" I cried, begging, "Cissie? What was it? Was it cancer?"

She looked up then with a faint line of annoyance between her eyes. "Good Lord, no. Doctor said he'd be up in no time. Left his number by the phone."

I ran to the kitchen and dialed the hospital, hooking up with the surgeon fairly quickly, an associate in the same practice with Dr. Azuri, as it turned out, who assured me it was a simple perforated ulcer, nothing to worry with, just a special diet, and no Antabuse, till the stomach lining healed.

I thanked him profusely and hung up, then rested my forehead to the wall a moment, till Cissie called through the house, "Clay's out back. Told him you'se here."

I made no reply, as I was having a nervous overload and just leaned there with my forehead to the wall, thinking maybe I'd put off seeing Clay a little longer, till Gabe was stronger, till *I* was stronger. But after a moment, curiosity got the best of me and I went to the window and cautiously lifted the curtain a few inches to look out on the yard, where, sure enough, Clay was working in jeans and a Nike T-shirt, clearing the fence.

I was standing there peering through the curtains when Cissie came up behind me and spoke at my back, just about making me jump through the window. "He's been at it all afternoon," she said. "Paying him *five dollars.*"

She lifted her face at the enormity of the sum, but I just edged away from the window and looked at my watch. "Gosh, it's late. I need to call Missy, go to the hospital — Can I borrow your car?"

But Cissie wasn't in the mood for any more of my waffling and just leaned against the stove and met my eye. "Missy's all right. She's at Joanna's, and Sim's with Gabe." She nodded toward the yard. "You go on out there, speak to thet boy. Like I was telling Case: it was time he was coming home. Canadasier'll have him a *Charismatic,* you don't warch."

She said the word with the same horror some mothers would say *homosexual,* making me glance nervously at the door, finally whisper, "I don't know what to say."

But she wasn't having any of it, just folded her arms and gave me the same level Mama-look she'd given Gabe. "Oh, you got plenty to say, sister — and if you doan say it, who will?"

Who, indeed? I thought, just glancing between her and the backyard, where Clay was working with an uncommon vengeance, yanking at the kudzu so ruthlessly that he was about to upend the old fence. Cissie didn't blink an eye, and I finally chose the yard as the lesser of two evils and crept out on the porch, quietly closing the screen at my back.

I paused a moment at the top of the steps to glance around the narrow old yard that had hardly changed over the years, the old oak gone, but the sweet gum still there, wearing new spring leaves the color of light grass. Even the little ditch was the same, bubbling merrily along with the run-off from the spring rains, a pretty little grass-grown thing, full of life, frogs and snakes and the small heronlike birds I still couldn't name.

Clay was working just this side of it, not a dozen feet from where Gabriel and I used to play as children, and as I watched him, it finally came to me why he reminded me so much of Ira: he had his slump. The *Sims Slump,* I called it, because I had it, too. I used to tell Michael it was the price I paid for marrying into a short family, till I'd noticed Ira standing in line at UCI, waiting to be unshackled, noticed he stood with the same little face-forward slump. Clay did, too, though when he noticed me standing there, he straightened up and gave me a little nod of greeting, as if he were a stranger passing on a sidewalk.

At least he hadn't spit or something, I thought, and with Cissie standing at the window, defying me to chicken out, I plunged right in, going down the steps and calling in a casual little voice, "Clay? Can we talk?"

He just lifted his face, which was hot and dirt-streaked, not as unfamiliar as I'd feared, but really just as I'd suspected: a combination of Ira and Gabriel, with the Tierney softness, but something of Ira's width. His voice was not hostile at all, just nervous and a little shy (with me!): "Let me move this camellia," he answered; then, maybe to save any offense, "Grannie's paying me."

I just nodded, then went to the fence to sit like God knows I'd sat many an evening before, trying not to plan anything, just wait and see what questions he had up his sleeve, this son of mine. Cissie was certainly getting her money's worth that day, as her camellias were ancient old things, notoriously difficult to transplant, with taproots half a mile long. Poor Clay grunted and sweated a good half hour getting the last one out of the ground, then spent another twenty minutes digging the new hole. He was about to plunge it in inches above the trunk line, when I finally had to intervene, standing, calling, "Claybird. Wait. Here."

I went over and adjusted the dirt level, then wrapped the looping tap roots around and round, fitting them nicely into the hole, then had him go to the creek bottom and dig up some black dirt to top it off. When I'd patted it all back in, he said, "Gosh, Mama, you got all dirty."

Alas, I had, the knees of my nice khaki Dockers dirt-black, my fingernails a sorry sight. "That's all right," I told him, slapping my hands on my butt. "Run get the hose."

But he was tired and dirty, wanting to take a break. "That's all right," he said. "I'll water it later. Didju wanta talk?"

I just came to my feet and told him, "Claybird, the roots'll dry out. Run get the hose. We'll leave it to drip. It won't take a minute."

He obeyed without argument, and once I set the hose, I washed my hands as best I could and sat down in the lengthening shade of the old sweet gum. He joined me there, sitting a little away, his back to a fencepost, not saying anything, and after a moment, I dove for an opening, some bit of trivia that would open the floodgate on that mysterious stranger, The Truth. "Gabriel and I used to play here, under the sweet gum, when we were children."

But Clay was tired and a little shy, not hostile, but cagey. "Really?" he asked, with nothing of interest about him, and if he wasn't so keen on The Ugly Truth, I wasn't going to push it, turning aside to speak of more routine matters, of baseball, and the team's chances in the city tournament.

"Not so good, with me on it," he said with a small deprecating sarcasm that brought out a little of that old Cissie-defensiveness in me.

"Well, you just started," I told him. "Your Daddy wasn't any good, either, first time he played." Though technically speaking, Michael probably hit his first home run while I was still in diapers in Louisiana.

But Claybird didn't know that and lifted his face warily. "Really?" he asked, with a little more interest, and once I had my opening, I went after it like gangbusters, telling him every bit of detail I'd ever heard, seen, or dreamed of Michael's baseball career, downplaying his obvious natural talent and making it sound like something that he'd perfected after a rocky start. It might not be a strict account of the matter, but I was learning from The Master that recorded history was a simple matter of *interpretation.*

Twilight was settling around us as I spoke, and once we were cast in kindly shadow, Clay grew more relaxed, letting me chatter on about family matters: Ryan and how big he was getting, Missy and her ironclad intention to return to France. Then, with full dark almost upon us, I mentioned Gabe's surgery and how it had gone all right.

He didn't look particularly relieved or disgusted, either one, just wiped his forehead, said, "Yeah. That's what Grannie said."

I finally screwed up my courage then and told him in a small, hesitant voice, "He's sorry, about what happened." Clay just nodded, didn't say a word, and I pressed forward nervously, "I just wish, baby, that you could accept it —"

On the *accept,* his face flew up in challenge, making me back up quickly, stammer, "— not *accept* — forgive. *Forgive* it."

Like the good Charismatic Candace was training him to be, he couldn't very well argue with this pious bit of advice and just shrugged and looked away while I hastened to clarify myself. "I don't mean you have to say it was all right, because, Claybird, *believe me,* nobody knows better than me that forgiveness isn't saying it was all right, it was fine, what happened. Forgiveness is just saying: that was the way it was, and letting it go. That's all it is, baby."

I paused then, wishing I had better words to explain this nearly inexplicable thing, though Clay didn't look argumentative as much as tired when he finally answered in a quiet, honest voice, "But I don't know how it was."

There was a terrible sadness about him when he said it that hurt me so much. I mean, Michael and I had worked so hard to give our children everything we'd never had: money and houses, cars and pools, college and self-esteem. How was it that unhappiness had crept in, on quiet feet?

"— you don't ever talk about him," he added with a fast little glance of reproach that made me sit up.

"*What?*"

"Daddy," he said in that sulky, sure voice. "Grannie and Aint Candace, Lori and Curtis — they all talk about him. *You* never do."

Of all the things I thought he'd accuse me of, this had to be the furthest from my mind, making me stammer, "Gosh, Clay, what d'you mean, I don't talk about him? Sure, I talk about him. I think about him all the time."

"You do *not*," he insisted with a trace of his old Clay-petulance. "It's like he never even lived, you forgot him so quick. You don't even go to his grave anymore."

Well, I didn't know what to say to this, how to explain that I *couldn't* go to his grave, not like I used to, that it'd be like Gabe hanging out at a bar, too much of a temptation. But damn, it was hard to explain the Rules of the Twilight to this child I'd raised in the Light.

All my careful explanations just congealed there in my head, a hopeless knot that I despaired of untangling. I finally just plunged right in, stammering, "Baby, it's just that it's hard for me to talk about him. I mean when people —" I closed my eyes then, actually took a breath, as if in preparation for a long dive, "— *die,* it's like they get, lost, in the telling. You know how it was at the funeral, when everybody kept going on and on about what a good guy Michael was. Remember how — *petty* — it all sounded — like we were throwing him a bone because he left us in his will. That's why I don't talk about him, baby, because —" I paused again, this time striking appreciably closer to the mark, so close that even my breath reflected it, short and choppy: "— because it *hurts.* And I ain't so good at it anyway."

I came to a halt then, I had to, because it really did hurt so bad, my chest burning with that old suffocating grief that I closed my eyes against, willing away. Clay didn't press me any further, just sat there against the fence in a long, unbroken silence, till the first stars of the evening began to peep out of the violet sky, shy and lovely, causing an unexpected memory to bubble up from the silent depths, a story of my own; a Michael-story.

"A star fell the night we got engaged," I heard myself say in a sudden, story-telling voice, "while we drove home through the flat woods." It was too dark to see Clay's expression, though I felt his interest, his pivoted attention, and pressed forward nervously. "I don't know that I'd have married him if it hadn't, because Mama was pitching a fit up in Birmingham, and shoot, we'd just met — I didn't even know his middle name. But then a star fell, like a comet, all the way across the sky — he told me to make a wish."

I paused then, for I could see his face so clearly, lifted to the night sky in wonder, then turning to me with that fast, Michael-grin ("Make a wish, baby"). The image was so vividly alive that I closed my eyes against it, because it really was so painful to remember — God, I didn't know how Gabriel could stand it. I finally took a ragged breath and opened my eyes, managed, "And Clay — that's what your father was — to me. He was that star. He came out of nowhere, he streaked across the darkness. He lit the sky for just a moment with this terrible beauty, this great love — then, just like that, he was gone — everything faded, back to black."

I cried when I said it, the tears rolling down my face unchecked, all the way to my neck and chest. I didn't bother to wipe them away, just let them fall, unable to see Clay in the darkness, or how he'd taken it, though after a moment, he asked in a quiet voice, "What'd you wish for, that night?"

It was a funny thing to ask, a Clay-thing, that made me laugh, even through my tears. "Aw, baby, I don't remember. Happiness, I guess. Or that Mama'd let up on me. It didn't matter, 'cause I didn't need to be wasting my time wishing anymore. I was heading back to Magnolia Hill, to Cissie and Mr. Simon. That's all me or Ira ever wanted, anyway."

I couldn't speak after that, just sat there and let the tears flow, not in grief as much as simple wonder, as the warm May evening really was so reminiscent of my childhood, the back of the Catts house lit just as it used to be, the screen door open to the breeze, wafting the heavenly scent of baked ham. I hardly ever saw it from this angle anymore, and twenty-seven years later, was still amazed that I'd actually jumped that damn fence and left the darkness of my mother's closet for the lighted kitchen next door.

There was a shuffling by the fence, then Clay sat down beside me, not saying anything, just putting his arm clumsily around my shoulders, not much of a stretch, as he'd grown so tall. I tried to rein in the tears then, and after a long silence, he finally allowed, "Aint Candace told me about — you know — when you lived here. Your father and all."

I just nodded, finally managed, "Yeah. It was tough."

"You doan ever talk about it," he pointed out, and I shrugged.

"What d'you want to know?" I asked, for that old house was the least of my worries. I'd write a book myself if he wanted and told him, "I've just come to that point, Clay, that I told you about, where you say: that was the way it was and you let it go. But if you need me to dig it back up, I will. I mean, I do it for Ira, every time they send me a subpoena. I'll do it for you, too, if you want."

But he just shook his head. "That's all right," he said.

I finally got my tears under control and looked at him levelly. "Because, one day, Claybird, that's what you'll have to do about Gabriel, and me. It'll be the hardest damn thing you ever do in your life."

He was quiet a moment, then said in a small, honest voice, "I don't think I can." He was quick to add: "Not about you. I understand about you — but not him. He loved him."

I don't know which *he* he meant, Michael or Gabe, but it really didn't matter. I just sniffed, "He did. That's what you need to remember, Clay. They did love each other, so much."

"Then how could he do it?"

I realized then that it was *Gabe* he was talking about: how did Gabe do it, and I swear to God I wanted to say: *read The Book*. But I just sat there a moment, then sighed. "He just stumbled into it, Clay. Like most people do. Just stumbled into stupidity. Ask him sometime, he'll tell you."

"Which did you love?" he asked, very quickly, and I turned a little to look at him in the close darkness.

"*Which* did I love?" I repeated. "What d'you want me to do here, flip a coin?"

He returned my flippancy with such a level-eyed, Michael-Catts look that I dispensed with the sarcasm enough to say, "Listen, Clay, I loved them *both*. I loved them all: Cissie and Mr. Simon, Candace and Michael and Gabe. You want a division?" I shook the old sagging fence at our back. "This is the division. Everything on that side of the fence, I hated — or, not hated — *feared*. Everything on this side," I waved at Cissie's kitchen, her newly clipped hedges, "I loved. That answer your question?"

I don't know if it did, as Clay just shrugged, then, just as Cissie came out and called us to supper, he finally got to the sixty-four-thousand-dollar question. "People say, he ain't my father."

"Who?" I asked. "Michael?"

He nodded a fast little nod and I made one of Gabe's old bear-grunts of annoyance as I came wearily to my feet. "Well, Claybird," I told him, "as you grow older, you'll come to find that, generally speaking, *people* don't know *shit.*"

His face took on a little of his aunt's prudishness at my profanity, though I was too aggravated to care, just wondering what jackass had thought to rub his nose in this? As he came to his feet beside me, I set him straight once and for all, facing him in the near darkness and telling him plainly: "Michael is your father."

He seemed amazed at my confidence, though maybe not believing, and as Cissie came to the porch and called us again, I tried to explain. "I mean, he's the one who fed you, changed your diapers, put a roof over your head. He loved you more than he loved me, Clay, and that's saying a lot. Gabe —" I paused a moment, then sighed. "He would have been your father, if I'd have let him. He'd have given you his eyes, Clay, he still would. But I picked Michael. I had to, I loved him so much. There never was a choice for me, as long as he was alive. You understand?"

I'm not sure that he did. I'm not sure I did, either, though one thing was for certain: Michael was his father, and no gossip-hound or blood test or paternity suit on Earth was going to take that from him. Clay just stood there digesting it, though I could sense a difference about him already, a palpable lightness, a hint of relief.

"You think it's watered in enough?" he finally asked, meaning the camellia.

"Let it drip," I told him, and with no more discussion than that, we went in to supper, up the path, up the steps, right into the lighted kitchen next door.

=== *41* ===

hen I finally made my way back to the
hospital that night, they'd already moved Gabriel from ICU to a private
room on the surgery floor, as I'd requested. I found Sim dozing on a
couch in the waiting room and sent him to his Grannie's for supper,
then made my way alone down the familiar halls, a little disconcerted by
the small clicks of memory: the hospital smell, the orderlies clearing
supper trays, the little block-lettered sign on the door that read: CATTS.

They were enough to get my heart pumping hard in my chest as I
carefully opened the door to find Gabe lying there face up in a bleached-
out hospital gown, his arm all stuck with IVs and tubes, his face slack
with an unearthly peace. For a moment, the image was purely terrifying,
making me stop at the door, though it passed quickly, as Gabe had heard
my step and opened his eyes.

"Did Sim come by?" he asked dimly. "I think I saw him."

"Yes, baby," I told him as I went to the bed and felt for the lever to
let down the side rails. "He stayed the whole time. Him and Candace and
Brother Folger."

"Brother Folger?" he asked lightly. "Who's that?"

"Carlym Folger? Why Gabriel, he married us."

"Oh, Knute," he grunted. "I'm glad I was unconscious."

But there was no heat in his voice, and I just flipped down the rails and nested in close beside him. "Why d'you have to be so nasty?" I asked, and he nuzzled my face absently, eyes closed, like a puppy.

"He wasn't visiting me, he was visiting my checkbook."

"Hush," I told him, taking his bad hand and lifting it for a kiss. "The doctor said you could go home Monday. Said everything went fine. He had to remove part of your stomach, but the part that's left will stretch out. You won't even miss it."

"Good riddance," he murmured. Then, in this light, casual voice, "Didju see Clay?"

I paused, unable to answer, as my usual little rebound reaction had set in, my whole conversation with Clay submerged for the moment into a numb, blunted void, irretrievable. I knew from experience that this was a temporary thing, and sooner or later — probably in bed later that night — little details would begin to work their way up from the silent depths to delight or disgust me, make me think: *damn, I wisht I hadn't have said that.*

But for the moment, I could only skim the surface and answer in a wondering little voice, "Yes. He's fine. His hair's not as bad as it sounds. Kind of a moussed-up flat top."

He didn't press me further with his old bull-dog aggressiveness, didn't say anything at all, and instead of being relieved by his newfound passivity, I was struck uneasy; told him that maybe we needed to get away, go on vacation to somewhere nice. "Maybe Jamaica," I offered, but he just sighed.

"I don't have much patience with the Third World."

"What about Virginia? You like Virginia. Or Chattanooga. We could visit the battlefields."

"I'd rather have my spleen removed," he murmured, though he was quickly repentant, saying, "That's all right, baby. I'll be all right."

Which was about as much as I could get out of him the whole time he was in the hospital. He simply wouldn't be drawn out, returning home kindly and courteous, with none of his usual spunk, even turning me down when I politely offered to resume my conjugal duties. "That's all right," he said, patting my leg as if I'd offered him a cup of tea. "My belly's still sore."

When I pointed out that an old porch-lolling, white-trash temptress like myself could probably work my way around a piffling complication like a belly full of stitches, he just smiled. "Don't worry about it."

That's when I began to get seriously concerned, alarmed at this strange new passivity, worried that he might not pull out of it. What if he started drinking? The Book had occupied him all year, compensated for the loss of Clay. What would he do now that it was done?

Late in the night, while he snored peacefully at my side, I turned it over and over in my mind, thinking maybe Cissie was right. Maybe it was time I brought Clay home, though God help me, I didn't know how. I mean, we'd broken the ice to conversation that night at Cissie's, but he'd made no offer to come home, given no indication that he ever meant to return.

I still didn't want to railroad him and went back and forth on it for the better part of a week, till Missy unexpectedly remedied the situation one night when she came home from softball in her grimy old practice uniform. She was too pooped to take the stairs and just kicked off her cleats and collapsed on the end of the couch. "So where's the Famous Author?" she asked, though with a little less sting than before, as she was worried herself with Gabe's new complacency.

She'd gone so far as to order him an ice-cream cake for his birthday (as he still wasn't allowed solids) but wasn't sure that'd do the trick, and sitting there slumped in her dirty leg-pants, came up with an even more fascinating idea. "Why don't we throw him a party?" she said. "A surprise party." Though I wasn't so enthusiastic.

"Catts men aren't too good with surprises. He probably wouldn't come down."

She sat up then and gave me a knowing little look. "He'd come down if Clay was here."

I returned her look evenly. "How would we get Clay here?" I asked carefully, knowing from her cagey expression that a Plan was being incubated in that wily red head. Sure enough, she jumped on it with her father's crazy enthusiasm, lining it all out for me: how we'd have a party by the pool, invite everyone in the family plus the old boys from Gabe's class so Clay could blend in, not be put on the spot.

"I don't know, Missy," I told her after a moment. "I've never been too good at this *satisfying a man* thing. I cain't even satisfy Gabe anymore, how can I satisfy Clay?"

Missy just rolled her eyes on that. "Who said anything about *satisfying a man?* Why don't you satisfy *yourself,* for once?"

"It ain't as easy as that," I said pensively. "I don't want Clay to feel — pressured."

"Pressured?" she breathed. "Pressured to what? Be cooked for, kissed over, waited on hand and foot? You sound like he's coming back to be executed. I mean, everybody *knows* he's dying to come home."

She said this as if it were a patented truth, and I looked at her levelly. "What did you say?"

"He's dying to come home," she repeated matter-of-factly. "I mean, he made his grand departure a long time ago and was eating up the attention for a while, *making a statement.* But face it, Mama, Aint Candace *never* cooks and Uncle Ed's like this lawn-care Nazi, has him out there mowing and mulching five times a week. I bet old Claybird's weeping into his pillow every night, wishing he was back in his little bed where he belongs."

I had begun to sit up. "You think so?" I asked, and she grinned her father's grin.

"I *know* so. 'Cause to tell you the truth, I been throwing a little fuel on the fire myself. Every morning when I pick him up for school, I kind of drop a hint about what we had for supper the night before: pork *chops* and chicken *tenders* and fried *okra.*" She lifted her face in an evil laugh. "And you should see his face. I tell you, Mama, they're living off Pop-Tarts and microwave popcorn over there. You show him a sausage biscuit and he'll be over here so fast it'll make your head spin."

"What about him — and Gabe?" I asked, but she just shrugged.

"I don't know, Mama. It'll eat at him just because he's *always* got something eating at him. But, you know, he's just like the rest of us — still searching for Daddy — and Daddy was never over there at Aint Candace's. He was here, with us," her smile faltered a little, but stayed intact, "and this is where he'll find him."

I didn't say anything for a moment, because there really was a strange Michael-magic about this daughter of mine, not just in her athleticism, but her honesty, her utter reasonableness. I just watched her a moment, then finally managed, "You're right."

"Of course I'm right," she said with all her old Missy-confidence, standing and stretching like a cat. "Go call the little turd, tell him to get his tail back home. Tell him I'm ordering an ice-cream cake and Grannie's frying shrimp. That'll git him here. And tell him Curtis is coming. Give him somebody to hang with."

In the end, that's exactly what I did. After nine months of agony, I just went to the kitchen and picked up the phone and called Candace's and told him it was time he came home.

He didn't say anything for a moment, just let the silence drag on long enough for my palms to begin to sweat, then answered in a calm, even voice, "But I'm babysitting this week, for Ryan. Can I wait till Saturday?"

"Saturday's your uncle's party," I told him smoothly. "You're invited." There was another silence at that, and I praised God Missy had provided a small contingency. "Missy ordered an ice-cream cake and we've got to go to Tallahassee to pick it up. You can ride with Candace, or Curtis."

There was yet another silence, and I was beginning to wilt when he finally said, "But I don't have a — present."

"That's all right," I assured him. "Missy ordered him a book. I'm sure she'll let you contribute." Then, in a small, desperate tag, "Cissie's frying shrimp."

There was a final pause, longer and more portentous than before; then in a voice as small as mine, he asked, "D'you think he'll mind? Me being there?"

"Mind?" I wanted to scream, "MIND?" But I just closed my eyes and managed, "I don't think so, Clay. I think he'll be . . . thrilled."

He digested this in silence, then, in an obvious try at sounding like a mature adult: "Well, I'll have to talk to Aint Candace — you know — about moving and all. Okay?"

"Sure," I said, and that was about the end of it. Candace called me from work a little later, and with no more discussion than when I'd released him, she let him go, just asking if she should bother to pack all his old clothes that he'd grown out of, or just the new stuff.

"Whatever he wants," I told her, too relieved and nervous and jumpy to make any more decisions, though before we hung up, I managed a small "Thank you, Candace."

She didn't belabor it, and once Clay's appearance was confirmed, Missy and I went into overtime, spending the next two days making phone calls and arrangements and deftly fielding RSVPs. We woke early on Saturday and crept around all morning cleaning house and stringing lights, trying not to arouse Gabe's old radar, not an easy task, as he'd run out of pain pills on Thursday night and was getting restless, biting at the bit to come downstairs.

"Put something in his ice cream," Missy kept whispering, and in the end, that's exactly what I did. Nothing toxic, just a little hit of Xanax before we left for the mall that afternoon, so he wouldn't go downstairs and see the sparkling kitchen and the punch bowl and the lights, a dead giveaway that something was up. When we got home that afternoon, later than I'd intended, nearing six, I began to worry that I'd overdosed him, as he was still knocked out like a light, lying face up in bed, still kind of pale and anemic-looking.

I paused to watch him sleep a moment, for in repose he really did favor his brother, the bones of his cheeks and forehead quite prominent, his hands folded quietly on his chest. Even at forty, he held to something of the innocence and wonder of the fast-talking, curly-haired boy who'd once so entranced me, especially in his hands, which were as brown and clever as always and had finally come into their early promise, the hands of a man.

I lifted one and kissed it, then went downstairs where Missy was having one of those last-minute party crises, as a carload of old men from Gabe's class had pulled up half an hour early, boisterous and hard-of-hearing, impossible to keep quiet. Fortunately, Case pulled up right behind them, and on Missy's orders, took them on an extended tour of the grounds.

"Twenty minutes, at least," she hissed. "Show 'em the dang camellias."

Sim arrived from Waycross shortly after, looking like a golf pro in what had become the uniform of Sanger management: a Polo shirt and pressed khaki pants, Tom Sanger's one (and only) lasting influence. He was carrying a huge unwrapped box, big enough for a television.

"What in the world?" I asked as he plunked it down on the kitchen counter.

"It's one of the old XTs from Waycross," he said. "Slow as Christmas, but the word processor's all right. Thought maybe Gabe could use it for The Book."

I was a little disconcerted by the way he said it, *The Book,* as if he were talking about the Bible or something. Sight unseen, the damn thing was taking on a life of its on, making me look at the box with distaste. "Take it up to the apartment," I told him, "and for God's sake, don't tell Clay."

Sim hoisted it up obediently and I followed him to the French door to open it for him, and told him to go around front when he was done, show people where to park. "Not in my roses!" I called in a light whisper, watching him lug the computer up the stairs, thinking with this odd bewilderment that this man was my son. That my husband and I had run out of condoms on our honeymoon, and now there was a grown man who looked like me parking cars in my front yard. It was all very strange, but there was no time to stop and ponder it. Seven o'clock was rapidly approaching, and with time running short, I gave Missy her last-minute instructions, then took a deep breath and went upstairs to con the best con of them all.

I found him still lying there with his eyes closed, so pale that for a moment I was afraid I'd given him a lethal mixture of drugs and ice cream, though when he heard me, he sat up and squinted at the clock. "What time is it?" he blinked.

"Seven," I told him, plunking my shopping bags on the bed as if we'd just come home. "You want me to wrap 'em, or just give 'em?"

"Just give them," he yawned. "Why waste paper?"

I dug around the bags and presented him with the present his loving niece had picked out at Parisian's that afternoon with many howls of delight: a two-hundred-sixty-dollar paisley print Pierre Cardin robe and pajama set. She would have been gratified to see his look of baffled outrage. "We're in Florida. Nobody sleeps in pajamas. I'll burn up."

Missy had given me explicit instructions on my comeback, and I just busied myself ripping open the cellophane. "Missy's sixteen now, too old for you to be walking around here in your underwear."

"I have never," he informed me icily, "walked around here in my underwear."

"Oh, go put 'em on," I told him. "Then I'll give you your next present. I promise you'll be *thrilled.*"

I was gratified to see a glint in his eye of purely sensual interest at this, the first since he'd come home from the hospital. It was clear he thought I was about to underscore my Redneck Temptress skills by proving the stitches were not an insurmountable problem, as he hobbled obediently to the bathroom to put on the pajamas, coming out all dressed and robed with a look of happy anticipation, obviously disappointed to find me sitting on the edge of the bed still dressed.

But hope must have sprung eternal in his wily little heart, as he made some attempt to be pleasant, sitting back on the edge of the bed and asking, "What?"

I smiled brilliantly. "I'll retype your story."

This was in the nature of a low blow on my part, as he had suddenly become as uncertain of The Book as I was. He wouldn't say much about it, but after that last careful reread, I think he'd finally realized that he'd bitten off a little more than he could chew, applying something as caustic as The Truth to something as fragile as Gabe-World. For by some fluke of storytelling, or historical integrity or what-have-you, he'd somehow ended up recounting his life and times a little too accurately for his own good, as the self-portrait that had emerged was disappointingly warty.

So instead of a cry of thanks, he just lay back on the bed like I'd shot him, murmured, "Wonderful."

"And you can go to baseball with me tomorrow night, lay down in the back seat. Candace says we can take a quilt to throw over you if Clay comes by."

Gabriel just lay there like a dead thing and repeated, "Wonderful."

He was falling for it so completely that I began to enjoy myself a little, bumping the bed with my knees like Ira used to do and affecting a tone of wifely bewilderment. "But I thought you'd be pleased. It's the city-wide tournament. Maybe he'll hit a homer."

He just made a grunt of disbelief at that and as the little squeaks of noise and conversation downstairs began to grow imperceptibly louder, I let go a little, grabbing up the cellophane and wadding it up, murmuring, "What a disagreeable man you've become. And poor Missy bought you an ice-cream cake, ordered it *special* in Tallahassee, and you're gone *lay up* here and *show yourself.*"

At my pale imitation of his and Missy's pained hillbilly sing-song, he began to bestir himself. "Hush," he said. "I'm coming. I'll behave."

"She also got you some old book," I said as I helped him to his feet, "and I'd *appreciate* it if you wouldn't *tear it apart* the whole time you *read* it."

"What book?" he asked warily, and I toyed with the idea of telling him *The Joy of Sex* but decided it was too obvious.

"On that war. The Civil War," I said, and maybe went too far, as he came to a complete halt just outside the door. You could tell he was teetering on the edge of refusing to go down, forcing me to go in for the kill. "Well, you stay up here and sulk," I told him, "We did fine without you a lot a years. I'm sure we'll make a few more."

"Hush," he said, and started moving again. "I'm coming." Then, as we made the corner, "Has she read it yet?"

"No," I said absently, trying to listen for any noise downstairs, but finding everything unnaturally silent.

Missy must have run them all out on the deck, I thought, till I took him around the corner and caught a glimpse of the silent, packed room, though Gabe was too busy fooling with the hem of his robe to look up. "Good," he said. "I can fake it."

"Gabriel —" I began, but got no further, as just then, a wall of sound hit us: Madonna's "Like a Virgin." This was yet another of my little inside jokes, though it started in the middle of the song and blasted out, indecipherable.

It brought Gabriel to a dead halt there on the third stair, though instead of looking down at the packed, expectant room, he just faced me levelly and said in a clear, petulant voice: "You run tell Missy I ain't sitting down here listening to her nigger music, I don't care what kind of cake she bought me."

The room exploded then, in spontaneously combustible laughter, as poor Gabe had spent the better part of two years rebuking the old men for their various sins, racism being the chief. He jumped like a cat at the shock of it, then stood there a moment, stunned, and for a woman who has spent her whole damn life searching for that perfect orgasmic break-through, I must say that this one came close. For aside from his Mama-boy ways, Gabriel really is a pretty good sport and just shook his head at the cackling old men, calling down a good-natured insult or two until he final-ly laid eyes on Clay standing just inside the door, Curtis at his side.

I knew the moment he saw him; could actually feel the moment of grace, Gabriel's face losing that good-natured, you-got-one-over-on-me grin, his body actually slumping a little, like runners do at the end of a race. He turned to me then and kissed me, his eyes very level, sending a wordless message, the kind Ira and I used to send as children. *Thank you* was the message, though I couldn't do anything but laugh; I couldn't help it. It was the same way I sometimes laughed during sex, because sometimes life is kind of laughably wonderful. Not often, but some-times. It was all I could do to help him down the stairs to the festooned living room where the old men engulfed him, slapping his back and wag-ging fingers, calling, "Now, whut was thet I heard?"

Gabe took their teasing and paid it back in kind, working the party with his old Tierney charm, making jokes and shoveling insults, so smooth that I told his mother over the din of music and chatter that he really missed his calling when he hadn't become a politician. "Called to be a preacher," she shouted back with a resigned little shake of her head. "Didn't work out."

But preacher or not, he could damn sure spin a congregation, everyone having the time of their lives, especially the old men, who greeted me on all sides with their winks and ancient come-ons ("Hey sweet thang!" "Hey, *good-lookin'!*") There was a time in my life that I would have found this a little wearing, but I was about to the age where I'd take my *good-lookin's* where I found them.

So I just passed punch and cut cake, Clay a tall, quiet stranger, though he told me the house looked nice. "Nothing changed," he said with a small perplexity, as he'd changed so much; how had it remained the same?

"You bring your stuff?" I asked, and he answered over the din.

"In Curtis' truck."

Other than that, we had little opportunity to talk, for the old men hadn't had such a blow-out in years. Hours after everyone (including their wives) had headed back to town, they hung on, paying not one whit of attention to Candace's not-so-subtle hints that the party was over.

"You're gonna have to blast them out of here with gunpowder," she predicted when she left, as they'd pinned Gabe in a lawn chair on the far end of the deck and fallen to discussing, of all things, Chappaquiddick.

I left them to it and helped Sim and Clay bring his stuff in, not much, as he'd outgrown his entire wardrobe, shoes and all. When we were finished, Missy took her Grannie back to town and Sim left for Waycross, but still, the old men stayed on. I finally told Clay it was hopeless, that I had to work on my lesson and was going to bed. I told him goodnight, just like usual, then asked if he wanted anything special for breakfast.

"Why?" he asked, as I'd historically offered my children two options on Sunday mornings: frosted flakes or nothing at all.

But I was getting to be pretty wily myself in my old age and just told him very nonchalantly. "Gabe'll be able to eat solids tomorrow. Thought I'd make something soft, like biscuits. *Sausage* biscuits."

A light of undisguised love shown a moment in his eyes, though he tried to be cool, looking at his feet, murmuring, "Sure. I mean, if you want to."

I just smiled and said goodnight, then went upstairs and took a shower and punched out my Noah-and-the-Ark, scattering the bed with horses and cats and peacocks, all marching to their salvation two-by-two, as the Lord commanded. I put them away in my folder and was skimming my lesson when Gabriel finally got shed of the old men and hobbled upstairs, late, past midnight. He didn't say anything, just took off his new robe and folded it over the chest, then sat on the edge of the bed and said in a perfectly normal voice: "I'm gonna have to cry."

"Well, go outside," I whispered with a weather glance at Clay's bedroom. "Don't let him hear you."

He didn't argue, just put his robe back on and ambled out with this elaborate nonchalance. I could hear his footsteps on the stairs, then the sound of the French doors, then the drag of the old metal garbage can over the marble deck. When he finally made the grass, the clanging was stilled, leaving the house suddenly quiet. I waited for him a long time, even got up to go see if he needed me to help him up the stairs, but thought better of it, hesitant to pass Clay's closed door, not wanting to bring him out in time to see Gabe returning with his tear-ravaged face.

I went to the window instead and quietly opened the sash, lifting my face to the soaking humidity of the brilliant night sky. The moon was on the wane, giving place to a host of constellations, none of which I could name, as for most of my life I hardly remember ever seeing the sky, the stars. I simply never thought to look up at the never-ending pageant of sunrise and sunset, stars and driving rain, till just this past year, when I'd begun this love affair with the heavens, waking up early every morning to watch the dawn break, or walking down to the highway at twilight just as the first stars of the evening were peeking out, tiny pinpoints of light that magically appeared, one at a time, to cover the flat, Florida skies with their intricate traces of light. It lifted my heart like nothing else, sometimes made me think of my father and the sagging old easy chair on the porch of his house in Sliddell where he'd sat that last year of his life to watch the sunset. I wondered if he, too, had become a sky-watcher in the end and was oddly comforted by the thought, my mind drifting on, inevitably returning to Michael.

For he was the reason I'd begun this sky-watching in the first place, at his grave every morning the first winter he was gone. That's why I'd go there so early, before dawn, to watch the stars dissolve one by one into the clear light of dawn, the irony of it sometimes making me smile. Because in life, he'd pestered me to attend to earthly things, children and laundry, ironing and groceries, while in death, he'd turned me into a sky-watcher, a mystic, a muser of the heavens.

It wasn't a small favor for a woman who'd spent her first seventeen years staring at her feet, and as I quietly regarded the vast and unknowable heavens, I thought that of all his gifts, perhaps that was the greatest — better than the diamonds or the Mercedes, the house or the millions, even Gabe or his generosity in raising my son. That from that very first night, when he'd driven across the flat woods to retrieve me and stopped dead still on the highway so I could wish on a star, he did me the most incredible favor of all: he lifted my head. My husband Michael.